The
Lawrenceville Stories

OWEN JOHNSON

SIMON AND SCHUSTER · NEW YORK

P. 1C

THIRD PRINTING

LIBRARY OF CONGRESS CATALOG CARD NUMBER: 67-25392
DESIGNED BY EVE METZ
MANUFACTURED IN THE UNITED STATES OF AMERICA
PRINTED BY MAHONY & ROESE, INC., NEW YORK
BOUND BY AMERICAN BOOK-STRATFORD PRESS, N.Y.

CONTENTS

INTRODUCTION

Cleveland Amory

Writing from the inside out, with high good humor but with depth and understanding too, with rare modern insight combined with plain, old-fashioned storytelling, Owen Johnson has here created, out of his own experiences at school, the truly classic stories of the American boy. Indeed through these portals pass a whole bygone host of not just characters—but living, breathing companions.

I find these companions even more enthralling today than when they first delighted me, so many years ago, when I was one of them. The Prodigious Hickey (original title, The Eternal Boy), The Varmint and The Tennessee Shad were all originally published circa 1910, but they had such vitality that they did not even reach the peak of their fame until a decade or more after publication, and they were constantly in print for almost half a century. In recent years, however, they have been unobtainable, and now publisher Peter Schwed—himself a Lawrenceville boy, of course—has here righted the wrong.

The author, Owen Johnson, who was later to become chairman of the Yale Literary Magazine, from whence stemmed his famous Stover at Yale, was also a Lawrenceville boy—in fact he was Lawrenceville's first postgraduate boy. Graduated at sixteen in the class of '95, he asked for and received permission to stay on a year and launch, at Lawrenceville, the Lit, the school's literary magazine. Years later Mr. Johnson recalled those days of early trial. "The first batch of contributions," he declared, "were mainly concentrated on the love entanglements of the upper crust of High Society and the lower crust of the desperadoes of the Underworld. I was frightfully depressed. The stories lacked the background of conviction."

vii

Mr. Johnson, even at sixteen, took stern measures. "I laid down the first law of the Lit," *he said. "Don't invent—interpret. Write from your own experience." And, he added, "The change was remarkable. The love life of High Society and Low disappeared."*

Having laid down the law to others, Mr. Johnson next had to follow it himself. He too began to interpret, not invent, and he interpreted what he knew best—his own school. Later indeed he would admit that not only was there "a base of fact in every story I wrote," but also that, with the exception of Dink Stover, who was "a composite character," all the others were "easily recognizable portraits." Incredibly enough, Mr. Johnson declared that even his nicknames were real—and among these he ticked off "the Coffee-Colored Angel," "the Triumphant Egghead," "the Gutter Pup," and "the Waladoo Bird."

Real nicknames! So they did really exist. But, if the Coffee-Colored Angel and the Triumphant Egghead existed, and the Gutter Pup and the Waladoo Bird, then so too did Lovely Mead and Hungry Smeed, Beauty Sawtelle and Brotherly Love Baldwin, Poler Fox and Pink Rabbit, Goat Finney and Turkey Reiter, Piggy Moore and Mucker Reilly, Sow Emmons and Slush Randolph, Vulture Watkins and Old Ironsides Smith, the Uncooked Beefsteak and Dennis de Brian de Boru Finnegan.

One thing is certain. For us as readers these characters do a great deal more than just exist. In the very second story in this volume, for example, you will not only meet Hungry Smeed, you will actually eat with him as he goes all out for "The Great Pancake Record." And when, halfway through, he plaintively asks for syrup— well, we won't spoil it for you. Later, in "The Future President," you will not only read the world's first Walter Mitty story, you will actually dream along with Snorky Green in the middle of his Latin class. And at the end you will be as furious as he was when, after he and the brave men under him have held off the entire German army all night long, he is clumsily bumped back to reality by Red Dog. "Red Dog, of all the world! Red Dog, whom he had just cheered into a hero's death!" And when the Varmint falls desperately in love with the sister of Tough McCarty, you too will say to yourself, as he did, over and over to himself, "She's twenty-four, only twenty-four. I'm sixteen, almost seventeen—that's only seven years difference."

Humorous these stories certainly are, but make no mistake about it, like all great humor stories they are underneath deadly serious. Just as in Stover at Yale, *in which Mr. Johnson wrote not only the classic story of the collegian but also the classic satire of the Secret Societies, so in these Lawrenceville stories he wrote not only the classic story of the prep school boy but also the classic satire of prep school life. But it should be noted that these stories were not, in the sense of the Frank Merriwell and the Tom Swift series, "boys' books." They were published in the* Saturday Evening Post, *and they were read by millions—by men of twelve and by boys of eighty.*

Even mere women loved them—although it goes without saying that those of you who intend to read parts of this volume aloud to your wives should do so sparingly. The moral in many of these stories is so subtle it is beyond the comprehension of all but a handful of women—even those fortunate enough to be blessed with prep school husbands.

Finally, understand that you are reading here, alas, of what was, not is. Mr. Johnson himself phrased it best—in a paragraph he wrote for the 50th anniversary issue of the Lit:

I wrote of the end of an era, before the lion had lain down with the lamb. Between masters and students there was an armed and exceedingly wary neutrality. Nothing was taken for granted on either side. It was a battle of wits and the rule of the master was sternness tempered with justice. Justice had to be impersonal. To lose his temper would have been fatal. This era passed, with the earlier one of the birch and the ruler. The monkey instincts of the young imagination are looked on with amused tolerance, so I am told. Better so. But it was not so in the 'nineties when the old traditions of discipline were as rigid as in the old-fashioned schoolhouses—the iron fist in the velvet glove.

The Prodigious Hickey

THE AWAKENING OF HICKEY

" 'HE FORGED a thunderbolt and hurled it at what? At the proudest blood in Europe, the Spaniard, and sent him home conquered; at the most warlike blood in Europe, the French . . .' "

Shrimp Davis, on the platform, piped forth the familiar periods of Phillips's oration on Toussaint L'Ouverture, while the Third Form in declamation, disposed to sleep, stirred fitfully on one another's shoulders, resenting the adolescent squeak that rendered perfect rest impossible. Pa Dater followed from the last bench, marking the position of the heels, the adjustment of the gesture to the phrase, and the rise and fall of the voice with patient enthusiasm, undismayed by the memory of the thousand Toussaints who had passed, or the certainty of the thousands who were to come.

" 'I would call him Napoleon, but Napoleon made his way to empire over broken oaths and through a sea of *blood*,' " shrieked the diminutive orator with a sudden crescendo as a spitball, artfully thrown, sang by his nose.

At this sudden shrill notice of approaching manhood, Hickey, in the front row, roused himself with a jerk, put both fists in his eyes and glanced with indignant reproach at the embattled disturber of his privileges. Rest now being impossible, he decided to revenge himself by putting forth a series of faces as a sort of running illustration to the swelling cadences. Shrimp Davis struggled manfully to keep his eyes from the antics of his tormentor. He accosted the ceiling, he looked sadly on the floor. He gazed east and west profoundly, through the open windows, seeking forgetfulness in the distant vistas. All to no purpose. Turn where he might, the mocking face of Hickey danced after him. At the height of his eloquence Shrimp choked, clutched at his mouth, exploded into laughter and tumbled ingloriously to his seat amid the delighted shrieks of the class.

Pa Dater, surprised and puzzled, rose with solemnity and examined the benches for the cause of the outbreak. Then taking up a position on the platform from which he could command each face, he scanned the roll thoughtfully and announced, "William Orville Hicks."

Utterly unprepared and off his guard, Hickey drew up slowly to his feet. Then a flash of inspiration came to him.

"Please, Mr. Dater," he said with simulated regret, "I chose the same piece."

Delighted, he settled down, confident that the fortunate coincidence would at least postpone his appearance.

"Indeed," said Mr. Dater with a merciless smile, "isn't that extraordinary! Well, Hicks, try and lend it a new charm."

Hickey hesitated with a calculating glance at the already snickering class. Then, forced to carry through the bravado, he climbed over the legs of his seatmates and up to the platform, made Mr. Dater a deep bow, and gave the class a quick bob of his head, accompanied by a confidential wink from that eye which happened to be out of the master's scrutiny. He glanced down, shook the wrinkles from his trousers, buttoned his coat, shot his cuffs and assumed the recognized Websterian attitude. Twice he cleared his throat while the class waited expectantly for the eloquence that did not surge. Next he frowned, took one step forward and two back, sank his hands in his trousers and searched for the missing sentences on the molding that ran around the edge of the ceiling.

"Well, Hicks, what's wrong?" said the master with difficult seriousness. "Haven't learned it?"

"Oh, yes, sir," said Hickey with dignity.

"What's the matter then?"

"Please, sir," said Hickey, with innocent frankness, "I'm afraid I'm a little embarrassed."

The class guffawed loud and long. The idea of Hickey succumbing to such an emotion was irresistible. Shrimp Davis sobbed hysterically and gratefully.

Hickey alone remained solemn, grieved and misunderstood.

"Well, Hicks," continued the master with the ghost of a smile, "embarrassment is something that you should try to overcome."

At this Turkey Reiter led Shrimp Davis out in agony.

"Very well," said Hickey with an injured look, "I'll try, sir. I'll do my best. But I don't think the conditions are favorable."

Mr. Dater commanded silence. Hickey bowed again and raised his head, cloaked in seriousness. A titter acclaimed him. He stopped and looked appealingly at the master.

"Go on, Hicks, go on," said Mr. Dater. "Do your best. At least, let us hear the words."

Another inspiration came to Hickey. "I don't think that this is quite regular, sir," he said aggressively. "I have always taken an interest in my work, and I don't see why I should be made to sacrifice a good mark."

Mr. Dater bit his lips and quieted the storm with two upraised fingers.

"Nevertheless, Hicks," he said, "I think we shall allow you to continue."

"What!" exclaimed Hickey as though loath to credit his ears. Then adding calm to dignity, he said, "Very well, sir—not prepared!"

With the limp of a martyr, he turned his back on Mr. Dater and returned to his seat, where he sat in injured dignity, disdaining to notice the grimaces of his companions.

Class over, the master summoned Hicks and bent his brows, boring him with a look of inquisitorial accusation.

"Hicks," he said, spacing his words, "I have felt, for the last two weeks, a certain lack of discipline here. Just a word to the wise, Hicks, just a word to *the wise!*"

Hickey was pained. Where was the evidence to warrant such a flat accusation? He had been arraigned on suspicion, that was all, absolutely on mere haphazard suspicion. And this was justice?

Moreover, Hickey's sensitive nature was shocked. He had always looked upon Pa Dater as an antagonist for whose sense of fair play he would have answered as for his own. And now to be accused thus with innuendo and veiled menace—then he could have faith in no master, not one in the whole faculty! And this grieved Hickey mightily as he went moodily along the halls.

Now, the code of a schoolboy's ethics is a marvelously fashioned thing—and by that each master stands or falls. To be accused of an offense of which he is innocent means nothing, for it simply demonstrates the lower caliber of the master's intelligence. But to be suspected and accused on mere suspicion of something which he has just committed—that is unpardonable, and in absolute violation of the laws of warfare, which decree that the struggle shall be one of wits, without recourse to the methods of the inquisition.

Hickey, disillusioned and shocked, went glumly down the brownstone steps of Memorial and slowly about the green circle, resisting the shouted invitations to tarry under the nourishing apple trees.

He felt in him an imperative need to strike back, to instantly break some rule of the tyranny that encompassed him. With this heroic intention he walked nonchalantly up the main street to the Jigger Shop, which no underformer may enter until after four. As he approached the forbidden haunt, suddenly the figure of Mr. Lorenzo Blackstone Tapping, the young assistant housemaster at the Dickinson, more popularly known as "Tabby," rolled up on a bicycle.

"Humph, Hicks!" Mr. Tapping said at once, with a suspicious glance at the Jigger Shop directly opposite. "How do you happen to be here out of hours?"

"Please, sir," said Hickey glibly, "I've got a nail that's sticking into my foot. I was just going to Bill Orum's to get it fixed."

"Humph!" Mr. Tapping gave him a searching look, hesitated, and mounting his wheel continued, unconvinced.

"He looked back," said Hickey wrathfully, peering through the misty windows of the cobbler's shop. Then smarting at the injury, he added, "He didn't believe me—the sneak!"

It was a second reminder of the tyranny he lived under. He

6

waited a moment, found the coast clear and flashed across to the Jigger Shop. Half drugstore, half confectioner's, the Jigger Shop was the property of Doctor Furnell, whose chief interest in life consisted in a devotion to the theory of the millennium, to the lengthy expounding of which an impoverished boy would sometimes listen in the vain hope of establishing a larger credit. On everyday occasions the shop was under the charge of "Al," a creature without heart or pity, who knew the exact financial status of each of the four hundred odd boys, even to the amount and date of his allowance. Al made no errors, his sympathies were deaf to the call, and he never (like the doctor) committed the mistake of returning too much change.

Al welcomed him with a grunt, carefully closing the little glass doors that protected the tray of éclairs and fruit cake, and leaning back, drawled, "What's the matter, Hickey? You look kind of discouraged."

"Give me a coffee jigger, with chocolate syrup and a dash of whipped cream—stick a meringue in it," said Hickey. Then as Al remained passively expectant, he drew out a coin, saying, "Oh, I've got the money!"

He ate gloomily and in silence, refusing to be drawn into conversation. Something was wrong in the scheme of things. Twice in the same hour he had been regarded with suspicion and an accusing glance—his simplest explanation discountenanced! Up to this time, he had been like a hundred other growing boys, loving mischief for mischief's sake, entering into a lark with no more definite purpose than the zest of an adventure. Of course he regarded a master as the Natural Enemy, but he had viewed him with the tolerance of an agile monkey for a wolf who does not climb. Now slowly it began to dawn upon him that there was an ethical side.

He vanished suddenly behind the counter as Mr. Tapping, returning, made directly for the Jigger Shop. Hickey, at the end of the long counter, crouching amid stationery, heard him moving suspiciously toward his hiding place. Quickly he flicked a pencil down behind the counter and vanished through the back entrance as Tapping, falling into the trap, sprang in the direction of the noise.

The adventure served two purposes: it gave Hickey the measure of the enemy, and it revealed to him where first to strike.

II

The President of the Dickinson, by virtue of the necessary authority to suppress all insubordination, was Turkey Reiter, broad of shoulder, speckled and battling of face, but the spirit of the Dickinson was Hickey. Hickey it was, lank of figure and keen of feature, bustling of gait and drawling of speech, with face as innocent as a choir boy's, who planned the revolts against the masters, organized the midnight feasts and the painting of water towers. His genius lived in the nicknames of the Egghead, Beauty Sawtelle, Morning Glory, Red Dog, Wash Simmons and the Coffee Cooler, which he had bestowed on his comrades with unfailing felicity.

Great was Hickey, and Macnooder was his prophet. Doc Macnooder roomed just across the hall. He was a sort of genius of all trades. He played quarter on the eleven and ran the half-mile close to the two-minute mark. He was the mainstay of Banjo, Mandolin and Glee Clubs. He played the organ in chapel and had composed the famous Hamill House March in memory of his requested departure from that abode. He organized the school dramatic club. He was secretary and treasurer of his class and of every organization to which he belonged. He received a commission from a dozen firms to sell to his likenesses, stationery, athletic goods, choice sets of books, fin de siècle neckties, fancy waistcoats, fountain pens and safety razors, all of which articles, if report is to be credited, he sold with ease and eloquence at ten per cent above the retail price. His room was a combination of a sorcerer's den and junk shop. At one corner a row of shelves held a villainous array of ill-smelling black, green and blue bottles, with which he was prepared to instantly cure anything from lockjaw to snake bite.

The full measure of Macnooder's activities was never known. Turkey Reiter had even surprised him drawing up a will for Bill Orum, the cobbler, to whom he had just sold a cure for rheumatism.

It was to Macnooder that Hickey opened his heart and his need of vengeance. It cannot be said that the ethical side of the struggle appealed to Macnooder, who had small predilection for philosophy and none at all for the moral sciences, but the love of mischief was strong. The encounter with Tapping in the morning had suggested

8

a victim near at hand and conveniently inexperienced.

Mr. Tapping, in advance of young Mr. Baldwin (of whom it shall be related), had arrived at Lawrenceville the previous year with latter-day theories on the education of boys. As luck would have it, Mr. Rogers, the housemaster, would be absent that evening at a little dinner of old classmates in Princeton, leaving the entire conduct of the Dickinson in the hands of his assistant. In passing, it must be noted that between the two masters there was little sympathy. Mr. Rogers had lived too long in the lair of the boy to be at all impressed with the new ideas on education that Mr. Tapping and later Mr. Baldwin advocated in the blissful state of their ignorance.

At three o'clock, Tapping departed to convey to a class of impatient boys, decked out in athletic costumes with baseballs stuffed in their pockets and tennis rackets waiting at their sides, the interesting shades of distinction in that exciting study, Greek prose composition. Then Hickey gleefully, while Macnooder guarded the stairs, entered the study, and with a screwdriver loosened the screw which held the inner doorknob, to the extent that it could later be easily removed with the fingers.

At half past seven o'clock, when study hour had begun, Hickey entered the sanctum ostensibly for advice on a perplexing problem in advanced algebra.

Mr. Tapping did not like Hickey. He regarded him with suspicion, with an instinctive recognition of an enemy. Also he was engaged in the difficult expression of a certain letter which, at that time, presented more difficulties than the binomial theorem. So he inquired with short cordiality, concealing the written page under a blotter:

"Well, Hicks, what is it?"

"Please, Mr. Tapping," said Hickey, who had perceived the move with malignant delight, "I wish you'd look at this problem—it won't work out." He added (shades of a thousand boys!), "I think there must be some mistake in the book."

Now, the chief miseries of a young assistant master center about the study hours—when theory demands that he should be ready to advise and instruct the discouraged boyish mind on any subject figuring in the curriculum, whatever be his preference or his prejudice. Mr. Tapping, who romped over the Greek and Latin page, had an hereditary weakness in the mathematics, a failing that the boys had discovered and instantly turned to their profit. He took the book, glanced at the problem and began to jot down a line of figures. Hickey, meanwhile, with his back to the door, brazenly extracted the loosened screw.

Finally, Mr. Tapping, becoming hopelessly entangled, raised his head and said with a disdainful smile, "Hicks, I think you had better put a little work on this—just a little work!"

"Mr. Tapping, I don't understand it," said Hickey, adding to himself, "Old Tabby is up a tree!"

"Nonsense—perfectly easy, perfectly simple," said Tapping, returning the book with a gesture of dismissal, "requires a little application, Hicks, just a little application—that's all."

Hickey, putting on his most injured look, bowed to injustice and departed at the moment that Turkey Reiter entered, seeking assistance in French. Upon his tracks, without an interval, succeeded Macnooder with a German composition, Hungry Smeed to discuss history, the Egghead on a question of spelling, and Beauty Sawtelle in thirst for information about the Middle Ages. Finally, Mr. Tapping's patience, according to Macnooder's prophetic calculation, burst on a question of biblical interpretation, and announcing wrathfully that he could no longer be disturbed, he ushered out the last tormentor and shut the door with violence.

Presently Hickey stole up on tiptoe and fastening a noose over the knob, gave a signal. The string, pulled by a dozen equally responsible hands, carried away the knob, which fell with a tiny crash and spun in crazy circles on the floor. The fall of the inner useless knob was heard on the inside of the door and the exclamation that burst from the startled master. The tyrant was caged—the house was at their pleasure!

Mr. Tapping committed the initial mistake of knocking twice imperiously on the door and commanding, "Open at once."

Two knocks answered him. Then he struck three violent blows and three violent echoes returned, while a bunch of wriggling, chuckling boys clustered at every crack of the door, listening with strained ears for the muffled roars that came from within.

While one group began a game of leapfrog, another, under the guidance of Hickey, descended into the housemaster's quarters and proceeded to attend to the rearrangement of the various rooms.

Working beaverlike with whispered cautions, they rapidly exchanged the furniture of the parlor with the dining room, grouping each transformed room exactly as the original had been.

Then they placed the six-foot water-cooler directly in front of the entrance with a tin pan balanced, to give the alarm, and shaking with silent expectant laughter extinguished all lights, undressed and returned to the corridors, white, shadowy forms, to wait developments. Meanwhile, the caged assistant master continued to pound upon the door with a fury that betokened a state of approaching hysteria.

At half past ten, suddenly the tin pan crashed horribly on the floor. A second later every boy was sleeping loudly in his bed. Astonished at such a reception, Mr. Rogers groped into the darkness and fell against the water-cooler, which in his excitement he embraced and carried over with him to the floor. Recovering himself, he lighted the gas and perceived the transformed parlor and dining room. Then he started for the assistant housemaster's rooms, with long, angry bounds, saying incoherent, expressive things to himself.

The ordeal that young Mr. Tapping faced from his superior, one hour later when the door had been opened, was distinctly unpleasant, and was not made the more agreeable from the fact that every rebuke resounded through the house and carried joy and comfort to the listening boys.

The housemaster would hear no explanation; in fact, explanations were about the last thing he wanted. He desired to express his disgust, his indignation and his rage, and he did so magnificently.

"May I say one word, sir?" said Mr. Tapping in a lull.

"Quite unnecessary, Mr. Tapping," cut in the still angry master. "I don't wish any explanations. Such a thing as this has never happened in the history of this institution. That's all I wish to know. You forget that you are not left in charge of a young ladies' seminary."

"Very well, sir," said the mortified Mr. Tapping. "May I ask what you intend to do about this act of insubordination?"

"That is what I intend to ask *you*, sir," replied his superior. "Good night."

The next day after luncheon, Mr. Tapping summoned the house to his study and addressed them as follows:

11

"Young gentlemen of the Dickinson House, I don't think you have any doubt as to why I have called you here. A very serious breach of discipline has taken place—one that cannot be overlooked. The sooner we meet the situation in the right spirit, gravely, with seriousness, the sooner will we meet each other in that spirit of harmony and friendly understanding that should exist between pupil and master. I am willing to make some allowance for the spirit of mischief, but none for an exhibition of untruthfulness. I warn you that I know, that I *know* who were the ringleaders in last night's outrage."

Here he stopped and glanced in succession at each individual boy. Then suddenly turning, he said, "Hicks, were you concerned in this?"

"Mr. Tapping," said Hickey, with the air of a martyr, "I refuse to answer."

"On what ground?"

"On the ground that I will not furnish any clue whatsoever."

"I shall deal with your case later."

"Very well, sir."

"Macnooder," continued Mr. Tapping, "what do you know about this?"

"I refuse to answer, sir."

At each demand, the same refusal.

Tapping, repulsed in his first attempt, hesitated and reflected. Above all things he did not wish to perpetuate last night's humiliation, and to continue the combat meant an accusation *en bloc* against the Dickinson House before the headmaster.

"Hicks, Macnooder and Reiter, wait here," he said suddenly; "the rest may go."

He walked up and down before the three a moment, and then said, "Reiter, you may go; you, too, Macnooder."

Hickey, thus deprived of all support, remained defiant.

"May I ask," he said indignantly, "why I am picked out?"

"Hicks," said Mr. Tapping sternly, without replying to the question, "I know pretty well who was the ringleader in this, and other things that have been going on in the past. I warn you, my boy, I shall keep my eye on you from this time forth. That's all I want to say to you. Look out for yourself!"

Hickey could hardly restrain the tears. He went out with deadly wrath boiling in his heart. The idea of signaling him out from the whole house in that way! So then every hand was against him; he had no security; he was marked for suspicion, his downfall determined upon!

For one brief moment his spirit, the spirit of indomitable, battling boyhood, failed him, and he felt the gray impossibility of contending against tyrants. But only a moment, and then with a return of the old fighting spirit he suddenly conceived the idea of single-handedly defying the whole organized, hereditary and entrenched tyranny that sought to crush him, of matching his wits against the hydra despotism, perhaps going down gloriously like Spartacus, for the cause, but leaving behind a name that should roll down the generations of future boys.

THE GREAT PANCAKE RECORD

LITTLE SMEED stood apart, in the obscure shelter of the station, waiting to take his place on the stage which would carry him to the great new boarding school. He was frail and undersized, with a long, pointed nose and vacant eyes that stupidly assisted the wide mouth to make up a famished face. The scarred bag in his hand hung from one clasp, the premature trousers were at half-mast, while pink polka dots blazed from the cuffs of his nervous sleeves.

By the wheels of the stage Fire Crackers Glendenning and Jock Hasbrouck, veterans of the Kennedy House, sporting the varsity initials on their sweaters and caps, were busily engaged in cross-examining the new boys who clambered timidly to their places on top. Presently, Fire Crackers, perceiving Smeed, hailed him.

"Hello, over there—what's your name?"

"Smeed, sir."

"Smeed what?"

"Johnnie Smeed."

The questioner looked him over with disfavor and said aggressively:

"You're not for the Kennedy?"

"No, sir."

"What house?"

"The Dickinson, sir."

"The Dickinson, eh? That's a good one," said Fire Crackers, with a laugh, and, turning to his companion, he added, "Say, Jock, won't Hickey and the old Turkey be wild when they get this one?"

Little Smeed, uncomprehending of the judgment that had been passed, stowed his bag inside and clambered up to a place on the top. Jimmy, at the reins, gave a warning shout. The horses, stirred by the whip, churned obediently through the sideways of Trenton.

Lounging on the stage were half a dozen newcomers, six well-assorted types, from the well-groomed stripling of the city to the aggressive, big-limbed animal from the West, all profoundly under the sway of the two old boys who sat on the box with Jimmy and rattled on with quiet superiority. The coach left the outskirts of the city and rolled into the white highway that leads to Lawrenceville. The known world departed for Smeed. He gazed fearfully ahead, waiting the first glimpse of the new continent.

Suddenly Fire Crackers turned and, scanning the embarrassed group, singled out the strong Westerner with an approving glance.

"You're for the Kennedy?"

The boy, stirring uneasily, blurted out, "Yes, sir."

"What's your name?"

"Tom Walsh."

"How old are you?"

"Eighteen."

"What do you weigh?"

"One hundred and seventy."

"Stripped?"

"What? Oh, no, sir—regular way."

"You've played a good deal of football?"

"Yes, sir."

Hasbrouck took up the questioning with a critical appreciation.

"What position?"

"Guard and tackle."

"You know Bill Stevens?"

"Yes, sir."

"He spoke about you; said you played on the Military Academy. You'll try for the varsity?"

"I guess so."

Hasbrouck turned to Fire Crackers in solemn conclave.

"He ought to stand up against Turkey if he knows anything about the game. If we get a good end we ought to give that Dickinson crowd the fight of their lives."

"There's a fellow came from Montclair they say is pretty good," Fire Crackers said, with solicitous gravity. "The line'll be all right if we can get some good halves. That's where the Dickinson has it on us."

Smeed listened in awe to the two statesmen studying out the chances of the Kennedy eleven for the house championship, realizing suddenly that there were new and sacred purposes about his new life of which he had no conception. Then, absorbed by the fantasy of the trip and the strange unfolding world into which he was jogging, he forgot the lords of the Kennedy, forgot his fellows in ignorance, forgot that he didn't play football and was only a stripling, forgot everything but the fascination of the moment when the great school would rise out of the distance and fix itself indelibly in his memory.

"There's the water tower," said Jimmy, extending the whip; "you'll see the school from the top of the hill."

Little Smeed craned forward with a sudden thumping of his heart. In the distance, a mile away, a cluster of brick and tile sprang out of the green, like a herd of red deer surprised in the forest. Groups of boys began to show on the roadside. Strange greetings were flung back and forth.

"Hello-oo, Fire Crackers!"

"How-de-do, Saphead!"

"Oh, there, Jock Hasbrouck!"

"Oh, you Morning Glory!"

"Oh, you Kennedys, we're going to lick you!"

"Yes you are, Dickinson!"

16

The coach passed down the shaded vault of the village street, turned into the campus, passed the ivy-clad house of the head-master and rolled around a circle of well-trimmed lawn, past the long, low Upper House where the Fourth Form gazed at them in senior superiority; past the great brown masses of Memorial Hall and the pointed chapel, around to where the houses were ranged in red, extended bodies. Little Smeed felt an abject sinking of the heart at this sudden exposure to the thousand eyes fastened upon him from the wide esplanade of the Upper, from the steps of Memorial, from house, windows and stoops, from the shade of apple trees and the glistening road.

All at once the stage stopped and Jimmy cried, "Dickinson!"

At one end of the red-brick building, overrun with cool vines, a group of boys were lolling in flannels and light jerseys. A chorus went up.

"Hello, Fire Crackers!"

"Hello, Jock!"

"Hello, you Hickey boy!"

"Hello, Turkey; see what we've brought you!"

Smeed dropped to the ground amid a sudden hush.

"Fare," said Jimmy aggressively.

Smeed dug into his pocket and tendered the necessary coin. The coach squeaked away, while from the top Fire Crackers' exulting voice returned in insolent exultation:

"Hard luck, Dickinson! Hard luck, you, old Hickey!"

Little Smeed, his hat askew, his collar rolled up, his bag at his feet, stood in the road, alone in the world, miserable and thoroughly frightened. One path led to the silent, hostile group on the steps, another went in safety to the master's entrance. He picked up his bag hastily.

"Hello, you—over there!"

Smeed understood it was a command. He turned submissively and approached with embarrassed steps. Face to face with these superior beings, tanned and muscular, stretched in Olympian attitudes, he realized all at once the hopelessness of his ever daring to associate with such demigods. Still he stood, shifting from foot to foot, eyeing the steps, waiting for the solemn ordeal of examination and classification to be over.

"Well, Hungry—what's your name?"

Smeed comprehended that the future was decided, and that to the grave he would go down as "Hungry" Smeed. With a sigh of relief he answered, "Smeed—John Smeed."

"Sir!"

"Sir."

"How old?"

"Fifteen."

"Sir!!"

"Sir."

"What do you weigh?"

"One hundred and six—sir!"

A grim silence succeeded this depressing information. Then someone in the back, as a mere matter of form, asked, "Never played football?"

"No, sir."

"Baseball?"

"No, sir."

"Anything on the track?"

"No, sir."

"Sing?"

"No, sir," said Smeed, humbly.

"Do anything at all?"

Little Smeed glanced at the eaves where the swallows were swaying and then down at the soft couch of green at his feet and answered faintly, "No, sir—I'm afraid not."

Another silence came, then someone said, in a voice of deepest conviction: "A dead loss!"

Smeed went sadly into the house.

At the door he lingered long enough to hear the chorus burst out:

"A fine football team we'll have!"

"It's a put-up job!"

"They don't want us to win the championship again—that's it!"

"I say, we ought to kick."

Then, after a little, the same deep voice:

"A dead loss!"

With each succeeding week Hungry Smeed comprehended more fully the enormity of his offense in doing nothing and weighing one hundred and six pounds. He saw the new boys arrive, pass through the fire of christening, give respectable weights and go forth to the gridiron to be whipped into shape by Turkey and the Butcher, who played on the school eleven. Smeed humbly and thankfully went down each afternoon to the practice, carrying the sweaters and shin-guards, like the grateful little beast of burden that he was. He watched his juniors, Spider and Red Dog, rolling in the mud or flung gloriously under an avalanche of bodies; but then, they weighed over one hundred and thirty, while he was still at one hundred and six—a dead loss! The fever of house loyalty invaded him; he even came to look with resentment on the Faculty and to repeat secretly to himself that they never would have unloaded him on the Dickinson if they hadn't been willing to stoop to any methods to prevent the House again securing the championship.

The fact that the Dickinson, in an extraordinary manner, finally won by the closest of margins, consoled Smeed but a little while. There were no more sweaters to carry, or pails of barley water to fetch, or guard to be mounted on the old rail fence, to make certain that the spies from the Davis and Kennedy did not surprise the secret plays which Hickey and Slugger Jones had craftily evolved.

With the long winter months he felt more keenly his obscurity and the hopelessness of ever leaving a mark on the great desert of school life that would bring honor to the Dickinson. He resented even the lack of the mild hazing the other boys received—he was too insignificant to be so honored. He was only a "dead loss," good for nothing but to squeeze through his recitations, to sleep enormously, and to eat like a glutton with a hunger that could never be satisfied, little suspecting the future that lay in this famine of his stomach.

For it was written in the inscrutable fates that Hungry Smeed should leave a name that would go down imperishably to decades of schoolboys, when Dibbles' touchdown against Princeton and Kafer's home run should be only tinkling sounds. So it happened, and the agent of this divine destiny was Hickey.

It so happened that examinations being still in the threatening distance, Hickey's fertile brain was unoccupied with methods of facilitating his scholarly progress by homely inventions that allowed formulas and dates to be concealed in the palm and disap-

pear obligingly up the sleeve on the approach of the Natural
Enemy. Moreover, Hickey and Hickey's friends were in straitened
circumstances, with all credit gone at the Jigger Shop, and the appetite for jiggers in an acute stage of deprivation.

In this keenly sensitive, famished state of his imagination,
Hickey suddenly became aware of a fact fraught with possibilities.
Hungry Smeed had an appetite distinguished and remarkable even
in that company of aching voids.

No sooner had this pregnant idea become his property than
Hickey confided his hopes to Doc Macnooder, his chum and partner in plans that were dark and mysterious. Macnooder saw in a
flash the glorious and lucrative possibilities. A very short series of
tests sufficed to convince the twain that in little Smeed they had a
phenomenon who needed only to be properly developed to pass
into history.

Accordingly, on a certain muddy morning in March, Hickey and
Doc Macnooder, with Smeed in tow, stole into the Jigger Shop at
an hour in defiance of regulations and fraught with delightful risks
of detection.

Al, the watchdog of the Jigger, was tilted back, near a farther
window, the parted tow hair falling doglike over his eyes, absorbed
in the reading of Spenser's *Faerie Queene,* an abnormal taste which
made him absolutely incomprehensible to the boyish mind. At the
sound of the stolen entrance, Al put down the volume and started
mechanically to rise. Then, recognizing his visitors, he returned to
his chair, saying wearily, "Nothing doing, Hickey."

"Guess again," said Hickey, cheerily. "We're not asking you to
hang us up this time, Al."

"You haven't got any money," said Al, the recorder of allowances; "not unless you stole it."

"Al, we don't come to take your hard-earned money, but to do
you good," put in Macnooder impudently. "We're bringing you a
little sporting proposition."

"Have you come to pay up that account of yours?" said Al. "If
not, run along, you Macnooder. Don't waste my time with your
wildcat schemes."

"Al, this is a sporting proposition," took up Hickey.

"Has *he* any money?" said Al, who suddenly remembered that
Smeed was not yet under suspicion.

"See here, Al," said Macnooder, "we'll back Smeed to eat the jiggers against you—for the crowd!"

"Where's your money?"

"Here," said Hickey; "this goes up if we lose." He produced a gold watch of Smeed's, and was about to tender it when he withdrew it with a sudden caution. "On the condition, if we win I get it back and you won't hold it up against my account."

"All right. Let's see it."

The watch was given to Al, who looked it over, grunted in approval, and then looked at little Smeed.

"Now, Al," said Macnooder softly, "give us a gambling chance. He's only a runt."

Al considered and Al was wise. The proposition came often and he had never lost. A jigger is unlike any other ice cream. It is dipped from the creamy tin by a cone-shaped scoop called a jigger, which gives it an unusual and peculiar flavor. Since those days the original jigger has been contaminated and made ridiculous by offensive alliances with upstart syrups, meringues and macaroons with absurd titles, but then the boy went to the simple jigger as the sturdy Roman went to the cold waters of the Tiber. A double jigger fills a large soda glass when ten cents has been laid on the counter, and two such glasses quench all desire in the normal appetite.

"If he can eat twelve double jiggers," Al said slowly, "I'll set them up and the jiggers for youse. Otherwise, I'll hold the watch."

At this there was a protest from the backers of the champion, with the result that the limit was reduced to ten.

"Is it a go?" Al said, turning to Smeed, who had waited modestly in the background.

"Sure," he answered, with calm certainty.

"You've got nerve, you have," said Al, with a scornful smile, scooping up the first jiggers and shoving the glass to him. "Ten doubles is the record in these parts, young fellow!"

Then little Smeed, methodically, and without apparent pain, ate the ten doubles.

Conover's was not in the catalogue that anxious parents study, but then catalogues are like epitaphs in a cemetery. Next to the Jigger Shop, Conover's was quite the most important institution in the school. In a little white Colonial cottage, Conover, veteran of the late war, and Mrs. Conover, still in active service, supplied pancakes and maple syrup on a cash basis, two dollars credit to second-year boys in good repute. Conover's, too, had its traditions. Twenty-six pancakes, large and thick, in one continuous sitting, was the record, five years old, standing to the credit of Guzzler Wilkins, which succeeding classes had attacked in vain. Wily Conover, to stimulate such profitable tests, had solemnly pledged himself to the delivery of free pancakes to all comers during that day on which any boy, at one continuous sitting, unaided, should succeed in swallowing the awful number of thirty-two. Conover was not considered a prodigal.

This deed of heroic accomplishment and public benefaction was the true goal of Hickey's planning. The test of the Jigger Shop was but a preliminary trying out. With medical caution, Doc Macnooder refused to permit Smeed to go beyond the ten doubles, holding very wisely that the jigger record could wait for a further day. The amazed Al was sworn to secrecy.

It was Wednesday, and the following Saturday was decided upon for the supreme test at Conover's. Smeed at once was subjected to a graduated system of starvation. Thursday he was hungry, but Friday he was so ravenous that a watch was instituted on all his movements.

The next morning the Dickinson House, let into the secret, accompanied Smeed to Conover's. If there was even a possibility of free pancakes, the House intended to be satisfied before the deluge broke.

Great was the astonishment at Conover's at the arrival of the procession.

"Mr. Conover," said Hickey, in the quality of manager, "we're going after that pancake record."

"Mr. Wilkins' record?" said Conover, seeking vainly the champion in the crowd.

"No—after that record of *yours*," answered Hickey. "Thirty-two pancakes—we're here to get free pancakes today—that's what we're here for."

"So, boys, so," said Conover, smiling pleasantly; "and you want to begin now?"

"Right off the bat."

"Well, where is he?"

Little Smeed, famished to the point of tears, was thrust forward. Conover, who was expecting something on the lines of a buffalo, smiled confidently.

"So, boys, so," he said, leading the way with alacrity. "I guess we're ready, too."

"Thirty-two pancakes, Conover—and we get 'em free!"

"That's right," answered Conover, secure in his knowledge of boyish capacity. "If that little boy there can eat thirty-two, I'll make them all day free to the school. That's what I said, and what I say goes—and that's what I say now."

Hickey and Doc Macnooder whispered the last instructions in Smeed's ear.

"Cut out the syrup."

"Loosen your belt."

"Eat slowly."

In a low room, with the white rafters impending over his head, beside a basement window flanked with geraniums, little Smeed sat down to battle for the honor of the Dickinson and the record of the school. Directly under his eyes, carved on the wooden table, a name challenged him, standing out of the numerous initials— Guzzzler Wilkins.

"I'll keep count," said Hickey. "Macnooder and Turkey, watch the pancakes."

"Regulation size, Conover," cried that cautious Red Dog, "no doubling now. All fair and aboveboard."

"All right, Hickey, all right," said Conover, leering wickedly from the door. "If that little grasshopper can do it, you get the cakes."

"Now, Hungry," said Turkey, clapping Smeed on the shoulder. "Here is where you get your chance. Remember, kid, old sport, it's for the Dickinson."

Smeed heard in ecstasy; it was just the way Turkey talked to the eleven on the eve of a match. He nodded his head with a grim little shake and smiled nervously at the thirty-odd Dickinsonians who formed around him a pit of expectant and hungry boyhood from the floor to the ceiling.

"All ready!" sang out Turkey, from the doorway.

"Six pancakes!"

"Six it is," replied Hickey, chalking up a monster 6 on the slate that swung from the rafters. The pancakes placed before the ravenous Smeed vanished like snowflakes on a July lawn.

A cheer went up, mingled with cries of caution.

"Not so fast."

"Take your time."

"Don't let them be too hot."

"Not too hot, Hickey!"

Macnooder was instructed to watch carefully over the temperature as well as the dimensions.

"Ready again," came the cry.

"Ready—how many?"

"Six more."

"Six it is," said Hickey, adding a second figure to the score. "Six and six are twelve."

The second batch went the way of the first.

"Why, that boy is starving," said Conover, opening his eyes.

"Sure he is," said Hickey. "He's eating 'way back in last week— he hasn't had a thing for ten days."

"Six more," cried Macnooder.

"Six it is," answered Hickey. "Six and twelve is eighteen."

"Eat them one at a time, Hungry."

"No, let him alone."

"He knows best."

"Not too fast, Hungry, not too fast."

"Eighteen for Hungry, eighteen. Hurrah!"

"Thirty-two is a long ways to go," said Conover, gazing apprehensively at the little David who had come so impudently into his domain. "Fourteen pancakes is an awful lot."

"Shut up, Conover."

"No trying to influence him there."

"Don't listen to him, Hungry."

"He's only trying to get you nervous."

"Fourteen more, Hungry—fourteen more."

"Ready again," sang out Macnooder.

"Ready here."

"Three pancakes."

"Three it is," responded Hickey. "Eighteen and three is twenty-one."

24

But a storm of protest arose.

"Here, that's not fair!"

"I say, Hickey, don't let them do that."

"I say, Hickey, it's twice as hard that way."

"Oh, go on."

"Sure it is."

"Of course it is."

"Don't you know that you can't drink a glass of beer if you take it with a teaspoon?"

"That's right, Red Dog's right! Six at a time."

"Six at a time!"

A hurried consultation was now held and the reasoning approved. Macnooder was charged with the responsibility of seeing to the number as well as the temperature and dimensions.

Meanwhile Smeed had eaten the pancakes.

"Coming again!"

"All ready here."

"Six pancakes!"

"Six," said Hickey. "Twenty-one and six is twenty-seven."

"That'll beat Guzzler Wilkins."

"So it will."

"Five more makes thirty-two."

"Easy, Hungry, easy."

"Hungry's done it; he's done it."

"Twenty-seven and the record!"

"Hurrah!"

At this point Smeed looked about anxiously.

"It's pretty dry," he said, speaking for the first time.

Instantly there was a panic. Smeed was reaching his limit—a groan went up.

"Oh, Hungry."

"Only five more."

"Give him some water."

"Water, you loon; do you want to end him?"

"Why?"

"Water'll swell up the pancakes, crazy."

"No water, no water."

Hickey approached his man with anxiety.

"What is it, Hungry? Anything wrong?" he said tenderly.

"No, only it's a little dry," said Smeed, unmoved. "I'm all right, but I'd like just a drop of syrup now."

The syrup was discussed, approved and voted.

"You're sure you're all right?" said Hickey.

"Oh, yes."

Conover, in the last ditch, said carefully, "I don't want no fits around here."

A cry of protest greeted him.

"Well, son, the boy can't stand much more. That's just like the Guzzler. He was taken short and we had to work over him for an hour."

"Conover, shut up!"

"Conover, you're beaten."

"Conover, that's an old game."

"Get out."

"Shut up."

"Fair play."

"Fair play! Fair play!"

A new interruption came from the kitchen. Macnooder claimed that Mrs. Conover was doubling the size of the cakes. The dish was brought. There was no doubt about it. The cakes were swollen. Pandemonium broke loose. Conover capitulated, the cakes were rejected.

"Don't be fazed by that," said Hickey, warningly to Smeed.

"I'm not," said Smeed.

"All ready," came Macnooder's cry.

"Ready here."

"Six pancakes!"

"Regulation size?"

"Regulation."

"Six it is," said Hickey, at the slate. "Six and twenty-seven is thirty-three."

"Wait a moment," sang out the Butcher. "He has only to eat thirty-two."

"That's so—take one off."

"Give him five, Hickey—five only."

"If Hungry says he can eat six," said Hickey, firmly, glancing at his protégé, "he can. We're out for big things. Can you do it, Hungry?"

And Smeed, fired with the heroism of the moment, answered in disdainful simplicity, "Sure!"

A cheer that brought two Davis House boys running in greeted the disappearance of the thirty-third. Then everything was forgotten in the amazement of the deed.

"Please, I'd like to go on," said Smeed.

"Oh, Hungry, can you do it?"

"Really?"

"You're goin' on?"

"Holy cats!"

"How'll you take them?" said Hickey, anxiously.

"I'll try another six," said Smeed, thoughtfully, "and then we'll see."

Conover, vanquished and convinced, no longer sought to intimidate him with horrid suggestions.

"Mr. Smeed," he said, giving him his hand in admiration, "you go ahead; you make a great record."

"Six more," cried Macnooder.

"Six it is," said Hickey, in an awed voice; "six and thirty-three makes thirty-nine!"

Mrs. Conover and Macnooder, no longer antagonists, came in from the kitchen to watch the great spectacle. Little Smeed alone, calm and unconscious, with the light of a great ambition on his forehead, ate steadily, without vacillation.

"Gee, what a stride!"

"By Jiminy, where does he put it?" said Conover, staring helplessly.

"Holy cats!"

"Thirty-nine—thirty-nine pancakes—gee!!!"

"Hungry," said Hickey, entreatingly, "do you think you could eat another—make it an even forty?"

"Three more," said Smeed, pounding the table with a new authority. This time no voice rose in remonstrance. The clouds had rolled away. They were in the presence of a master.

"Pancakes coming."

"Bring them in!"

"Three more."

"Three it is," said Hickey, faintly. "Thirty-nine and three makes forty-two—forty-two. Gee!"

In profound silence the three pancakes passed regularly from the plate down the throat of little Smeed. Forty-two pancakes!

"Three more," said Smeed.

Doc Macnooder rushed in hysterically.

"Hungry, go the limit—the limit! If anything happens I'll bleed you."

"Shut up, Doc!"

"Get out, you wild man."

Macnooder was sent ignominiously back into the kitchen, with the curses of the Dickinson, and Smeed assured of their unfaltering protection.

"Three more," came the cry from the chastened Macnooder.

"Three it is," said Hickey. "Forty-two and three makes—forty-five."

"Holy cats!"

Still little Smeed, without appreciable abatement of hunger, continued to eat. A sense of impending calamity and alarm began to spread. Forty-five pancakes, and still eating! It might turn into a tragedy.

"Say, bub—say, now," said Hickey, gazing anxiously down into the pointed face, "you've done enough—don't get rash."

"I'll stop when it's time," said Smeed. "Bring 'em on now, one at a time."

"Forty-six, forty-seven, forty-eight, forty-nine!"

Suddenly, at the moment when they expected him to go on forever, little Smeed stopped, gazed at his plate, then at the fiftieth pancake, and said:

"That's all."

Forty-nine pancakes! Then, and only then, did they return to a realization of what had happened. They cheered Smeed, they sang his praises, they cheered again, and then, pounding the table, they cried, in a mighty chorus, "We want pancakes!"

"Bring us pancakes!"

"Pancakes, pancakes, we want pancakes!"

Twenty minutes later, Red Dog and the Egghead, fed to bursting, rolled out of Conover's, spreading the uproarious news.

"Free pancakes! Free pancakes!"

The nearest houses, the Davis and the Rouse, heard and came with a rush.

Red Dog and the Egghead staggered down into the village and over to the circle of houses, throwing out their arms like returning bacchanalians.

"Free pancakes!"

"Hungry Smeed's broken the record!"

"Pancakes at Conover's—free pancakes!"

The word jumped from house to house, the campus was emptied in a trice. The road became choked with the hungry stream that struggled, fought, laughed and shouted as it stormed to Conover's.

"Free pancakes! Free pancakes!"

"Hurrah for Smeed!"

"Hurrah for Hungry Smeed!!"

THE RUN THAT TURNED THE GAME

IN THIS same fall of Hungry Smeed's arrival, when the Dickinson, the Cleve, the Woodhull, the Griswold, the Hamill, the Kennedy, and the Davis, were each separately convinced that the faculty was seeking to prevent its winning the football championship by filling the house with boys under weight and under size, there arrived at the Kennedy the now-celebrated "Piggy" Moore. He did not come on the top of the stage as new boys should, but drove up in a carriage, in the company of an aunt, who departed with misgivings after kissing him in the full sight of the campus.

For she had raised Piggy on the bottle of gentle manners and rocked him in the cradle of innocent and edifying ambitions until the manly age of sixteen. His hands were soft and manicured, he entered a room with grace and left it with distinction. His body was swathed in plumpness. His face was chubby and well nourished, with fat, indolent eyes and wide nostrils. He was five feet eight and weighed a hundred and fifty.

Without embarrassment or anxiety he went to his room, removed his coat, folded it neatly on a chair, turned up his sleeves and proceeded to spread on his bureau a toilet set of chaste silver. He was neatly arranging eight pairs of shoes, carefully treed, when his name was shouted from the hall.

"Oh, Moore! Hello there!"

He emerged hurriedly to find Captain Hasbrouck in football togs, eying him critically and without enthusiasm.

"Football practice, Moore!"

"It will take me an hour or so, I'm afraid," said Moore, smiling politely. "That is, to put my things in order and get thoroughly unpacked."

"Sir!"

Piggy was surprised. The voice was harsh, rude and ominous, and the figure of Hasbrouck quite obscured the doorway.

"Yes, sir!" he said hastily. "I'll be right down, sir."

"Have you got any football togs?" said Hasbrouck, looking at the toilet set.

"No, sir."

"A sweater?"

"No, sir."

"Well, we only want a little light practice. Get your things tonight in the village. On the jump now!"

Moore hastily trooped down with the others and followed across the long green stretches in the tingly September air, a little apprehensive of what the term "light practice" might mean. The veterans in scarred suits and rent jerseys marched gloriously in front, gamboling and romping with the ball, shouting out salutations to parties who swarmed over the campus from other houses on the way to the playgrounds. The newcomers in hastily patched-up costumes, incongruous and absurd, clustered together, talking in broken, forced monosyllables. Suddenly the advance halted and a shout went up.

"Here come the Dickinsons! Gee, look at the material they've got!"

Piggy, uncomprehending, beheld a group of thirty-odd boys swinging toward them, shouting and laughing as they came. From the advancing crowd came a challenging yell.

"We're going to wipe the earth up with you, Kennedy."

"Goodbye, Kennedy. Goodbye!"

From the Kennedys the challenge was flung back:

"We've got you where we want you."

"You'll be easy, Dickinson."

"We'll attend to the championship this year."

The two crowds halted while the leaders inspected their antagonists, sizing up the new material. Moore, in a tailor-cut suit of English tweed, a stiff collar and a derby hat, felt for the first time a little out of the picture when Hickey of the enemy paused in front of him and derisively asked, "Where did that come from?"

"Oh, that's been specially raised for us."

"He has? In a hothouse, yes! What'll *he* play?"

"He'll play all over the field. *He's* a regular demon!"

"Huh!"

"We'll twist your tail, Dickinson."

"We'll skin you, Kennedy."

"Yes, you will!"

"Yes, we will!"

The groups departed, each vowing that it was disheartening the way the faculty had favored the other.

On the playground Jock Hasbrouck and Fire Crackers Glendenning held a consultation while the old boys frolicked with the ball and the new arrivals huddled in an embarrassed group.

The new material was excellent, beyond expectation, but no joy appeared on the face of the captain.

"How in the deuce are we ever going to beat the Dickinsons with such a bunch as that?" he said, with a shake of his head. "What do we need anyhow?"

"Both ends, a tackle and the halves," said Fire Crackers gloomily.

"Well, we've got to do our best, that's all," said the captain, with a glance that made every newcomer miserable. "Let's see how we can line up. Fatty Harris, get in at center there. Keg, you'll have to go in at right guard. Buffalo, you stay at left."

The old boys, brawny and hard, formed into a center trio.

"If you take left tackle we'd better put Walsh in at right to face Turkey," said Fire Crackers. "Legs Brockett there plays end, he says."

Walsh and Brockett, eyes to the ground, took their places in the line at a nod from Jock.

"Duke Wilson, full; Fire Crackers, quarter. What then?" he said slowly to his counsel. "Suppose we give Pebbles Stone a chance at half this year?"

"What do you weigh, Pebbles?" asked Fire Crackers.

"One hundred and forty-five," brazenly answered the lithe but rather frail person addressed.

"Honest?"

"Honest to God, Jock."

"Stripped?"

"No—o-o. With ten pounds in me pockets."

"Well, get in there, you old liar; you've got the sand all right."

Pebbles, with a delighted whoop, sprang into line. Then Fire Crackers and Jock stopped before a trim, cleanly built boy with a suit that looked worthy.

"You're Francis, ain't you?"

"Yes, sir."

"Played half?"

"Yes, sir."

"What do you weigh?"

"One hundred and fifty, stripped, sir."

"Take right half."

Francis, quickly, but with an air of ease, took his place. Only one position remained vacant, left end. Hasbrouck glanced over the squad of slight, overgrown boys, and his eye by a process of elimination, rested on Moore, standing stiff and immaculate.

"Moore, get in to right end."

"Me?" said Moore in horror.

"Sir!"

"Sir."

"Quick!"

"But I—I've never played, sir!"

"Get into line!"

Piggy went sullenly, indignant and cherishing resistance. Hasbrouck gave a professionally pessimistic glance at the whole and said, "Well, fellows, we'll only take a little light practice today. Try a few starts."

The candidates in threes and fours crouched on a designated line, dug their toes in the sod, and raced forward at the clap of a hand for a good fifteen yards.

"Take your place, Moore," said Jock finally. "Dig down and get off with a jump."

Piggy, embarrassed by the stiffness of his collar and the difficulty of retaining his derby without loss of dignity, made a lumbering attempt.

"Try again. You're not racing a baby buggy! Get back on your marks," said Hasbrouck, and moving to a position directly behind him, he thundered, "Now, one—two—*three!*"

A stinging hand descended upon the crouching Piggy, who leaped forward in indignant amazement.

"That helped," said Jock, with an approving nod. "Once more."

Piggy, red to the ears, a second time was forced to humble himself and receive the indignity of such propulsion.

"Here, Piggy, catch!"

Moore had just time to spin around, when a football vigorously thrown, smote him full in the stomach.

"Oh, butterfingers!"

"Clumsy!"

"Get your arms into it!"

"Now!"

Warned by a chorus of instructions Moore strove a dozen times to retain the tantalizing spinning oval, which constantly slipped his grasp with a smart reminder as it bounded away.

"My boy, your education has been neglected," said Jock in disgust. "At least try and learn how to fall on the ball. Watch."

Rolling the pigskin in front of him, he dove for it, pounding on it as a beagle on a rabbit.

"Now, Piggy, let her go!"

Moore, who loved his tailor suit with the pride and affection which a father bestows only on the firstborn, desperately essayed to secure the pigskin with the minimum of danger possible.

A shriek of derision burst forth.

"No, my dear Miss Moore, I did not ask you to lie down and pillow your head upon it," said Jock in disgust. "That is *not* what is called falling on the ball. Go at it like a demon; chew it up, mangle it! Here, Morning Glory," he added, turning to a scrubby little urchin who was gamboling about, "take this young lady and show her how it's done."

To Piggy's culminating mortification, the diminutive Morning

Glory, with a contemptuous sneer, began to instruct him in the new art, with a rattling fire of insults which drew shrieks of laughter from the squad.

"Now then, old ice-wagon—get your nose in it."

"Don't spare the daisies, dearest."

"Jump, you Indian, jump!"

"Ah, watch me—like this."

The urchin hurled himself viciously on the ball, plowing up the soft turf, and bounding gloriously to his feet, with scornful, mud-stained face, cried, "Ah, what're you afraid of! Now then, old houseboat!"

Piggy's collar clung limply to his neck, half the buttons of his coat had gone, streaks of yellow and green decorated the suit a custom tailor had fashioned for fifty dollars cash, but still he was forced to go tumbling after the ball, down and up, up and down, head over heels, at the staccato shriek of the Morning Glory, like the one dog in the show who circles about the stage, tumbling somersaults.

"That's enough for today," came at last Jock's welcome command. "We must begin easily. Tomorrow we'll get into it. Practice over! Moore, jog around the circle six times and cut out pastry at supper."

During the dinner a great light dawned over Moore as he sat silently investigating his new masters with sidelong, calculated glances. He went to his room and with one sweep eliminated the solid silver toilet set, removed the trees from his boots, packed away the pink embroidered bedroom slippers so neatly arranged under the bed and pruned solicitously among the gorgeous cravats. Then he went to the village and, under skillful prompting, bought a pair of corduroy trousers, a cap, a red-and-black jersey, the softest pair of football trousers in stock, a jersey padded at the elbows and shoulders, a sweater, a pair of heavy shoes, a nose protector, and a pair of shin-guards. Encased in every possible protection he reported next day for the dreadful ordeal of tackling and being tackled.

"So you've all got your togs," said Fire Crackers, surveying the squad of freshmen on the field. "Let's see how you made out."

With Keg Smith and Jock, he passed them over in inspection, punching and poking the new suits with brief interjections, until Moore was reached. Before that swollen figure the three halted in mock amazement.

"Who's this?" said Keg, with a blank face.

"It's Moore, sir," said Piggy innocently.

"What's happened to you?" continued Fire Crackers with great seriousness.

Moore, perceiving he had blundered again, grew red with mortification, while Fire Crackers stripped the sweater from him and examined the jersey.

"Say, just see what Bill sold him!" he exclaimed. "Isn't it a shame how he'll impose on the green ones? Look at that bedticking! And those pads! Gee, I'll fix that!"

Before Moore could protest, Fire Crackers had ripped off the protections and flung them away.

"Now you'll feel easier,'" he said with a friendly smile. "Bill Appleby is an infernal old swindler, selling you shin-guards and a nose protecter! Huh! Throw 'em away."

'Thank you, sir," said Moore gratefully, "I'll make him take them back."

"That's right," said his inquisitor with a queer nod, "you're pretty green at this, aren't you?"

"I have never done much, sir."

"Well, let me give you a pointer; when you tackle, you want to grit your teeth and slam down hard, then you don't feel it at all."

"Thank you, sir."

"And when you're tackled," continued Fire Crackers with perfect seriousness, "just let yourself go limp; then you can't break any bones—see?"

"Yes, sir."

"You like the game, don't you?"

"Oh, very much."

Fire Crackers' advice did him scant good. On the whole it was probably the most painful afternoon he had ever known in his life. He had no instinct for tackling, that was certain. His arms slipped, his hands could not fasten to anything and he accomplished nothing more than to go sprawling, face downward.

"Funny you don't get on to that," said Jock, shaking his head.

36

"I tell you what you do. Run down the line and take a few tackles; then you'll see how it's done."

Moore stood balancing, looking down to where Jock's one hundred and sixty-five pounds were gathering for a model tackle. Every natural instinct in him bade him turn tail and run.

"Come on now!" cried Jock, spitting on his hands. "Hard as you can."

Piggy went as a horse goes to a road crusher, faltering and finally stopping dead. The next moment, Jock, cleaving the air in a perfect dive, caught him about the knees and threw him crashing to the ground. Piggy rose with difficulty.

"Do you get it now?" said Jock solicitously.

"I think I do," said Moore faintly.

"Well now, try one on me," said Jock, brightening. "Put your shoulder into it and squeeze it. Remember now."

Piggy remembered only the sensation of being tackled, and with the thought of that greater evil, improved astonishingly.

"That's the way to learn," said Jock approvingly. "Now, notice how I pull your legs from under you, and try to get that."

That evening after supper, Moore valiantly determined to take the bull by the horns. Seizing a favorable opportunity, he accosted his captain with the resolution of despair, and told him point blank that he would not be eligible for the team.

"Why not?" said Jock aggressively.

"I don't know anything about the game, sir," said Moore defiantly, "and I don't like it."

"Is that the only reason?"

"I don't want to play, sir—that ought to be enough."

"We're not *asking* you what you want to do."

"But, sir, I don't like it," said Moore, beginning to shrink under the cold, boring gaze of Hasbrouck.

"That has nothing to do with it, either."

"Nothing—"

"Certainly not. We don't want you; in fact, we're crying because we've got to take you. You're a flubdub and a quitter. But there's no one else, and so, Piggy, mark you—we're going to make a demon out of you, a regular demon. Mark my words!"

All of which was accomplished easily and naturally within a short two weeks by the discipline and tradition which has put courage into the hearts of generations of natural cowards.

The crisis came in the first game of the series, when, for the first time, Piggy beheld the terrifying spectacle of an end run started in his direction. At the sight of the solid front of bone and muscle ready to sweep him off his feet and send him tumbling head over heels, he shut his eyes and funked deliberately and ingloriously.

The next moment Jock had him by the small of the neck; Jock's hand jerked him to his feet and Jock's voice cried, "You cowardly little pup! You do that again and I'll tear the hide off you!"

Piggy, chilled to the bone, went to his position. The opposing team, with a shout of exultation, sent the same play crashing in his direction. Piggy, desperate with fear, tore through the advancing mass, found the runner and hurled him to the ground. Jock smiled contentedly. Moore was a coward, he knew, but from that time forth, no passing menace before him could compare with the abiding terror that waited behind.

Had Moore been possessed of even moderate courage the task would have been difficult, for then it would have resolved itself into a mere question of natural ability. But being an arrant and utter coward, his very cowardice drove him into feats of desperate recklessness. For always, in lull or storm, in the confusion of the melee or the open scramble down the field to cover a punt, Moore felt the ominous presence of Hasbrouck just at his shoulder and heard the sharp and threatening cry, "Get that man, you, Piggy!"

So blindly and rebelliously he served the tyrant, and unwilling and revolting learned to despise fear, little suspecting how many reckless spirits of other teams had been formed under the same rude discipline.

The earlier contests developed the strength of the two long-time rivals, the Kennedy and the Dickinson, between whom at last lay the question of supremacy. The last week approached with excitement at fierce heat. Every day a fresh rumor was served up; Hickey, the wily Dickinson quarter, had a weak ankle; Turkey, the captain, was behind in his studies; a Princeton varsity man was over, coaching the enemy; the signals were discovered and a dozen trick plays were being held in reserve, each good for a touchdown.

Each night on the Kennedy steps, the council of war convened and plans were discussed in utter gravity for temporarily crippling and eliminating from the contest Turkey, Slugger Jones, Hickey and the Butcher. For, of course, it was conceded that Jock, Tom Walsh and Fire Crackers would probably be maimed for life by the brutal and unscrupulous enemy.

Piggy, whose critical sense of humor had been under early disadvantages, took this as exact truth and beheld the horrible day arrive with an absolute conviction that it would be his last. He did not sleep during the night; he could eat nothing during the day; his fingers trembled and snarled up the lacings as he forced himself into his football clothes. Then he stood a long moment, viewing his white face in the mirror—the last look, perhaps—and went weakly to join the squad below. He heard nothing of the magnificent address of Jock to his followers. One idea only was in his head: to sell his life as dearly as possible.

While the captains conferred and tossed for position, the two teams, face to face at last, paced up and down, eying each other with contempt, breathing forth furious threats.

The Egghead assured Fatty Harris that the first scrimmage would be his last. Fatty Harris returned the compliment and suggested that the Egghead leave a memorandum for the hearse. The Coffee Cooler looked Buffalo Brown over and sneered; Keg Smith did as much to the Butcher and laughed. The diminutive Spider at right end, approached his dear friend Legs Brockett, his opponent, and muttered through his teeth, "I'm going to slug you!"

While these friendly salutations were taking place, Flea Obie and Wash Simmons, the Dickinson halves, approached Piggy, who, sick at heart, was stamping his feet and churning his arms to convey to Red Dog, opposite, the impression that he was thirsting for his blood.

Wash gave Piggy one withering glance and said loudly to the Red Dog, "This fellow's a quitter. He's got yellow in his eyes. Smash him good and hard, Red Dog. Don't waste any time about it, either."

"He's got a chicken liver," said Red Dog, who looked a reed beside the sturdy Piggy. "He shuts his eyes when he tackles! I'll fix him. Huh!"

"Ah, go on now, go on, go on," said Piggy, with a desperate attempt at lightheartedness.

Flea Obie, lovely no longer in mud-stained jacket and pirate band around his forehead, strode up to Piggy and added, "Old Sport, let me give you a word of advice. When we strike your end, the best thing you can do is to lie down *quick and soft. Savez?*"

Luckily for Piggy, whose imagination was panic-driven by this perfectly innocuous braggadocio, the torrent of conversation was checked by a cry of exultation.

The Kennedy had won the toss and chose the kickoff. Bat Finney, umpire from the Fourth Form, called the two teams together and said solemnly, "Now I want it understood by you fellows this is going to be a gentleman's game. No roughing it, no slugging, nothing bru-tal. Take your sides."

Immediately the air resounded with war cries:

"Get in there, Dickinson."

"Chew 'em up, Kennedy."

"Hit 'em hard, Buffalo."

"Sock 'em, Turkey."

"Knock 'em out, boys!"

Piggy, at left end with his eye on the ball, waited hopelessly for Jock to send the oval spinning into Dickinson territory. He was shivering, in a dead funk. The whistle blew, the run was on. Piggy went perfunctorily, helplessly, down the field to where the dreaded Hickey, ball under arm, was dodging toward him. Suddenly the vigorous form of Wash Simmons hove into view, headed directly for him. He wavered and the next moment was knocked off his feet, while Hickey, the way thus cleared for him, went bounding back for a run of forty yards.

Meanwhile Piggy was in the hands of Jock, who administered to him before the eyes of every spectator, a humiliating and well-placed kick.

"You funked, I saw you funk, you miserable shivery little coward!" he cried, shaking his fist in his face. "You jump in there now and cripple a few of those fellows or I'll massacre you!"

He added a few words which shall remain sacred between them and shoved him into place. The old fear awoke triumphant in Piggy. He rushed in like a demon, whirling over the field, upsetting play after play, making tackles that brought Flea Obie and Wash Simmons to their feet rubbing their sides. Nothing could stop him, for at last he was panic-stricken, utterly and horribly afraid.

The two teams, evenly matched, fought each other to a standstill. The first half closed without any perceptible advantage. The second half continued the deadlock, the precious minutes slipping away. Such a struggle had never been known in a House contest. Several eyes were closed, several bandages had appeared. The frenzy of battle had taken possession of the descendants of Goth and Viking. Challenges to future encounters were flung recklessly and recklessly accepted. After each melee little clusters of battling boyhood were disentangled with difficulty, while Bat Finney, the umpire, joyfully proclaimed, "No roughing it, fellows—remember, this is a *gentleman's* game."

The dusk began to cloud the field and the players, one of those tragic, melancholy mists that come only at the close of a desperate second half. Two minutes only to play and the ball in the Kennedy's possession, exactly at midfield, without a score.

"6-5-8-15-2-3!" shrieked Fire Crackers, grimy and unrecognizable.

The team, converging swiftly for a revolving mass play on tackle, strove wearily to make headway against the reeling Dickinsons, who, too fagged to upset the play, could only hold, surging and twisting. Piggy, scrambling and pushing, head down in the melee, whirled and spun with the revolving mass. Then his feet tripped and he went underneath, shielding his head from the vortex of legs that swirled above him. Suddenly, lying free, a scant five yards in front of him, he perceived to his horror the precious ball! With a lurch, he freed himself from the mass, scrambled to his feet, picked up the ball and set out, break-a-neck, for the faraway goal. Five yards behind was Hickey, the fleet quarter, bounding after him.

In a twinkling the whole scene had changed into the extraordinary spectacle of a stern chase, two figures well in front, striving for the mastery of the fates, and behind the futile, scrambling, exulting or desperate mass of players, sweeping helplessly on the tracks of destiny.

Forty yards to the interminable goal! Piggy remembered with dread the stories of Hickey's fleetness. He glanced back. His pursuer had not gained an inch. On the contrary, his freckled face was distorted, his arms were churning, his teeth were horribly displayed, biting at the stinging air, with the agony of the effort to increase his speed. So he was beating out Hickey, the famous Hickey! Then the touchdown was a fact! Above the uproar he heard a strident shriek:

"Piggy, oh, you damned Piggy!"

The terror of that familiar voice gave a new impetus to his chubby legs. Someone else must be gaining on him. Thirty yards still to go!

He ran and ran, hugging the ball in his arms, his head thrown back, gasping for breath. Twenty yards—fifteen yards! Suddenly swift, glorious visions rose before him, scenes of jubilation and exultation, of cheering comrades, celebrations that would wipe out the long record of humiliation. Hickey was closer now, but Piggy did not dare to turn his head; five yards more and the game would be over and the kingdom of the Kennedy in his grasp. He sped over the last white chalk line and dropped triumphant behind the goal posts. The next moment, Hickey, wily Hickey, screaming with laughter, flung himself on him.

Piggy gazed about wildly with a sudden horrible suspicion. He had run over his own goal line and scored a safety for the Dickinson.

Then Hasbrouck arrived.

THE FUTURE PRESIDENT

"Snorky" Green, at the fourth desk of the middle aisle, gazed dreamily at the forgotten pages of the divine Virgil. The wide windows let in the warm breath of June meadows and the tiny sounds of contented insects roaming in unhuman liberty. Outside were soft banks to loll upon, from which to watch the baseball candidates gamboling over the neat diamond, tennis courts calling to be played upon, and the friendly jigger ready to soothe the parched highway to the aching void. And for an hour the tugging souls of forty-two imprisoned little pagans would have to construe, and parse, and decline, secretly cursing the fossils who rediscovered those unnecessary Latin documents.

Eight rows of desks, nine deep, were swept by the Argus eye of the master from his raised pulpit. Around the room, immense vacant blackboards shut them in—dark, hopeless walls over which no convict might clamber, on which a thousand boys had blundered and guessed and writ in water.

Lucius Cassius Hopkins, the Roman, man of heroic and consular mold, flunker of boys and deviser of systems against which even the ingenuity of a Hickey hurled itself in vain, sat on the rostrum, pitilessly mowing down the unresisting ranks.

43

Snorky's tousled hair was more rumpled than ever, a smudge was on one cheek where his grimy, ball-stained hand had unknowingly left its mark. He was dirty, bored, and unprepared. The dickey at his throat, formed by the junction of a collar and two joined cuffs, saved the proprieties and allowed the body to keep cool. But the spirit of dreams was upon Snorky, and the hard, rectangular room began to recede.

He heard indistinctly the low, mocking rumble of the Roman as his scythe passed down the rows.

"Anything from the Simpson twins today? No, no? Anything from the Davis House combination? Too bad! Too bad! Nothing from the illuminating Hicks? Yes? No? Too bad! Too bad!"

Snorky did not hear him; his eyes were on the firm torsos of Flash Condit and Charley De Soto before him—Condit, wonder of the football field, hero of the touchdown against the Princeton varsity, and De Soto the phenomenal shortstop, both Olympian spirits doomed to endure the barbed shafts of Lucius Cassius Hopkins.

He, too—Snorky—would go down in the annals of school history. He remembered the beginning of an outcurve he had developed that morning in the lot back of the Woodhull—a genuine outcurve, Ginger Pop Rooker to the contrary notwithstanding. With a little practice he would master the perplexing incurve and the drop. And the Woodhull needed a pitcher badly. McCarty had no courage; the Dickinson would batter him all over the field in the afternoon's game, and then goodbye to the championship. In his mind he began the game, trotting hopelessly out into left field. He saw Hickey, first up for the Dickinson, get a base on balls—four wide ones in succession. Slugger Jones, four balls—heavens, to be beaten like that! Turkey Reiter, third man up, hit a two-bagger; two runs. Doc Macnooder knocked the first ball pitched for a clean single; a two-bagger for the Egghead! Again four balls for Butcher Stevens! The Red Dog, of all people in the world, to hit safely! And still they allowed the slaughter to go on! The Dickinson House was shrieking with joy, dancing war dances back of third, and singing derisive songs of triumph. Flea Obie went to first on another base on balls, filling the bases. And five runs over the plate! Hickey and Turkey on the line began to dance a cakewalk. From the uproarious Dickinsonians rose the humiliating wail:

We're on to his curves, we're on to his curves;
Long-legged McCarty has lost his nerves.

McCarty *had* lost his nerves. Five runs, the bases full, and Wash
Simmons, the Dickinson pitcher, to the bat. The infield, badly
rattled, played in to catch the runner at home in approved professional style. Snorky stole in closer and closer until he was almost
back of shortstop. Simmons, he knew, couldn't send it out of the
diamond. But Wash knocked what looked to be a clean single, clear
over the heads of the near infield. That was what he had been
waiting for; on the full run he made a desperate dive, caught the
ball one-handed, close to the ground, turned a somersault, scrambled to second base, and shot the ball to first before the runner
could even check himself!

Nothing like it had ever been seen in Lawrenceville. Even the
Dickinsons generously applauded him as he came up happy and
flushed.

"Snorky, that's the greatest play I ever saw pulled off. I wish I
had made it myself."

He looked up. The speaker was the dashing De Soto. That from
Charley, the greatest ballplayer who ever came to Lawrenceville!
Snorky's throat swelled with emotion. At last they knew his worth.

One run for the Woodhull. Again the Dickinsons to the bat, and
again the rout; one single, a base on balls, two bases on balls—oh,
if he only would get his chance! One ball, two balls, three balls.
Suddenly McCarty stopped and clutched his arm with an exclamation of pain. The team gathered about him. Snorky sniffed in
disdain; he knew that trick, pretending it was all on account of
his arm! What a quitter McCarty was, after all! Still, what was to
be done? The team gathered in grave discussion. No one else had
ever pitched.

"Give me a chance," he said suddenly to Rock Bemis, the captain.

"You!" said Rock, with a laugh. "You, Snorky!"

"Look at me! I can do it," he answered, and met the other's glare
with steady look as heroes do. Something of the fire in that look
convinced Bemis.

"Why not?" he said. "The game's gone, anyhow. Go into the
box, Snorky, and put them over if you can."

45

The teams lined up. With clenched teeth and a cold streak down his spine he strode into the box. An insulting yelp went up from the enemy.

Three balls, no strikes, and the bases full! Turkey at the plate stepped back scornfully to wait for the fourth ball.

"Strike one!"

Turkey advanced to the utmost limit of the batter's box, turned his back deliberately on Snorky, and called out, "You hit me, and I'll break your neck!"

"Strike two!"

Turkey turned in surprise, looked at him, and deliberated.

"He can't put it over," yelled the gallery. "Yi, yi, yi!"

Then Turkey seated himself Indian fashion, his back still to Snorky, and gazed up into the face of Tug Moffat, the catcher. A furious wrangle ensued, the Woodhull claiming that his position was illegal, the Dickinson insisting that nothing in the rules prohibited it. Stonewall Jackson, the umpire, a weak-minded fellow from the Rouse House, allowed the play.

"Strike three!"

Turkey, crestfallen and muttering, arose and dusted himself amid the jeers of the onlookers. Doc Macnooder smote high and low, and then forgot to smite—three strikes and out. The Egghead, despite the entreaties of the Dickinson to bring in his housemates, could only foul out. The Woodhulls went wild with delight. He heard Tug, the catcher, whispering excitedly to De Soto.

"Charley, just watch him! He's got everything—everything!"

Then the Woodhull tied the score on two bases on balls, and his own two-bagger.

When he walked lightly into the box for the third inning, Stonewall Jackson had been replaced by De Soto with the imperious remark: "Here, get out! I want to watch this."

He gave the great Charley a modest nod.

"When did you ever pitch?" said De Soto, critically.

"Oh, now and then," he answered.

"Well, Snorky, let yourself out."

"Tug can't hold me," he said impudently. "That's the trouble, Charley."

"Try him."

Tug signaled for an in-shoot. He wound himself up and let fly. Butcher Stevens flung himself from the plate, Moffat threw up his mitt in sudden fear. The ball caromed off and went frolicking past the backstop.

"Strike one!"

Tug, puzzled and apprehensive, came up for a consultation.

"Gee, Snorky, give me warning! What do you think I am—a Statue of Liberty?"

"Charley wants me to let myself out. I'll slow down on the third strike," he said loftily. "Let the others go if you want."

Tug, like a Roman gladiator, with undying resolve, squatted back of the plate and signaled for an outcurve. No use; no mitt of his could ever stop the frightful velocity of that shoot.

"Stri-ike two!"

"Now ease up a bit," cautioned De Soto.

He sent a floating outdrop that seemed headed for Butcher Stevens' head, and finally settled gently over the plate at the waistline.

"Striker out!"

Moffat no longer tried to hold him, admitting himself outclassed by the blinding speed of ins and outs, jump balls, and cross fire that Snorky hurled unerringly across the plate. The Red Dog and Flea Obie, plainly unnerved, died like babes in their tracks. Five strike-outs in two innings!

Then De Soto spoke.

"Here, Snorky, you get out of this!"

A cry of protest came from the Woodhull.

"Yell all you like," said De Soto; "Snorky is going with me where he belongs."

And, to the amazement of the two houses, he drew his arm under Snorky's and marched him right over to the varsity diamond.

How the school buzzed and chattered about the phenomenal rise of the new pitcher! He saw himself pitching wonderful curves to burly Cap Kiefer, the veteran backstop, built like a mastodon, who had all he could do to hold those frightful balls. He saw the crowds of boys, six deep, who stood reverentially between times to watch the amazing curves. He heard pleasurably the chorus of "Ahs!" and "Ohs!" and "Gees!" which followed each delivery. Then suddenly he was in the box on the great, clean diamond, with the eyes of hundreds of boys fastened prayerfully on him, and the orange-and-black stripes of a Princeton varsity man facing him at the plate. To beat the Princeton varsity—what a goal!

He saw each striped champion come up gracefully and retire

47

crestfallen to the bench, even as the Dickinson batters had done. Inning after inning passed without a score; not a Princeton man reached first. Then in the seventh an accident happened. The first Princeton man up deliberately stepped into the ball, and the umpire allowed him to take his base. It was outrageous, but worse was to follow. On the attempt to steal second, Cap lined a beautiful ball to the base, but no one covered it—a mistake in signals! And the runner kept on to third! Snorky settled down and struck out the next two batters. The Lawrenceville bleachers rose *en masse* and shrieked his praises. Then suddenly Kiefer, to catch the runner off third, snapped the ball to Waladoo a trifle, just a trifle, wild; but the damage was done. 1 to 0 in favor of Princeton. Even the great Princeton captain, Barrett, said to him, "Hard luck, Green! Blamed hard luck!"

But Snorky wasn't beaten yet. The eighth and ninth innings passed without another Princeton man reaching first. Nine innings without a hit—wonderful!—and yet to be beaten by a fluke. One out for Lawrenceville; two out. The third man up, Cap Kiefer himself, reached first on an error. "Green to the bat," sang out the scorer.

Snorky looked around, picked up his bat and calmly strode to the plate. He had no fear; he knew what was going to happen. One ball, one strike, two strikes. He let the drop pass. What he wanted was a swift in-shoot. Two balls—too high. Three balls—wide of the plate. He was not to be tempted by any such. Two strikes and three balls; now he must get what he wanted. He cast one glance at the bleachers, alive with the frantic red-and-black flags; he heard his comrades calling, beseeching, imploring. Then his eye settled on the far green stretch between right and center field and the brown masses of Memorial where no ball before had ever reached. A home run would drive in Kiefer and win the game! The chance had come. The Princeton pitcher slowly began to wind up for the delivery. Snorky settled into the box, caught his bat with the grip of desperation, gathered together all his sinews, and—

"Green!" called the sharp, jeering voice of Lucius Cassius Hopkins.

Snorky sprang to his feet in fright, clutching at his book. The great home run died in the air.

"Translate."

Snorky gazed helplessly at the page, seeking the place. He heard the muffled voice of Hickey behind him:

"The advance, the advance, you chump!"

But to find the place under the hawk eyes of the Roman was an impossibility. He stared at the page in a well-simulated attempt, shook his head, and sat down.

"A very creditable attempt, Green," said the master, now with a gentle voice. "De Soto?—Nothing from De Soto? Dear, dear! We'll have to try Macnooder then. What? Studied the wrong lesson? How sad! Mistakes will happen. Don't want to try that, either? No feeling of confidence today; no feeling of confidence." He began to call them by rows. "Dark, Davis, Denton, Dibble—nothing in the D's. Farr, Francis, Frey, Frick—nothing from the F's; nothing from the D. F's. Very strange! very strange! Little spring fever—yes? Too bad! too bad! Lesson too long? Yes? Too long to get any of it? Dear, dear! Everyone studied the review, I see. Excellent moral idea, conscientious; wouldn't go on until you have mastered yesterday's lesson. Well, well, so we'll have a beautiful recitation in the review."

How absurd it was to be flunking under the Roman! Next year he would show them. He would rise early in the morning and study hours before breakfast; he would master everything, absorb everything—declensions and conjugations, Greek, Roman, and medieval civilization; he would frolic in equations and toy with logarithms; his translation would be the wonder of the faculty. He would crush Red Dog and Crazy Opdyke; he would be valedictorian of his class. They would speak of him as a phenomenon, as a prodigy, like Pascal—was it Pascal? What a tribute the headmaster would pay him at commencement! There on the stage before all the people, the fathers and mothers and sisters, before the Red Dog, and Ginger Pop Rooker, and Hickey, and all the rest, sitting open-mouthed while he, Snorky Green, the crack pitcher and valedictorian of his class, a scholar such as Lawrenceville had never known—

"Green, Gay, and Hammond, go to the board. Take your books."

Snorky went hastily and clumsily, waiting as a gambler waits for his chance.

"Gay, decline *hic, haec, hoc;* Green, write out the gerundive

49

forms of all the verbs in the first paragraph top of page 163."

Snorky gazed helplessly at the chronicles of Aeneas, and then blankly at the inexorable blackboard, where so many gerundives had not been inscribed.

He drew his name in lagging letters exactly midway, at the top, with a symmetrical space above.

R. B. GREEN

Then he searched anxiously for the gerundives that lurked somewhere in the first paragraph, top of page 163. Then returning to the board he rubbed out the name with little reluctant dabs and wrote

ROGER B. GREEN

Abandoning the chase for gerundives, he stood off a few feet and surveyed his labors on the blackboard, frowned, erased it and wrote dashingly

ROGER BALLINGTON GREEN

Satisfied, he drew a strong line under it, added two short crosses and a dot or two, and returned to his seat.

Once more in the abode of dreams he was transported to college, president of his class, the idol of his mates, the marvel of the faculty. He hesitated on the borderline of a great football victory, where, single-handed, bruised, and suffering, he would win the game for his college—and then found higher levels. War had been declared swiftly and treacherously by the German Empire. The whole country was rising to the President's call to arms. A great meeting of the university was held, and he spoke with a sudden revelation of a power for oratory he had never before suspected.

That very afternoon a company was formed under his leadership. Twenty-four hours later they marched to the station, and, amid a whirlwind of cheers and godspeeds, embarked for the front. During the night, while others slept, he pored over books of tactics; he studied the campaigns of Caesar, Napoleon, Grant, and Moltke. In the first disastrous year of the war, when the American army was beaten back at every point and an invading force of Germans was penetrating from the coast in three sections, he rose to the command of his regiment, with the reputation of being the finest disciplinarian in the army. Their corps was always at the front, checking the resistless advance of the enemy, saving their comrades time after time at frightful loss. Then came that dreadful day when it seemed as though the Army of the South was doomed to be surrounded and crushed by the sudden tightening of the enemy's net before the Army of the Center could effect a junction. In the gloomy council he spoke out. One way of escape there was, but it meant the sacrifice of five thousand men. Clearly and quickly he traced his plan, while general, brigadier-general, and general-in-chief stared in amazement at the new genius that flashed before their minds.

"That is the plan," he said calmly, with the authority of a master mind. "It means the safety of a hundred thousand, and if a junction can be made with the Army of the Center, the Germans can be stopped and driven back at so-and-so. But this means the death of five thousand men. There is only one man who has the right to die so—the man who proposes it. Give me five regiments, and I will hold the enemy for thirty-six hours."

He threw his regiments boldly into the enemy's line of march, and by a sudden rush carried the spur that dominated the valley. The German army, surprised and threatened in its most vulnerable spot, forced to abandon the pursuit, turned to crush the handful of heroes.

All day long the desperate battalions flung themselves in vain against the little band. All day long he walked with drawn sword up and down the thinning ranks, stiffening their courage. Red Dog and Ginger Pop called to him, imploring him not to expose himself —Red Dog and Ginger Pop whose idol he now was; yes, and Hickey's and Condit's, too. But carelessly, defiantly, he stood in full view, his clothes pierced, his head bared. Then came the night—the long, fatiguing night, without an instant's cessation. The carnage was frightful. Half of the force gone, and twelve hours more to hold out! That was his promise. And the sickening dawn, with the shrouded clouds and the expectant vultures, came stealing out of the east. Until night came again they must cling to the spur-top and manage to live in that hurricane of lead. He went down the line, calling each man by name, rousing them like a prophet inspired. The fury of sacrifice seized them. They fought on, parched and bleeding, while the sun rose above them and slowly fell. A thousand lives; half that, and half that again. Five o'clock, and still two hours to go. He looked about him. Only a few hundred remained to meet the next charge. Red Dog and Ginger Pop were cold in death, Hickey was dying. Of all his school friends, only Flash Condit remained, staggering at his side. And then the great masses of the enemy swept over them like an avalanche, and he fell, unconscious but happy, with the vision of martyrdom shining above him.

Red Dog, on his way back to his seat, knocked against him, saying angrily, "Oh, you clumsy!"

Red Dog, of all the world! Red Dog, whom he had just cheered into a hero's death. Snorky, thus brought to earth, decided to resuscitate himself and read the papers, with their big page-broad scareheads of the fight on the spur. This accomplished, he decided to end the war. The President, driven by public clamor, put him in command of the Army of the South. In three weeks, by a series of rapid Napoleonic marches, he flung the enemy into morasses and wilderness, cut their line of communication and starved them into surrender; then flinging his army north, he effected a junction with the Army of the Center, sending a laconic message to the President: "I am here. Give me command, and I will feed the sea with the remnants of Germany's glory."

Official Washington, intriguing and jealous, cried out for a court martial; but the voice of the people, echoing from coast to coast, gave him his wish. In one month he swept the middle coast bare of resistance, fought three enormous battles, and annihilated the armies of the invaders, ending the war. What a triumph was his! That wonderful entry into Washington, with the frenzied roars of multitudes that greeted him, as he rode simply and modestly, but greatly, down the Avenue at the head of his old regiment, in their worn and ragged uniforms, with the flag shot to shreds proudly carried by the resuscitated Hickey and Flash Condit, seeing in the crowd the tear-stained faces of the Roman and the headmaster and all his old comrades, amid the waving handkerchiefs of frantic thousands.

At this point Snorky's emotion overmastered him. A lump was in his throat. He controlled himself with difficulty and dignity. He went over the quiet, stately years until a grateful nation carried him in triumph into the Presidential chair, nominated by acclamation and without opposition! He saw the wonderful years of his ascendancy, the wrongs righted, peace and concord returning to all classes, the development of science, the uniting into one system of all the warring branches of education, the amalgamation of Canada and Mexico into the United States, the development of an immense merchant fleet, the consolidation of all laws into one national code, the establishment of free concerts and theaters for the people. Then suddenly there fell a terrible blow, the hand of a maniac struck him down as he passed through the multitudes who loved him. He was carried unconscious to the nearest house. The greatest physicians flocked to him, striving in vain to fight off the inevitable end. He saw the street filled with tanbark and the faces of the grief-stricken multitude, with Hickey and Red Dog and Ginger Pop sobbing on the steps and refusing to leave all that fateful night, while bulletins of the final struggle were constantly sent to every part of the globe. And then he died. He heard the muffled peal of bells, and the sobs that went up from every home in the land; he saw the houses being decked with crepe, and the people, with aching hearts, trooping into the churches: for he, the President, the beloved, the great military genius, the wisest of human rulers, was dead—dead.

Suddenly a titter, a horrible, mocking laugh, broke through the stately dignity of the national grief. Snorky, with tears trembling in his eyes, suddenly brought back to reality, looked up to see Lucius Cassius Hopkins standing over him with mocking smile. From their desks Red Dog and Hickey were making faces at him, roaring at his discomfiture.

"So Green is dreaming again! Dear, dear! Dreaming again!" said the deliberate voice. "Dreaming of chocolate eclairs and the Jigger Shop, eh, Green?"

FURTHER PERSECUTION OF HICKEY

EVER SINCE the disillusioning encounter with Tabby, Hickey, like the obscure Bonaparte before the trenches of Toulon, walked moodily alone, absorbed in his own resolves, evolving his immense scheme of a colossal rebellion. Macnooder alone received the full confidence of the war *à outrance* with the faculty which he gradually evolved.

Macnooder was the man of peace, the Mazarin and the Machiavelli of the Dickinson. He risked nothing in action, but to his cunning mind with its legal sense of dangers to be met and avoided, were brought all the problems of conspiracies against the discipline of the school. Macnooder pronounced the scheme of a revolt heroic, all the more so that he saw an opportunity of essaying his strategy on large lines.

"We must begin on a small scale, Hickey," he said wisely, "and keep working up to something really big."

"I thought we might organize a secret society," said Hickey, ruminating, "something Masonic, all sworn to silence and secrecy and all that sort of thing."

"No," said Doc, "just as few as possible and no real confidants, Hickey; we'll take assistants as we need them."

"What would you begin with?"

"We must strike a blow at Tabby," said Macnooder. "We must show him that we don't propose to stand for any of his underhanded methods."

"He needs a lesson," Hickey asserted savagely.

"How about the skeleton?"

"Humph!" said Hickey, considering. "Perhaps, but that's rather old."

"Not up the flagpole—something new."

"What is it, Doc?"

Hickey looked at Macnooder with expectant admiration.

"I noticed something yesterday in Memorial, during chapel, that gave me an idea," said Macnooder profoundly. "There is a great big ventilator in the ceiling; now there must be some way of getting to that and letting a rope down." Macnooder stopped and looked at Hickey. Hickey returned a look full of admiration, then by a mutual movement they clasped hands in ecstatic, sudden delight.

That night they reconnoitered with the aid of a dark lantern, borrowed from Legs Brownell of the Griswold, and the passkeys, of which Hickey was the hereditary possessor.

They found to their delight that there was in fact a small opening through which one boy could wriggle with difficulty.

The attempt was fixed for the following night, and as a third boy was indispensable, it was decided that etiquette demanded that the owner of the lantern should have the first call.

At two o'clock that night Hickey and Macnooder stole down the creaking stairs, and out Sawtelle's window (the highway to the outer world). The night was misty, with a pleasant, ghostly chill that heightened measurably the delight of the adventure. In the shadow of the Griswold a third shivering form cautiously developed into the possessor of the dark lantern.

After a whispered consultation, they proceeded to Foundation

House, where they secured the necessary rope from the clothes line, it being deemed eminently fitting to secure the cooperation of the best society.

Memorial Hall entered, they soon found themselves, by the aid of the smelly lantern, in front of the closet that held the skeleton which twice a week served as demonstration to the class in anatomy, and twice a year was dragged forth to decorate the flagpole or some such exalted and inaccessible station. In a short time the door yielded to the prying of the hatchet Macnooder had thoughtfully brought along, and the white, chalky outlines of the melancholy skeleton appeared.

The three stood gazing, awed. It was black and still, and the hour of the night when dogs howl and bats go hunting.

"Who's going to take him?" said Legs in a whisper.

"Take it yourself," said Macnooder, unhooking the wriggling form. "Hickey's got to crawl through the air hole, and I've got to work the lantern. You're not superstitious, are you?"

"Sure I'm not," retorted Legs, who received the skeleton in his arms with a shiver that raised the gooseflesh from his crown to his heels.

"Come on," said Hickey in a whisper, "softly now."

"What's that?" exclaimed Legs, drawing in his breath.

"That's nothing," said Macnooder loftily; "all buildings creak at night."

"I swear I heard a step. There, again. Listen."

"Legs is right," said Hickey in a whisper. "It's outside."

"Rats! It's nothing but Jimmy," said Macnooder with enforced calm. "Keep quiet until he passes on."

They stood breathless until the sounds of the watchman on his nightly rounds died away. Then they started on tiptoe up the first flight for the chapel, Macnooder leading with the lantern, Legs next with the skeleton gingerly carried in his arms, Hickey bringing up the rear with the coil of rope.

"Here we are," said Macnooder at length. "Legs, you wait here —see, that's where we're going to hoist him." He flashed the bull's-eye upward to the perforated circle directly above the rostrum, and added, "I'll get Hickey started and then I'll be right back."

"Are you going to take the lantern?" said Legs, whose courage began to fail him.

"Sure," said Hickey, indignantly. "Legs, you're getting scared."

"No, I'm not," protested Legs faintly, "but I don't like to be left all alone with this thing in my arms!"

"Say, do you want my job," said Hickey, scornfully, "crawling down thirty feet of air hole with bugs and spiders and mice? Do you? 'Cause if you do just say so."

"No-o-o," said Legs with a sigh. "No, I'll stay here."

"You don't believe in ghosts and that sort of thing, do you?" said Macnooder solicitously.

" 'Course, I don't!"

"All right then, 'cause if you do we won't leave you."

"You chaps go on," said Legs bravely, "only be quick about it."

"All right?"

"All right."

Hickey and Macnooder stole away; then suddenly Hickey, returning, whispered, "Say, Legs!"

"What?"

"If you catch your coat don't think it's the dead man's hand grabbing you, will you?"

"Darn you, Hickey," said Legs, "if you don't shut up I'll quit."

"Sh-h—goodbye, old man."

"Hurry up!"

In the crawling, howling darkness Legs waited, holding the skeleton at arm's length, trembling like a leaf, listening tensely for a sound, vowing that if he ever got safely back into his bed he would never break another law of the school. At the moment when his courage was wavering, he heard the muffled, slipping tread of Macnooder returning. He drew a long comfortable breath, threw one leg nonchalantly over the back of a nearby seat and clasped the skeleton in an affectionate embrace.

"Hist—Legs."

The lantern flashed upon him. Legs yawned a bored, tranquil yawn.

"Is that you, Doc?"

"Were you scared?"

"Of what!"

"Say, you've got nerve for a youngster," said Macnooder admiringly. "Honestly, how did it feel hugging old Bonesy, all alone there in the dark?"

"You know, I rather liked it," said Legs with a drawl. "I tried to imagine what it would be like to see a ghost. Only, I could hardly keep awake. Good Lord! What's that?"

The coil of rope descending had brushed against his face and the start which he gave completely destroyed the effect of his narrative. Macnooder, seizing the rope, made it fast to the skeleton. Then, producing a large pasteboard from under his sweater, he attached it to a foot so that it would display to the morrow's audience the inscription, TABBY.

He gave two quick tugs, and the skeleton slowly ascended, twisting and turning in unnatural white gyrations, throwing grotesque shadows against the ceiling.

"Now, let's get up to see Hickey come out," said Macnooder with a chuckle. "He's a sight."

Ten minutes later, as they waited expectantly, listening at the opening of the narrow passage, a sneeze resounded.

"What's that?" exclaimed Legs, whose nerves were tense.

"That's Hickey," said Macnooder with a chuckle. "He'll be along in a minute. He's scattering red pepper after him so no one can crawl in to get the skeleton down. Gee, he must have swallowed half of it!"

A succession of sneezes resounded, and then with a scramble an unrecognizable form shot out of the opening, covered with cobwebs and the accumulated dust of years.

"For heaven's sake, Hickey, stop sneezing!" cried Macnooder in tremor. "You'll get us pinched."

"I—I—can't help it," returned Hickey between sneezes. "Great idea of yours—red pepper!"

"Just think of the fellow that goes in after you," said Macnooder, "and stop sneezing."

"It's in my eyes, down my throat, everywhere!" said Hickey helplessly.

They got him out of the building and down by the pond where he plunged his head gratefully into the cooling waters. Then they slapped the dust from him and rubbed the cobwebs out of his hair, until he begged for mercy.

"Never mind, Hickey," said Macnooder helpfully. "Just think of Tabby when he comes in tomorrow."

Fortified by this delicious thought, Hickey submitted to being cleaned. Then Macnooder examined him carefully, saying, "There mustn't be the slightest clue; if there is a button missing you'll have to go back for it." Suddenly he stopped. "Hickey, there's one gone—off the left sleeve."

"I lost that scrapping with the Egghead last week," explained Hickey, "and both of the left suspender ones are gone, too."

"Honest?"

"I swear it."

"There's been many a murder tracked down," said Macnooder impressively, "on just a little button."

"Gee, Doc." said Legs in chilled admiration. "Say, what a bully criminal you would make!"

And on this spontaneous expression of young ambition, the three separated.

The next morning, when the school filed in to Memorial for chapel, they beheld with rapture the uncanny figure suspended directly over the rostrum. In an instant the name was whispered over the benches—"Tabby." It was then a feat of the Dickinson House. Every Dickinsonian was questioned excitedly and professed the blankest ignorance, but with such an insistent air that twenty were instantly credited with the deed. Then, with a common impulse, the school turned to watch the entrance of the faculty. Each master on entering started, repressed an involuntary smile, looked to see the name attached, frowned, gazed fiercely at the nearest boys and took his seat.

Suddenly a thrill of excitement ran over the school and like a huge sigh the exclamation welled up, "Tabby!"

Mr. Lorenzo Blackstone Tapping had entered. His eyes met the skeleton and he colored. A smile would have saved him, but the young Greek and Latin expert understood nothing of the humanizing sciences. He tried to look unconcerned and failed; he tried to look dignified and appeared sheepish; he tried to appear calm and became red with anger. It was a moment that carried joy into the heart of Hickey, joy and the forgetfulness of red pepper, cobwebs and dust.

Then the headmaster arrived and a frightened calm fell over the awed assemblage. Did he see the skeleton? There was not the slightest evidence of recognition. He walked to his seat without a break and began the services without once lifting his eyes. The school was vexed, mystified and apprehensive. But at the close of the services the headmaster spoke, seeking the culprits among the four hundred, and under that terrifying glance each innocent boy looked guilty.

Such an outrage had never before occurred in the history of the institution, he assured them. Not only had a gross desecration been done to the sacredness of the spot, but wanton and cowardly insult had been perpetrated on one of the masters (Tapping thought the specific allusion might have been omitted). It was as cowardly as the miserable wretch who writes an anonymous letter, as cowardly as the drunken bully who shoots from the dark. He repelled the thought that this was a manifestation of the spirit of the school; it was rather the isolated act of misguided unfortunates who should never have entered the institution, who would leave it the day of their detection. And he promised the school that they would be detected, that he would neither rest nor spare an effort to ferret out this cancer and remove it.

Hickey drank in the terrific onslaught with delight. He had struck the enemy, he had made it wince and cry out. The first battle was his. He rose with the school and shuffled up the aisle. Suddenly at the exit, he beheld Mr. Tapping waiting. Their glances met in a long, hostile clash. There was no mistaking the master's meaning; it was a direct accusation that sought in Hickey's face to surprise a telltale look.

A great lump rose in Hickey's throat; all the joy of a moment ago passed, a profound melancholy enveloped him; he felt alone, horribly alone, fighting against the impossible.

"Why," he said, bitterly, "why should he always pick on me—the sneak!"

During the next few days a few minor skirmishes ensued which showed only too clearly to Hickey the implacable persecution he must expect from Tabby. The first day it was the question of breakfast.

At seven o'clock every morning the rising bell fills the air with its clamor from the belfry of the old gymnasium, but no one rises. There is half an hour until the gong sounds for breakfast, a long delicious half hour—the best half hour of the day or night to prolong under the covers. After twenty minutes a few effeminate members rise to prink, five minutes later there is a general tumbling out of the bed and a wild scamper into garments arranged in ingenious time-saving combinations.

At exactly the half hour, with the first sounds of the breakfast gong, Hickey would start from his warm bed, plunge his head into the already filled basin, wash with circumspection in eight seconds (drying included), thrust his legs into an arrangement of trousers, socks and unmentionables, pull a jersey over his head, stick his feet into the waiting pair of slippers, part and brush his hair, snap a dickey about his neck, and run down the stairs struggling into his coat, tying his tie and attending to the buttons, the whole process varying between twenty-one and one-eighth seconds and twenty-two and three-quarters.

But on the morning after the exposing of the skeleton Hickey had trouble with the dickey. The school regulations tyrannically demanded that each boy should appear at breakfast and chapel properly dressed, i.e., in collar and shirt. But as the appearance is accepted for the fact, the dickey comes to the rescue and permits not only dispatch in dressing, but, by suppressing a luxury from the wash list, to attend to the necessities of the stomach. The dickey is formed by the junction of two flat cuffs, held together by a stud, to which is attached a collar, and later a tie. When the coat is added even the most practiced eye may be deceived by the enclosed exhibition of linen.

On the aforesaid morning, as Hickey hastily donned his dickey, the stud snapped and he was forced to waste precious seconds in not only procuring another stud but in arranging the component parts. He tore down the stairs to find the door shut in his face—Tabby's orders, of course!

The next night the same malignant enemy surprised him at ten o'clock returning on tiptoe from the Egghead's room—marks and penal service on Saturday afternoon. Hickey soon perceived that he was to be subjected to a constant surveillance, that the slightest absence from his room after dark would expose him to detection and punishment. Macnooder counseled seeming submission and a certain interval of patient caution. Hickey indignantly repelled the advice; the more the danger the greater the glory.

On Friday morning a strange calm pervaded the school, a lethargy universal and sweet. Seven o'clock, half-past seven, a quarter of eight, and not a stir. Then suddenly in every house, exclamations of amazement burst from the rooms, watches were scanned incredulously and excited boys called from house to house. Gradually the wonder dawned, welcomed by cries of rejoicing—the clapper had been stolen!

In the Dickinson, Hickey and Macnooder were the first in the halls, the loudest in their questions, the most dumfounded at the occurrence. Breakfast, forty minutes late, was eaten in a buzz of excitement, interrupted by the arrival of a messenger from the headmaster with peremptory orders to convene at once in Memorial.

The Doctor was in no pleasant mood. The theft of the clapper, coming so soon upon the incident of the skeleton, had roused his fighting blood. His discourse was terse, to the point, and uncompromising. There could no longer be any doubt that individuals were in rebellion against the peace and discipline of the school. He would accept the defiance. If it was to be war, war it should be. It was for the majority to say how long they, the law-abiding, the studious, the decent, would suffer from the reckless outrages of a few without standards or seriousness of purpose. The clapper would not be replaced. All marks for tardiness and absence from recitations would be doubled, and the moment any total reached twenty, that boy would be immediately suspended from the institution. The clapper would not be replaced until the school itself replaced it!

Hickey drank in the sweet discourse, reveling in the buzz of conjecture that rose about him, concentrating all his powers on appearing innocent and unconcerned before the fusillade of admiring, alluring glances that spontaneously sought him out.

The school went to the recitation rooms joyfully, discussing how best to draw from the ultimatum all the amusement possible. By the afternoon every boy was armed with an alarm clock which he carried into each recitation, placing it in the aisle at his feet after a solicitous comparison of the time with his neighbors. Five minutes before the close of the hour the bombardment would begin, and as each clock exploded, the owner would grab it up frantically and depart for the next recitation in a gallop. Bright, happy days, when even the monotony of the classroom disappeared under the expectation of a sudden alarm!

With a perfect simulation of seriousness, expeditions known as clapper parties were organized to search for the missing clapper.

Orchards, gardens, streams—nothing was spared in the search. Complaints began to pour in from neighboring farmers with threats of defending their property with shotguns. The school gardener arrived in a panic to implore protection for his lawns. Then the alarm clocks became strangely unreliable. At every moment the sound of the alarm, singly, or in bunches, was heard in the halls of Memorial. Several of the older members of the faculty, who were addicted to insomnia and nervous indigestion, sent in their ultimatum. Thus forced to a decision, the headmaster compromised. He had the clapper replaced and assessed the school for the costs.

During those glorious, turbulent days, Hickey perceived with melancholy that Tabby still persisted in suspecting him. It was disheartening but there was no blinking the fact. Tabby suspected him!

At the table Tabby's eyes restlessly returned again and again in his direction. Tabby's ears were strained to catch the slightest word he might utter; in fact, everything in Tabby's bearing indicated a malignant determination to see in him the author of every escapade. This fresh injustice roused Hickey's ire to such an extent that, despite the cautious Macnooder, he determined upon a further deed of bravado.

One morning, Mr. Lorenzo Blackstone Tapping, exactly as Hickey planned, perceived a curious watch charm on Hickey's watch chain, which he soon made out to be a miniature silver clapper. Immediately suspicious, he noticed that every boy in the room was in a state of excitement. On examining them, he discovered that every waitscoat was adorned with the same suspect emblem. During the day, a chance remark overheard revealed to him the fact that Hickey was selling the souvenirs at a dollar apiece. Assuredly here was an important clue. That afternoon all his doubts were answered. He was seated at his study window when his attention was attracted by a group directly beneath. Against the wall Hickey was standing, with a large box under his arm, selling souvenirs as fast as he could make change to the breathless crowd which augmented at every moment.

Meanwhile, Hickey, fully aware of his enemy's proximity, took special pains that the conversation should carry. About him the excited crowd pressed in a frantic endeavor to purchase before the store was exhausted.

To all inquiries Hickey maintained a dark secrecy.

"I'm saying nothing, fellows, nothing at all," he said with a canny smile. "It isn't wise sometimes to do much talking. The impression has somehow got around that these little 'suveneers' are made out of the original clapper. I'm not responsible for that impression, gents, and I make no remarks thereupon. These little 'suveneers' I hold in my hand are silver-plated—*silver-plated*, gents, and when a thing is silver-plated there must be something inside. And I further remark that these 'suveneers' will sell for one dollar apiece only until five o'clock, that after that time they will sell at one dollar and a half, and I further remark that there are only forty-five left!" Then, rattling the box, he continued with simulated innocence, "Nothing but a 'suveneer,' gents, nothing guaranteed. We sell nothing under false pretenses!"

At half past four he had sold the last of a lot of two hundred and fifty amid scenes of excitement worthy of Wall Street.

At five o'clock, Hickey received a summons to Foundation House. There, to his delight, he found the headmaster in the company of Mr. Tapping.

Hickey entered with the candor of a cherub, plainly quite at loss as to the object of the summons.

"Hicks," said the headmaster in his solemnest tones, "you are under very grave suspicion."

"Me, sir?" said Hickey in ungrammatical astonishment.

"Hicks, it has come to my knowledge that you are selling as souvenirs bits of the clapper that was stolen from the gymnasium."

"May I ask, sir," said Hickey with indignation, "who has accused me?"

At this Mr. Tapping spoke up severely.

"I have informed the Doctor of facts which have come into my possession."

"Sir," said Hickey, addressing the headmaster, "Mr. Tapping has *honored* me with his enmity for a long while. He has not even hesitated to *threaten* me. I am not surprised that he should accuse me, only I insist that he state what evidence he has for bringing this accusation."

"Doctor, allow me," said Mr. Tapping, somewhat ill at ease. Then turning to Hickey he said, with the air of a cross-examiner: "Hicks, are you or are you not selling souvenirs at one dollar apiece, in the shape of small silver clappers?"

"Certainly."

"Made out of the original clapper?"

"Certainly *not!*"

"What!" exclaimed the amazed Tapping.

"Certainly not."

"Do you mean to say that two hundred and fifty boys would have bought those souvenirs at a dollar apiece for any other reason than that they contained a bit of the stolen clapper?"

Hickey smiled proudly.

"They may have been under that impression."

"Because you told them!"

"No, sir," said Hickey with righteous anger. "You have no right, sir, to say such a thing. On the contrary, I refused to answer one way or the other. You listened this afternoon from your window and you heard exactly my answer. If you will do me the *justice,* sir, to tell the Doctor what I did say, I shall be very much obliged to you."

"Enough, Hicks," said the headmaster with a frown. "Answer me directly. Are these watch charms made up out of the original clapper?"

"No, sir."

The Doctor, in his turn, looked amazed.

"Come, Hicks, that is not possible," he said. "I warn you I shall trace them without any difficulty."

Then Hickey smiled, a long delicious smile of culminating triumph. Slowly he drew forth from his pocket an envelope, from which he produced a legal document.

"If you will kindly read this, sir," he said, tending it with deepest respect.

The Doctor took it, glanced curiously at Hickey, and then began to read. Presently his face relaxed, and despite a struggle a smile appeared. Then he handed the document to Mr. Tapping, who read as follows:

I, John J. Goodsell, representing the firm of White, Brown and Bangs, jewelers, of Trenton, New Jersey, take oath that I have this day engaged to manufacture for William Orville Hicks of The Lawrenceville School 250 small clappers, design submitted, of iron plated with silver, and that the iron which forms the

foundation comes from scrap iron entirely furnished by us.
  Sworn to in the presence of notary.

JOHN J. GOODSELL.

Attached to the document was a bill as follows:

William Orville Hicks, Dr.,
        To White, Brown and Bangs.
250 silver gilt clappers, at 11c apiece.................. $27.50
                Received payment.

MAKING FRIENDS

"THAT WAS just before I licked Whitey Brown," said Lazelle, alias Gazelle, alias the Rocky Mountain Goat and the Gutter Pup. "Cracky, that was a fight!"

"How many rounds?" asked Lovely Mead, disrobing for the night.

"Eleven and a half. Knocked him to the count in the middle of the twelfth with a left jab to the bellows," said the Gutter Pup professionally. "He weighed ten pounds more than me. Ever do any fighting?"

"Sure," said the new arrival instantly.

"How many times?"

"Oh, I can't remember."

"You don't look it."

"Why not?"

"Your complexion's too lovely; and you're only a shaver, you know."

"I'm fifteen, almost sixteen," said Lovely, bridling up and surveying his new roommate with a calculating glance. "How old are you?"

"I've been three years at Lawrenceville, freshman," said the Gutter Pup severely. "That's the difference. What's your longest fight?"

"Twenty-one rounds," said Lovely, promptly.

"Oh," said the Gutter Pup in profound disappointment. "He licked you?"

"No."

"You licked him?"

"No."

"What then?"

"They stopped us."

"Huh!"

"We had to let it go over to the next day."

"And then?"

"Then I put him out in the thirteenth."

"Yes, you did!"

"Yes, I did."

The two fiery-haired champions stood measuring each other with their glances. Lovely Mead ran his eye over the wiry arms and chest opposite him and wondered. The Gutter Pup in veteran disdain was about to remark that Lovely was a cheerful liar when the tolling of the gym bell broke in on a dangerous situation. The Gutter Pup dove into bed and, reaching for a slipper, hurled it across the room, striking the candle fair and square and plunging the room into darkness.

"I learned that trick," he said, "the year I put the Welsh Rabbit to sleep in six." He stopped and ruminated over Lovely's story of his two-day fight, and then spoke scornfully from the dark: "I never fought anybody over eleven rounds. I never *had* to."

Lovely heard and possessed his soul in patience. He was on his second day at the school, his spirit not a whit subdued, though considerably awed, by the sacred dignities of the old boys. He liked the

Gutter Pup, with one reservation, and that was an instinctive antagonism for which there was no logical explanation. But at the first fistic reminiscence of the Gutter Pup he had sought in his soul anxiously and asked himself, "Can I lick him?" Each time the question repeated itself he felt an overwhelming impulse to throw down the gage and settle the awful doubt then and there. It was pure instinct, nothing more. The Gutter Pup was really a good sort and had adopted him in quite a decent way without taking an undue advantage. In fact, Lovely was certain that in his roommate he had met the congenial soul, the chum, the best friend among all friends for whom he had waited and yearned. His heart went out to the joyous, friendly Gazelle, but his fingers contracted convulsively. Theirs was to be an enduring friendship, a sacred, Three Musketeer sort of friendship—after one small detail was settled.

The next morning Lovely Mead bounded up with the rising bell and started nervously to dress. There was a lazy commotion in the opposite bed, and then, after a few languid movements of the covers, the Gutter Pup's reddish head appeared in surprise.

"Why, Lovely, what are you doing?"

"Dressing. Didn't you hear the bell?"

"Jiminy crickets, what a waste, what an awful waste of time," said the Gutter Pup, luxuriously, stretching his arms and yawning. "Say, Lovely, I like you. You're a good sort and that was a rattlin' plucky tackle you made yesterday. Say, we're going to get on famously together, only, Lovely, you *are* green, you know."

"I suppose I am."

"You are. Of course, you can't help it, you know. Everyone starts that way. Lordy, Lovely, you remind me of the first time I hit this old place, three weeks after I fought Mucker Dennis of the Seventy-second Street gang."

Lovely Mead's gorge swelled up with indignation. To hide his emotion, he plunged his head into the basin and emerged dripping.

"I say, Lovely, I must give you some pointers," said the Gutter Pup affably. "Everything depends, you know, on the start. You want to stand in with the masters, you know. Study hard the first week and get your lessons down fine, and work up their weak points, and you'll slide through the term with ease and pleasure."

"What are these weak points?" inquired Lovely from the depths of a clean shirt.

"Oh, I mean the side they're most approachable. Now the Roman, you know, when he makes a joke you always want to laugh as though you were going to die."

"Does he make many jokes?" asked Lovely.

"Cracky, yes. Then there's one very important one he makes around Thanksgiving that everyone watches for. I'll put you on, but you must be very careful."

"What? The same joke every year?" said Lovely.

"Regular. It's about Volturcius in Caesar—the 'c' is soft, you know, but you have to pronounce it—Vol-turk-ious."

"Why so?"

"So the Roman can say, 'No-o, no-o, not even the near approach of Thanksgiving will justify such a pronunciation.' See? That's the cue to laugh until the tears wet the page. It's most important."

"What about the Doctor?"

"Easy, dead easy; just ask questions, side-path questions that'll lead him away from the lesson and give him a chance to discourse. Say—another thing, Lovely, don't go and buy anything in the village; let me do that for you."

"Thanks."

"I'm on to their games, you know; I'm wise. Oh, say, another pointer—about the Jigger Shop. You want to build up your credit with Al, you know."

"How d'you mean?"

"The best way is to get trusted right off while you've got the chink and then pay up promptly at the end of a week, and repeat the operation a couple of times. Then Al thinks you're conscientious about debts and that sort of thing, and when the hard-up months come he'll let you go the limit."

"I say, Lazelle," said Lovely, admiringly, "you've got it down pretty fine, haven't you? It's real white of you to look after me this way."

"You're all right," said the Gutter Pup, still lolling in bed. "All you want is to lay low for a month or so and no one'll bother you. Besides, I'll see to that."

"Thank you."

"You see, Lovely, I've taken a fancy to you: a real, live, fat, young fancy. You remind me of Bozy Walker that was fired for introducing geese into the Muffin Head's bedroom; dear old Bozy, he stood up to me for seven rounds."

Lovely Mead dropped the hairbrush in his agitation and drew a long breath. How much longer could his weak human nature hold out? Downstairs the gong began to call them to breakfast. With the first sound the Gutter Pup was in the middle of the floor, out of his pajamas and into his clothes before the gong had ceased to ring. He plunged his head into the basin already filled with water, dried himself, parted the moist hair with one sweeping stroke of his comb, snapped a dickey about his neck and struggled into his coat while Lovely was still staring with amazement.

"That's the way it's done," said the Gutter Pup, triumphantly. "There's only one fellow in the school can beat me out, and that's that old Hickey, over in the Dickinson; but I'll beat him yet. Are you ready? Come on!"

The trouble was that the Gutter Pup was absolutely unaware of the disturbance in Lovely's mind, or that his reminiscences provoked such thoughts of combat. He took Lovely to the village and fitted him out, hectoring the tradesmen and smashing prices with debonair impudence that Lovely sneakingly envied. Certainly the Gutter Pup was unusually cordial and did not in the least make him feel the indignities of his position of newcomer, as he had a right to do.

After supper they worked on the arrangement of their room. The Gutter Pup grew ecstatic as Lovely produced his treasures from the bottom of the trunk.

"My aunt's cat's kittens!" he ejaculated as Lovely produced a set of pennants in gaudy arrangement. "Will we have the boss room, though! Lovely, you are a treasure! This will make the Waladoo Bird turn pale and weep for sorrow. Supposin' we ruminate."

They ranged their accumulated possessions on the floor, and sat back to consider.

"Well," said the Gutter Pup, "let's begin by putting the cushions on the window seat and the rugs on the floor. Now the question is —what's to have the place of honor?"

"What have you got?" asked Lovely, considering.

"I've got a signed photograph of John L. Sullivan," said the Gutter Pup, proudly producing it. "It used to be cleaner, but Butsey White blew up with a root beer bottle and spattered it."

"Is it his own signature?" inquired Lovely, gazing in awe.

"Sure. Dear old John L. He *was* a fighter. Now, what have *you* got?"

71

"I've got a picture of an actress."

"Honest?"

"Sure."

"Who is it?"

"Maude Adams."

"You don't say so!"

"Fact."

"It isn't signed, Lovely—it can't be?"

"It is."

"Cracky! That *is* a prize. Maude Adams! Think of it! What will the Waladoo Bird say?"

The Gutter Pup gazed reverently at the priceless photograph and said in a breath, "Maude Adams and John L.; think of it, Lovely!" He paused and added in a burst of gratitude, "Say, you can call me Gazelle or Razzle-dazzle now, if you want; afterward we'll see about Gutter Pup."

Lovely was too overcome by this advance to voice his feelings, but his heart went out to his new friend, all irritation forgotten. After long discussion it was decided that the two photographs, being of unique and equal value, should be hung side by side on the background of an American flag. The pennants were strung as a border around the walls, but were speedily hidden under an imposing procession of lightweight and middleweight champions, sporting prints, posters and lithographic reproductions of comic opera favorites, boxing gloves, fencing masks, lacrosse sticks, Japanese swords, bird nests, stolen signs, photographs of athletic teams, cotillion favors and emblems of the school and the Woodhull. They stopped and gazed in awe and admiration, and falling gleefully into each other's arms, executed a dance about the room. Then Lovely Mead, in an unthinking moment, standing before the photograph of the mighty John L., exclaimed, "Say, Gazelle, isn't he a wonder, though! How long have you had it?"

"I got it," said the Gutter Pup, putting his head on one side and reflecting, "right after I fought Whitey Brown—just before my mill with Doggie Shephard—a year and a half ago, I should say."

All the joy of the home-building left Lovely. He sat down on the bed and pulled at his shoestrings so viciously that they broke off in his hand.

"What's the matter?" said the Gutter Pup in surprise.

"Nothing."

"You look sort of put out."

"Oh, no."

"Whitey was a tough one," resumed the Gutter Pup, lolling on the window seat, "but Doggie was no great shakes. Too fat and overgrown. He did look big, but he had no footwork and his wind was bad—very bad."

Lovely Mead listened with averted eyes.

If he had only been an old boy he would have thrown down the gauntlet then and there; but he was a freshman and must check the tugging within. Besides, there must be some excuse. He could not openly, out of clear sky, provoke an old boy who had taken him under his protection and had done everything to make him feel at home. Such an act would be fresh, and would bring down on him the condemnation of the whole school.

"Why the deuce should I care, after all?" he asked himself gloomily that night. "What difference does it make how many fellows he's licked. I suppose it's because I'm a coward. That's it; it's because I'm afraid that he would lick me that it rankles so. Am I a coward, after all, I wonder?"

This internal questioning became an obsession. It clouded his days and took the edges from the keen joy of romping over the football field and earning the good word of Tough McCarty for his neat diving tackles. Could the Gutter Pup lick him, after all? He wondered, he debated, he doubted. He began to brood over it until he became perfectly unapproachable, and the Gutter Pup, without a suspicion of the real cause, began to assure Hasbrouck that Lovely was being overtrained.

Meanwhile, matters were approaching a crisis with Lovely. Each morning he calculated the strength of the Gutter Pup's chest and arms, and wondered what was the staying power of his legs. Sometimes he admitted to himself that he wouldn't last three rounds. At others he figured out a whole plan of campaign that must wear down the Gutter Pup and send him to a crashing defeat. Waking, he went through imaginary rounds, received without wincing tremendous, imaginary blows, and sent in sledge-hammer replies that inevitably landed the champion prone on his back. At night his dreams were a long conglomeration of tussling and battle in the most unexpected places. He fought the Gutter Pup at the top of the water tower and saw him vanish over the edge as the result of a smashing blow on the point of the jaw; he fought him on the football field and in the classroom, while the Roman held the watch and the headmaster insisted on refereeing.

The worst of it was, he knew he was going to pieces and moping in a way to render himself a nuisance to all his associates; and yet he couldn't help it. Try as he would to skip the mention of any subject that could be tagged to a date, every now and then an opening would come, and the Gutter Pup would begin: "Let me see; that must have been just after I fought—"

At last, one night, unable to bear the strain longer, Lovely went to his room resolved to end it. He bided his opportunity, gazing with unseeing eyes at the pages of the divine Virgil. Finally he raised his head and said, abruptly, "Say, Lazelle, what do you think of our chances for the football championship?"

"Fair, only fair," said the Gutter, glad for any excuse to stop studying. "The Davis and the Dickinson look better to me."

"How long has it been since we won?" said Lovely, scarcely breathing.

"Let me see," said the Gutter Pup, unsuspecting. "We won the fall I fought Legs Brownell behind the Davis house."

"Lazelle," said Lovely, rising desperately, "I can lick you!"

"What?"

"I can lick you!"

"Hello," said the Gutter Pup, considering him in amazement, "what does this mean?"

"It means I can lick you," repeated Lovely doggedly, advancing and clenching his fists.

"You want a fight?"

"I do."

"Why, bully for you!"

The Gutter Pup considered, joyfully, with a glance at the clock.

"It's too late now to pull it off. We'll let it go until tomorrow night. Besides, you'll be in better condition then, and you can watch your food, which is important. I'll notify Hickey. You don't mind fighting by lamplight?"

"Huh!"

"Of course, we'll fight under the auspices of the Sporting Club, with a ring and sponges and that sort of thing," said the Gutter Pup cheerfully. "You'll like it. It's a secret organization and it's a great honor to belong. Hickey, at the Dickinson, got it up. He's president, and referees. I'm the official timekeeper, but that don't matter. They'll arrange for seconds and all that sort of thing, and Doc Macnooder is always there for medical assistance. You're sure the light won't bother you?"

"No."

"It's a queer effect, though. First time I fought Snapper Bell—"

"Lazelle," said Lovely, choking with rage, "I can lick you, right now—here—and I don't believe you ever licked anyone in your life!"

"Look here, freshman," said the Gutter Pup, at once on his dignity; "I've stood enough of your impertinence. You'll do just as I say, and you'll act like a gentleman and a sport and not like a member of the Seventy-second Street gang. We'll fight like sportsmen, tomorrow, at midnight, under the auspices of the Sporting Club, in the baseball cage, and until then I'll dispense with your conversation! Do you hear me?"

Lovely Mead felt the justice of the reproof. Yes, he *had* acted like a member of the Seventy-second Street gang! He glanced up at the photograph (slightly spotted) of John L. and he thought of Ivanhoe and the Three Musketeers, and Sir Nigel of the White Company, and presently he said, tentatively, "I say—"

No answer.

"Lazelle—"

Still no answer.

"Say, I want to—to apologize. You're right about the Seventy-second Street gang. I'm sorry."

"All right," said the Gutter Pup, not quite appeased. "I'm glad you apologized."

"But we fight to-morrow—to the end—to the limit!"

"You're on!"

They spoke no more that night, undressing in silence, each covertly swelling his muscles and glancing with stolen looks at his opponent's knotted torso. By morning the Gutter Pup's serenity had returned.

"Well, how're you feeling? How did you sleep?" he asked, poking his nose over the coverlets.

"Like a log," returned Lovely, lying gloriously.

"Good. Better take a nap in the afternoon, though, if you're not used to midnight scrapping."

"Thanks."

"Mind the food—no hot biscuits and that sort of thing. A dish of popovers almost put me to the bad the first time I met Bull Dunham. Fact, and he didn't know enough to counter."

Lovely dressed and hurriedly left the room.

At two o'clock, to his amazement, Charley De Soto, the great quarterback, in person, waited on him in company with the gigantic Turkey Reiter, tackle on the eleven, and informed him that they had been appointed his seconds and anxiously inquired after his welfare.

"I—oh, I'm doing pretty well, thank you, sir," said Lovely, overcome with embarrassment and pride.

"Say, Charley," said Turkey, after an approving examination, "I kind of hanker to the looks of this here bantam. He's got the proper color hair and the protruding jaw. Danged if I don't believe he'll give the Gutter Pup the fight of his life."

"Can you lick him?" said De Soto, looking Lovely tensely in the eyes.

"I'll do it or die," said Lovely, with a lump in his throat.

"Good, but mind this, youngster: no funking. I don't stand second to any quitter. If I'm behind you, you've *got* to win."

Lovely thought at that moment that death on the rack would be a delight if it only could win a nod of approbation from Charley De Soto.

"How's your muscles?" asked Turkey. He ran his fingers over him, slapped his chest and punched his hips, saying, "Hard as a rock, Charley."

"How's your wind?" said De Soto.

"Pretty well, thank you, sir," said Lovely, quite overcome by the august presence.

"Now keep your mind off things. Don't let the Gutter Pup bluff you. Slip over to the Upper, right after lights, and I'll take charge of the rest. By the way, Turk, who's in the corner with the Gutter Pup?"

"Billy Condit and the Triumphant Egghead."

"Good. We'll just saunter over and lay a little bet. So long, youngster. No jiggers or eclairs. See you later."

"So long, old Sporting Life," added Turkey, with a friendly tap on the shoulder. "Mind now, keep cheerful."

76

Lovely's mood was not exactly cheerful. In fact he felt as if the bottom had fallen out of things. He tried his best to follow Charley De Soto's advice and not think of the coming encounter, but, do what he would, his mind slipped ahead to the crowded baseball cage, the small, ill-lighted ring, and the Gutter Pup.

"After all, will he lick me?" he said, almost aloud. His heart sank, or rather it was a depression in the pit of his stomach.

"Supposing he does?" he went on, pressing his knuckles against his teeth. What a humiliation after his boast! There would be only one thing to do—leave school at once, and never, never return!

He had wandered down to the football field where the candidates for the school eleven were passing and falling on the ball under the shouted directions of the veterans. The bulky figure of Turkey Reiter, gigantic with its padded shoulders and voluminous sweater, hove into view, and the tackle's rumbling voice cried out:

"Hi there, old Sockarooster, this won't do! Keep a-laughin'; keep cheerful; tumble down here and shag for me."

Lovely Mead went gratefully to fetch the balls that Turkey booted, far down the field, to the waiting halfbacks.

"Feeling a bit serious, eh?" said Turkey.

"Well—"

"Sure you are. That's nothing. Don't let the Gutter Pup see it, though. He's got to believe we are holding you in, chaining you up, keepin' you under the bars, 'cause you're barking to get at him. Savvy? Chuck in a bluff, old sport, and—keep cheerful. Better now?"

"Yes, thank you," said Lovely, who was in nowise suffering from an excess of hilarity.

He did not see the Gutter Pup until supper, and then had to undergo again his solicitous inquiries. By a horrible effort he succeeded in telling a funny story at the table, and laughed until his own voice alarmed him. Then he relapsed into silence, smiling furiously at every remark, and chewing endlessly on food that had no flavor for him.

"Lovely," said the Gutter Pup upstairs, shaking his head, "you don't look fit; you're getting nervous."

"Sure," said Lovely, remembering Turkey's injunction. "I'm a high-strung, *vicious* temperament!"

"Your eye acts sort of loose," said the Gutter Pup, unconvinced.

"You're new to fighting before a big assemblage. It's no wonder. I don't want any *accidental* advantages. Say the word and we'll put it over."

"No," said Lovely, quite upset by his friendly offer. "I only hope, Lazelle, I can hold myself in. I've got an awful temper; I'm afraid I'll kill a man some day."

"No, Lovely," said Gutter Pup, shaking his head. "You don't deceive me. You are ill—ill, I tell you, and you might as well own up."

The truth was, Lovely was ill and rapidly getting worse under the insouciance of the veteran of the ring.

"Why, my aunt's cat's pants, Lovely," said the Gutter Pup seriously. "That's nothing to be ashamed of. Didn't I get it the same way the first time I went up against Bloody Davis of the Murray Hill gang, on a bet I'd stick out three rounds?"

Lovely Mead drew a sigh of relief. The red blood seemed to rush back into his veins once more, and his lungs to resume their appointed functions.

"September's a good month for these little things," he said hopefully.

"October's better, more snap in the air," said the Gutter Pup. "September's muggy. I remember when I was matched against Slugger Kelly; it was so hot I lost ten pounds, and the fight only went five rounds at that."

The old provocation had roused up the old antagonism in Lovely. He hardly dared trust himself longer in the room, so he bolted and slipped down to the Waladoo's room and out into the campus.

"Gee," he said to himself, with a sigh of relief, "if I could only get at him *now!*"

At taps he went cautiously to the Upper, by the back way, and gained the room of Charley De Soto, where he was told to turn in on the window seat and take it easy.

Presently Turkey Reiter and Macnooder arrived to discuss the probabilities. Then Bojo Lowry, who could play anything, sat down at the piano and performed the most wonderful variations and medleys, until Lovely forgot any future engagement in the delight of gazing from his cushioned recess on real Fourth Formers, enjoying the perquisites and liberties of the Upper House.

Suddenly Macnooder glanced at his watch and announced that it was almost midnight. Lovely sprang up feverishly.

"Here, young Sporting Life," cried Turkey, "no champing on the bit! Just a dash of calm and tranquility."

"Easy, easy there," said De Soto, with a professional glance.

"Ready here," said Macnooder, picking up a brown satchel. "I'll bleed him if he faints."

They separated, and, on tiptoe, by various routes, departed from the Upper, making wide circles in the darkness before seeking the baseball cage, Lovely Mead supported on either side by Charley De Soto and Turkey.

They gave the countersign at the door, and were admitted noiselessly into the utter blackness of the baseball cage. Lovely waited in awe, unable to distinguish anything, clutching at Turkey's arm.

"Is the Gutter Pup here yet?" said De Soto's voice, in a whisper.

Another voice, equally guarded, replied: "Just in."

From time to time the door opened on the starry night and vague forms flitted in. Then other voices spoke:

"What time is it?"

"Midnight, Hickey."

"Lock the door; no admittance now. Egghead, show up with the light. Strike up, Morning Glory!"

A bull's-eye flashed out from one corner, and then two lanterns filled the gloom with their trembling flicker.

Out of the mist suddenly sprang forty-odd members of the Sporting Club, grouped about a vacant square in the middle of the cage which had been roped off. De Soto and Turkey pushed forward to their appointed stations, where chairs had been placed for the principals. Lovely seated himself and glanced across the ropes. The Gutter Pup was already in his corner, stripped to the waist, and being gently massaged by the Triumphant Egghead and Billy Condit, captain of the eleven.

In the middle of the ring, Hickey, in his quality of president and referee, was giving his directions in low, quick syllables. The assembled sporting gentlemen pressed forward for the advantage of position; the two front ranks assuming sitting or crouching positions, over which the back rows craned. Lovely gazed in awe at the select assembly. The élite of the school was there. He saw Glendenning, Rock Bemis and Tough McCarty of his own house, scattered among such celebrities as Crazy Opdyke, the Mugwump Politician, Goat Phillips who ate the necktie, and the Duke of Bilgewater, Wash Simmons, Cap Kiefer, Stonewall Jackson, Tug Moffat, Slugger Jones, Ginger-Pop Rooker, Cheyenne Baxter, Red Dog, Hungry Smeed, and Beauty Sawtelle, all silently estimating the strength of the freshman who had to go up against the veteran Gutter Pup.

Referee Hickey paid a quick visit to the contending camps, and was assured that each antagonist was restrained from flying at his opponent's throat only by the combined efforts of his seconds.

"Gentlemen of the Sporting Club," said Hickey, scraping one foot and shooting his collar, as referees do, "before proceeding with the evening's entertainment, the management begs to remind you that the labors incident to the opening of the school have been un-usually heavy—unusually so; and, as we particularly desire that nothing shall be done to disturb the slumbers of our overworked faculty, we will ask you to applaud only in the English fashion, by whispering to your neighbor, 'Oh, very well struck, indeed,' when you are moved to excitement. We gently remind you that anyone breaking forth into cheers will be first slugged and then expelled.

"Gentlemen of the Sporting Club, I have the honor to present to you the evening's contestants. On the right, our well-known sport-ing authority, Mr. Gutter Pup Lazelle, known professionally as the Crouching Kangaroo. On the left, Mr. Lovely Mead, the dark horse from Erie, Pennsylvania, who has been specially fed on raw beef in preparation for the encounter. Both boys are members of the Woodhull branch of this club. The rounds will be of three minutes each—one minute intermission. Mr. Welsh Rabbit Simpson will act as timekeeper, and will return the stop watch *immediately* on con-clusion of the exercises. Both contestants have signified their desire to abide strictly to the rules laid down by the late Marquis of Queensberry, bless him! No fouls will be tolerated, and only one blow may be struck in the breakaway.

"In the corner for the Gutter Pup, Mr. William Condit, the tiddledy-winks champion, and the only Triumphant Egghead in captivity.

"In the corner for Lovely, Mr. Turkey Reiter, the Dickinson Mud Lark, and Mr. Charles De Soto, the famous crochet expert. Doctor Macnooder, the Trenton veterinary, is in attendance, but will *not* be allowed to practice. The referee of the evening will be that upright and popular sportsman, the Honorable Hickey Hicks. Let the contestants step into the ring."

Lovely was shoved to his feet and propelled forward by a resounding slap on his shoulders from Turkey Reiter. He had sat in a daze, awed by the strange, imposing countenances of the school celebrities, duly submitting to the invigorating massage of his seconds, hearing nothing of the directions showered on him. Now he was actually in the ring, feeling the hard earth under his feet, looking into the eyes of the Gutter Pup, who came up cheerfully extending his hand. Surprised, Lovely took it, and grinned a sheepish grin.

"Ready—go!" came the command.

Instantly the Gutter Pup sprang back, assuming that low, protective attitude which had earned from Hickey the epithet of the Crouching Kangaroo. Lovely, very much embarrassed, extended his left arm, holding his right in readiness while he moved mechanically forward on the point of his toes. The Gutter Pup, smiling at him, churned his arms and shifted slightly to one side. Strangely enough, Lovely felt all his resentment vanish. He no longer had the slightest desire to hurl himself on his antagonist. Indeed, it would at that moment have seemed quite a natural act to extend his hand to the joyful Gutter Pup and close the incident with a laugh. But there he was, irrevocably destined to fight before the assembled Sporting Club, under penalty of everlasting disgrace. He made a tentative jab and sprang lightly back from the Gutter Pup's reply. Then he moved forward and backward, feinting with his left and right, wishing all the time that the Gutter Pup would rush in and strike him, that he might attack with anger instead of this weakening mental attitude to which he was at present a prisoner. Twice the Gutter Pup's blows grazed his head, and once landed lightly on his chest, without his being at all moved from his calm. The call of "Time" surprised him. He went to his seconds frowning.

"What's wrong, young'n?" said De Soto. "You're not in the game."

"No," said Lovely, shaking his head. "I—I've got to get mad first."

"All right, that'll come. Keep cool and play to tire him out," said De Soto, satisfied. "Make him do the prancing around; don't you waste any energy."

81

"Time!" whispered the Welsh Rabbit.

Again he was in the ring, experiencing once more that same incomprehensible feeling of sympathy for the Gutter Pup. The more he danced about, shaking his head and feinting with quick, nervous jabs, the more Lovely's heart warmed up to him. Wasn't he a jolly, genial chap, though? Desperately Lovely strove to remember some fault, a word or a look that had once offended him. In vain; nothing came. He liked the chap better than he had ever liked anyone before. He struck out as one strikes at his dearest friend, and a low groan of disgust rose from the Sporting Club.

"Ah, put some steam in it!"

"Do you think you're pickin' cherries?"

"That's it—be polite!"

"Sister, don't hurt little brother!"

The Welsh Rabbit spoke:

"Time!"

Not a real blow had yet been struck. Lovely went to his corner perplexed.

"That's the boy," said De Soto, with a satisfied shake of his head. "That's the game! Don't mind what you hear. Play the long game. The Crouching Kangaroo style is all very pretty, but it doesn't save the wind."

"Never mind the ballet steps, Sport," added Turkey, vigorously applying the towel. "Hold in, but when you do start, rip the in'ards out of things."

"They think I'm doing it on purpose," said Lovely to himself.

"Time!" called the Welsh Rabbit.

The Gutter Pup, changing his tactics, as though he had sufficiently reconnoitered, began to attack with rapid, pestiferous blows that annoyed Lovely as a swarm of gnats annoys a dog. He shook his head angrily and sought an opportunity to strike, but the fusillade continued, light but disconcerting. When he struck, the Gutter Pup slipped away or ducked and returned smiling and professional to attack. Lovely began to be irritated by the Gutter Pup's complacency. He wasn't serious enough—his levity was insulting. Also, he was furious because the Gutter Pup would not strike him a blow that hurt. His jaw set and he started to rush.

"Time!" said the Welsh Rabbit.

Lovely went to his corner unconvinced.

"Are the rounds three minutes?" he asked.

"Sure," said Turkey. "Don't worry; they'll get longer."

Lovely looked across at the opposite camp. The adherents of the Gutter Pup were patting him on the back, exulting over his work.

"What's he done?" said Lovely, angrily, to himself. "That sort of work wouldn't hurt a fly."

"Time!" said the Welsh Rabbit.

Lovely walked slowly to meet the Gutter Pup, bursting with irritation. He waited, and as the Gutter Pup attacked he plunged forward, taking a blow in the face, and drove his fist joyfully into the chest before him. The Gutter Pup went back like a tenpin, staggered, and kept his footing. When he came up there was no longer a smile in his eyes.

They threw boxing to the winds. It was give and take, fast and furious, back and forth against the ropes, and rolling over and over on the ground.

"Time!" announced the Welsh Rabbit, and Hickey had to pry them apart.

Lovely thought the intermission would never end. He sat stolidly, paying no heed to his seconds' prayers to go slow, to rest up this next round, to make the Gutter Pup work. He would fight his fight his own way, without assistance.

"Time!" said the Welsh Rabbit.

Lovely started from his corner for the thing that came to meet him without yielding, exchanging blows without attempt at blocking, rushing into clinches, locking against the heaving chest, looking into the strange, wild eyes, pausing for neither breath nor rest.

Once he was rushed across the ring, fighting back like a tiger, and jammed over the ropes into the ranks of the spectators. Then he caught the Gutter Pup off his balance, and drove him the same way, his arms working like pistons. The rounds continued and ended with nothing to choose between them.

Lovely felt neither the blows received nor the rough rubbing-down of his seconds. He heard nothing but the sharp cries of "Time!" and sometimes he didn't hear that; but a rough hand would seize him (was it Hickey's?) and tear him away from the body against him.

He went down several times, wondering what had caused it, remembered standing moments triumphantly, while the fallen Gutter Pup raised himself from the ground.

Then he lost track of the rounds; and the rows of sweaters and

83

funny white faces about the ring seemed to swell and multiply into crowds that stretched far back and up. The lights seemed to be going out—getting terribly dim and unsteady.

Once in his corner he thought he heard someone say: "Fifteenth round"—fifteen, and he could remember only six. In fact, he had forgotten whom he was fighting or what it was about, only that someone on whose knee he was resting was shrieking in his ear, "He's all out, Lovely. You've got him. Just one good soak—just one *lovely* one!"

That was a joke, he supposed—a poor joke—but he would see to that "one soak" the next round.

"Time!" cried the Welsh Rabbit.

For the sixteenth time the seconds raised their champions, steadied them, and sent them forth. One good blow would send either toppling over to the final count. So they craned forward in wild excitement, exhorting them in hoarse whispers.

The two contestants gyrated up and stood blankly regarding each other. About them rose a murmur of voices:

"Sail in!"

"Soak him, Lovely!"

"Clean him up, Gutter Pup!"

"One to the jaw!"

"Now's your time!"

With a simultaneous movement each raised his right and shot it lumberingly forward, past the hazy, confronting head, fruitlessly into the air. Renewed whispers, dangerously loud, arose:

"Now's your chance, Gutter Pup!"

"Draw off and smash him!"

"He's all yours, Lovely!"

"Oh, Lovely, hit him! Hit him!"

"Just once!"

They neither heard nor cared. Their arms locked lovingly about their shoulders, and they began to settle. New cries:

"Break away!"

"Don't let him pull you down!"

"Keep your feet, Lovely!"

"They're both going!"

With a gradual, deliberate motion, Lovely and the Gutter Pup sat down, still affectionately embraced; then, wavering a moment, careened over and lay blissfully unconscious. Amazement and perplexity burst forth.

"Why, they're done for!"

"They're out—they're both out!"

"Sure enough."

"What happens?"

"Who wins?"

"Well, did you ever—"

Suddenly Hickey, standing forward, began to count:

"One, two, three—"

"What's he doing that for?"

"Aren't they both down?"

"Four, five, six, seven—"

"But Lovely went first!"

"No, the Gutter Pup."

"Eight, nine, TEN!" cried Hickey. "I declare both men down and out. The Sporting Club will register one knockout to the credit of the Gutter Pup and one to Lovely Mead. All bets off. The Welsh Rabbit will proceed to return that watch!!"

At seven o'clock the next morning Lovely, from his delicious bed, gazed across at the swollen head of the Gutter Pup. At the same instant the Gutter Pup, opening his eyes, perceived the altered map of Lovely's features.

"Lovely," he said brokenly, "you're the finest ever. You're a man after my own heart!"

"Razzle-dazzle," replied Lovely, choking, "you're the finest sport and gentleman in the land. I love you better than a brother."

"Lovely, that was the greatest fight that has ever been fought," said the Gutter Pup. "You are *the* daisy scrapper!"

"Razzle-dazzle—"

"Call me Gutter Pup."

"Gutter Pup, you've got the nerve market cornered."

"Lovely, I haven't felt so happy since the day I stood up five rounds—"

Suddenly the Gutter Pup stopped and added apologetically: "Say, Lovely, honest, does my au-to-biography annoy you?"

And Lovely replied happily:

"No, Gutter Pup, honest—not now."

THE HERO OF AN HOUR

GEORGE BARKER SMITH was one of the four hundred-odd boys whose names figure in the school catalogue at the commencement of each year. He had passed from the shell into the first form, from the first form into the second, where he had remained an extra year, during the elongating, dormant period of his growth, and another year, during the dormant, elongating one. Then in the seventh year of his career he finally achieved the fourth form and entered the Upper House.

During this generous stay he had done nothing to distinguish himself from his neighbor. He had never accomplished anything heroic, attempted anything daring, or done anything ridiculous. After seven years his record was so blank that even the fertile imaginations of Hickey and Macnooder could find nothing on which to hang a nickname. Besides, it is doubtful if they ever stopped to think of George Barker Smith. He filled in, he was the average—a part of the great background of school life, which made up the second teams in athletic contests and substituted occasionally on the banjo and mandolin clubs, after borrowing a dress suit across the hall.

He ran in debt at the Jigger Shop, like everyone else, or he might have been called Miser. He flunked in Greek and mathematics sufficiently to escape the epithet of Poler. He had occasionally been read out at roll call for absence from bath, thus invalidating the right to Soapsuds or Wash.

Sometimes, when his neighbors dropped in on him in quest of stamps or a collar or a jersey, they called him affectionately Smithy, old Sockarooster. But he was not deceived, and loaned from his wardrobe with a full comprehension of the value of endearing terms. Smithy! After seven years he was just Smithy—his whole story was there.

And in the secret places of his heart, which no boy reveals, George Barker Smith grieved. Covertly he felt his obscureness and rebelled. After seven years' afflictions he would pass from Law-renceville and be forgotten. And all for the lack of a nickname! If Nature had only formed him so that he might have aspired to the appellation of the Triumphant Egghead. The Triumphant Egg-head—that was a name to be proud of! Who could ever forget that? There was fame secure and imperishable; neither years nor dis-tance could dim the memory!

No, Nature had not been considerate of him. His nose was just a nose, not a Beekstein; his ears were ordinary ears, not Flop Ears; his teeth were regular and all present. No one would ever call him Walrus or Tuskarora Smith, which sounds so well. He was not tall enough to be called Ladders or Beanpole; he was not small enough for Runt, Tiny, Wee-wee, or The Man. He was just average size, average weight, which barred a whole category, such as Skinny, Puff-Ball, Shanks, Slab-Sides, Jumbo, Flea, Bigboy and Razors.

To pass into the world and be forgotten! To fade from the mem-ory of his classmates or to linger indistinctly as one of the Smiths between Charles D. and George R.! And all for the lack of a nick-name! George Barker Smith, brooding thereon, envied the Gutter Pup, who likewise rejoiced in the appellation of Razzle-dazzle and the Rocky Mountains Gazelle; he envied the Waladoo Bird, the Coffee Cooler, the Morning Glory; he envied Two-Inches Brown, whose indiscreet remark that he needed but that to make the varsity nine had at least enrolled his name on the list of celebrities; but most of all he envied the Triumphant Egghead. With that glorious title as model, he sought in himself for something which might reclaim him—and found nothing. From Barker Smith might be made Doggie or Bow-wow Smith, but even that lacked naturalness and application. No, there was no turning his destiny; Smithy it was decreed and Smithy it would remain.

It was not fame Smith sought. His spirit was not of the sort that drags angels down. Naturally there had been periods in his youth when he had dreamed of reaching the Homeric proportions of Turkey Reiter or Slugger Jones; of scurrying over the gridiron, darting through a maze of frantic tacklers like Flash Condit, who had scored against the Princeton varsity in that glorious eight-to-four game; of knocking out dramatic home runs like Cap Kiefer, that bring joy out of sorrow and end in towering bonfires. These are glories which all may dream of but few attain.

Neither did he ask for the gifts of a Hungry Smeed, for to possess the ability to eat forty-nine pancakes at a sitting was a talent that is not lightly bestowed. No, he did not ask for fame; all he asked was to be remembered; for some incident or accident to come which would mark him with a glorious, fantastic nickname that would live with the Triumphant Egghead and the Duke of Bilgewater. And Fate, which sometimes listens to prayers, was kind and brought him not only a nickname but fame—real enduring fame. For in the most extraordinary way it came to pass that George Barker Smith unwittingly accomplished a feat which no boy had ever dared before and which it is extremely unlikely will ever be duplicated in the future. And this is the manner in which greatness was thrust upon him.

In the last days of the month of September the school returned from the fatiguing period of vacation to seek recuperation and needed sleep in the classrooms. George Barker Smith found himself at last a full-fledged fourth former, one of the lords of the school, member of a free governing body, with license to burn the midnight lamp unchallenged, to stray into the village at all hours, to visit the Jigger Shop during school and remain tranquilly seated when a master bore down from the horizon, instead of joining the palpitating under-formers that just at his back crouched, glasses in hand, behind the counter. No longer did he have to stand in file once a week before the Bursar to claim a beggarly half-dollar allowance. Instead, once a month he strolled in at his pleasure and nonchalantly tendered checks for fifty dollars, with which allowance his parents, for one blissful year only, fondly expected him to purchase all the clothes necessary—per agreement.

He could hire a buggy at ruinous rates and disappear in search of distant cider-mills or visit friends in Princeton, who had gone before. Finally, his room was his castle, where no imperious tapping of a lurking undermaster would come to disturb a little party at the national game, for chips only, of course.

George Barker Smith's room was on the third floor back and had attached to it certain communal rights. Even as the possession of the ground-floor rooms in the under-form houses entailed the obligation to assist at all hours of the night the passage to the outer world, and to assure the safe return therefrom, so room 67 was the recognized highway to the roof of the Upper, when the thermometer had mounted above seventy-eight degrees Fahrenheit.

Those who sought the cooling heights sought security and (be it confessed, now that an inconsiderate faculty's sanction has made smoking no longer a pleasure but a choice) the companionship of the Demon Cigarette or the "Coffin Nail," as it was more affectionately known. The guardianship of this highway, if it entailed responsibilities, also brought with it certain perquisites and tariffs in the shape of an invitation without expense.

Now, George Barker Smith did not like the odor of tobacco in the least, and he particularly disliked the effects produced by the cheap cigarette which the price rendered popular. But once a fourth former there were so few rules to break that this opportunity had to be embraced as an imperative duty, and so he resigned himself, pretending (like how many others!) to inhale and enjoy it.

The last weeks of September were unusually hot and distressing. The stiff collar disappeared. Two-piece suits became the fashion for full dress and fatigue uniform consisted of considerably less. The day was passed in long, grumbling siestas under the shade of apple trees or in a complete surrender to the cooling contact of peach and strawberry jiggers. Even games lost their attraction, and the only sign of life was the pleasant spectacle of the heavy squad on the football team, puffing protestingly about the circle under the cruel necessity of reducing weight.

After dark, bands were organized which stole away, through Negro villages, arousing frantic dogs, to the banks of the not-too-fragrant canal, where they spent a long, blissful hour frolicking in the moonlit water or raising their voices in close harmony on the bank. Other spirits, not so adventurous, contented themselves with lining up behind the Upper in white, shivering line, where the hose brought comfort as it played over grateful backs.

Naturally, at night, smoking up the flue, even with the whispered conversations with the boy below and the boy across, lost all charm. The roof became a veritable rookery. Mattresses were carried up and hot, suffocating boys lolled through the raging night swapping yarns and gazing at the inscrutable stars.

On a certain evening, hot among the hottest, George Barker Smith, in that costume which obtained before the publication of the first fashions, was sitting at his desk in a conscientious endeavor to translate one paragraph of Cicero, which he held in his right hand, for every chapter of *The Count of Monte Cristo,* which he held in his left.

At his door suddenly appeared the Triumphant Egghead and Goat Phillips, whose title at this time had been conveyed solely for the butting manner of his attack. Each had likewise reached that stage of dishabille where there is little more to shed.

"Hello, old Sockbutts," said Egghead, genially.

"Hello yourself," returned Smith, noncommittally.

"We're going up on the roof," continued the Egghead. "Anyone up yet?"

"Not yet."

"It's as hot as blazes," said the Goat. "Better come along."

"I ought to finish this Cicero," said Smith, wondering if he could leave his hero in a sack, ready to be plunged into the dizzy waters below.

"Oh, come on," said the Egghead; "I'll give you that when we come down. Have you any matches? I've got the coffin nails."

A slight shower had ended a few minutes before without bringing relief from the heat.

"Are you coming?" said the Egghead, already out of the window. "Don't be a grind, Smithy."

"Sure, I'm with you," replied Smith, thus forced to repel the insinuation.

The Goat had gone first, then the Egghead, with Smith bringing up the rear.

"Look out, fellows," whispered the pilot, lost in the darkness ahead. "It's slippery as the deuce!"

The way led up a gutter to the peak of one slope, down that, up another and over to a cranny which formed about the back chimneys. The still moist tiles were, in fact, slippery and treacherous, and their movements were made with calculation and solicitude.

Smith, arriving the last at the top of the first peak, waited until the Egghead had descended and climbed in safety to the next ridge, glanced down the twenty feet of slippery slate, and, tempted, called out, "Look out, fellows, I'm going to slide!"

The Goat and the Egghead, in unison, cried to him to desist, for the second ridge which ended the slope of the first had a downward inclination toward the edge of the roof that made it exceedingly dangerous.

Just how it happened has never been satisfactorily settled: whether Smith actually intended to slide or whether he lost his grip and started unwillingly. However it may be, Egghead and the Goat, astride the second ridge, were suddenly horrified to see Smith's naked body shoot down the slope, strike the moist incline at the bottom, and, bounding down that, with increased velocity disappear over the roof. They heard one thud and then another in the gravel path, three stories below.

The two clung to each other with a dreadful sinking feeling.

"He's dead," said the Goat, solemnly. "Poor old Smith is dead."

"Squashed like a bug," said the Egghead. "We won't even recognize his remains."

"Egghead, it's all our fault—all our fault."

"Shut up, Goat, and don't blubber!"

"I'm not."

"You are—for Heaven's sake, brace up! We've got to get down to him!"

They started fearfully over the treacherous return, reaching Smith's room thoroughly unnerved. Then they began to run down the stairs, calling out:

"Smithy's dead!"

"Smithy's fallen off the roof!"

On their trail came a motley assortment of excited boys, rushing out of every room. Without a single hope they tore around to the back of the Upper, and there, sitting bolt upright in the position in which he had fallen, they found George Barker Smith. They stopped, astounded.

"Smith, is that you!" Egghead said, in a hoarse, incredulous whisper, and the answer returned faintly:

"It's me, Egghead."

"Are you dying?"

"I don't know."

"Are your bones all broken?"

"I don't know—I'm full of gravel!"

The boys gazed astounded up at the dark outline three stories above them. Halfway, the slanting roof of the porch had broken the fall and saved him from certain death. They gazed in silence, and then the chorus arose:

"Holy cats!"

"Great snakes!"

"Marvelous!"

"Can you beat that!"

"Mamma!"

"Simply marvelous!"

Smith, still in a comatose condition, caught the sounds of astonishment, and suddenly comprehended, first, that he had done something without parallel in school history, and, second, that he was alive.

"You fellows, get me upstairs," he said, gruffly, "and send for Doctor Charlie. I want to get this gravel out of me."

Macnooder and Turkey reverently carried him to his room, while Shy Thomas, who was clothed in a dressing gown, went streaming across the campus for the doctor.

A quick examination revealed the amazing fact that not a bone had been fractured.

"You've got a few bruises, and that's all, by George!" said the doctor, looking at him in open-eyed wonder.

"It's the gravel that bothers me," said Smith, twisting on his side.

"You did sit down rather hard," remarked the doctor, with a twitch of his lips. In half an hour he had removed thirty-seven pieces of gravel, large and small, and departed, after ordering rest and a few days' sojourn in bed.

Hardly had the doctor departed when Hickey arrived, full of importance and enthusiasm. For a moment he stood at the foot of the bed surveying the bruised hero with the affectionate and fatherly joy of a Barnum suddenly discovering a new freak.

"My boy," he said, happily, "you're a wonder. You're great. You're it. There's been nothing like it ever happened. Smithy, my boy, you're a genius. You're the wonder of the age!"

"I suppose everyone's excited?" said Smith, faintly realizing that Fate had touched him in her flight and made him famous.

"Excited? Why, they're howling with curiosity," responded Hickey, who, having cautiously turned the key in the door, returned and continued with importance: "Say, but I suppose you don't realize what we can make of this, do you?"

"What do you mean?" said Smith.

"First, where are those thirty-seven pieces of gravel?"

"I threw them away."

"My boy, my boy!" said Hickey, sitting down and burying his head in his arms. "Pearls before swine."

"But they're over there in the basket."

Hickey, with a cry of joy, flung himself on them, counted them and thrust them into his pocket.

"Smith," he said, condescendingly, "you've got certain qualities, I'll admit, but what you need is a manager!"

"Why, what are you thinking of?" said Smith, who began to have a suspicion of Hickey's plan.

"I suppose you would expose your honorable scars," said Hickey, disdainfully, "to anyone who asks to see them?"

"Why not?"

"Just out of friendliness?"

"Yes."

"Smith, you *are* a nincompoop! Why, my boy, there's money in it—big money! Never thought of that, eh?"

"How so?"

"Exhibitions—paid exhibitions, my boy! We'll organize the greatest sideshow ever known."

Smith blushed at the thought.

"Won't it be rather undignified?" he said doubtfully.

"Dignity, rats!" said Hickey. "Talk to me of dignity when you hear the gold rattling in your pocket, when you lodge in a marble palace and drive fast horses up Fifth Avenue. My boy, you don't know what you're worth. I'll have Macnooder paper the campus tomorrow. I'll get up scareheads that'll bring every mother's son of them scampering here to see you."

"What do I get out of it?" said Smith cautiously.

"Half!"

"You low-down robber!"

"Who had the idea? Would you ever have made a cent if it hadn't been for me? Do you suppose any attraction ever makes as much as his manager? My boy, I'm generous! I oughtn't to do it! Come now—is it a go?"

"Well—yes!"

"Wait—till you see the posters," said Hickey, squeezing his hand joyfully, "and mind, no private exhibitions. Promise?"

"I promise."

"Under oath?"

"So help me."

"Ta, ta."

Left at last alone, George Barker Smith could hardly seize the full measure of his future. Hickey was right, it was the biggest thing that had ever happened. In one short hour everything had changed. Now he was of the elect—a part of history, a tale to be told over whenever one old graduate would meet another. Even Hungry Smeed's great pancake record would have to be placed second to this. Other more distinguished appetites might come who would achieve fifty pancakes, but no boy would ever go the path he had gone. He was famous at last. At Prom and Commencement he would be pointed out to visitors in the company of Hickey, Flash Condit, Cap Kiefer and Turkey Reiter. Only yesterday he was plain George Barker Smith, tomorrow he might be . . .

What would the morrow bring? Who would name him? Would it be Hickey, Macnooder or Turkey or the Egghead, or would some unsuspected classmate find the happy expression? He hoped that it would be something picturesque, but a little more dignified than the Triumphant Egghead. He tried to imagine what the nickname would be. Of course, there were certain obvious appellations that immediately suggested themselves, such as Roofie, Jumper, or, better still, Plunger Smith. There was also Tattoo and Rubber and Sliding, but somehow none of these seemed to measure up to the achievement, and in this delightful perplexity Smith fell asleep.

OLD IRONSIDES
THE GREATEST SIDESHOW ON EARTH ON EXHIBITION
AT ROOM 67 UPPER
MANAGEMENT—Hicks & Macnooder.

Come one, Come all! Come and View the HUMAN METEOR, THE YOUNG RUBBER PLANT, THE FAMOUS PLUNGING ROCKET, THE WORLD-RENOWNED SMITH, THE BOY GRAVEL YARD!

Come and see the honorable scars! No private exhibition. This afternoon only! Old Ironsides is under contract not to bathe in the canal this fall. This is your one and only opportunity to see the results of Old Ironsides' encounter with the gravel path!

Come and see the 37 original guaranteed and authentic bits of gravel which dented but could not penetrate!

ADMISSION, 5 CENTS   FRESHMEN, 10 CENTS

$500 REWARD $500

To anyone who will duplicate this mad, death-defying feat. MR. MACNOODER, on behalf of Old Ironsides, will offer the above reward. Doctor's or Undertaker's bills to be shared in case of failure.

ROOM 67   ROOM 67

Exhibition begins at 2 o'clock.

The above posters, prominently displayed, produced a furore. By two o'clock fully one hundred boys were in line before room 67. At two o'clock Hickey addressed the crowd.

"Gentlemen, unfortunately a slight delay has become necessary —only a slight delay. Mr. Ironsides Smith's sense of natural delicacy is at present struggling with Mr. Ironsides Smith's desire not to disappoint his many friends and admirers. Just a slight delay, gentlemen—just a slight delay."

A cry of protest went up and Hickey disappeared. At the end of five minutes he returned radiant, announcing:

"Gentlemen, I am very glad to announce to you that Old Ironsides will not disappoint his many admirers. Only we wish it to be understood that this is a strictly scientific exhibition with an educational purpose in view. No levity will be tolerated. The exhibition is about to begin. Have your nickels in hand, gentlemen; ten cents for freshmen, with the privilege of shaking hands with Old Ironsides himself! Absolutely unique, absolutely unique!"

When the last spectator had filed out, Hickey, Macnooder and Smith divided fifteen dollars and twenty cents as pure profit, of which sum the gravel stones had brought no less than a third.

When on the fourth day Smith was able painfully to descend the stairs and circulate in the world again he felt the full delight of his newly acquired fame. At the Jigger Shop, Al graciously waved aside his tendered money, saying:

"I guess it's up to me, Ironsides, to stand treat. Such things don't happen every day. Go ahead—do your worst."

Bill Appleby and "Mista" Laloo, the rival livery men, Bill Orum, the cobbler, Barnum of the village store, even Doc Cubberly, the bell-ringer, with his little dog, stopped to watch him pass. When he crossed the campus youngsters gamboled up to his side with solicitous inquiries and the inevitable, "Say, weren't you awfully scared?"

Even in the classroom the Roman, after flunking him, would say, "That will do now, Smith. You may sit down—gently."

So he was now "Old Ironsides." He liked the name and was proud of it. It had a certain grim, uncompromising sternness about it that lent it dignity. It sounded well and it had patriotic associations.

For a whole week he knew the intoxications of popularity, of being the celebrity of the hour, of the thrill that runs up and down the back when a dozen glances are following, and the music of a murmured name, admiringly pronounced. Then abruptly another hero was exalted and he fell.

One evening after supper, while the fourth form lounged on the esplanade of the Upper, Turkey Reiter and Slugger Jones amused themselves with teasing Goat Phillips, who, being privileged by his diminutive size, responded by butting his tormentors in vigorous fashion.

"My, what an awful, rambunctious, great big Goat," said Reiter, defending himself. "Do goats eat neckties?"

"I'll eat yours," responded the youngster recklessly.

"Ten double jiggers to one you can't do it," said Slugger Jones, lazily.

"Give me the tie," responded Phillips.

More to continue the joke than for any other reason, Turkey detached the green and yellow cross tie, which was his joy, and tendered it. What was his amazement to see Goat Phillips calmly set to work to devour it, and to devour it to the very last shred in the most classic goat fashion.

When he had swallowed the last mouthful he stood stock-still and gazed at his shrieking audience. Then he began to have doubts; then he began to have premonitions. Then he ended by having settled on rather the most unsettling convictions. The consideration of the act came after the accomplishment, but it came with terrifying force. What would happen now?

"Turkey," he said, grown very solmen, "you don't think I'm going to be poisoned, do you?"

Turkey became serious at once. Everyone became serious.

"What do you fellows think?" said Turkey, addressing the crowd.

No one had any opinions to volunteer. There were no precedents to go by.

"He might get ptomaine poisoning," finally suggested Shy Thomas.

"What's that?" said Goat, horrified. Shy was forced to confess that he did not know. Hungry Smeed thought it was when you cut your toe on an oyster shell.

"See here, Goat," said Turkey, decisively, "we can't fool with this any more. You come with me."

The now thoroughly demoralized and penitent Goat went meekly between Turkey and Slugger toward Foundation House. But on the way, encountering the Roman, they decided to consult him instead.

"Please, sir," said Phillips, with difficult calm, "I'd like to ask you something."

The master stopped and, prepared for any eventuality, said, "Well, Phillips, nothing serious, I hope?"

"Please, sir, I'm afraid it is," said Phillips, all in a breath. "I've just eaten a necktie, sir."

"A what?"

"A necktie, sir, and I want to know if you think I'm in any danger, sir."

The Roman stood stock-still for a long moment, with dropped jaw; then, recovering himself, he said, "A necktie, Phillips?"

"Yes, sir."

"A whole necktie?"

"Yes, sir."

"Well, Phillips, if you can eat a necktie I guess you can digest it!"

The next morning, when Ironsides Smith unsuspectingly strolled out into the campus, no soul did him honor, not a glance turned as he turned, not a first-form youngster, primed with curiosity and admiration, came rushing to his side. Instead, a knot of boys at the far end of the esplanade was clustered in excited contemplation about Goat Phillips, the boy who had heroically eaten a necktie rather than suffer a dare.

Then Ironsides understood—he was the hero of yesterday. A new celebrity had risen for the delectation of the fickle populace. The King was dead—long live the King!

He went to the classroom disillusioned and sat through the hour stolidly tasting the bitterness of Napoleonic isolation. So this was the favor of crowds. In a night to be dethroned and forgotten!

As he descended Memorial steps, Goat Phillips passed, radiant, saluted by capricornian acclamations.

Smith regarded him darkly.

"As though anyone couldn't eat a necktie," he said in righteous disgust.

Unacclaimed he went through the crowd toward the Upper—he who had risked life and limb to amuse them for a week!

From a tower window in the Upper the Triumphant Egghead, lolling on the cushioned window seat, called down lazily, "Oh, you —Ironsides!"

That was the answer. Let popularity run after a dozen unworthy lights. Other boys would come who would eat neckties, no one ever would go the way he had gone. He had nothing to do with transitory emotions. He must be superior to the voice of the hour. He, Ironsides, belonged to history. That, nothing could take from him!

THE PROTEST AGAINST SINKERS

THE FEELING of revolt sprang up at chapel during the headmaster's weekly talk. Ordinarily the school awaited these moments with expectation, received them with tolerance and drew from them all the humor that could be extracted.

These little heart-to-heart talks brought joy to many an over-weighted brain and obliterated momentarily the slow, dragging months of slush and hail. They also added, from time to time, picturesque expressions to the school vocabulary—and for that much was forgiven them. No one who heard it will ever forget the slashing that descended from the rostrum on the demon tobacco, in its embodied vice, the cigarette, nor the chill that ran over each of the four hundred cigarette smokers as the headmaster, with his boring glance straight on him, concluded:

"Yes, I know what you boys will say; I know what your plea will be when you are caught. You will come to me and you'll say with tears in your eyes, with tears, 'Doctor, think of my mother—my poor mother—it will kill my mother!'

"I tell you, *now* is the time to think of your mother; *now* is the time to spare her gray hairs. Every cigarette you boys smoke is a *nail in the coffin of your mother*."

It was terrific. The school was unanimous in its verdict that the old man had outdone himself. Boys, whom a whiff of tobacco rendered instantly ill, smoked up the ventilators that night with shivers of delight, and from that day to this a cigarette has never been called anything but a coffin nail.

Only the week before, in announcing the suspension of Cork-screw Higgins (since with the ministry), for, among other offenses, mistaking the initials on the hat of Bucky Oliver as his own, the headmaster in his determination to abolish forever such deadly practices, had given forth the following:

"Young gentlemen, it is my painful duty, my very painful duty, to announce to you the suspension of the boy Higgins. The boy Higgins was a sloth, the boy Higgins was the prince of sloths! The boy Higgins was a gambler, the boy Higgins was the prince of gamblers! The boy Higgins was a liar, the boy Higgins was the prince of liars! The boy Higgins was a thief, the boy Higgins was the prince of thieves! Therefore, the boy Higgins will no longer be a member of this community!"

The school pardoned the exaggeration in its admiration for the rhetoric, which was rated up to the oration against Catiline. But on the first Monday of that lean month of February the school rose in revolt. In a tirade against the alarming decline in the percentage of scholastic marks the headmaster, flinging all caution to the winds, had terminated with these incendiary words:

"I know what the trouble is, and I'll tell you. The trouble with you boys is *inordinate and immoderate eating*. The trouble with you boys is—*You Eat Too Much!*"

Such a groan as went up! To comprehend the monstrosity of the accusation it is not sufficient to have been a boy; one must have re-tained the memory of the sharp pains and gnawing appetites of those growing days! Four hundred-odd famished forms, just from breakfast, suddenly galvanized by that unmerited blow, roared forth a unanimous indignant:

"WHAT!"

"Eat too much!"—they could hardly believe their ears. Had the headmaster of the school, with years of personal experience, actually, in his sober mind, proclaimed that they ate too much! The words had been said; the accusation had to stand. And such a time to proclaim it—in the month of sliced bananas and canned vegetables! The protest that rumbled and growled in the under-form houses exploded in the Dickinson.

It so happened that for days there had been a dull grumbling about the monotony of the daily meals and the regularity and frequency of the appearance of certain abhorrent dishes known as "scrag-birds and sinkers." "Scrag-bird" was a generic term, allowing a wide latitude for conjecture, but "sinker" was an opprobrious epithet dedicated to a particularly hard, doughy substance that under more favorable auspices sometimes, without fear of contradiction, achieves the name of "dumpling."

The sinker was, undoubtedly, the deadliest enemy of the growing boy—the most persistent, the most malignant. It knew no laws and it defied all restraint. It languished in the spring, but thrived and multiplied amazingly in the canned, winter term. It was as likely to bob up in a swimming dish of boiled chicken as it was certain to accompany a mutton stew. It associated at times with veal and attached itself to corned beef; it concealed itself in a beefsteak pie and clung to a leg of lamb. What the red rag is to the bull, the pudgy white of the sinker was to the boys, who, in a sort of desperate hope of exterminating the species, never allowed one to return intact to the kitchen. Twice a week was the allotted appearance of the sinker; at a third visit grumbling would break out; at a fourth arose threats of leaving for Andover or Exeter, of writing home, of boycotting the luncheon.

Now, it so happened that during the preceding week the sinker had inflicted itself not four, but actually six, times on that community of aching voids. The brutal accusation of the headmaster was the spark to the powder. The revolt assumed head and form during the day, and a call for a meeting of protest was unanimously made for that very night.

The boys met with the spirit of the Boston Tea Party, resolved to defend their liberties and assert their independence. The inevitable Doc Macnooder was to address the meeting. He spoke naturally, fluently, with great sounding phrases, on any occasion, on any topic, for his own pure delight, and he always continued to speak until violently suppressed.

"Fellows," he began, without apologies to history, "we are met to decide once and for all whether we are a free governing body, to ask ourselves what is all this worth? For weeks we have endured, supinely on our backs, the tyranny of Mrs. Van Asterbilt, the matron of this House. We have, I say, supinely permitted each insult to pass unchallenged. But the hour has struck, the worm has turned, the moment has come and, without the slightest hesitation, I ask you . . . I ask you . . . what do I ask you?" He paused, and appealed for enlightenment.

The meeting found him guilty of levity and threatened him with the ban of silence.

Macnooder looked grieved and continued: "I ask you to strike as your fathers struck. I ask you to string the bow, to whet the knife, to sharpen the tomahawk, to loose the dogs of war—"

Amid a storm of whoops and catcalls, Macnooder was pulled back into his seat. He rose and explained that his peroration was completed and demanded the inalienable right to express his opinions.

The demand was rejected by a vote of eighty-two to one (Macnooder voting).

Butcher Stevens rose with difficulty and, clutching the shoulder of Red Dog in front of him, addressed the gathering as follows:

"Fellows, I am no silver-tongued orator and all I want to say is just a few words. I think we want to treat this thing seriously." (Cries of "Hear! hear!" "Right.") "I think, fellows, this is a very serious matter, and I think we ought to take some action. This food matter is getting pretty bad. I don't think, fellows, that we ought to stand for sinkers the way they're coming at us, without some action. I don't know just what action we ought to take, but I think we ought really to take some action."

The Butcher subsided into his seat amid immense applause. Lovely Mead arose and jangling the keys in his trousers pocket, addressed the ceiling in rapid, jerky periods:

"Fellows, I think we ought to begin by taking a vote—a vote. I think—I think the sentiment of this meeting is about made up— made up. I think my predecessor has very clearly expressed the—the —has voiced the sentiments of this meeting—very clearly. I think a vote would clear the air, therefore I move we take a vote."

He sighed contentedly and returned into the throng. Doc Macnooder sarcastically demanded what they were to vote upon. Lovely Mead, in great confusion, rose and stammered:

"I meant to say, Mr. Chairman, that I move we take a vote, take a vote to—to take some action."

"Action about what?" said the merciless Macnooder.

Lovely Mead remained speechless. Hungry Smeed interposed glibly:

"Mister Chairman, I move that it is the sense of this meeting that we should take some action looking toward the remedying of the present condition of our daily meals."

The motion was passed and the chairman announced that he was ready to hear suggestions as to the nature of the act, as contemplated. A painful silence succeeded.

Macnooder rose and asked permission to offer a suggestion. The demand was repulsed. Wash Simmons moved that at the next appearance of the abhorrent sinkers, they should rise and leave the room *en masse*. It was decided that the plan entailed too many sacrifices, and it was rejected.

Crazy Opdyke from the Woodhull developed the following scheme, full of novelty and imagination:

"I say, fellows, I've got an idea, you know. What we want is an object lesson, you know, something striking. Now, fellows, this is what I propose: We're eighty-five of us in these dining rooms; now, at two sinkers each, that makes one hundred and seventy sinkers every time; at six times that makes one thousand sinkers a week. What we want to do is to carry off the sinkers from table, save them up, and at the end of the week make a circle of them around the campus as an object lesson!"

Macnooder, again, was refused permission to speak in support of this measure, which had an instant appeal to the imagination of the audience. In the end, however, the judgment of the more serious prevailed, and the motion was lost by a close vote. After more discussion the meeting finally decided to appoint an embassy of three, who should instantly proceed to the headmaster's, and firmly lay before him the Woodhull's and the Dickinson's demand for unconditional and immediate suppression of that indigestible and totally ornamental article known as the sinker. Hickey, Wash Simmons and Crazy Opdyke, by virtue of their expressed defiance, were chosen to carry the ultimatum. Someone proposed that Macnooder should go as a fourth, and the motion passed without opposition. Macnooder rose and declined the honor but asked leave to state his reasons. Whereupon the meeting adjourned.

The Messrs. Crazy Opdyke, Hickey, and Wash Simmons held a conference and decided to shave and assume creased trousers in order to render the aspect of their mission properly impressive. After a short delay they united on the steps, where they received the exhortations of their comrades—to speak out boldly, to mince no words, and to insist on their demands.

The distance to Foundation House, where the headmaster resided, was short—thirty seconds in the darkness; and almost before they knew it the three were at the door. There, under the muffled lamp, they stopped, with spontaneous accord, and looked at one another.

"I say," said Hickey, "hadn't we better agree on what we'll say to the old man? We want to be firm, you know."

"That's a good idea," Opdyke assented, and Wash added, "We'll take a turn down the road."

"Now, what's your idea?" said Simmons to Hickey, when they had put a safe distance between them and the residence of the Doctor.

"We'd better keep away from discussion," replied Hickey. "The Doctor'll beat us out there, and I don't think we'd better be too radical either, because we want to be firm."

"What do you call radical?" said Opdyke, with a little defiance.

"Well, now, we don't want to be too aggressive; we don't want to go in with a chip on our shoulder."

"Hickey, you're beginning to hedge!"

Hickey indignantly denied the accusation, and a little quarrel arose between them, terminated by Wash, who broke in.

"Shut up, Crazy—Hickey is dead right. We want to go in friendly-like, just as though we knew the Doctor would side with us at once—sort of take him into our confidence."

"That's it," said Hickey; "we want to be good-natured at first, lay the matter before him calmly, then afterward we can be firm.

"Rats!" said Crazy. "Are we going to tell him, or not, that we represent the Dickinson and the Woodhull and that they have voted the extinction of sinkers?"

"Sure we are!" exclaimed Wash. "You don't think we are afraid, do you?"

"Well, then, let's tell him," said Crazy. "Come on, if you're going to."

They returned resolutely and again entered the dominion of the dreary lamp.

"Say, fellows," Wash suddenly interjected, "are we going to say anything about scrag-birds?"

"Sure," said Crazy.

"The deuce we are!" said Hickey.

"Why not?" said Crazy, militantly.

"Because we don't want to make fools of ourselves."

The three withdrew again and threshed out the point. It was decided to concentrate on the sinker. Crazy gave in because he said he was cold.

"Well, now, it's all settled," said Hickey. "We make a direct demand for knocking out the sinker, and we stand firm on that. Nothing else. Come on."

"Come on."

A third time they came to the terrible door.

"I say," said Wash, suddenly, "we forgot. Who's to do the talking?"

"Crazy, of course," said Hickey, looking hard at Simmons, "since that clapper episode, I'm not dropping in for the dessert!"

"Sure, Crazy, you're just the one," Simmons agreed.

"Hold up," said Crazy, whose fury suddenly cooled. "Let's talk that over."

Again they retired for deliberation.

"Now, see here, fellows," said Crazy, "let's be reasonable. We want this thing to go through, don't we?"

"Who's hedging now?" said Hickey, with a laugh.

"No one," retorted Crazy. "I'll talk up if you say. I'm not afraid, only I don't stand one, two, three with the Doctor and you know it. I've flunked every recitation in Bible this month. What we want is the strongest pull—and Wash is the one. Why, the old man would feed out of Wash's hand."

Wash indignantly repelled the insinuation. Finally it was agreed that Crazy should state the facts, that Hickey should say, "Doctor, we feel strongly, very strongly, about this," and that Wash should then make the direct demand for the suspension for one month of the sinker, and its future regulation to two appearances a week.

"And now, no more backing and filling," said Hickey.

"I'll lay the facts before him, all right," added Crazy, clenching his fists.

"We'll stick together, and we stand firm," said Wash. "Now for it!"

They had reached a point about thirty feet from the threshold when suddenly the door was flung violently open and a luckless boy bolted out, under the lamp, so that the three could distinguish the vehement gestures. The Doctor appeared in a passion of rage, calling after the retreating offender:

"Don't you dare, young man, to come to me again with such a complaint. You get your work up to where it ought to be, or down you go, and there isn't a power in this country that can prevent it."

The door slammed violently and silence returned.

"He's not in a very receptive mood," said Wash, after a long pause.

"Not precisely," said Hickey, thoughtfully.

"I'm catching cold," said Crazy.

"Suppose we put it over?" continued Wash. "What do you say, Hickey?"

"I shall not oppose the will of the majority."

"And you, Crazy?"

"I think so, too."

They returned to the Dickinson, where they were surrounded and assailed with questions: How had the Doctor taken it? What had he said?

"We took no talk from him," said Crazy, with a determined shake of his head, and then Wash added brusquely, "Just keep your eyes on the sinkers."

"You took long enough," put in the suspicious Macnooder.

"We were firm," replied Hickey, bristling at the recollection, "very firm!"

BEAUTY'S SISTER

His hair it is a faded white,
 His eye a watery blue;
He has no buttons on his coat,
 No shoe-strings in his shoe.

"BEAUTY" SAWTELLE, or Chesterton V. Sawtelle, as it was pronounced when each Monday the master of the form read the biweekly absences from bath, sat adjusting his skate on the edge of the pond with a look of ponderous responsibility on the freckled face, crowned by a sheaf of tow hair, like the wisp of a Japanese doll. Presently he drew from his pocket a dance card, glanced over it for the twentieth time, and replaced it with a sigh.

"Cracky!" he said, in despair. "Sixteen regulars and eight extras; sixteen and eight, twenty-four. Gee!"

Beauty's heart was heavy and his hope faint, for the sinister finger of the Prom had cast its shadow over the lighthearted democracy of boyhood. Into this free republic, where no thoughts of the outside society should penetrate, the demoralizing swish of coming petticoats had suddenly intruded its ominous significance of a world without, where such tyrannies as money and birth stand ready to divide the unsuspecting hosts.

Now Beauty's woes were manifold: he was only a second former, and the Prom was the property of the lords of the school, the majestic fourth formers, who lived in the Upper House and governed themselves according to the catalogue and a benevolent tempering of the exact theory of independence.

A few rash under-formers with pretty sisters were admitted on sufferance, and robbed of their partners if the chance arose. Beauty, scrubby boy of fourteen, with a like aversion to girls and stiff collars in his ugly little body, had been horrified to learn that his sister, at the invitation of Rogers, the housemaster, was coming to the Prom. On his shoulders devolved the herculean task of filling a card from the upper class, only a handful of whom he knew, at a moment when the cards had been circulated for weeks. So he stood dejectedly, calculating how to fill the twenty-four spaces that were so blank and interminable. Twenty-four dances to fill, and the Prom only two weeks off!

In the middle of the pond boys were darting and swaying in a furious game of hockey. Beauty lingered, biding his opportunity, searching the crowd for a familiar face, until presently Wash Simmons, emerging from the melee, darted to his side, grinding his skates and coming to a halt for breath, with a swift: "Hello, Venus! How's the Dickinson these days?"

Beauty, murmuring an inaudible reply, stood turning and twisting, desperately seeking to frame a demand.

"What's the secret sorrow, Beauty?" continued Wash, with a glance of surprise.

"I say, Wash," said Beauty, plunging, "I say, have you got any dances left?"

"I? Oh, Lord, no!" said the pitcher of the school nine, with a quick glance. "Gone long ago."

He drew the strap tight, dug his hands into his gloves again, and with a nod flashed back into the crowd. Beauty, gulping down something that rose in his throat, started aimlessly to skirt the edge of the pond. He had understood the look that Wash had given him in that swift moment.

In this abstracted mood, he suddenly came against something angular and small that accompanied him to the ice with a resounding whack.

"Clumsy beast!" said a sharp voice.

From his embarrassed position, Beauty recognized the Red Dog.

"Excuse me, Red Dog," he said hastily; "I didn't see you."

"Why, it's Beauty," said the Red Dog, rubbing himself. "Blast you, all the same."

"I say, Red Dog," said Beauty, "have you any dances left?"

"All gone, Beauty," answered Red Dog, stooping suddenly to recover his skate.

"Nothing left?"

"Nope—filled the last extra today," said Red Dog, with the shining face of prevarication. Then he added, "Why, Venus, are *you* going to the Prom?"

"No," said Sawtelle; "it's my sister."

"Oh, I'm sorry. I'd like to oblige you, but you see how it is," said Red Dog, lamely.

"I see."

"Ta, ta, Beauty! So long!"

Sawtelle shut his lips, struck a valiant blow at an imaginary puck, and began to whistle.

> 'Tis a jolly life we lead
> Care and sorrow we defy—

After piping forth this inspiring chorus with vigorous notes, the will gave way. He began another:

> To Lawrenceville my father sent me,
> Where for college I should prepare;
> And so I settled down,
> In this queer, forsaken town,
> About five miles away from anywhere.

The bellows gave out. Overcome by the mournfulness of the last verse, he dropped wearily on the bank, continuing doggedly:

> About five miles from anywhere, my boys,
> Where old Lawrenceville evermore shall stand;

For has she not stood,
Since the time of the flood—

Whether the accuracy of the last statement or the forced rhyme displeased him, he broke off, heaved a sigh, and said viciously, "They lied, both of 'em."

"Well, how's the boy?" said a familiar voice.

Beauty came out of the vale of bitterness to perceive at his side the great form of Turkey Reiter, preparing to adjust his skates.

"Oh, Turkey," said Beauty, clutching at the straw, "I've been looking everywhere—"

"What's the matter?"

"Turkey, I'm in an awful hole."

"Out with it."

"I say, Turkey," said Sawtelle, stumbling and blushing, "I say, you know, my sister's coming to the Prom, and I thought if you'd like—that is, I wanted to know if—if you wouldn't take her dance card and get it filled for me." Then he added abjectly, "I'm awfully sorry."

Turkey looked thoughtful. This was a commission he did not relish. Beauty looked particularly unattractive that afternoon, in a red tobogganing toque that swore at his faded white hair, and the orange freckles that stared out from every point of vantage.

"Why, Beauty," he began hesitatingly, "the way it is, you see, my card's already filled, and I'm afraid, honestly, that's about the case with all the others."

"She's an awfully nice girl," said Sawtelle, looking down in a desperate endeavor to control his voice.

"Nice girl," thought Turkey, "ahem! Yes, must be a good-looker, too, something on Venus's particular line of beauty."

He glanced at his companion and mentally pictured a lanky girl with sandy hair, a little upstart nose, and a mass of orange freckles. But between Turkey and Sawtelle relations had been peculiar. There had been many moments in the last year at the Dickinson when the ordinary luxuries of life would have been difficult had it not been for the superior financial standing of Chesterton V. Sawtelle. The account had been a long one, and there was a slight haziness in Turkey's mind as to the exact status of the balance. Also, Turkey was genuinely grateful, with that sense of gratitude which is described as a lively looking forward to favors to come.

"Oh, well, young 'un," he said with rough good humor, "give us the card. I'll do what I can. But, mind you, I can't take any myself. My card's full, and it wouldn't do for me to cut dances."

Jumping up, he started to escape the effusive thanks of the overjoyed Sawtelle, but suddenly wheeled and came skating back.

"Hello, Beauty!" he called out. "I say, what's your sister's name?"

"Sally—that is, Sarah," came the timid answer.

"Heavens!" said Turkey to himself as he flashed over the ice. "That settles it. Sally—Sally! A nice pickle I'm in! Wonder if she sports spectacles and old-fashioned frocks. A nice pickle—I'll be the laughingstock of the whole school. Guess I won't have much trouble recognizing Beauty's sister. Whew! That comes from having a kind heart!"

With these and similar pleasant reflections he threaded his way among the crowd of skaters until at length he perceived Hickey skimming over the ice, stealing the puck from a bunch of scrambling players, until his progress checked, and the puck vanishing into a distant melee, he came to a stop for breath. Turkey, profiting by the occasion, descended on his victim.

"Whoa there, Hickey!"

"Whoa it is!"

"How's your dance card?"

"A dazzling galaxy of beauty, a symposium of grace, a feast of—"

"Got anything left? I have a wonder for you if you have."

"Sure, twelfth regular and sixth extra—but the duchess will be awfully cut up."

"Twelfth and sixth," said Turkey, with a nod; "that's a go."

"Who's the heart-smasher?" asked Hickey, with an eye on the approaching puck.

"A wonder, Hickey; a screamer. There'll be nothing to it. Ta, ta! Much obliged."

"What's her name?"

"Sawtelle—some distant relative of the Beauty's, I believe. I'm filling out her card. Obliged for the dance. Ta, ta!"

"Hold up!" said Hickey, quickly. "Hold up! Jiminy! I almost forgot—why, I do believe I went and promised those two to Hasbrouck. Isn't that a shame! Sorry. To think of my forgetting that! Try to give you some other. Confound it! I have no luck." With the most mournful look in the world he waved his hand and sped ostentatiously toward the bunch of players.

111

"Hickey's on to me," thought Turkey as he watched him disengage himself from the crowd and skate off with Sawtelle; "no hope in that quarter."

Finally, after an hour's persistent work, during which he pleaded and argued, commanded and threatened, he succeeded in filling exactly six of the necessary twenty-four dances. Indeed, he would have had no difficulty in completing the card if he could have passed over that fatal name. But each time, just as he was congratulating himself on another conquest, his victim would ask, "By the way, what name shall I put down?"

"Oh—er—Miss Sawtelle," he would answer nonchalantly; "a distant relative of the Beauty—though nothing like him—ha! ha!"

Then each would suddenly remember that the dances in question were already half-promised—a sort of an understanding; but of course he would have to look it up—but of course, if he found they were free, why, then of course, he wanted, above all things in the world, to dance with Miss Sawtelle.

"Well, anyhow," said Turkey to himself, recapitulating, "I've got six, provided they don't all back out. Let me see. I can make the Kid take three—that's nine—and Snookers will have to take three—that's twelve—and, hang it! Butcher and Egghead have got to take two each—that would make sixteen. The other eight I can fill up with some harmless freaks: some will snap at anything."

That night at the supper table Turkey had to face the music.

"You're a nice one, you are," said Hickey, starting in immediately, "you arch-deceiver. You are a fine friend; I have my opinion of you. 'Handsome girl,' 'a wonder,' 'fine talker,' 'a screamer'—that's the sort of game you try on your friends, is it? Who is she? Oh—ah, yes, a *distant* relative of the Beauty."

"What's up now?" said the Kid, editor of the *Lawrence,* and partner of Turkey's secrets, joys, and debts.

"Hasn't he tried to deceive you yet?" continued Hickey, with an accusing look at Turkey. "No? That's a wonder! What do you think of a fellow who tries to pass off on his friends such a girl as the Beauty's sister?"

"No!" said Butcher Stevens.

"What!" exclaimed Macnooder, laying down his knife with a thud.

"Beauty's sister," said the Egghead, gaping with astonishment.

"Well, why not?" said Turkey, defiantly.

"Listen to that!" continued Hickey. "The brazenness of it!"

The four graduates of the Dickinson, after a moment of stupefied examination of Hickey and Reiter, suddenly burst into roars of laughter that produced a craning of necks and a storm of inquiries from the adjoining tables.

When the hilarity had been somewhat checked, Hickey returned to the persecution of the blushing Turkey.

"Bet you three to one she's a mass of freckles," he said. "Bet you even she wears glasses; bet you one to three she's cross-eyed; bet you four to one she won't open her mouth."

"Hang you, Hickey!" said Turkey, flushing, "I won't have her talked about so."

"Did you take any dances?" said the Kid to Hickey.

"Me?" exclaimed the latter, in great dudgeon. "Me! Well, I guess not! I wouldn't touch any of that tribe with a ten-foot pole."

"Look here, you fellows have got to shut up," said Turkey, forced at last into a virtuous attitude by the exigency of the situation. "I promised the Beauty I'd fill his sister's card for him, and I'm going to do it. The girl can't help her looks. You talk like a lot of cads. What you fellows ought to do is to join in and give her a treat. The girl is probably from the backwoods, and this ought to be made the time of her life."

"Turkey," said the malicious Hickey, "how many dances have you eagerly appropriated?"

Turkey stopped point-blank, greeted by derisive jeers.

"Oho!"

"That's it, is it?"

"Fake!"

"Humbug!"

"Not at all," said Turkey, indignantly. "What do you think I am?"

"Pass over your list and let's see the company you're going to introduce her to," said Hickey, stretching out his hand for the dance card. "Ah, I must congratulate you, my boy; your selection is magnificent; the young lady will be charmed." He flipped the card disdainfully to the Egghead, saying, "A bunch of freaks!"

"Hang it all," said the Egghead, "that's too hard on any girl. A fine opinion she'll have of Lawrenceville fellows! We can't stand for that."

"Look here," said the Kid, suddenly. "Turkey is at fault, and has got to be punished. Here's what we'll do, though: let's each take a dance on condition that Turkey takes her out to supper."

"Oh, I say!" protested Turkey, who had other plans.

The others acclaimed the plan gleefully, rejoicing in his discomfiture, until Turkey, driven to a corner, was forced to capitulate.

That evening on the esplanade he called Snookers to him, and resting his hand affectionately on the little fellow's shoulder, said, "Old man, do you want to do me a favor?"

"Sure."

"I'm filling up a girl's card for the Prom, and I want you to help me out."

"Certainly; give me a couple, if the girl's the real thing."

"Much obliged. I'll put your name down."

"Second and fifth. Say, who is she?"

"Oh, some relative of Sawtelle's—you remember you used to go with him a good deal in the Dickinson. It's his sister."

"Whew!" said Snookers, with a long-drawn whistle. "Say, give me three more, will you?"

"Hardly," answered Turkey, with a laugh; "but I'll spare you another."

"I didn't think it quite fair to the girl," he explained later, "to give her too big a dose of Snookers. Queer, though, how eager the little brute was!"

The last week dragged interminably in multiplied preparations for the great event. In the evenings the war of strings resounded across the campus from the gym, where the Banjo and Mandolin clubs strove desperately to perfect themselves for the concert. The Dramatic Club, in sudden fear, crowded the day with rehearsals, while from the window of Room 65, Upper, the voice of Biddy Hampton, soloist of the Glee Club, was heard chanting "The Pride of the House is Papa's Baby," behind doors stout enough to resist the assaults of his neighbors.

Oil stoves and flatirons immediately came into demand, cushions were rolled back from window seats, and trousers that were limp and discouraged grew smooth and well-creased under the pressure of the hot iron. Turkey and Doc Macnooder, who from their long experience in the Dickinson had become expert tailors, advertised on the bulletin board:

REITER AND MACNOODER
BON TON TAILORS

Trousers neatly pressed, at fifteen cents per pair; all payments
strictly cash—*in advance.*

Each night the dining room of the Upper was cleared, and the
extraordinary spectacle was seen of boys of all sizes in sweaters and
jerseys, clasping each other desperately around the waist, spinning
and bumping their way about the reeling room to the chorus of:
"Get off my feet!"
"Reverse, you lubber!"
"Now, *one,* two, three—"
"A fine lady you are!"
"Do you expect me to carry you around the room?"
"Darn you, fatty!"
"Hold tight!"
"Let 'er rip now!"
From the end of the room the cynics and misogynists, roosting
on the piled-up tables and chairs, croaked forth their contempt:
"Oh, you fussers!"
"You lady-killers!"
"Dance, my darling, dance!"
"Squeeze her tight, Bill!"
"That's the way!"
"Look at Skinny!"
"Keep a-hoppin', Skinny!"
"Look at him spin!"
"For heaven's sake, someone stop Skinny!"
Of evenings certain of the boys would wander in pairs to the
edge of the woods and confide to each other the secret attachments
and dark, forlorn hopes that were wasting them away. Turkey and
the Kid, who were going as stags, opened their hearts to each other
and spoke of the girl, the one distant girl, whose image not all the
fair faces that would come could for a moment dim.

"Kid," said Turkey, in solemn conclusion, speaking from the experience of eighteen years, "I am going to make that little girl—my
wife."

"Turkey, old man, God bless you!" answered the confidant, with
nice regard for old precedents. Then he added, a little choked,
"Turkey, I, too—I—"

"I understand, Kid," said Turkey, gravely clapping his shoulder; "I've known it all along."

"Dear old boy!"

They walked in silence.

"What's her name?" asked Turkey, slowly.

"Lucille. And hers?"

"Marie Louise."

Another silence.

"Kid, is it all right?"

The romanticist considered a moment, and then shook his head.

"No, Turk."

"Dear old boy, you'll win out."

"I must. And you, Turk, does she care?"

A heavy sigh was the answer. They walked back arm in arm, each fully believing in the other's sorrow, and almost convinced of his own. At the esplanade of the Upper they stopped and listened to the thumping of the piano and the systematic beat from the dancers.

"I wish it were all over," said Turkey, gloomily. "This can mean nothing to me."

"Nor to me," said the Kid, staring at the melancholy moon.

On the fateful day the school arose, so to speak, as one boy, shaved, and put on a clean collar. Every boot was blacked, every pair of trousers creased to a cutting edge. The array of neckties that suddenly appeared in gigantic puffs or fluttering wings was like the turn of autumn in a single night.

Chapel and the first two recitations over, the esplanade of the Upper was crowded with fourth formers, circulating critically in the dandified throng, chattering excitedly of the coming event. Perish the memory of the fashion there displayed! It seemed magnificent then: let that be the epitaph.

The bell called, and the group slowly departed to the last recitation. From each house a stream of boys came pouring out and made their lagging way around the campus toward Memorial. Slower and slower rang the bell, and faster came the unwilling slaves—those in front with dignity; those behind with dispatch, and so on down the line to the last scattered stragglers who came racing over the lawns. The last peal sounded, the last laggard tore up Memorial steps, and vanished within. A moment later the gong in the hall clanged, and the next recitation was on. The circle, a moment before alive with figures, was quiet and deserted. A group of seven or eight lounging on the esplanade were chatting indolently, tossing a ball back and forth with the occupant of a third-story window.

At this moment Turkey emerged from the doorway in shining russets, a Gladstone collar, a tie of robin's-egg-blue, and a suit of red and green plaids, such as the innocent curiosity of a boy on his first allowance goes to with the thirst of possession.

"Hurrah for Turkey!" cried the Kid. "He looks like a regular fashion plate."

In an instant he was surrounded, punched, examined, and complimented.

"Well, fellows, it's time to give ourselves them finishing touches," said the Egghead, with a glance of envy. "Turkey is trying to steal a march on us. The girls are coming."

"Hello!" cried the Kid, suddenly. "Who's this?"

All turned. From behind Foundation House came a carriage. It drove on briskly until nearly opposite the group on the steps, when the driver reined in, and someone within looked out dubiously.

"Turkey, you're in luck," said the Gutter Pup. "You're the only one with the rouge on. Go down gracefully and see what the lady wants."

So down went Turkey to his duty. They watched him approach the carriage and speak to someone inside. Then he closed the door and spoke to the driver, evidently pointing out his destination, for the cab continued around the circle.

Then Turkey made a jump for the esplanade, and, deaf to all inquiries, seized upon his roommate and dragged him aside.

"Great guns! Kid," he exclaimed, "I've seen her—Beauty's sister! She isn't like Beauty at all. She's a stunner, a dream! Look here! Get that dance card. Get it, if you have to lie and steal. He's in recitation now. You've got to catch him when he comes out. For heaven's sake, don't let anyone get ahead of you! Tell him two girls have backed out, and I want five more dances. Tell him I'm to take her to the debate tonight, and the Dramatic Club tomorrow. Kid, get that card!"

Releasing his astounded roommate, he went tearing across the campus to meet the carriage.

"What's happened to our staid and dignified president?" cried the Gutter Pup in wonder. "Is he crazy?"

"Oh, say, fellows," exclaimed the Kid, overcome by the humor of the situation, "who do you think that was?"

The carriage had now stopped before the Dickinson, and Turkey, arrived in time, was helping out a tall, slender figure in black. A light flashed over the group.

"Beauty's sister."

"No!"

"Yes."

"Impossible!"

"Beauty's sister it is," cried the Kid; "and the joke is, she's a stunner, a dream!"

"A dream!" piped up the inevitable Snookers. "Well, I guess! She's an all-round A-No. 1. Gee! I just got a glimpse of her at a theater, and I tell you, boys, she's a paralyzer."

But his remark ended on the air, for all, with a common impulse, had disappeared. Snookers, struck with the same thought, hastened to his room.

Ten minutes later they reappeared. Hickey, in a suit of pronounced checks, his trousers carefully turned up *à l'Anglais*, glanced approvingly at the array of manly fashion.

"And now, fellows," he said, pointing to the Chapel, which Turkey was entering with Miss Sawtelle, "that traitor shall be punished. We'll guard every entrance to Memorial, capture our friend, 'Chesterton V. Sawtelle (absent from bath),' relieve him of that little dance card, and then, Romans, to the victors belong the spoils!"

The Kid, having delayed over the choice between a red-and-yellow necktie or one of simple purple, did not appear until Hickey had stationed his forces. Taking in the situation at a glance, he chuckled to himself and picking up a couple of books, started for the entrance.

"Lucky it's Hungry and the Egghead," he said to himself as he passed them and entered the Lower Hall. "Hickey would have guessed the game."

He called Sawtelle from the second form, and, slipping his arm through his, drew him down the corridor.

"Sawtelle," he said, "I want your sister's dance card. There's some mistake, and Turkey wants to fix it up. Thanks; that's all. Oh, no, it isn't, either. Turkey said he'd be over after supper to take your sister to the debate, and that he had seats for the Dramatic Club tomorrow. Don't forget all that. So long! See you later."

In high feather at the success of this stratagem, he skipped downstairs, and avoiding Hickey, went to meet Turkey in the Chapel, where he was duly presented.

When Sawtelle emerged at length from the study room, he was amazed at the spontaneity of his reception. He was no longer "Beauty" or "Apollo" or "Venus."

"Sawtelle, old man," they said to him, "I want to see you a moment."

"Chesterton, where have you been?"

"Old man, have you got anything to do?"

Each strove to draw him away from the others, and failing in this, accompanied him to the Jigger Shop, where he was plied with substantial flattery, until having disposed of jiggers, soda, and éclairs, he cast one lingering glance at the tempting counters, and said with a twinkle in his ugly little eyes:

"And now, fellows, I guess my sister must be over at the house. Come around this afternoon, why don't you, and meet her?"—an invitation which was received with enthusiasm and much evident surprise.

When the Prom opened that evening, Beauty's sister made her entrée flanked by the smitten Turkey and the languishing Hasbrouck, while the stricken Kid brought up the rear, consoled by the responsibility of her fan. Five stags who had been lingering miserably in the shadow searching for something daring and imaginative to lay at her feet, crowded forward only to be stricken dumb at the splendor of her toilette.

Beauty's sister, fresh from a Continental season, was quite overwhelmed by the subtle adoration of the famous Wash Simmons and of Egghead, that pattern of elegance and *savoir-faire*—overwhelmed, but not at all confused. Gradually under her deft manipulation the power of speech returned to the stricken. Then the rout began. The young ladies from city and country finishing schools, still struggling with their teens, were quite eclipsed by the gorgeous Parisian toilette and the science of movement displayed by the sister of Chesterton V. Sawtelle. The ordinary ethics of fair play were thrown to the winds. Before the eyes of everyone, Turkey held up the worthless dance card, and tore it into shreds. Only the brave should deserve the fair. Little Smeed, Poler Fox, and Snorky Green struggled in vain for recognition, and retired crestfallen and defrauded, to watch the scramble for each succeeding dance, which had to be portioned among three and often four clamorers.

In fact, it became epidemic. They fell in love by blocks of five, even as they had sought the privileges of the measles. Each implored a memento to fix imperishably on his wall. The roses she wore consoled a dozen. The Gutter Pup obtained her fan; the Kid her handkerchief, a wonderful scented transparency. Glendenning and Hasbrouck brazenly divided the gloves while Turkey, trembling at his own blurting audacity, was blown to the stars by permission to express in a letter certain delicate thoughts which stifle in the vulgar scramble of the ballroom.

When the last dance had been fought for, divided, and redivided, and the lights peremptorily suppressed, the stags *en masse* accompanied Beauty's sister to the Dickinson, where each separately pressed her hand and strove to give to his "Good night" an accent which would be understood by her alone.

On that next morning that somehow always arises, Turkey and the Kid, envied by all, drove her to the station, listening mutely to her gay chatter, each plunged in melancholy, secretly wondering how she managed to conceal her feelings so well.

They escorted her to the car, and loaded her with magazines and candies and flowers, and each succeeded in whispering in her ear a rapid, daring sentence, which she received from each with just the proper encouragement. Then, imaginary Lucilles and Marie Louises forgot, they drove back, heavy of heart, and uncomprehending, viewing the landscape without joy or hope, suffering stoically as men of eighteen should. Not a word was spoken until from the last hill they caught the first glimmer of the school. Then Turkey hoarsely, flicking the air with the lash of the whip, said:

"Kid—"

"What?"

"That *was* a woman."

"A woman of the world, Turkey."

They left the carriage at the stable, and strolled up to the Jigger Shop, joining the group, all intent on the coming baseball season; and gradually the agony eased a bit. Presently a familiar little figure, freckled and towheaded, sidled into the shop, and stood with fists jammed in empty pockets, sniffing the air for succor.

"Oh, you Beauty! Oh, you astonishing Venus!" cried the inevitable persecutor. Then from the crowd Macnooder began to intone the familiar lines:

> His hair, it is a faded white,
> His eye a watery blue;
> He has no buttons on his coat,
> No shoe-strings in his shoe.

"Doc," said the Beauty, blushing sheepishly, "set me up to a jigger, will you? Go on, now!"

Then Macnooder, roaring, shouted back: "Not this year; next year—SISTER!"

THE GREAT BIG MAN

THE NOON bell was about to ring, the one glorious spring note of
that inexorable Gym bell that ruled the school with its iron tongue.
For at noon, on the first liberating stroke, the long winter term
died and the Easter vacation became a fact.

Inside Memorial Hall the impatient classes stirred nervously,
counting off the minutes, sitting gingerly on the seat edges for fear
of wrinkling the carefully pressed suits, or shifting solicitously the
sharpened trousers in peril of a bagging at the knees. Heavens!
How interminable the hour was, sitting there in a planked shirt
and a fashion-high collar—and what a recitation! Would Easter ever
begin, that long-coveted vacation when the growing boy, according
to theory, goes home to rest from the fatiguing draining of his
brain, but in reality returns exhausted by dinners, dances, and
theaters, with perhaps a little touch of the measles to exchange with

his neighbors. Even the masters droned through the perfunctory exercises, flunking the boys by twos and threes, by groups, by long rows, but without malice or emotion.

Outside, in the roadway, by the steps, waited a long, incongruous line of vehicles, scraped together from every stable in the country-side, forty-odd. A few buggies for nabobs in the Upper House, two-seated rigs (holding eight), country buckboards, excursion wagons to be filled according to capacity at twenty-five cents the trip, hacks from Trenton, and the regulation stage coach—all piled high with bags and suitcases, waiting for the bell that would start them on the scramble for the Trenton station, five miles away. At the horses' heads the lazy drivers lolled, drawing languid puffs from their cigarettes, unconcerned.

Suddenly the bell rang out, and the supine teamsters, galvanizing into life, jumped to their seats. The next moment, down the steps, pell-mell, scrambling and scuffling, swarming over the carriages, with joyful clamor, the school arrived. In an instant the first bug-gies were off, with whips frantically plied, disputing at a gallop the race to Trenton.

Then the air was filled with shouts.

"Where's Butsey?"

"Oh, you, Red Dog!"

"Where's my bag?"

"Jump in!"

"Oh, we'll never get there!"

"Drive on!"

"Don't wait!"

"Where's Jack?"

"Hurry up, you loafer!"

"Hurry up, you butterfingers!"

"Get in!"

"Pile in!"

"Haul him in!"

"We're off!"

"Hurrah!"

Wagon after wagon, crammed with joyful boyhood, disappeared in a cloud of dust, while back returned a confused uproar of broken cheers, snatches of songs, with whoops and shrieks for more speed dominating the whole. The last load rollicked away to join the mad race, where far ahead a dozen buggies, with foam-flecked horses, vied with one another, their youthful jockeys waving their hats, hurling defiance back and forth, or shrieking with delight as each antagonist was caught and left behind.

The sounds of striving died away, the campus grew still once more. The few who had elected to wait until after luncheon scattered hurriedly about the circle and disappeared in the houses, to fling last armfuls into the already bursting trunks.

On top of Memorial steps the Great Big Man remained, solitary and marooned, gazing over the fields, down the road to Trenton, where still the rising dust clouds showed the struggle toward vacation. He stood like a monument, gazing fixedly, struggling with all the might of his twelve years to conquer the awful feeling of homesickness that came to him. Homesickness—the very word was an anomaly: what home had he to go to? An orphan without ever having known his father, scarcely remembering his mother in the hazy reflections of years, little Joshua Tibbetts had arrived at the school at the beginning of the winter term, to enter the shell,* and gradually pass through the forms in six or seven years.

The boys of the Dickinson, after a glance at his funny little body and his plaintive, doglike face, had baptized him the "Great Big Man" (Big Man for short), and had elected him the child of the house.

He had never known what homesickness was before. He had had a premonition of it, perhaps, from time to time during the last week, wondering a little in the classroom as each day Snorky Green, beside him, calculated the days until Easter, then the hours, then the minutes. He had watched him with an amused, uncomprehending interest. Why was he so anxious to be off? After all, he, the Big Man, found it a pleasant place, after the wearisome life from hotel to hotel. He liked the boys; they were kind to him, and looked after his moral and spiritual welfare with bluff but affectionate solicitude. It is true, one was always hungry, and only ten-and-a-half hours' sleep was a refinement of cruelty unworthy of a great institution. But it was pleasant running over to the Jigger Shop and doing errands for giants like Reiter and Butcher Stevens, with the privileges of the commission. He liked to be tumbled in the grass by the great tackle of the football eleven, or thrown gently from arm to

* The "shell" is the lowest class.

arm like a medicine ball, quits for the privileges of pummeling his big friends *ad libitum* and without fear of reprisals. And then what a privilege to be allowed to run out on the field and fetch the nose-guard or useless bandage, thrown down haphazard, with the confidence that he, the Big Man, was there to fetch and guard! Then he was permitted to share their studies, to read slowly from handy, literal translations, his head cushioned on the Egghead's knee, while the lounging group swore genially at Pius Æneas or sympathized with Catiline. He shagged elusive balls and paraded the bats at shoulder-arms. He opened the mail, and sorted it, fetching the bag from Farnum's. He was even allowed to stand treat to the mighty men of the house whenever the change in his pocket became too heavy for comfort.

In return he was taught to box, to wind tennis rackets, to blacken shoes, to crease trousers, and sew on the buttons of the House. Nothing was lacking to his complete happiness.

Then lately he had begun to realize that there was something else in the school life, outside it, but very much a part of it—vacation.

At first the idea of quitting such a fascinating life was quite incomprehensible to him. What gorging dinner party could compare with the thrill of feasting at midnight on crackers and cheese, deviled ham, boned chicken, mince pie and root beer by the light of a solitary candle, with the cracks of the doors and windows smothered with rugs and blankets, listening at every mouthful for the tread of the master that sometimes (oh, acme of delight!) actually passed unsuspectingly by the door?

Still, there was a joy in leaving all this. He began to notice it distinctly when the trunks were hauled from the cellar and the packing began. The packing—what a lark that had been! He had folded so many coats and trousers, carefully, in their creases, under Macnooder's generous instructions, and, perched on the edge of the banisters like a queer little marmoset, he had watched Wash Simmons throw great armfuls of assorted clothing into the trays and churn them into place with a baseball bat, while the Triumphant Egghead carefully built up his structure with nicety and tenderness. Only he, the Big Man, sworn to secrecy, knew what Hickey had surreptitiously inserted in the bottom of Egghead's trunk, and also what, from the depths of Wash's muddled clothing, would greet the fond mother or sister who did the unpacking; and every time he thought of it he laughed one of those laughs that pain. Then gleefully he had watched Macnooder stretching a strap until it burst with consequences dire, to the complete satisfaction of Hickey, Turkey, Wash, and the Egghead, who, embracing fondly on the top of another trunk, were assisting Butcher Stevens to close an impossible gap.

Yet into all this amusement a little strain of melancholy had stolen. Here was a sensation of which he was not part, an emotion he did not know. Still, his imagination did not seize it; he could not think of the halls quiet, with no familiar figures lolling out of the windows, or a campus unbrokenly green.

Now from his lonely aerie on Memorial steps, looking down the road to vacation, the Great Big Man suddenly understood—understood and felt. It was he who had gone away, not they. The school he loved was not with him, but roaring down to Trenton. No one had thought to invite him for a visit; but then, why should anyone?

"I'm only a runt, after all," he said angrily to himself. He stuck his fists deep in his pockets, and went down the steps like a soldier and across the campus chanting valorously the football slogan:

> Bill kicked,
> Dunham kicked.
> They both kicked together,
> But Bill kicked mighty hard.
> Flash ran,
> Charlie ran,
> Then Pennington lost her grip;
> She also lost the championship—
> Siss, boom, ah!

After all, he could sleep late; that was something. Then in four days the baseball squad would return, and there would be long afternoon practices to watch, lolling on the turf, with an occasional foul to retrieve. He would read *The Count of Monte Cristo,* and follow *The Three Musketeers* through a thousand far-off adventures, and *Lorna Doone*—there was always the great John Ridd, bigger even than Turkey or the Waladoo Bird.

He arrived resolutely at the Dickinson, and started up the deserted stairs for his room. There was only one thing he feared; he did not want Mrs. Rogers, wife of the housemaster, to "mother" him. Anything but that! He was glad that after luncheon he would have to take his meals at the Lodge. That would avert embarrassing situations, for whatever his friends might think, he, the Great Big Man, was a runt in stature only.

To express fully the excessive gaiety he enjoyed, he tramped to his room, bawling out:

> 'Tis a jolly life we lead,
> Care and sorrow we defy.

All at once a gruff voice spoke:

"My, what a lot of noise for a Great Big Man!"

The Big Man stopped thunderstruck. The voice came from Butcher Stevens' room. Cautiously he tiptoed down the hall and paused, with his funny little nose and eyes peering around the door jamb. Sure enough, there was Butcher, and there were the Butcher's trunks and bags. What could it mean?

"I say," he began, according to etiquette, "is that you, Butcher?"

"Very much so, Big Man."

"What are you doing here?"

"The faculty, Big Man, desire my presence," said the Butcher, sarcastically. "They would like my expert advice on a few problems that are perplexing them."

"Ah," said the Great Big Man, slowly. Then he understood. The Butcher had been caught two nights before returning by Sawtelle's window at a very late hour. He did not know exactly the facts because he had been told not to be too inquisitive, and he was accustomed to obeying instructions. Supposing the faculty should expel him! To the Big Man such a sentence meant the end of all things, something too horrible to contemplate. So he said, "Oh, Butcher, is it serious?"

"Rather, youngster; rather, I should say."

"What *will* the baseball team do?" said the Big Man, overwhelmed.

"That's what's worrying me," replied the crack first baseman, gloomily. He rose and went to the window, where he stood beating a tattoo.

"You don't suppose Crazy Opdyke could cover the bag, do you?" said the Big Man.

"Lord, no!"

"How about Stubby?"

"Too short."

"They might do something with the Waladoo."

"Not for first; he can't stop anything below his knees."

"Then I don't see how we're going to beat Andover, Butcher."

"It does look bad."

"Do you think the faculty will—will—"

"Fire me? Pretty certain, youngster."

"Oh, Butcher!"

"Trouble is, they've got the goods on me—dead to rights."

"But does the Doctor know how it'll break up the nine?"

Butcher laughed loudly.

"He doesn't *ap*-preciate that, youngster."

"No," said the Big Man, reflectively. "They never do, do they?"

The luncheon bell rang, and they hurried down. The Big Man was overwhelmed by the discovery. If Butcher didn't cover first, how could they ever beat Andover and the Princeton freshmen? Even Hill School and Pennington might trounce them. He fell into a brown melancholy until suddenly he caught the sympathetic glance of Mrs. Rogers on him, and for fear that she would think it was due to his own weakness, he began to chat volubly.

He had always been a little in awe of the Butcher. Not that the Butcher had not been friendly; but he was so blunt and rough and unbending that he rather repelled intimacy. He watched him covertly, admiring the bravado with which he pretended unconcern. It must be awful to be threatened with expulsion and actually to be expelled, to have your whole life ruined, once and forever—the Big Man's heart was stirred. He said to himself that he had not been sympathetic enough, and he resolved to repair the error. So, luncheon over, he said with an appearance of carelessness, "I say, old man, come on over to the Jigger Shop. I'll set 'em up. I'm pretty flush, you know."

The Butcher looked down at the funny face and saw the kindly motive under the exaggerated bluffness. Being touched by it, he said gruffly, "Well, come on, then, you old billionaire!"

The Big Man felt a great movement of sympathy in him for his big comrade. He would have liked to slip his little fist in the great brown hand and say something appropriate, only he could think of

128

nothing appropriate. Then he remembered that among men there should be no letting down, no sentimentality. So he lounged along, squinting up at the Butcher and trying to copy his rolling gait.

At the Jigger Shop, Al lifted his eyebrows in well-informed disapproval, saying curtly, "What are you doing here, you Butcher, you?"

"Building up my constitution," said Stevens, with a frown. "I'm staying because I like it, of course. Lawrenceville is just lovely at Easter: spring birds and violets, and that sort of thing."

"You're a nice one," said Al, a baseball enthusiast. "Why couldn't you behave until after the Andover game?"

"Of course; but you needn't rub it in," replied the Butcher, staring at the floor. "Give me a double strawberry, and heave it over."

Al, seeing him not insensible, relented. He added another dab to the double jigger already delivered, and said, shoving over the glass, "It's pretty hard luck on the team, Butcher. There's no one hereabouts can hold down the bag like you. Heard anything definite?"

"No."

"What do you think?"

"I'd hate to say."

"Is anyone doing anything?"

"Cap Kiefer is to see the Doctor tonight."

"I say, Butcher," said the Big Man, in sudden fear, "you won't go up to Andover and play against us, will you?"

"Against the school! Well, rather not!" said the Butcher, indignantly. Then he added, "No; if they fire me, I know what I'll do."

The Big Man wondered if he contemplated suicide; that must be the natural thing to do when one is expelled. He felt that he must keep near Butcher, close all the day. So he made bold to wander about with him, watching him with solicitude.

They stopped at Lalo's for a hot dog, and lingered at Bill Appleby's, where the Butcher mournfully tried the new mitts and swung the bats with critical consideration. Then feeling hungry, they trudged up to Conover's for pancakes and syrup. Everywhere was the same feeling of dismay; what would become of the baseball nine?

Then it suddenly dawned upon the Big Man that no one seemed to be sorry on the Butcher's account. He stopped with a pancake poised on his fork, looked about to make sure no one could hear him, and blurted out, "I say, Butcher, it's not only on account of first base, you know; I'm darn sorry for *you*, honest!"

"Why, you profane little cuss," said the Butcher, frowning, "who told you to swear?"

"Don't make fun of me, Butcher," said the Great Big Man, feeling very little; "I meant it."

"Conover," said the Butcher, loudly, "more pancakes, and brown 'em!'"

He, too, had been struck by the fact that in the general mourning there had been scant attention paid to his personal fortunes. He had prided himself on the fact that he was not susceptible to "feelings," that he neither gave nor asked for sympathy. He was older than his associates, but years had never reconciled him to Latin or Greek or, for that matter, to mathematics in simple or aggravated form. He had been the bully of his village out in northern Iowa, and when a stranger came, he trounced him first, and cemented the friendship afterward. He liked hard knocks, give and take. He liked the school because there was the long football season in the autumn, with the joy of battling, with every sinew of the body alert and the humming of cheers indistinctly heard, as he rammed through the yielding line. Then the spring meant long hours of romping over the smooth diamond, cutting down impossible hits, guarding first base like a bulldog, pulling down the high ones, smothering the wild throws that came ripping along the ground, threatening to jump up against his eyes, throws that other fellows dodged. He was in the company of equals, of good fighters, like Charley De Soto, Hickey, Flash Condit, and Turkey, fellows it was a joy to fight beside. Also, it was good to feel that four hundred-odd wearers of the red and black put their trust in him, and that trust became very sacred to him. He played hard—very hard, but cleanly, because combat was the joy of his life to him. He broke other rules, not as a lark, but out of the same fierce desire for battle, to seek out danger wherever he could find it. He had been caught fair and square, and he knew that for that particular offense there was only one punishment. Yet he hoped against hope, suddenly realizing what it would cost him to give up the great school where, however, he had never sought friendships or anything beyond the admiration of his mates.

The sympathy of the Big Man startled him, then made him

uncomfortable. He had no intention of crying out, and he did not like or understand the new emotion that rose in him as he wondered when his sentence would come.

"Well, youngster," he said, gruffly, "had enough? Have another round?"

"I've had enough," said the Big Man, heaving a sigh. "Let me treat, Butcher."

"Not today, youngster."

"Butcher, I—I'd like to. I'm awfully flush."

"Not today."

"Let's match for it."

"What!" said the Butcher, fiercely. "Don't let me hear any more of that talk. You've got to grow up first."

The Big Man, thus rebuked, acquiesced meekly. The two strolled back to the campus in silence.

"Suppose we have a catch," said the Big Man, tentatively.

"All right," said the Butcher, smiling.

Entrenched behind a gigantic mitt, the Big Man strove valorously to hold the difficult balls. After a long period of this mitigated pleasure they sat down to rest. Then Cap Kiefer's stocky figure appeared around the Dickinson, and the Butcher went off for a long, solemn consultation.

The Big Man, thus relieved of responsibility, felt terribly alone. He went to his room and took down volume two of *The Count of Monte Cristo,* and stretched out on the window seat. Somehow the stupendous adventures failed to enthrall him. It was still throughout the house. He caught himself listening for the patter of Hickey's shoes above, dancing a breakdown, or the rumble of Egghead's laugh down the hall, or a voice calling, "Who can lend me a pair of suspenders?"

And the window was empty. It seemed so strange to look up from the printed page and find no one in the Woodhull opposite, shaving painfully at the window, or lolling like himself over a novel, all the time keeping an eye on the life below. He could not jeer at Two Inches Brown and Crazy Opdyke practicing curves, nor assure them that the Dickinson nine would just fatten on those easy ones. No one halloed from house to house, no voice below drawled out, "Oh, you Great Big Man! Stick your head out of the window!"

There was no one to call across for the time o' day, or for just a nickel to buy stamps, or for the loan of a baseball glove, or a sweater, or a collar button, scissors, button-hook, or fifty and one articles that are never bought but borrowed.

The Great Big Man let *The Count of Monte Cristo* tumble unheeded on the floor, seized a tennis ball, and went across the campus to the esplanade of the Upper House, where for half an hour he bounced the ball against the rim of the ledge, a privilege that only a fourth former may enjoy. Tiring of this, he wandered down to the pond where he skimmed innumerable flat stones until he had exhausted the attractions of this limited amusement.

"I—I'm getting homesick," he admitted finally. "I wish I had a dog—something living—around."

At suppertime he saw the Butcher again, and forgot his own loneliness in the concern he felt for his big friend. He remembered that the Butcher had said that if he were expelled he knew what he would do. What had he meant by that? Something terrible. He glanced up at the Butcher and, being very apprehensive, made bold to ask, "Butcher, I say, what does Cap think?"

"He hasn't seen the Doctor yet," said the Butcher. "He'll see him tonight. I guess I'll go over myself, just to leave a calling card accordin' to *et*-iquette!"

The Big Man kept his own counsel but when the Butcher, after dinner, disappeared through the awful portal of Foundation House, he sat down in the dark under a distant tree to watch. In a short five minutes the Butcher reappeared, stood a moment undecided on the steps, stooped, picked up a handful of gravel, flung it into the air with a laugh, and started along the circle.

"Butcher!"

"Hello, who's that!"

"It's me, Butcher," said the Big Man, slipping his hand into the other's; "I—I wanted to know."

"You aren't going to get sentimental, are you, youngster?" said Stevens, disapprovingly.

"Please, Butcher," said the Great Big Man, pleadingly, "don't be cross with me! Is there any hope?"

"The Doctor won't see me, young one," said the Butcher, "but the *at*-mosphere was not encouraging."

"I'm sorry."

"Honest?"

"Honest."

"You *damn* little runt!"

They went hand in hand over to the chapel, where they chose the back steps and settled down with the great walls at their back and plenty of gravel at their feet to fling aimlessly into the dusky night.

"Butcher?"

"Well, Big Man!"

"What will you do if—if they fire you?"

"Oh, lots of things. I'll go hunting for gold somewhere, or strike out for South America or Africa."

"Oh!" The Big Man was immensely relieved; but he added incredulously, "Then you'll give up football and baseball?"

"Looks that way."

"You won't mind?"

"Yes," said the Butcher, suddenly, "I will mind. I'll hate to leave the old school. I'd like to have one chance more."

"Why don't you tell the Doctor that?"

"Never! I don't cry out when I'm caught, youngster. I take my punishment."

"Yes," said the Big Man, reflecting. "That's right, I suppose; but, then, there's the team to think of, you know."

They sat for a long time in silence, broken suddenly by the Butcher's voice, not so gruff as usual.

"Say, Big Man—feeling sort of homesick?"

No answer.

"Just a bit?"

Still no answer. The Butcher looked down, and saw the Big Man struggling desperately to hold in the sobs.

"Here, none of that, youngster!" he exclaimed in alarm. "Brace up, old man!"

"I—I'm all right," said the Great Big Man with difficulty. "It's nothing."

The Butcher patted him on the shoulder, and then drew his arm around the little body. The Big Man put his head down and blubbered, just as though he had been a little fellow, while his companion sat perplexed, wondering what to do or say in the strange situation.

"So he's a little homesick, is he?" he said lamely.

"No-o-o," said the Great Big Man, "not just that; it's—it's all the fellows I miss."

The Butcher was silent. He, too, began to understand that feeling; only he, in his battling pride, fiercely resisted the weakness.

"You've got an uncle somewhere, haven't you, youngster?" he said gently. "Doesn't he look after you in vacation time?"

"I don't miss *him*," replied the Big Man, shaking his head. Then he pulled himself together and said apologetically, "It's just being left behind that makes me such a damned cry-baby."

"Youngster," said the Butcher, sternly, "your language is *atrocious*. Such words do not sound well in the mouth of a suckling of your size."

"I didn't mean to," said the Big Man, blushing.

"You must leave something to grow up for, young man," said the Butcher, profoundly. "Now tell me about that uncle of yours. I don't fancy his silhouette."

The Great Big Man, thus encouraged, poured out his lonely, starved little heart, while the Butcher listened sympathetically, feeling a certain comfort in sitting with his arm around a little fellow being. Not that he was sensible of giving much comfort; his comments, he felt, were certainly inadequate; nor did he measure in any way up to the situation.

"Now it's better, eh, Big Man?" he said at last when the little fellow had stopped. "Does you sort of good to talk things out."

"Oh, yes; thank you, Butcher."

"All right, then, youngster."

"All right. I say, you—you don't ever feel that way, do you—homesick, I mean?"

"Not much."

"You've got a home, haven't you?"

"Quite too much, young one. If they fire me, I'll keep away from there. Strike out for myself."

"Of course, then, it's different."

"Young one," said the Butcher, suddenly, "that's not quite honest. If I have to clear out of here, it will cut me up *con*-siderable."

"Honest?"

"A fact. I didn't know it before; but it will cut me up to strike out and leave all this behind. I want another chance; and do you know why?"

"Why?"

"I'd like to make friends. Oh, I haven't got any real friends, youngster; you needn't shake your head. It's my fault. I know it. You're the first mortal soul who cared what became of me. All the rest are thinking of the team."

"Now, Butcher—"

"Lord, don't think I'm crying out!" said the Butcher, in instant alarm. "It's all been up to me. Truth is, I've been too darned proud. But I'd like to get another whack at it."

"Perhaps you will, Butcher."

"No, no, there's no reason why I should." The Butcher sat solemnly a moment, flinging pebbles down into the dark tennis courts. Suddenly he said, "Look here, Big Man, I'm going to give you some good advice."

"All right, Butcher."

"And I want you to tuck it away in your thinker—*savez?* You're a nice kid now, a good sort, but you've got a lot of chances for being spoiled. Don't get fresh. Don't get a swelled head just because a lot of the older fellows let you play around. There's nothing so hateful in the sight of God or man as a fresh kid."

"You don't think—" began the Big Man in dismay.

"No; you're all right now. You're quiet, and don't tag around, and you're a good sort, darned if you aren't, and that's why I don't want to see you spoiled. Now a straight question: Do you smoke?"

"Why, that is—well, Butcher, I did try once a puff on Snookers' cigarette."

"You ought to be spanked!" said the Butcher, angrily. "And when I get hold of Snookers, I'll tan him. The idea of his letting you! Don't you monkey around tobacco yet a while. First of all, it's fresh, and second, you've got to *grow*. You want to make a team, don't you, while you're here?"

"O-o-oh!" said the Great Big Man with a long sigh.

"Then just stick to growing. 'Cause you've got work cut out for you there. Now I'm not preachin'; I'm saying that you want to fill out and grow up and do something. Harkee."

"All right."

"Cut out Snookers and that gang. Pick out the fellows that count, as you go along, and just remember this, if you forget the rest: if you want to put ducks in Tabby's bed or nail down his desk, do it because *you* want to do it, not because some other fellow wants you to do it. D'ye hear?"

"Yes, Butcher."

"Remember that, youngster; if I'd stuck to it, I'd kept out of a peck of trouble." He reflected a moment and added, "Then I'd study a little. It's not a bad thing, I guess, in the long run, and it gets the masters on your side. And now jump up and we'll trot home."

The following night the Big Man, again under his tree, waited for the result of the conference that was going on inside Foundation House between the Doctor and the Butcher and Cap Kiefer. It was long, very long. The minutes went slowly, and it was very dark there, with hardly a light showing in the circle of houses that ordinarily seemed like a procession of lighted ferryboats. After an interminable hour, the Butcher and Cap came out. He needed no word to tell what their attitudes showed only too plainly: the Butcher was expelled!

The Big Man waited until the two had passed into the night, and then, with a sudden resolve, went bravely to the doorbell and rang. Before he quite appreciated the audacity of his act, he found himself in the sanctum facing a much-perplexed headmaster.

"Doctor, I—I—" The Big Man stopped, overwhelmed by the awful majesty of the Doctor, on whose face still sat the grimness of the past conference.

"Well, Joshua, what's the matter?" said the headmaster, relaxing a bit before one of his favorites.

"Please, sir, I'm a little—a little embarrassed, I'm afraid," said the Great Big Man, desperately.

"Am I so terrible as all that?" said the Doctor, smiling.

"Yes, sir—you are," the Big Man replied frankly. Then he said, plunging in, "Doctor, is the Butcher—is Stevens—are you going to—expel him?"

"That is my painful duty, Joshua," said the Doctor, frowning.

"Oh, Doctor," said the Big Man all in a breath, "you don't know —you're making a mistake."

"I am? Why, Joshua?"

"Because—you don't know. Because the Butcher won't tell you, he's too proud, sir; because he doesn't want to cry out, sir."

"What do you mean exactly?" said the Doctor in surprise. "Does Stevens know you're here?"

"Oh, Heavens, no, sir!" said the Big Man in horror. "And you must never tell him, sir; that would be too terrible."

"Joshua," said the Doctor, impressively, "I am expelling Stevens because he is just the influence I don't want boys of your age to come under."

"Oh, yes, sir," said the Big Man, "I know you think that, sir; but really, Doctor, that's where you are wrong; really you are, sir."

The Doctor saw there was something under the surface, and he encouraged the little fellow to talk. The Big Man, forgetting all fear in the seriousness of the situation, told the listening head-master all the Butcher's conversation with him on the chapel steps the night before—told it simply and eloquently, with an ardor that bespoke absolute faith. Then suddenly he stopped.

"That's all, sir," he said, frightened.

The Doctor rose and walked back and forth, troubled and per-plexed. There was no doubting the sincerity of the recital; it was a side of Stevens he had not guessed. Finally he turned and rested his hand on the Big Man's shoulders.

"Thank you," he said; "it does put another light on the ques-tion. I'll think it over."

When, ten days later, the school came trickling home along the road from vacation, they saw, against all hope, the Butcher holding down first base, frolicking over the diamond in the old familiar way, and a great shout of joy and relief went up. But how it had happened no one ever knew, least of all Cap and the Butcher, who had gone from Foundation House that night in settled despair.

To add to Butcher's mystification, the Doctor, in announcing his reprieve, had added, "I've decided to make a change, Stevens. I'm going to put Tibbetts in to room with you. I place him in your charge. I'm going to try a little responsibility on you."

THE POLITICAL EDUCATION
OF MR. BALDWIN

If Hickey had not been woefully weak in mathematics the famous Fed and anti-Fed riots would probably never have happened. But as revolutions turn on minor axes, Hickey, who could follow a football like a hound, could not for the life of him trace X, the unknown factor, through the hedges of the simplest equation.

It was, therefore, with feelings of the acutest interest that he waited, in the upper corridor of Memorial Hall, on the opening morning of the spring term, for the appearance of Mr. Baldwin, the new recruit to the mathematics department. The Hall was choked with old boys chattering over the doings of the Easter vacation, calling back and forth, punching one another affectionately, or critically examining the returning stragglers.

"His name is Ernest Garrison Baldwin," said the Gutter Pup. "Just graduated, full of honors and that sort of thing."

"He ought to be easy," said Crazy Opdyke, hopefully.

"These mathematical sharks are always fancy markers," interposed Macnooder.

"If I'm stuck in the first row," said the Egghead gloomily, "it's all up—I never could do anything with figures."

"If we want short lessons," said Hickey, waking out of his reverie, "we've all got to flunk in the beginning."

At this Machiavellian analysis there was a chorus of assent.

"Sure."

"Hickey's the boy!"

"Red Dog and Poler Fox have got to be kept down."

"We're not packhorses."

"Say, is he green?"

"Sure—never taught before."

"Cheese it—he's coming."

The group stood aside, intent on the arrival of the new adversary. They saw a stiff young man, already bald, with a set, affable manner and a pervading smile of cordiality, who entered the classroom with a confident step, after a nodded, "Ah, boys—good morning."

The class filed in, eyeing the natural enemy closely for the first indications of value to aid them in the approaching conflicts.

"He's awfully serious," said the Egghead to his neighbor.

"He'll try to drive us," replied Macnooder, with instinctive resentment.

Hickey said nothing, absorbed in contemplation of a momentous question—how would the new master hear recitations? To solve a master's system is to be prepared in advance, and with the exception of the Roman's there was not a system which he had not solved. Popular masters, like Pa Dater, called you up every third day, which is eminently just and conducive to a high standard of scholarship. The Muffin Head, in stealthy craftiness, had a way of calling you up twice in succession after you had flunked and were expecting a brief period of immunity; but this system once solved gave ample opportunity to redeem yourself. The Doctor, wiser than the rest, wrote each name on a card, shuffled the pack and called for a recitation according to chance—but even the Doctor left the pack on his desk, nor counted the cards as all careful players should. Other masters, like Tapping and Baranson, trusted to their intuitions, seizing upon the boy whose countenance betrayed a lurking apprehension. Hickey took kindly to this method and had thrived amazingly, by sudden flagrant inattentions or noticeable gazing out of the windows, which invariably procured him a staccato summons to recite just as the recitation neared the limited portion he had studied.

So Hickey sat, examining Mr. Baldwin, and speculating into which classification he would fall.

"Now, boys," said Mr. Baldwin, with an expanding smile, "we're beginning the new term. I hope you'll like me—I know I shall like you. I'm quite a boy myself—quite a boy, you know. Now I'm going ahead on a new principle. I'm going to assume that you all take an interest in your work [the class sat up]. I'm going to assume that you look upon life with seriousness and purpose. I'm going to assume that you realize the sacrifices your parents are making to afford you an education. I'm not here as a taskmaster. I'm here to help you, as your friend, as your companion—as an older brother— that's it, as an older brother. I hope our interest in one another will not be limited to this classroom."

Hickey and the Egghead, who had prominently installed themselves in the front seats, led the applause with serious, responsive faces. Mr. Baldwin acknowledged it, noticing pleasantly the leaders of the demonstration.

Then he rapped for order and began to call the roll, seating the boys alphabetically. He ran rapidly through the F's, the G's and H's and, pausing, inquired, "Are there any J's in the class?"

At this excruciatingly witty remark, which every master annually blunders upon, the waiting class roared in unison, while Hinsdale was forced to slap Hickey mercilessly on the back to save him from violent hysterics.

Mr. Baldwin, who suddenly perceived he had made a pun, hastily assumed a roguish expression and allowed a considerable moment for laughter to die away. The session ended in a gale of cordiality.

Hickey and the Egghead paid a visit that afternoon to the Griswold, to make the new arrival feel quite at home.

"Ah, boys," said Mr. Baldwin, with a wringing handshake, "this is very friendly of you, very friendly."

"Mr. Baldwin," said Hickey seriously, "we were very much interested in what you said to us this morning."

"Indeed," said Baldwin, gratified. "Well, that pleases me very much. And I am glad to see that you take me at my word, and I hope you will drop in often. There are lots of things I want to talk over with you."

"Yes, sir," said the Egghead. "It's very kind of you."

"Not at all," said Baldwin, with a wave of his hand. "My theory is that a master should be your companion, and I have one or two ideas about education I am anxious to have my boys interested in. Now, for instance, take politics; what do you know about politics?"

"Why, nothing," said Hickey in acquiescent surprise.

"And yet that is the most vital thing you will have to face as men. Here's a great national election approaching, and yet, I am certain not one in four hundred of you has any clear conception of the political system."

"That's so, Egghead," said Hickey, nodding impressively at his companion. "It *is* so."

"I have a scheme I'm going to talk over with you," continued Baldwin, "and I want your advice. Sit down; make yourselves comfortable."

Later in the afternoon Mr. Baranson, Baldwin's superior in the Griswold, dropped in with a friendly inquiry. Young Mr. Baldwin was gazing out of the window in indulgent amusement. Mr. Baranson, following his gaze, beheld, in the far campus, Hickey and Egghead rolling over each other like two trick bears.

"Well, Baldwin, how goes it?" said Baranson genially.

"Splendidly. The boys are more than friendly. We shall get on famously."

" '*Danaos timeo et dona ferentes,*' " said Baranson shrewdly.

"Oh—" Baldwin objected.

"Yes, yes—I'm an old fogy—old style," said Baranson, cutting in, "but it's based on good scientific researches, Baldwin. I just dropped in for a hint or two, which you won't pay attention to—never mind. When you've lived with the young human animal as long as I have, you won't have any illusions. He doesn't want to be enlightened. He hasn't the slightest desire to be educated. He isn't educated. He never will be. His memory simply *detains* for a short while, a larger and larger number of facts—Latin, Greek, history, mathematics, it's all the same—facts, nothing but facts. He remembers when he is compelled to, but he is supremely bored by the performance. All he wants is to grow, to play and to get into sufficient mischief. My dear fellow, treat him as a splendid young savage, who breaks a rule for the joy of matching his wits against yours, and don't take him seriously, as you are in danger of doing. Don't let him take you seriously or he will lead you to a cropper."

Ernest Garrison Baldwin did not deign to reply—the voice of the older generation, of course! He was of the new, he would replace old prejudices with new methods. There were a great many things in the world he intended to change—among others this whole antagonistic spirit of education. So he remained silent, and looked very dignified.

Baranson studied him, saw the workings of his mind, and smiled.

"Never were at boarding school, were you?" he asked.

"No," said Baldwin, drily.

Baranson gave a glance at the study, remarked the advanced note in the shelves, and went to the door.

"After all," he said, with his hand on the knob, "the first year, Baldwin, we learn more than we teach."

"Gee! I think it's an awful bore," said the Gutter Pup.

"I don't see it either," said the Egghead.

"Who started it?" asked Turkey Reiter.

"Hickey and Elder Brother Baldwin," said the Egghead. "Hickey's improving his stand."

"Hickey, boy," said Butcher Stevens, professionally, "you're consorting with awful low company."

"Hickey, you are getting to be a greasy grind," said the Gutter Pup.

"I am, am I," said Hickey indignantly. "I'd like to know if I'm not a patriot. I'd like to know if I'm not responsible for the atmosphere of brotherly love and the dove of peace that floats around Baldwin's classroom. I'd like to know if I'm not responsible for his calling us up alphabetically, regular order, every other day, no suspicion, perfect trust—mutual confidence. Am I right?"

"You are right, Hickey, you are right," said Turkey apologetically. "The binomial theorem is a delight and a joy, when, as you say, the master has mutual trust in the scholar. But where in blazes, Hickey, did you get this political shindy into your thinker?"

"It's Elder Brother's theory of education," said Hickey carefully, "*one* of his theories. Elder Brother is very much distressed at the ignorance, the political ignorance, of the modern boy. Brother is right."

"Come off," said the Egghead, glancing at him suspiciously, but Hickey maintained a serious face.

"What's up?" said Macnooder, sauntering over to the crowd on the lawn.

"Hickey's fixed up a plan with Brotherly Love to have a political campaign," said the Gutter Pup, "and is trying to rouse our enthusiasm."

"A campaign here in the school, in the Lawrenceville School, John C. Green Foundation!" said Macnooder incredulously.

"The same!"

"No! I won't believe it. It's a dream—it's a beautiful, satisfying dream," said Macnooder, shaking his head. "A political campaign in school; Hickey, my bounding boy, I see your cunning hand!"

"Now Doc's gone nutty," said the unimaginative Egghead. "What the deuce do you see in it?"

"Hickey, you old rambunctious, foxy, prodigious Hickey, I knew something was brewing," said Doc, not deigning to notice the Egghead. "You have been quiet, most quiet of late. Hickey, how did you do it?"

"Sympathy, Doc," said Hickey blandly. "I've been most sympathetic with Elder Brother, sympathetic and most encouraging. Sympathy is a beautiful thing, Doc, beautiful and rare."

"Hickey, don't torture me with curiosity," said Doc. "Where are we at?"

"At the present moment, Brother is asking the Doctor for permission to launch the campaign, and the sympathetic, popular and serious Hickey Hicks is proceeding to select a preliminary conference committee."

"And what then?" said Turkey, with sudden interest.

"What then?" said Hickey. "Bonfires, parades, stump speeches, proclamations, et cetera, et ceteray."

"Oh, Hickey," said the now enthusiastic Gutter Pup, "do you think the Doctor ever will permit it?"

"What's the use of getting excited?" said the Egghead contemptuously. "You don't fancy for a moment, do you, there's a chance of fooling the Doctor?"

"Sure, Egghead's right," said Butcher Stevens; "you won't get the Doctor to bite. Baldwin is green, but the Doctor is quite ripe, thank you!"

Even Macnooder looked dubiously at Hickey, who assumed an air of superhuman wisdom and answered, "I have two chances, Baldwin and the De-coy Ducks!"

"The what?"

"Decoy Ducks—the committee that will confer tomorrow afternoon with the Doctor."

Turkey emitted a long, admiring whistle.

"I have given the matter thought—serious thought, as Baldwin would say," said Hickey. "The following collection of Archangels and young High Markers will be rounded up for the Doctor's inspection tomorrow."

"As Decoy Ducks?"

"As Decoy Ducks, you intelligent Turkey. High Markers: Red Dog, Poler Fox, Biddy Hampton and Ginger Pop Rooker, Wash Simmons—the Doctor would feed out of Wash's hand—Crazy Opdyke—he reads Greek like Jules Verne. Everything must be done to make this a strictly ed-u-cational affair. Now to demonstrate that it has the sanction of the religious element of this community the following notorious and flagrant Archangels will qualify: Halo Brown, Pink Rabbit, Parson Eddy, and Saphead and the Coffee Cooler—the Doctor is real affectionate with the Coffee Cooler."

"What a beoo-ti-ful bunch!" said the Gutter Pup rapturously.

"It is," said Hickey, proudly; "the Doctor would let any one of them correct his own examination papers and raise the mark afterward on the ground of overconscientiousness."

"Well, where's the fun?" said the Egghead obstinately. "If Crazy Opdyke and that bunch is to run the campaign, where do we come in?"

"There will be a small preliminary representation of professional politicians," said Hickey, smiling, "very small at present, limited to the handsome and popular Hickey Hicks, who will represent the large body of professional politicians who will be detained at home by hard work and serious application, but—"

"But what?" said Macnooder.

"But who will find time to ac-tively assist this quiet, orderly campaign of education, *after* their presence will not be misunderstood!"

At half-past one the next day, the Doctor, sympathetically inclined by the enthusiastic, if inexperienced, Mr. Baldwin, received the Decoy Ducks in his study at Foundation House.

The Doctor, while interested, had not been convinced, and had expressed a desire to know into whose guidance the nurturing of such a tender plant had been entrusted. As the impresssive gathering defiled before him, his instinctive caution vanished, his glance warmed with satisfaction, and assuming the genial and conversational attitude he reserved for his favorites, he began:

"Well, boys, this appears to be a responsible gathering, an unusually responsible one. It is gratifying to see you approaching such subjects with serious purpose and earnestness. It is gratifying that the leaders of this school" (here his glance rested fondly on Wash Simmons, Crazy Opdyke and the Coffee Cooler, prominently placed) "that the earnest, purposeful boys show this interest in the political welfare of the nation. Mr. Baldwin's plan seems to me to be a most excellent one. I am in hearty accord with its motive. We cannot begin too soon to interest the youth, the intelligent, serious youth of our country in honest government and clean political methods." (Hickey, in noble effacement by the window seat, here gazed dreamily over the campus to the red circle of houses.) "Much can be accomplished from the earnest and purposeful pursuit of this instructive experiment. The experiment should be educational in the largest sense; the more I study it the more worthy it appears. I should not be surprised if your experiment should attract the consideration of the educational world. Mr. Baldwin, it gives me pleasure to express to you my thanks and my gratification for the authorship of so worthy an undertaking. I will leave you to a discussion of the necessary details."

"Well, boys," said Baldwin briskly, "let me briefly outline the plan agreed upon. The election shall be for a school council, before which legislation affecting the interests of the school shall come. Each of the four forms shall elect two representatives, each of the ten houses shall elect one representative, making a deliberative body of eighteen. In view of the fact that the approaching national election might inject unnecessary bitterness if the election should be on national issues, we have decided, on the very excellent suggestion of Hicks, who has indeed given many valuable suggestions" (Hickey looked preternaturally solemn), "to have the election on a matter of school policy, and have settled upon the athletic finances as an issue of sufficient interest and yet one that can be calmly and orderly discussed. At present, the management of the athletic finances is in the hands of selected officers from the fourth form. The issue, then, is whether this method shall be continued or whether a member of the faculty shall administer the finances. I should suggest Federalists and Anti-Federalists as names for the parties you will form. One week will be given to campaigning and the election will take place according to the Australian ballot system. Now, boys, I wish you success. You will acquire a taste for public combat and a facility in the necessary art of politics that will nurture in you a desire to enter public life, to take your part in the fight for honest politics, clean methods, independent thinking, and will make you foes of intimidation, bribery, cheating and that demagoguery that is the despair of our present system. At present you may be indifferent, a little bored, perhaps, at this experiment, but you will like it—I am sure you will like it. I prophesy it will interest you once you get started."

Hickey lingered after the meeting to explain that the duties incident to the organizing of such an important undertaking had unfortunately deprived him of the time necessary to prepare his advanced algebra.

"Well, that is a little matter we'll overlook, Hicks," said the enthusiast genially. "I congratulate you on your selection, an admirable committee, one that inspires confidence. Keep me in touch with developments and call on me for advice at any time."

"Yes, indeed, sir."

"Good luck."

"Thank you, sir."

A half hour later Hickey announced the addition of the following professional politicians: Tough McCarty, Doc Macnooder, the Triumphant Egghead, Slugger Jones, Turkey Reiter, Cheyenne Baxter, Jock Hasbrouck, Butcher Stevens, Rock Bemis, and Bat Greer.

The reinforced committee then met, divided equitably, and having tossed for sides, announced their organization, as follows:

FEDERALIST PARTY
Chairman: THE HON. TOUGH MCCARTY
Vice-Chairman: THE HON. GINGER POP ROOKER
ANTI-FEDERALIST PARTY
Chairman: HON. CHEYENNE BAXTER
Vice-Chairman: HON. HICKEY HICKS

The school was at first apathetic, then mildly interested. The scheme was examined with suspicion as perhaps being a veiled attempt of the faculty to increase the already outrageous taxes on the mind. It looked prosy enough at first glance—perhaps an attempt to revive the interest in debating and so to be fiercely resisted.

For an hour the great campaign for political education hung fire and then suddenly it began to catch on. A few leading imaginations had seen the latent possibilities. In another hour apathy had disappeared and every house was discussing the momentous question whether to go Fed or Anti-Fed.

The executive committee of the Federalist party met immediately, on a call from the Honorable Cheyenne Baxter, in the Triumphant Egghead's rooms for organization and conference.

"We've got the short end of it, all right, all right," said Butcher Stevens gloomily. "The idea of our standing up for the faculty."

"That's right, Cheyenne," said Turkey, shaking his head. "We'll be left high and dry."

"We won't carry any house outside the Dickinson and the Woodhull," said Slugger Jones.

"I'd like to make a suggestion," said Crazy Opdyke.

"We've got to plan two campaigns," said Cheyenne, "one for the election from the forms and one for the control of the houses. Let's take up the forms—the fourth form will go solidly against us."

"Sure," said Doc Macnooder, "because if we win they lose control of the finances."

"I have a suggestion," said Crazy Opdyke for the second time.

"Now," said Cheyenne, "we've got to make this a matter of the school against the fourth form, and it oughtn't to be so hard, either. Now, how're we going to do it? First, what have we got?"

"The Dickinson and the Woodhull," said Hickey.

"Yes, we can be sure of those, but that's all. Now, those Feds, with Jock Hasbrouck and Tough McCarty, will swing the Kennedy and the Griswold."

"The Davis House will be against us," said Macnooder, with conviction. "They're just aching to get back at the Dickinson."

"That's so," said Turkey. "They're still sore because we won the football championship."

"The Davis will pull the Rouse House with it," said Hickey gloomily. "They're forty in the Davis and only twelve in the Rouse.

147

The Davis would mangle them if they ever dared go our way."

"We've got to counteract that by getting the Green," said Cheyenne. "They're only ten there, but it makes a vote. The fight'll be in the Hamill and the Cleve."

"The Cleve is sore on us," said Turkey of the Dickinson, "because we swiped the ice cream last year for their commencement dinner."

"I've got an idea," said Crazy Opdyke, trying to be heard.

"Shut up, Crazy," said Doc. "You've served your purpose; you're a Decoy Duck and nothing else."

"Harmony!" said Cheyenne warningly. "The way to get the Green is to give Butsey White, down there, the nomination from the second form, if he'll swing the house."

"And put up Bronc Andrews in the Hamill," added Macnooder.

"Where do I come in?" said Crazy Opdyke, who had aspirations.

"You subordinate yourself to the success of your party," said Cheyenne.

"The devil I do," said Opdyke. "If you think I'm a backwater delegate, you've got another think coming. I may be a Decoy Duck, but either I'm made chairman of a Finance Committee or I lead a bolt right out of this convention."

"A Finance Committee?" said Butcher Stevens, mystified.

"Sure," said Cheyenne Baxter. "That's most important."

"I'll take that myself, then," said Macnooder aggressively. "I'd like to know what claim Crazy's got to a position of trust and responsibility."

"Claim or no claim," said Opdyke, pulling his hat over his eyes and tilting back, "either I handle the funds of this here campaign or the Anti-Federalist party begins to split."

"Shall a half-plucked rooster from the Cleve House hold up this convention?" said Wash Simmons militantly. "If we're going to be blackjacked by every squid that comes down the road, *I'm* going to get out."

"I have spoken," said Crazy.

"So have I."

"Gentlemen, gentlemen," protested the Honorable Cheyenne Baxter, "we must have harmony."

"Rats!" said Opdyke. "I demand a vote."

"I insist upon it," said Wash.

The vote was taken and Macnooder was declared chairman of the Finance Committee. Crazy Opdyke arose and made them a profound bow.

"Gentlemen, I have the honor of bidding you farewell," he said, loftily. "The voice of freedom has been stifled. This great party is in the hands of commercial interests and private privilege. This is nothing but a Dickinson House sinecure. I retire, I withdraw, I shake the dust from my feet. I depart, but I shall not sleep, I shall not rest, I shall neither forget nor forgive. Remember, gentlemen of the Anti-Federalist party, this hour, and when in the stillness of the night you hear the swish of the poisoned arrow, the swirl of the tomahawk, the thud of the secret stone, pause and say to yourself, 'Crazy Opdyke done it!' "

"It is unfortunate," said Cheyenne, when Crazy had departed, "most unfortunate, but that's politics."

"Crazy has no influence," said Wash, contemptuously.

"He has our secrets," said Cheyenne gloomily.

"Let's get to work," said Macnooder. "You can bet Tough Mc-Carty's on the job; his father's an alderman."

At six o'clock the campaign was off with a rush. At seven the headmaster, all unsuspecting, stepped out from Foundation House, cast one fond glance at the familiar school, reposing peacefully in the twilight, and departed to carry the message of increased liberty in primary education to a waiting conference at Boston. Shortly after, a delegation of the school faculty, who had just learned of the prospective campaign, hurried over in amazed, indignant and incredulous protest. They missed the headmaster by ten minutes—but ten minutes make history.

"Jiminy crickets!"

"Suffering Moses!"

"Call Hickey!"

"Tell Hickey!"

"Hickey, stick your head out of the window!"

Hickey, slumbering peacefully, in that choicest period between the rising bell and breakfast, leaped to the middle of the floor at the uproar that suddenly resounded through the Dickinson.

He thrust his head out of the window and beheld from the upper stories of the Griswold an immense white sheet sagging in the breeze, displaying in crude red-flannel letters the following device:

NO APRON STRINGS FOR US
THE FEDERAL PARTY
WILL FIGHT TO THE END
FACULTY USURPATION

Hardly had his blinking eyes become accustomed to the sight when a fresh uproar broke out on the other side of the Dickinson.

"Hully Gee!"

"Look at the Kennedy!"

"Great cats and little kittens!"

"Snakes alive!"

"Look at the Kennedy, will you!"

"Hickey, oh you, Hickey!"

At the sound of Macnooder's voice in distress, Hickey realized the situation was serious and rushed across the hall. He found Macnooder with stern and belligerent gaze fixed out of the window. From the Kennedy House another banner insolently displayed this amazing proclamation:

DOWN WITH THE GOO-GOOS
LAWRENCEVILLE SHALL NOT BE
A KINDERGARTEN.
RALLY TO THE FEDERALISTS AND
DOWN THE DICKINSON GOO-GOOS

Hickey looked at Macnooder. Macnooder looked at Hickey.

"Goo-Goo," said Hickey, grieved.

"Goo-Goo," repeated Doc sadly. "Goo-Goo and Apron strings. Hickey, my boy, we have got to be up and doing."

"Doc," said Hickey, "that's Tough McCarty's work. We never ought to have let him get away from us."

"Hickey, we must nail the lie," said Doc solemnly.

"The Executive Committee of the Anti-Fed party will meet in my rooms," said Hickey determinedly, "directly after first recitation. We have been caught napping by a gang of ballot stuffers, but we will come back—Doc, we *will* come back!"

The Executive Committee met with stern and angry resolve, like battling football players between the halves of a desperate game.

"Fellows," said Hickey, "while we have slept the enemy has been busy. We are mutts, and the original pie-faced mutt is yours truly."

"No, Hickey, if there's going to be a competition for mutts," said Cheyenne Baxter, "I'm the blue ribbon."

"Before we bestow any more bouquets," said Macnooder sarcastically, "let's examine the situation. Let's see the worst. The Feds have the jump on us. They've raised the cry of 'Apron strings' on us, and it's going to be a mighty hard one to meet."

"We'll never answer it," said the gloomy Egghead; "we're beaten now. It's a rotten issue and a rotten game."

At this moment the Gutter Pup rushed in like a white fuzzy dog, his eyes bulging with importance as he delivered the bombshell, that Crazy Opdyke had organized a Mugwump party and carried the Cleve House for it.

"No."

"A Mugwump party!"

"What the deuce is he up to?"

"Order," said Hickey, stilling the tumult with a shoe vigorously applied to a wash-basin. "This meeting is not a bunch of undertakers. We are here to save the party."

"Hickey's right," said Turkey; "let's get down to business."

"First," said Hickey, "let's have reports. What has Treasurer Macnooder to report?"

The Mark Hanna of the campaign rose, tightened his belt, adjusted his glasses, and announced amid cheers that the Finance Committee had to report sixty-two dollars and forty cents in promissory notes, twelve dollars and thirty-eight cents in cash, three tennis rackets, two jerseys, one dozen caps, a bull's-eye lantern (loaned) and a Flobert rifle.

"We can always have a banquet, even if we're beaten," said the Triumphant Egghead. The gloom began to dissipate.

"What has the Honorable Gutter Pup to report?" said Cheyenne Baxter.

The Rocky Mountain Gazelle proudly announced the establishment of a thorough system of espionage, through the corrupting of Mr. Klondike Jackson, the cooperative gentleman who waited on the table at the Kennedy, and Mr. Alcibiades Bonaparte, who shook up the beds at the Griswold. He likewise reported that young Muskrat Foster, who was not overpopular at the Davis House, had perceived the great truths of Anti-Federalism. He then presented a bill of two dollars and forty-five cents for the corrupting of the

Messrs. Jackson and Bonaparte, with an addition of fifty cents for the further contaminating of young Muskrat Foster.

"The Honorable Wash Simmons will report," said Cheyenne Baxter.

"Fellows," said Wash, "I ain't no silver-tongued orator, and all I've got to say is that Butsey White, down at the Green House, is most sensible to the honor of representing this great and glorious party of moral ideas, as congressman from the second form, but—"

"But what?" said Slugger Jones.

"But he kind of fears that the other members of the Green House aren't quite up on Anti-Federalism, and he reckons it will take quite a little literature to educate them."

"Literature?" said Cheyenne, mystified.

"About eight volumes," said Wash. "Eight green-backed pieces of *literature!*"

"The robber!"

"Why, that's corruption."

"Gentlemen," said Cheyenne, rapping for order, "the question is, does he get the literature? Ayes or noes."

"I protest," interrupted Hickey. "Remember, gents, this is a campaign for clean politics. We will not buy votes, no! We will only encourage local enterprises. The Green is trying to fit themselves out for the baseball season. I suggest contributing toward a catcher's mitt and a mask, and letting it go at that."

On the announcement of a unanimous vote, the Honorable Wash Simmons departed to encourage local enterprises.

"And now, fellows," said Hickey, "we come to the serious proposition—the real business of the meeting. We have got to treat with Crazy Opdyke."

"Never!"

"Macnooder must sacrifice himself," said Hickey. "Am I right, Cheyenne?"

"You are," said Cheyenne. "The campaign has reached a serious stage. The Upper, the Kennedy, the Griswold, the Davis, are already Fed; the Rouse will go next. Even if we get the Green, we're lost if the Cleve goes against us, and Crazy is just holding out to make terms."

"We have misjudged Crazy," said Hickey. "His record was against him, but we have misjudged him. He's been the only live one in the bunch. Now we've got to meet his terms."

The door opened and Crazy Opdyke sauntered in.

"Hello, fellows," he drawled. "How's the campaign going? Are you satisfied with your progress?" He stretched languidly into an armchair. "Am I still welcome in the home of great moral ideas?"

"Crazy, our feelings for you are both of sorrow and of affection," said Cheyenne, conciliatingly. "You certainly are a boss politician. What's this new wrinkle of yours over in the Cleve?"

"I've been amusing myself," said Crazy with a drawl, "organizing the Mugwumps, the intelligent and independent vote, the balance of power, you know, the party that doesn't heel to any boss, but votes according to its, to its—"

"To its what, Crazy?" said Hickey, gently.

"To its conscience," replied Crazy firmly. "To its conscience, when its conscience is intelligently approached."

"Oh, you're for sale, are you?" said Turkey aggressively.

"No, Turkey, no-o-o! And yet we've organized the Blocks of Five Marching Club; rather significant, eh?"

"Well, what's your game; what have you come for?"

"Oh, just to be friendly," said Crazy, rising languidly.

"Stop," said Hickey. "Sit down. Let's have a few words."

Crazy slouched back, sank into the armchair and assumed a listening position.

"Crazy," said Hickey, "we've made a mistake. We didn't know you. You are the surprise of the campaign. We apologize. We are merely amateurs; you are the only original, professional politician."

"This is very gratifying," said Crazy, without a blush.

"Crazy, from this moment," said Hickey, firmly, "you are the treasurer of the Campaign Committee, and we're listening for any words of wisdom you have ready to uncork."

"No, Hickey, no," said Crazy, rising amid general dismay, "I no longer hanker to be a treasurer. It was just a passing fancy. Independence is better and more profitable; I appreciate your kind offer, I do appreciate it, Hickey, but I'm a Mugwump; I couldn't wear a dog collar, I couldn't!"

"Sit down again, Crazy," said Hickey, persuasively; "sit down. It's a pleasure to talk with you. You're right; your independent and intelligent nature would be thrown away in a matter of books and figures. We've been looking round for a fearless, upright, popular and eloquent figure to stand for the Cleve, and, Crazy, we're just aching to have you step up into the frame."

"Hickey, you mistake me, you mistake me and my motives," said Crazy, sadly. "My soul does not hanker for personal glorification or the flattery of the multitude. I'm a child of nature, Hickey, and my ambitions are few and simple."

"It's right to have ambitions, Crazy," said Hickey, soothingly, "and they don't need to be few or simple. We regret that we cannot honor your eminent qualities as we wish to, but we still have hopes, Crazy, that we may have the benefit of your guiding hand."

"Guiding hand?" said Crazy, looking at the ceiling.

"Exactly," said Hickey, magnanimously; "in fact, I realize how unworthy I am to fill the great position of trust and responsibility of vice-chairman of this committee, and I long to see it in the hands—"

"I thought you said guiding hand," said Crazy, interrupting.

The assembled committee looked in amazement at Crazy. Then the storm broke out.

"Why, you insolent, impudent pup!"

"Do you think we'll make you chairman?"

"Kick him out!"

"Roughhouse!"

"Order!" cried Cheyenne. "Crazy, out with it. You want to be chairman, don't you?"

"Have I made any demands?" said Crazy, coolly.

"Come now—yes or no!"

"Are you handing it to me?"

A fresh storm of indignation was interrupted by the sudden tumultuous reappearance of Wash Simmons, shouting, "Fellows, Butsey White and the Green have sold out to the Mugwumps!"

Crazy Opdyke sat down again.

A long silence succeeded. Then Cheyenne Baxter, mutely interrogating every glance, rose and said, "Crazy, you win. The chairmanship is yours. Will you take it on a silver platter or with a bouquet of roses?"

That evening, when Hickey went to report to Ernest Garrison Baldwin, he found that civic reformer in a somewhat perturbed condition.

"I'm afraid, Hicks," he said dubiously, "that the campaign is getting a wrong emphasis. It seems to me that those Federalist banners are not only in questionable taste, but show a frivolous and trifling attitude toward this great opportunity."

"It's just the humor of the campaign, sir," said Hickey reassuringly; "I wouldn't take them seriously."

"Another thing, Hicks; I'm rather surprised that the management of the campaign does not seem to be in the hands of the very representative committee you originally selected."

"Yes, sir," said Hickey; "we realize that; but we're making a change in our party at least which will please you. Opdyke is going to take control."

"Indeed! That is reassuring; that is a guarantee on your side, at least, of a dignified, honorable canvass."

"Oh, yes, sir," said Hickey.

He left gravely and scampered across the campus. Suddenly from the Woodhull Toots Cortell's trumpet squeaked out. At the same moment the first Anti-Fed banner was flung out, thus conceived:

TURN THE ROBBERS OUT
NO MORE GRAFTING
NO MORE GOUGING THE UNDER-FORMERS
FACULTY SUPERVISION MEANS
SAVING TO THE POCKET
OUT WITH THE BLACKMAILERS

The astute and professional hand of the Honorable Crazy Opdyke was felt at once. The Anti-Fed party, while still advocating faculty control of the athletic finances for purposes of efficiency and economy, now shifted the ground by a series of brilliant strokes.

The third day of the campaign had hardly opened when the four fusion houses displayed prominently the following proclamation:

ECONOMY AND JIGGERS
FACULTY MANAGEMENT OF THE FINANCES
MEANS RIGID ECONOMY
PROTECTION OF THE WEAK
FROM THE TYRANNY OF THE TAX GATHERER
EQUITABLE PRO-RATA
LEVYING OF CONTRIBUTIONS
ECONOMY MEANS MORE JIGGERS
MORE JIGGERS MEANS
MORE HAPPINESS FOR THE GREATER NUMBER
VOTE FOR THE FATTER POCKETBOOK

Hardly had this argument to the universal appetite been posted before the Feds retorted by posting a proclamation:

FACULTY PLOT

EVIDENCE IS PILING UP THAT THE PRESENT POLITI-
CAL CAMPAIGN IS A HUGE FACULTY CONSPIRACY TO
DEPRIVE THE SCHOOL OF ITS LIBERTIES BY UNDER-
GROUND DARK-LANTERN METHODS, WHERE IT DOES
NOT DARE TO ATTEMPT IT OPENLY

THE APRON STRINGS ARE IN POSSESSION OF A GI-
GANTIC CORRUPTION FUND   WHO IS PUTTING UP?

When this attack became public the Anti-Feds were in deep deliberation, planning a descent on the Hamill House. The news of the
outrageous charge was borne to the conference by Hungry Smeed,
with tears in his eyes.

"Crazy," said Doc, "we must meet the charge, now, at once."

There was a chorus of assent.

"We will," said Crazy, diving into his pocket and producing a
wad of paper. "This is what I've had up my sleeve from the beginning. This is the greatest state paper ever conceived."

"Let's have it," said Hickey, and Crazy proudly read:

THE FULL PROGRAM

The Campaign of Slander and Vilification Instituted by Tough
McCarty and His Myrmidons Will Not Deceive the Intelligent
and Independent Voter. Anti-Federalist Candidates Only Are
the Defendants of the Liberties of the School.

Anti-Fed Candidates Stand Solemnly Pledged to Work For Increased Privileges.

ACCESS TO THE JIGGER SHOP AT ALL TIMES
REMOVING THE LIMIT ON WEEKLY ALLOWANCES
ABOLITION OF THE HATEFUL COMPULSORY
BATH SYSTEM
BETTER FOOD   MORE FOOD
REGULATION OF SINKERS AND SCRAG-BIRDS
ESTABLISHMENT OF TWO SLEIGHING HOLIDAYS
CUSHIONED SEATS FOR CHAPEL

When this momentous declaration of principles was read there was an appalled silence, while Crazy, in the center of the admiring circle, grew perceptibly.

Then a shriek burst out and Crazy was smothered in the arms of the regenerated Anti-Feds.

"Crazy will be President of the United States," said Turkey admiringly.

"Wonderful!"

"The bathroom plank will win us fifty votes."

"And what about the jigger vote?"

At this moment an egg passed rapidly through the open window and spread itself on the wall, while across the campus the figure of Mucker Reilly of the Kennedy was seen zigzagging for safety, with his thumb vulgarly applied to his nose.

The Executive Committee gazed at the wall, watching the yellow desecration gradually trickling into a map of South America.

"This means the end of argument," said Cheyenne sadly. "The campaign from now on will be bitter."

"If the appeal to force is going to be made," said Crazy, applying a towel, "we shall endeavor—Doc, shut the window—we shall endeavor to meet it."

"We have now a chance," said Egghead, brightening, "to prove that we are not Goo-Goos."

"Egghead, you are both intelligent and comforting," said Hickey. "The first thing is to corner the egg market."

"The Finance Committee," said Crazy wrathfully, "is empowered to buy, beg or borrow every egg, every squashy apple, every mushy tomato that can be detected and run down. From now on we shall wage a vigorous campaign."

The publication of the Anti-Fed program roused the party cohorts to cheers and song. The panicky Feds strove desperately to turn the tide with the following warning:

HA! HA!

IT WON'T DO!

WE KNOW THE HAND!

Don't Be Deceived. Hickey is the Sheep in Wolf's Clothing. Stung to the Quick by Our Detection of the Criminal Alliance Between the Anti-Feds and the Faculty, Hickey, the King of the Goo-Goos, is Trying to Bleat Like a Wolf. It Won't Do! They Cannot Dodge the Issue. Stand Firm. Lawrenceville Must Not Be Made Into a Kindergarten.

But this could not stem the rising wave. The Hamill House turned its back on Federalism and threw in its lot with the foes of compulsory bath. Just before supper the Anti-Feds were roused to frenzy by the astounding news that the little Rouse House, isolated though it was from the rest of the school and under the very wing of the Davis, had declared Anti-Fed, for the love of combat that burned in its heroic band led by the redoubtable Charley De Soto and Scrapper Morrissey.

With the declaration of the different houses the first stage of the campaign ended. By supper every house was on a military footing and the dove of peace was hastening toward the horizon.

That night Mr. Baldwin waited in vain for the report of Hickey, waited and wondered. For the first time Baldwin, the enthusiast, began to be a little apprehensive of the forces he had unchained.

A little later Mr. Baranson chose to pay him a visit.

"Well, Baldwin, what news?" he said drily. "Thoroughly satisfied with your new course in political education?"

"Why, the boys seem to take to it with enthusiasm," said Baldwin rather dubiously. "I think they're thoroughly interested."

"Interested? Yes—quite so. By the way, Baldwin," Baranson stopped a moment and scanned his young subordinate with pitying knowledge, "I'm going to retire for the night. If I had a cyclone cellar I'd move to it. I put you in charge of the house. If any attempt is made to set it on fire or dynamite it, go out and argue gently with the boys, and above all, impress upon them that they are the hope of the country and must set a standard. Reason with them, Baldwin, and above all, appeal to their better natures. Good night."

Baldwin did not answer. He stood meditatively gazing out the window. From the Dickinson and the Kennedy magic lanterns were flashing campaign slogans on white sheets suspended at opposite houses. The uproar of catcalls and hoots that accompanied the exhibitions left small reason to hope that they were couched in that clear, reasoning style which would uplift future American politics.

As he looked, from the Upper House the indignant and now

thoroughly aroused fourth form started to parade with torchlights and transparencies. Presently the winding procession, clothed in superimposed night shirts, arrived with hideous clamor. Dangling from a pole were two grotesque figures stuffed with straw and decked with aprons; overhead was the inscription, "Kings of the Goo-Goos," and one was labeled Hickey and one was labeled Brother. Opposite his window they halted and chanted in soft unison:

> Hush, hush, tread softly,
> Hush, hush, make no noise,
> Baldwin is the King of the Goo-Goos,
> Let him sleep,
> Let him sleep.
> SHOUTED: LET HIM SLEEP!!!

Then the transparencies succeeded one another, bobbing over the rolling current of indignant seniors.

> BACK TO THE KINDERGARTEN!
> WE WANT NO BROTHERLY LOVE!
> GOODBYE, BALDWIN! GOODBYE!

Baldwin drew down the shade and stepped from the window. He heard a familiar step in the corridor, and quickly locked the door. Baranson knocked; then he knocked again; after which he moved away, chuckling.

When the fourth-form procession arrived on its tour around the circle the Dickinsonians were prepared to welcome it. Crazy Opdyke, head of the literary bureau, stood by the lantern directing the proclamations to be flashed on the sheet that hung from the opposite house.

Hickey and Macnooder posted the orators at strategic windows, supplying them with compressed arguments in the form of eggs and soft apples.

"All ready?" said Opdyke as Hickey returned, chuckling.

"Ready and willing," said Hickey.

"Here they come," said the Big Man.

"Is the Kennedy and the Woodhull with them?" asked Hickey.

"Sure, they're trailing on behind," said Turkey.

A yell of defiance burst from the head of the procession as it reached the headquarters of the enemy.

"Start the literature," said Crazy.

Egghead, at the lantern, slipped in the first slides, flashing them on the opposite sheet.

IT'S ALL OVER, BOYS
FEDERALISM IS IN THE SOUP
FEDERALISTS
THE UPPER HOUSE MYRMIDONS
THE DAVIS JAYHAWKERS
THE WOODHULL SORE HEADS
THE KENNEDY MUCKERS
ANTI-FEDERALISTS
THE ROUSE INVINCIBLES
THE CLEVE INDEPENDENTS
THE GRISWOLD INTELLECTUALS
THE GREEN MUGWUMPS
THE DICKINSON SCHOLARS
THE HAMILL MISSIONARIES
GOODBYE, FEDS! GOODBYE!

"Now for a few personal references," said Crazy, smiling happily at the howls that greeted his first effort. "Egghead, shove them right along."

Another series was put forth:

WHY, WOODHULL, DID WE STEAL
YOUR ICE CREAM?
IS TOUGH McCARTY'S GANG OF
BALLOT STUFFERS WITH YOU?
WE ARE NOT FOURTH-FORM PUPPY DOGS
HELLO, TOUGH, HOW DOES IT FEEL TO
BE A PUPPY DOG?

"What are they shouting now?" said Hickey, peering over at the turbulent chaos below.

"They are re-questing us to come out!" said the Egghead.

The night was filled with the shrieks of the helpless Feds.

"Come out!"

"We dare you to come out!"

"Come out, you Dickinson Goo-Goos."

"Why, they're really getting excited," said Hickey. "They're hopping right up and down."

"We will give them a declaration of principles," said Crazy. "Egghead, give them the principles; Hickey, notify the orators to prepare the compressed arguments. The word is 'BIFF.' "

Hickey went tumbling upstairs; the Egghead delivered the new series.

WHY, FEDS, DON'T GET PEEVISH
THIS IS AN ORDERLY CAMPAIGN
A QUIET, ORDERLY CAMPAIGN
REMEMBER, WE MUST UPLIFT THE
NATION

Outside, the chorus of hoots and catcalls gave way to a steady rhythmic chant:

GOO-GOOS, GOO-GOOS, GOO-GOOS!

"How unjust!" said Crazy, sadly. "We must clear ourselves; we must nail the lie—in a quiet, orderly way! Let her go, Egghead; Cheyenne, give Hickey the cue."

On the sheet suddenly flashed out:

WE ARE GOO-GOOS, ARE WE? BIFF!

At the same moment, from a dozen windows descended a terrific broadside of middle-aged eggs, assorted vegetables and squashy fruit.

The Federalist forces, utterly off their guard, dripping with egg and tomato, vanished like a heap of leaves before a whirlwind, while from the Anti-Federalist houses exultant shrieks of victory burst forth.

"If we are to be called Goo-Goos," said Crazy, proudly, "we have, at least, made Goo-Goo a term of honor."

"Tomorrow should be a very critical day in the campaign," said Macnooder, pensively.

"I suggest that on account of the uncertain state of the weather," said Hickey, wisely, "that all window blinds should be closed and locked."

"I think," said Cheyenne, "that we had better march to chapel in close formation."

"Are there any more arguments left?" said Crazy.

"Quite a number."

"They must be delivered tonight," said Crazy, firmly. "No egg shall be allowed to spoil—in this house."

At eleven o'clock that night, as the headmaster sat in his room in distant Boston, giving the last touches to the address which he had prepared for the following day on the "Experiment of Self-Government and Increased Individual Responsibility in Primary Education," the following telegram was handed to him:

> Come back instantly. School in state of anarchy. Rioting and pillaging unchecked. Another day may be too late. Baldwin's course in political education.
>
> BARANSON

When the Doctor, after a night's precipitous travel, drove onto the campus he had left picturesque and peaceful but a few days before, he could hardly believe his eyes. The circle of houses was stained and spotted with the marks of hundreds of eggs and the softer vegetables. From almost every upper window a banner (often ripped to shreds) or a mutilated proclamation was displayed. Proclamations blossomed on every tree, couched in vitriolic language. Two large groups of embattled boys, bearing strange banners, were converging across the campus with haggard, hysterical faces, fists clenched and muscles strung in nervous tension, waiting the shock of the approaching clash.

The Doctor sprang from the buggy and advanced toward chapel with determined, angry strides. At the sight of the familiar figure a swift change went over the two armies, on the point of flying at each other's throats. The most bloodthirsty suddenly quailed, the most martial scowls gave place to looks of innocence. In the twinkling of an eye every banner had disappeared, and the two armies, breaking formation, went meekly and fearfully into chapel.

The Doctor from his rostrum looked down upon the school. Under his fierce examination every glance fell to the hymn-book.

"Young gentlemen of the Lawrenceville School, I will say just one word," began the headmaster. "This political campaign will

STOP, NOW, *AT ONCE!*" He paused at the spectacle of row on row of blooming eyes and gory features, and, despite himself, his lips twitched.

In an instant the first ranks began to titter, then a roar of laughter went up from the pent-up, hysterical boys. They laughed until they sobbed, for the first time aware of the ridiculousness of the situation. Then as the Doctor, wisely refraining from further discourse, dismissed them, they swayed out on the campus where the Davis fell into the arms of the Dickinson, and Fed and Anti-Fed rolled with laughter on the ground.

When Hickey, that afternoon, brazenly sought out Mr. Baldwin, a certain staccato note in the greeting caused a dozen careful phrases to die on his tongue.

"Don't hesitate, Hicks," said Baldwin, smiling coldly.

"I came, sir," said Hicks, looking down, "I came—that is, I—Mr. Baldwin, sir, I'm sorry it turned out such a failure."

"Of course, Hicks," said Baldwin, softly, "of course. It must be a great disappointment—to you. But it is not a failure, Hicks. On the contrary, it has been a great success—this campaign of education. I have learned greatly. By the way, Hicks, kindly announce to the class that I shall change my method of hearing recitations. I have a new system—based on the latest discoveries in the laws of probability. Announce also an examination for tomorrow."

"Tomorrow?" said Hickey, astounded.

"On the review—in the interest of education—my education. Don't look down, Hicks—I cherish no resentment against you—none at all."

"Against me?" said Hickey, aggrieved.

"My feelings are of gratitude and affection only. You have been the teacher and I the scholar—but—" He paused and surveyed the persecuted Hicks with the smile of the anaconda for the canary, "but, Hicks, my boy, whatever else may be the *indifference* of the masters toward your education, when you leave Lawrenceville you will not be weak in—mathematics."

THE MARTYRDOM OF WILLIAM HICKS

HICKEY HAD now reached the height of his fame. Intoxicated by success, he forgot all prudence, or rather his revolt became an appetite that demanded constant feeding. He no longer concealed his past exploits; he even went so far as to announce the escapades he planned.

"You are running your head into the noose, Hickey, my boy," said Macnooder, sadly; "every master in the school has got his eye on you."

"I know it," said Hickey proudly, "but they've got to catch me."

"Your position is different," objected Macnooder, "now you are suspected. And do you want me to tell you the truth? Your trick about the clappers was too clever. If you could imagine that, you were at the bottom of other things. That's what the Doctor will say to himself when he thinks it over."

"The Doctor plays square," retorted Hickey; "he won't do anything on suspicion. Let him try and catch me, let them all try. If they get me fair and square, I'll take my punishment. I say, Doc, just you wait. I've got something up my sleeve that'll make them all sit up."

"Good Lord!" said the Egghead, who was of the party. "You don't mean you're going on?"

"Egghead," said Hickey, impressively, "I've made up my mind that I just can't live without doing one thing more!"

"Heavens, Hickey! What now?"

"I've got a craving, Egghead, to sleep in Tabby's bed."

"No!"

"Fact."

"What do you mean?"

"Just that. I intend to sleep, not just pop in and out, to *sleep* two hours in Tabby's nice white little bed."

"Gee whiz, Hickey! When?"

"Some night that's coming pretty soon."

"When Tabby's away——"

"No, sir, when Tabby's here—after Tabby himself has been in it. After that I'm going to get back at Big Brother."

"You're crazy!"

"I'm backing my feelings."

"You'll bet on it?"

"As much as you want."

The scornful Egghead, thus provoked, offered ten to one against him. Hickey accepted at once.

During the day the news spread and the bets came flying in. As to his plans, Hickey preserved a cloaked mystery, promising only that the feat should take place within the fortnight.

Each night toward midnight, he slipped out of Sawtelle's window (Sawtelle being sworn to deadly secrecy). He remained out an hour, sometimes two, and came back sleepy and chuckling. About this time the report began to spread that burglars were in the vicinity.

The Gutter Pup, who roomed on the first floor of the Woodhull, took a solemn oath that having been waked up by a strange scratching noise at his window, he had seen four masked figures with bull's-eye lanterns scurrying away. The next report came from

Davis with added picturesqueness. The school became wrought up to an extraordinary pitch of excitement in which even the masters joined after a period of incredulity.

When the proper stage of frenzy arrived, Hickey took into his confidence a dozen allies.

At exactly two o'clock on a moonless night, Beauty Sawtelle, waiting, watch in hand, gave a horrid shriek and sent a baseball bat crashing through his window, where he afterward swore four masked faces had glared in on him. At the same time the Egghead raised his window and emptied a revolver into the air, shouting, "Thieves, thieves, there they go!"

Immediately every waiting boy sprang out of bed armed with revolvers, shotguns, brickbats, Japanese swords and what not, and rushed downstairs, shouting, "Stop thief!"

Mr. Tapping, startled from his slumbers by the uproar, seized a bird gun and, guided by Hungry Smeed and the Red Dog, rushed out of doors and valorously took the lead of the searching party. By this time the racket had spread about the campus and boys in flimsy garments, ludicrously armed, came pouring out of the other houses and joined the wild hunt for the masked marauders. Suddenly, from the direction of Foundation House, a series of shots exploded amid yells of excitement. At once the mass that had been churning in the middle of the campus set off with a rush. The cry went up that the burglars had been discovered and were fleeing down the road to Trenton. Five minutes later the campus was silent, as boys and masters swept along the highway, their cries growing fainter in the distance.

Meanwhile, Hickey had not lost a second. Hardly had Mr. Tapping's pink pajamas rushed from the Dickinson when Hickey, entering the study, locked the door and set to work. In a jiffy he had the mattress and bedclothes out the window, down into the waiting hands of Macnooder and the Eggnead, who piled them on a ready wheelbarrow. In less than five minutes the iron bedstead, separated into its four component parts, followed. The whole, packed on the wheelbarrow, was hastily rushed into the darkness by the rollicking three. According to the plan, Hickey directed them past Memorial and into the baseball cage, where, by the light of the indispensable dark-lantern, they put the bed together, placed on it the bedding, and saw Hickey crawl blissfully under cover.

When Mr. Tapping returned after an hour's fruitless pursuit down the dutsy road, it had begun to dawn upon him, in common with other athletic members of the faculty, that he had been hoaxed. Mr. Tapping was very sensitive to his dignity, and dignity was exceedingly difficult in pajamas, in the chill of a night with a ridiculous bird gun over his shoulder and an assorted lot of semi-bare savages chuckling about him. Tired, covered with dust, and sheepish, he returned to the Dickinson, gave orders for everyone to return to his room and wearily toiled up to seek his comfortable bed.

The vacancy that greeted his eyes left him absolutely incredulous, then beside himself with rage. If in that moment he could have laid his hands on Hickey, he would have done him bodily injury. That Hickey was the perpetrator of this new outrage, as of the previous ones, he never for a moment doubted. His instinct needed no proofs, and in such enmities the instinct is strong. He went directly to Hickey's room, finding it, as he had expected, empty. He sat there half an hour, an hour, fruitlessly. Then he made the rounds of the house and returned to the room, seated himself, folded his arms violently, set his teeth and prepared to wait. He heard four o'clock strike, then five, and he began to nod. He rose, shook himself, returned to his seat and presently fell asleep, and in this condition Hickey, returning, found him.

The bell rang six, and Mr. Tapping, starting up guiltily, glanced hastily at the bed and assured himself thankfully that it was empty. Moreover, conclusive evidence, the counterpane had not been turned down, so Hickey had not gone to bed at all.

By prodigies of will power he remained awake, consoled by the fact that he held at last the evidence needed to debarrass himself of his tormentor. At seven o'clock the gym bell rang the rising hour. Mr. Tapping rose triumphant. Suddenly he stopped and looked down in horror. Something had moved under the bed. The next moment Hickey's face appeared under the skirts of the trailing bedspread—Hickey's face, a mirror of sleepy amazement, as he innocently asked, "Why, Mr. Tapping, what *is* the matter?"

"Hicks!" exclaimed Mr. Tapping, too astounded to gather his thoughts. "Is that you, Hicks?"

167

"Yes, sir."

"What are you doing under there?"

"Please sir," said Hickey, "I'm troubled with insomnia and sometimes this is the only way I can sleep."

At two o'clock Hickey was a second time summoned to Foundation House. He went in perfect faith. Nothing had miscarried, there was not the slightest evidence against him. If he was questioned he would refuse to answer—that was all. It had been a morning of exquisite triumph for him. Tabby's bed had not been discovered until ten o'clock, and the transferral to the Dickinson, made in full daylight, had been witnessed by the assembled school. He went across the campus, light of feet and proud of heart, aware of the scores of discreetly admiring eyes that followed him, hearing pleasantly the murmurs which buzzed after him:

"Oh, you prodigious Hickey—oh, you daredevil!"

Of course, the Doctor would be in a towering rage. Hickey was not unreasonable, he understood and expected a natural exhibition of vexation. What could the Doctor do, after all? Ask him questions which he would refuse to answer—that was all, but that was not evidence.

He found the Doctor alone, quietly writing at his desk, and received a smile and an invitation to be seated. Somehow the tranquillity of the headmaster's attitude did not reassure Hickey. He would have preferred a little more agitation, but this satisfied calm was disquieting.

He stood with his hands behind his back, twirling his cap, studying the photographs of Grecian architecture on the walls, finding it awfully still and wishing the Doctor would begin.

Presently the Doctor turned, put down his spectacles, shoved back from the desk and glanced at Hickey with a smile, saying, "Well, Hicks, we're going to let you go."

"Beg your pardon, sir," said Hickey, smiling frankly back, "you said—"

"We're going to let you take a vacation."

"Me?"

"You."

Hickey stood a long moment, open-mouthed, staring.

"Do you mean to say," he said, at last, with an effort, "that I am expelled?"

"Not expelled," said the Doctor, suavely, "we don't like that word; we're going to let you go, that's all."

"For what reason?" said Hickey, defiantly.

"For no reason at all," answered the Doctor, smoothly. "There is no reason, there can be no reason, Hicks. We're just naturally going to make up our minds to part with you. You see, Hicks," he continued, tilting back and gazing reminiscently at the ceiling, "we've had a rather agitated session here, rather extraordinary. The trouble seems to have broken out in the Dickinson about the time of the little surprise party at which Mr. Tapping did not assist! Then a few days later our chapel service was disturbed and our janitor put to considerable trouble; next the school routine was thrown into confusion by the removal of the clapper. We passed a very disagreeable period—much confusion, very little study, and the nerves of the faculty were thrown into such a state that even you, Hicks, were suspected. Then there was the political campaign, a subject too painful to analyze. Last night we lost a great deal of sleep—and sleep is most necessary to the growing boy. All these events have followed with great regularity, and while they have not lacked in picturesqueness, we have, we fear, been forgetting the main object of our life here—to study a little."

"Doctor, I—" broke in Hickey.

"No, Hicks, you misunderstand me," said the Doctor, reproachfully. "All this is true, but that is *not* why we are going to let you go. We are going to let you go, Hicks, for a much more conscientious reason; we're parting with you, Hicks, because we feel we no longer have anything to teach you."

"Doctor, I'd like to know," began Hickey, with a great lump in his throat. Then he stopped and looked at the floor. He knew his hour had sounded.

"Hicks, we part in sorrow," said the Doctor, "but we have the greatest faith in your career. We expect in a few years to claim you as one of our foremost alumni. Perhaps some day you will give us a library which we will name after you. No, don't be disheartened. We have the greatest admiration for your talents, admiration and respect. Anyone who can persuade two hundred and fifty keen-eyed Lawrenceville boys to pay one dollar apiece for silver gilt scrap-iron souvenirs worth eleven cents apiece because they may or may not be genuine bits of a stolen clapper—anyone who can do that is needed in the commercial development of our country."

"Doctor, do you—do you call this justice?" said Hickey, with tears in his voice.

"No," said the Doctor, frankly, "I call it a display of force. You see, Hicks, you've beaten us at every point, and so all we can do is to let you go."

"I'll hire a lawyer," said Hicks, brokenly.

"I thought you would," said the Doctor, "only I hope you will be easy on us, Hicks, for we haven't much money for damage suits."

"Then I'm to be fired," said Hickey, forcing back the tears, "fired just for nothing!"

"Just for nothing, Hicks," assented the Doctor, rising to close the painful interview, "and, Hicks, as one last favor, we would like to request that it be by the evening train. We have lost a great deal of sleep lately."

"Just for nothing," repeated Hickey, hoarsely.

"Just for nothing," replied the Doctor, as he closed the door.

At six o'clock, in the midst of indignant hundreds, Hickey climbed to the top of the stage, where his trunks had already been deposited. Nothing could comfort him, neither the roaring cheers that echoed again and again to his name, nor the hundreds of silent handshakes or muttered vows to continue the good fight. His spirit was broken. All was dark before him. Neither right nor justice existed in the world.

Egghead and Macnooder, visibly affected, reached up for the last handshakes.

"Keep a stiff upper lip, old man," said the Egghead.

"Don't you worry, Hickey, old boy," said Macnooder; "we'll attend to Tabby."

Then Hickey, bitterly, from the caverns of his heart, spoke, raising his fist toward Tabby's study window.

"He hadn't any proof," he said, brokenly, "no proof—damn him!"

The Varmint

ILLUSTRATED BY
F. R. GRUGER

TO

Alexander Lambert, M.D.
IN FRIENDSHIP, IN GRATITUDE,
AND IN MEMORY OF MY WIFE

I

WHEN YOUNG STOVER disembarked at the Trenton station on the fourth day after the opening of the spring term, he had acquired in his brief journey so much of the Pennsylvania rolling stock as could be detached and concealed. Inserted between his nether and outer shirts were two gilt "Directions to Travelers" which clung like mustard plasters to his back, while a jagged tin sign, wrenched from the home terminal, embraced his stomach with the painful tenacity of the historic Spartan fox. In his pockets were objects— small objects but precious and dangerous to unscrew and acquire.

Being forced to wait, he sat now, preternaturally stiff, perched on a heap of trunks, clutching a broken dress-suit case which had been reinforced with particolored strings.

There was about young Stover, when properly washed, a certain air of cherubim that instantly struck the observer; his tousled tow hair had a cathedral tone, his cheek was guileless, and his big blue eyes had an upward cast toward the angels which, as in the present moment when he was industriously transferring a check labeled Baltimore to a trunk bound for Jersey City, was absolutely convincing. But from the limit whence the cherub continueth not, the imp began. His collar was crumpled and smutty with the descent of many signs, a salmon-pink necktie had quarreled with a lavender shirt and retreated toward one ear, one cuff had broken loose and one sulked up the sleeve. His green serge pockets bulged in every direction, while the striped blue-and-white trousers, already outgrown, stuck to the knees and halted short of a pair of white socks that in turn disappeared into a pair of razor-pointed patent-leathers.

Young Stover's career at Miss Wandell's Select Academy for boys and girls had been a tremendous success, for it had ended in a frank confession on Miss Wandell's part that her limited curriculum was inadequate for the abnormal activities of dangerous criminals.

As Stover completed the transfer of the last trunk checks the stage for Lawrenceville plodded cumbrously up, and from the box Jimmy hailed him.

"Eh, there, young Sporting Life, bound for Lawrenceville? Step lively."

Stover swung up, gingerly pushing ahead of him the battered bag.

"Lawrenceville?" said the driver, looking at it suspiciously.

"Right the first time."

"What house?"

"Oh, the Green will be good enough for me."

"Well, tuck in above."

"Thanks, I'll cuddle here," said Stover, slipping into the seat next to him, "just to look over the way you handle the ribbons and see if I approve."

Jimmy, connoisseur of new arrivals, glanced behind at the only other passenger, a man of consular mold, and then looked at Stover in sardonic amusement.

"Don't look at me like that, old Sport," said Stover impressively; "I've driven real coaches, sixteen horses, rip-snorters, and all that sort of thing."

Jimmy, having guided the placid animals through the labyrinths of Trenton, gave them the rein on the long highway that leads to Lawrenceville and turned to examine Stover with new relish.

"Say, Bub," he said at length, "you're goin' to have a great time at this little backwoods school—you're going to enjoy yourself."

"Think I'm fresh, eh?"

"Fresh?" said Jimmy thoughtfully. "Why, fresh ain't at all the word."

"Well, I can take care of myself."

"What did they fire you for?" said Jimmy, touching up the horses.

"Who said they fired me?" said Stover, surprised.

"Well, what was it?" said Jimmy, disdaining an explanation.

"They fired me," said Stover, hesitating a moment—"they fired me for trying to kill a man."

"You don't say so!"

"I drew a knife on him," said Stover rapidly. "I'd 'a' done for him, too, the coward, if they hadn't hauled me off."

At this there was a chuckle from the passenger behind, who said with great solemnity, "Dear me, dear me, a dreadful state of affairs —quite thrilling."

"I saw red, everything—everything red," said Stover, breathing hard.

"What had he done to you?" said Jimmy, winking at Mr. Hopkins, alias Lucius Cassius, alias The Roman, master of the Latin line and distinguished flunker of boys.

"He insulted my—my mother."

"Your mother?"

"She—she's dead," said Stover in a stage voice he remembered.

At this Jimmy and Mr. Hopkins stopped, genuinely perplexed, and looked hard at Stover.

"You don't mean it! Dear me," said The Roman, hesitating before a possible blunder.

"It was long ago," said Stover, thrilling with the delight of authorship. "She died in a shipwreck to save me."

The Roman was nonplused. There was always the possibility that the story might be true.

"Ah, she gave her life to save yours, eh?" he said encouragingly.

"Held my head above water, breeches buoy and all that sort of thing," said Stover, remembering something in Dickens. "I was the only one saved, me and the ship's cat."

"Well, well," said The Roman, with a return of confidence; "and your father—is he alive?"

"Yes," said Stover, considering the distant woods; "but—but we don't speak of him."

"Ah, pardon me," said The Roman, gazing on him with wonder. "Painful memories—of course, of course. And what happened to your brother?"

Stover, perceiving the note of skepticism, turned and looked The Roman haughtily in the face, then, turning to Jimmy, he said in a half-whisper, "Who's the old buck, anyhow?"

Jimmy stiffened on the box as though he had received an electric shock; then, biting his lips, he answered with a vicious lunge at the horses, "Oh, he comes back and forth every now and then."

They were now in the open country, rolling steadily past fields of sprouting things, with the warm scent of new-plowed earth borne to them on the gentle April breeze.

All of a sudden Stover seemed to dive sideways from the coach and remained suspended by his razor-tipped patent-leathers.

"Hi, there!" cried Jimmy, bringing the coach to a stop with a jerk. "What are you trying to do?"

Stover reappeared.

"Seeing if there are any females inside."

"What's that to you?" said Jimmy indignantly.

"Keep your eye peeled and I'll show you," said the urchin, standing up, freeing his belt and unbuttoning his vest. In a moment, by a series of contortions, he drew forth the three signs and proudly displayed them.

"See these gilt ones," he said confidentially to the astounded Roman. "Got 'em in the open car; stood right up and unscrewed them—penal offense, my boy. The tin one was easier, but it's a beaut. 'No loitering on these premises.' Cast your eye over that," he added, passing it to The Roman, who, as he gravely received it, gave Jimmy a dig that cut short a fit of coughing.

"Pretty fine, eh?" said Stover.

"Em, yes, quite extraordinary—quite so."

"And what do you think of these?" continued Stover, producing two silver nickel-plated knobs ravished from the washbasin. " 'Pull and Push'—that's my motto. Say, Bill, how does that strike you?"

The Roman examined them and handed them back.

"You'll find it rather—rather slow at the school, won't you?"

"Oh, I'll put ginger into it."

"Indeed."

"What's your line of goods, old Sport?" said Stover, examining Mr. Hopkins with a knowing eye.

"Books," said The Roman with a slight jerk of his thin lips.

"I see!"

Jimmy stopped the horses and went behind, ostensibly to see if the door was swinging.

"Let me drive?" said Stover, fidgeting after a moment's contemplation of Jimmy's method. "I'll show you a thing or two."

"Oh, you will, will you?"

"Let's have 'em."

Jimmy looked inquiringly at Mr. Hopkins and, receiving a nod, transferred the reins and whip to Stover, who immediately assumed a Wild West attitude and said patronizingly, "Say, you don't get the speed out of 'em."

"I don't, eh?"

"Naw."

They were at that moment reaching the brink of a hill, with a sharp though short descent below.

"In my country," said Stover professionally, "we call a man who uses a brake a candy dude. The trick is to gallop 'em down the hills. Hang on!"

Before he could be stopped he sprang up with an ear-splitting war whoop, and brought the whip down with a stinging blow over the ears of the indignant horses, who plunged forward with a frightened leap. The coach rose and rocked, narrowly missing over-turning in its sudden headlong course. Jimmy clamped on the brakes, snatched the reins, and brought the plunging team to a stop after narrowly missing the gutter. Stover, saved from a headlong journey only by the iron grip of The Roman, had a moment of horrible fear. But immediately recovering his self-possession he said gruffly, "All right, let go of me."

"What in blazes were you trying to do, you young anarchist?" cried Jimmy, turning on him wrathfully.

"Gee! Why don't you drive a couple of cows?" said Stover in disgust. "Why, in my parts we always drive on two wheels."

"Two wheels!" said Jimmy scornfully. "Guess you never drove anything that did have four wheels but a baby buggy."

But Stover, as though discouraged, disdained to reply, and sat in moody silence.

The Roman, who was still interested in a possible brother or two, strove in vain to draw him out. Stover wrapped himself in a majestic silence. Despite himself, the mystery of the discoverer was upon him. His glance fastened itself on the swelling horizon for the school that suddenly was to appear.

"How many fellows have you got here?" he said all at once to Jimmy.

"About four hundred."

"As much as that?"

"Sure."

"Big fellows?"

"Sizable."

"How big?"

"Two-hundred-pounders."

"When do we see the school?"

"Top of next hill."

The Roman watched him from the corner of his eye, interested in his sudden shift of mood.

"What kind of a football team did they have?" said Stover.

"Scored on the Princeton Varsity."

"Jemima! You don't say so!"

"Eight to four."

"Great Heavens!"

"Only game they lost."

"The Princeton championship team, too," said Stover, who was not deficient in historical athletics. "Say, how's the nine shaping up?"

"It's a winner."

All at once Jimmy extended his whip. "There it is, over there—you'll get the water tower first."

Stover stood up reverentially. Across the dip and swell of the hills a cluster of slated roofs, a glimpse of red brick through the trees, a touch of brownstone, a water tower in sharp outline against the sky, suddenly rose from the horizon. A continent had been discovered, the land of possible dreams.

"It's ripping—ripping, isn't it?" he said, still standing eagerly.

The Roman, gazing on it for the thousandth time, shook his head in musing agreement.

Across the fields came the stolid ringing of the school bell, ringing a hundred laggards across the budding campus to hard seats and blackboarded walls, ringing with its lengthened, slow-dying, never varying note.

"That the bell?" said Stover, rebelling already at its summons.

"That's it," said Jimmy.

Stover sat down, his chin in his hands, his elbows on his knees, gazing eagerly forward, asking questions.

"I say, where's the Green House?"

"Ahead on your left—directly."

"That old, stone, blockhouse affair?"

"You win."

"Why, it's not on the campus."

"No, it ain't," said Jimmy, flicking the flies off the near horse; "but they've got a warm bunch of Indians all the same." Then, remembering the Wild Western methods of driving, he added, "Don't forget about the ginger. Sock it to them. Fare, please."

"I'll sock it," said Stover with a knowing air. "I may be tender, but I'm not green."

He slapped a coin into the outstretched hand and reached back for the battle-scarred valise, to perceive the keen eye of Mr. Hopkins set on him with amusement.

"Well, Sport, ta-ta, and good luck," said Stover, who had mentally ticketed him as a commercial traveler. "Hope you sell out."

"Thanks," said Mr. Hopkins, with a twitch to his lip. "Now just one word to the wise."

"What's that?"

"Don't get discouraged."

"Discouraged!" said Stover disdainfully. "Why, old Cocky-wax, put this in your pipe and smoke it—I'm going to own this house. In a week I'll have 'em feeding from my hand."

He sprang down eagerly. Before him, at the end of a flagged walk, under the heavy boughs of evergreens, was a two-story building of stone, and under the Colonial portico a group curiously watching the new arrival.

The coach groaned and pulled heavily away. He was alone at the end of the interminable stone walk, clutching a broken-down bag ridiculously mended with strings, face to face with the task of approaching with dignity and ease these suddenly discovered critics of his existence.

II

IN ALL his fifteen years Stover had never been accused of standing in awe of anything or anybody; but at the present moment, as he balanced from foot to foot, calculating the unending distance of the stone flags, he was suddenly seized with an overpowering impulse to bolt. And yet the group at the steps were only mildly interested. An urchin pillowed on the knees of a Goliath had shifted so as languidly to command the approach; a baseball, traveling back and forth in lazy flight, had stopped only a moment, and then continued from hand to hand.

Stover had thought of his future associates without much trepidation, as he had thought of the faculty as Miss Wandell in trousers —being inferior to him in mental agility and resourcefulness who, he confidently intended, should shortly follow his desires.

All at once, before he had spoken a word, before he had even seen the look on their countenances, he realized that he stood on the threshold of a new world, a system of society of which he was ignorant and by whose undivined laws he was suddenly to be judged.

Everything was wrong and strangely uncomfortable. His derby hat was too small—as it was—and must look ridiculous; his trousers were short, and his arms seemed to rush from his sleeves. He tried desperately to thrust back the cuff that had broken loose and stooped for his bag. It would have been wiser to have embraced it bodily, but he breathed a prayer and grasped the handle. Then he started up the walk; halfway, the handle tore out and the bag went down with a crash.

He dived at it desperately, poking back the threatened avalanche of linen, and, clutching it in his arms as a bachelor carries a baby, started blindly for the house.

A roar of laughter had gone up at his discomfiture, succeeded by a sudden, solemn silence. Then the White Mountain Canary pillowed against the knees of Cheyenne Baxter, spoke:

"No old clothes, no old clothes; nothing to sell today."

At this Butsey White's lathery face suddenly appeared at the second-story window.

"He doesn't want to buy—he wants to sell us something," he said. "Patent underwear and all that sort of thing."

Stover, red to the ears, advanced to the steps and stopped.

"Well?" said the Coffee-colored Angel as the guardian of the steps.

"I'm the new boy," said Stover in a gentle voice.

"The what?"

"The new boy."

"Impossible!"

"He's not!"

"New boys always say 'sir' and take off their hats politely."

The White Mountain Canary looked at Tough McCarty, who solemnly interrogated the Coffee-colored Angel, who shook his head in utter disbelief and said, "I don't believe it. It's a blind. I wouldn't let him in the house."

"Please, sir," said Stover hastily, doffing his derby, "I am."

"Prove it," said a voice behind him.

"Say, I'm not as green as all that."

Stover smiled a sickly smile, shifted from foot to foot and glanced hopefully at his fellow imps to surprise a look of amusement. But as every face remained blank, serious and extremely critical, the smile disappeared in a twinkling and his glance went abruptly to his toes.

"He certainly should prove it," said the Coffee-colored Angel anxiously. "Can you prove it?"

Stover gingerly placed the gaping valise on the top step and fumbled in his pockets.

"Please, sir, I have a letter from—from the Doctor," he blurted out, finally extracting a crumpled envelope and tendering it to the Coffee-colored Angel, who looked it over with well-simulated surprise and solemnly announced, "My goodness gracious! Why, it *is* the new boy!"

Instantly there was a change.

"Freshman, what's your name?" said little Susie Satterly in his deepest tones.

"Stover."

"Sir."

"Sir."

"What's your full name?"

"John Humperdink Stover, sir."

"Humper—what?"

"Dink."

"Say it again."

"Humperdink."

"Say it for me," said the Coffee-colored Angel, with his hand to his ear.

"Humperdink."

"Accent the last syllable."

"Humper—*Dink!*"

"Are you trying to bluff us, Freshman?" said Cheyenne Baxter severely.

"No, sir; that's my real name."

"Humperdink?"

"Yes, sir."

"Well, Rinky Dink, you've got a rotten name."

"Yes, sir," said Stover, who never before had felt such a longing to agree.

"How old?"

"Fifteen, sir."

"Weight?"

"One hundred and thirty, sir."

"Ever been in love?"

"No, sir."

"Ever served a penal sentence?"

"No, sir."

"Then where did you get these clothes?"

The group slowly circulated about the embarrassed Stover, scanning the amazing costume. Cheyenne Baxter took up the inquisition.

"Say, Dink, honest, are these your *own* clothes?" he said with a knowing look.

"Yes, sir."

"Now, honest," continued Cheyenne in a whisper, bending forward and putting his hand to his ear as though inviting a confidence.

Stover felt suddenly as though his own ears were swelling to alarming proportions—swelling and perceptibly reddening.

"What do they feed you on, Rinky Dink?" said the White Mountain Canary softly.

"Feed?" said Stover unwarily, not perceiving the intent of the question.

"Do they give you many green vegetables?"

Stover tried to laugh appreciatively, but the sound fizzled dolefully out.

"Because, Dink," said the White Mountain Canary earnestly, "you must not eat green vegetables, really you must not. You're green enough already."

"Why did they fire you?" said Tough McCarty.

Stover raised his eyes instinctively. There was a new accent to the inquisition, different from all the other questions he had run. He looked at Tough McCarty's stocky frame and battling eyes, and suddenly knew that he was face to face with a human being between whom and himself there could never be a question of compromise or quarter.

"Well, Freshman," said McCarty impatiently.

"What did you ask me?" said Dink purposely.

"Sir."

"Sir."

"What did they fire you for?"

"They fired me," began Stover slowly, and then stopped to reconsider. The story he had told on the coach, somehow, did not seem quite in place here. The role of firebrand and hothead, drawing villainous knives on frightened boys, would not quite convince his present audience. To tell the truth was impossible—to admit himself the product of Miss Wandell's and coeducation would be fatal—and likewise the truth was, in his philosophy (and be this remembered), only a lazy expedient to a man of imagination. So he said slowly, "They fired me for bringing in a couple of rattlesnakes and—and assaulting a teacher."

"My! You are a bad man, aren't you?" said Tough McCarty seriously. "I'm afraid you're too dangerous for the Green, Dink. Really I do."

"He does look devilishly wicked, Tough."

"Assaulting a teacher—how broo-tal."

"Why, Rinky Dink," said the Coffee-colored Angel sadly, "don't you know that was very wicked of you? You should love your teachers."

Stover suddenly perceived that his audience was unsympathetic.

"Don't you know you should love your teachers?"

Stover essayed a grin, then looked at the ground and stirred up a stone with his foot.

"So you're fond of rattlesnakes?" said McCarty, persisting.

"Ye-es, sir."

"Very fond?"

"I was brought up with them," said Stover, trying to fortify his position.

"You don't mean it," said McCarty, looking hard at Baxter. "Cheyenne, he's just the man to train up that little pet rattler of yours."

"Just the thing," said Cheyenne instantly; "we'll let him take out the fangs."

Stover smiled a superior smile; he was not to be caught on such tales.

"What are you smiling at, Freshman?" said McCarty immediately.

"Nothing, sir."

Butsey White, at the second-story window, scanning the road, perceived Mr. Jenkins approaching, and announced the fact, adding, "Send him up; he belongs to me."

"Make a nice bow, Freshman," said McCarty. "Take your hat off, keep your heels together. Oh, that wasn't a very nice bow. Try again."

At this moment Jimmy, returning on the stage, reined in with a sudden interest. Stover hastily executed a series of grotesque inclinations and, grasping the clumsy valise, disappeared behind the door, hearing, as he struggled up the stairs, the roar from without that greeted his departure.

"The freshest of the fresh."

"Green all over."

"Will we tame him?"

"Oh, no!"

"And Butsey's got him."

"Humper—*Dink!*"

"Wow!"

As Stover reached the head of the stairs a door was thrown open and Butsey White appeared in undress uniform. The next moment Stover found himself in a large double room gorgeously decorated with flags, pennants, sporting prints and souvenirs, while through the open window came a grateful feeling of quiet and repose.

Butsey White, a roly-poly comical fellow of sixteen or seventeen, with a shaving brush in one hand, held out the other with an expression of lathery solicitude.

"Well, Stover, how are you? How did you leave mother and the chickens? My name's White. Mr. White, please. I'm most particular."

"How do you do, Mr. White?" said Stover, recovering some of his composure.

"There's your kennel," said Butsey White, indicating the bed. "The washtrough's over here. Bath's down the corridor. Do you snore?"

"What?" said Stover, taken back.

"Oh, never mind. If you do I'll cure you," said White encouragingly. "What did they fire you for?"

Stover, smarting at his humiliation below, seized the opportunity for revenge.

"They fired me for drinking the alcohol out of the lamps," he said with his most convincing smile.

Butsey White, who had returned to the painful task of shaving, suddenly straightened up and extended the deadly razor in angry rebuke.

"There's a little too much persiflage around here," he said sternly. "We don't like it. We prefer to see young, unripe freshmen come in on their tiptoes and answer when they're spoken to. Young Stover, you've got in wrong. You're just about the freshest cargo we've ever had. You've got a lot to learn, and I'm going to start right in educating you. *Savez?*"

"It was only a joke," said Stover, looking down.

"A joke! I'll attend to any joking around here," said Butsey, with a reckless wave of his razor. "There may be a few patent nickel-plated jokes roaming around here, soon, you hadn't thought of. Now, what did they fire you for?"

"They fired me for kissing a teacher."

"A teacher?"

"The drawing teacher," said Stover hastily, perceiving the danger of the new assertion.

The old boy looked at him hard, gave a sort of grunt and, turning his back, took up again the interrupted task of shaving. Stover, a little dismayed at his own audacity, sought to conciliate his future roommate.

"Mister White, I say, where'll I stow my duds?"

No answer.

"I'm sorry—I didn't mean to be fresh. Which is my bureau?"

The razor, suddenly extended, pointed between the windows. Stover, crestfallen, hastily sorted out the contents of his bag and silently ranged collars and neckties, waiting hopefully for a word. Suddenly he remembered the properties of the Pennsylvania Railroad and, sorting out the signs, he advanced on Butsey White, saying, "I brought these along—thought they might help decorate the room, Mr. White."

Butsey White gazed at the three stolen signs and grunted a somewhat mollified approval.

"Got anything else?"

"A couple of sporting prints coming in the trunk, sir."

"You want to get everything you can lay your hands on when you go home. Now run on down and report to Fuzzy-Wuzzy—Mr. Jenkins. He'll be waiting for you. After lunch I'll take you up to the village and fit you out."

"I say, that's awfully good of you."

"Oh, that's all right."

"Say, I didn't mean to be fresh."

"Well, you were."

White, having carefully noted the ravages of the razor, turned from the looking glass and surveyed the penitent Stover.

"Well, what *did* they fire you for?" he said point-blank.

"They fired me—," began Stover slowly, and stopped.

"Out with it," said Butsey militantly.

But at that moment the voice of Mr. Jenkins summoned Stover below and left the great question unanswered.

III

THE INTERVIEW with the housemaster was not trying. Mr. Jenkins was a short, fuzzy little man, who looked him over with nervous concern, calculating what new strain on his temper had arrived, introduced him to Mrs. Jenkins, and seized the occasion of the luncheon bell to cut short the conversation.

At lunch Stover committed an unpardonable error which only those who have suffered can understand—he sent his plate up for a second helping of prunes.

"What in the name of peanuts did you do that for?" said Butsey in a whisper, while the Coffee-colored Angel jabbed him with his elbow and trod on his toes. "Now you *have* put your foot in it!"

Stover looked up to behold every countenance grim and outraged.

"What's wrong?" he said in a whisper.

"Wrong? Didn't you ever have prunes and skimmed milk before, thousands and thousands of times?"

"Yes, but—"

"You don't like 'em, do you?"

"Why, I don't know."

"Do you want to have them five times a week—in springtime?"

The plate, bountifully helped, returned from hand to hand down the table, laden with prunes and maledictions.

"I didn't know," Stover said apologetically.

"Well, now you know," said the Coffee-colored Angel vindictively, "don't you so much as stir 'em with your spoon. Don't you dare!"

Stover, being thus forbidden, calmly, wickedly, chuckling inwardly, emptied his plate, smacked his lips and exclaimed, "My! those are delicious. Pass my plate up for some more, will you, Mr. White?"

"Now, why did you do that?" said Butsey White when they were alone in their room.

"I couldn't help it. I just couldn't help it," said Stover truthfully. "It was such a joke!"

"Not from you," said Butsey White with Roman dignity. "You've got the whole darn house down on you already, and the Coffee-colored Angel will never forgive you."

"Just for that?"

Butsey White disdained an answer. Instead, he scanned Stover's clothes with critical disfavor.

"Say, if I'm going to lead you around by the hand you've got to come down on that color scheme of yours, or it's no go."

Stover, surprised, surveyed himself in the mirror.

"Why, I thought that pretty fine."

"Say, have you got a pair of trousers that's related to a coat?"

Stover dove into the trunk and produced a blue suit that passed the censor, who had in the meanwhile confiscated the razor-tipped patent-leathers and the red-visored cap, saying, "Now you'll sink into the landscape and won't annoy the cows. Stick on this cap of mine and hoof it; you're due at the Doctor's in half an hour, and I promised old Fuzzy-Wuzzy to show you the lay of the land and give you some pointers."

Outside, Cheyenne Baxter, who was pitching curves to Tough McCarty, stopped them. "Hello, there, Rinky Dink: turn up here sharp at four o'clock."

"What for—sir?" said Stover, surprised.

"We've got a game on with the Cleve. Play baseball?"

"I—I'm a little out of practice," said Stover, who loathed the game.

"Can't help it; you're it. You play in the field. Four o'clock sharp."

"You're the ninth man in the house," Butsey explained as they started for the school. "Everyone has to play. Are you any good?"

Stover was tempted to let his imagination run, but the thought of the afternoon curbed it.

"Oh, I used to be pretty fair," he said halfheartedly, plunging into the distant past.

But Stover had no desire to talk; he felt the thrill of strange sensations. Scarcely did he heed the chatter of his guide that rattled on.

The road lay straight and cool under the mingled foliage of the trees. Ahead, groups of boys crossed and recrossed in lazy saunterings.

"There's the village," said Butsey, extending his hand to the left. "First bungalow is Mister Laloo's, buggies and hot dogs. There's Bill Appleby's—say, he's a character, rolling in money— we'll drop in to see him. Firmin's store's next and the Jigger Shop's at the end."

"The Jigger Shop!" said Stover, mystified. "What's that?"

"Where they make jiggers, of course."

"Jiggers?"

"Oh, my beautiful stars, think of eating your first jigger!" said Butsey White, the man of the world. "What wouldn't I give to be in your shoes! I say, though, you've got some tin?"

"Sure," said Stover, sounding the coins in his change pocket.

Butsey's face brightened.

"You see, Al has no confidence in me just at present. It's a case of the regular table d'hôte for me until the first of the month. Say, we'll have a regular gorge. It'll be fresh strawberry jiggers, too."

They began to pass other fellows in flannels and jerseys, who exchanged greetings.

"Hello, you, Butsey!"

"Why, Egghead, howdy-do?"

"Ah, there, Butsey White!"

"Ta-ta, Saphead."

"See you later, old Sport."

"Four o'clock sharp, Texas."

Under the trees, curled in the grass, a group of three were languidly working out a Greek translation.

"Skin your eyes, Dink," said Butsey White, waving a greeting as they passed. "See the fellow this side? That's Flash Condit."

"The fellow who scored on the Princeton varsity?"

"Oh, you knew, did you?"

"Sure," said Stover with pride. "Gee, what a peach of a build!"

"Turn to your left," said Butsey suddenly. "Here's Foundation House, where the Doctor lives. Just look at that doorway. Wouldn't it give you the chills?"

They were in front of a red-brick house, hidden under dark trees and overgrown with vines that congregated darkly over the porte-cochère and gave the entrance a mysterious gloom that still lives in the memory of the generations.

"It swallows you up, doesn't it?" said Dink, awed.

"You bet it does, and it's worse inside," said Butsey comfortingly. "Come on; now I'll show you the real thing."

They passed the surrounding trees and suddenly halted. Before them the campus burst upon them.

"Well, Dink, what do you think of that?" said Butsey proudly.

Stover plunged his hands in his trousers pockets and gazed awed. Before him extended an immense circle of greensward, dotted on the edge with apple trees in blossom, under which groups of boys were lolling, or tumbling over one another in joyous cublike romping. To the left, across the circle, half a dozen red-coated, slate-topped, portly houses, overgrown with ivy, were noisy with urchins hanging out of myriad windows, grouped on steps, chasing one another in twisting spirals over the lawns. Ahead, a massive brownstone chapel with pointed tower rose up, and to its right, in mathematical bulk, was the abode of Greek and Latin roots, syntax and dates, of blackboards, hard seats and the despotism of the faculty. To the right, close at hand, was a large three-storied building with wonderful dormer windows tucked under the slanted slate roof, and below was a long stone esplanade, black with the grouped figures of giants. At the windows, propped on sofa cushions, chin in hand, some few conned the approaching lesson, softening the task by moments of dreamy contemplation of the scuffle below or stopping to catch a tennis ball that traveled from the esplanade to the window. Meanwhile, a constant buzz of inquiry and exclamation continued:

"Say, Bill, how far's the advance?"

"Middle page ninety-two."

"Gee, what a lesson!"

"You bet—it's tough!"

"Hi, there, give me a catch."

"Look out! Biff!"

"Oh, you, Jack Rabbit, come up and give me the advance!"

"Can't. I'm taking my chances. Get hold of Skinny."

"What time's practice?"

That's the Upper House, House of Lords, Abode of the Blessed," said Butsey with envious eyes. "That's where we'll land when we're fifth formers—govern yourself, no lights, go to the village any time, and all that sort of thing. Say!" He swept the circle comprehensively with his arm. "What do you think of it? Pretty fine, eh—what?"

"Gee!" said Stover with difficulty, then after a moment he blurted out, "It's—it's terrific!"

"Oh, that's not all; there's the Hamill House in the village and the Davis and Rouse up the street. The baseball fields are past the chapel."

"Why, it's like a small college," said Stover, whose gaze returned to the giants on the esplanade.

"Huh!" said Butsey in sovereign contempt. "We'll wipe up anything in the shape of a small college that comes around here! Do you want to toddle around the circle?"

"Oh, Lord, no!" said Stover, cold at the thought of running the inspection of hundreds of eyes. "Besides, I've got to see the Doctor."

"All right. Stand right up to him now. Don't get scared," said Butsey, choosing the one method to arouse all latent fears.

"What's he like?" said Stover, biting his nails.

"There's nothing like him," said Butsey reminiscently. "He's got an eye that gives you the creeps. He knows everything that goes on—everything."

Stover began to whistle, keeping an eye on the windows as they approached.

"Well, ta-ta! I'll hang out at Laloo's for you," said Butsey, loping off. "Say, by the way, look out—he's a crackerjack boxer."

Stover, like Æneas at the gates of Avernus, stood under the awful portals, ruminating uneasily on Butsey's last remark. There certainly was something dark and terrifying about the place that cast cold shadows over the cheery April day. Then the door opened, he gave his name in blundering accents to the butler, and found himself in the parlor sitting bolt upright on the edge of a gilded chair. The butler returned, picking up his steps, and, after whispering that the Doctor would see him presently, departed, stealing noiselessly away. Abandoned to the classic stillness, nothing in the room reassured him. The carpets were soft, drowning out the sounds of human feet; the walls and corridors seemed horribly stilled as if through them no human cry might reach the outer air. All about were photographs of broken columns—cold, rigid, ruined columns, faintly discerned in the curtained light of the room. The Doctor's study was beyond, through the door by which the butler had passed. Stover's glance was riveted on it, trying to remember whether the American Constitution prohibited headmasters from the brutal English practice of caning and birching; and, listening to the lagging tick of the mantel clock, he solemnly vowed to lead that upright, impeccable life that would keep him from such another soul-racking visit.

The door opened and the Doctor appeared, holding out his hand.

Stover hastily sprang up, found himself actually shaking hands and mumbling something futile and idiotic. Then he was drawn to the horror of horrors, and the door shut out all retreat.

"Well, John, how do you like the school?"

Stover, more terrified by this mild beginning than if the Doctor had produced a bludgeon from behind his back, stammered out that he thought the buildings were handsome, very handsome.

"It's a pretty big place," said the Doctor, throwing his nervous little body back in an easy chair and studying the four-hundred-and-second problem of the year. "You'll find a good deal in it—a great many interests."

"He certainly has a wicked eye," thought Stover, watching with fascination the glance that confronted him like a brace of pistols suddenly extended from under shaggy bushes. "Now he's sizing me up—wonder if he knows all?"

"Well, John, what was the trouble?" said the Doctor from his easy, reclining position.

"The trouble, sir? Oh," said Stover, sitting bolt upright with every sinew stiffened. "You mean why they fired—why they expelled me, sir?"

"Yes, why did they fire you?" said the Doctor, trying to descend.

"For getting caught, sir."

The Doctor gazed at him sharply, seeking to determine whether the answer was from impertinence or fright or a precocious judgment of the morals of the nation. Then he smiled and said, "Well, what was it?"

"Please, sir, I put asafetida in the furnace," said Stover in frightened tones.

"You put asafetida down the furnace?"

"Yes, sir."

"That was a very brilliant idea, wasn't it?"

"No, sir," said Stover, drawing a long breath and wondering if he could possibly stay after such a confession.

"Why did you do it?"

Stover hesitated, and suddenly, yielding to an unaccountable impulse toward the truth that occasionally surprised him, blurted out, "I did it to make trouble, sir."

"You didn't like the school?"

"I hated it! There were a lot of girls around."

"Well, John," said the Doctor with heroic seriousness, "it may be that you didn't have enough to do. You have evidently an active brain—perhaps imagination would be a fitter word. As I said, you'll find this a pretty big place, just the sort of opening an ambitious boy should delight in. You'll find here all sorts of boys—boys that count, boys you respect and want to respect you, and then there are other boys who will put asafetida in the furnace if you choose to teach them chemistry."

"Oh, no, sir," said Stover, all in a gasp.

"Your parents think you are hard to manage," said the Doctor, with the wisp of a smile. "I don't. Go out; make some organization; represent us; make us proud of you; count for something! And remember one thing: if you want to set fire to Memorial Hall or to dynamite this study, do it because *you* want to, and not because some other fellow puts it into your head. Stand on your own legs." The Doctor rose and extended his hand cordially. "Of course, I shall have my eye on you."

Stover, dumfounded, rose as though on springs. The Doctor, noticing his amazement, said, "Well, what is it?"

"Please, sir—is that all?"

"That's all," said the Doctor seriously.

Stover drew a long breath, shook hands precipitately and escaped.

IV

THE SPELL was still on him as he stumbled over the resounding steps. But, twenty feet from the door, the spirit of irreverence overtook him. Then, at the thought of the waiting Butsey, he began to pipe forth voluminously the martial strains of "Sherman's March to the Sea," kicking enormous pebbles victoriously before him.

Butsey White, sitting on the doorstep of Laloo's, gazed at him from the depths of a steaming frankfurter sandwich.

"Well, you look cheerful," he said in surprise.

"Why not?"

"How was he?"

"Gentle as a kitten."

"Come off! Were you scared?"

'Scared! Lord, no! I enjoyed myself."

"You're a cheerful liar, you are. What did he say to you?"

"Hoped I'd enjoy the place and all that sort of thing. And—oh, yes, he spoke about you."

"He did, did he?" said Butsey, precipitately leaving the frankfurter sandwich.

"He hoped I'd have a good influence on you," said Stover, whose imagination had been too long confined.

Butsey rose wrathfully, but the answer he intended could not be made, for, reckoning on his host, he was already in his third frankfurter, and there was the Jigger Shop yet to be visited.

"Dink, if you ever have to tell the truth," he said, "it'll kill you. Come in and meet Mr. Laloo."

Mr. Laloo was leaning gratefully on the counter—as, indeed, he was always leaning against something—his legs crossed, lazily plying the afternoon toothpick.

"Laloo, shake hands with my friend, Mr. Stover," said Butsey White professionally. "Mr. Stover's heard about your hot dogs, way out in California."

Laloo transferred the toothpick and gave Stover his hand in a tired, unenthusiastic way.

"Well, now, they do be pretty good hot dogs," he drawled out. "Suppose you want one?" He looked at Stover in sleepy reproachfulness, and then slid around the counter in the shortest parabola possible.

"Pick him out a nice young Pomeranian," said Butsey, peering into the steaming tin.

Laloo forked a frankfurter, selected a roll and looked expectantly at Stover.

"What's the matter?" said Dink, mystified.

"Mustard or no mustard?" Butsey said in explanation. "He likes to talk, but the doctor won't let him."

"I'll have all that's coming to me," said Dink loudly.

A second later his teeth had sunk into the odorous mass. He shut his eyes, gazed seraphically at the smooty ceiling and winked at Butsey.

"Umm?" said Butsey.

"Umm! Umm!"

"Isn't he the fancy young dogcatcher?"

"Well, I should rather!" said Dink, lost in the vapors. "I say, have another?"

"Thanks, old chap, but I had a couple while you were chucking the Doctor under the chin," said Butsey glibly. "Save up now; we've got a couple more places to visit."

"How much?" said Dink.

Laloo, who was reclining against the nearest wall, elevated four fingers and gazed out the window.

"Four!" said Stover.

"One and three."

"Three!" said Butsey in feigned surprise. "Oh, come, I didn't eat three—well, I never; what do you think of that?"

Dink rubbed his ear thoughtfully, looked hard at Butsey and paid. Laloo followed them to the door, leaned against the jamb and gazed down the road.

"Now for Bill Appleby's," said Butsey cheerily. "He's rolling—

rolling in wealth. We'll go in later for lamps and crockery and all that sort of thing. I thought we might sort of wash down the hot dogs before we go up to the Jigger Shop—eh, what?"

In Appleby's general merchandise store Stover gravely shook hands with a quick businesslike little man with a Western mustache, a Down East twang and a general air of being on the trigger.

"Well, Bill, how's business?" said Butsey affably, nudging Stover.

"It's bad, boys, it's bad," said Bill mournfully.

"Bad, you old robber," said Butsey; "why, that little iron safe of yours is just cracking open with coin. How's the root beer to-day?"

"It's very nice, Mr. White. Just come in this morning."

"Yes, it did! Bet it came in with the Ark," said Butsey, to Stover's great admiration. "Well, are you going to set us up to a couple of bottles, or have we got to pay for them?"

"We've got some very fine Turkish paste, Mr. White," said Bill, producing the root beer.

"Well?" said Butsey, looking at Stover.

"Sure!"

"I'd like to show you some of our new crockery sets, Mr. Stover," said Appleby softly. "Just came in this morning. Want a student's lamp?"

"No time now, Bill," said Butsey, hastily consulting the clock. "See you later."

Other groups came in; Appleby moved away. Stover, quenching the hot dogs in root beer, heard again the opening salutations:

"Well, Bill, how's business?"

"It's bad, Mr. Parsons. It's bad."

"Well, Bill, ta-ta," said Butsey, as they moved off. "Seen Doc Macnooder this morning?"

"No, Mr. White, I haven't saw him today."

"Always make him answer that," said Butsey chuckling, "and always ask him about business. We all do. It's e-tiquette. There's Firmin's," he said, with a wave of his hand—"post office, country store, boots and shoes and all that sort of thing. And here's the Jigger Shop!"

Stover had no need of the explanation. Before a one-story glass-fronted structure a swarm of boys of all ages, sizes and colors were clustered on steps and railings, or perched on posts and backs of chairs, all ravenously attacking the jigger to the hungry clink of the spoon against the glass. They elbowed their way in through the joyous, buzzing mass to where, by the counter, Al, watchdog of the jigger, scooped out the fresh strawberry ice cream and gathered in the nickels that went before. At the moment of their arrival Al was in what might be termed a defensive formation. One elbow was leaning on the counter, one hand caressed the heavy, drooping mustache, one ear listened to the promises of a ravenous, impecunious group, but the long pointer nose and the financial eyes were dreamily plunged on the group without.

"Gee, did you ever see such an eye?" said Butsey, who had reasons of his own for quailing before it. "It's almost up to the Doctor's. You can't fool him—not for a minute. Talk about Pierpont Morgan! Why, he knows the whole blooming lot of us, just what we're worth. Why, that eye of his could put a hole right through any pocket. Watch him when he spots me." Pushing forward he exclaimed, "Hello, Al; glad to see me?"

Al turned slowly, fastening his glance on him with stony intentness.

"Don't bother me, you Butsey," he said shortly.

"Al, I've sort of set my sweet tooth on these here strawberry jiggers of yours."

The Guardian of the Jigger made a half motion in the air, as though to brush away an imaginary fly.

"Two nice, creamy, double strawberry jiggers, Al."

Al's eyes drooped wearily.

"My friend, Mr. Vanastorbilt Stover, here's setting up," said Butsey in conciliating accents.

The eyes opened and fastened on Stover, who advanced saying, "That goes."

"Ring a couple of dimes down, Astorbilt," said Butsey, "Al's very fond of music."

"Give me change for that," said Stover, rising to the occasion with a five-dollar bill.

"And, for the love of Mike, hustle 'em," said Butsey White. "I've only got a second."

The shop began to empty rapidly as the hour of the two o'clock recitation neared. Stover gazed into the pink fruity depths of his first strawberry jigger, inserted his spoon gingerly and took a nibble. Then he drew a long, contented breath, gazed into the land of dreams, and gave himself up to the delights of a new, of an incomparable, sensation.

Butsey White, gobbling against time, flung out occasional, full-mouthed phrases:

"Got to run—'xcuse us—jemima! Isn't it the stuff—see you at three—better bring some back in box—don't tell anyone, though —especially the Coffee-colored Angel."

Across the fields the bell suddenly, impatiently, brutally clanged out. With a last convulsive gulp, Butsey White finished his glass and burst from the shop in the helter-skelter company of the last laggards. Stover, left alone, looked inquiringly at Al.

"Recitation," said Al. "They've got a two-twenty sprint before the bell stops. We're out of hours, now, except for the Upper House."

"Meaning me?" said Stover, rising.

"Sit where you are," said Al. "You're all right for today. Where do you hang out?"

"Green House," said Dink, who, beginning to feel hungry, ordered another jigger and selected a chocolate éclair.

"You're not rooming with Butsey White?"

"The same."

"You are?" said Al pityingly. "Well, just let me give you one word of advice, young fellow. Sew your shirt to your back, or he'll have it off while you're getting into your coat."

"I wasn't born yesterday," said Dink impudently, gesturing with his spoon. "And I rather fancy I'm a pretty cute little proposition myself."

"So!"

"If any of these smart alecks can get the best of me," said Dink grandiloquently, egged on by the other's tone of disbelief, "he'll have to get up with the chickens!"

"You're pretty slick?"

"As slick as they make 'em."

"Say, bub," said Al, with his dreamy drawl, "is this the line of talk you've been putting out to that bunch of Indians down in the Green?"

"Oh, I'll put it out."

"Say, you're going to have a wonderful time here!"

"Watch me," said Dink, cocking his head; but with less confi-

"WHY, SOME OF 'EM ARE SO SLICK THAT WHEN THEY COME IN I LOCK THE
CASH DRAWER AND STUFF COTTON IN MY EARS."

dence than when he had announced his intentions on the stage-
coach.

"Young fellow," said Al, leaning back and looking at him from
under his eyelids, "you're in wrong. You don't know what you've
come to. Why, there's a bunch of young stock jobbers around here
that would make a Wall Street bunco-steerer take to raising chickens! Slick? Why, some of 'em are so slick that when they come in
I lock the cash drawer and stuff cotton in my ears."

"Bring 'em on," said Dink disdainfully.

At this moment there was a loud flop by the window in the rear,
and the Tennessee Shad rose slowly from the floor. At the same
moment Doc Macnooder, ambling innocently by on the farther
sidewalk, turned, dashed across the street, bounded into the shop
and, returning to the door, carefully surveyed the approaches.

"All clear," said the Tennessee Shad from the window.

"All's well on the Rappahannock," returned the scout at the door.

Macnooder, with a well-executed double shuffle, the Tennessee Shad, with a stiff-jointed lope of his bony body, advanced and shook hands.

"Al, we come not to take your hard-earned money, but do you good," said Macnooder as usual, genially shaking an imaginary hand.

The Tennessee Shad camped on the back of a chair, drew up his thin, long legs, laid one bony finger against a bony nose and looked expectantly at Macnooder.

Meanwhile Al, without turning his back, carefully moved over to the glass counter that sheltered appetizing trays of éclairs, plum cakes and cream puffs and, whistling a melancholy note, locked the door, scanned the counter, and placed a foot on the cover of the jigger tub.

Doc Macnooder, whose round, bullet head and little rhinoceros eyes had followed the hostile preparation, said sorrowfully, "Albert, your conduct grieves us."

"Go ahead, now," said Al in a tired voice.

"Go ahead?" said Macnooder, looking in surprise at the equally impassive Tennessee Shad.

"What's the flimflam to-day?"

"Al," said Macnooder, in his most persuasive tones, "you wrong me. My motives are honorable. At four o'clock this very afternoon Turkey Reiter will proceed to cash a check and settle for a fountain pen, a pair of suspenders and a safety razor I sold him. Just trust me till then—will you?"

"Nothing doing," said Al.

"Honor bright, Al!"

"No use."

"You *must* trust me till then."

Al, producing a patent clipper, began to pare his nails.

"Al?"

"What?"

"Won't you trust me?"

"Don't make me laugh!"

"Al's right, Doc," said the Tennessee Shad, entering the discussion. "You ought to put up some guarantee."

Al slowly turned his gaze on the Tennessee Shad and waited hopefully for the real attack.

"Well, what?" said Macnooder.

"How about your watch?"

"It's loaned."

"You haven't got a stickpin on you?"

"Left 'em at home—never thought Al would go back on me."

Al smiled.

"That's a very nice spring coat you've got on," said the Tennessee Shad, as though struck by an inspiration. "Why don't you put that up for a couple of hours?"

"Not on your life," said Macnooder indignantly. "This coat's brand new, worth thirty dollars."

Al, suddenly shifting, leaned forward, both elbows on the counter, and studied the coat with a reminiscent air.

"Oh, put it up," said the Tennessee Shad.

"Never. I've got associations about this coat and, besides, I've got to make a swell call in Princeton to-morrow."

"What's the diff?" said the Tennessee Shad, yawning. "It's only a couple of hours; and you know you said you were going to clean off the whole slate with Al, sure as Turkey boned up."

Macnooder seemed to hesitate.

"It's idiotic to put up a real, high-life coat for a couple of jiggers."

"Hurry up; I'm hungry."

"Stop," said Al, drawing back satisfied. "I wouldn't bother about that coat if I were you."

"Why not?" exclaimed the two partners.

" 'Cause I remember that coat gag now," said Al with a far-off look. "I bit once—way back in '89. It's a good game, specially when the real owner comes ramping in the next day."

"What do you mean?" said Doc Macnooder indignantly.

"I mean that it don't button, you young pirate," said Al scornfully, but without malice. "When you try anything as slick as that again you want to be sure the real owner ain't been around. That coat belongs to Lovely Mead."

Doc Macnooder looked at the Tennessee Shad.

"Have we really got to pay for them?" he said mournfully.

"Looks that way."

"Oh, well," said Doc, slapping down a quarter, "fill 'em up."

Al heaped up the glasses, adding an appreciative extra dab with the magnanimity of the victor, and said, "Say, you boys want to rub up a little. Here's Stover, over there, just come. He's about your size."

The Tennessee Shad and Doc Macnooder about faced and stared at Stover, who all the while had remained in quiet obscurity, dangling his legs over the counter.

"Just come, Stover?" said Macnooder at last.

"Yes, sir."

"On the noon stage?"

"Yes, sir."

"What form?"

"Second, sir."

"Why, shake, then, brother," said the Tennessee Shad, offering his hand. "Shake hands with Doc Macnooder."

Doc Macnooder grasped his hand with extra cordiality, saying, "What house?"

"Green House, sir," said Stover, awed by the sight of a Varsity jersey. "I'm rooming with—with Mr. White."

"What'll you have?"

"I beg pardon."

"What'll you have?"

"Why," said Stover, quite taken back by the offer, "I think it's up to me, sir."

"Rats!" said Macnooder. "If you've been in tow of Butsey, I'll bet you've been paying out all day. Butsey White's a low-down, white-livered cuss, who'd take advantage of a freshman. Step up."

"I'll have another one of these," said Stover gratefully, feeling his heart warm toward the unexpected friends.

"Bet Butsey's stuck you pretty hard," said the Tennessee Shad, nodding wisely. "He's just loaded with the spondulix, too."

"Well, he did sort of impose on me," said Stover, thinking of the frankfurters at Laloo's.

"It's a shame," said Macnooder indignantly. "Here, Al, make that a triple. Don't think we're all like that, though."

Al, listening, was sorely puzzled at this sudden cordiality, knowing of old the firm of Doc Macnooder and the Tennessee Shad.

"I say, let me set up for éclairs or something," said Stover, exceedingly moved.

"Not a cent," said Macnooder firmly.

"I hope Butsey hasn't been steering you around to Firmin's and Appleby's for crockery and all that sort of thing," said the Tennessee Shad, with a look that at once convinced Stover of his roommate's criminal complicity.

"Why, he was going to do that after this recitation."

"He was, was he?" said Doc. "Think of that! He's going to stick you for everything first hand."

"What can I do?"

"Do? Save half your chink, get everything secondhand, the way we do."

Al, comprehending, leaned back and smiled.

"I'll bet he gets a rake-off," said Stover indignantly.

"I don't say that," said Macnooder, with the air of insinuating as much.

"I wish I knew the ropes."

"That's easy enough. Anyone can tell you."

"I wish you fellows'd put me on."

"Glad to do it," said Macnooder, without enthusiasm. "Finish up and we'll fit you out in a jiffy."

When the three went shuffling down the street Al did an unusual, an unprecedented thing. He actually made the turn of the counter and stationed himself at the door, watching the group depart—Macnooder with his arm on Stover's shoulder, the Tennessee Shad guarding the other side.

When they disappeared beyond Bill Orum's, the cobbler's, in the direction of the Dickinson, he said slowly, in profound admiration, "Well, I'll be jiggered! If those body snatchers don't get electrocuted, they'll own Fifth Avenue!"

V

―――――――――

"COME UP to my room and we'll see what's on hand," said Doc, entering the Dickinson. "Too bad you're stuck down in the Green —no house spirit there—you must get in with us next year."

"Doc's a great fellow," said the Tennessee Shad, as Macnooder went quickly ahead, "a great business man. He's a sort of clearing-house for the whole school. Say, he's taken a regular fancy to you."

"What did he get his 'L' for?" said Stover, as the Tennessee Shad, to gain time, showed him the lower floor.

"Quarter on the eleven last fall. Here's the Triumphant Egg-head's room. Isn't it a peach? They've got a good crowd here; you must be with them or us next year. Here's Turkey Reiter's and Butcher Stevens' quarters. They're crackerjacks, too; on the eleven and the nine. Come on, now. We'll strike Doc. You know he stud-ies medicine and all that sort of thing. Wait till I give the counter-sign. Doc's most particular."

Stover found himself in a den, a combination of drugstore, taxi-dermist's shop and general warehouse. All about the room were ranged an extraordinary array of bottles—green bottles that lurked under the bed, red, blue and white bottles that climbed the walls and crowded the mantelpiece, tops of bottles that peered out of half-opened boxes, all ticketed and mustered in regiments. From the ceiling a baby alligator swung on a wire, blinking at them hor-ribly with shining glass eyes; a stuffed owl sat in one corner; while opposite, a muskrat peered into a crow's nest. The closet and all available floor space were heaped high with paper boxes and wooden cases, while over all were innumerable catalogues.

"Pretty fine, isn't it?" said the Tennessee Shad.

"It's wonderful," said Stover, not quite at ease.

"It's not bad," said Doc. "I'd like to have a nice white skeleton over there in that corner; but they're hard to get, nowadays. Now let's get down to business. Sit down."

Stover took the only chair; the Tennessee Shad curled up languidly on the bed, after brushing aside the débris; while Macnooder, perched on a dry-goods box, poised a pencil over a pad of paper.

"You want a crockery set, first; a student lamp, and an oil can to keep your oil in."

"Especially the can," said the Tennessee Shad gravely. "Better get a padlock with it, or the whole Green House will be stealing from you."

"I don't know whether I have a can on hand," said Macnooder anxiously. "But here's a lamp."

He placed a rather battered affair in the middle of the floor, saying, "It's a little squeegeed, but you don't care about looks. They ask you all kinds of prices for them when they're new; but you can have this for two twenty-five. There's a bite out of the shade, but you can turn that side to the wall. They're rather hard to get secondhand."

"All right," said Stover.

"Better light it up first," said the Tennessee Shad professionally.

"That's businesslike," said Macnooder, who lit a match and, after an unsuccessful attempt, said, "There's no oil in it. Still, if Stover wants—"

"Never mind that," said Stover loudly, to show his confidence.

"Now for the toilet set."

"Say, how about the can?"

"Oh, the can. Let me look," said Macnooder, disappearing among the packing boxes in the closet.

"You want that," said the Tennessee Shad confidentially.

"Hope he's got one," said Stover.

Macnooder reappeared with an ordinary kerosene can and a padlock, announcing, "This is the only one I've got on hand. It's my own."

"Let him have it," said the Tennessee Shad. "No one can get in here; you're always locked and bolted."

Macnooder hesitated.

"How does it work?" said Stover, interested.

"The spigot is plugged up and the top cover is padlocked to the side. See? Now no one can get it. I don't particularly care about selling it, but if you want it, take it at one twenty-five."

"That's too much," said the Tennessee Shad. "One plunk's enough."

"You're paying cash?" said Macnooder, considering.

"Sure!" said Stover.

"Well, call it one bone, then."

Stover looked gratefully at the Tennessee Shad, who winked at him to show him he was his friend.

"Now, about a crockery set," said Macnooder, scratching his head. "I've got two, plain and fancy, what we call a souvenir set—but you wouldn't understand that. I'll show you the regular kind."

"What's a souvenir set?" said Dink, mystified.

"Oh, it's a sort of school fad," said the Tennessee Shad as Doc disappeared. "Every piece is different, collected from all sorts of places—swap 'em around like postage stamps, don't you know. We've got rather tired of the ordinary thing, you know."

"Say, that's a bully idea," said Dink, whose imagination was appealed to.

"Some of the fellows have perfect beauts," said the Tennessee Shad, yawning; "got at hotels, and house parties, and all that sort of thing."

"Why, that beats hooking signs all hollow," said Dink, growing enthusiastic.

"I didn't know you'd be interested," said the Tennessee Shad carelessly. "Like to see one?"

"You bet I would."

"I say, Doc, old boy," said the Tennessee Shad, "bring out the souvenir set, too, will you, like a good fellow?"

"Wait till I get this out," said Macnooder, who, after much rummaging, puffed back with a blue-and-white set which he ranged on the floor.

"How's that appeal to you?" he said with a flourish of his hand. "Good condition, too; only the soap dish has a nick. You can have it for two fifty."

But Dink had no eyes for the commonplace.

"Could I see the other," he said, "before I decide?"

Macnooder appeared loath to exert himself to no purpose.

"You wouldn't cotton to it, bub," he said, with a shake of his head.

"I'm not so sure about that," said the Tennessee Shad. "This chap's no bottle baby; he's more of a sport than you think. I'll bet you he's got a few swagger trophies in the line of signs himself."

"I've got two or three might strike your fancy," said Dink with a reckless look.

"Come on, Doc, don't be so infernally lazy. You're the deuce of a salesman. Out with the crockery."

"What's the use?" said Doc halfheartedly, moving back into the litter of the closet.

"Don't get it unless you can afford it," said the Tennessee Shad in a friendly whisper.

When at length the souvenir set had been carefully displayed on the top of a box, cleared for the occasion, Stover beheld a green-and-white pitcher, rising like a pond lily from the depths of a red-and-white basin, while a lavender tooth mug, a blue cup, and a pink soap dish gave the whole somewhat the effect of an aurora borealis.

The Tennessee Shad sprang up and examined each piece with a connoisseur's enthusiasm. The lavender tooth mug, especially, attracted his curiosity. He looked it over, handled it gingerly, holding it to the light.

"Don't think this is up to the rest," he said finally, looking at Doc. "It's cracked."

"Suppose it is!" said Doc scornfully. "Do you know whose that is? That was swiped out of the set of Brother Baldwin."

"No?"

"Fact. Last day of spring term, when he was giving a math exam."

"You don't say so!"

"What are the rest?" said Stover, wondering what sum could possibly compensate for such treasures.

"The rest are not so much; from the other houses, but they're good pieces. The water pitcher was traded by Cap Kiefer, catcher of the nine, you know. But there's one article," said Doc, pointing melodramatically, "that's worth the whole lot. Only I'll have to put you under oath—both of you."

The Tennessee Shad, puzzled, looked hard at Macnooder and raised his right hand. Stover, blushing, followed suit.

"That," said Macnooder, "came *direct* from Foundation House. That belonged to his Nibs himself!"

"Come off!" said the Tennessee Shad, not daring to look at Macnooder. "That's a bunco game."

"I didn't say it was swiped," said Macnooder indignantly. "Just give me a chance, will you? It was smashed up at the fire scare and thrown away with a lot of other things. Tough McCarty, down at the Green, I think, has got the slop jar."

"Excuses!" said the Tennessee Shad. "I did think for a moment you were trying to impose on my young confidence. Gee! Just think of it! Cracky, what a prize! The Doctor himself—well—well! Say, I'd like to make a bid myself."

"It goes with the set," said Macnooder. "It ain't mine; I'm only getting the commission."

Stover, having caressed each article, drew a long breath and said falteringly, "I suppose it comes pretty high!"

"Of course it's worth more than the other set."

"Oh, of course."

"The price set on it was four flat."

"That's a good deal of money," said the Tennessee Shad. "Specially when you've got to fit yourself out."

"Well, the other's cheaper at two fifty," said Macnooder.

"Stover's sort of set his heart on this," said the Tennessee Shad. "Haven't you, Sport?"

Stover confessed that he had.

"Come on; make him a better price, Doc."

"I'd have to consult my client."

"Well, consult your old client."

Macnooder disappeared.

"Stand firm now," said the Tennessee Shad, "you can beat him down. Doc wants to make his commish. I tell you what I'd do if I were you."

"What?"

"If I were looking for a real trophy I'd make him a bid on this. This is the best thing in the whole caboodle. Come over here. Say, just cast your eyes on this!"

Stover gazed in awe. On the wall, suspended on the red-and-black flag of the school, were a pair of battered and torn football shoes, while underneath was a photograph of Flash Condit and the score—Princeton Varsity, 8; Lawrenceville, 4.

"Gee!" said Stover, "He wouldn't sell those!"

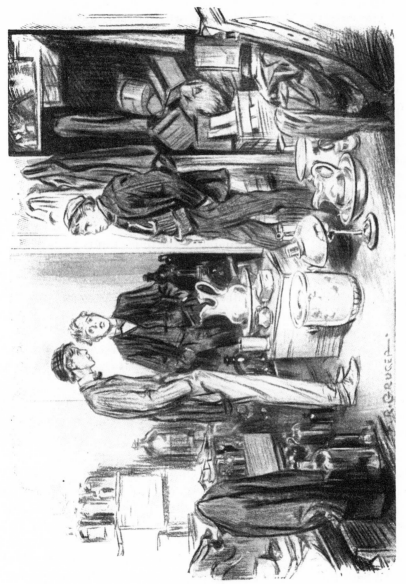

"CRACKY, WHAT A PRIZE! SAY, I'D LIKE TO MAKE A BID MYSELF."

"He might," said the Tennessee Shad. "Between you and me and the lamppost, Doc is devilishly hard up. Offer him a couple of dollars and see."

"The shoes that made the touchdown," said Dink reverentially. The Tennessee Shad did not contradict him.

Half an hour later Dink Stover sallied forth with the ecstasy of a collector who has just discovered an old master. Klondike Jackson, who shook up the beds at the Dickinson, preceded him, drawing in an express wagon the lamp, the padlocked kerosene can and the souvenir set, slightly reduced. Wrapped in tissue paper, tucked under Stover's arm, were the precious shoes, which he had purchased on the distinct understanding that Macnooder should have the right to redeem them at any time before the end of the term, on the payment of costs and fifty-per-cent interest. In Stover's pocket were a new fountain pen, a box of elastics, a pair of Boston garters and a patent nail clipper. Only the limits of his exchequer had prohibited his availing himself of the opportunity to purchase, at a tremendous bargain, a pair of snowshoes, a toboganning cap and a pair of corduroy trousers, slightly spotted.

Luckily for Dink, marching warily behind the vanguard, the three-o'clock recitation had begun, and but a scattering of his schoolmates were abroad to witness his progress.

He arrived thus, virtually unnoticed, at the Green and, with the help of Klondike, arranged his possessions so as to make the greatest display.

He was standing in the middle of the floor, clutching the historic shoes and searching the walls for the proper place of honor, when Butsey White blew in.

"Where in thunder have you been?" he exclaimed, and then stopped at the sight of the twisted lamp. He looked at Dink, gave a grunt, and examined the new purchase.

"Broken-winded, spavined, has the rickets—bet it leaks and won't burn. Where in—"

All at once he perceived the kerosene can with its attached padlock.

"What's this thing?" he said, in genuine surprise, picking it up with two fingers and regarding it with a look of blank incomprehension.

"That's the safety can," said Stover, yielding to a vague feeling of uneasiness.

"What's this?"

"That's a padlock."

"What for?"

"Why, for the kerosene."

"What kerosene?"

"The kerosene for the lamp."

"Why, you nincompoop, we don't furnish the kerosene."

"We don't?" said Stover faintly, with a horrible sinking feeling. "Don't furnish the kerosene?"

"Who got hold of you?" said Butsey, too astounded to laugh.

"I met Macnooder—"

"And the Tennessee Shad, I'll bet my pants on it," said Butsey.

"Yes, sir."

"What else did they unload on you?"

"Why—why, I bought a souvenir set."

"A what?"

"A souvenir toilet set."

Butsey wheeled to the washstand, uttered a shriek and fell in convulsions on the bed.

Stover stook stockstill, gazing in horror from the variegated crockery to Butsey, who was thrashing to and fro in hysterical flops, holding both the pillows where they would most ease the agony. Then, with a sudden deft movement, Dink dropped the historic shoes, sent them under the bed with a savage kick and, rushing to the window, threw the safety can into the tall grass of the fields beyond. Then he returned solemnly, sat down on the edge of the bed, took his head in his hands and began to do some rapid thinking. Butsey White, prone on the bed, burying his head in the covers, by painful degrees returned, gasping, to self-control.

"Mr. White," said Dink solemnly.

There was a slight commotion opposite and a hand fluttered beseechingly, while Butsey's weak voice managed to say, "Take it away—take it away."

Dink rose and cast a towel over the set of seven colors, and then resumed his seat.

"It's all right; I've hidden it," he said.

Butsey rolled from the bed, tottered over to his own washstand and drank deeply from the water pitcher. Then he turned on the melancholy Stover.

"Say!"

"Go ahead! Soak it to me!"

"I thought you were old enough to go out alone."

"They lied to me," said Stover, kicking a chair.

"Say that again."

"They lied," repeated Dink, but with a more uncertain note.

"This from you!" said Butsey maliciously.

A great ethical light burst over Dink. He scratched his head and then looked at Butsey, grinning a sheepish grin.

"Well, I guess it was coming to me—but they are wonders!" he said, with reluctant admiration. "I'll take my medicine, but I'll get back at them, by jiminy! You see if I don't."

"For the love of Mike, give us the story!"

"You'll keep it twenty-four hours?"

"So help me—"

"I'm a sucker, all right," said Dink ruefully. Then he stopped and blurted out, "Say, White, I guess it was about what I needed. I guess I'm not such a little wonder worker, after all. I've been fresh—rotten fresh. But, say, from now on I'm holding my ear to the ground; and when it comes to humbly picking up a few crumbs of knowledge you'll find me ready and willing. I'm reformed. Now, here's the tale:"

VI

DINK, UNDER the influence of the new emotion, made a fairly full confession, merely overlooking the shoes that Flash did not carry over the Princeton goal line, and suppressing that detail of the Foundation House's supposed contribution which had lent such a peculiar value to the souvenir crockery set. By four o'clock Butsey White had sufficiently recovered to remember the afternoon baseball match.

Ten minutes later Dink, lost in a lapping baseball suit lent by Cheyenne Baxter, reinforced with safety pins, stationed himself in the outfield behind a catcher's mitt for preliminary practice with little Susie Satterly and Beekstein Hall, who was shortsighted and wore glasses.

The result of five minutes' frantic chasing was that Dink, who surprised everyone by catching a fly that somehow stuck in his glove, was promoted to center field; Susie Satterly, who had stopped two grounders, took left; while Beekstein was ignominiously escorted to a far position in right field and firmly requested to stop whatever he could with his chest.

The Cleve cohorts arrived, thirty strong, like banditti marching to sack a city, openly voicing their derision for the nine occupants of the Green House. The contest, which at first sight seemed unequal, was not in reality so, Tough McCarty and Cheyenne Baxter being an unusually strong battery, while the infield, with Butsey White at first, the White Mountain Canary at second, Stuffy Brown shortstop and the Coffee-colored Angel at third, quite outclassed the invaders. The trouble was in the outfield—where the trouble in such contests are sure to congregate.

Stover had never been so thoroughly frightened in his life. His imagination, boylike, was aghast at the unknown. A great question was to be decided in a few minutes, when his turn would come to

213

step up to the box and expose himself to the terrific cannonade of Nick Carter, the lengthy pitcher of the Cleve. The curious thing was that on this point Stover himself was quite undecided. Was he a coward, or was he not? Would his legs go back on him, or would he stand his ground, knowing that the stinging ball might strike anywhere—on the tender wrist bones, shattering the point of the elbow, or landing with a deadly thud right over his temple, which he remembered was an absolutely fatal spot?

His first two innings in the field were a complete success—not a ball came his way. With his fielding average quite intact he came in to face the crisis.

"Brown to the bat, Stover on deck, Satterly in the hole," came the shrill voice of Fate in the person of Shrimp Davis, the official scorer.

Stover nervously tried one bat after another; each seemed to weigh a ton. Then Cheyenne Baxter joined him, crouching beside him for a word of advice.

"Now, Dink," he said in a whisper, keeping his eye on Stuffy Brown, who, being unable to hit the straightest ball, was pawing the plate and making terrific preparatory swings with his bat. "Now, Dink, listen here. (Pick out an easy one, Stuffy, and bang it on the nose. Hi-yi, good waiting, Stuffy.) Nick Carter's wild as a wet hen. All he's got is a fast outcurve. Now, what you want to do is to edge up close to the plate and let him hit you. (Oh, robber! That wasn't a strike! Say, Mr. Umpire, give us a square deal, will you?) Walk right into it, Dink, and if it happens to hit you on the wrist, rub above the elbow like the mischief."

"Above the elbow?" said Dink in a hollow voice.

"That's it. You've got a chance to square yourself with the House. Step right into it. What? Three strikes? Say, Mr. Umpire, you're not taking Nick Carter's word for it, are you?"

Amid a storm of execrations Stuffy Brown retired, appealing frantically to the four quarters of the globe for justice and a judge.

Impelled by a resounding whack, Dink approached the plate as a balky horse tries his hoofs in a pool of water. He spread his feet and shouldered his bat, imitating the slightly crouching position of Cheyenne Baxter. Then he looked out for a favorable opening. The field was thronged with representatives of the Cleve House. He turned to first base—it was miles away. He looked at Nick Carter, savagely preparing to mow him down, and he seemed to loom over him, infringing on the batter's box.

"Why the devil don't they stick the pitcher back and give a fellow a chance?" he thought, eying uneasily the quick, jerky preparations. "Why, at this distance a ball could go right through you."

"Come on, Nick, old boy," said a voice issuing from the iron mask at his elbow. "We've got an umpire that can't be bluffed. This is nothing but a Statue of Liberty. Chop him right down."

Dink shivered from the ground up, Carter's long arms gyrated spasmodically, and the ball, like the sweep of a swallow from the ground, sprang directly at him. Stover, with a yell, flung himself back, landing all in a heap.

"Ball one," said the umpire.

A chorus of taunts rose from the Green House nine.

"Trying to put him out, are you?"

"Mucker trick!"

"Put him out!"

"Good eye, Dinky!"

"That's the boy."

Stover rose, found his bat and ruthfully forced himself back to his position.

"I should have let it hit me," he said angrily, perceiving Baxter's frantic signals. "It might have broken a rib, but I'd have showed my nerve."

Clenching his bat fiercely he waited, resolved on a martyr's death. But the next ball coming straight for his head, he ducked horribly.

"Ball two—too high," said the umpire.

Stover tightened his belt, rapped the plate twice with his bat, as Butsey had done, and resumed his position. But the memory of the sound the ball had made when it had whistled by his ears had unnerved him. Before he could summon back his heroic resolves, Carter, with a sudden jerk, delivered the ball. Involuntarily Stover stepped back, the ball easily and slowly passed him and cut the corner of the plate.

"Ball three," said the umpire hesitatingly.

The Cleve catcher hurled his mask to the ground, Carter cast down his glove and trod on it, while the second baseman fell on his bag and wept.

When order was restored Stover dodged the fourth wild ball and went in a daze to first, where to his amazement he was greeted with jubilant cheers.

"You're the boy, Dinky."

"You've got an eye like Charley De Soto."

"They can't fool Rinky Dink."

"Why, he's a wonder."

"Watch him steal second."

Stover slapped his foot on first base with the joy of unhoped-for victory. He glowered about his own possessions. The perspective had suddenly changed; the field was open, all his, the Cleve House representatives were a lot of dubs, butterfingers and fumblers, anyhow! Under Cheyenne Baxter's directions he went plunging down to second, slid, all arms and legs, safely on to the bag, thanks to a wild pitch, and rose triumphantly, blowing the dust from his mouth.

There he remained, as Susie Satterly and Beekstein methodically struck out.

But the joy of that double voyage was still on him as he went back to center field, ready to master the hottest liner or retrieve the sky-scraping fly. It was a great game. He felt a special aptitude for it and wondered why he had never discovered the talent before. He began to dream of sizzling two-baggers and long home runs over the fence.

"I wish I'd get a chance," he said, prancing about digging vicious holes in the glove, that looked like a chest protector. "I'd show 'em what I can do out here."

But no chance came. The battle was between pitchers, and to the surprise of everyone the Green House came up to the last inning with the score of 2 to 1 in their favor, the solitary run of the Cleve being due to a fly that Beekstein had failed to notice.

The Green House nine went jubilantly out into the field for the last half of the ninth inning, determined to shut out the Cleve and end the season with at least one victory.

Dink ran out on his tiptoes, encased himself in his mitt and turned, tense and alert. He had gone through his first ordeal triumphantly. No chances had come to him in the field, but at bat he had accidently succeeded in being hit, and though he had struck out the next time he had hit a foul and knew the jubilant feeling that came with the crack of the bat.

"Give me a week and I'll soak 'em out," he said, moving restlessly, and he added to himself, "Strike 'em out, Cheyenne, old man! They're easy."

But the Cleves suddenly woke up and began to fight. One man beat out a grounder, and one struck out; another error of the temperamental White Mountain Canary put a man on third and one on second. Then Cheyenne, pulling himself together, made his second strikeout.

"Two out, play for the batter," came Cheyenne Baxter's warning hallo.

"Two out," said Dink to his fellow fielders. "One more and we spink 'em. Come on, now!"

Both sides settled for the final play, the man on second leading well up toward third.

"Steady!" said Cheyenne.

Stover drew in his breath and rose to his toes, as he had done thirty times already.

Suddenly there was a sharp crack, and the ball, meeting the bat, floated fair and free, out toward center field.

Dink did not have to move a step; in fact, the ball rose and fell straight for the massive mitt as though it had chosen his glove from all the other gloves in the field. It came slowly, endlessly, the easiest, gentlest, most perfect fly imaginable, directly for the large brown mitt that looked like a chest protector.

Stover, turned to stone, saw it strike fair in the middle, and then, irresistibly, slowly, while, horribly fascinated, he stood powerless, slowly trickle over the side of the mitt and drop to the ground.

Dink did not stop for a look, for a second thought, to hesitate or to deliberate. He knew! He gave a howl and broke for the House, and behind him, pell-mell, shrieking and murderous, like a pack of hounds in full cry, came the vanquished, thirsting body of the Green.

He cleared the fence with one hand, took the road with two bounds, fled up the walk, burst through the door, jumped the stairs, broke into his room, slammed the door, locked it, backed the bed against it and seized a chair.

Then the Green House struck the door like a salvo of grapeshot.

"Open up, you robber!"

"Open the door, you traitor!"

BEHIND HIM, PELL-MELL,

SHRIEKING AND MURDEROUS . . .

CAME THE VANQUISHED.

"You Benedict Arnold!"

"Open up, you white-livered pup!"

"You quitter!"

"You chickenheart!"

"You coward!"

Stover, his hair rising, seized the wooden chair convulsively, waiting for the door to burst in.

All at once the transom swung violently and the wolfish faces of Tough McCarty, the White Mountain Canary, Cheyenne and the Coffee-colored Angel crowded the opening.

"Get back or I'll kill you," said Dink in frantic fear, and, advancing, he swung the chair murderously. In a twinkling the transom was emptied.

The storm of voices rose again.

"The freshest yet!"

"The nerve of him!"

"Let's break in the door!"

"Come out!"

"Come out, Freshman!"

"He did it on purpose!"

"He chucked the game!"

"Wait till I get my hands on him!"

"I'll skin him!"

All at once the face of Butsey White appeared at the transom.

"Dink, you let me right in, you hear?"

No answer.

"You let me in right off!"

Still no answer.

"It's my room; you let me in to my room, do you hear?"

Stover continued silent.

"Dink," said Butsey in his loudest tones, "I'm coming right over the transom. Don't you dare to touch me!"

Stover again seized the chair.

Butsey White, supported from behind, carefully drew up one foot, and then convulsively disappeared as Stover charged with the chair.

There was a whispered consultation and then the battling face of Tough McCarty appeared with a new threat:

"You lay a hand on me and I'll rip the hide off you!"

EACH MEMBER OF THE OUTRAGED NINE CLIMBED TO THE TRANSOM AND
EXPRESSED HIS UNFLATTERING OPINION.

"Keep back!" said Stover hoarsely.

"Put down that chair, you little varmint; do you hear me?"

"Don't you come over!"

"Yes, I'm coming over, and you don't dare to touch me. You
don't—"

Stover was neither a coward nor a hero; he was simply in a panic and he was cornered. He rushed wildly to the breach and delivered the chair with a crash, Tough McCarty barely saving himself.

This open defiance of the champion angered the attacking party.

"He ought to be lynched!"

"The booby!"

"Wait till tomorrow!"

Tough McCarty reappeared for a brief second.

"I'll get you yet," he said, pointing a finger at the embattled Stover. "You're a muff, a lowdown muff, in every sense of the word!"

Then succeeded the Coffee-colored Angel: "Wait till I catch you, you Rinky Dink!"

Followed the White Mountain Canary: "You'll reckon with *me* for this!"

Down to Beekstein Hall, with his black-rimmed spectacles, each member of the outraged nine climbed to the transom and expressed his unflattering opinion.

Stover sat down, his chin in his hands, his eyes on the great, lumbering mitt that lay dishonored on the floor.

"I'm disgraced," he said slowly, "disgraced. It's all over—all over. I'm queered—queered forever!"

VII

UNTIL DUSK, like Gilliatt in Victor Hugo's *Toilers of the Sea*, waiting for the tide to swallow him up, Stover sat motionless, brooding. There was only one thing to do—to run away. His whole career had been ruined in a twinkling. He knew. There could be no future for him in the school. What he had done was so awful that it could never be forgiven or forgotten. Why had he run? If only he had made a quick dive at the ball as it had trickled off the glove and caught it before it reached the ground, instead of standing there, horrified, hypnotized. Yes, he would escape, run off to sea somewhere—anywhere! But he wouldn't go home; no, never that! He would ship around the Horn, like the hero in that dreadful book, *Two Years Before the Mast*. He would run away that night, before the story spread over the whole school. He would never face them. He hated the school, he hated the Green, he hated everyone connected with it!

A tap came on the door, and the voice of Butsey White said coldly, "Open up! Fuzzy-Wuzzy's in the House; you're safe. Open up. I've got to get ready for supper."

Stover drew back the bed, unlocked the door and waited with clenched fists for Butsey to spring at him. Butsey White, whose tempestuous rage had long since spent itself in hilarious laughter, as, indeed, had been the case with the rest, thought it best, however, for the purposes of authority, still to preserve a grave face.

"You're a fine specimen!" he said curtly. "You've had a beautiful day of it."

"Yes, I have," said Dink miserably, "a beautiful day!"

Butsey, to whom the tragedy of the century was nothing but an incident, had not the slightest suspicion of Stover's absolute, overwhelming despair. Yet Butsey too had suffered, and profited by the suffering.

"You better square up with Tough McCarty," he said, failing to read the anguish in Stover's eyes. "You certainly were the limit."

"I hate him!" said Dink bitterly.

"Why?"

"He's a bully."

"Tough McCarty? Not a bit of it."

"He tried to bully me."

"Why didn't you let them in?" said Butsey, putting the part in the middle of his hair with a dripping comb.

"Let them in?"

"Why, what do you think they'd have done to you?"

Stover had never thought of that. After all, what could they have done to him?

"I didn't think—"

"Rats!" said Butsey. "They might have pied you on the bed; but that's nothing if you lie face down and keep your elbows in. That's all you'd have got. Then it would have been over; now you've got to square yourself. Well, brush up and come down to supper, and for the love of Mike smile a little."

Butsey White's sentiments neither consoled nor convinced. Stover was too firmly persuaded of the enormity of his offense and the depth of his ignominy.

In all his life he had never done a more difficult thing than to follow Butsey into the dining room and face the disdainful glances of those from whom he had so lately fled.

He sat in abject mental and physical suffering, his eyes on his plate, tasting nothing of what went into his mouth, chewing mechanically.

Mr. Jenkins, to be affable, asked him how he had enjoyed the day. He mumbled some reply, he never knew what, hearing only the dreadful snicker that ran the table. He refused the dessert and left the table. It had been a nightmare.

He stayed in his room, watching from behind the curtains his fellow beings romping and shrieking over a game of baby-in-the-hat. The bottom had, indeed, dropped out of things—the universe was topsy-turvy. More keenly than in the afternoon he felt the utter hopelessness of his disgrace. If he could only get away—escape from it all. If he only had had five dollars in his pocket he could have reached Trenton and worked his way to some seaport town. He looked at the now ridiculous souvenir toilet set and bitterly thought where the precious dollars had gone—that story, too, would be abroad by the morrow. The whole school would probably rise and jeer at him when he entered chapel the next morning. That night he crept into his bed to the stillness of the black room, to suffer a long hour that first overwhelming anguish that can only be suffered once, that no other suffering can compare to, that is complete, because the knowledge of other suffering has not yet come, and he who suffers suffers alone. Then the imagination came to the rescue. He fell into blissful unconsciousness by a process of consoling half dreams in which he vindicated himself by feats of extraordinary valor, carrying the suffocating Tough Mc-Carty and the Coffee-colored Angel out of burning houses at the risk of his own life, and earning the plaudits of the whole school.

Suddenly a peal of thunder shook the building; he landed all in a heap in the midst of the sunlit floor, rubbing his eyes. Outside, the morning came in with warm embrace; green things stirred against the windowpanes; the flash of a robin's wing cut a swift shadow on the floor and was gone. Below, the horrid clanging of the gong rattled the walls and called on the dead to rise.

Dink gazed at the opposite bed. Butsey, with the covers wound around him, with his knees under his chin, was actually asleep. In great alarm he went over and shook him gently. One eye opened and reproachfully fastened on him.

"I say, the gong—the gong's rung, Mr. White," said Dink.

"The rising gong?"

"Yes, sir."

"Well, when the breakfast gong explodes wake me up."

The eyes shut, but presently reopened and a muffled voice added:

"Pour out water—washbasin—stick my shoes over here."

Dink obeyed, mystified. Then, going to the window, he drank in all the zest and glory of green fields and blue skies with woolly clouds drifting over the tingling air. Joyfully he turned for a plunge in cold water and the unspeakable crockery set met his eye. Then he remembered. A shadow fell across the room; the day went into eclipse. Mechanically, heavily, he dressed, and the fever of yesterday sprang up anew.

Meanwhile, not a sound in the House except down the hall a snore—a glorious, triumphant note. A second time the gong took up its discordant march. Then from the cocoon on the bed a flash of legs and arms sprang out and into the waiting garments. There was a splash in the basin that spattered the water far and near, and Butsey, enveloped in a towel, rushed into his upper garments, flung back his hair with a masterful swooping stroke of the comb, and bolted out of the door, buckling his belt and struggling into a sweater. Down the stairs they went in the midst of floating coats, collars to be buttoned and neckties to be tied; and when the last note of the gong had ended not a place was vacant, though every eye still drooped with drowsiness.

Breakfast over, Dink followed Butsey to their room and, after the more permanent preparations had been attended to, they left for chapel.

The much dreaded breakfast had passed with but one incident; the Coffee-colored Angel, in passing him the sugar, had said in a terrific whisper, "I'll get you to-day. I'll tame you!"

But, being still in a nodding state, his anger was contented with this slight expression. Tough McCarty had given him just one look, but somehow he remembered nothing else. The instinctive hostility he had felt at the first meeting of their eyes rose anew. The Coffee-colored Angel and the White Mountain Canary were but incidents; the enemy, *le sacré* Albion, was Tough McCarty.

He went in the current of boyhood past Foundation House and around the circle toward chapel. For the first time the immensity of the school was before him in the hundreds that, streaming across the campus in thin, dotted lines, swelled into a compact, moving mass at the chapel steps. It was more than an institution; it was a world, the complex, marvelously ordered World of Youth.

Somehow, he did not attract the attention he had expected. His entrance into the pew was attended by no hilarious uprising *en masse*. He found his place in the gallery, between Pebble Stone and Duke Straus, who sleepily asked his name and went off for a supplementary nap on the shoulder of D. Tanner. Stone evidently had heard nothing of his disgrace, or else was too absorbed in a hurried conning of the Latin lesson to make remarks.

Dink lifted his head a little and stole a glance—strange, no one seemed to be paying the slightest attention to him. Somewhat astonished and unutterably relieved, he gazed down at the body of the school marshaled below, at the enormous fifth formers who seemed—and never was that illusion to fade—the most terrifically immense and awesome representatives of manhood he had ever seen. The benches were hard, decidedly so; but he lost himself pleasantly in the vaulted roof, and gazed with respect at the distant pulpit.

The Doctor ascended and swept the school with that glance peculiar to headmasters which convinces each separate boy it is directed at him. Stover felt the impact on his own forehead and dropped his eyes uneasily. When the hymn began he looked curiously among his classmates, located Doc Macnooder and caught the eye of the Tennessee Shad, who winked at him to show him he was still his friend.

Somehow, his awful disgrace seemed to slip from him—the Green House was but a grain in the sand. There were friends, undiscovered friends, in the mass before him, to be won and held. An easier feeling came to him. When the school shuffled out he sought the Tennessee Shad and, holding out his hand said, "Say, you are wonders; and I'm the only living sucker!"

"Dink, you're a real sport," said the Tennessee Shad, pleased; "but we did come it pretty strong. Now, if you want to turn in those shoes—"

"Not on your life!" said Dink. "I deserved it, but—but look out for next year!"

"All right," said the Tennessee Shad with an approving look. "If you do us we'll take you into the firm. Tack on to me, and I'll pilot you to The Roman's."

Following his lanky guide Stover went in the churning, lagging mass across to Memorial Hall, rubbing elbows with the heroes, who stalked majestically in their voluminous bulk, with the coveted Varsity caps riding on the backs of their cropped heads, or being jostled by the freckled imps who ran zigzag, shrieking chases past him.

At the steps they divided, some surging upward and others crowding into the lower corridor.

"Below for us," said the Tennessee Shad, pushing his way forward.

Dink found himself outside of one of the dozen classrooms in a throng that waited hopefully, as other classes waited hopefully every hour of every day, in the hopes of an improbable cut.

"The Roman," said the Tennessee Shad wisely, "is the one master you want to stand in with. Study like the devil the first two weeks; and say, get up on the gerund and the gerundive—they're his pets."

"I will," said Dink.

"You can't bluff him and you can't beat his system," continued the Tennessee Shad. "If you guess, don't hesitate; jump at it. The only thing you can do is to wait for his jokes, and then grab the desk and weep for salvation—it's his one weak spot."

"I will," said Dink.

A cry of dismay went up from the sentinels at the window.

"Oh, rats! Here he comes."

"Oh, peanuts!"

"Oh, melancholy!"

"All in!"

Dink modestly took a seat in the back, at the end of the row of S's where he must sit. On four sides, like prison walls that no convict might hope to scale, the slippery blackboards rose up and bound them in. On a raised stand was the master's pulpit where presently The Roman would come and sit, like the watcher of the galley slaves in *Ben Hur,* with his eagle glance sweeping the desks that, in regimental file, ran back from him.

Outside, through two open windows, was the warm, forbidden month of April, and the gateway to syntax-defying dreams. At this moment Dink's copy of Cæsar's *Gallic Wars* slid onto the floor. He bent down, laboriously collecting the scattered pages and straightened up. Then he glanced at the pulpit. Directly in front of him, his eyes on his eyes, sat the big consular frame of his stage companion of the day before.

Dink gasped in horror; twice his hand went instinctively toward his lip, stopped halfway and dropped. Then his mouth opened, set, and galvanically he rose to his feet, while the room seemed to tip up.

He grasped the desk to keep from slipping, never taking his eyes from the Ciceronian countenance and the twinkling orbits above the slightly twitching lips.

"Dear me," said a low, mocking voice with a curious rising and falling infection, "who's here? Another delegate to this congress of scintillating intelligences?"

"Yes, sir," said Dink in a whisper.

"Quite a valuable addition, I hope. Yes? What is the name?"

"John."

"Well—well?"

"John Humperdink Stover," said Dink with difficulty.

"Ah, yes, Stover: the name is familiar—very familiar," said The Roman, with a twitch to his lip and a sudden jump of the eyebrow. "Haven't we met before?"

Dink, suffocating, nodded. The class, at a loss, turned from one to the other, watching for the cue.

"Well, Stover, come a little nearer. Take the seat between Stone and Straus. Straus will be better able to take his little morning nap. A little embarrassed, Stover? Dear me! I shouldn't have thought that of you. Sit down now and—try to put a little ginger into the class, Stover."

Dink looked down and blushed until it seemed as though his hair would catch on fire. The class, perceiving only that there was a point for laughter, burst into roars.

"There—there," said The Roman, stilling the storm with one finger. "Just a little joke between us two; just a little confidential joke. Now for a bee-ootiful recitation. Splendid spring weather— yesterday was a cut; of course you all took the hour to study conscientiously—eager for knowledge. Fifth and sixth rows go to the board."

While The Roman's modulated accents doled out conjugations and declensions Stover sat without a thought in his head, his hands locked, staring out at the green and yellow necktie that rose on Pebble Stone's collar.

"Oh, Lord! Oh, Lord!" he said at last. "Dished! Spinked! He'll flunk me every day. I certainly am in wrong!"

He raised his eyes at the enthroned Natural Enemy and mentally threw down the gage of battle with a hopeless, despairing feeling of the three years' daily conflict that was to come. For, of course, now there could be no question of The Roman's mortal and unsparing enmity. But after the first paralyzing shock Dink recovered himself. It was war, but the war he loved—the war of wits.

The Roman, having flunked a dozen by this time, had Channing, the Coffee-colored Angel, on his feet, on delicate matters of syntax.

"Top of page, third word, Channing—gerund or gerundive?" said The Roman.

"Gerund, sir."

"Too bad!" said The Roman musically, and on a lower octave repeated, "Too bad! Third line, fifth word—gerund or gerundive?"

"Gerund, sir," said the Coffee-colored Angel with more conviction.

"No luck, Channing, no luck. Tenth line, last word—gerund, Channing, or gerundive?"

"Gerund-ive," said the Coffee-colored Angel hesitatingly.

"Poor Channing, he didn't stick to his system. The laws of probability, Channing—"

"I meant gerund," said the Coffee-colored Angel hastily.

"Dear me! Really, Channing?"

"Yes, sir."

"Positive?"

"Absolutely, sir."

"It *was* the gerundive, Channing."

The Coffee-colored Angel abruptly sat down.

"Don't want to speculate any more, Channing?"

"No, sir."

"No feeling of confidence—no luck today? Try the gerundive tomorrow."

The discouraged began to return from the boards, having writ in water. The Roman, without malice, passed over the rows and, from flunking them individually, mowed them down in sections.

"Anything from the Davis House today? No, no? Anything from the Rouse House combination? Nothing at all? Anything from the Jackson twins? Alas! How about the D's this morning? Davis, Dark, Denton, Deer, Dickson, nothing from the D's. Let's try the F's. Farr, Fenton, Foster, Francis, Finch? Nothing from the F's—nothing from the D F's! Nothing at all?"

Dink burst into laughter, and laughed alone. The Roman stopped. Everyone looked surprised.

"Ah, Stover has been coached—well coached," said The Roman.

"But, Stover, this is not the place to laugh. The D F's are not a joke; they are painful, everyday facts. Well, well, it has been a beautiful recitation in the review—not exceptional, not exceptional at all. Has anyone the advance? Don't all rise at once. Strange what trying weather it is—too sunny, not enough rain—everyone rises exhausted. Will Macnooder kindly lead the massacre?"

Macnooder disdained to rise; one or two faltered and tripped along for brief spaces and then sat down. The Roman, counting his dead, hesitated and called, "Stover."

"Me, sir?" said Dink, too astonished to rise. "Why, I'm unprepared, sir."

"Unprepared?" said The Roman with a wicked smile. "I never thought you would be unprepared, Stover."

The smile decided Stover.

"I'll try, sir," he said.

"Very kind of you, Stover."

Dink rose slowly, put the book on his desk, tightened his belt, buttoned his coat and took up the prosy records of Cæsar. Pebble Stone showed him the place. He straightened up and, glancing at the first line, saw *"Ubi eo ventum est, Cæsar initio orationis . . ."*

"Cæsar," began Dink in a firm voice.

"Excellent!" said The Roman.

"Cæsar, wherever the wind blew him, initiated the orators . . ." Dink continued smoothly, after a rapid glance.

The Roman, from a listless attitude, gripped the desk, pivoted clear on one leg of his chair, staring at the familiar text as though it had suddenly taken on life and begun to crawl about the page.

Dink, resolved not to be bested, gravely and fluently continued to glide on, without pause or hitch, turning syllables into words, building sentences wherever he met an acquaintance. On and on he went, glib and eloquent, weaving out of the tangled text a picture that gradually, freeing itself from the early restraints, painted in vivid detail a spirited conference between Cæsar and the German envoys. The class, amazed, resorted to their books; many of the unprepared, quite convinced, stared at him as though a new rival to the high markers had suddenly appeared.

The Roman, fascinated, never quitted the text, marveling as the tale ran on, leaping adverbs and conjunctions, avoiding whole phrases, undismayed by the rise of sudden, hostile nouns, impressing into service whatever suited it, corrupting or beating down all obstacles.

Once or twice he twitched spasmodically, twice he switched the leg of his chair, murmuring all the while to himself. Finally he rose and, slowly approaching to where Stover stood, glanced incredulously at his book.

"Shall I stop, sir?" said Stover.

"Heaven forbid!"

Stover completed the page with a graphic, rushing account of the athletic exercises of the ancient Germans, and sat down without a smile.

The Roman, back at his post, wiped his eyes with his handkerchief and spoke:

"Very well run, indeed, Stover; excellently well run. Take your breath. Very fluent, very vivid, very persuasive—a trifle free, a trifle —but, on the whole, a very creditable performance. Very! I was sure, whatever you did, Stover, you wouldn't bore us. Now, let us see how the same passage will appeal to a more prosaic, less richly endowed mind."

Then Red Dog rose and unfeelingly brought the scene back to Rome and the deliberations of the Senate.

But this was a detail that did not interest Dink in the least. He had clashed with The Roman and not retreated. He had his first moment of triumph, attested by the admiring glances of the class and the muffled whisper of Straus, saying, "Gee, you're a peach!"

The session ended with a solemn warning from The Roman.

"One word," he said in his deepest tones, "just one word to the wise. We have journeyed together for two whole terms; there is only one more between you and reassignment. Candor compels me to say that you have acquired not even a flunking knowledge." He turned and raked the awed ranks with the sweep of a pivot gun, and then took up again in cutting, chilling, spaced syllables: "I have, in the course of my experience as a teacher, had to deal with imbeciles, had to deal with mere idiots; but for sheer, determined, *monumental* asininity I have never met the equal of this aggregation. I trust this morning's painful, disgraceful, disheartening experience may never, never be repeated. You may go."

And Stover, who had brazenly planned to remain and converse, went swiftly out with the rest, little imagining that he whom he had ranked as a deadly, unforgiving foe sat a long while chuckling over the marvelous route Dink had gone, murmuring gratefully to himself, "Wherever the wind blew him, Cæsar initiated the orators."

VIII

IN THE hallway the Coffee-colored Angel jabbed him with his elbow, muttering, "You laughed at me, you miserable Rinky Dink. I'll fix you for that."

He disappeared swiftly. Before Dink could frame a reply he was surrounded by an admiring chorus. The Tennessee Shad and Macnooder shook hands with ceremony.

"You'll do," said the Tennessee Shad.

"You certainly will!" said Doc Macnooder.

"You've made a hit with Lucius Cassius," said the Tennessee Shad.

Dink shook his head; he knew better.

"You must always recite—always," said Doc Macnooder, from his great knowledge of the nature of masters. "Whether you're prepared or not—recite."

"I will," said Dink.

"And say, Dink," said Macnooder, "keep that outfit we sold you. There'll be more hayseeds in the fall."

Dink had thought of that; he had thought of something else, too, which he craftily hid in his own memory.

"Next fall I'll show them a thing or two," he said gleefully. "I'll make souvenir crockery sets the rage."

The Coffee-colored Angel and the petty annoyances of the Green House forgot, he went with a hitch and a kick, loping along, while his delicately balanced imagination, now soaring above the gloomy descents of the morning, swam joyfully in the realms of future triumphs.

In this abstracted mood he passed Foundation's gloomy portals and Laloo standing in his door gazing down the road, and took the leafy path that led to the Green.

All at once he heard a battle cry and, turning, beheld the Coffee-colored Angel and the White Mountain Canary spring from their concealment and bear down upon him with unmistakable intent. Now, whether in a former existence Dink had been parent to the fox, or whether the purely human instinct was quicker than the reason, before he knew what he had done he had bounded forward and burst for home in full flight, with his heart pumping at his ribs. Easily distancing his pursuers, he arrived at the Green House before it dawned upon him that he had been challenged and run away.

He stopped abruptly with clenched fists, breathing deep.

"Now let them come," he said, turning.

But the Coffee-colored Angel and the White Mountain Canary, having abandoned the hopeless chase, had gone another way.

Angry and ashamed, Dink went to his room, vowing terrific vengeance. He planted himself before the mirror and, doubling up either arm, felt the well-hardened muscles.

"There were two of them, and I didn't have time to think," he said. "I'll fight 'em—any of 'em."

Reassured by the scowling ferocity of his reflected countenance, he turned away. But, passing near the window, he saw the Coffee-colored Angel and the White Mountain Canary come militantly up the stone walk. A moment later their steps sounded on the stairs. He went hastily to the door and shot the key. An instant later the door was tried, and then the contemptuous face of the Coffee-colored Angel loomed through the transom.

"I knew you were yellow the moment I looked at you," he said scornfully. "Pah!"

Dink did not answer. He was all in a whirl. His action in locking the door, so contrary to his heroic resolutions, left him in confusion.

"I wonder if I really am afraid," he said, sitting down all in a heap. The look in the Coffee-colored Angel's eye had brought him an unpleasant creeping sensation in the region of the back.

And yet the Coffee-colored Angel, bone for bone and inch for inch, was just what he was—only he had fled from him, inadvertently, instinctively, it is true, yet feeling the running menace at his back.

"I'm a coward!" he said, staring at the opposite wall. "I must be a coward! If I weren't I would have opened that door."

Now, Dink had never fought a real fight. He had had a few

rough-and-tumble skirmishes, but a fight where you stood up and looked a man in the whites of the eyes, a deliberate, planned-out fight, was outside his knowledge, in the mists of the unknown. And so his imagination—which later should be his strength—recoiled before that unknown as it had recoiled the moment he stepped from the stage to face his new judges; as it had recoiled in the hushed parlor before the closed door of the headmaster's den, and again at the thought of stepping into the batter's box and risking his head against the deadly shoots of Nick Carter, of the Cleve. He had never fought, therefore he was aghast at the fear of being afraid.

"Well, I won't run again," he said desperately. "I'll have it over with—he can only lick me."

But he did run again, and often, despite all his resolves, impelled always by the psychological precedent that he had run before.

The Coffee-colored Angel and the White Mountain Canary made a regular ceremony of it, raising a hue and cry at the sight of him and bursting into derisive laughter after short chases.

Dink was miserable and now thoroughly frightened. He slunk into the solitude of his own company, avoiding the disdainful looks of his Housemates. He knew now he was a coward and should never be anything else. He did not blame Butsey, who scarcely spoke to him. All he thought of was, by roundabout ways, to put off the dreadful hour when either the Coffee-colored Angel or the White Mountain Canary should catch him and beat him to a quivering, senseless pulp.

Then the unexpected happened. One day, cutting across fields to avoid his persecutors, he was suddenly shut off by the White Mountain Canary, who rose from ambush, jeering horribly. Cut off from the Green, Dink returned posthaste up the village, when all at once the Coffee-colored Angel closed in on him. Only one way of escape was open to him, down an alley between two houses. With the Coffee-colored Angel at his heels he dashed ahead, turned the corner of the house and found himself caught in a blind area.

Whereupon he turned on the Coffee-colored Angel and slathered him, drove him hither and thither with terrific blows, knocked him head over heels, caught him by the throat and beat him against a wall, rolled him on the ground and rubbed him in the dust, tore his clothes, blacked his eyes and left him beaten and supinely, passively wallowing.

He walked out on his tiptoes, like a terrier, head erect, his chest out, fists still clenched, tears in his eyes—tears of pride and relief. He had fought a fight, he had received terrific blows and minded them not. He had thrashed the Coffee-colored Angel; he could thrash or take a thrashing from anyone. He had his first thrill, the thrill of conscious rage, comparable only to first love and first sorrow. He had licked the Coffee-colored Angel—he was not a coward!

At this highly auspicious moment the unsuspecting White Mountain Canary perceived the despised object of his chase and, raising a shout, triumphantly bore down down upon him. With a rush he cleared the intervening space and then, catching sight of the new Dink, stopped as though he had been jerked in by a rope.

A few moments later the group on the Green House steps were lazily working out a French translation, which Beekstein, the Secretary of the Department of Education, was reading to them, when suddenly, in the fields opposite, two figures appeared, zigzagging wildly.

"Here comes the Dink again," said Stuffy Brown. "They'll get him this time."

"Who's after him?" said Tough McCarty. "He's a disgrace to the House."

"It's the White Mountain Canary," said Susie Satterly.

"Hello!" said Cheyenne.

"What?"

"I'll be darned—no—yes—dinged if it isn't the Dink chasing the Canary!"

As they sprang up, amazed, Stover dove at the fleeing tormentor, caught him, and the two went down in a heap, thrashing to and fro.

"Well, I'll be jig-swiggered!" said Cheyenne.

"I'll eat my pants!"

"The Dink!"

At this moment the awful wreck of the Coffee-colored Angel limped up. A chorus broke out:

"The Coffee-colored Angel!"

"Shot to pieces!"

"Massacred!"

"Kicked by a horse!"

"What hit you?"

"Dink," said the Coffee-colored Angel, taking a tooth out of his muddy mouth. "I caught him."

Presently they saw Stover arise and loose the battered White Mountain Canary, who broke wildly for shelter.

"Well, anyhow," said the Coffee-colored Angel, "Dink's swallowed the Canary."

"What's he up to now?" said Cheyenne.

They watched him approach the fence, deliberately take off his coat, remove his collar and necktie, tighten his belt and methodically, slowly roll up his sleeves.

"Here he comes," said the Coffee-colored Angel, moving swiftly away. "Why, he's crying!"

Dink came up the path, choking with rage and the knowledge of his own tears, and in front of them all threw down his coat.

"You thought I was afraid, did you? You thought I was a coward!" he sobbed. "Well, I'll show you whether I'm afraid of you, any of you, you big bullies! You big stuff, you, come on!"

And suddenly advancing, he squared off and struck Tough Mc-Carty a wild blow, crash on the nose.

IX

THEY ADJOURNED to a sheltered spot back of the stump willows and chose a bare space of soft, green turf. At their sides the brook ran splashing over the cool stones.

"Who'll be Dink's second?" said Cheyenne Baxter, the referee.

There was an embarrassed pause.

"Go on, any of you," said Tough McCarty generously.

"I'll be," said the Coffee-colored Angel. "He licked me square." He stepped over and held out his hand.

"I don't want you—I don't want your hand!" said Dink with a scream. "I don't want any second; I won't have any! I hate you—I hate the whole lot of you!"

Cheyenne Baxter consulted with Tough McCarty and came over.

"Say, Dink," he said kindly, "Tough doesn't want to fight you now; it isn't fair. He'll give you a fight any time you want—when you're fresh."

"I don't want to wait," cried Stover, blubbering despite himself. "I'll fight him now. I'll show him if I'm afraid, the big bully!"

"What rounds do you want?" said Cheyenne, seeing it was wisest not to interfere.

"I don't want any rounds," cried Dink wildly. "I want to get at him, the great, big mucker!"

Cheyenne went over to Tough, who stood apart, looking very uncomfortable.

"Better go on, Tough. Don't hurt the little varmint any more than you have to."

It was a strange fight. They stood around in silence, rather frightened at Stover's frenzy. Tough McCarty, overtopping his antagonist by four good inches, stood on the defensive, seeking only to ward off the storm of frantic blows that rained on him. For

238

Dink cared not a whit what happened to him or how he exposed himself.

Blinded by rage, crying from sheer excess of emotion, shrieking out inarticulate denunciations, he flung himself on McCarty with the recklessness of a mad dervish, crying, "You thought I was a coward—darn you! You great, fat slob! You thought I was afraid of a licking, did you? I'll show you. Lick me now if you can, you big brute! Lick me every day! I'm not afraid of you!"

"Confound the lunatic!" said Tough McCarty, receiving a solid thump in the ribs. "I can't stand here, getting pummeled all day. Got to hit him—ouch!"

Dink, in his frantic rush, throwing himself under his enemy's guard, almost bore him to the ground by the shock of his on-slaught. McCarty, angrily brushing the blood from his already out-raged nose with the cuff of his sleeve, shook himself like an angry bear and, catching Stover with a straight-arm blow, sent him roll-ing on the turf.

Back again and again came Stover, hurling himself wildly onto the scientific fists that sent him reeling back. The green arms of the trees, the gray faces of the onlookers, the blue of the tilting sky rushed into the reeling earth, confounded together. He no longer saw the being he was fighting, a white film slipped over everything, and then all went out in blank unconsciousness.

When he opened his eyes again he was on his back, looking up through the willows at a puffy cloud that turned against the blue. At his side the brook went softly, singing in whispers the note that stirred the leaves.

Something wet fell on his face and trickled uncomfortably down his neck. Someone was applying a dripping cloth.

"Coming to?" said Cheyenne Baxter.

Then Dink remembered.

"Where is he?" he cried, trying to spring up. "Fight him—fight him to the end!"

A strong hand pressed him down.

"There, there, you fire-eater!" said Cheyenne. "Go easy. You've had enough blood for one afternoon. Lie back. Shut your eyes."

He heard whispering and the sound of voices going, and lost consciousness again.

When he saw the face of the day once more he was alone with

Cheyenne, who was kneeling by his side, smiling as he watched him.

"Better now?"

"I'm all right."

"Let me carry you."

"I can stand."

Cheyenne's good right arm caught him as he tottered and held him.

"I'm all right," said Dink gruffly.

Aided by Cheyenne, he went weakly back to the Green. At the steps Tough McCarty sprang up and advanced with outstretched hand, saying, "Put her here, Dink; you're dead game!"

Stover put his hand behind his back.

"I don't want to shake hands," he said, flushing and gazing at Tough McCarty until the pupils of his eyes seemed to dwindle, "with you or any of you. I hate you all; you're a gang of muckers. I'll fight you now: I'll fight you tomorrow. You're too big for me now, but I'll lick you—I'll lick you next year—you, Tough Mc-Carty—or the year after that; you see if I don't!"

Tough McCarty stood back, rightfully offended. Cheyenne led Dink up to his room and lectured him.

"Now, young bantam, listen to me. You've shown your colors and we respect you for it. But you can't fight your way into being liked—put that in your pipe and smoke it. You've got to keep a civil tongue in your head and quit thinking this place was built for your special benefit. *Savez?* You've got to win your way if you want to be one of us. Now, when you get your head clear, go down and apologize to Tough McCarty and the Angel, like a man."

The advice, which a day later would have been gratefully received, came inopportunely for Dink's overwrought nerves. He gave an angry answer—he did not want to be friends—he hated them all—he would never apologize—never.

When Butsey White came with friendly offers he cut him short.

"Don't *you* come rubbering around now," he said scornfully. "You went back on me. You thought I was afraid. I'll do without your friendship now."

When a calmer view had come to him he regretted what he had done. He eliminated Tough McCarty—that was a feud of the in-stincts—but it certainly had been white of the Coffee-colored Angel to offer to be his second; Cheyenne was every inch a leader, and Butsey really had been justified. Unfortunately, his repentance came too late; the damage had been done. Only one thing could right him—an apology to the assembled House; but as the courage to apologize is the last virtue to be acquired—if it ever is acquired —Dink in his pride would rather have chopped off his hand than admit his error. They had misjudged him; they would have to come to him. The breach, once made, widened rapidly—due, principally, to Dink's own morbid pride. Some of the things he did were simply ridiculous and some were flagrantly impudent.

He was one against eight—but one who had learned his strength, who feared no longer the experiences he knew. He stood ready to back his acts of belligerency with his fists against anyone—except, of course, Butsey White; for roommates do not fight unless they love one another.

He had always in him the spirit of the rebel. To be forbid a thing, with him, was to do it instantly. He refused all the service a Freshman should do. At table he took a malignant delight in demanding loudly second and third helps of the abhorrent prunes— long after he had come to feel the universal antagonism. He would not wake Butsey in the morning, fill his basin or arrange his shoes. He would run no errands. He refused to say sir or doff his hat to his superiors in the morning; and, being better supplied with money, he took particular pleasure in entering the House with boxes of jiggers or tins of potted meats and a bottle of root beer, with which he openly gorged himself at night, while Butsey squirmed over the unappetizing pages of the *Gallic Wars*.

Finally, the blow came. Cheyenne Baxter, as president of the House, appeared one evening and hurled on him the ban of excommunication—from that hour he was to be put in Coventry.

From that moment no one spoke to him or by the slightest look noticed his existence. Dink at first attempted to laugh at this exile.

At every opportunity he joined the group on the steps. No one addressed him. If he spoke no one answered. At table the Coffee-colored Angel no longer asked him to pass his plate, but passed it around the other way. He went out in the evenings and placed his cap in line with the other boys', but the ball never went into his hat. If he stood, hoping to be hit, no one seemed to notice that he was standing there. For several days he sought to brazen it out with a miserable, sinking feeling, and then he gave it up. He had thought he cared nothing for the company of his Housemates—he soon discovered his error and recognized his offending. But apology was now out of the question. He was a pariah, a leper, and so must continue—a thing to be shunned.

The awful loneliness of his punishment threw him on his own resources. At night he lay in his bed and heard Butsey steal out to a midnight spread behind closed doors, or to join a band that, risking the sudden creak of a treacherous step, went down the stairs and out to wend their way with other sweltering bands across the moonlit ways, through Negro settlements, where frantic dogs bayed at the sticks they rattled over the picket fences, to the banks of the canal for a cooling frolic in the none too fragrant waters.

In the morning he could not join the group that congregated to listen to Beekstein—Secretary of Education—straighten out the involved syntax or track an elusive x to its secret lair. In the afternoon he could not practice on the diamond with them, learning the trick of holding elusive flies or teaching himself to face thunderous outshoots at the plate.

This enforced seclusion had one good result: left to his own devices his recitations improved tremendously, though this was scant consolation.

He kept his own company proudly, reading long hours into the land of Dumas and Victor Hugo; straying up to the Varsity diamond, where he cast himself forlornly on the grass, apart from the groups, to watch Charley De Soto dash around the bases, and wonderful Jo Brown on third base scrape up the grounders and shoot them to first.

He was too proud to seek other friends, for that meant confession. Besides, his own classmates were all busy on their own diamonds, working for the success of their own House nines.

Only when there was a Varsity game and he was swallowed up in the indiscriminate mass that whooped and cheered back of first, thrilling at a sudden crisis, did he forget himself a little and feel a part of the great system. Once when, in a game with the Princeton Freshmen, Jo Brown cleared the bases with a sizzling three-bagger, a fourth former he didn't know thumped him ecstatically on the back and he thrilled with gratitude.

But the rest was loneliness, ever recurrent loneliness, day in and day out. His only friends were Charley De Soto and Butcher Stevens at first, whom he could watch and understand—feeling, also, the fierce spirit of battle cooped up and forbidden within him.

One night in the second week of June, when Butsey White had gone to a festal spread in Cheyenne Baxter's rooms, Dink sat cheerlessly over the Latin page, seeing neither gerund nor gerundive.

The windows were open to the multiplied chorus of distant frogs and the drone of nearby insects. The lamp was hot, his clothes steamed on his back. He thought of the root beer and sarsaparilla being consumed down the hall and, going to the closet, consulted his own store of comforting things.

But to feast alone was no longer a feast at all. He went to the window and sniffed the warm air, trying to penetrate the outer darkness. Then, balancing carefully, he let himself out and, dropping on the yielding earth, went hungrily up to the campus.

He had never been on the Circle before at night, with all the lights about him. It gave him a strange, breathless feeling. He sat down, hugging his knees, in the center of the Circle, where he could command the blazing windows of the Houses and the long, lighted ranks of the Upper, where the fourth formers were singing on the Esplanade. The chapel at his back was only a shadow; Memorial Hall, a cloud hung lower than the rest.

From his position of vantage he could hear scraps of conversation through the open windows, and see dark figures flitting before the mellow lamps. The fellowship in the Houses, the good times, the feeling of home that hung about each room came to him with acute poignancy as he sat there, vastly alone. In the whole school he had made not a friend. He had done nothing; no one knew him. No one cared. He had blundered from the first. He saw his errors now—only too plainly—but they were beyond retrieving.

There was only a week more and then it would be over. He would never come back. What was the use? And yet, as he sat there outside the life and lights of it all, he regretted, bitterly regretted, that it must be so. He felt the tug at his heartstrings. It was something to win a place in such a school, to have the others look up to you, to have the youngsters turn and follow you as you passed, as they did with Charley De Soto or Flash Condit or Turkey Reiter or a dozen of others. Instead, he would drop out of the ranks, and who would notice it? A few who would make a good story out of that miserable game of baseball. A few who would speak of him as the freshest of the fresh, the fellow who had to be put in Coventry —if, indeed, any one would remember Dink Stover, the fellow who hadn't made good.

The bell clanged out the summons to bed for the Houses. One by one the windows dropped back into the night; only the Upper remained ablaze.

At this moment he heard somewhere in the dark near him the sound of scampering feet. The next moment a small boy tripped over his legs and went sprawling.

"What in the name of Willie Keeler!" said a shrill voice. "Is that a master or a human being?"

"Hello!" said Stover gruffly, to put down the lump that had risen in his throat. "Who are you."

"Me? Shall we tell our real names?" said the voice approaching and at once bursting out into an elfish chant:

> *Wow, wow! Wow, wow, wow!*
> *Oh, me father's name was Finnegan,*
> *Me mother's name was Kate,*
> *Me ninety-nine relations*
> *To you I'll now relate.*

"Oh, you're Dennis de Brian de Boru Finnegan, are you?" said Dink, laughing as he dashed his cuff across his eyes. "The kid that wrote the baseball story."

"Sir, you do me honor," said Finnegan. "Who are you?"

"I'm Stover."

"The Dink?"

"Yes, the Dink."

"The cuss that translates at sight?"

"You've heard of it?"

"Cracky, yes! They say The Roman was knocked clean off his pins, first time in his life. I say—"

"What?"

"Then you're the fellow down in the Green, aren't you?"

"Yes," said Dink, thinking only of the ban of excommunication.

"Why, you're a regular cross-sawed, triple-hammered, mule-kick, beef-fed, rarin'-tearin' John L. Sullivan, ain't you?" said the exponent of the double adjective in rapid admiration.

"What do you mean?"

"Why, you're the cuss that smeared the Angel, swallowed the Canary, and bumped Tough McCarty, all at once."

"Oh, yes."

"My dear boy, permit me—you're it, you're the real thing."

Dink, with a feeling of wonder, shook hands, saying, "Well, they don't think so much of it at the Green."

"Anything wrong?"

"Nothing much."

Finnegan, perceiving the ground was shaky, switched.

"I say, you want to get into the Kennedy next year; we've got the A No. 1 crowd there. I'm there, the Tennessee Shad, the Gutter Pup—he's the president of the Sporting Club, you know; prizefights and all that sort of thing—and King Lentz and the Waladoo Bird, the finest guards Lawrenceville ever had. And say, you'n' I and the Tennessee Shad could strike up a combine and get out a ripsnorting, muzzle-off, all-the-news, sporting-expert, battle-cry-of-freedom newspaper that would put the *Lawrence* out of biz. I say, you must get in the Kennedy."

"I'm not coming back."

"What!"

"I guess my par-ticular style of talent isn't suited around here."

"What's wrong?"

"Well, everything."

"I say, Dink, confide in me!"

Stover, at that moment, in his loneliness, would have confided in anyone, especially the first human being who had given him a thrill of conscious pride.

"It's just this, youngster," he said, wondering how to begin. "They don't like me."

"You like the school, don't you?" said Finnegan in alarm.

Dink had never had the question put to him before. He was silent and his look went swiftly over to the coveted House of Lords. He drew a long breath.

"You bet I do. I love it!"

"What then?"

"I started wrong; didn't understand the game, I guess. They've put me in Coventry."

"You must have been pretty fresh."

"What!"

"Oh, don't mind me," said Dennis cheerfully. "I'm fresher than you ever thought of being. I was the freshest bit of verdure, as the poet says, that ever greened the place. I'm the freshest still. But I'm different. I'm under six inches—that's the cinch of it."

"Yes, I was fresh," said Dink, intensely relieved.

"You're always fresh if you're any good, the first term," said Finnegan. "Don't mind that. Next year you'll be an old boy, and then they'll follow you around for sugar."

"I hadn't thought of that," said Dink slowly.

"Keep a-thinking. I'm off now. Ta-ta! Got to slink in Fatty Harris' room before The Roman makes his rounds. Proud to have met you. *Au revoir!*"

Dink sat a long while thinking, and a lighter mood was on him. After all, he was not a blank. Someone had recognized him; someone had taken his hand in admiration. He rose and slowly made his way toward the singers on the Esplanade, and by the edge of the road camped under the shadows of an apple tree and leaned his back against the trunk.

The groups of the Esplanade stood out in cut outlines against the warm windows of the reading room. Above, the open windows were tenanted by boys who pillowed their heads on one another and sent their treble or bass notes down to swell the volume below.

Led by a tenor voice that soared clear and true above the rest came the melody to Stover huddled under the apple tree:

> *At evening, when twilight is falling*
> *And the birds to their nests are all gone,*
> *We'll gather around in the gloaming,*
> *And mingle our voices in song.*
> *Yes, in song.*
> *The bright stars are shining above us,*

Keeping their watch and ward.
We'll sing the old songs that we love, boys.
Out on the Esplanade.

Stover listened, pressing his knuckles to his lips, raised out of himself by the accord of voices and the lingering note of melancholy that was in the hour, the note of the dividing of the ways.

Again in deeper accents a song arose:

We sing the campus, green and fair.
  We sing the 'leven and nine
Who battle for the old school there
  An guard the base and line.
No cause for fear when they appear
  And the school flag floats above our head.
When the game begins 'tis Lawrence wins,
  While we cheer the Black and Red.
When the game begins 'tis Lawrence wins,
  While we cheer the Black and Red.

The song ended in lingering accents. Dink shut his eyes, clenching his fists, seeing wonderful days when the school should gather to cheer him, too, and lay its trust in him.

Suddenly near him in the road came the crunching sound of footsteps, and a voice said, "Is that you, Bill?"

"Yes."

"Bill, I wanted to say a word to you."

"Well?"

"We've only got a few days more in the old place. I don't want to go out with any hard feelings for anybody, do you?"

"No."

"Let's call it off! Shake hands."

Stover listened breathless, hearing little more, understanding only that a feud had ceased, that two enemies on the verge of the long parting had held each other's hands, slapped each other's backs with crude, embarrassed emotion, for the sake of the memories that lived in the shadow of a name. And something like a lump rose again in Dink's throat. He no longer thought of his loneliness. He felt in him the longing to live as they had lived through the glorious years, to know the touch of a friend's arm about his shoulders, and to leave a name to stand with the names that were going out.

He raised his fists grotesquely, unconsciously, and swore an oath:

"No, I won't give up; I'll never give up. I'll come back. I'll fight it out!" he said almost aloud. "I'll make 'em like me. I'll make 'em proud of me."

X

My father sent me here to Lawrenceville,
And resolved that for college I'd prepare;
And so I settled down
In this ancient little town,
About five miles away from anywhere.

Five miles away from anywhere, my boys,
Where old Lawrenceville evermore shall stand.
For has she not stood since the time of the flood.
About five miles away from anywhere?

THE SCHOOL was returning after the long summer vacation, rollicking back over the dusty, Trenton highway, cheering and singing as they came.

Jimmy, on the stage, was swallowed up in the mass of exultant boyhood that clustered on the top like bees on a comb of honey, and clung to step and strap. Inside, those who had failed of place stuck long legs out of the windows, and from either side beat the time of the choruses.

"Next verse!" shouted Doc Macnooder as leader of the orchestra.

The First Form then I gayly entered,
And did so well, I do declare,
When they looked my record o'er
All the masters cried "Encore!"
About five miles away from anywhere.

"Chorus!" cried Macnooder. "Here, you legs, keep together! You're spoiling the effect."

Dink Stover sat quietly on the second seat, joining in the singing, but without the rollicking abandon of the others. He had shot up amazingly during the vacation and taken on some weight, but the change was most marked in his face. The roundness was gone and with it the cherubic smile. The oval had lengthened, the mouth was straighter, more determined, and in the quiet set of eyes was something of the mental suffering of the last months. He had returned, wondering a little what would be his greeting. The first person he had met was the Coffee-colored Angel, who shook hands with him, pounded him on the back and called him "Good old Dink." He understood—the ban was lifted. But the lesson had been a rude one; he did not intend to presume. So he sat, an observer rather than a participant, not yet free of that timidity which, once imposed, is so difficult to shake off.

The stage, which was necessarily making slow progress, halted at the first hill with a sudden rebellion on the part of the long-suffering horses.

"All out!" shouted Macnooder.

In a jiffy every boy was on the ground.

"All push!"

The stage, propelled by dozens of vigorous hands, went up the hill on a run.

"Same places!"

"All ready?"

"Let her go!"

Mamie Reilly, being discovered on the roof and selfishly claimed below, was thrust kicking and wriggling over the side and into the ready hands at the window.

"All ready, orchestra?" said Macnooder.

"Aye, aye, sir."

"All legs in the air!"

"Aye, me Lord!"

"One, two, three!"

> *And then the Second Form received me,*
> *Where I displayed such genius rare,*
> *That they begged me to refrain,*
> *It was going to my brain.*
> *About five miles away from anywhere!*

Meanwhile, at the approach of the astounding coach, which looked like a drunken centipede, the farmers stopped their plows or came to the thresholds, shading their eyes; while the cattle in the fields put up their tails and bolted, flinging out their heels, amid triumphant cheers from the students.

All the while, the bulk of the school in two-seaters, and three-seaters, the fifth formers, the new Lords of Creation, in buggies specially retained, went swirling by exchanging joyful greetings.

"Oh you, Doc Macnooder!"

"Why, Gutter Pup! You old son-of-a-gun!"

"Look at the Coffee-colored Angel!"

"Where's Lovely Mead?"

"Coming behind."

"Hello, Skinny."

"Why, you Fat Boy!"

"See you later."

"Meet me at the Jigger Shop."

"There's Stuffy!"

"Hello, Stuffy! Look this way!"

"Look at the Davis House bunch!"

"Whose legs are those?"

> Hallegenoo, nack, nack!
> Hallegenoo, nack, nack!
> Hooray! Hooray!
> Lawrenceville!

"Next verse," shouted Doc Macnooder. "Legs at attention. More action there! La-da-da-dee! One, two, three!"

> In course of time, I reached the Third Form,
> But was caught in examination's snare.
> Reassignment played its part,
> And it almost broke my heart,
> About five miles away from anywhere.

"What house are you in?" said the Coffee-colored Angel to Stover, between breaths.

"Kennedy."

"The Roman, eh?"

"Yes, he reached out and nabbed me," said Stover, who was persuaded that his new assignment was a special mark of malignant interest.

"Who are you rooming with?"

"The Tennessee Shad."

"Well, you'll be a warm bunch!"

A shout burst out from the back of the coach.

"A race, a race!"

"Here come the Tennessee Shad and Brian de Boru."

"Turn out, Jimmy!"

"Give 'em room!"

"Go it, Dennis!"

"Go it, Shad!"

Two runabouts came up at a gallop, neck and neck, four boys in each, the Tennessee Shad standing at the reins in one, Dennis de Brian de Boru Finnegan in the other, each firmly clutched about the waist by the boy on whose knees he jolted and jostled.

"Push on the reins!"

"Home run, Dennis!"

"Swim out, you Shad!"

"Pass him, Dennis! Pass him!"

"Shad wins!"

"Look at his form, will you!"

"Oh, you jockey!"

"Shad wins!"

"Hurrah!"

"Hurray!"

"Hurroo!"

But at this moment, when it seemed as though the race was to go to the Tennessee Shad's nag, which had that superiority which one sacrificial horse in a Spanish bullfight ring has over another, Dennis de Brian de Boru suddenly produced the remnants of a bag of cream puffs and, by means of three well-directed squashing shots on the rear quarters of his coal-black steed, plunged ahead and won the road, amid terrific cheering.

"Dennis forever!"

"Oh, you, Brian de Boru!"

"Get an éclair, Shad!"

"Get an omelet!"

"Get a tomato!"

"Get out and push!"

The racers disappeared in mingled clouds of dust.

Macnooder, whirling around like a dervish on the stage top,

conducted the next verse. Suddenly another shout went up.

"Here comes Charley De Soto and Flash Condit."

"Three cheers for the football team!"

"How are you, Charlie?"

"Flash, old boy!"

"What do you weigh?"

"Pretty fit?"

"Too bad you can't run, Flash!"

"What'll we do to Andover?"

De Soto and Condit passed, acknowledging the salutations with joyful yelps.

"Give 'em the Fifty-six to Nothing, boys," shouted Macnooder. "All you tenor legs get into this. Oom-pah! Oom-pah! Oom-pah! One, two, three!"

> *There is a game called football,*
> *And that's the game for me.*
> *And Lawrenceville can play it,*
> *As you will shortly see.*
> *She goes to all the schools about,*
> *And with them wipes the ground.*
> *For it's fifty-six to nothing, boys,*
> *When Lawrenceville's around.*
>
> *She has a gallant rush-line*
> *That wears the Red and Black.*
> *Each man can carry the ball through*
> *With six men on his back.*
> *They carry it through the middle*
> *And then they touch it down.*
> *For it's fifty-six to nothing, boys,*
> *When Lawrenceville's around.*

Little by little Stover was drawn into the spirit of the song. He forgot his aloofness, he felt one of them, thrilling with the spirit of the coming football season.

"Gee, it's great to be back," he found himself saying to Butcher Stevens next to him.

"You bet it is!"

"Charley De Soto looks fit, doesn't he?"

"He's eight pounds heavier, Doc tells me."

"By George, that's fine!"

They stopped to sing the third verse.

"It won't be any fifty-six to nothing when Andover comes around," said Butcher gruffly.

"We've got to hustle?" asked Stover respectfully of the Varsity left tackle.

"We certainly have!"

"What's the prospects?"

"Behind the line, corking. It's the line's the trouble—no weight."

"There may be some new material."

"That's so." Stevens looked him over with an appraising eye. "Played the game?"

"No, but I'm going to."

"What do you strip at?"

"Why, about 140—138."

"Light."

"I thought I might try for the second eleven."

"Perhaps. Better learn the game, though, with your House team."

Hearing them talk football the crowd eagerly began to ask questions.

"Who's out for center?"

"Will they move Tough McCarty out to end?"

"Naw, he's too heavy."

"I'd play him at center, and stick the Waladoo Bird in at tackle."

"You would, would you? Shows what you know about it."

"Butcher, you'll be in at tackle, won't you?"

"Hope so," said Stevens laconically.

Stover, who had entered the observant stage of his development, noted the laconic, quiet answer and stored it away for classification and meditation among the many other details that his new attitude of watchful analysis was heaping up.

"There's the water tower! I see the water tower!" cried a voice.

"I see the Cleve!"

"All up!"

"Long cheer for the school!"

"All together!"

"Rip her out!"

They gave a cheer and then two more.

"Now, fellows," said Doc Macnooder shrilly, as master of ceremonies, "we want to pull this off in fine shape. We're going to drive around the Circle. And I want this orchestra to keep together. Whose legs are those with the canon-cracker socks?"

"Beekstein's," cried several voices from inside.

"Well, he's rotten. He gums the whole show. Now, get together, fellows, will you?"

"We will!"

As they turned to enter the campus the voice of the master spoke, clanging its inexorable note from the old Gym. Instantly a shout broke out:

"Hang the old thing!"

"Drown it!"

"Down with the Gym bell!"

"Murder!"

"Oh, Melancholy!"

"Silence!" cried the bandmaster. "Give 'em 'The Gym Bell'— all ready below! La-da-da-dee!"

"Too high!"

"La-da-da-*dum*. Slow and melancholy. One, two, three!"

> *When the shades of night are falling*
> *Round our campus, green and fair,*
> *All the drowsy sons of Lawrence*
> *To their couches then repair.*
> *Soon the slumber god has bound them*
> *With his spell of magic power,*
> *And he holds them thus enchanted*
> *Till the early morning hour.*

"Up legs and at 'em now, Rip her out—chorus!"

> *Till awakened*
> *By the clanging*
> *And the banging*
> *And the whanging*
> *From the cupola o'erhanging,*
> *Of that ancient Gym bell!*

Cheered by the new fifth formers, who came laughing to the windows to hail them, the stage went gloriously around the Circle and came to a stop.

"Here we are back at the same old grind," said Butcher Stevens.

"Frightful, isn't it?" said Stover; and the rest made answer:

"Back at the grindstone!"

"Hard luck!"

"We're all slaves!"

"Nothing to eat!"

"Nothing to do!"

"Stuck in a mudhole!"

XI

AT THE KENNEDY steps The Roman was waiting for him. Stover shook hands or, rather, allowed The Roman to pump him, as was the custom.

"Why, dear me—dear me—this is actually Stover!" said The Roman. "Well, well! How you have grown—shouldn't have known you. Had a pleasant vacation? Yes? Glad to have you in the Kennedy. It's a good House—good boys—manly, self-reliant, purposeful. You'll like 'em."

The Roman released Stover's hand, which had grown limp in the process, and said with a twinkle to his quick little eyes, "Don't put too much ginger into them, Stover."

This remark confirmed Stover's darkest suspicions.

"I'll scatter a little ginger around all right," he said under his breath, as he climbed the stairs to his room. "He thinks he has the laugh on me, does he? Well, we'll see who laughs last!"

On the third floor the Tennessee Shad and Dennis de Brian de Boru Finnegan, from their respective trunks, were volubly debating the merits of Finnegan's victory—the Tennessee Shad claiming that the external application of cream puffs was equivalent to doping and invalidated the result.

"Hello!" said Dink.

"Why, it's my honorable roommate," said the Tennessee Shad, emerging with a load of flannels.

"It's the Dink himself," said Dennis, gamboling up. "Welcome to our city!"

"I hear I'm rooming with you," said Stover, shaking hands with the Shad.

"You certainly are, my bounding boy."

"Where's the room?"

"Straight ahead, turret room, finest on the campus, swept by ocean breezes and all that sort of thing."

"Why, Dink," said Dennis de Brian de Boru in affectionate oc-
taves, "you old, slab-sided, knock-kneed, baby-cheeked, wall-eyed,
battling Dink. You've grown ee-normously."

"How's your muscle?" said the Tennessee Shad, with an ulterior
motive.

"Feel it," said Stover, who had consecrated the summer to the
same.

"Hard as a goat," said Dennis after an admiring whistle. "All
nice little cast-iron, jerky bunches, ready and willing. Been in
training, Dink?"

"Yes, just so."

"Feels sort of soft to me," said the Tennessee Shad pensively.

"Oh, it does?"

"Question: What can you do with it? Lift a trunk as heavy as
this?"

"Huh!" said Stover, bending down. "Where do you want it?"

"Gee! I do believe he can carry it almost to the room," said the
Tennessee Shad, whose theory of life was to admire others into
doing his work for him.

Stover bore it proudly on his shoulders and set it down. Dennis,
planting himself arms akimbo, surveyed him with melancholy disapproval.

"Too bad, Dink! I had expected better things from you. You're
still green, Dink. Been too much with the cows and chickens.
Don't do it; don't do it!"

Stover glanced at the Tennessee Shad, who, satisfied, had curled
himself up on the bed, to rest himself after the exertion of walking.

"I guess I am still a sucker," he said, scratching his head with a
foolish grin. "I'll not be so easy next time."

"Never mind, Dink," said Dennis comfortingly. "Your education's been neglected, but I'm here. Remember that, Dennis is
here, ready and willing."

Presently the Gutter Pup and Lovely Mead came tumbling in,
and then the lumbering proportions of P. Lentz, King of the Kennedy, crowded through the doorway, and the conversation continued in rapid crossfire.

"Who's seen the Waladoo Bird?"

"Jock Hasbrouck's dropped into the third form."

"What do you think of the electric lights they've given us?"

"They've stuck an arc light in the Circle, too."

"We'll fix that."

"How's the new material, King?"

"Rotten!"

"Think we've a chance for the House championship?"

"A fine chance—to finish last."

"Say, who do you think they've stuck us with?"

"Who?"

"Beekstein."

"Suffering Moses!"

"Never mind. We've got the Dink."

"What's he do?"

"He's the champion truckman—carry your trunk for you any-where you want."

Dink, thus brought unwillingly into the conversation, blushed a warm red.

"Truckman?" said P. Lentz, mystified.

"Champion," said Finnegan. "The mysterious champion truck-man of Broad Street Station, Philadelphia. Stand up, Dink, my man, and twitch your muscles."

Stover squirmed uneasily on his chair. There was no malice in the teasing, and yet he was at a loss how to turn it.

The Gutter Pup, as president of the Sporting Club and chief authority on the life and works of the late Marquis of Queens-berry, examined the embarrassed Stover, running professional fingers over his legs and arms.

"You're the fellow who tried to fight the whole Green House aren't you?" he said, immensely interested.

"Why, yes."

"Good nerve," said the Gutter Pup. "You've got something the style of Beans Middleton, who stood up to me for ten rounds in the days of the old Seventy-second Street gang. I'll train you up some time. You'd do well with the crouching style—good reach, quick on the trigger and all that sort of thing. Like fighting?"

"Why, I—I don't know," said Stover helplessly, unable to make out whether the Gutter Pup spoke in jest.

"Modest and brave!" said the irrepressible Finnegan.

The conversation drifted away. Stover, with a sigh of relief, obliterated himself in a corner, feeling immense distances between himself and the laughing group that continued to exchange rapid banter.

"Dennis, they tell me you're fresher than ever."

"Sir, you compliment me."

"Say, Boru, have they put you on the bottle yet?"

"Not yet, Lovely. Waiting for you to drop it."

It was not particularly brilliant, but it was good-natured, and there was a certain trick to it that he had lost in the long weeks of Coventry.

Presently the group departed to take the keen edge off the approaching luncheon pangs by a trip to the Jigger Shop, the center of social life.

"Coming, Dink?" said the Gutter Pup.

"I—I'll be over a little later," said Stover, who did and did not want to go.

Left alone, half angry at his own enforced aloofness, and yet desiring solitude, Stover stood among the litter of boxes and gaping trunks and surveyed the four bare walls that spelled for him the word home.

"It's a bully room—bully," he said to himself with a tender feeling of possession. "The Shad's a bully fellow—bully! Dennis is a corker! I'm going to make good; see if I don't! But I'm going slow. They've got to come to me. I won't break in until they want me. Gee! What a peach of a room!"

He went to the window and looked out at the whole panorama of the school that ran beneath him, from the long, rakish lines of the Upper, by Memorial Hall, to the chapel and the circle of Houses that ended at the rear with the Dickinson. Below, boys were streaking across the green depths like water bugs over limpid surfaces, or hallooing joyfully from window to terrace, greeting one another with bearlike hugs, tumbling about in frolicking heaps. He was on the mountain, they on the plain. His was the imaginative perspective and the troubled vision of one who finds a strange city at his feet.

"It's all there," he said lamely, confused by his own impressions. "All of it."

"Homesick?" said a thin voice behind him.

He turned to find Finnegan eyeing him uncertainly.

"Why, you wild Irishman," Dink said, surprised. "Thought

you'd gone with the crowd. Hello, what's up now?"

Finnegan, with an air of great mystery, locked the door, extracted the key and, returning, enthroned himself on a chair which he had previously planted defiantly on a trunk.

"That's so you can't throw me out."

"Well?"

"I'm going to be fresh as paint."

"You are?" said Stover, mystified and amused.

"Fact," said Finnegan, who, having crossed his legs, plunged his hands into his pockets and cocked one eye, said impressively, "Dink, you're wrong."

"I am—am I?"

"But never mind; I'm here. Dennis de Brian de Boru Finnegan —ready and willing."

"Irishman, I do believe you're embarrassed," said Stover, surprised.

"I'm not," said Finnegan indignantly. "Only—only, I want to be impressive. Dink, you're getting in wrong again."

"What in thunder—?"

"You are, Dink, you are. But don't worry; I'm here. In the first place, you can't forget what everyone else has forgotten."

"Forget what?"

"The late unpleasantness," said Finnegan, with an expelling wave of his hand. "That's over, spiked, dished, set back, covered up, cobwebbed, no flowers and no tombstone."

"I know."

"No, you don't—that's just it. You've got it on your mind— brooding and all that sort of thing."

Stover sat down and stared at the Lilliputian philosopher.

"Well, I like your nerve!"

"Don't—don't start in like that," said Finnegan, rolling up his sleeves over his funny, thin forearms, "'cause I shall have to thrash you."

"Well, go on," said Stover suddenly.

"You're not in Coventry—you never have been. You're one of us," said Dennis glibly. "*But*—I repeat *But*—you can't be one of us if you don't believe in your own noodle that you are one of us! Get that? That's deep—no charge, always glad to oblige a customer."

"Keep on," said Stover, leaning back.

"With your kind permission, directly. It's all in this—you haven't got the trick."

"The trick?"

"The trick of conversation. That's not just it. The trick of answering back. Aha, that's better! Scratch out first sentiment. Change signals!"

"There's something in that," said Stover, genuinely amazed.

"You blush."

"What?"

"The word was blush," said Finnegan firmly. "I saw you—Finnegan saw you and grieved. And why? Because you didn't have the trick of answering back."

"Dennis de Brian de Boru Finnegan," said Stover slowly, "I believe you are a wholehearted little cuss. Also, you're not so far off, either. Now, since this is a serious conversation, this is where I stand: I went through Hades last spring—I deserved it and it's done me good. I've come back to make good. *Savez?* And that's a serious thing, too. Now if you have one particular theory about your art of conversation to elucidate—eluce."

"One theory!" said Finnegan, chirping along as he perceived the danger-point passed. "I'm a theorist, and a real theorist doesn't have one theory; he has dozens. Let me see; let me think, reflect, cogitate, tickle the thinker. Best way is to start at the A, B, C—first principles, all that sort of thing. Supposin', supposin' you come into the room with that hat on—it's a bum hat, by the way—and some one pipes up, 'Get that at the fire sale?' What are you going to answer?"

"Why, I suppose I'd grin," said Stover slowly, "and say, 'How did you guess it?' "

"Wrong," said Finnegan. "You let him take the laugh."

"Well, what?"

"Something in this style: 'Oh, no, I traded it for luck with a squint-eyed, humpbacked biter-off of puppy-dog tails that got it out of Rockefeller's ashcan.' See?"

"No, Dennis, no," said Stover, bewildered. "I see, but there are some things beyond me. Every one isn't a young Shakespeare."

"I know," said Finnegan, accepting the tribute without hesitation. "But there's the principle. You go him one better. You make him look like a chump. You show him what you could have said in his place. That shuts him up, makes him feel foolish, spikes the gun, corks the bottle."

"By Jove!"

"It's what I call the Superiority of the Superlative over the Comparative."

"It sounds simple," said Stover pensively.

"When you know the trick."

"You know, Dennis," said Stover, smiling reminiscently, "I used to have the gift of gab once, almost up to you."

"Then let's take a few crouching starts," said Dennis, delighted. "Go ahead."

"Room full of fellows. You enter."

"I enter."

"I speak: 'Dink, I bet Bill here a quarter that you used a toothbrush.' "

"You lose," said Stover; "I use a whiskbroom."

"Good!" said Dennis professionally, "but a little quicker on the jump, get on the springboard. Try again. 'Why, Dink, how *do* you get such pink cheeks?' "

"That's a hard one," said Dink.

"Peanuts!"

"Let me think."

"Bad, very bad."

"Well, what would you say?"

"Can't help it, Bill; the girls won't let me alone!"

"Try me again," said Stover, laughing.

"Say, Dink, did your mamma kiss you goodby?"

"Sure, Mike," said Stover instantly. "Combed my hair, dusted my hands, and told me not to talk to fresh little kids like you."

"Why, Dink, come to my arms," said Dennis, delighted. "A Number 1. Mark 100 for the term. That's the trick."

"Think I'll do?"

"Sure pop. Of course, there are times when the digestion's jumping fences and you get sort of in the thunder glums. Then just answer, 'Is that the best you can do to-day?' or 'Why, you're a real funny man, aren't you?' sarcastic and sassy."

"I see."

"But better be original."

"Of course."

"Oh, it's all a knack."

"And to think that's all there is to it!" said Stover, profoundly moved.

"When you know," said Dennis in correction.

"Dennis, I have a thought," said Stover suddenly. "Let's get out and try the system."

"Presto!"

"The Jigger Shop?"

"Why tarry?"

On the way over Dink stopped short with an exclamation.

"What now?" said Finnegan.

"Tough McCarty and a female," said Stover in great indignation.

They stood aside, awkwardly snatching off their caps as McCarty and his companion passed them on the walk. Stover saw a bit of blue felt with the white splash of a wing across, a fluffy shirtwaist, and a skirt that was a skirt, and nothing else. His glance went to McCarty, meeting it with the old, measuring antagonism. They passed.

"Damn him!" said Stover.

"Why, Dink, how shocking!"

"He's grown!"

In the joy of his own increased stature he had never dreamed that like processes of Nature produce like results.

"Ten pounds heavier," said Dennis. "He ought to make a peach of a tackle this year!"

"Bringing girls around!" said Stover scornfully, to vent his rage.

"More to be pitied than blamed," sang Dennis on a popular air. "It's his sister. Luscious eyes—quite the figure, too."

"Figure—huh!" said Stover, who hadn't seen.

At the Jigger Shop the Gutter Pup, looking up from a meringue entirely surrounded by peach jiggers, hailed them. "Hello, Rinky Dink! Changed your mind, eh? Thought you were homesick."

"Sure I was, but Dennis came in with a bucket and caught the tears," said Stover gravely. "I'll call you in next time. Al, how be you? Here's what I owe you. Set 'em up."

"*Très bien!*" said Dennis de Brian de Boru Finnegan.

That night, as they started on the problem of interior decorations, Stover threw himself on the bed rolling with laughter.

"Well, I'm glad you've decided to be cheerful; but what in blazes are you hee-hawing at?" said the Tennessee Shad, mystified.

"I'm laughing," said Stover, loud enough for Dennis down the hall to hear, "at the Superiority of the Superlative over the Comparative."

XII

"WHY, LOOK AT the Dink!" said Lovely Mead the next afternoon, as Stover emerged in football togs which he had industriously smeared with mud to conceal their novelty.

"He must be going out for the Varsity!" said Fatty Harris sarcastically.

"By request," said the Gutter Pup.

"Why, who told you?" said Stover.

"You trying for the Varsity?" said Lovely Mead incredulously. "Why, where did you play football?"

"Dear me, Lovely," said Stover, lacing his jacket, "thought you read the newspapers."

"Huh! What position are you trying for?"

"First substitute scorer," said Stover, according to Finnegan's theory. "Any more questions?"

Lovely Mead, surprised, looked at Stover in perplexity and remained silent.

Dink, laughing to himself at the ease of the trick, started across the Circle for the Varsity football field, whither already the candidates were converging to the first call of the season.

He had started joyfully forth from the skeptics on the steps, but once past the chapel and in sight of the field his gait abruptly changed. He went quietly, thoughtfully, a little alarmed at his own daring, glancing at the padded figures that overtopped him.

The veterans with the red L on their black sweaters were apart, tossing the ball back and forth and taking playful tackles at one another. Stover, hiding himself modestly in the common herd, watched with entranced eyes the lithe, sinuous forms of Flash Condit and Charley De Soto—greater to him than the faint heroes of mythology—as they tumbled the Waladoo Bird gleefully on the ground. There was Butcher Stevens of the grim eye and the laconic word, a man to follow and emulate; and the broad span of

266

Turkey Reiter's shoulders, a mark to grow to. Meanwhile, Garry Cockrell, the captain, and Mr. Ware, the new coach from the Princeton championship eleven, were drawing nearer on their tour of inspection and classification. Dink knew his captain only from respectful distances—the sandy hair, the gaunt cheekbones and the deliberate eye, whom governors of states alone might approach with equality, and no one else. Under the dual inspection the squad was quickly sorted, some sent back to their House teams till another year brought more weight and experience, and others tentatively retained on the scrubs.

"Better make the House team, Jenks," said the low, even voice of the captain. "You want to harden up a bit. Glad you reported, though."

Then Dink stood before his captain, dimly aware of the quick little eyes of Mr. Ware quietly scrutinizing him.

"What form?"

"Third."

The two were silent a moment, studying not the slender, wiry figure but the look in the eyes within.

"What are you out for?"

"End, sir."

"What do you weigh?"

"One hundred and fifty—about," said Dink.

A grim little twinkle appeared in the captain's eyes.

"About one hundred and thirty-five," he said, with a measuring glance.

"But I'm hard, hard as nails, sir," said Stover desperately.

"What football have you played?"

Stover remained silent.

"Well?"

"I—I haven't played," he said unwillingly.

"You seem unusually eager," said Cockrell, amused at this strange exhibition of willingness.

"Yes, sir."

"Good spirit; keep it up. Get right out for your House team—"

"I won't!" said Stover, blurting it out in his anger and then flushing. "I mean, give me a chance, won't you, sir?"

Cockrell, who had turned, stopped and came back.

"What makes you think you can play?" he said, not unkindly.

"I've got to," said Stover desperately.

"But you don't know the game."

"Please, sir, I'm not out for the Varsity," said Stover confusedly. "I mean, I want to be in it, to work for the school, sir."

"You're not a Freshman?" said the captain, and the accents of his voice were friendly.

"No, sir."

"What's your name?" said Cockrell, a little thrilled to feel the genuine veneration that inspired the "sir."

"Stover—Dink Stover."

"You were down at the Green last year, weren't you?"

"Yes, sir," said Stover, looking down with a sinking feeling.

"You're the fellow who tried to fight the whole House?"

"Yes, sir."

"Well, Dink, this is a little different—you can't play football on nothing but nerve."

"You can if you've got enough of it," said Stover, all in a breath. "Please, sir, give me a chance. You can fire me if I'm no good. I only want to be useful. You've got to have a lot of fellows to stand the banging and you can bang me around all day. I do know something about it, sir; I've practiced tackling and falling on the ball all summer, and I'm hard as nails. Just give me a chance, will you? Just one chance, sir."

Cockrell looked at Mr. Ware, whose eye showed the battling spark as he nodded.

"Here, Dink," he said gruffly, "I can't be wasting any more time over you. I told you to go back to the House team, didn't I?"

Stover, with a lump in his throat, nodded the answer he could not utter.

"Well, I've changed my mind. Get over there in the squad."

The reversal of feeling was so sudden that tears came into Stover's eyes.

"You're really going to let me stay?"

"Get over there, you little nuisance!"

Dink went a few steps, and then stopped and tightened his shoe-laces a long minute.

"Too bad the little devil is so light," said Cockrell to Mr. Ware.

"Best player I ever played against had no right on a football field."

"But one hundred and thirty-five!"

"Yes, that's pretty light."

"What the deuce were you chinning so long about?" said Cheyenne Baxter to Dink, as he came joyfully into the squad.

"Captain wanted just a bit of general expert advice from me," said Dink defiantly. "I've promised to help out."

The squad, dividing, practiced starts. Stover held his own, being naturally quick; and though Flash Condit and Charley De Soto distanced him, still he earned a good word for his performances.

Presently Mr. Ware came up with a ball and, with a few words of introduction, started them to falling on it as it bounded grotesquely over the ground, calling them from the ranks by name.

"Hard at it, Stevens."

"Dive at it."

"Don't stop till you get it."

"Oh, squeeze the ball!"

Stover, moving up, caught the eye of Mr. Ware intently on him, and rose on his toes with the muscles in his arms strained and eager.

"Now, Stover, hard!"

The ball, with just an extra impetus, left the hand of Mr. Ware. Stover went at it like a terrier, dived and came up glorious and muddy with the pigskin hugged in his arms. It was the extent of his football knowledge, but that branch he had mastered on the soft summer turf.

Mr. Ware gave a grunt of approval and sent him plunging after another. This time as he dived the ball took a tricky bounce and slipped through his arms. Quick as a flash Dink, rolling over, recovered himself and flung himself on it.

"That's the way!" said Mr. Ware. "Follow it up. Can't always get it the first time. Come on, Baxter."

The real test came with the tackling. He waited his turn, all eyes, trying to catch the trick, as boy after boy in front of him went cleanly or awkwardly out to down the man who came plunging at him. Some tackled sharply and artistically, their feet leaving the ground, and taking the runner off his legs as though a scythe had passed under him; but most of the tackling was crude, and often the runner slipped through the arms and left the tackler prone on the ground to rise amid the jeers of his fellows.

"Your turn, Stover," said the voice of the captain. "Wait a minute." He looked over the squad and selected McCarty, saying, "Here, Tough, come out here. Here's a fellow thinks all you need in this game is nerve. Let's see what he's got."

Dink stood out, neither hearing nor caring for the laugh that went up. He glanced up fifteen yards away where Tough McCarty stood waiting the starting signal. He was not afraid, he was angry clean through, ready to tackle the whole squad, one after another.

"Shall I take it sideways?" said Tough, expecting to be tackled from the side as the others had been.

"No, head on, Tough. Let's see if you can get by him," said Cockrell. "Let her go!"

McCarty, with the memory of past defiances, went toward Stover head down, full tilt. Ordinarily in practice the runner slackens just before the tackle; but McCarty, expecting slight resistance from a novice, arrived at top speed.

Stover, instead of hesitating or waiting the coming, hurled himself recklessly forward. Shoulder met knee with a crash that threw them both. Stunned by the savage impact, Stover, spilled head over heels, dizzy and furious, instinctively flung himself from his knees upon the prostrate body of McCarty, as he had followed the elusive ball a moment before.

"That's instinct, football instinct," said Mr. Ware to Cockrell, as they approached the spot where Dink, still dazed, was clutching Tough McCarty's knees in a convulsive hug.

"Let go! Let go there, you little varmint," said Tough McCarty, considerably shaken. "How long are you going to hold me here?"

Someone touched Dink on the shoulder; he looked up through the blur to see the captain's face.

"All right, Dink, get up."

But Stover released his grip not a whit.

"Here, you young bulldog," said Cockrell with a laugh, "it's all over. Let go. Stand up. Sort of groggy, eh?"

Dink, pulled to his feet, felt the earth slip under him in drunken reelings.

"I missed him," he said brokenly, leaning against Mr. Ware.

"H'm, not so bad," said the coach gruffly.

"How do you feel?" said Garry Cockrell, looking at him with his quiet smile.

Dink saw the smile and misjudged it.

"Give me another chance," he cried furiously. "I'll get him."

"What? Ready for another tackle?" said the captain, looking at him intently.

"Please, sir."

"Well, get your head clear first."

"Let me take it now, sir!"

"All right."

"Hit him harder than he hits you, and grip with your hands," said the voice of Mr. Ware in his ear.

Dink stood out again. The earth was gradually returning to a state of equilibrium, but his head was buzzing and his legs were decidedly rebels to his will.

The captain, seeing this, to give him time, spoke to McCarty with just a shade of malice.

"Well, Tough, do you want to take it again?"

"Do I?" said McCarty, sarcastically. "Oh, yes, most enjoyable! Don't let me interfere with your pleasure. Why don't you try it yourself?"

"Would you rather watch?"

"Oh, no, of course not. This is a real pleasure, thank you. The little devil would dent a freight train."

"All ready, Stover?" said Cockrell.

The players stood in two lines, four yards apart. No one laughed. They looked at Stover, thrilling a little with his communicated recklessness, grunting forth their approval.

"Good nerve."

"The real stuff."

"Pure grit."

"Little devil."

Stover's face had gone white, the eyes had dwindled and set intensely, the line of the mouth was drawn taut, while on his forehead the wind lifted the matted hair like a banner. In the middle of the lane, crowding forward, his arms out, ready to spring, his glance fixed on McCarty, he waited like a champion guarding the pass.

"All right, Stover?"

Someone near him repeated the question.

"Come on!" he answered.

McCarty's one hundred and seventy pounds came rushing down. But this time the instinct was strong. He slacked a bit at the end as Stover, not waiting his coming, plunged in to meet him. Down they went again, but this time it was the force of Stover's impact that threw them.

When Cockrell came up, Dink, altogether groggy, was entwined around one leg of McCarty with a gaunt grin of possession.

They hauled him up, patted him on the back and walked him up and down in the cool breeze. Suddenly, after several minutes, the mist rose. He saw the fields and heard the sharp cries of the coaches prodding on the players. Then he looked up to find Garry Cockrell's arm about him.

"All right now?" said the captain's voice.

Stover hastily put the arm away from him.

"I'm all right."

"Did I give you a little too much, youngster?"

"I'm ready again," said Stover instantly.

Cockrell laughed a short, contented laugh.

"You've done enough for today."

"I'll learn how," said Dink doggedly.

"You know the real things in football now, my boy," said the captain shortly. "We'll teach you the rest."

Dink thought he meant it sarcastically.

"You will give me a chance, won't you?" he said.

"Yes," said the captain, laying his hand on his shoulder with a smile. "You'll get chance enough, my boy. Fact is, I'm going to start you in at end on the scrub. You'll get all the hard knocks you're looking for there. You won't get any credit for what you do —but you boys are what's going to make the team."

"Oh, sir, do you mean it?"

"I'm in the habit of meaning things."

"I'll—I'll—" began Stover, and then stopped before the impossibility of expressing how many times his life should be thrown to the winds.

"I know you will," said the captain, amused. "And now, you young bulldog, back to your room and shake yourself together."

"But I want to go on; I'm feeling fine."

"Off the field," said the captain with terrific sternness.

Dink went like a dog ordered home, slowly, unwillingly, turning from time to time in hopes that his captain would relent.

When he had passed the chapel and the strife of the practice had dropped away he felt all at once sharp, busy pains running up his back and over his shoulders. But he minded them not. At that moment with the words of the captain—*his* captain forever now—ringing in his ears, he would have gone forth gratefully to tackle the whole team, one after another, from wiry little Charley De Soto to the elephantine P. Lentz.

Suddenly a thought came to him.

"Gee, I bet I shook up Tough McCarty, anyhow," he said grimly. And refreshed by this delightful thought he went briskly across the Circle.

At the steps Finnegan, coming out the door, hailed him excitedly, "Hi, Dink, we've got a Freshman who's setting up to jiggers and éclairs. Hurry up!"

"No," said Dink.

"What?" said Dennis faintly.

"I can't," said Dink, bristling. "I'm in training."

XIII

THE TENNESSEE SHAD, reclining in an armchair softened by sofa cushions, gave critical directions to Dink Stover and Dennis de Brian de Boru Finnegan, to whom, with great unselfishness, he had surrendered all the privileges of the hanging committee.

"Suppose *you* agitate yourself a little," said Dink, descending from a rickety chair which, placed on a table, had allowed him to suspend a sporting print from the dusty molding.

"The sight of you at hard labor," said Finnegan, from a bureau on the other side of the room, "would fill me with cheer, delectation and comfort."

The Tennessee Shad, by four convulsive processes, reached his feet.

"Oh, very well," he said carelessly. "Thought you preferred to run this show yourselves."

Picking up a poster, he selected with malicious intent the most unsuitable spot in the room and started to climb the bureau, remarking, "This is about it, I should say."

The artistic souls of Dink and Dennis protested.

"Murder, no!"

"You chump!"

"Too big for it."

"Well, if you know so much," said the Tennessee Shad, halting before the last upward struggle and holding out the poster, "where would you put it?"

Stover and Dennis indignantly bore the poster away and with much effort and straining tacked it in an appropriate place.

"Why, that is better," said the Tennessee Shad admiringly, regaining his chair, not too openly. "Much better. Looks fine! Great! Say, I've got an idea. Stick the ballet girl under it."

"What?"

"You're crazy!"

"Well, where would you put it?"

"Here, you chump."

"Why, that's not half bad, either," said the Tennessee Shad, once more back among the cushions. "A trifle more to the left, down—now up—good—make fast. First rate; guess you have the best eye. Now where are you going to put this?"

By this process of self-debasement and generous exterior admiration the Tennessee Shad successfully perceived the heavy hanging and arranging brought to a satisfactory conclusion.

The vital touches were given, the transom was hung with heavy black canvas; a curtain of the same was so arranged as to permit its being drawn over the telltale cracks of the door. Dennis and Stover, sent to reconnoiter from the hall, waited while the Tennessee Shad passed a lighted candle back and forth over the sealed entrance. One traitor crack was discovered and promptly obliterated.

"Now we're secure," said the Tennessee Shad. "Cave of Silence and all that sort of thing. The Old Roman would have to smell us to get on."

"How about the windows?" said Dink.

"They're a cinch," said the Shad. "When you get the shade down and the shutters closed a blanket will fix them snug as a bug in a rug. Now, at nine o'clock we can go to bed without suffering from drafts. Ha, ha—joke."

"Burn the midnight oil, etceteray—etcetera."

"Tomorrow," said the Tennessee Shad, "Volts Mashon is going to install a safety light for us."

"Elucidate," said Dink.

"A safety light is a light that has a connection with the door. Shut door, light; open door, where is Moses? Midnight reading made a pleasure."

"Marvelous!"

"Oh, I've heard of that before," said Finnegan.

The Tennessee Shad, meanwhile, had been busy stretching a string from his bed to the hot-air register and from a stick at the foot of his bed to a pulley at the top.

Stover and Finnegan waited respectfully until the Shad, having finished his operations, deigned to give a practical exhibition.

"This thing is simple," said he, stretching out on his bed and pulling a string at one side. "Opens hot-air register. No applause necessary. But this is a little, comforting idea of my own. Protection from sudden change of temperature without bodily exposure." Extending his hand he pulled the other rope, which, running through the pulley over his head, brought the counterpane quickly over him. "How's that? No sitting up, reaching down, fumbling about in zero weather."

"That's good as far as it goes," said Dennis, whose natural state was not one of reverence; "but how about the window? Someone has to get up and shut the window."

"Simple as eggs," said the Shad, yawning disdainfully. "A string and a pulley do the trick, see? Down comes the window. All worked at the same exchange. Well, Dink, you may lead the cheer."

Now, Stover suddenly remembered a device he had been told of, and, remembering it, to give it the appearance of improvisation he pretended to deliberate.

"Well," said the Tennessee Shad, surprised, "my humble little inventions don't seem to impress you."

"Naw."

"They don't, eh! Why not?"

"Oh, it's the right principle," said Stover, assuming a deliberate look, "but crude, very crude, backwoods, primitive, and all that sort of thing."

The Tennessee Shad, amazed, looked at Finnegan, who spoke. "Crude, Dink?"

"Why, yes. All depends on whether the Shad wakes up or not. And then, why hand labor?"

"I suppose you have something more recherché to offer," said the Tennessee Shad cuttingly, having recovered.

"Why, yes, I might," said Stover coolly. "A real inventor would run the whole thing by machinery. Who's got an alarm clock?"

Dennis, mystified, returned running with his.

Stover, securing it with strings, fastened it firmly on the table, which he moved near the scene of operations. He then lowered the upper half of the window, assuring himself that a slight impetus would start it. To the sash he attached a stout string which he ran through a pulley fixed to the top of the window frame; to the string he fastened a weight which he carefully balanced on the edge of a chair; to the weight, thus fastened, he attached another string which he led to the clock and made fast to the stem that wound the alarm. Then he straightened up, cast a glance over the Shad's handiwork and went to the register.

"When the window shuts it should open the register, of course —first principles," he said crushingly. He disconnected the string from the bed and arranged it on the window. Having wound the clock he addressed his audience:

"It's a simple little thing," he said with a wave of his hand. "I happened to remember that the key of an alarm clock turns as the alarm works. That's all there is to it. Set the alarm when you want to wake up—see—like this. Alarm goes off, winds up spring, throws weight off balance, weight falls, shuts the window, opens the register and you stay under the covers. Practical demonstration now proceeding."

The mechanism worked exactly as he had predicted. The Tennessee Shad and the Wild Irishman, transfixed with awe, watched with dropped mouths the operation. Finnegan, the first to recover, salaamed in true Oriental fashion.

"Mr. Edison," he said in a whisper, "don't take advantage of two innocent babes in the wood. Did you honestly just work this out?"

"Oh, no, of course not," said Dink loftily. "My father told me— it cost him a fortune; he gave years of his life to perfecting it!"

"And this to me!" said the exponent of the superlative reproachfully.

The Tennessee Shad rose and offered his hand with a gesture worthy of Washington.

"Sir to you. I am your humble servant. Wonderful! Marvelous! Smashing! Terrific! Sublime!"

"Do it again," said Dennis de Brian de Boru.

The alarm being wound and set, the operation was repeated with the same success, while Dennis danced about excitedly and the Tennessee Shad contemplated it with dreamy absorption.

"Jemima!" said Dennis. "And it works for any time?"

"Any time," said Dink, with one hand gracefully resting on his hip.

"Cracky!" exclaimed Dennis, prancing excitedly toward the door. "I'll get the whole House up."

"Dennis!"

Finnegan stopped, surprised at the note of authority in the Tennessee Shad's voice.

"Dennis de Brian de Boru Finnegan; back and sit down."

"What's wrong?"

"You would call in the whole House, would you?"

"Why not?" said Dink, thirsting for the applause of the multitude.

"Dink, oh, Dink!" said the Shad, in profound sorrow. "You would throw away a secret worth millions, would you?"

Dink looked at Dennis, who returned the look, and then with a simultaneous motion they sat down.

"This invention has millions in it, millions," said the Tennessee Shad, promoter. "It is simple, but revolutionary. Every room in the school must be equipped with it."

"Then there's all the apartment houses," said Dennis eagerly.

"That will come later," said the Tennessee Shad.

"We'll patent it," said Stover, seeing clouds of gold.

"Certainly," said the promoter. "We will patent the principle."

"Let's form a company."

The three rose and solemnly joined hands.

"What shall we call it?"

"The Third Triumvirate?" said Dennis.

"Good!" said the Tennessee Shad.

"What shall we charge?" said Dink.

"We must make a dollar profit on each," said the Tennessee Shad. "That means—four hundred fellows in the school—allowing for roommates; we should clear two hundred and ten dollars at the lowest. That means seventy dollars apiece profit."

"Let's begin," said Dennis.

"I'm unalterably opposed," said Dink, "to allowing Doc Macnooder in the firm."

"Me, too," said Dennis.

"Doc is strong on detail," said the Tennessee Shad doubtfully.

"I'm unalterably opposed," said Dink, "to allowing Doc Macnooder to swallow this firm."

"Me, too," said Dennis.

"Doc has great business experience," said the Tennessee Shad; "wonderful, practical mind."

"I'm unalterably—" said Dink and stopped, as the rest was superfluous.

"Me, too," said Dennis.

"Someone's got to work for us in the other Houses."

"Make him our foreign representative," said Stover.

"And give him a commission?"

"Sure—ten per cent."

"No more," said Dennis. "Even that cuts down our profits."

"All right," said the Tennessee Shad. "As you say, so be it. But still I think Doc Macnooder's business sagacity—"

At this moment Doc Macnooder walked into the room. The three future millionaires responded to his greeting with dignity, keeping in mind that distance which should separate a board of directors from a mere traveling man.

"Hello," said Macnooder glibly. "All shipshape and ready for action. Tea served here and chafing dish ready for the midnight rabbit. Ha, ha, Dink, still got the souvenir toilet set, I see."

"Still, but not long," said Dink. "But that story comes later. Sit down, Doc, and pay attention."

"Why so much chestiness?" said Doc, puzzled. "I haven't sold anything to any of you, have I?"

"Doc," said Stover, "we have formed a company and we want to talk business."

"What company?"

"The Third Triumvirate Manufacturing Company," said Dennis.

"This," said Stover, indicating the appliance. "A combined window closer and alarm clock that also opens the register."

"Let's see it," said Macnooder, all excitement.

The demonstration took place. Macnooder the enthusiast was conquered, but Macnooder the financier remained cold and controlled. He sat down, watched by three pairs of eyes, took from his pocket a pair of spectacles, placed them on his nose and said indifferently, "Well?"

"What do you think of it?"

"It's a beaut!"

"I say, Doc," said Finnegan, "now, won't every fellow in the school be crying for one, won't be happy till he gets it, and all that sort of thing?"

"Every fellow in the school will have one," said Macnooder carefully, making a distinction which was perceived only by the Tennessee Shad.

"Now, Doc," said Dink, still glowing with his triumph over the Tennessee Shad, "let's talk business."

Macnooder took off the glasses and minutely polished them with his handkerchief.

"You've formed a company, eh?"

"The Third Triumvirate—the three of us."

"Well, where do I come in?"

"You're to be our foreign representative."

"Commission ten per cent," added Finnegan carefully.

The Tennessee Shad said nothing, waiting expectantly. Macnooder rose whistling through his teeth and stood gazing down at the alarm clock.

"Foreign representative, commission ten per cent," he said softly.

"We thought we'd give you first whack at it," said Stover in a careless, businesslike way.

"So. What's your idea of developing it?"

"Why, we thought of installing it for a dollar."

"With the clock?"

"Oh, no! The clock extra."

"Charging a dollar for string and pulley?"

"And the invention."

"Humph!"

"Well, Doc, is it a go?" said Dink, watching him fall into a reverie.

"No, I guess I'm not much interested in this," said Macnooder, taking up his hat. "There's no money in it."

"Why, Doc," said Finnegan, aghast, "you said yourself every fellow would have to have it."

"Would have it," said Macnooder in correction. "The invention's all right, but it's not salable."

"Why not?"

"Nothing to sell. First fellow who sees it can do it himself."

Finnegan looked at Stover, who suddenly felt his pockets lighten.

"Doc is very strong on detail," said the Tennessee Shad softly, in a reminiscent way.

"You might sell it to one fellow," said Macnooder, "without telling him. But soon as you set it up everyone will copy it."

"Great business head," continued the Tennessee Shad.

"It's a good idea," said Macnooder condescendingly. "You might get a vote of thanks, but that's all you would get. Do you see the rub?"

"I see," said Dink.

"Me, too," said Dennis.

"And a wonderful practical mind," concluded the Tennessee Shad dreamily.

"Well, let's be public benefactors then," said Dennis in a melancholy tone.

"And such a beautiful idea," said Dink mournfully.

"I move the Third Triumvirate disband," said the Tennessee Shad; and there was no objection.

"Now," said Doc Macnooder briskly, sitting down, "I'll put my own proposition to you amateurs. There's only one way to make the thing go, and I've got the way. I take all responsibility and all risks. All I ask is control of the stock—fifty-one per cent."

Ten minutes later the Third Triumvirate Manufacturing Company was reformed on the following basis:

PRESIDENT . . . . Doc Macnooder, 51 shares.
ADVISORY BOARD . . . . The Third Triumvirate.
TREASURER . . . . Doc Macnooder.

PAID-UP CAPITAL

Macnooder $5.10
The Tennessee Shad 1.70
Dink Stover 1.70
Dennis de B. de B. Finnegan 1.50

"Now," said Macnooder, when the articles were safely signed and the capital paid up, "here's the way we work it. We've got to do two things: first, conceal the way it's done until we sell it; and second, keep those who buy from letting on."

"That's hard," said the Tennessee Shad.

"But necessary. I'm thinking out a plan."

"Of course the first part is a cinch," said Dennis. "A few extras, etcetera, etceteray. It's putting the ribbons in the lingerie, that's all."

"Exactly."

"You don't think it's selling goods under false pretenses?"

"Naw," said Macnooder. "Same principle as the patent medicine—the only wheel that goes round there is a nice, fat temperance measure of alcohol, isn't it? We'll have the first public demonstration tomorrow afternoon. I'll distribute a few more pearls tonight. Ta-ta."

The three sat quietly, listening to the fall of his departing steps.

"If we'd asked him in the first place," said the Tennessee Shad, gazing out the window, "we'd only given up twenty-five per cent. Great business head, Doc; great mind for detail."

XIV

MACNOODER, THAT night, formed the Eureka Purchasing Company, incorporated himself, and secured, at jigger rates, every secondhand alarm clock on which he could lay his hands—but more of that hereafter.

At five o'clock the next afternoon the combined Kennedy House packed itself into the Tennessee Shad's room, where Doc Macnooder rose and addressed them:

"Gentlemen of the Kennedy: I will only detain you an hour or so; I have only a few thousand words to offer. We are gathered here on an auspicious occasion, a moment of history—the moment *is* historical. Your esteemed Housemate, Mr. Dink Stover, has completed, after years of endeavor, an invention that is destined to be a household word from the northernmost wilds of the Davis House to the sun-kissed fragrance of the Green, from the Ethiopian banks of the fur-bearing canal to the Western Tins of Hot-dog Land! Gentlemen, I will be frank—"

"Cheese it!" said a voice.

"I will be frank," repeated Macnooder, turning on them a countenance on which candor struggled with innocence. "I did not wish or encourage the present method of procedure. As a member of the Dickinson House I combated the proposition of Mr. Stover and his associates to make this invention a Kennedy House sinecure. I still combat it—but I yield. If they wish to give away their profits they can. Gentlemen, in a few moments I shall have the pleasure of placing before you an opportunity to become shareholders in one of the most epoch-making inventions the world has ever known."

"What's it called?" said a voice.

"It's called," said Macnooder slowly, secure now of the attention of his audience, "it's called The Complete Sleep Prolonger. The title itself is a promise and a hope. I will claim nothing for this wonderful little invention. It not only combats the cold, but it encourages the heat; it prolongs not only the sleep, but the existence; it will increase the stature, make fat men thin, thin men impressive, clear the complexion, lighten the eye and make the hair long and curly."

"Let's have it," cried several voices.

"Gentlemen," said Macnooder, seeing that no further delay was possible, "our first demonstration will be entitled The Old Way."

Dennis de Brian de Boru Finnegan, in pajamas, appeared from a closet, went to the window, opened it, shut the register, yawned, went to his bed and drew the covers over his head. The faint sounds of a mandolin were heard from the expert hands of the Tennessee Shad.

"Scene," said Macnooder, fitting his accents to low music as is the custom of vaudeville—"scene represents the young Lawrenceville boy, exhausted by the preparation of the next day's lessons, seeking to rest his too conscientious brain. The night passes, the wind rises. It grows cold. Hark the rising bell. He hears it not. What now? He rises in his bed, the room is bitter cold. He bounds to the window over the frozen ground. He springs to the register and back to his bed. He looks at his watch. Heavens! Not a moment to lose. The room is bitter cold, but he must up and dress!"

Finnegan, completing the pantomime, returned with thunders of applause.

"Gentlemen," cried Macnooder, "is this picture a true one?"

And the roar came back: "You bet!"

"Our next instructive little demonstration is entitled The Scientific Way or The Sleep Prolonger Watches Over Him. Observe now the modest movements of the Dink, the Kennedy House Edison."

Dink, thus introduced, connected the hot-air register to the window sash, the window sash to the weight—specially covered with tinfoil—and brought forth the table on which was the now completed Sleep Prolonger. Only the face of the clock appeared, the rest was buried under an arrangement of cardboard boxes and perfectly useless spools, that turned with the rope that took a thrice devious way to the alarm key. In front, two Kennedy House flags were prominently displayed.

"Is everything ready, Mr. Stover?" said Macnooder, while the crowd craned forth, amazed at the intricacy of the machine.

"Ready, Mr. President."

"Second demonstration," said Macnooder.

Finnegan again entered, fixed the register, lowered the window and, going to the clock, set the alarm.

"He sets the alarm for half-past seven," said Macnooder in cadence. "One half-hour gained. The night passes. The wind rises. It grows cold. Hark the rising bell. He hears it not; he doesn't have to. The Sleep Prolonger is there."

The alarm shot off with a suddenness that brought responsive jumps from the audience, the weight fell, and to the amazement of all, the window closed and the register opened.

"Watch him now, watch him," cried Macnooder, hushing the tumult of applause. "Observe the comfort and the satisfaction in his look. He has not stirred, not a limb of his body has been exposed, and yet the room grows warm. His eye is on the clock; he will rise in time, and he will rise in comfort!

"Gentlemen, this great opportunity is now before you. This marvel of human ingenuity, this baffling example of mechanical intricacy is now within your reach. It can do anything. It is yours. It is yours at prices that would make a miner turn from picking up gold nuggets. It is yours for one dollar and twenty-five cents— twenty-five cents is our profit, gentlemen, and you get one profit-sharing bonus. And, furthermore, each of the first fifteen purchasers who will pay the sum of one fifty will receive not one, but three eight per cent accumulative preferred bonuses."

"Bonus for what?" said an excited voice.

"Twenty-five per cent of the net profits," cried Macnooder, thumping the table, "will be set aside for pro rata distribution. The device itself remains for three days a secret, until the completion of the patents. Orders from the model set up and installed in twenty-four hours now acceptable, cash down. No crowding there, first fifteen get three bonuses—one at a time; keep back there—no crowding, no pushing—no pushing, boys. Here, stop! Owing to the extraordinary demand, have I the advisory board's consent to give every purchaser present who pays one fifty three bonuses? I have? Let her go! Mr. Finnegan, take down the names. Cash, right over here!"

"I don't like this idea of bonuses," said Finnegan, when the rooms had returned to their quiet again.

"Twenty-five per cent Doc!" said the Tennessee Shad reproachfully.

"Why, you chump," said Macnooder proudly, "that's what's called the profit-sharing system. It keeps 'em quiet, and it also keeps 'em from going out and giving the game away. Mark my words."

"But twenty-five per cent," said the Tennessee Shad, shaking his head.

"Of the profits—net profits," said Macnooder. "There's a way to get around that. I'll show you later."

"We must get to work and round up some alarm clocks," said Stover.

"I've already thought of that," said Doc, as he took his leave. "Don't worry about that. Now I'll canvass the Dickinson."

"A slight feeling of uneasiness—" said the Tennessee Shad solemnly, when Macnooder had departed—"a slight feeling of uneasiness is stealing over me, as the poet says."

"Let's have a look at the articles of incorporation," said Stover, who sat down with Dennis to study them.

"We're the advisory board," said Dennis stoutly.

"He's got fifty-one per cent of the stock, though," said Dink.

"But we've got forty-nine!"

The Tennessee Shad, who had not risen from his chair as it involved extraordinary exertion, was heard repeating in a lonely sort of way to himself:

"A slight feeling of uneasiness."

By the next nightfall every room in the Kennedy was equipped with a Complete Sleep Prolonger. Their reception was exactly as Macnooder had foreseen. At first a roar went up as soon as the simplicity of the device was unearthed, but the thought of the precious bonuses soon quelled the revolt.

Besides, there was no doubt of the great humanizing effects of the invention, and the demand that it would awaken throughout the whole school.

But an obstacle arose to even the deep-laid plans of Macnooder himself. As the Third Triumvirate Manufacturing Company had bought its stock from the Eureka Purchasing Company—which had cornered the alarm-clock market—it followed that the alarm clocks were distinctly second-rate.

The consequence was that, though all were set for half-past seven, the first gun went off at about quarter-past two in the morning, bringing Mr. Bundy, the assistant housemaster, to the middle of the floor in one terrified bound, and starting a giggle that ran the darkened house like an epidemic.

At half-past three another explosion took place, aggravated this time by the fact that, the window pulleys being worn, the sash flew up with enough force to shatter most of the glass.

At four o'clock, when three more went off in friendly conjunction, The Roman met Mr. Bundy in the hall in light marching costume, and made a few very forcible remarks on the duties of subordinates—the same being accentuated by the wailing complaint of the youngest Roman which resounded through the house.

From then on the musketry continued intermittently until half-past seven, when such a salvo went off that the walls of the house seemed jarred apart.

The Third Triumvirate went down to breakfast with small appetite. To add to their apprehension, during the long wakeful reaches of the night there had been borne to their ears faint but unmistakable sounds from the opposite Dickinson and the Woodhull, which had convinced them that there, too, the great invention of the age had been betrayed by defective supplies.

The Roman looked haggard; Mr. Bundy haggard and aggressive.

"Northwester coming," said the Tennessee Shad under his breath. "I know the signs."

"It's all Macnooder," said Stover bitterly.

At first recitation The Roman flunked Stover on the review, on the gerund and gerundive, on the use of hendiadys—a most unfair exhibition of persecution—on several supines, and requested him to remain after class.

"Ahem, John," he said, bringing to bear the batteries of his eyes on the embattled Dink, "you were, I take it, at the bottom, so to speak, of last night's outrage. Yes? Speak up."

"May I ask, sir," said Dink, very much aggrieved—for masters should confine themselves to evidence and not draw deductions—"I should like to know by what right you pick on me?"

The Roman, knowing thoroughly the subject under hand, did not condescend to argue, but smiled a thin, wan smile.

"You were, John, weren't you?"

"I was—that is, I invented it."

"Invented it?" said The Roman, sending one eyebrow toward the ceiling. "Invented what?"

"The Sleep Prolonger," said Dink very proudly.

"Prolonger!" said The Roman, with the jarring memories of the night upon him. "Explain, sir!"

Dink went minutely over the detailed construction of the invention of the age. By request, he repeated the same while The Roman followed, tracing a plan upon his pad. At the conclusion Dink waited aggressively, watching The Roman, who continued to stare at his sketch.

"One question, John," he said, without raising his eyes. "Was the Kennedy the only house thus favored?"

"No, sir. Macnooder installed them in the Dickinson and the Woodhull."

"Ah!" As though finding comfort in this last statement, The Roman raised his head and said slowly, "Dear me! I see, I see now. Quite a relief. It is evident from your recital, John, that at least there was no concerted effort to destroy the property of the school. I withdraw the term outrage, in so far as it may suggest outrages of pillage or anarchy. As to the continued usefulness of what you so felicitously term the Sleep Prolonger, that will have to be a subject of consultation with the Doctor, but—but, as your friend, I should advise you, for the present, not to risk any further capital in the venture. Don't do it, John, don't do it."

"Tyrant!" said Stover to himself. Aloud he asked, "Is that all, sir?"

"One moment—one moment, John. Are you contemplating any further inventions?"

"Why, no, sir."

"On your honor, John?"

"Why, yes, sir."

"Good—very good. You may go now."

At noon, by virtue of an extraordinary order from headquarters, all alarm clocks were confiscated and ordered to be surrendered.

"It's all the Old Roman," said Stover doggedly. "He knew it was my invention. He's got it in for me, I tell you."

"Anyhow," said Finnegan, "since Doc planted a few Prolongers in the Dickinson and the Woodhull we ought to be able to stack up a few nice, round plunks."

The Tennessee Shad looked very thoughtful.

At this moment the Gutter Pup and P. Lentz, representing the profit-sharing stockholders, called to know when the surplus was to be divided.

"Macnooder is now at work on the books," said Dink. "We expect him over at any time."

But when at eight o'clock that evening no word had been received from the president, the Third Triumvirate held a meeting and sent the Tennessee Shad over to the Dickinson, with orders to return only with the bullion, for which purpose he was equipped with a small, black satchel.

Just before lights the Tennessee Shad's dragging step was heard returning.

"I don't like the sound," said Dink, listening.

"He always shuffles his feet," said Dennis, clinging to hope.

The door opened and the Tennessee Shad, carrying the black satchel, solemnly entered. Dink flung himself on the bag, wrenched it open and let it drop, exclaiming, "Nothing!"

"Nothing?" said Dennis, rising.

"Nothing," said the Tennessee Shad, sitting down.

"But the profits?"

"The profits," said the Tennessee Shad, pointing sarcastically to the bag, "are in there."

"Do you mean to say—?" began Dink and stopped.

"I mean to say that the Third Triumvirate Manufacturing Company is insolvent, bankrupt, busted, up the spout."

"But then, who's got the coin?"

"Doc Macnooder," said the Tennessee Shad, "and it's all legal."

"Legal?"

"All legal. It's this way. Our profits depended upon the price we paid for alarm clocks. See? Well, when Doc Macnooder, as president of the Third Triumvirate Manufacturing Company looked around for clocks, he found that Doc Macnooder, as president of the Eureka Purchasing Company, had cornered the market and could dictate the price."

"So that?" said Stover indignantly.

"So that each clock was charged up to us at a rate ranging from one dollar and forty cents to one dollar and fifty."

"By what right?" said Dennis.

"It's what is called a subsidiary company," said the Tennessee Shad. "It's quite popular nowadays."

"But where's the stock we subscribed?" said Dennis, thinking of his one dollar and fifty cents. "We get that back?"

"No."

"What!" said the two in unison.

"It's this way. Owing to executive interference, the Third Triumvirate Manufacturing Company is liable to the Eureka Purchasing Company for ten alarm clocks, which it has ordered and can't use."

"But then, out of the whole, blooming mess," said Dennis, quite overcome, "where do I stand?"

The Tennessee Shad unfolded a paper and read:

"You owe the Eureka, as your share of the assessment, two dollars and forty cents."

"Owe!" said Finnegan with a scream.

"Just let him come," said Dink, doubling up his fists. "Let him come and assess us!"

The three sat in long silence. Finally the Tennessee Shad spoke: "I am afraid Doc was sore because we tried to freeze him out at first. It was a mistake."

No one noticed this.

"Great Willie Keeler!" said Dennis suddenly. "If this thing had been a success we'd have been ruined!"

"But what right," said Dink, unwilling to give up the fight, "had he to pay the Eureka such prices. Who authorized him?"

"A vote of fifty-one per cent of the stock," said the Tennessee Shad.

"But he never said anything to us—the forty-nine per cent. Has the minority no rights?"

"The minority," said the Tennessee Shad, speaking beyond his horizon, "the minority has only one inalienable right, the right to endorse."

"I'll get even with him," said Dink, after a blank period.

"I suppose," said Dennis de Brian de Boru Finnegan, "that's what's called Finance."

And the Tennessee Shad nodded assent. "Higher Finance, Dennis."

XV

DURING THE busy October week Dink found little time to vent the brewing mischief within him. The afternoons were given over to the dogged pursuit of the elusive pigskin. In the evenings he resolutely turned his back on all midnight spreads or expeditions to the protecting shadows of the woods to smoke the abhorrent cigarette, for the joy of the risk run. At nine o'clock promptly each night he dived into bed, wrapped the covers about his head and, leaving the Tennessee Shad deep in the pages of Dumas, went soaring off into lands where goals are kicked from the center of the field, winning touchdowns scored in the last minute of play and bonfires lighted for his special honor. He was only end on the scrub, eagerly learning the game; but with the intensity of his nature that territory, which each afternoon he lined up to defend, was his in sacred trust; and he resolved that the trust of his captain should not be misplaced if it lay in his power to prevent it.

However, the busy mind was not entirely inactive. With the memory of his financial disappointment came the resolve to square himself with The Roman and turn the tables on Doc Macnooder.

The opportunity to do the first came in an unexpected way.

One evening P. Lentz came in upon them in great agitation.

"Why, King," said Dennis, who was lolling around, "you're excited, very, very much excited!"

"Shut up!" said the King of the Kennedy, who was in anything but a good humor. "It's the deuce to pay. I've had a first warning."

At this everyone looked grave, and Dink, the loyalist, said, "Oh, King, how could you!"

For another warning meant banishment from the football team and all the devastation that implied.

"That would just about end us," said Dennis. "Might as well save Andover the traveling expenses."

"I know, I know!" said P. Lentz furiously. "I've had it all said to me. Beautifully expressed, too. Question is, what's to be done? It's all the fault of old Baranson. He's been down on me ever since we licked the Woodhull."

"We must think of something," said the Tennessee Shad.

"How about a doctor's certificate?"

"Rats!"

"We might get up a demonstration against Baranson."

"Lot's of good that'll do me!"

Various suggestions were offered and rejected.

"Well, King," said the Tennessee Shad at last, "I don't see there's anything to it but you'll have to buckle down and study."

"Study?" said P. Lentz. "Is that the best you can produce?"

"It seems the simplest."

"I came here for consolation," said P. Lentz, who thereupon departed angrily.

"Still, it'll come to that," said the Tennessee Shad.

"P. Lentz study?" said Finnegan contemptuously. "Can a duck whistle?"

"Then we'll have to tutor him."

"What says Dink?"

"Don't bother me, I'm thinking."

"Gracious, may I watch you?"

"Shad," said Stover, ignoring Dennis, "did it ever occur to you how unscientific this whole game is?"

"What game?"

"This chasing the Latin root, wrestling with the unknown equation, and all that sort of thing."

"Proceed."

"Why are we smashed up? Because we are discouraged, all fighting alone, unscientifically. Does the light dawn?"

"Very slowly," said the Tennessee Shad. "Keep dawning."

"I am thinking of organizing," said Stover impressively, "The Kennedy Co-operative Educational Institute."

"Aha!" said the Tennessee Shad. *"Video, je vois,* I see. All third formers in the house meet, divide up the lesson and then fraternize."

"Where do I come in?" said Finnegan, who was two forms below.

"A very excellent idea," said the Tennessee Shad in final approval.

"I've a better one now," said Stover.

"Why, Dink!"

"It begins by chucking the Co-operative idea."

"How so?"

"There's no money in that," said Stover. "We must give the courses ourselves, see?"

"Give?" said the Tennessee Shad. "We two shining marks!"

"No," said Stover contemptuously. "We hire the lecturers and collect from the lectured."

"Why, Shad," said Finnegan, in wide-eyed admiration, "our boy is growing up!"

"He is, he certainly is. I love the idea!"

"Why, I think it's pretty good myself," said Dink.

"It has only one error—the lecturers."

"Why, that's the finest of the fine," said Dink indignantly. "You see what I do. Here's Beekstein and Gumbo Binks been laying around as waste material and the whole house kicking because we've been stuck with two midnight-oilers. Now what do I do? I utilize them. I make them a credit to the house, useful citizens."

"True, most true," said the Tennessee Shad. "But why pay? Never pay anyone anything."

Stover acknowledged the superior financial mind, while Finnegan remained silent, his greatest tribute.

"I suppose we might lasso them," said Stover, "or bring them up in chains."

"That's only amateurish and besides reprehensible," said the Tennessee Shad. "No, the highest principle in finance, the real cream de la crème, is to make others pay you for what you want them to do."

Stover slowly assimilated this profound truth.

"We'll charge twenty-five cents a week to students and we'll make Beekstein and Gumbo disgorge half a plunk each for letting us listen to them."

"I am ready to be convinced," said Dink, who still doubted.

"I'll show you how it's done," said the Tennessee Shad, who, going to the door, called out, "Oh, you Beekstein!"

"Profound, profound mind," said Dennis de Brian de Boru Finnegan. "Doc Macnooder is better on detail, but when it comes to theory the Tennessee Shad is the Willie Keeler boy every time!"

"I've another idea," said Stover, "a way to get even with **The Roman**, too."

"What's that?"

"To signal the gerund and the gerundive."

"Magnificent and most popular!" said the Tennessee Shad. "We'll put that in as a guaranty. Who'll signal?"

"I'll signal," said Stover, claiming the privilege. "It's my right!"

Beekstein, who might be completely described as a pair of black-rimmed spectacles riding an aquiline nose, now shuffled in with his dictionary under his arm, his fingers between the leaves of a Cicero to which he still clung.

"Mr. Hall," said the Tennessee Shad with a flourish, "take any chair in the room."

Beekstein, alarmed by such generosity, sat down like a ramrod and cast a roving, anxious glance under the beds and behind the screen.

"Beekstein," said the Tennessee Shad, to reassure him, "we have just organized the Kennedy Educational Quick Lunch Institute. The purpose is fraternal, patriotic and convivial. It will be most exclusive and very secret." He explained the working scheme and then added anxiously, "Now, Beekstein, you see the position of First Grand Hot Tamale will be the real thing. He will be, so to speak, Valedictorian of the Kennedy and certainly ought to be elected secretary of the House next year. Now, Beekstein, what we got you here for is this. What do you think of Gumbo for the position? Well, what?"

Beekstein, in his agitation, withdrew his finger from the Orations of Cicero.

"What's the matter with me?" he said directly. "Gumbo is only a second-rater."

"He's very strong in mathematics."

"That's the only thing he beats me on!"

"Yes, but, Beekstein, there is another thing—a delicate subject. I don't know how to approach it. You see, we don't know how you're fixed for the spondulix," said the Tennessee Shad, who knew perfectly well the other's flourishing condition. "You see, this is not only educational, but a very select body, quite a secret society—with a midnight spread now and then. Of course there are dues, you see. It would cost you a half a week."

"Is that all?" said Beekstein, who had never belonged to a secret society in his life. "Here's the first month down. Right here."

"I don't know how far we are committed to Gumbo," said the Tennessee Shad, not disdaining to finger the two-dollar bill. "But I'll do everything I can for you."

Gumbo Binks, being consulted as to the qualifications of Beekstein, fell into the same trap. He was a monosyllabic, oldish little fellow, whose cheeks had fallen down and disturbed the balance of his already bald head. He had but one emotion and one enthusiasm, a professional jealousy of Beekstein, who was several points ahead of him in the race for first honors. Under these conditions the Tennessee Shad proceeded victoriously. Having made sure of each, he next informed them that, owing to a wide divergence of opinion, a choice seemed impossible. Each should have two months' opportunity to lecture before the Quick Lunchers before a vote would be taken.

Under these successful auspices the Institute met enthusiastically the following day, both the lecturers and the lectured ignoring the financial status of the others. It was found on careful compilation that, by close and respectful attention to Professors Beekstein and Gumbo, twenty minutes would suffice for the rendering of the Greek and Latin test; while only ten minutes extra were needed to follow the requirements of mathematics.

The clause in the constitution which pledged defiance to The Roman and guaranteed protection on the gerund and gerundive was exceedingly popular. The signals were agreed upon. Absolute rigidity on Stover's part denounced the gerund, while a slight wriggling of his sensitive ears betrayed the approach of the abhorrent gerundive.

In his resolve to destroy forever the peace of mind of The Roman, Dink sat an extra period under Beekstein, stalking and marking down the lair of these enemies of boykind.

On the following morning The Roman lost no time in calling up P. Lentz, who, to his amazement, recited creditably.

"Dear me," said The Roman, quite astonished, "the day of miracles is not over—most astounding! Bring your book to the desk, Lentz—hem! Everything proper! Profuse apologies, Lentz, profuse ones! The suspicion is the compliment. I'm quite upset, quite so. First time such a thing has happened." He hesitated for a moment, debating whether to allow him to retire with the honors, but his curiosity proving strong he said, "And now, Lentz, third line, second word—gerund or gerundive?"

"Gerundive, sir," said P. Lentz promptly, observing Stover's ears in a state of revolution.

"Fortunate youth! Next line, third word, gerund or gerundive?"

"Gerund, sir."

"Still fortunate! Once more, make your bet, Lentz, red or black?" said The Roman, smiling, believing Lentz was risking his fortunes on the alternating system. "Once more. Sixth line, first word, gerund or gerundive?"

"Gerund, sir."

"Is it possible—is it possible?" said The Roman. "Have I lived to see it! Sit down, *Mr.* Lentz, sit down."

He sat silent a moment, his lips twitching, his eyebrows alternately jumping, gazing from the text to P. Lentz and back.

Stover, in the front row, was radiant.

"Gee, that's a stiff one for him to swallow!" he said, chuckling inwardly. "P. Lentz, of all mutts!"

As luck would have it, the next boy called up, not being from the Kennedy, flunked and somewhat restored The Roman's equanimity.

"Now he feels better," thought Dink. "Wait till the next jolt comes, though!"

"Lazelle," said The Roman.

The Gutter Pup rose, translated fluently and, with his eyes on Dink's admonitory ears, grappled with the gerund and threw the gerundive.

"Mead," said The Roman, now thoroughly alert.

Lovely, with a show of insouciance, bagged three gerunds and one gerundive.

The Roman thought a moment and, carefully selecting the experts, sent Beekstein, Gumbo Binks, the Red Dog and Polar Fox to the blackboards. Having thus removed the bird dogs, The Roman called up Fatty Harris.

Stover, struggling to maintain his seriousness, grudgingly admired the professional manner with which The Roman attacked the mystery, the more so as it showed the wisdom of his own planning; for, had the signals been left with either Beekstein or

Gumbo, the plot would have been instantly exposed.

As it was, The Roman, to his delighted imagination, at each successful answer seemed to rise under an electric application.

Stover went out radiant, to receive the delighted congratulations of the Institute and the recognition of those who were not in the secret.

"We've got him going," he said, skipping over the campus arm in arm with the Tennessee Shad. "He's nervous as a witch! It's broken him all up. He won't sleep for a week."

"He'll spot it tomorrow," said the Tennessee Shad.

"I'll lay a bet on it."

The next day The Roman, at the beginning of the lesson, ordered all the books to the desk and fruitlessly examined them. Macnooder, as spokesman for the justly indignant class, at once expressed the pain felt at this evidence of suspicion and demanded an explanation. This highly strategic maneuver, which would have tripped up a younger master, received nothing but a grim smile from The Roman who waved them to their seats and called up P. Lentz.

"Gerund or gerundive?" he began directly, at the same time rising and scanning the front ranks.

"Why, gerund, sir," said P. Lentz instantly.

"What, again?" said The Roman, who then called upon Stover.

Dink arose, watched with some trepidation by the rest; for being in the front row he could receive no signal.

"First paragraph, third word, gerund or gerundive, Stover?"

Dink took a long time, shifting a little as though trying to glance from side to side, and finally named haltingly, "Gerund, sir."

"Next line, first word, gerund or gerundive? Look in front of you, Stover. Look at me."

Dink purposely called it wrong, likewise the next, thereby completing the mystification of The Roman, who now concentrated his attention on Macnooder and the Tennessee Shad, as being next in order of suspicion. The day ended victoriously.

"He won't live out the week," announced Dink. "There are circles under his eyes already."

"Better quit for a day or two," said the Tennessee Shad.

"Never!"

Now the advantage of Dink's method of signaling was in its absolute naturalness. For the growing boy wiggles his ears as a pup tries his teeth or a young goat hardens his horns. Moreover, as Dink held to his plan of judicious flunking, The Roman's suspicions were completely diverted. For three days more the lover of the gerund and the gerundive sought to localize and detect the sources of information without avail.

Finally on the sixth day The Roman arrived with a briskness that was at once noted and analyzed. P. Lentz was called and translated.

"We will now take up our daily recreation," said The Roman, in a gentle voice. "It has been a matter of pleasure to me—not unmixed with a little surprise, incredulous surprise—to note the sudden affection of certain members of this class for those elusive forms of Latin grammar known as the gerund and the gerundive. I had despaired, in my unbelief I had despaired, of ever satisfactorily impressing their subtle distinctions on certain, shall we say athletic, imaginations. It seems I was wrong. I had not enough faith. I am sorry. It is evident that these Scylla and Charybdis of prosody have no longer any terrors for you, Lentz. Am I right?"

"Yes, sir," said P. Lentz hesitatingly.

"So—so—no terrors? And now, Lentz, take up your book, take it up. Direct your unfailing glance at the first paragraph, page sixty-two. Is it there?"

"Yes, sir."

"Pick out the first gerund you see."

P. Lentz, beyond the aid of human help, gazed into the jungle and brought forth a supine.

"Is it possible, Lentz?" said The Roman. "Is it possible? Try once more, but don't guess. Don't guess, Lentz; don't do it."

P. Lentz closed the book and sat down.

"What! A sudden indisposition? Too bad, Lentz, too bad. Now we'll try Lazelle. Lazelle won't fail. Lazelle has not failed for a week."

The Gutter Pup rose in a panic, guessed and fell horribly over an ordinary participle.

"Quite mysterious!" said The Roman, himself once more. "Sudden change of weather. Mead, lend us the assistance of your splendid faculties. What? Unable to rise? Too bad. Dear me—dear me —quite the feeling of home again—quite homelike."

The carnage was terrific, the scythe passed over them with the old-time sweep, laying them low. Once, maliciously, when Fatty Harris was on his feet, The Roman asked, "Top of page, fifth word, gerund or gerundive?"

"Gerund," said Harris instantly.

"Ah, pardon—" said The Roman, bringing into play both eyebrows. "My mistake, Harris, entirely my mistake. Go down to the next paragraph and recognize a gerundive. No? Sit down—gently. Too bad—old methods must make way for new ideas. Too bad, then you did have one chance in two and now, where in the whole wide world will you find a friend to help you? Class is dismissed."

"I told you you couldn't beat The Roman," said the Tennessee Shad.

"I made him change his system, though," said Dink gloriously, "and he never caught me."

"Well, if you have, how are you going to spot the gerund and the gerundive?"

"I don't need to; I've learned 'em," said Dink, laughing.

XVI

THE KENNEDY House Educational Quick Lunch Institute broke up in wrath a week later when an innocent inquiry of Beekstein's for the passwords revealed the direction of the club's finances.

Meanwhile, true to his resolve, Dink, with the assistance of Finnegan and the Tennessee Shad, had started the fad of souvenir toilet sets; which, like all fads, ran its course the faster because of its high qualities of absurdity and uselessness. Dink's intention of recouping himself by selling his own set of seven colors at a big advance was cut short by a spontaneous protest to the Doctor from the housemasters, whose artistic souls were stirred to wrath at the hideous invasion. The subject was then so successfully treated from the pulpit, with all the power of sarcasm that it afforded, that the only distinct artistic movement of New Jersey expired in ridicule.

Dink took this check severely to heart and, of course, beheld in this thwarting of his scheme to dispose of the abhorrent set with honor a fresh demonstration of the implacability of The Roman.

He wandered gloomily from Laloo's and Appleby's to the Jigger Shop, where, after pulling his hat over his eyes, folding his arms inconsolably, he confided his desires of revenge on Doc Macnooder to the sympathetic ears of the guardian of the Jigger.

"Why not get up a contest and offer it as a prize?" said Al.

"Have you seen it?" said Dink, who then did the subject full justice.

Al remained very thoughtful for a long while, running back dreamily through the avenues of the past for some stratagem.

"I remember way back in the winter of '88," he said at last, "there was a slick coot by the name of Chops Van Dyne, who got strapped and hit upon a scheme for decoying the shekels."

"What was that?" said Dink hopefully.

"He got up a guessing contest with a blind prize."

"A what?"

"A blind prize all done up in tissue paper and ribbons, and no one was to know what was in it until it was won. It certainly was amazing the number of suckers that paid a quarter to satisfy their curiosity."

"Well, what was inside?" said Dink at once.

"There you are!" said Al. "Why, nothing, of course—a lemon, perhaps—but the point is, everyone just had to know."

"Not a word!" said Dink, springing up triumphantly.

"Mum as the grave," said Al, accepting his handshake.

Dink went romping back like a young spring goat, his busy mind seizing all the ramifications possible from the central theory. He found the Tennessee Shad and communicated the great idea.

"I don't like the guessing part," said the Tennessee Shad.

"Nor I. We must get up a contest."

"A championship."

"Something devilishly original."

"Exactly."

"Well, what?"

"We must think."

The day was passed in fruitless searching but the next morning brought the answer in the following manner: Dink and the Tennessee Shad—as the majority of trained Laurentians—were accustomed to wallow gloriously in bed until the breakfast gong itself. At the first crash they would spring simultaneously forth and race through their dressing for the winning of the stairs. Now this was an art in itself and many records were claimed and disputed. The Tennessee Shad, like most lazy natures, when aroused was capable of extraordinary bursts of speed and was one of the claimants for the authorized record of twenty-six and a fifth seconds from the bed to the door, established by the famous Hickey Hicks who—as has been related—had departed to organize the industries of his country. Of a consequence Stover was invariably still at his collar button when the thin shadow of the Shad glided out of the door. But on the present morning, the shoelaces of the Tennessee Shad snapping in his hand, Dink reached the exit a bare yard in advance. Suddenly he stopped, clasped the Tennessee Shad by the middle and flung him toward the ceiling.

"I have it," he cried. "We'll organize the dressing championship of the school!"

That very evening a poster was distributed among the Houses, thus conceived:

FIRST AMATEUR DRESSING CHAMPIONSHIP
OF THE SCHOOL
under the management of that well-known
Sporting Promoter
MR. DINK STOVER
FOR THE BELT OF THE SCHOOL
and
A SEALED MYSTERIOUS PRIZE
Guaranteed to be Worth Over $3.50
Entrance Fee 25c   Books Close at 6 P.M.
To-morrow
For Conditions and Details Consult
MR. DENNIS DE B. DE B. FINNEGAN, SECRETARY.

While the announcement was running like quicksilver through the school the souvenir toilet set was encased in cotton, packed in the smallest compass, stowed in a wooden box, which was then sewed up in a gunny sacking. This in turn was wrapped in colored paper, tied with bows of pink ribbon and sealed with blue sealing wax stamped with the crest of the school—VIRTUS SEMPER VIRIDIS. The whole was placed on a table at the legs of which were grouped stands of flags.

By noon the next day one-half of the school had passed around the table, measuring the mysterious package, touching the seals with itching fingers and wanting to know the reason for such secrecy.

"There are reasons," said Stover, in response to all inquiries. "Unusual, mysterious, excellent reasons. We ask no one to enter. We only guarantee that the prize is worth over three dollars and fifty cents. No one is coaxing you. No one will miss you. The entrance list is already crowded. We are quite willing it should be closed. We urge nobody!"

Macnooder came among the first, scratching his head and walking around the prize as a fox about a tainted trap. Stover, watching from the corner of his eye, studiously appeared to discourage him. Macnooder sniffed the air once or twice in an alarmed sort of way, grunted to himself and went off to try to pump Finnegan.

Finally, just before the closing of the entries, he shambled up with evident dissatisfaction and said, "Here's my quarter. It's for the championship, though, and not on account of any hocus-pocus in the box."

"Do I understand?" said Dink instantly, "that if you win you are willing to let the prize go to the second man?"

"What are you making out of this?" said Doc hungrily, disdaining an answer.

The contest, which began the next afternoon with thirty-one entries, owing to certain features unusual to athletic contests produced such a furor of interest that the limited admissions to the struggle brought soaring prices.

Everything was conducted on lines of exact formality.

Each contestant was required to don upper and lower unmentionables, two socks, two shoes, which were to be completely laced and tied, a dickey—formed by a junction of two cuffs, a collar and one button—one necktie, one pair of trousers and one coat. Each contestant was required satisfactorily to wash and dry both hands and put into his hair a recognizable part.

The contestants were allowed to arrange on the chair their wearing apparel according to their own theories, were permitted to fill the washbasin with water, leaving the comb and towel on either side. In order to prevent the formation of two classes, pajamas were suppressed and each contestant, clothed in a nightshirt, was inducted under the covers and his hair carefully disarranged.

Time was taken from the starting gun to the moment of the arrival of the fully clothed, reasonably washed and apparently brushed candidate at the door. Each time was to be noted and the two lowest scores were to compete in the finals. A time limit of forty-five seconds was imposed, after which the contestant was to be ruled out.

The first heat began with the Triumphant Egghead in the bed for the Dickinson, Mr. Dennis de Brian de Boru Finnegan on the stopwatch, Mr. Dink Stover as master of ceremonies and Mr. Turkey Reiter, Mr. Cheyenne Baxter and Mr. Charley De Soto as jurors.

The entries were admitted by all to be the pick of the school; while the champions most favored were the Tennessee Shad for the Kennedy, Doc Macnooder for the Dickinson, and the White Mountain Canary for the Woodhull.

A certain delay took place on the third heat owing to Susie Satterly, of the Davis House, refusing to compete unless there was less publicity, and being peremptorily ruled out on a demand for a screen.

"The next on the program," said Stover, as master of ceremonies, "is the champion of the Dickinson, the celebrated old-clothes man, Doctor Macnooder."

Macnooder gracefully acknowledged the applause which invariably attended his public performances, and asked leave to make a speech, which was unanimously rejected.

"Very well, gentlemen," said Macnooder, taking off his coat and standing forth in a sudden blaze of rainbow underwear, "I will simply draw attention to this neat little bit of color that I have the honor to present to your inspection. It is the latest thing out in dainty fancies and I stand ready to fill all orders. It is rather springy, but why fall when you can spring? Don't applaud—you'll wake the baby. It is light, it is warm, it gives a sense of exhilaration to the skin. It endears you to your friends, and not even a Lawrenceville suds-lady would bite a hole in it—"

"If you don't get into bed," said Dink, "I'll rule you out."

Macnooder, thus admonished, hastened to his post, merely remarking on the distinction of his garters and impressionistic socks and the fact that he had incurred great expense to afford his schoolmates an equal opportunity.

"Are you ready?" said Turkey Reiter, for the indignant jury.

"One moment."

Macnooder, in bed, glanced carefully at the preparations without, turned on his side and brought his knees up under his chin.

"All ready?"

"Go!"

With a circular kick, something like the flop of a whale's tail, Macnooder drove the covers from him and sprang into the doubled trousers.

A cheer went up from the spectators.

"Gee, what a dive!"

"Faster, Doc!"

"Wash carefully!"

"Behind the ears!"

"Don't forget the buttons!"

"That's the boy!"

"Come on, Doc, come on!"

"Oh, you Dickinson!"

"Hurray!"

"Time—twenty-seven seconds flat," said Dennis de Brian de Boru Finnegan. "Best yet. Twenty-seven and four-fifths seconds, next on the list, made by the White Mountain Canary and the Gutter Pup."

"Next contestant," said Dink, in sing-song, "is the champion of the Rouse, Mr. Peanuts Biddle."

But here a difficulty arose.

"Please, sir—" said the candidate, who as a freshman was visibly embarrassed at the ordeal before him—"Please, sir, I don't part my hair."

Every eye went to the pompadour, cropped like a scrubbing brush, and recognized the truth of this assertion.

"Please, sir, I don't see why I should have to touch a comb."

A protest broke forth from the other candidates.

"Rats!"

"Penalize him!"

"Why part my hair?"

"I always do that with my fingers when I'm skating down the stairs."

"Why wash till afterward?"

"No favoritism!"

The jury retired to deliberate and announced amid cheers that to equalize matters Mr. Peanuts Biddle would be handicapped two-fifths of a second. The candidate took this ruling very much to heart and withdrew.

The Tennessee Shad, closing the list on entries, slouched up to the starting line, amid great excitement, to better the record of Doc Macnooder.

He first inspected the washstand, filling the basin higher than customary and exchanging the stiff face towel for a soft bath towel which would more quickly absorb the moisture.

Doc Macnooder, who followed these preparations with a hostile eye, protested against this last substitution, but was overruled.

The Tennessee Shad then divested himself of his coat and undergarments amid cries of:

"Oh, you ribs!"

"What do they feed you?"

"Oh, you wishbones!"

"Oh, you shad bones!"

Macnooder then claimed that the undershirt was manifestly sewed to the coat. The allegation was investigated and disproved, without in the slightest ruffling the composure of the Tennessee Shad, who continued his calculations while making a toothpick dance through his lips. By means of safety pins, he next fastened the back and one wing of his collar to his coat so that one motion would clothe his upper half.

"I protest," said Doc Macnooder.

"Denied," said Turkey Reiter, as foreman of the jury.

The Tennessee Shad, donning the nightshirt, carefully unloosened the laces of his low shoes, drew them off and arranged the socks inside of them so as to economize the extra movement.

"The socks aren't his!" said Macnooder. "They're big enough for P. Lentz."

"Proceed," said Turkey Reiter.

The Tennessee Shad then unloosened his belt and the trousers slipped down him as a sailor down a greased pole.

Macnooder once more protested and was squelched.

The Tennessee Shad arranged the voluminous trousers, cast a final glance, placed the toothpick on the table and went under the covers.

"All ready?" said Dink.

"Wait!" With the left hand he clutched the covers, with the right his nightshirt, just back of the neck. "Ready now."

"Go!"

With one motion the Tennessee Shad flung the covers from him, tore off his nightshirt and sprang from the bed like Venus from the waves.

The audience burst into cheers:

"Holy Mike."

"Greased lightning!"

"Oh, you Shad!"

"Gee, right through the pants!"

"Suffering Moses!"

"Look at him stab the shoes!"

"Right into the coat!"

"Go it, Shad!"

"Out for the record!"

"Gee, what a wash!"

"Come on, boy, come on!"

"Now for the part!"

"Hurray!"

"Hurrah!"

"Hurroo!"

"Time—twenty-six and one-fifth seconds," cried the shrill voice of Dennis de Brian de Boru. "Equalizing the world's unchallenged professional, amateur and scholastic record made by the late Hickey Hicks! The champion's belt is now the Tennessee Shad's to have and to hold. According to the program the champion and Doc Macnooder, second-best score, will now run another heat for the mysterious sealed prize, guaranteed to be worth over three dollars and fifty cents!"

Macnooder, adopting the Shad's theories of preparation, made an extraordinary effort and brought his record down to twenty-six and four-fifths seconds. The Tennessee Shad then, according to the plan agreed upon with Stover, purposely broke a shoelace and lost the match.

Dink, in a speech full of malice, awarded the mysterious sealed prize to Doc Macnooder, with a request to open it at once.

Now, Macnooder, who had been busy thinking the matter over, had sniffed the pollution in the air and, perceiving a wicked twinkle in the eye of Stover, shifted the ground by carrying off the box despite a storm of protests to his room in the Dickinson, where, strategically proving his title to Captain of Industry, he charged ten cents admission to all who clamored to see the clearing up of the mystery.

Having thus provided a substantial consolation against a discomfiture and joined twenty other curiosity seekers to his own fortunes, he opened the box and beheld the prodigal souvenir set. At the same moment Dink stepped forward and presented him with his own former bill for three dollars and seventy-five cents.

That night, after Stover had returned much puffed up with the congratulations of his schoolmates on the outwitting of Macnooder, the Tennessee Shad took him to task from a philosophical point of view.

"Baron Munchausen, a word."

"Lay on."

"You must come down to earth."

"Wherefore?"

"You must occasionally, my boy, just as a matter of safeguarding future ventures, start in and scatter a few truths."

"Pooh!" said Stover, with the memory of cheers. "Any fool can tell the truth."

"Yes, but—"

"It's such a lazy way!"

"Still—"

"Enervating!"

"But—"

"Besides, now they expect something more from me."

"True," said the Tennessee Shad, "but don't you see, Dink, if you do tell the truth no one will believe you?"

XVII

Oh, we'll push her over
Or rip the cover—
    Too bad for the fellows that fall!
They must take their chances
Of a bruise or two
    Who follow that jolly football.

So SANG the group on the Kennedy steps, heralding the twilight;
and beyond, past the Dickinson, a chorus from the Woodhull defiantly flung back the challenge. For that week the Woodhull
would clash with the Kennedy for the championship of the Houses.

The football season was drawing to a close, only the final game
with Andover remained, a contest awaited with small hopes of
victory. For the season had been disastrous for the Varsity; several
members of the team had been caught in the toils of the octopus
examination, and, what was worse among the members, ill feeling
existed due to past feuds.

Stover, in the long, grueling days of practice, had won the respect of all. Just how favorable an impression he had made he did
not himself suspect. He had instinctive quickness and no sense of
fear—that was something that had dropped from him forever. It
was not that he had to conquer the impulse to flinch, as most boys
do; it simply did not exist with him. The sight of a phalanx of
bone and muscle starting for his end to sweep him off his feet
roused only a sort of combative rage, the true joy of battle. He
loved to go plunging into the unbroken front and feel the shock
of bodies as he tried for the elusive legs of Flash Condit or Charley
De Soto.

This utter recklessness was indeed his chief fault; he would
rather charge interference than fight it off, waiting for others to
break it up for him and so make sure of his man.

Gradually, however, through the strenuous weeks, he learned

the deeper lessons of football—how to use his courage and the control of his impulses.

"It's a game of brains, youngster, remember that," Mr. Ware would repeat day after day, hauling him out of desperate plunges. "That did no good; better keep on your feet and follow the ball. Above all, study the game."

His first lesson came when, at last being promoted to end on the scrub, he found himself lined up against Tough McCarty, the opposing tackle. Stover thought he saw the intention at once.

"Put me against Tough McCarty, eh?" he said, digging his nails into the palms of his hands. "Want to try out my nerve, eh? I'll show 'em!"

Now McCarty did not relish the situation either, foreseeing as he did the long weeks of strenuous contact with the one boy in the school who was vowed to an abiding vengeance. The fact was that Tough McCarty, who was universally liked for his good nature and sociable inclination, had yielded to the irritation Stover's unceasing enmity had aroused and had come gradually into something of the same attitude of hostility. Also, he saw in the captain's assigning Stover to his end a malicious attempt to secure amusement at his expense.

For all which reasons, when the scrub first lined up against the Varsity, the alarum of battle that rode on Stover's pugnacious front was equaled by the intensity of his enemy's coldly calculating glance.

"Here's where I squash that fly," thought McCarty.

"Here's where I fasten to that big stuff," thought Dink, "and sting him until the last day of the season!"

The first direct clash came when the scrubs were given the ball and Dink came in to aid his tackle box McCarty for the run that was signaled around their end.

Tough made the mistake of estimating Stover simply by his lack of weight, without taking account of the nervous dynamic energy which was his strength. Consequently, at the snap of the ball, he was taken by surprise by the wild spring that Stover made directly at his throat and, thrown off his balance momentarily by the frenzy of the impact, tripped and went down under the triumphant Dink, who, unmindful of the fact that the play had gone by, remained proudly fixed on the chest of the prostrate tackle.

311

"Get off," said the muffled voice.

Stover, whose animal instincts were all those of the bulldog, pressed down more firmly.

"Get off of me, you little blockhead," said McCarty growing furious as he heard the jeers of his teammates at his humiliating reversal.

"Hurry up there, you Stover!" cried the voice of the captain, unheeded, for Dink was too blindly happy with the thrill of perfect supremacy over the hated McCarty to realize the situation.

"Stover! ! !"

At the shouted command Dink looked up and at last perceived the play was over. Reluctantly he started to rise, when a sudden upheaval of the infuriated McCarty caught him unawares and Tough's vigorous arm flung him head over heels.

Down went Dink with a thump and up again with rage in his heart. He rushed up to McCarty as in the mad fight under the willows and struck him a resounding blow.

The next moment not Tough, but Cockrell's own mighty hand caught him by the collar and swung him around.

"Get off the field!"

"What?" said Dink, astounded, for in his ignorance he had expected complimentary pats on his back.

"Off the field!"

Dink, cold in a minute, quailed under the stern eye of the supreme leader.

"I did sling him pretty hard, Garry," said Tough, taking pity at the look that came into Dink's eyes at this rebuke.

"Get off!"

Dink, who had stopped with a sort of despairing hope, went slowly to the sidelines, threw a blanket over his head and shoulders and squatted down in bitter, uttery misery. Another was in his place, plunging at the tackle that should have been his, racing down the field under punts that made the blood leap in his exiled body. He did not understand. Why had he been disgraced? He had only shown he wasn't afraid—wasn't that why they had put him opposite Tough McCarty, after all?

The contending lines stopped at last their tangled rushes and straggled, panting, back for a short intermission. Dink, waiting under the blanket, saw the captain bear down upon him and, shivering like a dog watching the approach of his punishment, drew the folds tighter about him.

"Stover," said the dreadful voice, loud enough so that everyone could hear, "you seem to have an idea that football is run like a slaughterhouse. The quicker you get that out of your head the better. Now, do you know why I fired you? Do you?"

"For slugging," said Dink faintly.

"Not at all. I fired you because you lost your head; because you forgot you were playing football. If you're only going into this to work off your private grudges, then I don't want you around. I'll fire you off and keep you off. You're here to play football, to think of eleven men, not one. You're to use your brains, not your fists. Why, the first game you play in someone will tease you into slugging him and the umpire will fire you. Then where'll the team be? There are eleven men in this game on your side and on the other. No matter what happens, don't lose your temper, don't be so stupid, so brainless—do you hear?"

"Yes, sir," said Dink, who had gradually retired under his blanket until only the tip of the nose showed and the terror-stricken eyes.

"And don't forget this. You don't count. It isn't the slightest interest to the team whether someone whales you or mauls you! It isn't the slightest interest to you, either. Mind that! Nothing on earth is going to get your mind off following the ball, sizing up the play, working out the weak points—nothing. Brains, brains, brains, Stover! You told me you came out here because we needed someone to be banged around—and I took you on your word, didn't I? Now, if you're going out there as an egotistical, puffed-up, conceited individual who's thinking only of his own skin, who isn't willing to sacrifice his own little, measly feelings for the sake of the school, who won't fight for the team, but himself—"

"I say, Cap, that's enough," said Dink with difficulty; and immediately retired so deep that only the mute, pleading eyes could be discerned.

Cockrell stopped short, bit his lip and said sternly, "Line up now. Get in, Stover, and don't let me ever have to call you down again. Tough, see here." The two elevens ran out. The captain continued: "Tough, every chance you get today give that little firebrand a jab, understand? So it can't be seen."

The Varsity took the ball and for five minutes Dink felt as though he were in an angry sea, buffeted, flung down and whirled about by massive breakers. Without sufficient experience his weight was powerless to stop the interference that bore him back. He tried to meet it standing up and was rolled head over heels by the brawny shoulders of Cheyenne Baxter and Doc Macnooder. Then, angrily, he tried charging into the offenses and was drawn in and smothered while the back went sweeping around his unprotected end for long gains.

Mr. Ware came up and volunteered suggestions:

"If you're going into it dive through them, push them apart with your hands—so. Keep dodging so that the back won't know whether you're going around or through. Keep him guessing and follow up the play if you miss the first tackle."

Under this coaching Dink, who had begun to be discouraged, improved and when he did get a chance at his man he dropped him with a fierce, clean tackle, for this branch of the game he had mastered with instinctive delight.

"Give the ball to the scrubs," said the captain, who was also coaching.

Stover came in close to his tackle. The third signal was a trial at end. He flung himself at McCarty, checked him and, to his amazement, received a dig in the ribs. His fists clenched, went back and then stopped as, remembering, he drew a long breath and walked away, his eyes on the ground; for the lesson was a rude one to learn.

"Stover, what are you doing?" cried the captain, who had seen all.

Dink, who had expected to be praised, was bewildered as well as hurt.

"What are you stopping for? You're thinking of McCarty again, aren't you? Do you know where your place was? Back of your own half. Follow up the play. If you'd been there to push there'd been an extra yard. Think quicker, Stover."

"Yes, sir," said Stover, suddenly perceiving the truth. "You're right, I wasn't thinking."

"Look here, boy," said the captain, laying his hand on his shoulders. "I have just one principle in a game and I want you to tuck it away and never forget it."

"Yes, sir," said Dink reverently.

"When you get in a game get fighting mad, but get cold mad—play like a fiend—but keep cold. Know just what you're doing and know it all the time."

"Thank you, sir," said Dink, who never forgot the theory, which had a wider application than Garry Cockrell perhaps suspected.

"You laid it on pretty strong," said Mr. Ware to Cockrell, as they walked back after practice.

"I did it for several reasons," said Garry; "first, because I believe the boy has the makings of a great player in him; and second, I was using him to talk to the team. They're not together and it's going to be hard to get them together."

"Bad feeling?"

"Yes, several old grudges."

"What a pity, Garry," said Mr. Ware. "What a pity it is you can't only have second and third formers under you!"

"Why so?"

"Because they'd follow you like mad dervishes," said Mr. Ware, thinking of Dink.

Stover, having once perceived that the game was an intellectual one, learned by bounds. McCarty, under instructions, tried his best to provoke him, but met with the completest indifference. Dink found a new delight in the exercise of his wits, once the truth was borne in on him that there are more ways of passing beyond a windmill than riding it down. Owing to his natural speed he was the fastest end on the field to cover a punt, and once within diving distance of his man he almost never missed. He learned, too, that the scientific application of his one hundred and thirty-eight pounds, well timed, was sufficient to counterbalance the disadvantage in weight. He never loafed, he never let a play go by without being in it, and at retrieving fumbles he was quick as a cat.

Meanwhile the house championships had gone on until the Woodhull and the Kennedy emerged for the final conflict. The experience gained in these contests, for on such occasions Stover played with his House team, had sharpened his powers of analysis and given him a needed acquaintance with the sudden, shifting crises of actual play.

Now, the one darling desire of Stover, next to winning the fair opinion of his captain, was the rout of the Woodhull, of which Tough McCarty was the captain and his old acquaintances of the miserable days at the Green were members—Cheyenne Baxter, the Coffee-colored Angel and Butsey White. This aggregation, counting as it did two members of the Varsity, was strong, but the Kennedy, with P. Lentz and the Waladoo Bird and Pebble Stone, the Gutter Pup, Lovely Mead and Stover, all of the scrub, had a slight advantage.

Dink used to dream of mornings, in the lagging hours of recitation, of the contest and the sweet humiliation of his ancient foes. He would play like a demon, he would show them, Tough Mc-Carty and the rest, what it was to be up against the despised Dink—and dreaming thus he used to say to himself, with suddenly tense arms, "Gee, I only wish McCarty would play back of the line so I could get a chance at him!"

But on Tuesday, during the Varsity practice, suddenly as a scrimmage ended and sifted open a cry went up. Ned Banks, left end on the Varsity, was seen lying on the ground after an attempt to rise. They gathered about him with grave faces, while Mr. Ware bent over him in anxious examination.

"What is it?" cried the captain, with serious face.

"Something wrong with his ankle; can't tell yet just what."

"I'll play Saturday, Garry," said Banks, gritting his teeth. "I'll be ready by then. It's nothing much."

The subs carried him off the field with darkened faces—the last hopes of victory seemed to vanish. The gloom spread thickly through the school; even Dink, for a time, forgot the approaching hour of his revenge in the great catastrophe. The next morning a little comfort was given them in the report of Doctor Charlie that there was no sprain but only a slight wrenching, which, if all went well, would allow him to start the game. But the consolation was scant. What chance had Banks in an Andover game? There would have to be a shift; but what?

"Turkey Reiter will have to go from tackle to end," said Dink, that afternoon, as in football togs they gathered on the steps before the game, "and put a sub in Turkey's place."

"Who?"

"I don't know."

"I guess you don't."

"Might bring Butcher Stevens back from center."

"Who'd go in at center?"

"Fatty Harris, perhaps."

"Hello—here's Garry Cockrell now," said P. Lentz. "He don't look particular cheerful, does he?"

The captain, looking indeed very serious, arrived, surveyed the group and called Stover out. Dink, surprised, jumped up, saying, "You want me, sir?"

"Yes."

Cockrell put his arm under his and drew him away.

"Stover," he said, "I've got bad news for you."

"For me?"

"Yes. I'm not going to let you go in the Woodhull game this afternoon."

Stover received the news as though it had been the death of his entire family, immediate and distant. His throat choked, he tried to say something and did not dare trust himself.

"I'm sorry, my boy—but we're up against it, and I can't take any risks now of your getting hurt."

"It means the game," said Dink at last.

"I'm afraid so."

"We've no one to put in my place—no one but Beekstein Hall," said Stover desperately. "Oh, please, sir, let me play; I'll be awfully careful. It's only a House game."

"Humph—yes, I know these House games. I'm sorry, but there's no help for it."

"But I'm only a scrub, sir," said Stover, pleading hard.

"We're going to play you at end," said Cockrell suddenly, seeing he did not understand, "just as soon as we have to take Banks out; and Heaven only knows when that'll be."

Dink was aghast.

"You're not going—you're not going—" he tried to speak, and stopped.

"Yes, we've talked it over and that seems best."

"But—Turkey Reiter—I—I thought you'd move him out."

"No, we don't dare weaken the middle; it's bad enough now."

"Oh, but I'm so light."

The captain watched the terror-stricken look in his face and was puzzled.

"What's the matter? You're not getting shaky?"

"Oh, no sir," said Dink, "it's not that. It—it seems so awful that you've got to put me in."

"You're better, my boy, than you think," said Cockrell, smiling a little, "and you're going to be better than you know how. Now you understand why you've got to keep on the sidelines this afternoon. You're too fragile to take risks on."

"Yes, I understand."

"It comes hard, doesn't it?"

"Yes, sir, it does; very hard."

When the Kennedy and the Woodhull lined up for play an hour later little Pebble Stone was at end in place of Stover, who watched from his post as linesman the contest that was to have been his opportunity. He heard nothing of the buzzing comments behind, of the cheers or the shouted entreaties. Gaze fixed and heart in throat, he followed the swaying tide of battle, imprisoned, powerless to rush in and stem the disheartening advance.

The teams, now more evenly matched, both showed the traces of tense nerves in the frequent fumbling that kept the ball changing sides and prevented a score during the first half.

In the opening of the second half, by a lucky recovery of a blocked kick, the Kennedy scored a touchdown, but failed to kick the goal, making the score four to nothing. The Woodhull then began a determined assault upon the Kennedy's weak end. Stover, powerless, beheld little Pebble Stone, fighting like grim death, carried back and back five, ten yards at a time as the Woodhull swept up the field.

"It's the only place they can gain," he cried in his soul in bitter iteration.

He looked around and caught the eye of Captain Cockrell and sent him a mute, agonizing, fruitless appeal.

"Kennedy's ball," came the sharp cry of Slugger Jones, the umpire.

Dink looked up and felt the blood come back to his body again— on the twenty-five yard line there had been a fumble and the advance was checked. Twice again the battered end of the Kennedy was forced back for what seemed certain touchdowns, only to be saved by loose work on the Woodhull's part. It was getting dark and the half was ebbing fast—three minutes more to play. A fourth time the Woodhull furiously attacked the breach, gaining at every rush over the light opposition, past the forty-yard line, past the twenty-yard mark and triumphantly, in the last minute of play, over the goal for a touchdown. The ball had been downed well to the right of the goal posts and the trial for goal was an unusually difficult one. The score was a tie, everything depended on the goal that, through the dusk, Tough McCarty was carefully sighting. Dink, heartbroken, despairing, leaning on his linesman's staff, directly behind the ball, waited for the long, endless moments to be over. Then there was a sudden movement of McCarty's body, a wild rush from the Kennedy and the ball shot high in the air and, to Stover's horror, passed barely inside the farther goalpost.

"No goal," said Slugger Jones. "Time up."

Dink raised his head in surprise, scarcely crediting what he had heard. The Woodhull team were furiously disputing the decision, encouraged by audible comments from the spectators. Slugger Jones, surrounded by a contesting, vociferous mass, suddenly swept them aside and began to take the vote of the officials.

"Kiefer, what do you say?"

Cap Kiefer, referee, shook his head.

"I'm sorry, Slugger, it was close, very close, but it did seem a goal to me."

"Tug, what do you say?"

"Goal, sure," said Tug Wilson, linesman for the Woodhull. At this, jeers and hoots broke out from the Kennedy.

"Of course he'll say that!"

"He's from the Woodhull."

"What do you think?"

"Justice!"

"Hold up, hold up, now," said Slugger Jones, more excited than anyone. "Don't get excited; it's up to your own man. Dink, was it a goal or no goal?"

Stover suddenly found himself in a whirling, angry mass—the decision of the game in his own hands. He saw the faces of Tough McCarty and the Coffee-colored Angel in the blank crowd about him and he saw the sneer on their faces as they waited for his answer. Then he saw the faces of his own teammates and knew what they, in their frenzy, expected from him.

He hesitated.

"Goal or no goal?" cried the umpire, for the second time.

Then suddenly, face to face with the hostile mass, the fighting blood came to Dink. Something cold went up his back. He looked once more above the riot, to the shadowy posts, trying to forget Tough McCarty, and then, with a snap of his jaws, he answered, "Goal."

XVIII

DINK RETURNED to his room in a rage against everything and everyone, at Slugger Jones for having submitted the question, at Tough McCarty for having looked as though he expected a lie, and at himself for ever having acted as linesman.

If it had not been the last days before the Andover match he would have found some consolation in rushing over to the Woodhull and provoking McCarty to the long-deferred fight.

"He thought I'd lie out of it," he said furiously. "He did; I saw it. I'll settle that with him, too. Now I suppose everyone in this House'll be down on me; but they'd better be mighty careful how they express it."

For as he had left the field he had heard only too clearly how the Kennedy eleven, in the unreasoning passion of conflict, had expressed itself. At present, through the open window, the sounds of violent words were borne up to him from below. He approached and looked down upon the furious assembly.

"Damn me up and down, damn me all you want," he said, doubling up his fists. "Keep it up, but don't come up to me with it."

Suddenly, back of him, the door opened and shut and Dennis de Brian de Boru Finnegan stood in the room.

"I say, Dink—"

"Get out," said Stover furiously, seizing a pillow.

Finnegan precipitately retired and, placing the door between him and the danger, opened it slightly and inserted his freckled little nose.

"I say, Dink—"

"Get out, I told you!" The pillow struck the door with a bang. "I won't have anyone snooping around here!"

The next instant Dennis, resolved on martyrdom, stepped inside, saying, "I say, old man, if it'll do you any good, take it out on me."

Stover, thus defied, stopped and said, "Dennis, I don't want to talk about it."

"All right," said Dennis, sitting down.

"And I want to be alone."

"Correct," said Dennis, who didn't budge.

They sat in moody silence, without lighting the lamp.

"Pretty tough," said Dennis at last.

Stover's answer was a grunt.

"You couldn't see it the way the umpire did, could you?"

"No, I couldn't."

"Pretty tough!"

"I suppose," said Dink finally, "the fellows are wild."

"A little—a little excited," said Dennis carefully. "It was tough—pretty tough!"

"You don't suppose I wanted that gang of muckers to win, do you?" said Stover.

"I know," said Dennis sympathetically.

The Tennessee Shad now returned from the wars, covered with mud and the more visible marks of combat.

"Hello," he said gruffly.

"Hello," said Stover.

The Tennessee Shad went wearily to his corner and stripped for the bath.

"Well, say it," said Stover, who, in his agitation, had actually picked up a textbook and started to study. "Jump on me, why don't you?"

"I'm not going to jump on you," said the Tennessee Shad, who weakly pulled off the heavy shoes. "Only—well, you couldn't see it as the umpire did, could you?"

"No!"

"What a day—what an awful day!"

Dennis de Brian de Boru Finnegan, with great tact, rose and hesitated. "I'm going—I—I've got to get ready for supper," he said desperately. Then he went lamely over to Stover and held out his hand. "I know how you feel old man, but—but—I'm glad you did it!"

Whereupon he disappeared in blushing precipitation.

Stover breathed hard and tried to bring his mind to the printed lesson. The Tennessee Shad, sighing audibly, continued his ablutions, dressed and sat down.

"Dink."

"What?"

"Why did you do it?"

Then Stover, flinging down his book with an access of rage, cried out, "Why? Because you all, every damn one of you, expected me to *lie!*"

The next day Stover, who had firmly made up his mind to a sort of modified ostracism, was amazed to find that overnight he had become a hero. By the next morning, the passion and the bitterness of the struggle having died away, the House looked at the matter in a calmer mood and one by one came to him and gripped his hand with halting, blurting words of apology or explanation.

Utterly unprepared for this development, Stover all at once realized that he had won what neither courage nor wit had been able to bring him, the something he had always longed for without being quite able to name it—the respect of his fellows. He felt it in the looks that followed him as he went over to chapel, in the nodded recognition of fifth formers, who had never before noticed him, in The Roman himself, who flunked him without satire or aggravation. And not yet knowing himself, his impulses or the strange things that lay dormant beneath the surface of his everyday life, Stover was a little ashamed, as though he did not deserve it all.

That afternoon as Dink was donning his football togs, preparing for practice, a knock came at the door which opened on a very much embarrassed delegation from the Woodhull—the Coffee-colored Angel, Cheyenne Baxter and Tough McCarty.

"I say, is that you, Dink?" said the Coffee-colored Angel.

"It is," said Stover, with as much dignity as the state of his wardrobe would permit.

"I say, we've come over from the Woodhull, you know," continued the Coffee-colored Angel, who stopped after this bit of illuminating news.

"Well, what do you want?"

"I say, that's not just it; we're sent by the Woodhull, I meant to say, and we want to say, we want you to know—how white we think it was of you!"

"Old man," said Cheyenne Baxter, "we want to thank you. What we want to tell you is how white we think it was of you."

"You needn't thank me," said Stover gruffly, pulling his leg through the football trousers. "I didn't want to do it."

The delegation stood confused, wondering how to end the painful scene.

"It was awful white!" said the Coffee-colored Angel, tying knots in his sweater.

"It certainly was," said Cheyenne.

As this brought them no further along, the Coffee-colored Angel exclaimed in alarm, "I say, Dink, will you shake hands?"

Stover gravely extended his right.

Cheyenne next clung to it, blurting out, "Say, Dink, I wish I could make you understand—just—just how white we think it was!"

The two rushed away leaving Tough McCarty to have his say. Both stood awkwardly, frightened before the possibility of a display of sentiment.

"Look here," said Tough firmly, and then stopped, drew a long breath and continued, "Say, you and I have sort of formed up a sort of vendetta and all that sort of thing, haven't we?"

"We have."

"Now, I'm not going to call that off. I don't suppose you'd want it, either."

"No, I wouldn't!"

"We've got to have a good, old, slam-bang fight sooner or later and then, perhaps, it'll be different. I'm not coming around asking you to be friends, or anything like that sort of rot, you know, but what I want you to know is this—is this—what I want you to understand is just how darned *white* that was of you!"

"All right," said Stover frigidly, because he was tremendously moved and in terror of showing it.

"That's not what I wanted to say," said Tough, frowning terrifically and kicking the floor. "I mean—I say, you know what I mean, don't you?"

"All right," said Stover gruffly.

"And I say," said Tough, remembering only one line of all he

324

had come prepared to say, "if you'll let me, Stover, I should consider it an honor to shake your hand."

Dink gave his hand, trembling a little.

"Of course you understand," said Tough, who thought he comprehended Stover's silence, "of course we fight it out some day."

"All right," said Stover gruffly.

Tough McCarty went away. Dink, left alone, clad in his voluminous football trousers, sat staring at the door, clasping his hands tensely between his knees, and something inside of him welled up, dangerously threatening his eyes—something feminine, to be choked instantly down.

He rose angrily, flung back his hair and filled his lungs. Then he stopped.

"What the deuce are they all making such a fuss for?" he said. "I only told the truth."

He struggled into his jersey, still trying to answer the problem. In his abstraction he drew a neat part in his hair before, perceiving the faux pas, he hurriedly obliterated the effete mark.

"I guess," he said, standing at the window still pondering over the new attitude toward himself, "I guess, after all, I don't know it all. Tough McCarty—well, I'll be damned!"

Saturday came all too soon and with it the arrival of the stocky Andover eleven. Dink dressed and went slowly across the campus—every step seemed an effort. Everywhere was an air of seriousness and apprehension, strangely contrasted to the gay ferment that usually announced a big game. He felt a hundred eyes on him as he went and knew what was in everyone's mind. What would happen when Ned Banks would have to retire and he, little Dink Stover, weighing one hundred and thirty-eight, would have to go forth to stand at the end of the line. And because Stover had learned the lesson of football, the sacrifice for an idea, he too felt not fear but a sort of despair that the hopes of the great school would have to rest upon him, little Dink Stover, who weighed only one hundred and thirty-eight pounds.

He went quietly to the Upper, his eyes on the ground like a guilty man, picking his way through the crowds of fifth formers, who watched him pass with critical looks, and up the heavy stairs to Garry Cockrell's room, where the team sat quietly listening to the final instructions. He took his seat silently in an obscure corner, studying the stern faces about him, hearing nothing of Mr. Ware's staccato periods, his eyes irresistibly drawn to his captain, wondering how suddenly older he looked and grave.

By his side Ned Banks was listening stolidly and Charley De Soto, twisting a paperweight in his nervous fingers, fidgeted on his chair with the longing for the fray.

"That's all," said the low voice of Garry Cockrell. "You know what you have to do. Go down to Charley's room; I want a few words with Stover."

They went sternly and quickly, Mr. Ware with them. Dink was alone, standing stiff and straight, his heart thumping violently, waiting for his captain to speak.

"How do you feel?"

"I'm ready, sir."

"I don't know when you'll get in the game—probably before the first half is over," said Cockrell slowly. "We're going to put up to you a pretty hard proposition, youngster." He came nearer, laying his hand on Stover's shoulder. "I'm not going to talk nerve to you, young bulldog, I don't need to. I've watched you and I know the stuff that's in you."

"Thank you, sir."

"Not but what you'll need it—more than you've ever needed it before. You've no right in this game."

"I know it, sir."

"Tough McCarty won't be able to help you out much. He's got the toughest man in the line. Everything's coming at you, my boy, and you've got to stand it off, somehow. Now, listen once more. It's a game for the long head, for the cool head. You've got to think quicker, you've got to out-think every man on the field and you can do it. And remember this: No matter what happens never let up—get your man back of the line if you can, get him twenty-five yards beyond you, get him on the one-yard line—but get him!"

"Yes, sir."

"And now one thing more. There's all sorts of ways you can play the game. You can charge in like a bull and kill yourself off in ten minutes, but that won't do. You can go in and make grand-stand plays and get carried off the field, but that won't do. My boy, you've got to last out the game."

"I see, sir."

"Remember there's a bigger thing than yourself you're fighting for, Stover—it's the school, the old school. Now, when you're on the sidelines don't lose any time; watch your men, find out their tricks, see if they look up or change their footing when they start for an end run. Everything is going to count. Now, come on."

They joined the eleven below and presently, in a compact body, went out and through Memorial and the chapel, where suddenly the field appeared and a great roar went up from the school.

"All ready," said the captain.

They broke into a trot and swept up to the cheering mass. Dink remembered seeing the Tennessee Shad, in his shirt sleeves, frantically leading the school and thinking how funny he looked. Then someone pulled a blanket over him and he was camped among the substitutes, peering out at the gridiron where already the two elevens were sweeping back and forth in vigorous signal drill.

He looked eagerly at the Andover eleven. They were big, rangy fellows and their team worked with a precision and machinelike rush that the red-and-black team did not have.

"Trouble with us is," said the voice of Fatty Harris, at his elbow, "our team's never gotten together. The fellows would rather slug each other than the enemy."

"Gee, that fellow at tackle is a monster," said Dink, picking out McCarty's opponent.

"Look at Turkey Reiter and the Waladoo Bird," continued Fatty Harris. "Bad blood! And there's Tough McCarty and King Lentz. We're not together, I tell you! We're hanging apart!"

"Lord, will they ever begin!" said Dink, blowing on his hands that had suddenly gone limp and clammy.

"We've won the toss," said another voice. "There's a big wind, we'll take sides."

"Andover's kick-off," said Fatty Harris.

Stover sunk his head in his blanket, waiting for the awful moment to end. Then a whistle piped and he raised his head again. The ball had landed short, into the arms of Butcher Stevens, who plunged ahead for a slight gain and went down under a shock of blue jerseys.

Stover felt the warm blood return, the sinking feeling in the pit of his stomach left him, he felt, amazed, a great calm settling over him, as though he had jumped from out his own body.

"If Flash Condit can once get loose," he said quietly, "he'll score. They ought to try a dash through tackle before the others warm up. Good!"

As if in obedience to his thought, Flash Condit came rushing through the line, between end and tackle, but the Andover left half-back, who was alert, caught him and brought him to the ground after a gain of ten yards.

"Pretty fast, that chap," thought Dink. "Too bad, Flash was almost clear."

"Who tackled him?" asked Fatty Harris.

"Goodhue," came the answer from somewhere. "They say he runs the hundred in ten and a fifth."

The next try was not so fortunate, the blue line charged quicker and stopped Cheyenne Baxter without a gain. Charley De Soto tried a quarterback run and someone broke through between the Waladoo Bird and Turkey Reiter.

"Not together—not together," said the dismal voice of Fatty Harris.

The signal was given for a punt and the ball lifted in the air went soaring down the field on the force of the wind. It was too long a punt for the ends to cover, and the Andover back with a good start came twisting through the territory of Ned Banks who had been blocked off by his opponent.

"Watch that Andover end, Stover," said Mr. Ware. "Study out his methods."

"All right, sir," said Dink, who had watched no one else.

He waited breathless for the first shock of the Andover attack. It came with a rush, compact and solid, and swept back the Lawrenceville left side for a good eight yards.

"Goodbye!" said Harris in a whisper.

Dink began to whistle, moving down the field, watching the backs. Another machinelike advance and another big gain succeeded.

"They'll wake up," said Dink solemnly to himself. "They'll stop 'em in a minute.

But they did not stop. Rush by rush, irresistibly the blue left their own territory and passed the forty-five-yard line of Lawrenceville. Then a fumble occurred and the ball went again with the gale far out of danger, over the heads of the Andover backs who had misjudged its treacherous course.

"Lucky we've got the wind," said Dink, calm amid the roaring cheers about him. "Gee, that Andover attack's going to be hard to stop. Banks is beginning to limp."

The blue, after a few quick advances, formed and swept out toward Garry Cockrell's end.

"Three yards lost," said Dink grimly. "They won't try him often. Funny they're not onto Banks. Lord, how they can gain through the center of the line. First down again." Substitute and coach, the frantic school, alumni over from Princeton, kept up a constant storm of shouts and entreaties:

"Oh, get together!"

"Throw 'em back!"

"Hold 'em!"

"First down again!"

"Hold 'em, Lawrenceville!"

"Don't let them carry it seventy yards!"

"Get the jump!"

"There they go again!"

"Ten yards around Banks!"

Stover alone, squatting opposite the line of play, moving as it moved, coldly critical, studied each individuality.

"Funny nervous little tricks that Goodhue's got—blows on his hands—does that mean he takes the ball? No, all a bluff. What's he do when he does take it? Quiet and looks at the ground. When he doesn't take it he tries to pretend he does. I'll tuck that away. He's my man. Seems to switch in just as the interference strikes the end about ten feet beyond tackle, running low—Banks is playing too high; better, perhaps, to run in on 'em now and then before they get started. There's going to be trouble there in a minute. The fellows aren't up on their toes yet—what is the matter, anyhow? Tough's getting boxed right along, he ought to play out further, I should think. Hello, someone fumbled again. Who's got it? Looks like Garry. No, they recovered it themselves—no, they didn't. Lord, what a butterfingered lot—why doesn't he get it? He has—Charley De Soto—clear field—can he make it?—he ought to—where's that Goodhue?—looks like a safe lead; he'll make the twenty-yard line at least—yes, fully that, if he doesn't stumble—there's that Goodhue now—someone ought to block him off, good work—that's it—that makes the touchdown—lucky—very lucky!"

Someone hit him a terrific clap on the shoulder. He looked up in surprise to behold Fatty Harris dancing about like a crazed man. The air seemed all arms, hats were rising like startled coveys of birds. Someone flung his arms around him and hugged him. He flung him off almost indignantly. What were they thinking of?—That was only one touchdown—four points—what was that against that blue team and the wind at their backs, too? One touchdown wasn't going to win the game.

"Why do they get so excited?" said Dink Stover to John Stover, watching deliberately the ball soaring between the goalposts; "6 to 0—they think it's all over. Now's the rub."

Mr. Ware passed near him. He was quiet, too, seeing far ahead.

"Better keep warmed up, Stover," he said.

"Biting his nails, that's a funny trick for a master," thought Dink. "He oughtn't to be nervous. That doesn't do any good."

The shouts of exultation were soon hushed; with the advantage of the wind the game quickly assumed a different complexion. Andover had found the weak end and sent play after play at Banks, driving him back for long advances.

"Take off your sweater," said Mr. Ware.

Dink flung it off, running up and down the sidelines, springing from his toes.

"Why don't they take him out?" he thought angrily, with almost a hatred of the fellow who was fighting it out in vain. "Can't they see it? Ten yards more, oh, Lord! This ends it."

With a final rush the Andover interference swung at Banks, brushed him aside and swept over the remaining fifteen yards for the touchdown. A minute later the goal was kicked and the elevens again changed sides. The suddenness with which the score had been tied impressed everyone—the school team seemed to have no defense against the well-massed attacks of the opponents.

"Holes as big as a house," said Fatty Harris. "Asleep! They're all asleep!"

Dink, pacing up and down, waited the word from Mr. Ware, rebelling because it did not come.

Again the scrimmage began, a short advance from the loosely knit school eleven, a long punt with the wind and then a quick, businesslike lineup of the blue team and another rush at the vulnerable end.

"Ten yards more; oh, it's giving it away!" said Fatty Harris.

Stover knelt and tried his shoelaces and rising, tightened his belt.

"I'll be out there in a moment," he said to himself.

Another gain at Banks's end and suddenly from the elevens across the field the figure of the captain rose and waved a signal.

"Go in, Stover," said Mr. Ware.

He ran out across the long stretch to where the players were moving restlessly, their clothes flinging out clouds of steam. Back of him something was roaring, cheering for him, perhaps, hoping against hope.

Then he was in the midst of the contestants, Garry Cockrell's arm about his shoulders, whispering something in his ear about keeping cool, breaking up the interference if he couldn't get his man, following up the play. He went to his position, noticing the sullen expressions of his teammates, angry with the consciousness that they were not doing their best. Then taking his stand beyond Tough McCarty, he saw the Andover quarter and the backs turn and study him curiously. He noticed the halfback nearest him, a stocky, close-cropped, red-haired fellow, with brawny arms under his rolled-up jersey, whose duty it would be to send him rolling on the first rush.

"All ready?" cried the voice of the umpire. "First down."

The whistle blew, the two lines strained opposite each other. Stover knew what the play would be—there was no question of that. Fortunately the last two rushes had carried the play well over to his side—the boundary was only fifteen yards away. Dink had thought out quickly what he would do. He crept in closer than an end usually plays and at the snap of the ball rushed straight into the starting interference before it would gather dangerous momentum. The back, seeing him thus drawn in, instinctively swerved wide around his interference, forced slightly back. Before he could turn forward, his own speed and the necessity of distancing Stover and Condit drove him out of bounds for a four-yard loss.

"Second down, nine yards to go!" came the verdict.

"Rather risky going in like that," said Flash Condit, who backed up his side.

"Wanted to force him out of bounds," said Stover.

"Oh—look out for something between tackle and guard now."

"No—they'll try the other side now to get a clean sweep at me," said Stover.

The red-haired halfback disappeared in the opposite side and, well protected, kept his feet for five yards.

"Third down, four to gain."

"Now for a kick," said Stover, as the Andover end came out opposite him. "What the deuce am I going to do to this coot to mix him up. He looks more as though he'd like to tackle me than to get past." He looked over and caught a glance from the Andover quarter. "I wonder. Why not a fake kick? They've sized me up for green. I'll play it carefully."

At the play, instead of blocking, he jumped back and to one side, escaping the end who dove at his knees. Then, rushing ahead, he stalled off the half and caught the fullback with a tackle that brought him to his feet, rubbing his side.

"Lawrenceville's ball. Time up for first half."

Dink had not thought of the time. Amazed, he scrambled to his feet, half angry at the interruption, and following the team went over to the room to be talked to by the captain and the coach.

It was a hangdog crowd that gathered there, quailing under the scornful lashing of Garry Cockrell. He spared no one, he omitted no names. Dink, listening, lowered his eyes, ashamed to look upon the face of the team. One or two cried out:

"Oh, I say, Garry!"

"That's too much!"

"Too much, too much, is it?" cried their captain, walking up and down, striking the flat of his hand with the clenched fist. "By heavens, it's nothing to what they're saying of us out there. They're ashamed of us, one and all! Listen to the cheering if you don't believe it! They'll cheer a losing team, a team that is being driven back foot by foot. There's something glorious in that, but a team that stands up to be pushed over, a team that lies down and quits, a team that hasn't one bit of red fighting blood in it, they won't cheer; they're ashamed of you! Now, I'll tell you what's going to happen to you. You're going to be run down the field for just about four touchdowns. Here's Lentz being tossed around by a fellow that weighs forty pounds less. Why, he's the joke of the game. McCarty hasn't stopped a play, not one! Waladoo's so easy that they rest up walking through him. But that's not the worst, you're playing wide apart as though there wasn't a man within ten miles of you; not one of you is helping out the other. The only time you've taken the ball from them is when a little shaver comes in and uses his head. Now, you're not going to win this game, but by the Almighty you're going out there and going to hold that Andover team! You've got the wind against you; you've got everything against you; you've got to fight on your own goal line, not once, but twenty times. But you've got to hold 'em; you're going to make good; you're going to wipe out that disgraceful, cowardly first half! You're going out there to stand those fellows off! You're going to make the school cheer for you again as though they believed in you, as though they were proud of you! You're going to do a bigger thing than beat a weaker team! You're going to fight off defeat and show that, if you can't win, you can't be beaten!"

Mr. Ware, in a professional way, passed from one to another with a word of advice: "Play lower, get the jump—don't be drawn in by a fake plunge—watch Goodhue."

But Dink heard nothing; he sat in his corner, clasping and unclasping his hands, suffering with the moments that separated him from the fray. Then all at once he was back on the field, catching the force of the wind that blew the hair about his temples, hearing the halfhearted welcome that went up from the school.

"Hear that cheer!" said Garry Cockrell bitterly.

From Butcher Stevens' boot the ball went twisting and veering down the field. Stover went down, dodging instinctively, hardly knowing what he did. Then as he started to spring at the runner an interferer from behind flung himself on him and sent him sprawling, but not until one arm had caught and checked his man.

McCarty had stopped the runner, when Dink sprang to his feet, wild with the rage of having missed his tackle.

"Steady!" cried the voice of his captain.

He lined up hurriedly, seeing red. The interference started for him, he flung himself at it blindly and was buried under the body of the red-haired half. Powerless to move, humiliatingly held under the sturdy body, the passion of fighting rose in him again. He tried to throw him off, doubling up his fist, waiting until his arm was free.

"Why, you're easy, kid," said a mocking voice. "We'll come again."

The taunt suddenly chilled him. Without knowing how it happened, he laughed.

"That's the last time you get me, old rooster," he said, in a voice that did not belong to him.

He glanced back. Andover had gained fifteen yards.

"That comes from losing my head," he said quietly. "That's over."

It had come, the cold consciousness of which Cockrell had spoken, strange as the second wind that surprises the distressed runner.

"I've got to teach that red-haired coot a lesson," he said. "He's a little too confident. I'll shake him up a bit."

The opportunity came on the third play, with another attack on his end. He ran forward a few steps and stood still, leaning a little forward, waiting for the red-haired back who came plunging at him. Suddenly Dink dropped to his knees, the interferer went violently over his back, something struck Stover in the shoulder and his arms closed with the fierce thrill of holding his man.

"Second down, seven yards to gain," came the welcome sound.

Time was taken out for the red-haired halfback, who had had the wind knocked out of him.

"Now he'll be more respectful," said Dink, and as soon as he caught his eye he grinned. "Red hair—I'll see if I can't get his temper."

Thus checked, and to use the advantage of the wind, Andover elected to kick. The ball went twisting, and, changing its course in the strengthening wind, escaped the clutches of Macnooder and went bounding toward the goal where Charley De Soto saved it on the twenty-five-yard line. In an instant the overwhelming disparity of the sides was apparent.

A return kick at best could gain but twenty-five or thirty yards. From now on they would be on the defensive.

Dink came in to support his traditional enemy, Tough McCarty. The quick, nervous voice of Charley De Soto rose in a shriek: "Now, Lawrenceville, get into this, 7—52—3."

Dink swept around for a smash on the opposite tackle, head down, eyes fastened on the back before him, feeling the shock of resistance and the yielding response as he thrust forward, pushing, heaving on, until everything piled up before him. Four yards gained.

334

A second time they repeated the play, making the first down.

"Time to spring a quick one through us," he thought.

But again De Soto elected the same play.

"What's he trying to do?" said Dink. "Why don't he vary it?"

Someone hauled him out of the tangled pile. It was Tough Mc-Carty.

"Say, our tackle's a stiff one," he said, with his mouth to Stover's ear. "You take his knees; I'll take him above this time."

Their signal came at last. Dink dived, trying to meet the shifting knees and throw him off his balance. The next moment a powerful arm caught him as he left the ground and swept him aside.

"Any gain?" he asked anxiously as he came up.

"Only a yard," said McCarty. "He got through and smeared the play."

"I know how to get him next time," said Dink.

The play was repeated. This time Stover made a feint and then dived successfully after the big arm had swept fruitlessly past. Flash Condit, darting through the line, was tackled by Goodhue and fell forward for a gain.

"How much?" said Stover, rising joyfully.

"They're measuring."

The distance was tried and found to be two feet short of the necessary five yards. The risk was too great, a kick was signaled and the ball was Andover's, just inside the center of the field.

"Now, Lawrenceville," cried the captain, "show what you're made of."

The test came quickly, a plunge between McCarty and Lentz yielded three yards, a second four. The Andover attack, with the same precision as before, struck anywhere between the tackles and found holes. Dink, at the bottom of almost every pile, raged at Tough McCarty.

"He's doing nothing, he isn't fighting," he said angrily. "He doesn't know what it is to fight. Why doesn't he break up that interference for me?"

When the attack struck his end now it turned in, slicing off tackle, the runner well screened by close interference that held him up when Stover tackled, dragging him on for the precious yards. Three and four yards at a time, the blue advance rolled its way irresistibly toward the red-and-black goal. They were inside the twenty-yard line now.

Cockrell was pleading with them. Little Charley De Soto was running along the line, slapping their backs, calling frantically on them to throw the blue back.

And gradually the line did stiffen, slowly but perceptibly the advance was cut down. Enmities were forgotten with the shadow of the goalposts looming at their backs. Waladoo and Turkey Reiter were fighting side by side, calling to each other. Tough Mc-Carty was hauling Stover out of desperate scrimmages, patting him on the back and calling him "good old Dink." The fighting blood that Garry Cockrell had called upon was at last there—the line had closed and fought together.

And yet they were borne back to their fifteen-yard line, two yards at a time, just losing the fourth down.

Stover at end was trembling like a blooded terrier, on edge for each play, shrieking, "Oh, Tough, get through—you must get through!"

He was playing by intuition now, no time to plan. He knew just who had the ball and where it was going. Out or in, the attack was concentrating on his end—only McCarty and he could stop it. He was getting his man, but they were dragging him on, fighting now for inches.

"Third down, one yard to gain!"

"Watch my end," he shouted to Flash Condit, and hurling himself forward at the starting backs, dived under the knees, and grabbing the legs about him went down buried under the mass he had upset.

It seemed hours before the crushing bodies were pulled off and someone's arm brought him to his feet and someone hugged him, shouting in his ear, "You saved it, Dink, you saved it!"

Someone rushed up with a sponge and began dabbing his face.

"What the deuce are they doing that for?" he said angrily.

Then he noticed that an arm was under his and he turned curiously to the face near him. It was Tough McCarty's.

"Whose ball is it?" he said.

"Ours."

He looked to the other side. Garry Cockrell was supporting him.

"What's the matter?" he said, trying to draw his head away from the sponge that was dripping water down his throat.

"Just a little wind knocked out, youngster—coming to?"

"I'm all right."

He walked a few steps alone and then took his place. Things were in a daze on the horizon, but not there in the field. Everything else was shut out except his duty there.

Charley De Soto's voice rose shrill: "Now, Lawrenceville, up the field with it. This team's just begun to play. We've got together, boys. Let her rip!"

No longer scattered, but a unit, all differences forgot, fighting for the same idea, the team rose up and crashed through the Andover line, every man in the play, ten—fifteen yards ahead.

"Again!" came the strident cry.

Without a pause the line sprang into place, formed and swept forward. It was a privilege to be in such a game, to feel the common frenzy, the awakened glance of battle that showed down the line. Dink, side by side with Tough McCarty, thrilled with the same thrill, plunging ahead with the same motion, fighting the same fight, no longer alone and desperate, but nerved with the consciousness of a partner whose gameness matched his own.

For thirty yards they carried the ball down the field before the stronger Andover team, thrown off its feet by the unexpected frenzy, could rally and stand them off. Then an exchange of punts once more drove them back to their twenty-five-yard line.

A second time the Andover advance set out from the fifty-yard line and slowly fought its way to surrender the ball in the shadow of the goalposts.

Stover played on in a daze, remembering nothing of the confused shock of bodies that had gone before, wondering how much longer he could hold out—to last out the game as the captain had told him. He was groggy; from time to time he felt the sponge's cold touch on his face or heard the voice of Tough McCarty in his ear.

"Good old Dink, die game!"

How he loved McCarty fighting there by his side, whispering to him, "You and I, Dink! What if he is an old elephant, we'll put him out of the play."

Still, flesh and blood could not last forever. The half must be nearly up.

"Two minutes more time."

"What was that?" he said groggily to Flash Condit.

"Two minutes more. Hold 'em now!"

It was Andover's ball. He glanced around. They were down near the twenty-five-yard line somewhere. He looked at McCarty, whose frantic head showed against the sky.

"Break it up, Tough," he said, and struggled toward him.

A cry went up, the play was halted.

"He's groggy," he heard voices say, and then came the welcome splash of the sponge.

Slowly his vision cleared to the anxious faces around him.

"Can you last?" said the captain.

"I'm all right," he said gruffly.

"Things cleared up now?"

"Fine!"

McCarty put his arm about him and walked with him.

"Oh, Dink, you will last, won't you?"

"You bet I will, Tough!"

"It's the last stand, old boy!"

"The last."

"Only two minutes more we've got to hold 'em! The last ditch, Dink."

"I'll last."

He looked up and saw the school crouching along the line—tense, drawn faces. For the first time he realized they were there, calling on him to stand steadfast.

He went back, meeting the rush that came his way, half knocked aside, half getting his man, dragged again until assistance came. De Soto's stinging hand slapped his back and the sting was good, clearing his brain.

Things came into clear outline once more. He saw down the line and to the end where Garry Cockrell stood.

"Good old captain," he said. "They'll not get by me, not now."

He was in every play, it seemed to him, wondering why Andover was always keeping the ball, always coming at his end. Suddenly he had a shock. Over his shoulder were the goalposts, the line he stood on was the line of his own goal.

He gave a hoarse cry and went forward like a madman, parting the interference. Someone else was through; Tough was through; the whole line was through, flinging back the runner. He went down clinging to Goodhue, buried under a mass of his own tacklers. Then, through the frenzy, he heard the shrill call of time.

He struggled to his feet. The ball lay scarcely four yards away from the glorious goalposts. Then, before the school could sweep them up, panting, exhausted, they gathered in a circle with incredulous, delirious faces, and leaning heavily, wearily on one another gave the cheer for Andover. And the touch of Stover's arm on McCarty's shoulder was like an embrace.

XIX

At nine o'clock that night Stover eluded Dennis de Brian de Boru Finnegan and the Tennessee Shad and went across the dusky campus, faintly lit by the low-hanging moon. Past him hundreds of gnomelike figures were scurrying, carrying shadowy planks and barrels, while gleeful voices crossed and recrossed.

"There's a whole pile back of Appleby's."

"We've got an oil barrel."

"Burn every fence in the county!"

"Who cares?"

"Where did you get that plank?"

"Up by the Rouse."

"Gee, we'll have a bonfire bigger'n the chapel!"

"More wood, Freshmen!"

"Rotten lot, those Freshmen!"

"Hold up your end, Skinny. Do you think I'm a pack mule?"

Dink pulled the brim of his hat over his eyes and slunk away, not to be recognized. He went in a roundabout way past the chapel. He had just one desire, to stand under the goalposts they had defended and to feel again the thrill.

"Who's that?" The voice was Tough McCarty's.

"It's me. It's Dink," said Stover.

"I came down here," said McCarty, appearing from under the goalposts and hesitating a little, "well, just to feel how it felt again."

"So did I."

Dink stood by the posts, taking one affectionately in his hand, and said curiously, "They tell me, Tough, we held 'em four times inside the ten-yard line."

"Four times, old boy."

"Funny I don't remember but two. Guess I was groggy."

"You didn't show it."

340

"It was you pulled me through, Tough."

"Rats!"

"It was. There at the last, I remember when you gripped me."
As this was perilously near sentiment, he stopped. "I say, how
many of us tackled that fellow the last time?"

"The whole bunch. I say, Dink."

"Yes?"

"Stand out here—that's it, knee to knee. Can't you just feel it behind you?"

"Yes," said Dink, surprised that in the big body there was an
imagination akin to his own. Then he said abruptly, "Tough, I
guess there won't be any fight."

"No—not after this."

"What the deuce did we get a grudge for, anyway?"

"I always liked you, Dink, but you wouldn't have it."

"I was a mean little varmint!"

"Rats! I say, Dink, we've got two years more on the old team.
There's nothing going to get around our end, is there, old boy?"

"You bet there isn't!"

All at once a flame ran up the towering bonfire and belched toward the sky.

"Are you going to let them get you?" said McCarty.

"Me? Oh, Lord, no—I can't make a speech!"

"Neither can I!" said Tough mendaciously. "I wouldn't go back
there for the world!"

The thin posts stood out against the sheet of flame, gaunt, rigid,
imbued with a certain grandeur.

"I say, Dink," said McCarty.

"Yes?"

"I say, we were going to have some great old fights together. But,
do you know, I sort of feel, after all, this will be the best."

Then a chorus of thin shrieks rose about them. They started
halfheartedly to run, pretending fury. A swarm of determined boyhood rushed over them and flung them kicking, struggling into the
air.

"Tough McCarty and Dink Stover!"

"We've got 'em!"

"On to the bonfire!"

"They're ours!"

341

"Hurray!"

"Help!"

"Help! We've got McCarty and Stover!"

Boys by the score came tearing out. The little knot under Dink became a thick, black shadow, rushing forward with hilarious, triumphant shouts. Then all at once he landed all fours on a cart before the flaming stack, greeted by fishhorns and rattles, his name shrieked out in a wild acclaim.

"Three cheers for good old Dink!"

"Three cheers for honest John Stover!"

"Three cheers for the little cuss!"

He drew himself up, fumbling at his cap, terrified at the multiplied faces that danced before his eyes.

"I say, fellows—"

"Hurray!"

"Good boy!"

"Orator!"

"I say, fellows, I don't see why you've got me up here."

"You don't?"

"We'll show you!"

"Dink, you're the finest ever!"

"You're the stuff!"

"Three cheers for good old Rinky Dink!"

"Fellows, I'm no silver-tongued orator—"

"Don't believe it!"

"You are!"

"Fellows, I haven't got anything to say—"

"That's the stuff!"

"Hurray!"

"Keep it up!"

"Oh, you bulldog!"

"Fellows, they were good—"

A derisive shout went up.

"Fellows, they were very good—"

"Yes, they were!"

"Fellows, they were re-markably good—but *they didn't beat the old school team!* That's all."

He dived headlong into the crowd, unaware that he had repeated for the sixth time the stock oration of the evening.

"Good old Dink! Good old Rinky Dink!"

The cry stuck in his memory all through the jubilant night and long after, when in his delicious bed he tossed and worried over the tackles he had missed.

"It's a bully nickname—bully!" he repeated drowsily again and again. "It sounds as though they liked you! And Tough McCarty, what a bully chap—bully! We're going to be friends—pals—what a bully fellow! Everything is bully—everything!"

With the close of the football season and the advent of December, with its scurries of snow and sleet, what might be termed the open season for masters began.

A school of four hundred fellows is a good deal like a shaky monarchy: the football and baseball seasons akin to foreign wars; so long as they last the tranquility of the state is secure, but with the return of peace a state of fermentation and unrest is due.

The three weeks that lead to the Christmas vacation are too filled with anticipation to be dangerous. It is the long reaches after January fifth, the period of arctic night that settles down until the passing of the muddy month of March, that tries the souls of the keepers of these caged menageries.

Since those days a humane direction has built a gymnasium to lighten the condition of servitude, preserve the health and prolong the lives of the faculty. But at this time, with the shutting of the door on the treadmills of exercise, the young assistant master arranged his warm wrapper and slippers at the side of his bed and went to sleep with one ear raised.

Dink Stover entered this season of mischief with all the ardor and intensity of his nature, the more so because, owing to his weeks of strict training and his virtual isolation of the year before, it was all strange to him. And at that period what is forbidden, dangerous and, above all, untried, must be attempted at least once.

Now, owing to the foresight of a wise father, Dink had never been forbidden to smoke. Of a consequence when, at an early age, he practiced upon an old corncob pipe and found it violently disagreed with him, the desire abruptly ceased and, as the athletic ardor came, he consecrated his years to the duty of growing, with not the slightest regret.

But between smoking under permission and squeezing close to a cold-air ventilator, stealthily, in the pin-drop silences of the

343

night, with frightful risks of detection, was all the difference in the world. One was a disagreeable, thoroughly unsympathetic exercise; the other was a romantic, medieval adventure.

So when Slops Barnett, who roomed below and was the proprietor of a model air flue with direct, perpendicular draught, said to him with an air of mannish insouciance, "I say, old man, I've got a fat box of 'Gyptians—glad to have you drop in tonight if you like the weed," Dink answered with blasé familiarity, "Why, thankee, I've been aching for just a good old coffin nail."

He slipped down the creaking, nervous stairs and found Slops luxuriously reclining before the ventilator, on a mattress reinforced by yellow and green sofa pillows that gave the whole somewhat of the devilishly dissipated effect of the scenes from Oriental lands that fascinated him on the covers of cigarette boxes.

Slops made him a sign in the deaf-and-dumb language to extinguish the light and creep to his side.

"Comfy?" said Slops, whispering from the darkness.

"Out of sight!"

"Here's the filthy weed."

"Thanks."

"Always keep the cig in front of the ventilator," said Slops, applying his lips to Dink's ear. "Get a light from mine. Talk in whispers."

Stover filled his cheeks cautiously and blew out after a sufficient period.

"You inhale?"

"Sure."

"Inhale a cigar?"

"Always."

"It's awful the way I inhale," said Slops with a melancholy sigh. "I'm undermining my constitution. Ever see my hand? Shakes worse'n jelly. Can't help it, though; can't live without the weed. I'm a regular cig fiend!"

Stover, holding his cigarette gingerly, keeping the sickly smoke at the end of his tongue, looked over at Slops' stupid little face, flashing out of the darkness at each puff. He was no longer the useless Slops Barnett, good only to fetch and carry the sweaters of the team, but Barnett, man of the world, versed in deadly practices.

"I say, Slops—"

"Hist—lower."

"I say, Slops, what would they do if they caught us?"

"Bounce us."

"For good?"

"Sure! P. D. Q."

The cigarette suddenly had a new delight to Dink. He was even tempted to inhale a small, very small puff, but immediately conquered this enthusiastic impulse.

"Isn't this the gay life, though?" said Slops carelessly.

"You bet," said Dink.

From down the flue came three distinct taps.

"That's the Gutter Pup signaling," said Slops, putting his finger over Dink's mouth. "Bundy is snooping around. Mum's the word."

Presently, as Dink sat there in the darkness, trying desperately to breathe noiselessly, the sound of slipping footsteps was heard in the hall. Slops' hand closed over his. The steps stopped directly outside their door, waited a long moment and went on.

"Bundy?" said Dink in a whisper.

"Yes."

"Why did he stop?"

"He's got me spotted. He's seen the nicotine on my finger," said Slops, showing a finger under a sudden glow of his cigarette.

A half-hour later, when Dink crept up the stairs, homeward bound, he swelled with a new sensation. Yesterday was months away. Then he was a boy; now that he had smoked up a cold-air ventilator, with Bundy outwitted by the door, he had aged with a jump—he must be at last a man.

The next week he added to his stature by going to P. Lentz's room for a midnight session of the national game, where, after a titanic struggle of three hours, he won the colossal sum of forty-eight cents.

Having sunk to these depths he began to listen to the Sunday sermons with a thrill of personal delight—there being not the slightest doubt that they were directly launched at him. Sometimes he wondered how the Doctor and The Roman could remain ignorant of the extent of his debauches, his transgressions were so daring and so complete. He stood shivering up the Trenton road, under the shadow of an icy trunk, of Sunday mornings, and met

Blinky, the one-eyed purveyor of illicit cigarettes and the forbidden Sunday newspapers, which had to be wrapped around his body and smuggled under a sweater.

Secretly he rubbed iodine on his fingers to simulate the vicious stain of nicotine that was such a precious ornament to Slops' squat fingers. Only one thing distressed him, and that was his invincible dislike for the cigarette itself.

Being now a celebrity, many doors were thrown invitingly open to him, invitations that flattered him, without his making a distinction. He went over to the Upper at times and into rooms where he had no business, immensely proud that he was called in to share the delights and liberties of the lords of the school.

At the Kennedy he was in constant rebellion against established precedent, constantly called below to be lectured by The Roman. In revenge for which at night he made the life of Mr. Bundy one of constant insomnia, and, by soaping the stairs or strewing tacks in the hall, seriously interfered with that inexperienced young gentleman's nightly exercises.

The deeper he went the deeper he was determined to go, doggedly imagining that the whole faculty, led by The Roman, were bending every effort to bring him down and convict him.

The Tennessee Shad had no inclinations toward sporting life —greatly to Stover's surprise. When Dink urged him to join the clandestine parties he only yawned in a bored way.

"Come on now, Shad, be a sport," said Dink, repeating the stock phrase.

"You're not sports," said the Tennessee Shad in languid derision, "you're bluffs. Besides, I've been all through it, two years ago. Hurry up with your dead-game sporting phase, if you've got to, but get through it, 'cause now you're nothing but a nuisance."

Dink felt considerably grieved at his roommate's flippant attitude toward his career of vice. Secretly, he felt that a word of kindly remonstrance, some friendly effort to pull him back from the frightful abyss into which he was sinking, would have been more like a friend and a roommate.

This same callous indifference to the fate of his roommate's soul so incensed Stover that, to bring before the Shad's eyes the really desperate state of his morals, he appointed a Welsh-rabbit party in their room for the following night.

"Don't mind, do you?" he said carelessly.

"Not if I don't have to eat it!"

"It's going to be a real one," said Stover, making a distinction.

"Come off!"

"Fact. It is not going to be flavored with root beer, toothwash, condensed milk or russet polish; it is going to be the genuine, satisfaction guaranteed, or you get your money back."

"With beer?"

"Exactly."

"Yes, it is!"

"It is."

"Where'll you get it?"

"I have ways."

"Oh," said the Tennessee Shad sarcastically, "this is one of your real sporting-life parties, is it?"

Stover disdained to answer.

"Is that bunch of slums going to be here?"

"Are you referring to my friends?" said Stover.

"I am," said the Tennessee Shad, "and all I ask while this feast of bacchanalian orgies is going on, is that *I* be allowed to sleep."

At eleven o'clock Stover, holding his shoes in his hand, went down the stairs to meet Slops in Fatty Harris' room and thence into the outlawed night. They stole over the crinkling snow, burying their noses in their sweaters, until, having climbed several fences, they arrived behind a shed of particularly cavernous appearance.

"Make the signal," said Slops, sheltering himself behind Stover.

Blinky appeared like a monster of the night.

"Hist, Blinky, O. K.?" said Slops, who, having his shoulder to Dink's recovered his sporting manner. "Got the booze?"

"I got it," said Blinky in husky accents, with his hand behind his back. "What's youse got?"

"The cash is here all right. How many bots did you bring?"

Blinky slowly brought forward one bottle.

"What, only one?" said Slops the bacchanalian in dismay.

"All's left," said Blinky, with a double meaning.

"How much?"

"One dollar."

"What? You robber!"

"Take it or leave it—don't care," said Blinky, who sat down and hugged the bottle to him like a baby.

347

They paid the extortion and slunk back.

"We'll have to cook up a story," said Dink.

"Sure!"

"Still, it's beer."

"It certainly is!"

"It's expulsion if we're caught."

"And a penal offense, don't forget that!"

Somewhat consoled by this delightful thought they cautiously tapped on Fatty Harris' window and, removing their boots, tiptoed upstairs like anarchists with a price on their heads.

In Stover's room three more desperate characters were waiting about the chafing dish, Fatty Harris, Slush Randolph and Pee-wee Norris, all determined on a life of crime—but all slightly nervous.

The Tennessee Shad, rolled into a ball on his bed, was venting his scorn with an occasional snore.

Stover held up the lonely bottle.

"Is that all?" exclaimed the three in indignant whispers.

"All, and mighty lucky to get that," said Dink valiantly. "We were chased by the constable, terrific time, pounced on us, desperate struggle, just got away with our skins."

At this a distinct snort was heard from the direction of the Tennessee Shad's bed.

"I say, isn't it rather—rather dangerous?" said Pee-wee Norris, with his ears horribly strained.

"What of it?"

"Suppose he goes to the Doctor?"

"We'll have to take the risk."

"I say, though, let's be quick about it."

An uncongenial chill began to pervade the room. Fatty Harris, as master cook, visibly hastened the operations.

The Tennessee Shad was now heard to say in a mumbled jumble:

"Hurrah for crime! Never say die, boys—dead-game sports— give us a drink, bartender!"

The revelers stood at the bed looking wrathfully down at the cynic, who snored heavily and said drowsily, "Talks in his sleep, he talks in his sleep, poor old Pol!"

"Don't pay any attention to him," said Stover angrily. "He's a cheap wit. What are you doing at the door, Pee-wee?"

"I'm listening," said Norris, turning guiltily.

"You're afraid!"

"I'm not; only let's hurry it up."

Fatty Harris, watching the swirling yellow depths of the rabbit with evident anxiety, emptied a third of the beer into it and held out the bottle, saying, "Here, sports, fill up the glasses with the good old liquor."

When the three glasses and two toothmugs had received their exact portion of the bitter stuff, which had been allowed to foam copiously in order to eke out, the five desperadoes solemnly touched glasses and Slops Barnett, who had visited in Princeton, led them in that whispered toast that is the acme of devilment:

> *Then stand by your glasses steady,*
> *This world is a world full of lies.*
> *Then here's to the dead already dead,*
> *And here's to the next man who dies!*

It was terrific. Stover, quite moved, looked about the circle, thought that Pee-wee looked the nearest to the earthworm and repeated solemnly: "To the next man who dies."

At this moment the Tennessee Shad was heard derisively intoning:

> *Ring around a rosie,*
> *Pocket full of posie.*
> *Oats, peas, beans and barley grows.*
> *Open the ring and take her in*
> *And kiss her when you get her in!*

They paid no heed. They felt too acutely the solemnity of life and the fleeting hour of pleasure to be deterred by even the lathery aspect of their own faces, which emerged from the suds of the beer ready for the barber.

"Dish out the bunny," said Slops, putting down his mug with a reckless look.

Suddenly there came an impressive knock and the voice of Mr. Bundy saying, "Open the door, Stover!"

In a thrice the revelry broke up, the telltale bottle and glasses were stowed under the window seat, the visiting sporting gentlemen precipitately groveled to places of concealment, while Stover extinguished the lights and softly stole into bed.

"Open the door at once!"

"Who's there?" said Dink with a start.

"Open the door!"

All sleepy innocence Dink opened the door, rubbing his eyes at the sudden glow.

"Up after lights?" said Mr. Bundy, marching in.

"I, sir?" said Dink, astounded.

All at once Mr. Bundy perceived the chafing dish and descended upon it. Stover's heart sank—if he tasted it they were lost; no power could save them. Mr. Bundy turned and surveyed the room; one by one the terrified roués were dragged forth and recognized, while the Tennessee Shad sat on the edge of his bed, reflectively sharpening his fingers on the pointed kneecaps.

Then, to the horror of all, Mr. Bundy, sniffing the chafing dish, inserted a spoon and tasted it. Immediately he set the spoon down with a crash, gave a furious glance at Stover and departed, after ordering them to their rooms.

The dead-game sports, white and shaky, went without stopping.

"They're a fine sample of vicious bounders, they are!" said the Tennessee Shad. "Bet that Slops Barnett is weeping to his pillow now!"

"I'm sorry I got you into this," said Stover gloomily.

"You've brought my gray hairs in sorrow to the grave!" said the Tennessee Shad solemnly.

"Don't jest," said Dink in a still voice. "It's all up with me, but I'll square you."

"Don's worry," said the Tennessee Shad smiling. "I may not be a tin sport, but I keep my thinker going all the time."

"Why, what do you mean?"

"I mean you'll get twigged for a midnight spread, that's all."

"But the beer. Bundy tasted the beer."

"Taste it yourself," said the Tennessee Shad, with a wave of his hand.

Stover hurriedly dipped in a spoon, tasted it and uttered an execration.

"Murder, what did you put in it?"

"About half a bottle of horse liniment," said the Tennessee Shad, crawling back into bed. "Only don't tell the others if you want to see how much dead-game sportiness there is in them by tomorrow morning."

The affair made a great noise and, as Stover suppressed the transformation worked by the Tennessee Shad, Slops Barnett and his companions did not exactly show those qualities of Stoic resignation which might be expected from brazen characters with their view of life.

Meanwhile, the skies cleared and the earth hardened, and the air resounded with the cries of baseball candidates.

Much to his surprise, Dink found at the end of the strenuous day no impelling desire to plunge into fast life. Still the conviction remained for a long time that his soul had been surrendered, that not only was he destined for the gallows in this world, but that only the prayers of his mother might save him from being irrevocably damned in the next. It was a terrific thought, and yet it brought a certain pleasure. He was different from the rest. He was a man of the world. He had known—Life!

The episode ended as episodes in the young days end—in a laugh.

"I say, Dink," said the Tennessee Shad one afternoon in April, as, gloriously reveling on the warm turf, they watched the Varsity nine.

"Say it."

"In your dead-game sporting days did you ever, by chance, paint your nicotine fingers with iodine?"

"How in blazes did you know?"

"Used to do it myself," said the Shad reminiscently. Then he added, "Thought yourself a lost soul?"

Stover began to laugh.

"All alone in a cold, cold world—wicked, very wicked?"

"Perhaps."

"And it was rather a nice feeling, too, wasn't it?"

"I didn't know you—" said Dink, blushing to find himself back in the common herd.

"Me, too," said the Tennessee Shad, sucking a straw. "Good old sporting days!" Presently he began mischievously:

> *Then stand by your glasses steady,*
> *This world is a—*

But here Dink, rising up, tumbled him over.

351

XX

WITH THE complete arrival of the spring came also a lessening of Dink's requested appearances at faculty meetings, his little evening chats in The Roman's study on matters of disciplinary interpretation and the occasional summons through the gates of Avernus to quail before the all-seeing eye.

It was not that the spirit of Spartacus was faint, or that his enmity had weakened toward The Roman—who, of course, without the slightest doubt, was always the persecutor responsible for his summons before the courts of injustice. The truth was, Stover had suddenly begun to age and to desire to put from himself youthful things. This extraordinary phenomenon that somehow does happen was in some measure a reflex action.

Ever since the stormy afternoon on which he had decided against his own eleven, he had slowly come to realize that he had won a peculiar place in the estimation of the school—somewhat of the dignity of the incorruptible judges that existed in former days. He became in a small way a sort of court of arbitration before which questions of more or less gravity were submitted. This deference at first embarrassed, then amused, then finally pleased him with an acute, mannish pleasure.

The consequence was that Stover, who until this time had only looked forward and up at the majestic shadows of the fourth and fifth formers, now looked backward and down, and became pleasurably aware that leagues blow him was the large body of the first and second forms. Having perceived this new adjustment he woke with a start and, rubbing his eyes, took stock of his amazing knowledge of life and again said to himself that now, finally, he certainly must have arrived at man's estate.

On top of which, having been asked to referee several disputes in his character of Honest John Stover, Dink, while holding himself in reserve to direct operations on a dignified and colossal scale against the Natural Enemy, decided that it was unbecoming of a man of his position, age and reputation, who had the entrée of the Upper House, to go skipping about the midnight ways, in undignified costume, with such rank shavers as Pebble Stone and Dennis de B. de B. Finnegan.

So when Dennis arrived after lights, like a will-o'-the-wisp, with a whispered "I say, Dink, all ready," Stover replied, "Already in bed."

"What?" said Dennis aghast. "You're not with us?"

"No."

"Aren't you feeling well?"

"First-rate."

"But I say, Dink, there's half a dozen of us. We've got all the laundry bags in the house heaped up just outside of Beekstein's door and, I say, we're going to pile 'em all up on top of him and then jump on and pie him, and scoot for our rooms before old Bundy can jump the stairs and nab us. It'll be regular touch and go—a regular lark! Come on!"

A snore answered him.

"You won't come?"

"No."

"Are you mad at me?"

"No, I'm sleepy!"

"Sleepy!" said Dennis in such amazement that he no longer had any strength to argue, and left the room convinced that Stover was heroically concealing an agony of pain.

Stover immediately settled his tired body, sank his nose to the level of the covers and floated blissfully off into the land of dreams. The next night and the next it was the same. For a whole month Dink slept, wasting not a one of the precious moments of the night, sleeping through the slow-moving recitations, sleeping on the green turf of afternoons, pillowed on Tough McCarty or the Tennessee Shad, and watching others scampering around the diamond in incomprehensible activity; but the month was the month of April and his years sixteen. In the first week of May Stover awakened, the drowsiness dropped from him and the spirit of perpetual motion again returned. Still, the distance between himself and his past remained. He had changed, become graver, more laconic, moving with sedateness, like Garry Cockrell, whose tricks of speech and gestures he imitated, holding himself rather aloof from the populace, curiously conscious that the change had come, and sometimes looking back with profound melancholy on the youth that had now passed irrevocably away.

During this period of somewhat fragile self-importance, the acquaintance with Tough McCarty had strengthened into an eternal friendship in a manner that had a certain touch of humor.

McCarty, after the close of the football season, had repeatedly sought out his late antagonist, but, though Dink at the bottom of his soul was thrilled with the thought that here at last was the friend of friends, the Damon to his Pythias, the chum who was to stand shoulder to his shoulder, and so on, still there was too much self-conscious pride in him to yield immediately to this feeling.

McCarty perceived the reserve without quite analyzing it, and was puzzled at the barriers that still intervened.

During the winter, when Dink was resolutely set in the pursuit of that beau ideal, which had a marked resemblance with a certain creation of Bret Harte's, Mr. Jack Hamlin, "gentleman sport," as Dennis would have called him, McCarty found little opportunity for friendly intercourse. He disapproved of many of Dink's friendships, not so much from a moralistic point of view as from Stover's not exercising the principle of selection. As this phase was intensified and Stover became the object of criticism of his classmates for hanging at the heels of fifth formers and neglecting his own territory, McCarty resolved that the plain duty of a friend required him to administer a moral lecture.

This heroic resolve threw him into confusion for a week, for, in the first place, he had been accustomed to receive rather than to give words of warning and, in the second place, he was fully aware of the difficulties of opening up the subject at all.

After much anxious and gloomy cogitation he hit upon a novel plan and, approaching Stover at the end of the last recitation, gave him a mysterious wink.

"What's up?" said Dink instantly.

McCarty pulled him aside. "I've got a couple of A. No. 1 millionaire cigars," he said in a whisper. "If you've got nothing better, why, come along."

"I'm yours on the jump," said Dink, trying to give to his words a joy which he was far from feeling in his stomach.

"You smoke cigars?"

"Do I!"

"Come on, then!"

It was the last day of March, which had gone out like a lamb, leaving the ground still chill and moist with the memory of departed snows. They went down by the pond in the shelter of the grove and McCarty proudly produced two cigars coated with gilt foil.

"They look the real thing to me," said Dink, eying the long projectiles with a rakish, professional look.

Now, Dink had never smoked a cigar in his life and was alarmed at the thought of the task before him; but he was resolved to die a lingering death rather than allow that humiliating secret to be discovered.

"You bet they're the real thing," said Tough McCarty, slipping off the foil. "Real black beauties! Get the flavor?"

Dink approached the ominous black cigar to his nose, sniffed it rapturously and cocked a knowing eye.

"Aha!"

"Real Havanas!"

"They certainly smell good!"

"Swiped 'em off my brother-in-law, forty-five centers."

"I believe it. Say, what do you call 'em?"

"Invincibles."

The name threw a momentary chill over Stover, but he instantly recovered.

"I say, we ought to have a couple of hatpins," he said, turning the cigar in his fingers.

"What for?"

"Smoke 'em to the last puff!"

"We'll use our penknives."

"All right—after you."

Stover cautiously drew in his first puff. To his surprise nothing immediate happened.

"How is it?" said McCarty.

"Terrific!"

"Do you inhale?"

"Sometimes," said Stover, with an inconsequential wave of his hand.

This gave McCarty his opening; besides, he was deceived by Stover's complete manner.

"Dink, I'm afraid you're smoking too much," he said earnestly, puffing on his cigar.

"Oh, no," said Dink, immensely flattered by this undeserved accusation from McCarty, who smoked forty-five-cent cigars.

"Yes, you are. I know it. Trouble with you is, old boy, you never do anything by halves. I know you."

"Oh, well," said Stover loftily.

"You're smoking too much, and that's not all, Dink. I—I've wanted to have a chance at you for a long while, and now I'm going for you."

"Hello—"

"Now, look here, boy," said Tough McCarty, filling the air with the blue smoke, "I'm not a mammy boy nor a goody-goody, and I don't like preaching; but you've got too much ahead of you, old rooster, to go and throw it away."

"What do you mean?" said Dink, champing furiously on his cigar, as he had seen several stage villains do.

"I mean, old socks," said Tough, frowning with his effort, "I mean there are some fellows here who are worthwhile and some who are not, who won't do you any good, who don't amount to a row of pins and aren't up to you in any way you look at it."

"Are you criticizing my friends?" said Stover, who had just passed an even more unflattering judgment, due to the Welsh-rabbit episode.

"I am," said McCarty, passing his hand over his forehead with difficulty.

Stover was just about to make an angry reply when he looked at McCarty, who suddenly leaned back against the tree. At the same moment a feeling of insecurity overtook him. He started again to make an angry answer and then all pugnacious thoughts left him. He sat down suddenly, his head swam on his shoulders and about him the woods danced in drunken reelings, sweeping grotesque boughs over him. Only the earth felt good, the damp, muddy earth, which he all at once convulsively embraced.

"Dink!"

The sound was far off, weak and fraught with mortal distress.

"Has it hit you, too?"

Dink's answer was a groan. He opened one eye; McCarty, prone at his side, lay on his stomach, burying his head in his arms.

At this moment a light patter sounded about them.

"It's beginning to rain."

"I don't care!"

"Neither do I."

Stover lay clutching the earth that somehow wouldn't keep still, that moved under him, that swayed and rose and fell. Then things began to rush through his brain: armies of football-clad warriors, The Roman whirling by on one leg of his chair, Dennis de Brian de Boru Finnegan prancing impishly, sticking out his tongue at him, whole flocks of Sunday preachers gesticulating in his direction, crowds of faces, legs, arms, an old, yellow dog with a sausage in his mouth—

Suddenly near him McCarty began to move.

"Where are you going?" he managed to say. "For Heaven's sake, don't leave me."

"To the pond—drink."

McCarty, on his hands and knees, began to crawl. Stover raised himself up and staggered after. The rain came down unheeded—nothing could add to his misery. They reached the pond and drank long copious drinks, plunging their dripping heads in the water.

Gradually the vertigo passed. Faint and weak they sat propped up opposite each other, solemnly, sadly, glance to glance, while unnoticed the rain spouted from the ends of their noses.

"Oh, Dink!" said Tough at last.

"Don't!"

"I thought I was going to die."

"I'm not sure of it yet."

"I had a lot I wanted to say to you," said Tough painfully, feeling the opportunity was slipping away.

"You said I was smoking too much," said Dink maliciously.

"Ugh! Don't—no, that wasn't it."

"Shut up, old cockalorum," said Dink pleasantly. "I know all you want to say—found it out myself—it's all in one word—swelled head!"

"Ah!" said Tough deprecatingly, now that Dink had turned accuser.

357

"I've been a little, fluffy ass!" said Dink, marvelously stimulated to repentance by the episode which had gone before. "But that's over. My head's subsiding."

"What?"

The two burst into sympathetic laughter.

"You—you didn't mind my sailing into you, old horse?" said Tough.

"Not now."

McCarty looked mystified.

"Tough," said Dink with a queer look, "if you had smoked that black devil and I hadn't—all would have been over between us. As it is—"

"Well?" said Tough.

"As it is—Tough, here's my hand—let's swear an eternal friendship!"

"Put it there!"

"I say, Tough—"

"What?"

"Now, on your honor—did you ever smoke a cigar before?"

"Never," said McCarty. "And I'll never smoke another. So help me."

"Nor I. I say, what was that name?"

"Invincibles."

"That's where we should have stopped!"

"Dink, I begin to feel a little chilly."

"Tough, that's a good sign; let's get up."

Arm in arm, laughing uproariously, they went, still a little shaky, back toward the school.

"I say, Tough," said Dink, throwing his arm affectionately about the other's shoulders, "I've been pretty much of a jackass, haven't I?"

"Oh, come, now!"

"I'm afraid I'm not built for a sport," said Dink, with a lingering regret. "But I say, Tough—"

"What?"

"I may be the prodigal son, but you're the devil of a moral lecturer, you are!"

XXI

ONE WEDNESDAY afternoon, as Dink was lolling gorgeously on his window seat, sniffing the alert air and waiting for the moment to go skipping over to the Varsity field for the game with a visiting school, a voice from below hailed him:

"Oh, you, Rinky Dink!"

Stover languidly extended his head and beheld Tough McCarty.

"Hello there, Dink."

"Hello yourself."

"Come over to the Woodhull and meet my family."

"What?" said Dink in consternation.

"They're over for the game. Hurry up now and help me out!"

Dink tried frantically to call him back, but Tough, as though to shut off a refusal, disappeared around the house. Dink returned to the room in a rage.

"What's the matter?" said the Tennessee Shad.

"I've got to go over and meet a lot of women," said Dink in disgust. "Confound Tough McCarty! That's a rotten trick to play on me. I'll wring his neck!"

"Go on now, make yourself beautiful!" said the Tennessee Shad, delighted. "Remember the whole school will be watching you."

"Shut up!" said Dink savagely, making the grand toilet, which consisted in putting on a high collar, exchanging his belt for a pair of suspenders and donning a pair of patent-leathers. "The place for women is at home! It's an outrage!"

He tied his necktie with a vicious lunge, ran the comb once through the tangled hair, glanced at his hands, decided that they would pass muster, slapped on his hat and went out, kicking the door open.

At the Woodhull, Tough hailed him from his window. Dink went up, bored and rebellious. The door opened, he found him-

359

self in Tough McCarty's room in the vortex of a crowd of fellow sufferers. Over by the window seat two fluffy figures, with skirts and hats on, were seated. He shook hands with both; one was Mrs. McCarty, the other was the daughter, he wasn't quite sure which. He said, something about the delight which the meeting afforded him, and, gravitating into a corner, fell upon Butsey White, with whom he gravely shook hands.

"Isn't this awful?" said Butsey in a confidential whisper.

"Frightful!"

"What the deuce's got into Tough?"

"It's a rotten trick!"

"Let's hook it."

"All right. Slide toward the door."

But at this moment, when deliverance seemed near, Tough bore down and, taking Stover by the arm, drew him aside.

"I say, stick by me on this, old man," he said desperately. "Take 'em to the game with me, will you?"

"To the game!" cried Dink in horror. "Oh, Tough, come now, I say, I'm no fusser. I'm tongue-tied and pigeon-toed. Oh, I say, old man, do get someone else!"

But as Tough McCarty kept a firm grip on the lapel of his coat Dink suddenly found himself, with the departure of the other guests, a helpless captive. The first painful scraps of conversation passed in a blur. Before he knew it he was crossing the campus, actually walking, in full view of the school, at the side of Miss McCarty.

Her unconsciousness was paralyzing, perfectly paralyzing! Dink, struggling for a word in the vast desert of his brain, was overwhelmed with the ease with which his companion ran on. He stole a glance under the floating azure veil and decided, from the way the brilliant blue parasol swung from her hand, that she must be a woman of the world—thirty, at least.

He extracted his hands precipitately from the trousers pockets in which they had been plunged and buttoned the last button of his coat. Somehow, his hands seemed to wander all over his anatomy, like jibs that had broken loose. He tried to clasp them behind his back, like the Doctor, or to insert one between the first and second button of his coat, the characteristic pose of the great Corsican, according to his history. For a moment he found relief by slipping them, English fashion, into his coat pockets; but at the thought of being detected thus by the Tennessee Shad he withdrew them as though he had struck a hornet's nest.

The school, meanwhile, had gamboled past, all snickering, of course, at his predicament. In this state of utter misery he arrived at last at the field, where, to his amazement, quite a group of fifth formers came up and surrounded Miss McCarty, chattering in the most bewildering manner. Dink seized the opportunity to drop back, draw a long sigh, reach madly behind for his necktie, which had climbed perilously near the edge of his collar, and shoot back his cuffs. He saw the Tennessee Shad and Dennis de Boru grinning at him from the crowd, and showed them his fist with a threatening gesture.

Then the game began and he was seated by Miss McCarty, unutterably relieved that the tension of the contest had diverted the entire attention of the school from his particular sufferings.

The excitement of the play for the first time gave him an opportunity to study his companion. His first estimate was undoubtedly correct; she was plainly a woman of the world. No one else could sit at such perfect ease, the cynosure of so many eyes. Her dress was some wonderful creation, from Paris no doubt, that rustled with an alluring sound and gave forth a pleasant perfume.

The more he looked the more his eye approved. She was quite unusual—quite. She had style—a very impressive style. He had never before remembered anyone who held herself quite so well, or whose head carried itself so regally. There was something Spanish, too, about her black hair and eyes and the flush of red in her cheeks.

Having perceived all this, Dink began to recover from his panic and, with a desire to wipe out his past awkwardness, began busily to search for some subject with which gracefully to open up the conversation.

At that moment his eye fell upon his boot carelessly displayed and, to his horror, beheld there a gaping crack. This discovery drove all desire for conversation at once out of his head. By a covert movement he drew the offending shoe up under the shadow of the other.

"You hate this, don't you?" said a laughing voice.

He turned, blushing, to find Miss McCarty's dark eyes alive with amusement.

"Oh, now, I say, really—" he began.

"Of course, you loathe being dragged out this way," she said, cutting in. "Confess!"

Dink began to laugh guiltily.

"That's better," said Miss McCarty approvingly. "Now we shall get on better."

"How did you know?" said Dink, immensely mystified.

Miss McCarty wisely withheld this information, and before he knew it Dink was in the midst of a conversation, all his embarrassment forgot. The game ended—it had never been really important —and Dink found himself, actually to his regret, moving toward the Lodge.

There, as he was saying goodbye with a Chesterfieldian air, Tough plucked him by the sleeve.

"I say, Dink, old man," he said doubtfully, "I'd like you to come over and grub with us. But I don't want to haul you over, you know—"

"My dear boy, I should love to!" said Dink, squeezing his arm eagerly.

"Honest?"

"Straight goods!"

"Bully for you!"

He had three-quarters of an hour to dress before dinner. He went to his room at a gallop, upsetting Beekstein and Gumbo on his volcanic way upward. Then for half an hour the Kennedy was thrown into a turmoil as the half-clothed figure of Dink Stover flitted from room to room, burrowed into closets, ransacked bureaus and departed, bearing off the choicest articles of wearing apparel. Meanwhile, the corridors resounded with such unintelligible cries as these:

"Who's got a collar, fourteen and a half?"

"Darn you, Dink, bring back my pants!"

"Who swiped my blue coat?"

"Who's been pulling my things to pieces?"

"Hi there, bring back my shoes!"

"Dinged if he hasn't gone off with my cuff buttons, too!"

"Oh, you robber!"

"Body snatcher!"

"Dink, the fusser!"

"Who'd have believed it!"

Meanwhile, Dink, returning to his room laden with the spoils of the house, proceeded to adorn himself on the principle of selection, discarding the Gutter Pup's trousers for the gala breeches of the Tennessee Shad, donning the braided cutaway of Lovely Mead's in preference to an affair of Slush Randolph's which was too tight in the chest.

The Tennessee Shad, the Gutter Pup and Dennis de Brian de Boru watched the proceedings, brownie fashion, across the transom, volunteering advice.

"Why, look at Dink wash!"

"It's a regular annual, isn't it?"

"Look out for my pants!"

"I say, Dink, your theory's wrong. You want to begin by parting your hair—soak it into place, you know."

Stover, struck by this expert advice, approached the mirror and seized his comb and brush with determination. But the liberties of a rebellious people, unmolested for sixteen years, were not to be suddenly abolished. The more he brushed the more the indignant locks rose up in revolt. He broke the comb and threw it down angrily.

"Wet your hair," said the Tennessee Shad.

"Soak it in water," said the Gutter Pup.

"Soak it in witch hazel," said Dennis. "It will make it more fragrant."

Dink hesitated. "Won't it smell too much?"

"Naw. It evaporates."

Stover seized the bottle and inundated his head, made an exact part in the middle and drew the sides back in the fashion of pigeon wings.

"Now clap on a dicer," said the Gutter Pup approvingly, "and she'll come up and feed from your hand."

"Are you really in love?" said Dennis softly.

Stover, ignoring all comments, tied a white satin four-in-hand with forget-me-not embossings, which had struck his fancy in Fatty Harris' room, and inserted a stickpin of Finnegan's.

"You ought to have a colored handkerchief to stick in your breast pocket," said the Gutter Pup, who began to yield to the excitement.

"Up his sleeve is more English, don't you know," said Dennis.

Stover stood brazenly before the mirror, looking himself over. The scrubbing he had inflicted on his face had left red, shining spots in prominent places, while his hair, slicked back and plastered down, gave him somewhat the look of an Italian barber on a Sunday off. He felt the general glistening effect without, in his innocence, knowing the remedy.

"Dink, you are bee-oo-tiful!" said Dennis.

"Be careful how you sit down," said the Tennessee Shad, thinking of the trousers.

"How are the shoes?" asked the Gutter Pup solicitously.

"Tight as mischief," said Dink, with a wry face.

"Walk on your heels."

Stover, with a last deprecating glance, opened the door and departed, amid cheers from the contributing committee.

When he arrived at the Lodge the dusky waitress who opened the door started back, as he dropped his hat, and sniffed the air. He went into the parlor, spoiling his carefully planned entrance by tripping over the rug.

"Heavens!" said Tough, "what a smell of witch hazel. Why, it's Dink. What have you been doing?"

Stover felt the temperature rise to boiling.

"We had a bit of a shindy," he said desperately, trying to give it a tragic accent, "and I bumped my head."

"Well, you look like a skinned rat," said Tough to put him thoroughly at his ease.

The angel, however, came to his rescue with solicitous inquiries and with such a heavenly look that Stover only regretted that he could not appear completely done up in bandages.

They went in to dinner, where Dink was so overwhelmed by the vision of Miss McCarty in all her transcendent charms that the effort of swallowing became a painful physical operation.

Afterward, Tough and his mother went over to Foundation House for a visit with the Doctor, and Dink found himself actually alone, escorting Miss McCarty about the grounds in the favoring dusk of the fast closing twilight.

"Let's go toward the Green House," she said. "Will you take my cloak?"

The cloak settled the perplexing question of the hands. He wondered uneasily why she chose that particular direction.

"Are you sure you want to go there?" he said.

"Quite," she said. "I want to see the exact spot where the historic fight took place."

Stover moved uneasily.

"Dear me, what's the matter?"

"I never go there. I hate the place."

"Why?"

"I was miserable there," said Dink abruptly. "Hasn't Tough told you about it?"

"Tell me yourself," said the angelic voice.

Stover felt on the instant the most overpowering desire to confide his whole life's history, and being under the influence of a genuine emotion as well as aided by the obliterating hour, he began straightforwardly to relate the story of his months of Coventry in tense, direct sentences, without pausing to calculate either their vividness or their effect. Once started, he withheld nothing, neither the agony of his pride nor the utter hopelessness of that isolation. Once or twice he hesitated, blurting out, "I say, does this bore you?"

And each time she answered quickly, "No, no—go on."

They went back in the fallen night to the campus, and there he pointed out the spot where he had stood and listened to the singing on the Esplanade and made up his mind to return. All at once, his story ended and he perceived, to his utter confusion, that he had been pouring out his heart to someone whose face he couldn't see, someone who was probably smiling at his impetuous confidence, someone whom he had met only a few hours before.

"Oh, I say," he said in horror, "you must think me an awful fool to go on like this."

"No."

"You made me tell you, you know," he said miserably, wondering what she could think of him. "I never talked like this before— to anyone. I don't know what made me confide in you."

This was untrue, for he knew perfectly well what had led him to speak. So did she and, knowing full well what was working in the tense, awkward boy beside her, she had no feeling of offense, being at an age when such tributes, when genuine, are valued, not scorned.

"I can just feel how you felt—poor boy," she said, perhaps not entirely innocent of the effect of her words. "But then, you have won out, haven't you?"

"I suppose I have," said Stover, almost suffocated by the gentleness of her voice.

"Charlie's told me all about the rest," she said. "Everyone looks up to you now—it's quite a romance, isn't it?"

He was delighted that she saw it thus, secretly wondering if she really knew every point that could be urged in his favor.

"I suppose I'll kick myself all over the lot tomorrow," he said, choosing to be lugubrious.

"Why?" she said, stopping in surprise.

"For talking as I've done."

"You don't regret it?" she said softly, laying her hand on his arm.

Stover drew a long breath—a difficult one.

"No, you bet I don't," he said abruptly. "I'd tell you anything!"

"Come," she said, smiling to herself, "we must go back—but it's so fascinating here, isn't it?"

He thought he had offended her and was in a panic.

"I say, you did not understand what I meant."

"Oh, yes, I did."

"You're not offended?"

"Not at all."

This answer left Stover in such a state of bewilderment that all speech expired. What did she mean by that? Did she really understand or not?

They walked a little way in silence, watching the lights that fell in long lines across the campus, hearing through the soft night the tinkling of mandolins and the thrumming of guitars, a vibrant, feverish life that suddenly seemed unreal to him. They were fast approaching the Lodge. A sudden fear came to him that she would go without understanding what the one, the only night had been in his life.

"I say, Miss McCarty," he began desperately.

"Yes."

"I wish I could tell you—"

"What?"

"I wish I could tell you just what a privilege it's been to meet you."

"Oh, that's very nice."

He felt he had failed. He had not expressed himself well. She did not understand.

"I shall never forget it," he said, plunging ahead.

She stopped a little guiltily and looked at him.

"You queer boy," she said, too pleasantly moved to be severe. "You queer, romantic boy! Why, of course you're going to visit us this summer, and we're going to be good chums, aren't we?"

He did not answer.

"Aren't we?" she repeated, amused at a situation that was not entirely strange.

"No!" he said abruptly, amazed at his own audacity; and with an impulse that he had not suspected he closed the conversation and led the way to the Lodge.

When at last he and Tough were homeward bound he felt he should die if he did not then and there learn certain things. So he began with Machiavellian adroitness, "I say, Tough, what a splendid mother you've got. I didn't get half a chance to talk to her. I say, how long will she be here?"

"They're going over to Princeton first thing in the morning," said Tough, who was secretly relieved.

A button on the borrowed vest popped with Stover's emotion. "How did you get on with Sis?"

"First-rate. She's—she's awful sensible," said Dink.

"Oh, yes, I suppose so."

"I say," said Dink, seeing that he made no progress, "she's been all around—had lots of experience, hasn't she?"

"Oh, she's bounded about a bit."

"Still, she doesn't seem much older than you," said Dink craftily.

"Sis—oh, she's a bit older."

"About twenty-two, I should say," said Dink hopefully.

"Twenty-four, my boy," said Tough unfeelingly. "But I say, don't give it away; she'd bite and scratch me all over the map for telling."

Stover left him without daring to ask any more questions—he knew what he wanted to know. He could not go to his room, he could not face the Tennessee Shad, possessor of the trousers. He wanted to be alone—to wander over the unseen earth, to gulp in the gentle air in long, feverish breaths, to think over what she had said, to grow hot and cold at the thought of his daring, to reconstruct the world of yesterday and organize the new.

He went to the back of chapel and sat down on the cool steps, under the impenetrable clouds of the night.

"She's twenty-four, only twenty-four," he said to himself. "I'm sixteen, almost seventeen—that's only seven years' difference."

XXII

————————

WHEN STOVER awoke the next morning it was to the light of the blushing day. He thought of the events of the night before and sprang up in horror. What had he been thinking of? He had made an ass of himself, a complete egregious ass. What had possessed him? He looked at himself in the glass and his heart sunk at the thought of what she must be thinking. He was glad she was going. He did not want to see her again. He would never visit Tough McCarty. Thank Heaven it was daylight again and he had recovered his senses.

Indignant at everyone, himself most of all, he went to chapel and to recitations, profoundly thankful that he would not have to face her in the mocking light of the day. That he never could have done, never, never!

As he left second recitation Tough McCarty joined him.

"I say, Dink, they both wanted to be remembered to you, and here's a note from Sis."

"A note?"

"Here it is."

Stover stood staring at a violet envelope, inscribed in large, flowing letters: "Mr. John H. Stover."

Then he put it in his pocket hastily and went to his room. Luckily the Tennessee Shad was poaching in the village. He locked the door, secured the transom and drew out the note. It was sealed with a crest and perfumed with a heavenly scent. He held it in his hand a long while, convulsively, and then broke the seal with an awkward finger and read:

DEAR MR. STOVER:

Just a word to thank you for being my faithful cavalier. Don't

369

forget that you are to pay us a good, long visit this summer, and that we are to become the best of chums.

Your very good friend,

JOSEPHINE MCCARTY.

P. S. Don't dare to "kick yourself about the place," whatever that may mean.

When Dink had read this through once he immediately began it again. The second reading left him more bewildered than ever. It was the first time he had come in contact with a manifestation of the workings of the feminine mind. What did she intend him to understand?

"I'll read it again," he said, perching on the back of a chair. "Dear Mr. Stover!" He stopped and considered. "My dear Mr. Stover—'Dear Mr. Stover'—well, that's all right. But what the deuce does she mean by 'faithful cavalier'—I wonder now, I wonder. She wants me to visit her—she can't be offended then. 'Your very good friend,' underlined twice, that sounds as though she wanted to warn me. Undoubtedly I made a fool of myself and this is her angelic way of letting me down. 'Friend'—underlined twice —of course that's it. What a blooming, sentimental, moonstruck jay I was. Gee, I could kick myself to Jericho and back!" But here his eye fell on the postscript and his jaw dropped. "Now how did she guess that? That sounds different from the rest, as though—as though she understood."

He went to the window frowning, and then to the mirror, with a new interest in this new Mr. John H. Stover who received perplexing notes on scented paper.

"I must get some decent collars," he said pensively. "How the deuce does Lovely Mead keep his tie tight?—mine's always slipping down, showing the stud." He changed his collar, having detected a smirch, and tried the effect of parting his hair on the side, like Garry Cockrell.

"She's a wonderful woman—wonderful," he said softly, taking up the letter again. "What eyes! Reminds me of Lorna Doone. Josephine—so that's her name, Josephine—it's a beautiful name. I wish the deuce I knew just what she did mean by this!"

By nightfall he had written a dozen answers which had been torn up in a panic as soon as written. Finally, he determined that the craftiest way would be to send her his remembrances by Tough—that would express everything as well as show her that he could be both discreet and dignified.

In the afternoon he added a dozen extra high collars to his wardrobe and examined hesitatingly the counter of Gent's Bon-Ton socks, spring styles, displayed at Bill Appleby's.

The collars, the latest cut, he tried on surreptitiously. They were uncomfortable and projected into his chin, but there was no question of the superior effect. Suddenly a new element in the school came to his notice—fellows like Lovely Mead, Jock Hasbrouck and Dudy Rankin, who wore tailor-made clothes, rainbow cravats, who always looked immaculate and whose trousers never bagged at the knees.

No sooner was this borne in upon him than he was appalled at the state of his wardrobe. He had outgrown everything. Everything he had bagged at the elbows as well as the knees. His neckties were frazzled and his socks were all earthy browns and oatmeal grays.

His first step was to buy a blacking brush and his next to press his trousers under his mattress, with the result that, being detected and diverted by Dennis, they appeared next morning with a cross-gartered effect.

At nights, especially moonlight nights, under pretense of insomnia, he drew his bed to the open window and gazed sentimentally into the suddenly discovered starry system.

"What the deuce are you mooning about?" said the Tennessee Shad on the first occasion.

"I'm studying astronomy," said Dink with dignity.

The Tennessee Shad gave a snort and soon went loudly off to sleep.

Dink, unmolested, soared away into his own domain. It is true that, having read *Peter Ibbetson*, he tried for a week to emulate that favored dreamer, throwing his arms up, clasping his hands behind his head and being most particular in the crossing of the feet. He dreamed, but only discouraging, tantalizing dreams, and the figure his magic summoned up was not the angelic one, but invariably the elfish eyes and star-pointing nose of Dennis de Brian de Boru Finnegan.

But the dreams that lay like shadows between the faltering eyelids and the shut were real and magic. Then all the difficulties were swept away, no cold chill ran up his back to stay the words that rushed to his lips. Conversations to defy the novelist were spun out and, having periodically saved her from a hundred malignant deaths, he continued each night anew the heroic work of rescue with unsatiated delight. At times, in the throbs of the sacred passion, he thought with a start of his blackened past and the tendencies to crime within him.

"Lord!" he said with a gasp, thinking of the orgy in beer, "what would have become of me—it's like an act of Providence. I wish I could let her know what a—what a good influence she's been. I don't know what I'd 'a' done—if I hadn't met her! I was in a dreadful way!"

By this time, having had the advantage of countless midnight walks, not to mention the familiarizing effect of several scores of desperate adventures, the character of Miss Lorna Doone Mc-Carty had been completely unfolded to the reverential Dink. He saw her, he conversed with her, he knew her. She was a sort of heavenly being, misunderstood by her family—especially her brother, who had not the slightest comprehension. She was like Dante's Beatrice, as the pictures, not the dreadful text, represent that lady—and only seven years older than Mr. John H. Stover. There was Napoleon, who had married a woman older than he was—Napoleon and hosts of others.

With the sudden fear of being dropped a year he began to study with such assiduity that, as is the way with newly sprouted virtue in a cynical world, his motives were suspected by the masters, who, of course, could know nothing of the divine transformation, and by his classmates, who secretly credited him with some new method of cribbing.

Meanwhile, as the year neared its close, the inventive minds of Dennis de Brian de Boru Finnegan and the Tennessee Shad conceived the idea of a monster mass meeting and illustrative parade, which should down the hereditary foe—the steam laundry.

Up to this time the columns of *The Lawrence* had been flooded with communications couched in the style of the oration against Catiline, demanding to know how long the supine Lawrenceville boy would bear in silence the return of his shirt with added entrances and exits, and collars that enclosed the neck with a cheval-de-frise.

This verbal, annual outbreak was succeeded, as usual, by House to House mutinies on the occasion of the arrival of the weekly boxes, without the protest taking further head or front. But at the opening of the last week of the school year, whether a machine had suddenly jumped its fences or whether the ladies of the wash-tubs desired to open the way for the new summer styles—however it may have been—the laundry returned like the battle flags of the republic to the outraged school. Windows were flung open and indignant boys appeared, with white shreds in hand, and vociferously appealed to the heavens above and the green lands below for justice and indemnification.

A meeting of determined spirits was speedily held under the leadership of the Tennessee Shad and Doc Macnooder, and it was decided that a demonstration should take place instanter, the Houses to form and march with complete exhibits to the Upper House, where the fifth formers should likewise display their grievances and join them in a mammoth protest.

Dink, at the first sounds of martial organization, pricked up his ears and summoned the Tennessee Shad and Dennis de Brian de Boru Finnegan to explain why he had been left out of such an important enterprise.

"Why have we left you out?" said the Tennessee Shad indignantly. "What's happened to you these last three weeks? You've had a fighting grouch—no one dared to speak to you for fear of being bitten!"

"In fact," said Dennis, with his sharp, little glance, "you are under the gravest suspicion."

Seeing his secret in peril, Stover assumed a melancholy, injured air.

"You don't know what I've had to worry me," he said, looking out the window, "family matters—financial reverses."

"Oh, I say, Dink, old boy," said the Tennessee Shad, in instant contrition.

"You don't mean it's anything that might keep you from coming back next year?" said Dennis, aghast. "Oh, Dink!"

"I had rather not talk about it," said Stover solemnly.

Dennis and the Shad were overwhelmed with remorse—they offered him at once the Grand Marshalship, which he refused with still offended dignity, but promised his fertile brain to the common cause.

Now Dink's sentimental education, which had progressed with a rush, had just begun to languish on insufficiency of food and a little feeling of staleness on having exhausted the one thousand and one possible methods of saving a heroine's life and wringing the consent of her parents.

He felt a species of guilt in the accusation of his roommate and a sudden longing to be back among mannish pursuits. In an hour, with delighted energy, he had organized the banner and effigy committees of the demonstration and had helped concoct the fiery speech of protest that Doc Macnooder, as spokesman, was so solemnly pledged to deliver for the embattled school.

Four hours later the Kennedy House, led by Toots Cortell and his famous Confederate bugle, defiled and formed the head of the procession. Each member carried a pole attached to which was some article that had been wholly or partly shot to pieces. The Dickinson contingent, led by Doc Macnooder, marched in a square, supporting four posts around which ran a clothesline decked out with the dreadful debris of the house laundry.

The Woodhull proudly bore as its battle flag a few strings of linen floating from a rake, with this inscription underneath:

THE GRAND OLD SHIRT OF THE WOODHULL!
WASHED 16 TIMES AND STILL IN THE GAME!

Several poles, adorned with single hosing in the fashion of liberty caps, were labeled:

WHERE IS MY WANDERING SOCK TONIGHT?

The Davis House was headed by Moses Moseby in a tattered nightshirt, backed up by an irreverent placard:

HOLY MOSES!

But the premier exhibit of the parade was admitted by all to be the Kennedy float, conceived and executed by the Honorable Dink Stover.

On a platform carried by eight hilarious members was displayed Dennis de Brian de Boru Finnegan, clothed in a suit of dark gymnasium tights, over which were superimposed a mangled set of upper and lower unmentionables, whose rents and cavities stood admirably out against the dark background, while the Irishman sat on a chair and alternately stuck a white foot through the bottomless socks that were fed him.

Above the platform was the flaring ensign:

RATHER FRANK NUDITY THAN THIS!

Now it happened that at the auspicious moment when Dink Stover led the apparently scantily clothed Finnegan and the procession of immodest banners around to the Esplanade of the Upper, the Doctor suddenly appeared through the shrubbery that screens Foundation House from the rest of the campus, with a party of ladies, relatives, as it unfortunately happened, of one of the trustees of the school.

One glance of horror and indignation was sufficient for him to wave back the more modest sex and to advance on the astounding procession with fury and determination.

Before Jove's awful look the spirit of '76 vanished. There was a cry of warning and the hosts hesitated, shivered and scampered for shelter.

Now, at any other time the Doctor—who suffered, too, from the common blight—would have secretly if not openly enjoyed the joke; but at that moment the circumstances were admittedly trying. Besides, there was the delicate explanation to be offered to the ladies, who were relatives of one of the influential members of the board of trustees of the Lawrenceville School, John C. Green Foundation. As a consequence, in a towering rage, he summoned the ringleaders, chief among whom he had recognized Dink Stover and, corraling them in his study that night, exposed to them the enormity of their offense against the sex of their mothers and sisters, common decency, morals and morality, the ideals of the school, and the hope that the nation had a right to place in a body of young men nurtured in such homes and educated at such an institution.

The ringleaders, being veterans, viewed the speech from the point of view of artists, and were unanimous in their appreciation. The episode had for Stover, however, unfortunate complications. With the closing of the scholastic season came the elections in the Houses. The Kennedy House, unanimously and with much enthusiasm, chose the Honorable Honest John Stover to succeed the

375

"NOTHING IN YOUR CAREER HAS INDICATED TO ME YOUR FITNESS FOR SUCH A
PLACE OF RESPONSIBILITY."

Honorable King Lentz as administrator and benevolent despot
for the ensuing year.

This election, coming as it did as a complete surprise to Stover,
was naturally a source of deep gratification. His enjoyment, however, was rudely shocked when, the next morning after chapel, the
Doctor stopped him and said, "Stover, I am considerably surprised
at the choice of the Kennedy House and I am not at all sure that
I shall ratify it. Nothing in your career has indicated to me your
fitness for such a place of responsibility. I shall have a further talk
with Mr. Hopkins and let him know my decision."

The Roman! Of course it was The Roman! Of course he had been raging at the thought of his elevation to the presidency! Dink, forgetting the hundred and one times he had met the faculty in the Monday afternoon deliberations, rushed out to spread the news of The Roman's vindictive persecution. Everyone was indignant, outraged at this crowning insult to a free electorate. The whole House would protest *en masse* if the despot's veto was exercised.

At the hour of these angry threats The Roman, persecutor of Dink, was actually saying to the tyrant, "Doctor, I think it would be the best thing—the very best. It will bring out the manliness, the serious earnestness that is in the boy."

"What, you say that?" said the Doctor, a little impatiently, for it was only the morrow of the parade. "I should think your patience would be exhausted. The scamp has been in more mischief than any other boy in the school. He's incorrigibly wild!"

"No—no. I shouldn't say that. Very high-spirited—excess of energy—too much imagination—that's all. There's nothing vicious about the boy."

"But as president, Hopkins, not as president!"

"No one better," said The Roman firmly. "The boy is bound to lead. I know what's in him—he will rise to his responsibility. Doctor, you will see. I have never lost confidence in him."

The Doctor, unconvinced, debated at length before acceding. When he finally gave his ratification he added with a smile, "Well, Hopkins, I do this on your judgment. You may be right, we shall see. By the way, Stover must have led you quite a dance over in the Kennedy. What is it you like in him?"

The Roman reflected and then, his eye twitching reminiscently, "Fearlessness," he said, "and—and a diabolical imagination."

When The Roman returned to the Kennedy he summoned Stover to his study. He knew that Dink misunderstood his attitude and he would have liked to enlighten him. Unfortunately, complete confidence in such cases is sometimes as embarrassing as the relations between father and son. The Roman, pondering, twisted a paper cutter and frowned in front of him.

"Stover," he said at last. "I have talked with the Doctor. He has seen best to approve of your election."

Dink, of course, perceiving the hesitation, went out gleefully, persuaded that the decision was gall and wormwood to his inveterate foe.

The last day of school ended. He drove to Trenton in a buggy with Tough McCarty as befitted his new dignity. He passed the Green House with a strange thrill. The humiliation of a year before had well been atoned, and yet the associations somehow still had power to rise up and wound him.

"Lord, you've changed!" said Tough, following his thoughts.

"Improved!" said Dink grimly.

"I was an infernal nuisance myself when I landed," said Tough, President of the Woodhull, evasively. "I say, Dink, next year we'll be licking the cubs into shape ourselves."

"That's so," said Stover. "Well, by this time next year I probably won't be so popular."

"Why not?"

"I'm going to put an end to a lot of nonsense," said Dink solemnly. "I'm going to see that my kids walk a chalk line."

"So am I," said McCarty, with equal paternity. "What a shame we can't room together, old boy!"

"That'll come in the Upper, and afterward!"

They drove sedately, amid the whirling masses of the school that went hilariously past them. They were no longer of the irresponsible; the cares of the state were descending on their shoulders and a certain respect was necessary.

"Goodbye, old Sockbuts," said Tough, departing toward New York. "Goodbye, old geezer!"

"Au revoir."

"Mind now—fifteenth of July and you come for one month."

"You bet I will!"

"Take care of yourself!"

"I say, Tough," said Dink, with his heart in his mouth.

McCarty, laden with valises, stopped. "What is it?"

"Remember me to your mother, will you?"

"Oh, sure."

"And—and to all the rest of the family!" said Dink, who thereupon bolted, panic-stricken.

XXIII

WHEN JOHN STOVER, President of the Kennedy House, arrived at the opening of the new scholastic year, he arrived magnificently in a special buggy, his changed personal appearance spreading wonder and incredulity before him. He was stylishly encased in a suit of tan whipcord, with creases down his trousers front that cut the air like the prow of a ship. On his head, rakishly set, was a Panama hat, over his arm was a natty raincoat and he wore gloves.

"Who is it?" said the Tennessee Shad faintly.

"It's the gas inspector," said Dennis de Brian de Boru, who, though now long of trousers, continued short of respect.

"Goodness gracious," said the Tennessee Shad, "can it be the little Dink who came to us from the Green House?"

Stover approached serenely and shook hands.

"Heavens, Dink," said the Gutter Pup, "what has happened? Have you gone into the clothing business?"

"Like my jibs?" said Stover, throwing back his coat. "Catch this!"

The front rank went over like so many ninepins. Stover, pleased with the effect, waved his hand and disappeared to pay his militant respects to The Roman, who led him to the light and looked him over with unconcealed amazement.

When Dink had gone to his old room, the Tennessee Shad, the Gutter Pup and Dennis de Brian de Boru Finnegan were already awaiting him, with heads critically slanted.

"Tell us the worst," said the Gutter Pup.

"Are you married?" said the Tennessee Shad.

"Let's see her photograph," said Dennis de Brian de Boru Finnegan.

Now, Stover had foreseen the greeting and the question and had

379

"LIKE MY JIBS?" SAID STOVER.

come prepared. He opened his valise and, taking out a case, arranged a dozen photographs on his bureau, artfully concealing the one and only in a temporarily subordinate position.

The three village loungers arose and stationed themselves in front of the portrait gallery.

"Why, he must be perfectly irresistible!" said the Gutter Pup.

"Dink," said Dennis, "do all these girls love you?"

Stover, disdaining a reply, selected another case.

380

"Razors!" said the Tennessee Shad.

"What for?" said Dennis.

"Oh, I shave, too," said the Gutter Pup, in whom the spirit of envy was beginning to work.

"And now, boys," said Stover briskly, taking off his coat, folding it carefully over a chair and beginning to unpack, "sit down. Don't act like a lot of hayseeds on a rail, but tell me what the Freshmen are like."

The manner was complete—convincing, without a trace of embarrassment. The three wits exchanged foolish glances and sat down.

"What do you weigh?" said the Gutter Pup faintly.

"One hundred and fifty-five, and I've grown an inch," said Stover, ranging on a ring a score of flashy neckties.

"I wish Lovely Mead could see those," said the Gutter Pup with a last appearance of levity.

"Call him up. Look at them yourself," said Stover, tendering the neckwear. "I think they're rather tasty myself."

Before such absolute serenity frivolity died of starvation. They made no further attempt at sarcasm, but sat awed until Stover had departed to carry the glad news of his increased weight to Captain Flash Condit.

"Why he's older than The Roman," said the Tennessee Shad, the first to recover.

"He's in love," said Dennis, who had intuitions.

"No, be-loved," said the Gutter Pup with a sigh, who was suffering from the first case, but not from the second.

The amazement of rolling old Sir John Falstaff at the transformation of Prince Hal was nothing to the consternation of the Kennedy House at the sudden conversion of Dink Stover, the fount of mischief, into a complete disciplinarian.

Now the cardinal principle of House government is the division of the flock by the establishing of an age line. The control of the youngsters is almost always vigorously enforced, and though the logical principles involved are sometimes rather dubious, they are adequate from the fact that they are never open to argument. Occasionally, however, under the leadership of some president either too indolent or incapable of leadership, this strict surveillance over the habits and conduct of youth is relaxed, with disastrous results to the orderly reputation of the House.

Stover, having been the arch-rebel and fomenter of mischief, had the most determined ideas as to the discipline he intended to enforce and the respect he should exact.

The first clash came with the initial House Meeting, over which he presided. Now in the past these occasions had offered Dennis de Brian de Boru Finnegan and his attendant imps unlimited amusement, as King Lentz had been almost totally ignorant of the laws of parliamentary procedure.

Of a consequence, no sooner was a meeting fairly under way, than some young scamp would rise and solemnly move the previous question, which never failed to bring down a storm of hoots at the complete mystification of the perplexed chairman, who never to his last day was able to solve this knotty point of procedure.

Now, Dennis, while he had been impressed by Stover's new majesty, retained still a feeling of resistance. So the moment the gavel declared the meeting open he bobbed up with a wicked gleam and shrilly announced, "Mr. Chairman, I move the previous question."

"Mr. Finnegan will come to order," said Stover quietly.

"Oh, I say, Dink!"

"Are you addressing the chair?" said Stover sternly.

"Oh, no," said Finnegan, according to his usual manner, "I was just whistling through my teeth, gargling my larynx, trilling—"

Crash came the gavel and the law spoke forth: "Mr. Finnegan will come to order."

"I won't!"

"Mr. Finnegan either apologizes to the chair, or the chair will see that Mr. Finnegan returns to short trousers and stays there. Mr. Finnegan has exactly one minute to make up his mind."

Dennis, crimson and gasping, stood more thoroughly amazed and nonplused than he had ever been in his active existence. He opened his mouth as though to reply, and beheld Stover calmly draw forth his watch. Had it been anyone else, Dennis would have hesitated; but he knew Stover of old and what the chilly, metallic note was in his voice. He chose the lesser of two evils and gave the apology.

"The chair will now state," said Stover, replacing his watch, "for the benefit of any other young, transcendent jokers that may care to display their side-splitting wit, that the chair is quite capable of handling the previous question, or any other question, and that these meetings are going to be orderly proceedings and not one-ring circuses for the benefit of the Kennedy Association of Clowns. The question before the House is the protest against compulsory bath. The chair recognizes Mr. Lazelle to make a motion."

The cup of Finnegan's bitterness was not yet filled. Stover's first act of administration was to forbid the privileges of the cold-air flues and the demon cigarette to all members of the House who had not attained, according to his judgment, either a proper age or a sufficient display of bodily stature. Among the proscribed was Dennis de Brian de Boru Finnegan, whose legs, clothed in new dignity, fairly quivered under the affront, as he tearfully protested, "I say Dink, it's an outrage!"

"Can't help it. It's for your own good."

"But I'm fifteen."

"Now, see here, Dennis," said Stover firmly, "your business is to grow and to be of some use. No one's going to know about it unless you yell it out, but I'm going to see that you turn out a decent, manly chap and not another Slops Barnett."

"But you went with Slops yourself."

"I did—but you're not going to be such a fool."

"Why, you're a regular tyrant!"

"All right, call it that."

"And I elected you," said Dennis, the aggrieved and astounded modern politician. "This is Goo-gooism!"

"No, it isn't," said Stover indignantly. "I'm not interfering with any fellow who's sixteen—they can do what they darn please. But I'm not going to have a lot of kids in this House starting sporting life until they've grown up to it, *savez?* They're going to be worth living with and having around, and not abominations in the sight of gods and men. Pass the word along."

The revolt, for a short while, was furiously indignant, but the prestige of Stover's reputation forestalled all thought of disobedience. In such cases absolute power is in the hands of him who can wield it, and Stover could command.

In short order he had reduced the youngsters to respect and usefulness, with the following imperial decrees:

1. All squabs are to maintain in public a deferential and modest attitude.

2. No squab shall talk to excess in the presence of his elders.

3. No squab shall habitually use bad language, under penalty of an application of soap and water.

4. No squab shall use tobacco in any form.

5. No squab shall leave the House after lights without express permission.

These regulations were not simply an exercise of arbitrary authority, for in the House itself were certain elements which Dink perfectly understood, and whose spheres of influence he was resolved to confine to their own limits.

"How're you going to enforce, Sire, these imperial decrees? asked the Tennessee Shad, who, however, thoroughly approved.

"I have a method," said Stover, with an interior smile. "It's what I call a Rogues' Gallery."

"I don't see," said the Tennessee Shad, puzzled.

"You will."

The first rebel was a Freshman, Bellefont, known as the Millionaire Baby, who, due to a previous luxurious existence, had acquired manly practices at an early age. Bellefont was detected with the odor of tobacco.

"Young squab, have you been smoking?" said Stover.

"Well, what are you going to do about it?" said the youngster defiantly.

"Gutter Pup, get your camera," said Stover.

The Gutter Pup, mystified, returned. The autocrat seized the young rebel, slung him paternally across his knee and with raised hand spoke:

"Gutter Pup, snap a couple of good ones. We'll make this Exhibit A in our Rogues' Gallery."

Bellefont, at the thought of this public perpetuation, set up a howl and kicked as though mortally stung. Stover held firm. The snapshots were taken, developed and duly posted.

From that moment, in public at least, Stover's slightest gesture was obeyed as promptly as the lifting of an English policeman's finger.

The yoke once accepted became popular alike with the older members, who ceased to be annoyed, and with the squabs themselves, who, finding they were protected from bullying or unfair exactions, soon adopted toward Stover an attitude of reverent idolatry that was not without its embarrassments. He was called upon at all hours to render decisions on matters political and philosophical, with the knowledge that his opinion would instantly be adopted as religion. Before him were brought all family quarrels, some serious, some grotesque; but each class demanding a settlement in equity.

One afternoon Dennis maliciously piloted to his presence Pee-wee Norris and his new roommate, a youngster named Berbacker, called Cyclops from the fact that one eye was glass, a gift that brought him a peculiar admiration and envy.

Stover, observing the cunning expression on Finnegan's face, scented a trap. The matter was, indeed, very grave.

"See here, Dink," said Pee-wee indignantly; "I leave it to you. How would you like to stumble upon a loose eye all over the room?"

"A what?"

"A loose eye. This fellow Cyclops is all the time leaving his glass eye around in my diggin's and I don't like it. It's the deuce of a thing to find it winking up at you from the table or the window seat. It gives me the creeps."

"What have you got to say, Cyclops?" said Stover, assuming a judicial air.

"Well, I've always been used to takin' the eye out," said Cyclops, with an injured look. "Most fellows are glad to see it. But, I say, I'm the fellow who has the kick. The whole thing started by Norris hiding it on me."

"Did you swipe his eye?" said Stover severely.

"Well, yes, I did. What right's he got to let it out loose?"

"I want him to leave my eye alone," said Cyclops.

"I want him to keep his old eye in his old socket," said Pee-wee.

"Oh, Solomon, what is thy judgment?" said Dennis, who had engineered it all.

"I'll give my judgment and it'll settle it," said Dink firmly. "But I'll think it over first."

True to his word, he deliberated long and actively and, as the judgment had to be given, he called the complaining parties before him and said, "Now, look here, Pee-wee and Cyclops; you fellows are rooming together and you've got to get on. If you fight, keep it to yourselves; don't shout it around. But get together—agree. You've got to go on, and the more you agree—ahem—the less you'll disagree, see? It's just like marriage. Now you go back and live like a respectable married couple, and if I hear any more about this glass eye I'll spank you both and have you photographed for the Rogues' Gallery."

Among the members of the Kennedy House there were two who defied his authority and gave him cause for dissatisfaction—the Millionaire Baby, who was a nuisance because he had been pampered and impressed with his own divine right, and a fellow named Horses Griffin, who was unbearable because, owing to his size and strength, he had never had the blessing of a good thrashing.

Now when Stover promulgated his laws for the protection of squabs he had served notice on the sporting centers that he expected their adherence. Fellows like Slops Barnett and Fatty Harris, who, to do them justice, approved of segregation, made no defiance. Griffin, though, who was a hulking, rather surly, self-conscious fellow, secretly rebelled at this act of authority, and gave asylum to Bellefont, from whom he was glad to accept the good things that regularly arrived in boxes from a solicitous mother.

Stover had seen from the first how the issue would have to be met, and met it at the first opportunity. Griffin having defied his authority by openly inviting the Millionaire Baby up for the nefarious practice of matching pennies, Dink marched up the stairs and entered the enemy's room.

A moment later the group expectantly gathered in the hall heard something within that resembled an itinerant cyclone, then the door blew open and Griffin shot out and raced for the stairs, while behind him—like an angry tomcat—came Stover, in time to give to the panicky champion just that extra impetus that allowed him, as Dennis expressed it, to establish a new record—flying start—for the twenty-six steps. After this little explanation Griffin showed a marked disinclination for the company of Bellefont, and became, indeed, quite a useful member of the community, though he always retained such acute memories that an angry tone from Stover would cause him to fidget and calculate the distance to the door.

Griffin subdued, the Millionaire Baby still remained. The problem was a knotty one, for as Bellefont was still of substature the means of correction were limited.

"What worries your Majesty?" said Dennis de Brian de Boru, perceiving Stover in stern meditation. "Is it that beautiful specimen of flunky-raised squab entitled the Millionaire Baby?"

"It is," said Dink. Between him and Dennis peace had long since been concluded.

"He is a very precious hothouse flower," said Dennis sarcastically.

"He is the most useless, pestiferous, conceited little squirt I ever saw," said Dink.

"I love him not."

"But I'll get that flunky smell out of him yet!"

"The pity is he has such fat, juicy boxes from home."

"He has—how often?"

"Every two weeks."

"It oughtn't to be allowed."

"What are you going to do? You can't take 'em by force."

"No—that wouldn't do."

"Still," said Dennis regretfully, "he's so young it is just ruining his little digestion."

They sat a moment deliberating. Finally Dink spoke rapturously. "I have it. We'll organize the Kennedy Customs House."

"Aha!"

"Everything imported must pass the Customs House."

"Pass?"

"Certainly; everything must be legal."

"What am I to be?"

"Appraiser."

"I'd rather be first taster."

"Same thing."

"You said pass," said Dennis obstinately. "I don't like that word."

"Purely technical sense."

"But there will be duties imposed?"

"Certainly."

"Aha!" said Dennis brightening. "Very high duties?"

"The maximum duty on luxuries," said Dink. "We're all good Republicans, aren't we?"

"I am, if I can write the tariff schedule," said Dennis, who, as may be seen, was orthodox.

When, on the following week, young Bellefont received his regular installment of high-priced indigestibles he was amazed to see the Gutter Pup and Lovely Mead appear with solemn demeanor.

"Hello," said the Millionaire Baby, placing himself in front of the half-open box.

"See these badges," said Lovely Mead, pointing to their caps, around which were displayed white bandages inscribed "inspector."

"Sure."

"We're in the Customs House."

"Well, what?"

"And we have received information that you are systematically smuggling goods into this territory."

The Millionaire Baby looked as though a ghost had arisen.

"Aha!" said the Gutter Pup, perceiving the box. "Here's the evidence now. Officer, seize the goods and the prisoner."

"What are you going to do to me?" said the culprit in great alarm.

"Take you before the Customs Court."

The Customs Court was sitting, without absentees, in Stover's room—appraisers, weighers, adjusters and consulting experts, all legally ticketed and very solemn. The prisoner was stood in a corner and the contents of the box spread on the floor.

"First exhibit—one plum cake," announced Beekstein, who was in a menial position.

"Duty sixty-five per cent," said Dennis de Brian de Boru Finnegan, consulting a book. "Raisins and spices."

"Two bottles of anchovy olives."

"Duty fifty per cent, imported fruits."

"Only fifty per cent?" said Stover, who had a preference for the same.

"That's all."

"What's it on?"

"Imported fruits."

"How about spiced fish?" said the Tennessee Shad, coming to the rescue, "and, likewise, Italian glass?"

The Millionaire Baby gave a groan.

"Imported fish, forty per cent," said Dennis, "glass—Venetian glass—thirty-five per cent. He owes us thirty per cent on this."

"Continue," said Stover, casting a grateful glance at the Tennessee Shad.

"Two boxes of candied prunes, that's vegetables, twenty-five per cent."

"They're preserved in sugar, aren't they?"

"Sure."

"There's a duty of fifty per cent on sugar."

"Long live the Sugar Trust."

"Doggone robbers!" said the Millionaire Baby tearfully.

"Three boxes salted almonds, one large box of chocolate bon-bons, one angel cake and six tins of candied ginger."

The judges, deliberating, assessed each article. Stover rose to announce the decree.

"The clerk of the court will return to the importer thirty-five per cent of the plum cake, twenty-five per cent of the candied prunes, one box of salted almonds and two tins of ginger."

The Millionaire Baby breathlessly contained his wrath.

Dennis de Brian de Boru Finnegan addressed the court. "Your Honor."

"Mr. Finnegan."

"I beg to call to your Honor's attention that these goods have been seized and are subject to a fine."

"True," said Stover, glancing sternly at the frothing Bellefont. "I would be inclined to be lenient, but I am informed that this is not the defendant's first offense. The clerk of the court will, there-fore, confiscate the whole."

The Millionaire Baby, with a howl, began to express himself in the language of the stables.

"Gag him," said Stover, "and let him be informed that the duties will be lightened if in the future he declares his imports."

The government then applied the revenues to the needs of the department of the interior.

"The duty on anchovy olives is too high," said Finnegan, look-ing fondly down a bottle.

"How so?"

"It will stop the imports."

"True—we might reduce it."

"We must encourage imports," said the Gutter Pup firmly.

And the chorus came full-mouthed:

"Sure!"

The Millionaire Baby received three more boxes—that is, he

received the limited portion that a paternal government allowed him. Then, being chastened, he took a despicable revenge—he stopped the supply.

"Well, it was sweet while it lasted," said Dennis regretfully.

"We've stopped toadyism in the House," said Stover virtuously. "We have eliminated the influence of money."

"That is praiseworthy, but it doesn't fill me with enthusiasm."

"Dink," said the Tennessee Shad, "I must say I consider this one of your few failures. You're a great administrator, but you don't understand the theory of taxation."

"I don't, eh? Well, what is the theory?"

"The theory of taxation," said the Tennessee Shad, "is to soak the taxed all they'll stand for, but to leave them just enough so they'll come again."

XXIV

No sooner had Mr. John H. Stover returned from the serious developments of the summer, arranged his new possessions and
brought forward the photograph of Miss McCarty to a position on
the edge of his bureau, where he could turn to it the last thing at
night and again behold it with his waking glance, than a horrible
coincidence appeared.

Among the festive decorations that made the corporate home of
Dink and the Tennessee Shad a place to visit and admire was, as
has been related, a smashing poster of a ballet dancer in the costume of an amazon parader. Up to now Dink had shared the just
pride of the Tennessee Shad in this rakish exhibit that somehow
gave the possessor the reputation of having an acquaintance with
stage entrances. But on the second morning when his faithful
glance turned to the protecting presence of Miss McCarty resting
among the brushes, it paused a moment on the representative of
the American dramatic profession, who was coquettishly trying to
conceal one foot behind her ear.

Then he sat bolt upright with a start. By some strange perversion
of the fate that delights in torturing lovers, the features of the
immodestly clothed amazon bore the most startling resemblance to
that paragon of celestial purity, Miss Josephine McCarty.

The more he gazed the more astounding was the impression. He
gazed and then he did not gaze at all—it seemed like a profanation.
The resemblance, once perceived, positively haunted him; stand
where he might, his eyes could see nothing but the seraphic head
of Miss McCarty upon the unspeakable body of the amazon—and
then those legs!

For days this centaurian combination tortured him without his
being able to evolve a satisfactory method of removing the blas-
phemous poster. A direct attack was quite out of the question, for
manifestly the Tennessee Shad would demand an adequate expla-

nation for the destruction of his treasured possession. There could be no explanation except the true one, and such a confession was unthinkable, even to a roommate under oath.

For two solid weeks Stover, brooding desperately, sought to avert his glance from the profane spectacle before chance came to his rescue. One Saturday night, after a strenuous game with the Princeton Freshmen, Dink, afraid of going stale, decided to quicken his jaded appetite by an application of sardines, deviled ham and root beer.

The feasting table happened to be directly beneath the abhorrent poster so that Stover, as he lifted the bottle to open it, beheld with fury the offending tights. He gave the bottle instinctively a shake and with that disturbing motion suddenly came his plan.

"This root beer has been flat as the deuce lately," he said.

"They're selling us poor stuff," said the Tennessee Shad, with the tail of a sardine disappearing within.

"I wonder if I could put life in the blame thing if I shook it up a bit," said Stover, suiting the action to the word.

Now, the Tennessee Shad knew from experience what that result would be, but as Stover was holding the bottle he dissembled his knowledge.

"Give it a shake," he said.

Stover complied.

"Shake her again."

"How's that?"

"Once more. It'll be just like champagne."

Stover gave it a final vigorous shake, pointed the nozzle toward the poster and cut the cork. There was an explosion and then the contents rose like a geyser and spread over the ceiling and the luckless ballet dancer who dared to resemble Miss McCarty.

By the next morning the poster was unrecognizable under a coating of dried reddish spots and was ignominiously removed, to the delight of Stover, whose illusions were thus preserved, as well as his secret.

Now, the month spent at the McCartys' had strengthened his honorable intentions and given them that definite purpose that is sometimes vulgarly ticketed "object matrimony."

It is not that Dink could return over the romantic days of his visit and lay his finger on any particular scene or any definite word that could be construed as binding Miss McCarty. But, on the other hand, his own actions and expressions, he thought, must have been so capable of but one interpretation that, as a man of honor, he held himself morally as well as willingly bound. Of course, she had understood his attitude; she must have understood. And, likewise, there were events that made him believe that she, in her discreet way, had let him see by her actions what she could not convey by her words. For, of course, in his present position of dependence on his father, nothing could be said. He understood that. He would not have changed it. Still, there were unmistakable memories of the preference he had enjoyed. There had been, in particular, an ill-favored dude, called Ver Plank, who had always been hanging around with his tandem and his millions, who had been sacrificed a dozen times by the mercenary angel to him, John H. Stover's, profit. That was clear enough, and there had been many such incidents.

The only thing that disappointed Dink was the polite correctness of her letters. But then something, he said to himself, must be allowed for maiden modesty. His own letters were the product of afternoons and evenings. The herculean difficulty that he experienced in covering four sheets of paper—even when writing a flowing hand and allowing half a page for the signature—secretly worried him. It seemed as though something was lacking in his character or in the strength of his devotion.

On the day after the final disappearance of the brazen amazon Dink pounced upon a violet envelope in the well-known handwriting and bore it to a place of secrecy. It was in answer to four of his own painful compositions.

He gave three glances before reading, three glances that estimate all such longed-for epistles. There were five pages, which brought him a thrill; it was signed "as ever, Josephine," which brought him a doubt; and it began "Dear Jack," which brought him nothing at all.

Having thus passed from hot to cold, and back to a fluctuating temperature, he began the letter—first, to read what was written, and second, to read what might be concealed between the lines:

DEAR JACK:
Since your last letter I've been in a perfect whirl of gaiety—

dances, coaching parties and what-not. Really, you would say that I was nothing but a frivolous butterfly of fashion. Next week I am going to the Ver Planks' with quite a party and we are to coach through the Berkshires. The Judsons are to be along and that pretty Miss Dow, of whom I was so jealous when you were here, do you remember? I met a Mr. Cockrell, who, it seems, was at Lawrenceville. He told me you were going to be a phenomenal football player, captain of the team next year, and all sorts of wonderful things. He *admires* you *tremendously*. I was so pleased! Don't forget to write soon.

As ever,
JOSEPHINE.

This letter, as indeed all her letters did, left Dink trapezing, so to speak, from one emotion to another. He had not acquired that knowledge, which indeed is never acquired, of valuing to a nicety the intents, insinuations and complexities of the feminine school of literature.

There were things that sent him soaring like a Japanese kite and there were things, notably the reference to Ver Plank, that tumbled him as awkwardly down.

He immediately seized upon pen and paper. It had, perhaps, been his fault. He would conduct the correspondence on a more serious tone. He would be a little—daring.

At the start he fell into the usual inky deliberation. "Dear Josephine" was so inadequate. "My dear Josephine" had—or did it not have—just an extra little touch of tenderness, a peculiar claim to possession. But if so, would it be too bold or too sentimental? He wrote boldly:

"My dear Josephine":

Then he considered. Unfortunately, at that time the late lamented Pete Daly, in the halls of the likewise lamented Weber and Fields, was singing love songs to a questionable lady likewise entitled "My Josephine." The connection was unthinkable. Dink tore the page into minute bits and, selecting another, sighed and returned to the old formula.

Here another long pause succeeded while he searched for a sentiment or a resolve that would raise him in her estimation. It is a mood in which the direction of a lifetime is sometimes bartered

394

for a phrase. So it happened with Dink. Suddenly his face lit up
and he started to write:

DEAR JOSEPHINE:

Your letter came to me just as I was writing you of a plan I
have been thinking of for weeks. I have decided not to go to
college. Of course, it would be a great pleasure, and perhaps I
look upon life too seriously, as you often tell me; but I want to get
to work, to feel that I am standing on my own feet, and four years
seems an awful time to wait—for that. What do you think? I do
hope you understand just *what* I mean. It is very serious to me,
the most serious thing in the world.

I'm glad you're having a good time.

Don't write such nonsense about Miss Dow; you know there's
nothing in that direction. Do write and tell me what you think
about my plan.

Faithfully yours,

JACK.

P. S. When are you going to send me that new photograph?
I have only three of you now, a real one and two Kodaks. I'm
glad you're having a good time.

No sooner was this letter dispatched and Stover had realized
what had been in his mind for weeks than he went to Tough Mc-
Carty to inform him of his high resolve.

"But, Dink," said Tough in dismay, "you can't be serious! Why,
we were going through college together!"

"That's the hard part of it," said Dink, looking and, indeed,
feeling very solemn.

"But you're giving up a wonderful career. Everyone says you'll
be a star end. You'll make the All-American. Oh, Dink!"

"Don't," said Dink heroically.

"But, I say, what's happened?"

"It's—it's a family matter," said Stover, who on such occasions, it
will be perceived, had a strong family feeling.

"Is it decided?" said Tough in consternation.

"Unless stocks take a turn," said Dink.

McCarty was heartbroken, Dink rather pleased, with the new
role that, somehow, lifted him from his fellows in dignity and

395

seriousness and seemed to cut down the seven years. All that week he waited hopefully for her answer. She must understand now the inflexibility of his character and the intensity of his devotion. His letter told everything, and yet in such a delicate manner that she must honor him the more for the generous way in which he took everything upon himself, offered everything and asked nothing. He was so confidently happy and elated with the vexed decision of his affairs that he even took the Millionaire Baby over to the Jigger Shop and stood treat, after a few words of paternal advice which went unheeded.

Toward the beginning of the third week in the early days of November, as the squad was returning from practice Tough said casually, "I say, did you get a letter from Sis?"

"No," said Dink with difficulty.

"You probably have one at the house. She's engaged."

"What?" said Dink faintly. The word seemed to be spoken from another mouth.

"Engaged to that Ver Plank fellow that was hanging around. I think he's a mutt."

"Oh, yes—Ver Plank."

"Gee, it gave me quite a jolt!"

"Oh, I—I rather expected it."

He left Tough, wondering how he had had the strength to answer.

"Look out, you're treading on my toes," said the Gutter Pup next him.

He mumbled something and his teeth closed over his tongue in the effort to bring the sharp sense of pain. He went to his box; the letter was there. He went to his room and laid it on the table, going to the window and staring out. Then he sat down heavily, rested his head in his hands and read:

DEAR JACK:

I'm writing to you among the first, for I want you particularly to know how happy I am. Mr. Ver Plank—

He put the letter down; indeed, he could not see to read any further. There was nothing more to read—nothing mattered. It was all over, the light was gone, everything was topsy-turvy. He could not understand—but it was over—all over. There was nothing left.

Some time later the Tennessee Shad came loping down the hall, tried the door and, finding it locked, called out, "What the deuce—open up!"

Dink, in terror, rose from the table where he had remained motionless. He caught up the letter and hastily stuffed it in his desk, saying gruffly, "In a moment."

Then he dabbed a sponge over his face, pressed his hands to his temples and, steadying himself, unlocked the door.

"For the love of Mike!" said the indignant Tennessee Shad, and then, catching sight of Dink, stopped. "Dink, what is the matter?"

"It's—it's my mother," said Dink desperately.

"She's not dead?"

"No—no—" said Dink, now free to suffocate. "Not yet."

XXV

THIS PROVIDENTIAL appearance of his mother mercifully allowed Dink an opportunity to suffer without fear of disgrace in the eyes of the unemotional Tennessee Shad.

That very night, as soon as the Shad had departed in search of Beekstein's guiding mathematical hand, Dink sat down heroically to frame his letter of congratulations. He would show her that, though she looked upon him as a boy, there was in him the courage that never cries out. She had played with him, but at least she should look back with admiration.

"Dear Miss McCarty," he wrote—that much he owed to his own dignity, and that should be his only reproach. The rest should be in the tone of levity, the smile that shows no ache.

DEAR MISS McCARTY:

Of course, it was no surprise to me. I saw it coming long ago. Mr. Ver Plank seems to me a most estimable young man. You will be very congenial, I am sure, and very happy. Thank you for letting me know among the first. That was *bully* of you! Give my very best congratulations to Mr. Ver Plank and tell him I think he's a very lucky fellow.

Faithfully yours,

JACK.

He had resolved to sign formally, "Cordially yours—John H. Stover." But toward the end his resolution weakened. He would be faithful, even if she were not. Perhaps when she read it and thought it over she would feel a little remorse, a little acute sorrow. Imbued with the thought, he stood looking at the letter, which somehow brought a little consolation, a little pride into the night of his misery. It was a good letter—a very good letter. He read it over three times and then, going to the washstand, took up the

398

sponge and pressed out a lachrymal drop that fell directly over the "Faithfully yours."

It made a blot that no one could have looked at unmoved.

He hastily sealed the letter and, slipping out of the House, went over and mailed it with his own hands. It was the farewell—he would never toil out his heart over another. And with it went John Stover, the faithful cavalier. Another John Stover had arisen, the man of heroic sorrows.

For a whole week faithfully he was true to his grief, keeping his own company, eating out his heart, suffering as only that first deception can inflict sorrow. And he sought nothing else. He hoped —he hoped that he would go on suffering for years and years, saddened and deceived.

But, somehow—though, of course, deep down within him nothing would ever change—the gloom gradually lifted. The call of his fellows began to be heard again. The glances of the under formers that followed his public appearances with adoring worship began to please him once more.

Finally, one afternoon, he stopped in at Appleby's to inspect a new supply of dazzling cravats.

"You've got the first choice, Mr. Stover," said Appleby in his caressing way. "No one's had a look at them before you."

"Well, let's look 'em over," said Stover, with a beginning of interest.

"Look at them," said Appleby. "You're a judge, Mr. Stover. You know how to dress in a tasty way. Now, really, have you ever seen anything genteeler than them?"

Stover fingered them and his eye lit up. They certainly were exceptional and just the style that was becoming to his blond advantages. He selected six, then added two more and, finally, went to his room with a dozen, where he tried them, one after the other, before his mirror, smiling a little at the effect.

Then he went to his bureau and relegated the photograph of the future Mrs. Ver Plank to the rear and promoted Miss Dow to the place of honor.

"That's over," he said; "but she nearly ruined my life!"

In which he was wrong, for if Miss McCarty had not arrived, Appleby, purveyor of Gents' Fancies, would never have sold him a dozen most becoming neckties.

When the Tennessee Shad came in, he looked in surprise.

"Hello, better news today?" he said sympathetically.

"News?" said Dink in a moment of abstraction.

"Why, your mother."

"Oh, yes—yes, she's better," said Dink hastily, and to make it convincing he added in a reverent voice, "thank God!"

The next day he informed McCarty that he had changed his mind. He was going to college; they would have four glorious years together.

"What's happened?" said Tough mystified. "Better news from home?"

"Yes," said Dink, "stocks have gone up."

But the tragedy of his life had one result that came near wrecking his career and the school's hope for victory in the Andover game. During the early weeks of the term Dink had been too engrossed with his new responsibilities to study, and during the later weeks too overwhelmed by the real burden of life to think of such technicalities as lessons. Having studied the preferences and dislikes of his tyrants, he succeeded, however, in bluffing through most of his recitations with the loyal support of Beekstein. But The Roman was not thus to be circumvented, and as Dink, in the Byronic period of grief, had no heart for florid improvisations of the applause of the multitude he contented himself, whenever annoyed by his implacable persecutor, The Roman, by rising and saying with great dignity, "Not prepared, sir."

The blow fell one week before the Andover game, when such blows always fall. The Roman called him up after class and informed him that, owing to the paucity of evidence in his daily appearances, he would have to put him to a special examination to determine whether he had a passing knowledge.

The school was in dismay. A failure, of course, meant disbarment from the Andover game—the loss of Stover, who was the strength of the whole left side.

To Dink, of course, this extraordinary decree was the crowning evidence of the determined hatred of The Roman. And all because he had, years before, mistaken him for a commercial traveler and called him "Old Cocky-wax"!

He would be flunked—of course he would be flunked if The Roman had made up his mind to do it. He might have waited another week—after the Andover game. But no, his plan was to keep him out of the game, which, of course, meant the loss of the captaincy, which everyone accorded him.

These opinions, needless to say, were shared by all well-wishers of the eleven. There was even talk, in the first moments of excitement, of arraigning The Roman before the Board of Trustees.

The examination was to be held in The Roman's study that night. Beekstein and Gumbo hurried to Dink's assistance. But what could that avail with six weeks' work to cover?

In this desperate state desperate means were suggested by desperate characters. Stover should go to the examination padded with interlinear friendly aids to translation. A committee from outside should then convey the gigantic water cooler that stood in the hall to the upper landing. There it should be nicely balanced on the topmost step and a string thrown out the window, which, at the right time, should be pulled by three patriots from other Houses. The water cooler would descend with a hideous clatter, The Roman would rush from his study, and Stover would be given time to refresh his memory.

Now, Stover did not like this plan. He had never done much direct cribbing, as that species of deception made him uncomfortable and seemed devoid of the high qualities of dignity that should attend the warfare against the Natural Enemy.

At first he refused to enter this conspiracy, but finally yielded in a halfhearted way when it was dinned in his ears that he was only meeting The Roman at his own game, that he was being persecuted, that the school was being sacrificed for a private spite—in a word, that the end must be looked at and not the means and that the end was moral and noble.

Thus partly won over, Dink entered The Roman's study that night with portions of interlinear translations distributed about his person and whipped up into a rage against The Roman that made him forget all else.

The study was on the ground floor—the conspirators were to wait at the window until Stover should have received the examination paper and given the signal.

The Roman nodded as Stover entered and, motioning him to a seat, gave him the questions, saying, "I sincerely hope, John, you are able to answer these."

"Thank you, sir," said Stover with great sarcasm.

He went to the desk by the window and sat down, taking out his pencil.

There was a shuffling of feet and the scraping of a chair across the room. Stover looked up in surprise.

"Take your time, John," said The Roman, who had risen. Then, without another word, he turned and left the room.

Stover smiled to himself. He knew that trick. He waited for the sudden reopening of the door, but no noise came. He frowned and, mechanically looking at the questions, opened his book at the place designated. Then he raised his head and listened again.

All at once he became very angry. The Roman was putting him on his honor—he had no right to do any such thing! It changed all their preparations. It was a low-down, malignant trick. It took away all the elements of danger that glorified the conspiracy. It made it easy and, therefore, mean.

At the window came a timid scratching. Stover shook his head. The Roman would return. Then he would give the signal willingly. So he folded his arms sternly and waited—but no footsteps slipped along outside the door. The Roman had indeed left him to his honor.

A great, angry lump came in his throat, angry tears blurred his eyes. He hated The Roman, he despised him; it was unfair, it was malicious, but he could not do what he would have done. There *was* a difference.

All at once the bowels of the House seemed rent asunder, as down the stairs, bumping and smashing, went the liberated water cooler. Instantly a chorus of shrieks arose, steps rushing to and fro, and then quiet.

Still The Roman did not come. Stover glanced at the paragraphs selected, and oh, mockery and bitterness, two out of three happened to be passages he had read with Beekstein not an hour before. His eye went over them, he remembered them perfectly.

"If that ain't the limit!" he said, choking. "To know 'em after all. Of course, now I can't do 'em. Of course, now if I hand 'em in the old rhinoceros will think I cribbed 'em. Of all the original Jobs I am the worst! This is the last straw!"

When half an hour later The Roman returned Stover was sitting erect, with folded arms and lips compressed.

"Ah, Stover, all through?" said The Roman, as though the House had not just been blown asunder. "Hand in your paper."

Stover stiffly arose and handed him the foolscap. The Roman took it with a frowning little glance. At the top was written in big, defiant letters: "John H. Stover."

Below there was nothing at all.

Stover stood, swaying from heel to heel, watching The Roman.

"What the deuce is he looking at?" he thought in wonder, as The Roman sat silently staring at the blank sheet.

Finally he turned over the page, as though carefully perusing it, poised a pencil, and said in a low voice, without glancing up, "Well, John, I think this will just about pass."

XXVI

THE FOOTBALL season had ended victoriously. The next week brought the captaincy for the following year to Stover by unanimous approval. But the outlook for the next season was of the weakest; only four men would remain. The charge that he would have to lead would be a desperate one. This sense of responsibility was, perhaps, more acute in Stover than even the pleasure-giving sense of the attendant admiration of the school whenever he appeared among them.

Other thoughts, too, were working within him. Ever since the extraordinary outcome of his examination at the hands of The Roman, Stover had been in a ferment of confusion. The Roman's action amazed, then perplexed, then doubly confounded him.

If The Roman was not his enemy, had not been all this time his persistent, malignant foe, what then? What was left to him to cling to? If he admitted this, then his whole career would have to be reconstructed. Could it be that, after all, month in and month out, it had been The Roman himself who had stood as his friend in all the hundred and one scrapes in which he had tempted Fate? And pondering on this gravely, Dink Stover, in the portion of his soul that was consecrated to fair play, was mightily exercised.

He consulted Tough McCarty, as he consulted him now on everything that lay deeper than the lip currency of his fellows. They were returning from a long walk over the early December roads in the grays and drabs of the approaching twilight. Stover had been unusually silent, and the mood settled on him, as, turning the hill, they saw the clustered skyline of the school through the bared branches.

"What the deuce makes you so solemncholy?" said Tough.

"I was thinking," said Dink with dignity.

"Excuse me."

"I was thinking," said Dink, rousing himself, "that I've been all wrong."

"I don't get that."

"I mean The Roman."

"How so?"

"Tough, you know down at the bottom I have a sneaking suspicion that he's been for me right along. It's a rotten feeling, but I'm afraid it's so."

"Shouldn't wonder. Have you spoken to him?"

"No."

"Why not?"

"I'm not sure. And then, I don't know just how to get to it."

"Jump right in and tackle him around the knees," said Tough.

"I think I will," said Dink, who understood the metaphor.

They went up swinging briskly, watching in silence the never stale spectacle of the panorama of the school.

"I say, Dink," said Tough suddenly, "Sis is going to put the clamps on that T. Willyboy, Ver Plank."

"Really—when?" said Dink, surprised that the news brought him no emotion.

"Next month."

Stover laughed a little laugh.

"You know," he said with a bit of confusion, "I fancied I was terribly in love with Josephine myself—for a little while."

"Sure," said Tough without surprise. "Jo would flirt with anything that had long pants on."

"Yes, she's a flirt," said Stover, and the judgment sounded like the swish of shears cutting away angels' wings.

They separated at the campus and Stover went toward the Kennedy. Halfway there, an excited little urchin came rushing up, pulling off his cap.

"Well, what is it, youngster?" said Stover, who didn't recognize him.

"Please, sir," said the young hero worshiper, producing a photograph of the team from under his jacket, "would you mind putting your name on this? I should be awfully obliged."

Stover took it and wrote his name.

"Who is this?"

"Williams, Jigs Williams, sir, over in the Cleve."

405

"Well, Jigs, there you are."

"Oh, thank you. Say—"

"Well?"

"Aren't you going to have an individual photograph?"

"No, of course not," said Stover with only outward gruffness.

"All the fellows are crazy for one, sir."

"Run along, now," said Stover with a pleased laugh. He stood on the steps, watching the elated Jigs go scudding across the Circle, and then went into the Kennedy. In his box was a letter of congratulation from Miss Dow. He read it smiling, and then took up the photograph and examined it more critically.

"She's a dear little girl," he said. "Devilish smart figure."

Miss Dow, of course, was very young. She was only twenty.

That night, after an hour's brown meditation, he suddenly rose and, descending the stairs, knocked at the sanctum sanctorum.

"Come in," said the low, musical voice.

Stover entered solemnly.

"Ah, it's you, John," said The Roman with a smile.

"Yes, sir, it's me," said Stover, leaning up against the door.

The Roman glanced up quickly and, seeing what was coming, took up the paper cutter and began to twist it through his fingers. There was a silence, long and painful.

"Well?" said The Roman in a queer voice.

"Mr. Hopkins," said Dink, advancing a step. "I guess I've been all wrong. I haven't come to you before, as I suppose I ought, because I've had to sort of think it over. But now, sir, I've come in to have it out."

"I'm glad you have, John."

"I want to ask you one question."

"Yes?"

"Have you, all this time, really been standing by me, yanking me out of all the messes I got in?"

"Well, that expresses it, perhaps."

"Then I've been way off," said Stover solemnly. "Why, sir, all this time I thought you were down on me, had it in for me, right from the first."

"From our first meeting?" said The Roman, with a little chuckle. "Perhaps, John, you didn't give me credit—shall I say, for a sense of humor?"

"Yes, sir." Stover looked a moment at his polished boot and then resolutely at The Roman. "Mr. Hopkins, I've been all wrong. I've been unfair, sir; I want to apologize to you."

"Thank you," said The Roman, and then because they were Anglo-Saxons they shook hands and instantly dropped them.

"Mr. Hopkins," said Stover after a moment, "I must have given you some pretty hard times?"

"You were always full of energy, John."

"I don't see what made you stand by me, sir."

"John," said The Roman, leaning back and caging his fingers, "it is a truth which it is, perhaps, unwise to publish abroad, and I shall have to swear you to the secret. It is the boy whose energy must explode periodically and often disastrously, it is the boy who gives us the most trouble, who wears down our patience and tries our souls, who is really the most worthwhile."

"Not the high markers and the gospel sharks?" said Stover, too amazed to choose the classic line.

"Sh!" said The Roman, laying his finger on his lips.

Stover felt as though he held the secret of kings.

"And now, John," said The Roman in a matter-of-fact tone, "since you are behind the scenes, one thing more. The real teacher, the real instructor, is not I, it is you. We of the faculty can only paint the memory with facts that are like the writing in the sand. The real things that are learned are learned from you. Now, forgive me for being a little serious. You are a leader. It is a great responsibility. They're all looking up at you, copying you. You set the standard; set a manly one."

"I think, sir, I've tried to do that—lately," said Stover, nodding.

"And now, in the House—bring out some of the younger fellows."

"Yes, sir."

"There's Norris. Perhaps a little serious talk—only a word dropped."

"You're right, sir; I understand what you mean."

"Then there's Berbecker."

"He's only a little fresh, sir; there's good stuff in him."

"And then, John, there's a boy who's been under early disadvantages, but a bright boy, full of energy, good mind, but needs to be taken in hand, with a little kindness."

407

"Who, sir?"

"Bellefont."

"Bellefont!" said Stover, exploding. "I beg your pardon, sir. You're wrong there. That kid is hopeless. Nothing will do him any good. He's a perfect little nuisance. He's a thoroughgoing, out-and-out little varmint!"

The Roman tapped the table and, looking far out through the darkened window, smiled the gentle smile of one who has watched the ever recurrent miracle of humanity, the struggling birth of the man out of the dirtied, hopeless cocoon of the boy.

And Stover, suddenly beholding that smile, all at once stopped, blushed and understood!

The Tennessee Shad

ILLUSTRATED BY

F. R. GRUGER

I

THE RISE OF DOC MACNOODER

AT THE TIME when the celebrated Doc Macnooder, that amateur practitioner but most professional financier, first dawned upon the school, he found the Tennessee Shad the admiration and the envy of the multitude. He had not been a week in the school before he, too, was moved to enthusiasm by the Shad's productive imagination—productive in the sense of its consequences to others. Macnooder, at that time unknown, with only the consciousness of greatness within him, conceived at once the mighty ambition to unite this Yankee fertility of ideas to his own practical but imaginative sense of financial returns. This ambition he did not achieve in a day for the firm of Macnooder and the Tennessee Shad was not finally established until Macnooder, by a series of audacious moves, forced himself to that position where he could compel the Shad to choose between a partner and a rival.

When the Tennessee Shad leaned against a wall his empty trousers wrapped themselves like damp sheets around his ankles. When he strode forth like a pair of animated scissors his coat hung from the points of his shoulder blades as though floating from a rake, while his narrow, lengthened head seemed more like a cross-section than a completed structure.

Hickey The Prodigious, after a long period of mental wrestling, had given him the nickname, and the same was agreed to be Hickey's *magnum opus*. It expressed not simply a state of inordinate thinness, but one of incredible, preposterous boniness such as could only have been possessed by that antediluvian monster that did or did not sharpen its sides on the ridges of Tennessee.

The Tennessee Shad frankly confessed his ambition to be a philosopher, his idea of the same being that of a gloriously languid person who resided in a tub and thought out courses of action over which other people should toil.

His first efforts were naturally directed to the greatest saving of personal energy. His window opened, his door shut, his lamp was extinguished by a series of ropes which he operated from his bed. On retiring he drew his undergarments through his trousers, tucked the legs carefully in the socks which in turn were placed in his slippers, and leaned the whole against the chair, on the back of which his undershirt in his shirt, his shirt in his vest, his vest in his coat lay gaping for the morrow. As a result of this precocious grasping of the principles of economics, he was able to spring from his bed fully clothed with but two motions, an upward struggle and a downward kick.

The physical inertia was not, however, accompanied by any surrender of the imagination. On the contrary he liked nothing better than to propose ideas; to lie back, lazily turning a straw in his lips, and to throw out suggestions that would produce commotions and give him the keen intellectual enjoyment of watching others hustle. These little ideas of the Tennessee Shad's, so rapturously hailed at the inception, were not always so admired in the retrospect; especially after the rise of Macnooder to the practical partnership had introduced the element of aggressive financeering.

Now Doc Macnooder came with no surrounding haze of green, but fully equipped with the most circumstantial manner.

It lies in the annals of the Hamill House that within six hours after the opening of his trunks, he had sold a patent bootjack to the Triumphant Egghead, and a folding toothbrush to Turkey Reiter, disinfected and bandaged the foot of Peewee Davis, who had stepped on a tack, and begun the famous Hamill House March which was a blend of the vibrant reiterations of a Chinese orchestra and the beatings of a tom-tom man.

Macnooder's early days, as well as his age, remained closely wrapped in mystery and speculation. Many stories moved about; he had shipped before the mast and fought Chinese pirates off Malay; he had been an enforced pirate himself; he had been an actor, touring the country with barn stormers; he had been a dentist's assistant, a jockey, and a Pinkerton detective. Macnooder never absolutely affirmed any of these reports, and he certainly would never have denied one.

He shortly became secretary and treasurer of his House, of his Form, and of each organization to which he was admitted. He

THE FAMOUS HAMILL HOUSE MARCH

played the organ in chapel, represented twenty firms, and plied so thriving a trade in patent and ingeniously useless goods that he was able to refuse a cash offer from the village tradesmen to abandon the field.

But Macnooder was not content. He wished a reputation not simply for ubiquity, but as a hero of some desperate deed of valor and cunning, and so to enter the company of that Machiavellian spirit, the Tennessee Shad, of Turkey Reiter and of Hickey, the incarnation of mischief.

In the days of which I write smoking had still the charm of Eden's apple. Thundering assaults were directed from the pulpit at the Demon Cigarette, which was further described as a Coffin Nail; and boys whose stomachs rebelled smoked with a thrill at the thought of detection, immediate expulsion, disgrace, and a swift downward career which nothing could check but the gallows.

Macnooder, either in Chinese junks or as a detective to screen his features behind a cloud of smoke, had acquired the deathly practice of inhaling the obnoxious weed, and soon began to cast about for a more safely luxurious method of enjoyment than a mattress beside an air-flue.

Now, the Hamill House, relic of the old school, was a rambling structure which had been patched and altered a dozen times, with the result that each story was composed of several levels.

Macnooder was hastening down the back steps from the third floor one afternoon when the lacrosse stick he carried at shoulder arms came in smart contact with a beam, with the result that he reached the landing without the formality of the remaining steps.

He picked himself up wrathfully, and gazed at the offending beam. It was totally unnecessary, in quite an absurd position, impending over a flight of narrow stairs. The more Macnooder studied it, the more curious he became. If it was only a beam, it was of extraordinary thickness and height. If it was not a beam, it must be a sort of blind passage leading directly from his room. But leading where?

Macnooder went softly up the steps and, stretching on tiptoes, gently sounded the plastered obstruction. It certainly gave forth a most promising hollow sound.

Twenty minutes later, Jay Gould who had waited patiently below, rushed up in a swearing mood.

"Where in blazes is that impudent, cheeky, all-fired, nervy freshman?" he cried, stamping up in pursuit of the greenhorn who had dared to keep him waiting. But at Macnooder's room he stopped in amazement.

"What in the name of peanuts are you doing?"

"Hush!" said Macnooder, pacing the floor. "Twelve feet from the door and six over."

"He's gone dippy," said Jay, not completely surprised at this solution of Macnooder's many-sided personality.

"HE HAD SHIPPED BEFORE THE MAST AND FOUGHT PIRATES."

"Twelve feet minus four leaves eight. Allowing, say, two-and-a-half feet for the width of the passage, it must strike in here somewhere."

Jay Gould, keeping a chair in front of him, carefully advanced, studying first the floor and then the abstracted, concentrated gaze of Macnooder.

"I say, Doc."

"Don't bother me."

"I say, dear boy, is anything wrong?"

"Come here," said Macnooder, suddenly straightening with a look of triumph.

"What do you want?"

"Lift your right hand and solemnly swear."

"Swear what?"

"Never to reveal the secret mysteries I am about to unfold to you."

"Come off. What's the answer?"

"Swear."

"Sure."

"I have discovered that the Hamill House hides a secret chamber, a den of horrors perhaps," said Macnooder darkly.

"How did you find that out?"

"I first suspected it," said Macnooder, rapidly dramatizing the bare facts, "by a strange, pungent, ghoulish odor that has come to me in the dead of the night."

"Poor Doc," said Jay Gould, shaking his head; "he is dippy, after all."

Macnooder, perceiving the time for simple words had arrived, rapidly imparted the accident of his discovery, ending excitedly:

"Jay, that passage starts right above the floor of my closet or you can take your pick of anything I sell, at fifty per cent off."

Gould was convinced at once.

"But where does it lead?"

"Straight over *back* of your room!"

"Back!"

"Exactly. I've worked it all out. There's a blind hole about six feet square directly back of your closet. What do you think of that?"

"Holy cats!" said Jay Gould who immediately bolted for his room with Macnooder at his heels. A short comparison of distances, with a craning survey of the shelving roof, convinced them that, in fact, the greatest discovery of the age was at hand.

"You see, my room is a couple of feet higher than yours," said Macnooder excitedly. "I'll dig for it low down in the wall. You saw a trapdoor through the floor of your closet and we'll have it cinched."

"This must be a profound secret," said Jay Gould slightly pale.

"Your hand!" said Macnooder.

Two minutes later, having locked and barred the door, the wide-eyed discoverers were flat on their bellies in Macnooder's closet,

MACNOODER STANDING ON TIPTOES SOUNDED THE PLASTERED OBSTRUCTION.

417

Doc stealthily applying a chisel to the plaster which Jay Gould carefully stuffed into a washbag, illegally borrowed from the Pink Rabbit.

"It's hollow, sure enough," said Macnooder, when the plaster had fallen. "Where's the saw?"

"Here you are. Down with the laths."

"Not a sound."

Through the dull rasping of the saw the laths gradually yielded an aperture for the passage of the human body.

"Let's look," said Jay Gould eagerly.

Through the jagged entrance lay a passage mysterious, adventurous, and gloomy, formed by the meeting of the sloping roof and the floor.

"Let's explore it," said Jay Gould, all for action.

"You bet."

"Think of finding it!"

"It's a wonder!"

"Start ahead, Doc."

"Take the honor," said Macnooder magnanimously; "I have had all the fun so far."

"I wouldn't think of it," said Gould resolutely, "you have every right. After you."

"Are you afraid?"

"Are you?"

"Let's toss."

"Beans! I'll go first," said Jay Gould, who feared neither man nor master.

"There may have been a murder," said Macnooder, when Gould was safely in. "If you strike any bones, don't rattle them."

Jay Gould at once lit a match.

"The bite of some rats is peculiarly poisonous," continued Macnooder, wriggling like a snake amid the cobwebs.

The first match was immediately succeeded by a second.

"Great Lalapazoozas!"

"What is it?"

"Look at this."

Macnooder hastily hauling himself upon the passage, found a blind enclosure above five feet square with a chimney at one side.

"Have a coffin nail," said Jay Gould, with perfect calm.

"What shall we call it?" said Macnooder instantly.

"The Holy of Holies."

"Your hand again."

"We'll bring rugs and sofa cushions and crackers and cheese. Eh, what?"

"Sure, Mike."

"Say, who'll we let in on this?"

"It must be a secret locked in the breasts of only a few," said Jay Gould firmly. "Sport McAllister is my roommate, he'll have to go in."

"Of course. But not the Waladoo Bird—no elephants that will stick their feet through the ceiling."

"Well, how about Shingle-Foot Harris?"

"Agreed; and Tinkles Bell—five; no more!"

"We must take a separate oath of secrecy."

"Sure."

"Sealed with blood."

"Quite so."

"And brand the arms with a burning cigarette."

"What!" said Macnooder; "all of us?"

"No—o, the fellows we let in."

"Oh, absolutely!"

The discovery of the Holy of Holies, destined to be passed down for four successive generations (this is not fiction), unsuspected by masters or uninitiated housemates, still left Macnooder short of the national reputation which he felt was his due. Of course, among the midnight brethren his standing was enormous. But this left him as restless as the right hand when the left hand knoweth not its doing.

From the floor of Jay Gould's closet a trapdoor was constructed, fitting cunningly in natural grooves with a bolt to be drawn below. The only moment of dire peril occurred one afternoon when Shingle-Foot, having gone into the Holy of Holies alone, fell asleep and gave forth snores that shook the House. Luckily, no masters were within, and Macnooder hastily diverted suspicion to himself while Jay Gould, scrambling into the den, seized Shingle-Foot by the throat and brutally throttled the disturber.

Still, the veneration of the inner brotherhood sufficed not. Often of evenings, when lights were out, and they were huddled by the warm bricks in whispered ecstasy lit by the winking sparks of their cigarettes, Macnooder would lapse into reverie.

"What's the matter?" one would inquire from time to time.

"I'm working out something—an idea," Macnooder would answer, lapsing into taciturnity.

But the great idea delayed unconscionably. Macnooder's suave good humor turned into a fidgeting irritability. He was only the big man of a House. The nation was beyond these sectional limits with its call to ambition.

Dink Stover had not yet arrived with his Sleep Prolonging Devices but Hickey who had not yet left (by request) had already preempted the lists of history with his nocturnal exploits and above all there was the Tennessee Shad, the fertile originator of busy schemes from recumbent positions. About this time a faculty decree was promulgated against the right of every future American citizen to acquire influenza, bronchitis and the catarrhal substitutes, and it was solemnly announced that henceforth, under odious penalties, every boy should wear a hat.

On the following morning, while the indignation was at its height, a joyful ripple spread over the school, which rushing to the fountain of rumors, beheld the Tennessee Shad lazily slouching across the Circle, equipped with what might legally be termed a hat. The rim of a derby, stripped of every vestige of a crown, reposed upon the indignant upright of his two flanking ears. It had been a hat and it was a hat. It complied with and it defied the tyrannous injunction. A roar of joy and freedom went up and in ten minutes every $3 to $5 derby in the school was decapitated and the brim defiantly riding on the exposed head of each rebellious imitator.

The incident concentrated the already passionate longings of the young Macnooder. He must pass over the limits of the House. He must rise to national scope. He must prove himself worthy of the complexities of the Tennessee Shad. For Macnooder had that critical enthusiasm for the Shad that the man of practical perceptions has for the irresponsibilities of a man of genius. The imagination of the Tennessee Shad must be turned to practical results as Niagara, stupendous in itself, has waited for centuries to be harnessed to the pockets of business. He, Macnooder, would prove his right, capitalize the Tennessee Shad, form the firm of Macnooder and the Tennessee Shad, and putting it on a sound business basis, develop it into a source of revenue.

In this mood he was bumping up the stairs one afternoon, when he came to an alarmed and sudden halt. Directly opposite, from the crack of the Pink Rabbit's door, came a faint, but unmistakable odor of tobacco.

Now the Pink Rabbit was among the cherubim and seraphim of the school. Macnooder could hardly believe his senses. He advanced a few steps, cocked his head on one side and drew in a deep breath. The odor was strange, but distinctly of the Demon Tobacco.

Macnooder, hastily sliding around the door, beheld, in fact, the Pink Rabbit, propped up in bed, reading a novel, devouring a box of taffy, and smoking a cigarette.

"For the love of Mike, Rabbit! What are you doing?" he exclaimed.

"What's the matter?" said the invalid hoarsely from his couch.

But here Macnooder suddenly sniffed the air.

"Cubebs!" he said.

"Sure."

"But that's smoking."

"Not at all. Doctor Charlie prescribed them—cure asthma, and all that sort of thing."

"Cubebs are not tobacco?" said Macnooder, who had missed the preliminary stages.

"No, you chump."

"And they're good for colds, you say."

"Hay fever and asthma."

"Well, I'll be jig-swiggered."

Macnooder continued to his room in a state of scientific speculation, halted by the window and, digging his fists into his pockets, stared out at the Circle, around which a dozen fellows were laboriously plodding in penance.

"Cubebs aren't tobacco," he repeated for the tenth time. "By the great horned spoon, there certainly is something in that idea."

That night, in the Holy of Holies, Macnooder was more silent than usual, though this time it was with a purpose.

"Doc's in love," said Shingle-Foot, suspiciously.

"I believe he is."

"He certainly acts off his feed."

This sally failed to awaken Macnooder.

"She doesn't love him."

"She loves another."

"Poor old Doc."

Macnooder calmed them with a disdainful flutter of his hand.

"I'll tell you," he said impressively, "what's been occupying me."

"Go ahead."

"I'm tired of local reputations."

"Oh, you are," said Sport McAllister critically; for he thought it was time that even Macnooder should be discouraged.

"I am."

"Indeed, and what will satisfy you, you conceited, brassy, top-heavy squirt?"

"Nothing but an international reputation," said Macnooder, disdaining to notice the mere flight of epithets.

"You don't say so!"

"And now I've got it."

"Dear me!"

"I've got the greatest stunt that was ever pulled off in any school, at any time, in any country."

"Well, we're listening."

"I'll put it this way. What would happen if the faculty got on to the Holy of Holies?"

"I'd be guiding a plow in South Idaho," said McAllister frankly.

"The use of tobacco in any form is prohibited."

"And punishable by suspension," said Jay Gould. "So says the catalog. Pass the coffin nails."

"Well, this is what I propose to do," said Macnooder, "I propose to go two times around the Circle, in full sight of every master in the whole place, smoking a cigarette."

"Repeat that," said Jay Gould.

Macnooder firmly complied.

"Oh, at night!" said Tinkles Bell scornfully; "that's an easy one."

"No, in full daylight."

"And remain in the school?"

"And remain in the school."

"Repeat the whole proposition again."

"Are you a betting man?" said Sport McAllister when Macnooder had stated the proposition the third time.

"First, last and always."

"I will bet you," said Sport McAllister, trying to still the eagerness in his voice, "I will bet you my monthly allowance from now until the close of the year. Take it, it's yours."

"I'll attend to that bet."

"What?" said McAllister, hardly believing his good fortune. "You take it?"

"The word was 'Attend.'"

"To smoke a cigarette while walking twice around the Circle in full daylight, and not get suspended."

"Exactly."

"Will you write that down?" said McAllister, who began to plan how he should enjoy the blessings of Providence.

"We have witnesses."

"When will you do it?" said Jay Gould.

"Within one week."

The next day Macnooder caught a cold which thickened considerably by the following morning. Despite this, he announced to the expectant House that the attempt would be made at one-thirty that afternoon.

Promptly at that hour Sport McAllister, Jay Gould, Tinkles and Shingle-Foot, according to agreement, repaired to the Dickinson House, armed with opera glasses, and spreading the great news. The word having circulated, the five Houses that bordered the Circle, as well as the long outline of the Upper, were suddenly and theatrically alive with spectators, carefully masked (also according to request) by hand screens and window curtains.

"Aw, he'll never dare," said Sport McAllister to the Tennessee Shad, who was furnishing the window.

"Perhaps he's been fired already."

"I'll bet there's a catch in it."

"Why, every master in the place is around now."

"Sure; he couldn't go ten yards before Robinson in the Cleve would nab him."

"Aw, he'll never dare," repeated Sport McAllister. In the misfortune of his friend, he found not only a certain pleasure but a promised easing of the money stringency.

"What's that?"

"Where?"

"Just coming behind the trees."

"It's Macnooder!"

"No!"

"It certainly is!"

It was Macnooder, stepping briskly forward. His throat, to emphasize its delicate condition, was wrapped around with several knitted scarfs; while, besides a sweater, he wore in the warm month of October a winter overcoat.

When precisely opposite the Upper, and in full sight of the Houses, Macnooder deliberately halted and bringing forth a box, lighted a cubeb cigarette.

Then, puffing it forth voluminously, he started around the Circle. The nearest House was the Cleve, wherein dwelt not only the Muffin Head but Brotherly Love Baldwin, the young assistant who had new ideas on education.

As luck would have it, at that precise moment Baldwin was on the threshold, preparing to cross the Circle.

At the sight of Macnooder, steaming briskly along his way, he stiffened one moment with horror, and the next, shot violently after the offender. He did not exactly leap forward, but there was in his advance all the growling rush of a bounding dog.

Macnooder, from the tail of his eye, beheld the sweeping approach and blew forth a particularly voluminous cloud.

"Stop!"

Macnooder came to a halt in gentle surprise.

"How dare you?" exclaimed Baldwin, almost incapable of speech.

"What's wrong, sir?" said Macnooder thickly.

Among the spectators in the Houses there was a sudden terrified craning forward.

"Throw that cigarette down this instant—you young reprobate!"

Macnooder was seized with a fit of coughing.

"Please, sir," he said finally, "I'm trying to work off a cold. It's only a cubeb."

"A what?"

"A cubeb, sir."

Mr. Baldwin began to suspect that he had bounded into a trap. So he said with dignity, "Were these prescribed by Dr. Jackson?"

"Oh yes indeed, sir. Of course, a cubeb isn't tobacco."

"But smoking is forbidden."

"Oh, no, sir."

"What!"

"Catalog only forbids use of tobacco. Cubebs are a medicine."

Mr. Baldwin stood rubbing his chin, thoroughly perplexed. Macnooder, with serious face, waited patiently the outcome of his dilemma. Now, of course, Mr. Baldwin could have ordered him to desist from any public display so liable to misconstruction and so upsetting of discipline. But he did not; and the reason was the very human motive that actuates the oppressor and the oppressed. He had been caught, and he wanted someone else to share the ignominy.

When the spying school (who of course saw only a cigarette) actually beheld Mr. Baldwin retire and Macnooder continue on his way, smoking, a spasm of horrified amazement swept the audience, in the midst of which young Peewee Davis fell from the second story, carrying away the vines.

Nothing more happened until the first turn had been completed when Macnooder encountered Mr. Jenkins, popularly known as Fuzzy-Wuzzy. Mr. Jenkins was nearsighted; and though he taught mathematics, his perceptions were not those of a lightning calculator.

When, on the pleasant meandering speculation of his mind, Macnooder suddenly intruded, he stopped dead, raising his hand to his spectacles to assure himself that he actually saw.

Macnooder, rounding the turn, saluted respectfully and continued his nonchalant way.

"Macnooder?"

"Yes, sir," said Macnooder, stopping at once.

"Er—er."

Macnooder inclined his head in an expectant sort of way until Mr. Jenkins was quite able to frame his words.

"Are you smoking a cigarette?" said the master slowly.

"A cubeb, sir, not tobacco," answered Macnooder. "Breaks up colds, sir."

Mr. Jenkins fidgeted with his eyeglasses and stared very hard at him.

"A cubeb, sir, no tobacco," continued Macnooder, allowing the aromatic odor to drift in his direction.

"A cubeb—" repeated Mr. Jenkins slowly, pulling his beard.

"Yes, sir," said Macnooder.

He waited a moment and tipping his hat went on his way, leaving the perplexed master fairly rooted in his tracks.

Mr. Smith, the Muffin Head, the next to be encountered, was

425

older in experience and cannier. Likewise, he had witnessed the last encounter so, instead of risking his reputation by rushing madly forth, he took up a book and started ostensibly for the library, carefully calculating his time and distance so as to cross Macnooder's path without seeming to have sought the meeting.

That there was a trap somewhere, he was convinced. So, carefully repressing the instinctive desire to spring upon the flaunter of the scholastic red rag, he approached all alert. A slight wind brought him the unmistakable odor of the cubeb. Now, as it happened, he, too, had suffered from bronchial affliction and was no stranger to this remedy. So when Macnooder came to a stop, he said with a superior smile:

"Yes, what is it, Macnooder?"

"Please, sir, did you want to speak to me?" said Macnooder himself surprised.

"About what?"

"I thought—"

"Oh, about smoking a cubeb? Not at all."

"I beg pardon, sir."

"You have a bad cold, I see."

"Yes, sir! Yes, sir!"

"That's very good for it."

The Muffin Head, chuckling with satisfaction, continued on his way. He, too, in the natural course should have sent Macnooder to his room; but again the little human strain prevented. At the entrance to Memorial, he turned and looked back to see who would fall into the trap he had evaded.

This was too much for the now utterly flabbergasted school—the Muffin Head, of all masters; the strictest of disciplinarians; the most relentless of taskmasters! In rapid succession the school then beheld a dozen more masters take the bait, some fairly galloping down with rage, others suspiciously sniffing the air. By the time Macnooder had completed four rounds, there remained only Mr. Baranson, of the Griswold, who had not been tempted out to investigate.

Macnooder made one more round with his eye on the study of the Griswold, hoping against hope. Finally he said, "Well, here goes! Someone has put him on—he's too cute to come out!"

Then, secure and triumphant, he discarded the stump of the

cubeb and lit a real cigarette, completing, without mishap, twice the rounds of the Circle.

Now Mr. Baranson, who rightly bore the title of the craftiest of the crafty, had witnessed the whole performance, chuckling hugely at the successive discomfitures of his associates and finally guessing the explanation.

The Muffin Head, on his return from the library, hoping that he had not been seen, dropped in for an artful call; and at the proper moment paused before the window, exclaiming, "By George, what's that!"

Mr. Baranson doubled up with laughter at the obviousness of the trap. When he had finally wiped the tears from his eyes, he said in a slightly superior manner, "Smith, if you're going to deal with boys, you must use your imagination. You must out-think them. That's the only way, Smith; the only way. Don't walk into their traps, don't do it. Every time a master lets himself be fooled, he loses some of his authority. Imagination, Smith, imagination!"

But an hour later, at dusk, he began to consider, to weigh and to speculate; and the more he analyzed the situation, the more he began to wonder if he had seen the last curtain. He left the House and went slowly toward the road Macnooder had traveled, and his eyes were on the ground where the last cigarette stump had fallen. Suddenly behind him a voice said solicitously, "Have you lost anything, Mr. Baranson?"

It was Macnooder.

The two stood a long moment, master and boy, the craftiest of the crafty and the ambitious Macnooder, glance to glance, one of those silent interrogatories that can not be described.

"Your cold seems to have gone," said Mr. Baranson at length, dealing out his words. Then he added, with a slightly twitching, generous smile, "I *congratulate you!*"

II

INTRODUCING THE TENNESSEE SHAD

MACNOODER'S SUCCESS in performing the impossible feat of circling the Circle smoking a genuine, bona fide non-cubeb cigarette, brought him at once the national reputation he had yearned for, but still left him short of his ambition. The Tennessee Shad had been too long entrenched in his own particular position of public admiration to relinquish a foot of his vantage simply because a new and ingenious claimant had arrived. He considered Macnooder carefully, even solicitously, and listened with deliberation to his crafty schemes of profitable promoting. He was interested but he was not convinced. Once or twice before he admitted Macnooder's equality he would have put him to the test.

Such was the condition of affairs when one Sunday afternoon the House was gathered in Lovely Mead's rooms recuperating from the fatigues of a categorical sermon preached that morning by a visiting missionary.

"Gee, Sunday's a bore!" said the Egghead, on the window seat, sticking a pin in Lovely Mead's leg to make room for his own.

"Ouch!" said Lovely in surprised indignation. "I've a mind to lick you, Egghead."

"Wish you would—anything for excitement!"

"What let's do?" said Macnooder from under the desk lamp, where he was pretending to read.

"Let's do something devilish."

"Ah, December's too cold."

"I have an idea," drawled out the Tennessee Shad from the fire rug, where he lay pillowed on the Gutter Pup's sleepy form. "Let's eat something."

At this there was a mild commotion on the window seat, where four forms lay curled, puppy fashion.

428

"Eat what?"

"I was sort of speculating on a Welsh rabbit," said the Shad in a nasal drawl.

"That's about up to your usual brand of ideas, you thin, elongated, bony Tennessee Shad," said the Gutter Pup contemptuously. "Where are we going to get anything on a Sunday evening?"

"I have a hunch," said the Tennessee Shad languidly. "I have a most particular hunch that Poler Fox was seen Saturday afternoon buying a luscious, fat and juicy piece of cheese at Doc Forman's. Question to the jury: Is or is not that cheese?"

Four figures sat up.

"Poler Fox?"

"What right has he to a piece of cheese?"

"This should be investigated!"

"It should."

"It will be!"

The Tennessee Shad and the Gutter Pup went softly down one flight of the House and along the corridor where Poler Fox burned the midnight oil. They paused and consulted.

"Had we better swipe it or invite him?"

"Let's try to swipe it first—we can always invite him."

"Whoever heard of keeping a cheese overnight, anyway?"

"That's right; it's positively unhealthy."

"We really ought to complain."

"Who'll swipe it?"

"I'll get him out of his room," said the Tennessee Shad, "and you rush in and capture the milkweed."

The Gutter Pup, for good reason, did not trust to the purity of the Tennessee Shad's intentions.

"Why don't you do the lifting?" he said suspiciously.

"You ungrateful Gutter Pup, don't you see?—you won't be seen. He'll know I was only a blind. But have it your own way."

"No," said the Gutter Pup. "You go ahead and get him out of the room."

He waited, ensconcing himself on the shadowy steps, until he saw the Shad and Poler Fox emerge and disappear down the resounding corridor. Then, quickly gliding to the abandoned room, he stepped through the door, elevated his nose, sniffed and considered.

Cheeses are not usually left unexposed or permitted to lend their aroma to articles that are to be worn. He could discard the bureau drawers and the trunk. He peered through the window; it was not on the sill. He opened the closet and drew a long, ineffectual breath. Then getting down on his hands and knees he started under the bed.

At this moment the Tennessee Shad returned with Poler Fox.

"Why, Gutter Pup," said the Shad blandly, "what are you doing under the bed?"

"I came down to borrow a trot," said the Gutter Pup, looking steadily at the Shad; "and I dropped a dime. I think it rolled under the bed."

"You weren't trying to steal Poler's cheese, were you?" said the Tennessee Shad reproachfully.

"Of course I wasn't," said the Gutter Pup indignantly.

" 'Cause Poler wants to give a Welsh rabbit party," said the Shad softly, "and he mightn't feel like inviting you if you were abusing his confidence."

The procession returned, the Tennessee Shad keeping a safe distance from the Gutter Pup, with Poler Fox clutching the cheese as his passport into the feast.

Then a crisis arose.

"What're you going to put in it?" said the Egghead skeptically.

"You can't make a Welsh rabbit without beer," said Turkey Reiter.

"Rats!" said the Tennessee Shad. "That's all you know. You can put a dozen things in."

The assembly divided radically.

"Come off!"

"What else?"

"Who ever heard of a rabbit without beer?"

"I've eaten them with condensed milk."

"We made 'em in the Dickinson with ginger pop."

"Anything'll do, so long as there's alcohol in it."

"Oh, murder!"

"Poison!"

"Not at all—they're not half bad."

"Order!" said the Tennessee Shad, rapping on the chafing dish. "I guess I've eaten and made more Welsh rabbits than any one in this bunch of amateurs. Hungry Smeed is right—you can make them with anything that's got a drop of alcohol in it."

Turkey and the Egghead put up their noses and bayed at the ceiling.

"Contrary-minded can exit."

The protest subsided at once.

"The next best thing to beer is imported ginger ale," said the Tennessee Shad. "Who's got ginger ale?"

A silence.

"Who's got ginger pop?"

Another silence.

"Root beer?"

More silence.

"Sarsaparilla?"

"I have," said the Gutter Pup, jumping up and disappearing under the window seat.

A cheer went up.

Suddenly the Gutter Pup bounded out.

"I put three bottles of sarsaparilla there Friday night," he said wrathfully. "If I knew the low-livered sneak that would steal—"

"Stealing is contemptible," said the Tennessee Shad softly, while everyone looked indignant. "I continue, who's got any cider? Who's got any lemon squash?"

"It's no use," said the gloomy Egghead. "No rabbit for us!"

"We have still our friends," said the persistent Shad. "I move we begin to sleuth. Remember, ginger ale first—but anything after."

The party went off in couples, all except the Tennessee Shad, the Gutter Pup, who didn't trust the Shad, and Poler Fox, who didn't trust the Gutter Pup.

In ten minutes the Triumphant Egghead and Hungry Smeed returned.

"Anything?" said the Tennessee Shad, ceasing to coax the melting mass of cheese.

"Nope."

Lovely Mead came back, and then Macnooder and Turkey Reiter empty-handed. The gloom spread.

"What a beastly shame!"

"And such a sweet cheese!"

431

"My, what a lovely smell!"

"Well, we're beaten—that's all."

"I have an idea," said the Tennessee Shad. "Let's try witch hazel."

A howl went up.

"You Indian!"

"You assassin!"

"Eat it yourself!"

"Witch hazel hasn't got alcohol in it, you ignoramus!"

"Why not?" said the Tennessee Shad militantly.

Everyone looked at the Egghead.

"Why not?"

The Egghead found the answer too difficult and remained silent.

"Give me the witch hazel," said the Tennessee Shad stirring the rabbit with determined swoops. "Now just let me give you a point or two. It's only the alcohol that counts, you jayhawkers; the rest evaporates—goes up in steam."

"Hold up," said the Egghead, who had recovered.

"What's wrong?"

"I don't stand for that scientific explanation of yours."

"Nor I," said Lovely Mead, whose father was a chemist. "Say, Doc, you ought to know. How about it?"

Now Doc Macnooder had more than a doubt, but he worshiped the fertility of the Tennessee Shad and moreover was seeking an opportunity to make a direct offer of partnership. So he looked wise and said, "The Tennessee Shad is right with this important distinction. The witch hazel will resolve itself into a modicum, ahem, of alcohol if heated separately and kept from contact with the cheese which you understand, in a state of transmutation, has certain lacto-bacillic qualities that arrest vaporization. It's quite simple if you understand it."

The Tennessee Shad gave him a grateful look.

"Say, Sport," said Turkey, only half reassured, "you may be right, but go slow—sort of coddle that witch hazel. Let it taste more of Doc Forman's grocery, if it's the same to you."

"Sure!" said the Tennessee Shad. "I'll put in an extra load of mustard and cayenne. Get those plates ready, you loafers. Dish out the crackers. Here goes!"

Eight plates stood untasted.

"Strange how my appetite's gone," said the Egghead dreamily.

"I don't feel a bit hungry."

"Someone taste it."

"Taste it yourself."

"Here, this won't do," said the Shad, frowning. "Let's all begin together."

Eight spoons made a feint toward the new species of rabbit.

The Tennessee Shad looked thoughtful, then spoke.

"Fellows, I've got an idea! Let's make it sweepstakes."

"Good idea."

"Why, Shad, you're getting intelligent."

"We'll each chip in a nickel and the first one through takes the pot," said the Shad. "Hungry, pass the toothmug."

The nickels fell noisily.

"One, two, three!" said the Tennessee Shad.

Eight spoons brandished in the air and rose again empty.

"Well, let's make it worthwhile," said the Shad. "Let's sweeten it with a quarter apiece. Sweepstakes, two dollars and forty cents. Hungry, lead the mug around again."

Each, as he dropped in a quarter, gazed deep into the mug, drew a breath and set his teeth—two dollars and forty cents was a fortune two weeks before Christmas.

"Everyone in?" said the Tennessee Shad. "No hunchin', Gutter Pup and Hungry, start fair—one, two, three, go!"

Not a boy faltered—Hungry Smeed won from the Gutter Pup by several strings and dove for the pot.

Then they sat and looked at one another.

"Gee, I feel queer!" said Turkey, with an expression of inward searching on his face.

"So do I."

"I believe we're poisoned."

"I know I am!"

"Honest, no joking, I do feel devilish queer."

"What in the deuce did we do it for?"

"Who suggested witch hazel?" said the Gutter Pup, clutching at his indignant digestion. "I'll fix him."

"Yes, who did?" said Turkey, rising with difficult wrath.

"Tennessee Shad!"

Seven writhing forms sprang up furiously.

The Tennessee Shad, with a perfect comprehension of dramatic values, had slipped away, leaving his plate untouched.

433

III

THE BEGINNING OF THE FIRM

Doc Macnooder bore no grudge. Even the recollected spasms of what might properly be termed his youthful *In*digestion, brought with them no feeling of malice toward the Tennessee Shad. On the contrary though his attempts at a mercantile union were continually repulsed, the determination held fast within him to turn to profit what was now only turned to mischief, and accident finally supplied the welding touch in the following manner.

In those days when the Gymnasium was still an oft-promised land, the winter term, from January to April, was to the embattled faculty what the Indian season was to the early pioneers. Four hundred-odd, combustible boys, deprived of outlet, cooped up for days by slush and sleet, presented in miniature that same state of frothy unrest from which spout forth South American somersaults and Balkan explosions.

It takes usually two weeks for the exhausted boy to recuperate from the Christmas vacation, but from about the twentieth of January the physical body overtakes the imagination and things begin to happen.

Toward the first week of February there gathered in the Triumphant Egghead's room ten disgusted members of the House, utterly wearied with life, especially bored with the present and without the slightest hope for the future.

Outside a steady, sleety downpour brought feeble icicles from the roof and ran rivulets through the muddied snowbanks.

"Now, it's turned to rain again," announced Hungry Smeed, with his nose applied to the windowpane while his waving heels cast shadows on the wall. Nice, wet, oozy, luscious rain."

"Let's all go bicycling," said Lovely Mead facetiously.

"What time is it?" asked the Gutter Pup from the crowd on the couch.

"Just two o'clock."

A groan went up.

"Is that all?"

"Thought it was after four."

"What is there to do?"

"It's still raining, fellows," said Smeed from the window, and the conversation ceased.

"Do you think Yale'll beat Princeton?" asked Turkey Reiter at last.

"Stop trying to make conversation," said Doc Macnooder resentfully, "and don't move any more; you're the deuce of a soft pillow."

"Who's going to the Prom?" inquired Crazy Opdyke feebly.

"Crazy, you annoy me," said Butcher; "you annoy me and disturb my rest. Don't propound questions."

"Say, fellows!" said Smeed in great excitement.

"What?"

"It's snowing!"

The door opened a crack and the Tennessee Shad slipped in.

"What's doing, fellows?"

"We're exhausted with excitement!" said Old Ironsides Smith sarcastically. "We're trying to rest up for the next debauch, you precocious young skeleton."

"Say, fellows, I've got an idea," said the Tennessee Shad, draping himself over the desk.

"Oh, go away!"

"It's a corker!"

"Huh! Another of those witch hazel rabbits?"

"No, no," said the Tennessee Shad, hurriedly skipping that disastrous episode. "This is a sensation!"

"Of course!"

"Never mind—let him speak his piece."

"Let's form," said the Tennessee Shad slowly, "let's form a Criminal Club."

"A what?"

Macnooder, with an awakening hope, sat up, wondering if the brain factory was again working.

"Criminal Club—convicts and that sort of thing. We'll shave off our heads and go about lockstep."

"And initiate new members?" cried Goat Finney.

435

"Sure."

"And go into chapel tomorrow morning lockstep?"

"Of course!"

"Gee, what a peach of an idea!"

"Can you see the Doctor's face?"

"Oh, mother!"

"Hurray!"

"Hurrah!"

"Hurroo!"

Into the dry pit of baffled energy an idea had fallen, and in a moment all was flame and fury.

"Shad, this is a good one," said Turkey, rousing himself. "We'll call it quits on that rabbit—only—only, remembering the past, we would like to have assurances from you, assurances and guarantees."

"I second the motion most emphatically," said the Gutter Pup revengefully.

The fate of the Criminal Club hung in the balance.

"Look at this," said the Tennessee Shad. And he removed his sombrero.

From ear to ear, from the nape of his neck to the blade of his nose, he was as smooth as a china egg. The day was won in a rollicking cheer.

"Oh, look at him! Look at him!"

"Isn't he wonderful?"

"Bee-oo-tiful!"

"Me for a convict!"

"Can you see the sensation?"

"Bully for the Shad!"

"Let's do it now."

"Come on!"

Five minutes of scurrying to and fro for scissors and shaving kits, and the Triumphant Egghead's room presented the spectacle of an improvised barber shop.

"How'll we begin?" said the Gutter Pup.

"Who goes first?"

"Supposin' we draw for it."

"Who does the shaving?"

"We can't shave back of our own ears."

"The way to do it," said Macnooder, looking at the Tennessee Shad, "is for one-half of us to shave the other half."

"That's it."

"Let her go at that."

"Who first?"

But here a difficulty arose. No one cared to go first.

"This won't do," said the fiery-headed Gutter Pup, repulsing the offers of Doc Macnooder. "If I'm going to shed my shade trees—I don't trust any man, least of all Doc Macnooder."

"What do you mean?"

"I mean no one scalps any of my hair till I get a guarantee off his."

"Rats!" said the Tennessee Shad. "Gutter Pup's a natural-born kicker. Go ahead, Doc, and give him an object lesson."

But Macnooder, though sympathetic to the Tennessee Shad, was on the defensive as far as it concerned the Gutter Pup.

"In the present state of the Gutter Pup's mind—no!" he said thoughtfully. "No, I've got to see a nice white boulevard on those red lands before I consent to laying out mine."

"Will someone else start her up?"

In the silence that ensued Old Ironsides noisily dropped a pin.

"Shad," said the pessimistic Egghead, "it's a good scheme of yours, a bully good scheme; the only trouble is there doesn't seem to be enough mutual confidence. I guess the verdict'll have to be premature death."

"Shad, old sporting print," said Turkey, "have you any suggestion for harmony?"

"Nothing easier," said the Tennessee Shad, locking the door and pocketing the key. "There's one guarantee and here's another. Stand up, form a circle, everyone face the man to his right, grab the shoulders of the man in front of you, sit down slowly on the knees of the fellow behind you, the fellow in front sits down on yours, slowly, *slowly*. There you are. That's the way the Zouaves do it."

The ten found themselves in a circle, comfortably seated and seating.

"There's the answer," said the ringmaster triumphantly; "you shave and get shaved, no first and no last; the happy family; safety razors only. Now, get up, stick on the towels and start with the scissors first."

437

The Tennessee Shad enthroned himself on a table as master of ceremonies, while the hilarious circle formed about him in a bedlam of exclamation.

"How the deuce is Hungry Smeed going to reach up to Turkey?"

"Stick him on a chair, you chump!"

"I don't want the Gutter Pup."

"Aw, send him over here."

"Stop bobbing that head, you Butcher."

"Shorten the circle."

"I can't get Crazy's scalp lock."

"When do we begin?"

"Say when, Shad."

"All ready."

"Let her go!" said the Tennessee Shad from his perch.

Pretty soon protests broke out.

"Ouch!"

"Do you think you're biting them off?"

"Be a little less careless back there."

"Say, who's got the Gutter Pup? Murder him!"

"Moses!"

"Kezowy!"

"Help!"

"Better be careful," said the Tennessee Shad warningly; "in a moment you're going to face the other way."

The shears snipped more gently.

"What do we do when we get through the back?" said Goat Finney.

"You lather it and shave."

"What about the rest?"

"The front's easy enough; anyone can do that."

In an hour every head was as bald as a sapling in a hurricane. They stood and gazed at one another, shrieking with laughter. They hugged one another, rolled on the floor in joyful battling groups, and blessed the imagination that had turned a slough of despond into a vaudeville. On the last stroke of the dinner-bell, solemnly, in lockstep, led by Hungry Smeed and grading up to the mighty Turkey Reiter, eleven glistening heads in sequence descended on the dining room. At the same moment, from the north entrance, appeared a chain gang of eight, equally void of hair, led by Mucker Reilly, followed by Snorky Green, Beauty Sawtelle,

Tough McCarty, Charley De Soto, Piggy Moore, Pink Rabbit and the Waladoo Bird!

The duplicity of the Tennessee Shad was forgotten in the masterly climax he had imagined. The rival clubs met and agreed to proselyte and divide the school.

At eight o'clock the next morning, when the Doctor, all unaware, stood in his pulpit, rubbing his glasses and shooting careful glances along the crowded pews, suddenly a shriek went up. Marching proudly with gleeful faces, two gangs of baldheaded boys suddenly appeared abreast, and in rhythmic step came down the aisles amid the gasps, the shrieks and roars of the school.

Now, there are two things a headmaster must control: his temper and, above all, his sense of humor. The situation was serious; a smile would have been fatal. Something had to be done at once or within a day there would not be enough hair left in the excited school to tuft the head of a Japanese doll. He set his teeth and stared his most terrific stare at a point where the double row of bald heads faded from the vision. Luckily the service allowed him to stifle his amusement and fan up his wrath by calling up the horrible vision of the threatening epidemic.

"Never in my experience, in my whole experience as a scholar or a teacher," he began, glaring with painful ferocity at the denuded culprits, "never have I known such willful, malicious and outrageous desecration of the house of the Lord as you young scalawags have shown today. I do not know whether I shall expel you outright or deprive you of your diplomas; I shall wait until I can consider the matter more calmly. But this I can say right now, if any other incipient imbecile in this school dares to imitate this exhibition of monumental asininity, that boy will leave this school within an hour and never return. I will see these deluded boys in my study after lunch."

The members of the newly formed Housebreakers' Union went out quietly, stealing apprehensive glances at one another.

At two o'clock, as they huddled together in the solemn study, each striving to occupy an unexposed position, T. Dean Smith, secretary, appeared, and, after gazing in fascination at them, said, "Well, boys, you certainly have riled the Doctor this time. You'd better go back quietly."

"Oh, Smithy, won't he see us?" said the Pink Rabbit in a panic, while others exclaimed:

439

"Is he going to fire us?"

"Will he take away our dips?"

"What does he say?"

"Is he mad as a hornet?"

"He says he won't trust himself to see you now," said Smith gravely, without mentioning the reason why the mirth-tortured Doctor wouldn't trust himself to face that sidesplitting spectacle. "I'd lay pretty quiet for a while, if I were you fellows. Let it blow over a little."

"Gee!" said the Tennessee Shad in disgust, as they filed through the gloomy portals. "Can't he have a sense of humor?"

T. Dean Smith glanced at the curtains of the Doctor's sanctum, but did not reply. Instead he stood on the top step gazing down on them with a sardonic smile.

"You'll be a beautiful sight at the Prom, you will!" he said and entered the house. His words fell like a bomb.

"Geewhilikens!"

"Holy cats and mice!"

"I never thought of that!"

"Give me the dunce cap!"

"Of all the fools!"

"Goats!"

"Asses!"

"Idiots!"

"My whole family's coming."

"The family's not what's worrying me."

"Who started us on this fool stunt?"

"The Tennessee Shad."

"Roughhouse him!"

"Hold up! I'm in the same boat," cried the Tennessee Shad. "Don't lose your blooming heads; the Prom's two weeks off!"

"Two weeks?" shouted the Gutter Pup, with a glitter in his eye. "What's two weeks going to do? Do you think we can get respectable in two weeks?"

"Nothing easier," said the Tennessee Shad. "Hair tonic!"

"Fall in line," said Macnooder, seizing instantly the suggestion.

The eleven convicts and the eight Housebreakers assumed a chain gang formation.

"About face!"

"Mark time!"

"Right, left!"

"Forward, march!"

Lockstep, pounding the ground, they went swiftly toward the village and descended on the vendors of hair lotions.

That night the commercial Macnooder appeared at the rooms of the Tennessee Shad and found the door barricaded. He knocked gently in a coaxing friendly way.

"Who's that?" said the Tennessee Shad after their eyes had met through the keyhole.

"Hist! It's Doc Macnooder. Open up."

"I'm studying," said the Tennessee Shad, too tired to choose his lies.

"Shad I come not to take your hard-earned money but to do you good," said Macnooder soothingly, using his well-known formula. "Will you listen?"

"Elucidate," said the Tennessee Shad, drawing up a chair on his side of the door.

Macnooder, camping down, said with the confidence that a great idea alone can inspire:

"Shad, I've approached you many a time and oft with a few little suggestions for adding a few coupons and bonds to our worldly possessions. You have rejected my partnership."

"I have a soul above money," said the Shad, moving his ear, however, a little closer to the keyhole.

"This is my last, positively last offer," said Macnooder firmly. "Accept it and we sign articles of partnership, share and share alike, in a month you will drive your own horse and carriage, wear diamond studs and sport a jewel-studded gold pencil. Refuse and—"

"And what?" said the Tennessee Shad.

"You won't refuse, you can't refuse! Now listen."

Three minutes later the bolts slipped and the Tennessee Shad led Doc Macnooder to the easy chair and propped him up with cushions.

That night the joyful Macnooder transformed his room into a barber shop, with rows of lotions and glassy ointments, announced the Tennessee Shad as partner and hung out this shingle:

441

THE IMPERIAL TONSORIAL PARLORS
MACNOODER AND THE TENNESSEE SHAD
BOSS BARBERS
CASH, MORE CASH, AND NOTHING BUT CASH!

Massage	$ *.03*
Friction with any hair encourager	*.05*
Vaselining	*.03*
Three-in-One	*.10*
Two weeks' treatment	*1.25*

No towels supplied.

The Macnooder treatment coaxes forth the hair, seizes and stretches it, makes it long and curly. Long and curly hair means social success at the Prom; social success means retaining the affections of the fair!

Don't hesitate, don't calculate, do it now!
Come early, come often and bring the children!

Two weeks to cover their nakedness, two weeks to meet the all-seeing feminine eye. That night, each greased hopeful went to bed with a prayer for the morrow.

At the stroke of the rising bell the Gutter Pup catapulted out of bed and flung himself anxiously before his mirror and remained transfixed with despair at the sight of two elephantine ears flanking a snow-white cranium that had not been covered overnight with hair. At this moment a groan arose from Lovely Mead's room across the study.

"Is that you, Lovely?" said the Gutter Pup, fascinated by the horrible caricature in the mirror.

"It is."

"What luck?"

"Nothing!"

"Nothing here."

The door opened on the Triumphant Egghead and Hungry Smeed in pajamas.

"What luck, you fellows?"

"Don't ask!"

"I've got a couple of shoots on top," said the Egghead; "but that's where Butcher Stevens' razor missed me. Isn't it awful?"

"When do you suppose it'll come out again?"

"There must be something tomorrow morning."

"What will we look like at the Prom?"

"I'm desperate," said the Triumphant Egghead. "I've got an Apollo Belvedere rival who stays at home. Jerusalem, where will I be now when she sees this!"

"We must load up with starchy food and drink lots of phosphates at the Jigger Shop," said Hungry Smeed wisely.

"Do you think anything'll show up by tomorrow?"

"Oh, Lovely, it must!"

"How're the others?"

"Smooth as a rink."

Every spare hour was spent in following a new theory; if persistency and ingenuity could have done it they would have succeeded, or had there been any faith in newspaper advertisements or honor in the labels of patent hair-restorers.

They rubbed and greased and dosed themselves, they caught at the first shoots and shut their jaws and pulled, morning, afternoon and night, and at last, when the inexorable Prom came galloping in, they went in hangdog fashion, balking and blushing, to meet the shrieks that greeted their first bow.

.   .   .   .   .   .

That night the Tennessee Shad sat among the lonely anti-fussers who roosted on the chilly edges of the Esplanade and scoffed at the gaiety within.

It was cold, uncomfortably cold, and one by one the frost-nipped spectators slipped away until only the Tennessee Shad remained, fascinated. As each stubble-covered, flap-eared dupe bumped his embarrassed way into view he half closed his eyes and smiled a contented, faraway smile.

The Tennessee Shad had never danced!

IV

FIRST JOINT OPERATION

THE RETURNS from the two weeks of rushing business of the Imperial Tonsorial Parlors made quite a respectable dividend to celebrate the inception of the firm, especially as the Triumphant Egghead, who was in difficult competition for the affections of a blonde, had plunged desperately in the vaselining and the massage.

The formation of the firm was still a matter of secrecy, unsuspected by the public, a fact which alone made possible the next operation.

When January and February have been endured, the limbo month of March is certainly the most fatiguing of the whole year. It belongs neither to the winter family nor to the aristocracy of the spring. It is peevish, malicious and the spirit of negation. When it shines overhead, with vaulted blues and lazy clouds that invite soaring baseballs to them, it is treacherous and foul underfoot. When it snows it brings no sleighing. When it freezes it is not to spread the pond for skating but to harden the mud ruts and delay the opening of the diamonds. Month of corduroys and leathern boots, of waiting and longing, when sinkers overrun the table and the vegetables taste of the can, when the greatest boon is a case of pinkeye or German measles (real or feigned) which gives you the right to doze and browse and play games with other fortunate inmates of the infirmary on the Hill.

The Triumphant Egghead sat on the ledge of the Esplanade and expressed these sentiments in more direct terms, while his whole conception of existence was centered in making a tennis ball strike the shoulder of an opposite ledge so as to bound back into his hands. From an upper window the Gutter Pup and Lovely Mead looked out in disgust at the sky because it had no sun, at the earth because it was unfit to gambol on, and more particularly at the Triumphant Egghead for having enough energy to sit there and bounce a ball.

444

Presently the Egghead's fingers slipped and the ball, escaping, rolled away. He watched it streak wetly down the Esplanade, hesitate and then topple down the steps and trickle languidly along the slimy surface, coating itself with rich yellow ooze. Then, falling off the ledge, he stretched himself and shuffled heavily up to join the Gutter Pup in Turkey Reiter's room.

"My, you're energetic!" said Lovely Mead.

The Egghead grunted, selected a soft spot and lay down.

The Gutter Pup continued gazing out the window with malicious joy at Cap Keefer and the candidates returning from their mud bath in the baseball cage.

"Hello!" he said suddenly. "There goes Doctor Charlie into the Dickinson with his little green bag."

"Wonder who's sick," said the Egghead. "Lucky fellow!"

"Wish I were," said Turkey Reiter.

"Same here," said the Gutter Pup.

"It's such a pleasure to be ill with Doctor Charlie," said Lovely Mead ruminatively. "He has such nice little white pills and such round brown pills and such great big black pills that decorate a mantelpiece so nicely!"

"Think of sleeping two luscious weeks at the infirmary."

"Hum!"

"Don't Turkey, don't—it's cruel."

"Why, here comes the Tennessee Shad," said the lookout, "just as fast as he can come. My, just see how he hops along!"

"He'd better keep away from here," said the Egghead, running his head over the still prickly hairs.

"He will, if he knows what's good for him," remarked Turkey Reiter.

"I only wish he would drop in!" said the Gutter Pup, doubling up his fists and annihilating a sofa pillow.

"I think, fellows," said the Egghead, squirming to and fro so as to scratch his back, "I say I think the Tennessee Shad's usefulness in this community is just about over."

"He won't catch me again," said the Gutter Pup. "If he brought me a ten-dollar guaranteed goldpiece on a solid silver platter I wouldn't so much as reach out my hand for it."

"His murder would be quite justifiable," said the Egghead, thinking of the Prom. "It will take me a couple of natural lives to

445

live down the effect of that haircut. I was not beautiful."

"Ugh!"

"Don't—don't recall it!"

"Gee, my girl's stopped corresponding."

At this moment the Tennessee Shad opened the door, inserted a cautious portion of his sharp features and said genially:

"Ah, there!"

Three vicious sofa cushions slam-banged against the door, accompanied by an explosion of wrath.

"Get out!"

"Cut loose!"

"Vanish!"

"Hold up," said the Tennessee Shad, opening the door again. "I've got an idea!"

Two books and a couple of slippers came smashing through the air.

"You'll regret it," said the Shad, bobbing in and out.

The Gutter Pup banged the door and locked it. Outside was heard the scraping of a chair along the hall, then the transom turned and the glittering eyes of the Tennessee Shad appeared over the door.

"Shad, you are a brave man," said Turkey Reiter ominously. "Go away—do go away while we can still control ourselves."

"Fellows, I have come to apologize," said the Tennessee Shad, while the chair squeaked protestingly.

"Keep your apologies," said Lovely Mead. "We loathe the sight of you. Get out!"

"To apologize and atone," added the Tennessee Shad, keeping a watchful eye on the Gutter Pup who was reaching out for a baseball bat.

"Atone!" said the Egghead with a bitter laugh. "Much good that'll do me."

"Yes, atone, Egghead," said the Shad firmly. "I'm sorry; I feel bad—I do feel bad. I'll admit that my ideas sometimes miscarry, but I have had good ones—you know I've had good ones, and this idea is a good one!"

The Gutter Pup raised the baseball bat, but Turkey Reiter restrained him.

"No, Gutter Pup; let's hear it," he said; "let's know the depth of his depravity. Let's have no illusions about him."

"I'll back my idea," said the Tennessee Shad stoutly.

"How'll you back it?"

"I'll tell you how I'll back it. I'll back it against all you fellows—the whole longeared lot of you. You let me in and promise to keep your hands off me till you hear my idea and, if you don't fall down and kiss my hand and say: 'Shad you're a public benefactor; can you ever, ever forgive us?'—if you don't say that, well, I'm willing to be massacred any time or anyhow. Now, can you imagine what sort of an idea it is?"

The four looked mutely at one another. Finally Turkey spoke.

"Tennessee Shad, you always did have a persuasive, silvery voice, and as my fondest hope for the future is to be associated with you in selling anything to anybody I'm going to let you in. Pup, let down that bat. Egghead, open the door."

The Tennessee Shad glided in, locked the door in turn and shut the transom with much mystery.

"First," he said, "give me your word of honor that you'll keep this a dead secret. No blabbing and no one else to be let in on it. Promise."

"Hold up, this wasn't in the agreement," said the Egghead stubbornly.

"No promise, no secret!"

"That's fair," said Turkey.

They raised their right hands and solemnly swore.

"And no mental reservations," said the Tennessee Shad severely, looking at the Gutter Pup, "if you're gentlemen!"

"Of course not. Say, what do you think we are?"

"All right."

The Tennessee Shad climbed on a chair and roosted on the back in his familiar manner, plucked forth a pencil, chewed it meditatively and said, "Are you happy?"

"What the deuce has that got to do with it?" said the Gutter Pup, tightening his grip on the baseball bat, while the Egghead added irately, "Turkey, it's a con game—he's kidding us."

"Oh, let him tell it his own way," said Turkey.

"Are you happy? Are you cheerful?" continued the Tennessee Shad pursuing the Socratic method. "Do you enjoy your meals? Do the words fresh vegetables mean anything to your jaded appetites? Do they?"

"Go on, and don't be idiotic."

447

"Does the prospect of wallowing two weeks in the mud fill your soul with rapture? Are you still eager to rise at an unearthly hour, to eat the deadly sinker and the scrag bird?"

"What are you driving at?" said Turkey, mystified. "You know the answers as well as we do. What's your scheme?"

"How would the idea of spending these next two weeks like this appeal to you?" said the Tennessee Shad, point-blank: "Sleeping late, eating cream in your coffee—not cream, but *real* cream—thick, lumpy, soggy cream—no chapel, no recitations—nothing! Would two weeks in the infirmary appeal to you as an idea?"

"Would it?" said Lovely Mead, opening his eyes. "Jemima!"

The Gutter Pup put away the baseball bat, leaning it gently in the corner.

"Think of nothing to do all day long," continued the Tennessee Shad, half shutting his eyes, "but to read novels and play cards and games! Think of having special steaks and nice, juicy chops to build up your delicate bodies!"

"Oh, Shad!" cried the converted Gutter Pup. "How are you going to work it?"

The Tennessee Shad came back to earth, gave a vicious last bite on his pencil, pocketed it, slapped his knee and cried:

"German measles!"

"German measles?" repeated the four.

"Shad!"

"You don't mean it!"

"Who's got 'em?"

"Oh, joy!"

Now, German measles are not an affliction but a dispensation of Providence, and the boy who in the month of March is thus blessed and discovers it before the doctor does is in honor bound to share his good fortune with his neighbors.

"I know," said the Gutter Pup suddenly. "It's over in the Dickinson. I saw Doctor Charlie trotting in."

"Naw!" said the Tennessee Shad disdainfully. "I've looked into that—that's nothing but Wee-Wee Logan faking up a case of pinkeye. Mine's the real, genuine article. Are you on?"

"Are we on?"

"Say, just lead us up to him!"

"Quick!"

"It's Doc Macnooder, on the second floor," said the Tennessee Shad. "But, mind, only we four get in on this. We don't want to sleep two in a bed."

"But, Shad, how do you know?"

"How can you be sure?"

"Doc knows the symptoms," said the Shad. "He's had 'em before; besides, he's going to be a doctor."

"For Heaven's sake, fellows, let's get to him."

"We mustn't lose a minute."

"Come on."

"Hold up," said the Tennessee Shad. "There's a condition attached to it."

The four seekers after infection drew up and eyed the glib impresario.

"There generally is a string to your ideas," said the Gutter Pup; "and we're getting very much to dislike those strings."

"That's dead right!"

"I wouldn't get too careless this time, young sporting life!"

"I never saw such a distrustful bunch," said the Tennessee Shad; "and the whole thing is to protect you, too."

"What do you mean?"

"I mean this," said the Tennessee Shad with an injured air. "I drew up a contract with Doc that we get exclusive rights and have to pay him a dollar down. Do you want the whole House started for the infirmary before we can get a look-in? If you don't think it's worth a quarter—oh, well —I guess I can find—"

"Excuse me," said Turkey Reiter, pulling out a coin, "you are a miracle of foresight."

"Pardon me," said the Gutter Pup, making change.

"Will this bright new quarter do?" said Egghead.

"You fellows ought to think twice before you shout," said Lovely Mead, completing the dollar.

"I had German measles second-form year," said the Egghead as they descended the stairs. "They're delightful!"

"How long does it take to catch 'em?" asked the Gutter Pup.

"About a week."

"That's an awful time to wait!"

"Hush, here we are," said the Tennessee Shad, stopping and knocking on door 48.

A slight swishing sound was heard on the other side and a catarrhal voice said, "Who's there?"

"It's me," said the Tennessee Shad. "It's all right, Doc; open up."

The key turned and they filed into a room encased with green, black and blue bottles arranged on shelves, heaped in corners, scattered everywhere.

Macnooder, swathed in neck cloths, dressed in a green-and-blue bathgown, red Mephistopheles slippers and violet garters, sank back into an easy chair and disappeared a moment behind a voluminous handkerchief.

The four proselytes stood by the door.

"Say, old sporting Tootlets," said the cautious Turkey, "German measles is most pleasant, but real measles isn't what we're looking for. What's to guarantee us we get what we pay our money for and not a gold brick?"

"You can't have measles twice, you ignoramus," said Macnooder with a sneeze. "I had 'em four years ago."

"You'll guarantee us?" said the Gutter Pup.

"Not to have measles? Sure, I will. I'll post a forfeit, five apiece."

"That's good, straight talk," said the Tennessee Shad briskly. "Don't be an ass, Gutter Pup. Now, Doc, if you'll give us your word not to let anyone else in on this, here's that dollar we agreed upon."

"So help me!" said Macnooder, jingling the coins in his pocket.

"Hold up there," broke in Lovely Mead; "all very well, but how're we going to know you'll carry out the bargain?"

"He's going to Trenton this afternoon," said the Tennessee Shad. "He's got an aunt living there."

"Is that so, Doc?"

"Just as soon as I get through with you fellows and get in Doctor Charlie."

"Well," said Turkey, "I don't see but what it's a go."

Macnooder rose, drew a carpet over the crack under the door, stuffed the keyhole with cotton and lit an alcohol lamp.

"What's that for?" said the Egghead, whom the presence of so many labeled bottles rendered uneasy.

"Cold kills germs, heat develops them," said Doc with a superior air. "Come on, Shad, you first!"

The Tennessee Shad seated himself opposite, touching knees and foreheads, while the others looked on in fascinated admiration.

450

"Grab my hands," said Doc solemnly, "and take long breaths."

One week later the Gutter Pup began to cough, Lovely Mead to sneeze and Turkey Reiter and the Triumphant Egghead to snuff and sniffle; only the Tennessee Shad remained disconsolate. Doctor Charlie, joyfully summoned, found the five waiting in Turkey Reiter's room, applied a thermometer and looked very solemn.

"Catarrhal symptoms and febrile disturbance," he said. "Pack up your things and get right up to the infirmary." Then, considering the Tennessee Shad thoughtfully, he added, "You have a slightly heightened temperature, but that may be only imagination. However, I think I won't risk it; you go up, too."

An hour later the five were shaking hands and slapping one another on the back in the cozy parlor of the infirmary.

"Well, you old growlers," said the Tennessee Shad proudly, "are my ideas always useless?"

"Shad," said Turkey, "you are reinstated in our affections. We love you. You are our pride and joy."

"I hope," said the Egghead, drawing up by the crackling fire, "that it'll rain and slush the whole time we're here."

"Gee, it certainly is good indoors," said Lovely Mead, squatted before the bookshelves.

"What'll come next?" said the Gutter Pup with thick speech. "I certainly have got you all beat on the snuffles."

"Look out for a little pink rash tomorrow morning," said the Egghead wisely.

"Does it itch bad?"

"Naw, it only tickles for a day."

"I suppose we'll have to stay in bed one day at least."

The Tennessee Shad stood, legs akimbo, gazing into the fire.

"Why so silent, old Shad?" said the Triumphant Egghead.

"I don't understand it."

"Understand what?"

"Why I didn't take," said the Shad dejectedly, "I haven't any symptoms at all. I faked up a temperature, but I can't keep that up."

"Old sporting life," said Turkey with a grin, "this is one on you!"

"It certainly is, Shad," said the Egghead with a chuckle.

"Poor old Shad!" said the Gutter Pup, winking at the others. "What an awful sell. But it was coming to you, old hoss; it certainly was coming to you."

"You ungrateful, spiteful little beast," said the Tennessee Shad.

There never was such a dinner as they sat down to that night.

"My, what a steak," said the Gutter Pup languidly, "soft and red and juicy."

"Say, are these mashed potatoes?"

"A little more, please."

"Um—if there's anything I love it's creamed onions."

"Ice cream for dessert."

"No?"

"Fact—coffee ice cream."

"Say, was that a tomato soup, eh?"

"Think of a week of this!"

"Pass my plate."

"Let's begin all over again."

"Hope you stay with us, Shad."

"Shut up," said Shad, "and be a gentleman with those onions!"

They slept late, had breakfast in bed and rose just in time to drop in to lunch.

"Why, where's the Shad?" said Turkey Reiter.

"He's gone."

"Fired!"

"Thrown out!"

"Hurray!"

They took their knives and forks and beat a gleeful tattoo on the table, then burst into peals of laughter.

"This is where we score."

"Oh, mamma, what a story to tell on the Shad!"

"Will we tell it?"

"Oh, no!"

"Are we it?"

They rose and shook hands, then sat down and looked at one another critically.

"Say, where's the little pink rash?"

"Search me."

"I haven't got it."

"Nor me."

"It ought to have come," said the Egghead thoughtfully.

"I feel bum enough to have a dozen, all right."

"Shut up!" said the Egghead, jumping up so as to catch the first view, "here comes lunch!"

"What is it?"

"Veal cutlet."

"With brown sauce?"

"Brown sauce—fresh peas and tomatoes!"

"Say, sports," said Turkey Reiter suddenly, "is this cutlet tough to you?"

"It certainly is."

"It cuts all right."

"Well, it hurts me to chew it."

The Egghead laid down his knife and fork with a clatter.

"Why, Egghead, what's wrong?"

"Do your jaws ache?"

"Sure!"

"They do."

"Have you ever had the mumps?"

"No!" cried in horror Turkey, the Gutter Pup and Lovely Mead.

"Well, you have them!"

.   .   .   .   .   .

They not only had the mumps, but they had them violently, outrageously, swollen to ridiculous proportions. On the third day, while the Gutter Pup from his bed was gazing in the opposite mirror at a face that looked like a chipmunk with a coconut in either cheek, a word of consolation came to him in the shape of the following scrawl:

Say, Gutter Pup, it was all Macnooder. I didn't know—honest, I didn't. Square me with Turkey.

Yours,

SHAD.

P. S.—I've had the mumps.

453

V

THE FIRM FINDS A NEW VICTIM

SHORTLY AFTER the firm of Macnooder and the Tennessee Shad had been established on a dividend basis, they discovered to their alarm that the scope of the future operations was exactly limited by the luster of their past successes. Not that there was any stop in the output of fertile ideas or astute practical financiering. The trouble was, to use Wall Street phraseology, with the market and the lambs. If Macnooder sought to launch an idea he was greeted with derisive smiles and the cry, "Fine, tell it to the Tennessee Shad!"

When the Tennessee Shad languidly and artfully proposed, the reply was similar and more insulting:

"Try it on Macnooder, you assassin and bunco steerer!"

Famine set in relentlessly and there is no telling what might have happened had not chance, as shall be related, brought them a victim made to order and a field of exploitation which for a time seemed more inexhaustible than the diamond field of Africa. Had either the avarice of Doc Macnooder or the mischievous imagination of the Tennessee Shad been capable of restraint, the firm might have gone the full course in fattening prosperity; but as both were but mortal, the speculation was profitable but unfortunately short. Here endeth the parenthesis.

When Montague Skinner had completed sixteen gentle and luxurious years in the hansoms and continuous vaudevilles of New York City, it chanced that the select private school which he reluctantly graced, becoming unduly elated with the phenomenally triumphant eleven which represented it, issued a challenge and bore down on The Lawrenceville School, Lawrenceville, New Jersey, with a betting commissioner and faces which they desperately strove to render without malice or guile.

As the hospitality of their hosts saw them to the Trenton depot, they reached New York on their return-trip tickets and arrived at their homes, delaying the cabdriver no longer than the time required to borrow the fares from their sympathetic butlers. The Metropolitan papers obligingly concealed the score in obscure corners while the business manager hurriedly revised the schedule for the ensuing season, excusing himself to the Lawrenceville Football Association on the ground that the two hours required to make the trip was unfortunately found to be a serious infringement on the scholarly routine of the school.

The experience was exceedingly upsetting to young Skinner who, being a very large frog in a very small pond, could not remember without profound unrest the very much larger frogs he had seen disporting themselves on the surface of the considerably larger waters.

Now Skinner had not simply been born with a gold spoon in his mouth, but literally amid a shower of golden spoons, forks and knives. Joshua M. Skinner, proprietor and manager of The Regal Hotel, blissfully regarded himself as but a humble instrument in the advancement of his only child's career, and secretly rejoiced when his son lectured him on the proprieties of masculine attire and the vernacular of select society.

At fifteen, Montague was installed in his private suite and given his particular valet, likewise a coachman and coupé to be at his orders all hours of the day. Accounts were opened at the best of tailors and haberdashers, and Joshua M. Skinner doubled an exceedingly elastic allowance, resolved that money should never be lacking to the proper equipment of Montague's genteel sporting proclivities. Mrs. Skinner was all that a fond and perfect mother should be and the only time that the semblance of a disagreement had arisen between her and her son was on one vulgar occasion when she had beheld Montague and three companions returning from school in a *hired* cab.

Despite this tender paternal solicitude, Montague had passed through so much of the disillusionment of worldly existence that he had quickly come to assume that air of complete boredom which goes with a stockade collar and a limply pendant cigarette. He never burst into roars of laughter. The most excruciatingly mirth-provoking turns of the vaudeville headliners never stirred him to

455

more than a tolerantly amused smile. He never applauded. At the age of sixteen he had never fallen in love. He spoke of the chorus as "homes for old women," and from his superior knowledge, smiled down at his more impulsive comrades who, blinded by the flood of lights and a painted cheek, occasionally borrowed from him the price of a timid bouquet. He had never lost his temper as he was surrounded by those who never quarreled with his choice of The Regal Hotel Special Cigars or the daintily served dinners, and generously left him the choice of the evening's entertainment —and the buying of the seats. He had never been guilty of anything so vulgar as a rough-and-tumble fight. He had never saved up to purchase something that gave him the thrill of unhoped-for possession. His trousers had never bagged at the knees. His glossy hair was never ruffled and Bucks, the devoted valet, saw to it that his cravats were never allowed to fade upon the constantly renewed shirts of specially imported French lawn.

He was just over the five-foot line, very carefully washed, reddish hair well subdued, a slightly raw countenance, perpendicular ears and a short chin which hung on the brink of a three-inch Piccadilly collar. Despite a creaseless coat that ran over the stoop of his shoulders and the distinction of his racing vest, he still had the look of one who had been forced into long trousers by hothouse processes.

On Saturday morning he rose promptly at ten, extended his unmuscular arms to Bucks who solicitously encased them in a wadded wrapper and opened the door to the already prepared bath.

By half-past-eleven he went out on the avenue dragging a bamboo cane, for a visit to his shirtmakers whose obsequious attention gave him a little lukewarm satisfaction. Later he met his cronies at an expensive restaurant where the headwaiter in person placed him in his chair with a deferential, "What can I do for you today, Mr. Skinner?"

Sometimes he ordered from his profound and nice knowledge of how such delectable repasts should be ordered and sometimes he said in a bored way, "Just shake us up something tasty, will you?"

Then he initialed the bill without looking at it, to the sidelong admiration of his guests.

In the evening, if the matinee had been too fatiguing, they ensconced themselves in Montague's private salon and sat into the early hours about a green table laden with different colored chips of the sort that on other tables are used in a sport entitled tiddledy-winks.

And yet, because way down beneath all the sham and superficiality with which doting parents were trying to smother the real impulses, because the spark of the boy is invincible and cannot be completely extinguished, young Skinner began to wonder and to dream. He saw again, beyond the heavy, crowded, towering buildings the glimpse of a strange life that ran joyously over green fields and around ivy-clad houses of brick and tile, a life where the boy and the man were strangely joined, where the world was the world of that youth of which he had known nothing and toward which he began strangely to yearn.

And so it happened to the amazement of his precious cronies, of Bucks the flabbergasted valet, of Skinner's father and mother, and most of all to himself, that at the beginning of his seventeenth year, in the month of September, Montague Skinner of Broadway and Fifth Avenue, renounced the metropolis and took his way toward The Lawrenceville School in Lawrenceville, New Jersey.

Doc Macnooder, perched like a sentinel hawk, sat in the open window of the Triumphant Egghead's room surveying the arrival of the appetizing freshmen. His legs hung out, his heels rapped an occasional tattoo around the clinging ivy, but his glance was distant and circling upward in the speculative heights of financial dreams.

Across the way, from Dick Stover's room in the turret of the Dickinson, the thin shanks of the Tennessee Shad protruded in a similar attitude. From time to time their carnivorous glances sought the front porches below them and fastened intently on the stir of an incoming freshman.

About the long, green reaches of the Circle, the last stages were discharging their vociferous or bashful occupants—a last belated buggy was streaking toward the distant Cleve, *ventre-à-terre*. Below on the stone steps the committee on introduction was catechizing a rumpled candidate who clasped a valise to him with a despairing loneliness.

"Oh you Macnooder man!"

Macnooder, screening his eyes, discovered under the pendant legs of the Tennessee Shad the wolfish eyes and star-pointing nose of Dennis de Brian de Boru Finnegan.

The call was repeated.

"Hello yourself," said Macnooder.

"What luck?"

"What luck over there?" said Macnooder who from theory always reserved the last word.

"Gilt-edged, premium-down, bang-up—strictly fresh and all that sort of thing," said Finnegan, who (as has been related) considered himself the discoverer of the double adjective.

"What have you got?"

"Two brutal sluggerinos who played professional feet-ball in the slums of Chicago."

Macnooder received this with a languid yawn.

"The champion peroxide blond halfback of Des Moines, Iowa."

"How interesting!"

"A millionaire baby from Philadelphia wrapped up in green-backs, and Cyclops Berbecker, the one-eyed wonder of the wandering eye."

"Fact?" said Macnooder, the impresario at once keenly alert and addressing the Tennessee Shad, the senior partner of the firm of Macnooder and Self.

"Fact," said the Shad solemnly, "glass eye, detachable and most sociable."

Macnooder's glance was a glance of envy. Seeing which Finnegan chirped up, "Well, old pawnbroker, what have you got to boast of?"

"Nothing," said Macnooder sadly. "Supplies very poor this year, boys."

At this moment back of him burst forth a chorus of exclamations.

"Keeroogalum!"

"Holy Cats!"

"What is it?"

"Hold me up!"

"Have I lived to see it!"

Below, two suburbanally distinguished horses, drawing Trenton's proudest hackney coach, had stopped and from the front seat a being, obsequious and mechanical, had sprung to his heels, touched his hat and waited at attention.

"Hush!" said the Triumphant Egghead, "don't frighten it, it'll fly away."

"It's a beadle," said Turkey Reiter.

"It's a dentist."

"It's a butler."

"A butler your grandmother—it's a valet."

"My word!"

"So it is."

"A real live young valet."

"What's he going to do now?"

"Hush!"

Bucks, in obedience to a command, came toward the steps, perceived Macnooder suspended from the sill, like a wooden monkey on a stick, and bringing his heels to attention, touched his finger to his hat and said, "Beg pardon, sir, but is this the Dickinson House?"

Macnooder put his hand to his throat, gulped and nodded, incapable of speech. The silence everywhere had fallen like the crash of thunder. Even Dennis de Brian de Boru Finnegan was clinging to the window frame awed and speechless.

Bucks returning, imparted the reassuring information, the door opened, and Montague Skinner emerged, supporting his languid body on a light bamboo cane, slapping the annoying dust from his beautiful trousers, and, leaving the vulgarities of the baggage to Bucks, sauntered, not too eagerly and in no wise embarrassed, up the stone flags to the house.

Upstairs, the pent-up indignation burst forth with a roar.

"Murder!"

"Desecration!"

"Outrage!"

"Lynch him!"

"Pie him!"

"Strip the hide off him!"

"Mangle him!"

The door resounded with the impact of furious bodies.

"Stop!"

The voice was the voice of Macnooder, the mastermind. The mob paused in suspense.

"Come back—sit down!"

"Sit down?" thundered the Triumphant Egghead. "Sit down! When we're disgraced—laughing stock of the campus—sit down?"

"Exactly. Would you kill the goose that lays the golden egg, you nincompoop!"

A light began to dawn. The Triumphant Egghead scratched one

459

ear, loosened his collar and collapsed in a chair.

"What this house needs is style," said Macnooder firmly, "style and proper banking facilities."

"Aha!"

"When a young Van Astorbilt arrives, you'd make a noise, would you, and frighten him away."

At this moment Hungry Smeed at the window announced shrilly, "The valet, the valet, he's driving away!"

"Let him go," said Macnooder with great calm.

"I say," said Butcher Stevens wrathfully, "are you going to let a fashion plate, a candy dude, insult us in this way and do nothing about it?"

"Butcher, you're so crude," said Macnooder crushingly, sitting down and gazing out of the window with the eye of a cat who knows what is waiting on the sill. "Just think—this belongs to us—all of us!"

The Great Big Man came scooting through the door, his little knickerbockered legs shaking with excitement.

"His name is Skinner and his father owns The Regal Hotel, New York City."

"Wire at once to reserve the bridal suite," said Macnooder triumphantly. "Where's Klondike?"

A moment later Klondike, the houseman who was advertised to shake up the beds of the Dickinson, was found and brought in grinning, while the mystified veterans gazed at Macnooder expectantly.

"No, he doesn't look like a valet," said Macnooder sadly. "Not at all like a valet."

"But we can dress him up," exclaimed Turkey Reiter, the first to seize the idea.

Ten minutes later, Klondike encased in a battered stovepipe, supplied with white mittens and a selected pigeon's blood cravat received on a salver a dozen calling cards which he was instructed to present one at a time, and departed in search of Montague Skinner after the stovepipe had been decorated with a chicken feather in lieu of a cockade.

"Remember," said Macnooder imperiously before the gathering dispersed, "nothing brutal, nothing coarse, we must do nothing to discourage capital, we must be kind to Van Astorbilt, we must educate him—gently, for he belongs to us—all of us!"

Skinner's first days were replete with disturbing surprises. He, the big frog, had sunk with a splash, dwindled into a very small tadpole among a myriad of other little tadpoles.

Of course he had expected a certain amount of ragging. When Klondike, in his circus paraphernalia had appeared with the calling cards, he had recognized the patness of the caricature. Still, this had surprised him. He had never thought of the incongruity of arriving with a valet, nor that it would be an isolated phenomenon. It was rather upsetting to find himself in a world where valets failed to impress.

Another thing that rather puzzled him was the studied attitude of deference assumed toward him by the Dickinson House. He was not always quite sure of this attitude. At times it seemed to him that a lip twitched or that a roguish gleam lurked in eyes that were set for gravity.

Now, of course, this was all rather ridiculous, for they were nothing but children, whereas he—he had lived. He had known things beyond their ken, had lived the life of a man of fashion, a cosmopolite, and of course if they found his costumes rather individual, equally of course he could not be expected to descend to jerseys and corduroy "pants."

He had had quite an interesting experience with that minor detail of scholastic life—the curriculum. He had hesitated a long while in deliberation over the requirements for admission into the Fifth Form and then modestly decided to lengthen his sojourn amid pleasant places. The day following his arrival he spent an annoying morning and afternoon being examined for the Fourth. The following morning he was assigned to the Third, where his recitations commanded such solicitous interest from the Natural Enemy that he agreed to descend another rung on the ladder. There he remained long enough to become pleasantly acquainted and wearily acquiesced in his final drop into the First Form, where all travel ceases.

Luckily, he did not regard the curriculum seriously. One thing, though, annoyed him. He had passed through the fire of baptism and had been renamed the Uncooked Beefsteak. Whether this was a tribute to himself as a product of The Regal Hotel or whether it was an attempt to express felicitously the red hair and singularly raw hue of his complexion, the fact remained that he, Montague Skinner, cosmopolite, was publicly known as the Uncooked Beefsteak. The worst of it was that he could not see the humor of it. It hurt his pride that he of all men, before whom headwaiters and haberdashers bowed down, should be so misunderstood.

Now there are only two ways to treat a nickname; either to grin and hope for some future coincidence that will substitute a more acceptable name, or to place a chip on your shoulder and announce publicly in the fashion of Sow Emmons and Vulture Watkins that any use of the abhorred name will have to be accomplished by an exhibition of the manly art.

The first alternative was beyond the knowledge of Montague Skinner and the second was brutal and mussing.

He fell back on his knowledge of the weaknesses of human nature. He would do what he had always done—open the pocketbook and win by Roman display.

Doc Macnooder roomed across the hall in that secret place into which few were allowed to penetrate. Montague liked the ubiquitous Macnooder. He was so natural and friendly and he showed him the deference that proved that Macnooder at least realized the difference between a tumbling cub and a man of experience. About this time the distinction of Macnooder's cravats became a matter of public comment; likewise a variegated vest that materially added to the charm of his personal appearance.

One afternoon as the Uncooked Beefsteak was sitting forlornly on his window seat, there came a knock and the round, guileless face of Doc Macnooder beamed through the doorway.

"Ah there, old sporting life," said Macnooder in a sympathetic way, "feeling pretty chipper?"

"Fine," said the Uncooked Beefsteak with a painful smile.

"Food's better in Little Old New York, isn't it?" said Macnooder, his eye roving among the gay cravats that hung from the bureau corner. Skinner sighed; a famished gluttonous sigh.

"I'd like to take you out for a little snap or two at some places I know of," he said regaining his worldly air.

"Caviar and asparagus?"

"*A vol-au-vent* with a cold salmon trout first."

"And a real *beefsteak*," said Macnooder, opening a bureau drawer hungrily.

Montague shrank back, glancing at Macnooder suspiciously.

"I say, Doc."

"Hello!"

"I wish you fellows wouldn't call me the Uncooked Beefsteak."

"Why, that's a stunning nickname."

"Well, I wish you wouldn't."

"Does it worry you?"

"It does."

"All right, Beefsteak, I'll try not to."

Montague bit his lip but Macnooder's face showed only the zest of the explorer.

"I don't see any," said Macnooder after a minute.

"Any what?"

"Any filthy weeds."

Montague, slipping to the door, shot the key and proceeding to his trunk brought forth a long, low box decorated with custom stamps and foreign gilt.

"This is what I smoke," he said carelessly, extending the box.

Macnooder's glance trembled in spite of himself.

"Black as ink and half-a-mile long. Fifty Centers?"

"They're private stock," said Montague in a bored way. "Take one if you like."

"Not now," said Macnooder, with visions of bigger game as he sat and watched with wolfish eyes Skinner return the box under lock and key.

"Gee, Beefsteak, pardon me, Montague old chap, you certainly are a dead game one."

"Oh, I've knocked about a bit," said Skinner, stretching his arms languidly.

"I say you really are a devil of a fellow," said Br'er Rabbit with his imagination centering on the miraculous cigars. "There are a couple of champion smokers around these modest little diggin's but my aunt's cat's pants, I believe you could smoke them to a finish!"

"Champion smokers!" said Skinner pricking up his ears.

"Oh, we pull off a couple of smoking championships a year," said Macnooder, stooping to tighten his shoelaces, "secret Ku Klux Klan, dead-of-midnight affairs."

"That interests me," said Skinner, approaching.

"They're great old powwows," said Macnooder, skillfully dropping the subject. "Got any grub?"

"We might wander over to the village," said Skinner, now intensely alert.

"Why not?"

"I say Doc," said Skinner as they shuffled over to Laloo's Hot Dog Palace, "when do they hold these championships?"

"Championships?" said Macnooder, pretending ignorance.

"Smoking championships."

"One's due now."

"I'd like to get into that, you know."

"Hm, rather difficult. They're quite select—the Tennessee Shad —old fellows—inner gang—crème de la crème and all that."

"Oh," said Skinner in great disappointment, "couldn't you work me in?"

"Hardly."

"I'd like a go at it."

"Let me think," said Macnooder whose fertile brain had already achieved daylight.

With the object of stimulating a favorable mental process, Skinner not only ordered up a pack of steaming frankfurters but forced down two indigestibles himself.

"Well, have you thought up anything?" he said anxiously, after they had consumed a jelly roll and steered for Appleby's, the second station on the road from the Aching Void.

"I'm thinking hard," said Macnooder, who gave the high signal to Appleby and soon was floundering among the pastries.

Skinner, to be democratic, after considerable epicurean hesitation, chose a Turkish Paste as the least of many evils and nibbled a little on the edge.

"Beefsteak," said Macnooder, in a friendly way as Skinner paid up, "you're really quite the bounding boy. Really now—we'll just cool off at the Jigger Shop—really now, you ought to get into the swim here."

"That's just what I want to do," said Skinner a little too eagerly. "I'd like to know the real crowd you know."

"I see, sort of break into high society," said Macnooder, who bit his tongue to keep from choking.

"Well," said the Uncooked Beefsteak, blushing a little.

"Oh, that's all right—perfectly proper—just a little expression of mine. Besides you belong—you're it—you're the real thing—you're a sport, you know."

"I say, have you been thinking up a scheme?" said Skinner, not only anxious but a little suspicious of Macnooder's admiration.

"I have a glimmer," said Macnooder, nodding to Al, the guardian of the Jigger, and elevating three fingers as a signal for the maximum, "yes, I may say a twinkle. I wish the Tennessee Shad were around. Try half-a-dozen éclairs, you old gormandizer. Shut your eyes and imagine you're denting the menu at dear old Del's. No? Well, thinking it over, I think I will. Al, transport the éclairs."

"You said a twinkle," said Skinner patiently figuring out Macnooder's greatest possible cubic capacity.

"Exactly that," said Macnooder, who continued to assist his stomach to stimulate his mind.

"Well, what have you hit upon?" said Skinner, expectantly.

"A good one," said Macnooder, leaving with one hand upon the belt and a lingering backward glance.

"Let's go back to the room and talk it over."

"Never!" said Doc in alarm. "We might be overheard—we'll just roll up to Conover's and get a quiet corner, and eat a few pancakes while we're discussing the details."

"I'm not hungry," said Skinner defensively.

"That's all right," said Macnooder cheerfully. "I am."

"You think you can work me in, then," said Skinner, after waiting for Doc to open the subject.

"Not in the championships," said Doc. "You have to be elected to the Sporting Club and all that—most select. I have another way, though, but it's expensive. You get the word—expensive."

Skinner handed Mrs. Conover a ten-dollar gold certificate.

"You reassure me," said Doc with a summery smile.

Skinner had a sudden feeling of uneasiness.

"We were speaking of breaking into society," said Macnooder. "That's the idea."

"How so?" said the Uncooked Beefsteak, looking decidedly raw.

"You give a banquet—an introductory banquet—a sort of débutante affair, you know."

"How could it be pulled off?" said the Beefsteak, caressing the idea.

"Terrific secrecy, dead of midnight, banks of the canal, and all that."

"But the smoking championship?"

"Aha!" said Macnooder, looking very subtle. "That's where the real idea comes in. For the entertainment of your guests you give an invitation smoking meet."

"I see," said Skinner joyfully.

"And put up as first prize a nice, long, fat, juicy box of *expensive* cigars."

"But suppose I win?"

"You won't."

"Oh, I don't know."

"Well, are you fond of my idea?" said Macnooder proudly.

"I am," said Skinner, resting his hand on Doc's shoulder as a mark of special favor. "But I say, how do you work a smoking championship?"

"Leave that to me."

"Who'll I invite?"

"Likewise to me. I'm the little social secretary."

"What'll I get?"

"Caviar," said Doc firmly.

"Something in the line of pâtés?"

"Truffled pheasants and all that sort of thing."

"A lot of sweets."

"But no *beefsteaks*," said Macnooder who departed hastily to roll off his laughter on the soft lawn behind the Kennedy, where he and the Tennessee Shad sat long in gleeful consultation.

Skinner was complacently elated at the new prospect. After all, big schools were very much like small ones and the way into high society lay clear, whatever the geography. The more he thought over Macnooder's scheme, the more it appealed to him. He had no vulgar envy in his nature. He did not aspire to be a hero—all he asked was to be the patron of heroes.

Full of confident expectations, he wrote a letter to Bucks, the marooned valet, outlining a program of Lucullan prodigality. After Doc Macnooder had dropped in for a few words of suggestion, two large boxes stuffed with The Regal Hotel's transported best duly arrived and were placed in safe keeping.

Finally, the great social night arriving, Skinner received the first real thrill of his misdirected little existence—the thrill of forbidden fruit. At ten o'clock the shivering Beefsteak, completely dressed, beheld a thin, roving bar of light trickling under the crack of his door. The next moment, Doc Macnooder preceded by a bull's-eye lantern stole noiselessly into the darkness.

"Who's that?" said the Uncooked Beefsteak in a chilly whisper.

"Hush," said Macnooder hoarsely, "not a breath!"

"What's that for?" said the Beefsteak, alarmed at the sight of a black cloth that shrouded the mysterious face, burglar-fashion.

"We must never be recognized!"

"Is there any danger?"

"Heaps. Old Greek-roots sleeps on a trigger. Put on this handkerchief. Get off those shoes. All ready now?"

"I say, what'll we do if he nabs us?"

"Soak him on the point of the chin," said Macnooder very solemnly. "If you miss him, I'll get him and then scud for your room. Come on now, on your tiptoes."

Guided by Macnooder, the now thoroughly alarmed Beefsteak slipped along the horribly proclaiming halls and through Hungry Smeed's window out into the steaming night.

"Gee!" said Montague, using that vulgar exclamation for the first time. "Gee, that was great!"

"First time?"

"You bet."

"Danger's not over yet. What's that? Down on your pantry!"

"Someone's moving towards us."

"Grab my hand. Come on now. Run for your life."

Guided by Macnooder, stumbling and swaying, Skinner felt the soft turf rush under him. They dodged between the chapel and the accursed abode of Compulsory Bath, skirted the baseball diamonds, and stopped to draw breath behind the safe confines of the laundry.

"Narrow squeak."

"Great," said the palpitating Beefsteak.

They passed through Negro settlements, dimly emerging in the suffused light of the approaching moon, rattling their sticks along picket fences to the indignation of furious dogs that came bounding after them, while from ahead came faint echoes of other parties similarly engaged. Gradually their group was augmented until as they reached the banks of the canal they mustered a dozen in free marching order. Another dozen under the leadership of the Tennessee Shad were splashing in the none-too-fragrant waters or drying their ghostly limbs ashore. Answering shouts went up.

467

"Here we are."

"Where's the grub?"

"Oh, Turkey Reiter!"

"Hello there, Butcher Stevens!"

"Have you got Van Astorbilt?"

"You bet we have."

"Open the boxes."

"Give us the grub."

"Am I hungry?"

"Oh, no!"

The strange zest of adventure disappeared in Skinner. He was again in his element, he the purveyor of banquets and the patron of heroes. The swimmers came in dripping, hastily scrambling for places in the festive ring.

At this moment there was a disturbance near the provender, and Finnegan came rushing up to Macnooder.

"I say, Doc! Here is the Coffee-colored Angel who's sneaked up on us and wants a share of the swag."

"Throw him out!"

"He says he is on to the game and will give the whole shooting match away. What's to be done?"

"Welcome him with open arms," said Macnooder, who had the instincts of the politician, "and kick the slats out of him tomorrow."

"Start her up!" cried a score of voices.

"Give us the truffles!"

"Trot out your venison!"

"Little girls and little boys," said Macnooder, who loved to speak, but was seldom allowed to finish, "when the evening star, swimming across the sun-kissed horizon—"

"Cut it out!"

"No elocution!"

"Come down to earth!"

"My friends," said Macnooder, complacently yielding, "before opening this evening's entertainment, I would draw your attention to a few articles of daily necessity which I am prepared to furnish at prices—"

"No business!"

"You can't flimflam us tonight."

"Come to the point."

"Gentlemen," said Macnooder, looking about him doubtfully, "you forget. Where are your manners? Remember this is a débutante affair. Gentlemen, I have the honor to socially introduce to you Mr. Montague Skinner, the Fifth Avenue Narcissus, one of the leaders of the crême de la crême of Metropolitan fashion. Mr. Skinner's perfect pants are the feature of the famous annual poultry exhibition. Mr. Skinner's socks are the limit—of gentility. Mr. Skinner's neckties are destined to revolutionize local styles."

"You ought to know, Doc!" said a voice.

"I do know," said Macnooder, with an evil look into the crowd, "and I know likewise the skulking author of that aspersion. I resume. Mr. Montague Skinner in making his début into the crême de la crême of Lawrenceville society comes before you, not simply as the spoiled favorite of the lobster palaces, but as an athlete!"

"A what?" cried a dozen mystified voices.

"I said athlete," said Macnooder. "Mr. Montague Skinner is the holder of all Metropolitan junior smoking records, from the one-minute cigarette dash to the one-hour record on cigars. As a preliminary to the opening of the evening's banquet, Mr. Skinner will meet in friendly competition the leather-lunged champions of the school. In order to add a little sportiness to the evening, as well as to soften the edge of his munificence, Mr. Skinner will supply each guest with three cigars. You start on a crouching start, and the first to finish, the first at the grub. Two prizes will be offered—one open to all present for the first to finish these same diamond-backed goldplated cigars; the second for the contest of champions."

"What's that?"

"It will be a finish fight—no quarter asked or given! Each contestant has nominated his particular brand of leather. There are five Would-Bes. There will be five distinctly different poisonous rounds. In deference to our host, the first round will be at cigars known as the Pride of The Regal Hotel; second round at corncob pipes specially loaded; third round at stogies; fourth round at political cigars, and fifth round at a final death-defying test proposed by Butcher Stevens—the terrible Hubble-Bubble—the Hookah or Persian Water Pipe!"

"Supposin' they live through it!" said a voice.

"They won't," said Macnooder. "But if they do, a new series will begin at once until a decisive knockout shall be scored."

469

"A regular ten-second knockout?"

"Each contestant, as he drops by the wayside, will be allowed one hour and twenty minutes to recover and then a doctor will be summoned."

"What doctor?"

"Doctor Macnooder."

"I resign," cried a dozen voices.

Macnooder, whose soul was above mosquito bites, continued, "The Hon. Rinky Dink Stover, Tough McCarty, the champion gum chewer of the Woodhull; Mr. Dennis de Brian de Boru Finnegan, our little silent boy, and the Tennessee Shad, the Apollo Belvedere of the Blue Ridges, have unselfishly agreed to serve as judges, spongers, and ambulance corps."

"Cheese it!" said the voice of the rebel.

"Why don't they smoke up?" cried another.

"Mr. Stover and Mr. McCarty," said Macnooder suavely, "as far as can be discovered, are bound by a secret oath never again to touch tobacco. Mr. Finnegan is desisting in the hope of ultimately reaching five feet, and the Tennessee Shad refrains from fear of scorching his bones."

"Gee, Doc, but you are a peach!" said the voice of one who was still cramped by the facts.

"Any more questions?"

There were none.

"I will now introduce to you Mr. Montague Skinner, the pet of the lobster palaces and the Prince of Wales of New Jersey fashions."

As Skinner rose to bow his blushing acknowledgments, Macnooder, with a wave of his hand, transferred the box of cigars to the Tennessee Shad who emerged from the shadows and proceeded to distribute. Just what took place in that shadow is locked in the secret archives of the firm of Macnooder and the Tennessee Shad, but the answer might explain much that proceeded to happen.

Quite deceived by the vociferousness of the false applause that greeted him, Skinner felt again the pleasant tickling sensations that recalled the prodigal days of the metropolis. He withdrew with all the old gorgeousness to join the group of champions. The risen moon flung leafy shadows over the half-naked circle of contestants, where each novice was resolved to die a martyr's death rather than miss the opportunity of smoking a genuine one-dollar cigar. At a command from Macnooder, the matches crackled into flames like the points of distant picket fires, accompanied at once by a gradually increasing chorus of coughs and choking. Still not a descendant of Eve, lover of the forbidden, flinched at his awful task.

"I will now present the champion of champions," said Macnooder in cadence. "Mr. Montague Skinner, the conqueror of the Rockfellerite, the cigar that the Czar of Russia calls for with his morning coffee, you have just had presented to you. The second contestant is Mr. Butcher Stevens, who smokes the terrible Hubble-Bubble as a baby swallows a hatpin. Mr. Stevens is absolutely confident of success."

Butcher Stevens arose amidst applause and performed a bow by means of a scraping motion of his left foot.

"The third contestant is Mr. Slush Randolph, known as the White Terror or King of the Cigarette Fiends. Mr. Randolph takes great pride in his yellow-tipped fingers, which he waggishly calls his Meerschaums. Mr. Randolph is absolutely confident of success."

Slush Randolph smiled a sickly smile and tumbled backward to a place beside Butcher Stevens.

"Our fourth contestant," continued Macnooder, "is Mr. Stubbs, the White Mountain Canary. Mr. Stubbs' speeches for the Democratic ticket not only defeated Mr. Bryan but wrecked his party. Mr. Stubbs bases his hopes for victory on the training he received in smoking political cigars, five of which, the gift of a Prohibitionist candidate for dogcatcher, he is confident no man can smoke and live to tell the tale. The White Mountain Canary is absolutely confident of success."

Stubbs, who had listened to this biography in awestruck amazement, gasped and sat down, still keeping a fascinated glance on the orator of the evening.

"The fifth and last contestant," continued Macnooder, "is Gomez, the Black Beauty, the Dark Horse from Cuba. Beauty, although a freshman just arrived, has a reputation second to none. In Cuba it is said he smoked his first cigar at the age of three years and two months. He is absolutely confident of success."

As the fifth contestant awkwardly slouched forward and bobbed his head, a suppressed murmur ran the rounds of the burning circle while Tough McCarty and Dink Stover were seen to bend warningly over the form of the Coffee-colored Angel, who had been making remarks.

"First Round, on Mr. Montague Skinner's suggestion, at the Rockfellerite coupon-bearing cigar. Ready! Go! All other contestants are reminded that three cigars must be finished before denting the grub, the sooner the finish, the more the grub! Smoke up, you gormandizers!"

Skinner drew in his first puff with complacency, assuming a position of ease and dignity against a tree. He studied his rivals, discounting at once Slush Randolph and the White Mountain Canary, who already were smoking lip-deep, but considering uneasily the professional precision of Butcher Stevens and the Black Beauty.

He finished his favorite cigar with a slight but noticeable feeling of heaviness, due, no doubt, to the distance from the last feeding hour. Butcher and Black Beauty were already waiting, having ended together. The White Mountain Canary was permitted to continue, after a slight altercation with the judges as to the amount consumed, while the White Terror, coughing through the last heated puffs, unbuckled his belt and removed his upper garments with gladiatorial resolution.

"Round Two, contribution of Mr. Slush Randolph, corncob pipes with Mr. Randolph's special mixture, known as The Blacksmith's Delight."

Skinner received his pipe with less elation. The first puff made him glance up sharply, half suspecting a practical joke. To his surprise the White Mountain Canary, albeit with an expression of pain, was resolutely at work, while the White Terror's face showed an expression of malignant ecstasy.

At the conclusion of Round Two the honors were plainly with the Black Beauty who had drawn slightly ahead of Butcher Stevens, while a considerable interval separated Skinner and Slush Randolph from the White Mountain Canary.

"Round Three," said the cold, unfeeling voice of Doc Macnooder; "political cigars, name unknown, at suggestion of the White Mountain Canary."

The cigar was worse than the pipe. A slight haze began to rock slowly down from the overhanging boughs. In desperation Skinner tried quick, short puffs, expelled as soon as taken, but at that he began to cough uneasily. The outer circle of contestants had disappeared from his consciousness, he saw only his little area, the tense faces of Slush and Stubbs, the determined jaws of Stevens, and the indolent figure of the Black Beauty, who, as regular as a teakettle, was enjoying every puff.

At Round Four, Slush Randolph had crawled away and the White Mountain Canary lay on his back with one leg elevated in token of the surrender he was unable to utter.

"Round Four," said the joyful voice, "resignations of the White Mountain Canary and Slush, the King of the Cigarette Fiends, received and accepted. Still resolved on asphyxiation, Butcher Stevens, Montague Skinner, and the Black Beauty. Round Four, suggested by the Dark Horse from Cuba, will be at the famous Seaman's Stogy, a charming little thing used either as a pastime or to lash the tiller. Are you ready? Go!"

Butcher Stevens took two short, jerky puffs, glanced very hard at Macnooder, and immediately threw up the sponge. The sight brought no feeling of joy to Skinner—he had tried the Stogy, with a pain like an electric needle shooting through his lungs. Still he would not give in. He would show them that courage was a relative thing, that they could fail where he could rise superior. His head rocked and weird forms danced before his eyes, but still he kept on. Suddenly he looked about him. Of the dozen who had started in the common race, not one was left upright. He had the feeling of a conqueror on the battlefield of his own defeat. Muttered curses and objurgations seemed to buzz about him in indistinct gasps. He heard them not at all. His flickering energies were concentrated on keeping alive the red spark at the end of the thing that burned like a wet rope coated with tar.

Halfway through, the haze cleared, and he suddenly perceived the Black Beauty deliciously on his back, legs crossed, expelling huge volumes of smoke, INHALING every breath! At this sight all resolution oozed from him. He tried one last discouraged pull, then allowed the reeking weed to slip from his limp fist, and digging his fingers in the warm turf, desperately strove to steady the careening world.

Once only he opened his dizzy eyes—at the sound of a clattering plate. In the middle of the circle, laughing ghoulishly, Macnooder the traitor, Stover, McCarty, Finnegan, and the Tennessee Shad were literally stuffing themselves with the banquet that was to have fed the score, that now lay in groaning groups vowing vengeance on him, Skinner, who had sought only popularity.

In this one horrid glance he had a vision of the Black Beauty, who, disdaining food, still gloriously on his back, was burning up the delicious cigars with the rapidity of a prairie fire.

"I hear you had a party," said Al, watchdog of the Jigger, when the next morning Skinner had stolen over during forbidden hours.

"They tell me I did," said Skinner, weakly ordering a bromo-seltzer.

"I hear quite a few young bruisers are laying for you."

"I am not very popular," said the Uncooked Beefsteak slowly, reflecting with a new enlightenment how ungrateful republics may be.

"I suppose you know how Macnooder and the Tennessee Shad flimflammed you," said Al, who harbored a little professional jealousy.

"No."

"Worked in a lot of doped cigars and cornered the grub."

"I don't care," said Skinner, to whom even French cooking would never mean anything again.

"They tell me, though, you are pretty good at the weed," said Al to console him.

"I thought I was till I struck that fellow Black Beauty."

"Who?"

"The fellow from Cuba—Gomez," said the Uncooked Beefsteak with reluctant admiration.

"Huh—there goes your Gomez now," said Al with a short, barking laugh.

"Why, that's Blinky!" said Skinner, perceiving the one-eyed purveyor of illicit Sunday papers slouching across the street.

"Sure," said Al, looking pityingly at the young innocent. "Macnooder worked him in to take no chances. Blinky could set fire to a rubber hose and smoke it with ease and pleasure."

VI

A SLIGHT DISPUTE IN THE FIRM

IF THE smoking championship had blighted Montague Skinner's young and tender illusions, it had also its sting for its promoters. The immediate consequence was an abrupt and violent rupture in the firm of youthful promoters on the following abstruse point of moral and financial etiquette.

When the final division had been made of cigars, slightly damaged sandwiches, mixed meat pastes, half-filled bottles of root beer and ginger ale, uneaten éclairs and French pastry turning slightly to the sour, and the same had either been forced into the Aching Void or sold to rank outsiders for cash considerations, the Tennessee Shad discovered by accident that Macnooder had actually collected from Blinky and each of the challenging smokers the sum of twenty-five cents for the privilege of smoking the miraculous cigars. The Tennessee Shad demanded an equitable accounting of all sums gained from whatever source. Macnooder refused, claiming certain perquisites as financier and underwriter and on this point an instant estrangement took place.

The Tennessee Shad, nursing the bitterness a creative genius feels for the pettinesses of a commercial partner, was curled up on the window seat of his high station at the Kennedy when a sudden outburst of shrieks sounded opposite.

"Beefsteak, this way!"

"Come on, you son of The Regal Hotel!"

"Beefsteak, clean my shoes!"

"Beefsteak, shake up this coat!"

"Beefsteak, tidy up my room!"

"Shake a leg!"

"On the jump!"

"Oh, you Beefsteak!"

The Tennessee Shad uncoiled as a snake uncoils, and lifting his head listened curiously to the insistent chorus that was borne to

475

him from the open windows of the Dickinson opposite. From time to time the frantic figure of Montague Skinner could be seen rushing through the rooms in a confused attempt to serve many masters.

"That's quite a speedy valet service they've organized over there," said the Gutter Pup enviously.

"It's a mistake," said the Tennessee Shad in lazy disapproval.

"How so?"

"The Beefsteak won't stand it. He'll run away—ship before the mast and all that sort of thing. They're overdoing it."

"Well, can you blame the crowd?" said the Gutter Pup, thinking of the smoking fiasco. "Why, I can taste those cigars yet."

As this was a delicate subject and the Shad was quite aware that his own motives were under the gravest suspicion, he turned the conversation with a yawn.

"All the same I'd like to swipe that young gold mine for one little week," he remarked.

The expression was casual and without malice, but no sooner uttered than it became a moving idea. Unseen by the Gutter Pup, the Tennessee Shad experienced almost a physical shock. His head rose eagerly and his eyes focusing on the noisy Dickinson fixed themselves in a dreamy stare.

"Supposin' I did swipe him?" he said softly to himself.

Now, of course such an act was in direct defiance of all law and precedent which forbids poaching beyond territorial limits. The Tennessee Shad, however, was one who bequeathed precedents rather than followed them.

With this predatory scheme in mind the Tennessee Shad became keenly alive to the turbulent course of the Uncooked Beefsteak's education in the Dickinson.

Shortly afterward Skinner, voyaging toward the Jigger Shop, was agreeably surprised to perceive the thin, elongated body of the Tennessee Shad bearing across his path with the most friendly intentions.

"Why, it's the Pet of the Lobster Palaces!" said the Shad, seemingly surprised by the encounter.

Skinner who had had nicknames showered upon him like flowers about a prima donna, accepted the title without demur.

"Going over to the village?" said the Shad cheerily.

"A SPEEDY VALET SERVICE THEY HAVE ORGANIZED OVER THERE."

"Yes."

"Come on. How are things going?"

"Oh, all right," said the Beefsteak wearily adopting the answer *de rigueur*.

"Not very chipper, though?"

"Oh, well—"

"The merry little sunshine smile not exactly working, eh?"

"No—o."

477

They had now come to that short and narrow dash that leads to the Jigger Shop, and the Uncooked Beefsteak, not only seeking sympathy, but willing to buy it, said, "How about a few jiggers?"

The Tennessee Shad, who was always subtle, brushing aside an immediate advantage in order to launch more securely his future maneuvers, replied, "Thanks, old Hippopotamus, but I'm out for exercise."

Now, had Skinner been anything but a newcomer the monstrosity of this statement would have put him at once on the *qui vive*. As it was, he was overwhelmed by a stranger sentiment. For the first time since his advent to the school he had offered and received a refusal. With this unexpected shock all defiance and suspicion died away.

"Who's putting you through the paces?" said the Tennessee Shad, observing the result with satisfaction.

"Why, it's no particular one," said Skinner sadly.

"But Macnooder is the worst!" said the Shad, striving for an advantage.

"Perhaps."

"Pretty strenuous, eh? what?"

Skinner passed his hand over his moist forehead and admitted without qualification the justice of the observation.

"That's the trouble with Macnooder—he's so coarse!"

Skinner, thus artfully encouraged, blurted out, "I don't mind the rest, but it's the scrubbing-up the shoes, the blacking, that gets my nerves."

"You've got good nerve though," said the Shad, examining critically the stained fingers.

"Oh, I'll stick it out."

"Good boy. Too bad you're not with us."

"I say, how long—" said Skinner, who then balked and stopped.

"How long will you have to be the Merry Little Bootblack?"

"Yes—that's about it."

"Um—m. That depends. Now I'll tell you what to do," said the Tennessee Shad, carefully choosing the best means to prolong the period of servitude that now seemed to promise him such fair returns. "Jolly right up with them!"

"What?" said Skinner amazed.

"Sure. Show you're one of them. Walk right up and swat 'em on the back!"

"No!"

"Jump in and tickle 'em right under the ribs—be playful."

"Playful?"

"That's the game. Start a few jokes at 'em yourself."

"What kind?"

"Crease the trousers the wrong way—a little mucilage in their shoes, camphor balls down the lamp chimney, and all that sort of thing."

"But what'll they do?"

"Do? Why, they'll discharge you for a bum valet!" said the Tennessee Shad with tears in his eyes.

"By George, I'll try it."

"Do, and say—"

"What?"

"Start on Macnooder."

"Why Macnooder?"

"You see, Doc's got more sense of humor than the rest."

Skinner, longing for company, suggested Conover's and pancakes. The Tennessee Shad refused. On the return Skinner pleaded again the attractions of the Jigger Shop. The Tennessee Shad refused again but it was an awful wrench. They parted, Skinner made gorgeously happy by an invitation to visit the treasure rooms of the Tennessee Shad who dove around a corner to give liberty to his true feelings.

When the Dickinson scouts reported for the fifth successive time that the Uncooked Beefsteak, property and perquisite of the House, had met the Tennessee Shad and led him from one gormandizing result to another, paying all bills—great was the indignation thereof.

"Look here, boy," said Turkey Reiter to Doc Macnooder at the hastily summoned council of war, "what are we going to do about it? Supposin' we let up a bit? The Beefsteak isn't so worse, after all."

"There's no use in letting the Tennessee Shad get away with the goods," said the Triumphant Egghead, who also felt defrauded by Skinner's constant excursions with a member of a foreign state.

Now Macnooder had been the chief victim of the Tennessee Shad's artful advice to Skinner, but he had no intention of publishing the fact. Equally he was resolved not to allow the Tennessee Shad to force him to a change of policy.

479

"The trouble with you cheap sports is your accounts are busted, and you want to be fed," he remarked witheringly.

"Well what of it?" said the Egghead brazenly.

"Don't you see it's all the Tennessee Shad's doings? He's put it into the Beefsteak's head that he can starve us out."

"Of course he has got to be kept in subjection," said Turkey Reiter, "but couldn't we relent a little?"

"Never!" said Vulture Watkins. "The trouble with that New York dude is the moment you treat him decent, he gets unbearable."

"He certainly has been fresh enough lately!"

"Still," said Turkey Reiter, "I don't see why we couldn't relent a little."

"Why should our import trade be deflected," added the Triumphant Egghead. "Skinner belongs to us, doesn't he? Well, then, what right has he to fatten up the Tennessee Shad?"

"In the first place," said Macnooder, raising his voice to quell the mutiny, "the Tennessee Shad won't fatten. In the second place, just sit back and wait. When the Beefsteak really gets to know the Tennessee Shad he'll come limping straight back to us. In the third place, I will have a few fat little words with the Tennessee Shad and tell him what we think of him."

In pursuance of which, choosing his time, Macnooder crossed the path of the Tennessee Shad at the moment when his late partner, having left Skinner, was returning languidly home, well fed and rejoicing.

"Hello," said Macnooder, assuming a critical position.

"Why, it's Macnooder isn't it?" said the Shad blandly. "Have you come to divvy up on that little graft of yours?"

"I've come," said Macnooder wrathfully, "to tell you just what we think of you, you low-down, body snatching nursery maid!"

"What strong words!"

"See here! What right have you got to interfere with the business of the Dickinson?"

"I, interfere? Gracious goodness! Do you mean little Montague?"

"I do. What right have you got to come poaching over on our grounds?"

"Are you vexed because Beefsteak buys me hot dogs and jiggers and Turkish paste and éclairs and root beer and pancakes?" said the Shad smiling, "and lots and lots of other juicy things?"

"Look here, the Beefsteak is fresh as paint. It's up to us to educate him and it's up to you to keep off!"

"Why, hasn't he improved?" said the Shad looking at Macnooder with a malicious eye. "Doesn't he attend to your boots as a real valet should?"

"Will you let him alone?"

"Why don't you be kind and gentle with him? If you're hungry ask him po-litely!"

"Shad, if you weighed a hundred pounds I'd whang the life out of you!"

"Thank you, I weigh just ninety-eight and a half."

"If you weighed a hundred, I'd kick the slats out of you!"

"Don't boast," said the Shad softly. "If I weighed a hundred, you'd settle up with me."

"Then you won't keep off?"

"Alas!"

"Look out!"

"Threats?"

"We'll get you yet!"

"Try."

"Anyhow, you bunco steerer, I'll bet you can't keep him a week!"

"Why, Doc," said the Shad brightening, "that is the first real word of sense you've spoken. But do remember that I'm doing it all because I am so very fond of Montague, and not because I'm trying to even up matters with you. Oh, dear no! Ta! Ta!"

"Just the same," said the Tennessee Shad to himself as he left the infuriated Macnooder. "There's a good deal in what Doc says. I wonder how long I can keep my hands out—really out of that stuffed bank from New York."

Three days later, Dennis de Brian de Boru Finnegan, gamboling in, found the Tennessee Shad on the window seat in the reflective attitude of Sherlock Holmes, the character he most admired, mumbling to himself. Finnegan, listening, heard strange muffled words.

"Why not end it all—sooner or later? What's the dif?"

"End what?" said Finnegan, mystified. "What's wrong?"

"It's the Beefsteak," said the Tennessee Shad perceiving him. "Irishman, did you ever try to resist temptation?"

Finnegan sat down and tried to remember.

"I'm resisting—but oh, it hurts!" said the Shad.

"The Beefsteak is some fresh vegetables, isn't he?" said Finnegan understanding.

"It isn't that," said the Shad, "though that is bad enough. It's the thought of all the green goods he is just itching to buy."

"Why don't you?"

"But then he'll go back to the Dickinson."

"Well, why do you?"

"But if I don't, then Macnooder will."

Finnegan ceased to offer suggestions.

"It's wrong," he said.

"Of course."

"You're interfering in his kindergarten education."

"I know."

"And the Beefsteak has just got to be educated out of those sporting ideas of his."

"Don't I have to listen to them?"

"My advice," said Dennis who was all for discipline, having signally evaded it, "is to wrap up one beautiful gold brick, an eighteen-karat smasher, coupon buster, soak it to him and quit the game."

"I am such a creature of habit," said the Tennessee Shad, thinking of the pleasant, refreshing trips to the village.

At this moment from below came a timid hallo.

"Oh, Tennessee Shad!"

Finnegan, hanging over the window sill, perceived below the irresolute figure of the Uncooked Beefsteak and summoned him up. Now Skinner had never yet gathered his courage to the point of a visit to the distinguished room. As it was, he shifted a long moment from foot to foot before daring to enter.

"Look at the Dickinson," said the Tennessee Shad gleefully. "Why, the whole house is boiling up."

Opposite, every window seemed tenanted with indignant spectators.

"Now is your time," said Finnegan hurriedly. "Sell him the whole blooming shooting match."

"No."

"Yes!"

"I mustn't."

"You must."

The door opened gently and Skinner, visibly overcome, stole in on his tiptoes and bumped down into the nearest chair. As Finnegan had calculated, no sooner had this first temperamental weakness passed than Skinner's gaze clearing, fastened in wonder upon the strange collection of real and bogus trophies which literally choked the walls from floor to ceiling. Each article recalled a chapter in the mercantile progress of the Tennessee Shad and Dink Stover, and some were reminders of youthful gullibility. Notably was this the case in a souvenir toilet set of seven colors which Stover in his salad days had bought from Macnooder with the joy of a Pittsburgh millionaire stumbling on an original Rembrandt. With his rise to fame, Stover, turning philosopher, had refused to part with this reminder of past enthusiasm, keeping it prominently displayed as a sort of anchor to common sense when too great a satisfaction with self should tend to raise his feet from the ground.

No sooner did the Beefsteak perceive this variegated assortment of odd china than he sat erect and asked.

"Gee, what's that?"

Dennis, with a triumphant glance at the Tennessee Shad, assumed an auctioneering attitude and rapturously detailed the many imaginary points of interest that could lend value to such a collection.

Propped up on the window seat, the Tennessee Shad watched through half-closed eyes the responsive eager flush on Skinner's face.

"He would buy it, he would, he certainly would," he said to himself, mastering his emotions with difficulty. "Think of selling it back, right under the nose of Old Macnooder!"

At this moment, as though to add to his trials, Skinner having listened enraptured to Finnegan's recital, exclaimed, "You don't say so! By jingo, wouldn't I like to have that, though!"

Finnegan yawned, as is customary when a strong emotion is to be concealed, and said in a sort of haphazard way, "Why, you can always fling out a nice juicy young bid. You never can tell. Perhaps Stover's hard up."

"Really?" said the Uncooked Beefsteak, turning to the joint proprietor.

The Tennessee Shad swallowed hard, glanced out the window to resist temptation, and said almost angrily,

"Not for sale."

"Perhaps Skinner here would like a chance at the football shoes," said Finnegan who at first believed the Shad was simply working up the scene for a slaughter *en masse*.

"What's that?" said the Beefsteak at once.

"The identical, historic, specially preserved shoes that Flash Condit wore when he scored on the Princeton Varsity," said Finnegan, who disappeared in quest.

Of course Skinner listened, admired and wanted to buy. The Tennessee Shad again refused, but with difficulty and in a weaker voice. Finnegan scratched his head, sorely vexed, and led the Beefsteak up to the consideration of several articles of fabulous history, including a watch charm supposed (but not guaranteed) to be made of that clapper whose theft had once thrown the school into such a turmoil. The Uncooked Beefsteak admired everything without reserve, coveted everything, and showed extreme willingness to pay spot cash.

The Tennessee Shad, had he been tied to a stake to the accompaniment of twenty howling savages, could have suffered no more. Finally almost overcome, he rose and hastened from the room. Finnegan, quite amazed, followed and last of all, Skinner with the reluctant step of the disappointed collector. Halfway down the second flight of stairs the Tennessee Shad could go no further. He turned, leaning against the banister, facing the Uncooked Beefsteak.

"Say, you don't really want to buy?" he said faintly, hoping against hope that Skinner would return a contrary answer.

"You bet I do!"

"Cash?" continued the Tennessee Shad still hoping. "It's got to be cash down."

Skinner, back in a familiar way, flashed a bundle of bills and said, "Why boy, just look these over."

"Go back!" said the Tennessee Shad.

He watched Skinner spring up the stair, the roll of bills carried insolently in his hand.

"Well, it's sending him back to Macnooder," he thought wistfully, "making him a present, but I can't resist my nature!"

Dennis de Brian de Boru Finnegan, who, of course, could sus-

THE IDENTICAL SHOES THAT FLASH CONDIT WORE

pect only a little of the inner conflict, pressed his hand covertly in admiration of what he at once considered the highest mercantile strategy.

When, half an hour later, the Tennessee Shad and the ebullient Skinner again descended the stairs to seal the compact in the usual way (Finnegan being detained by the annoyance of a recitation) the Tennessee Shad felt not the slightest elation. He glanced gloomily at Skinner's immaculate creases going before him on the narrow walk and a feeling of remorse came over him, the flat, heavy, tasteless feeling that succeeds the plunge into temptation.

"It's the last time," he thought, glancing back at the Dickinson where several wolfish eyes still watched his progress. "It's the last time that walking safe deposit will ever open for me. Well, there's only one thing to be done. If it is the last, I'll eat till I bust!"

With this colossal heroism in mind he said to prepare the Beefsteak for the hecatombs that were to come.

"Skinner, Old Sporting Tootlets, I feel rather hungry."

"My boy," said the exultant purchaser, "go as far as you like."

The tone was the tone that answered obsequious headwaiters in expensive metropolitan restaurants. The patronage decided the Tennessee Shad. The Beefsteak was really impossible when you treated him like a human being. He would show him no mercy.

"Well, Old Gazello," said the Uncooked Beefsteak, in imitation of Turkey Reiter, "pick out anything you want. You can't scare me, I've got the wad!"

He clapped him on the shoulder as a patron of gladiators might. The Tennessee Shad winced as from a blow and the last grumbling of his thin conscience died away.

"Shad, old boy!" said Skinner, throwing back his coat and allowing the tips of his pink fingers to slide along the blazing vest into the pockets. "You don't know what a real gorge is. I can't stand with you on this food here. It really is dyspeptic, you know. But say, wait till Thanksgiving, come up to the hotel with me and I'll show you what a real blowout is. I'll put you up against some real sports, I will."

The Tennessee Shad swallowed his wrath, glancing about to make sure no one was within hearing distance.

"My boy," continued Skinner, forgetting himself, "you young ones here don't know me!"

"We don't, eh?"

"Not a bit. Why, when I come in, every headwaiter in New York comes up on the jump. They have named a couple of dishes after me."

"You don't say so!"

"Fact."

"You're a little tin wonder, aren't you!" said the Tennessee Shad, beginning to be angry.

The constant opening of the pocketbook had stripped Skinner of the last semblance of awe toward the Tennessee Shad. He laughed a short, disagreeable laugh.

"A wonder? I'm a real sport—no ten-cent article like you put up with around here—the real dead game variety!"

This last indiscretion was too much for the Tennessee Shad. He left abruptly and dashing across the street, plunged through the doors of the Jigger Shop, straight into the arms of Mr. Lucius Cassius Hopkins, the Old Roman himself. For a second, face to face with that supreme flunker of boys, all thought deserted him. Then, assuming a look of combined grief and terror, he cried, "A roll of court plaster and a bandage Al, quick's you can! Fellow at house cut his foot!"

But at this moment the Uncooked Beefsteak all unprepared, flopped in, crying hilariously, "Lord, Al, open up a whole can!"

Then he saw the Roman.

"A can of—court plaster? Yes?" said the Roman with a little joyful burbling sound. "Well, speak up."

"No, sir."

"Not court plaster?"

"No, sir."

"Just the ordinary destructive, daily poison—well?"

"Yes, sir," said the Tennessee Shad slowly.

"So."

The Roman paused and, shooting up an eyebrow, fixed them with his long glance as though to petrify them first and punish them after. Montague Skinner was chilled to the bone, a sensation further enhanced by perceiving from his angle of observation, a more fortunate pair of legs, *en cachette,* behind the counter.

Now the Roman ruled not simply by the weight of an iron hand, but by the terrors of an imagination endowed with humor and satire. And so, remembering that it was the Tennessee Shad who waited before him, he decided to fit the punishment to the criminal.

"No excuse—no further excuse—none at all? Imagination numbed—not working today? Too bad. Ten times around the Circle. Do it now."

The Tennessee Shad was thunderstruck. He went out in high indignation. Of course the Roman had done it on purpose. There were a dozen punishments he might have selected—sent him to Penal for an afternoon—but to choose this, knowing his aversion to muscular strains! It was an outrage.

"Why, ten times around the Circle is over two miles," he said furiously as they tramped away. "I've never walked that in my life. The old rhinoceros, he did it on purpose! It's unfair. It's discrimination—persecution—tyranny. I've a mind to go right up to the Doctor."

"The Old Roman's down on you," said Skinner, who had learned a number of the routine formulas.

"Course he is, always has been. Nice mess you've got me in."

"How was I to know?" said Skinner.

The Tennessee Shad relapsed into gloomy meditation. What he did not voice aloud was that the real humiliation threatened was the spectacle of himself, yoked to the Beefsteak, parading before the hilarious audience of the school. Of course, Macnooder, of all persons, and the Dickinson cohorts, with the memory of defrauded threats, would come piling out to hoot him—caught in his own trap, publicly exposed as the boon companion, the bosom friend of the stolen Beefsteak.

The moment was critical, one of those public trials that changes in a twinkling a reputation and fastens a label of ridicule to a career of honor. What is more, the Tennessee Shad knew the peril.

In this state of immense mental perturbation and excited brain effort, the Tennessee Shad, heeled by the contrite Skinner, arrived at the edge of that vast area known as the Circle and gazed in horror, as the adventurous sailors of Columbus gazed at the limitless waters.

But fortune favored him. Directly in front stood a wheelbarrow waiting the reappearance of the gardener. His gaze left the stretches of the Circle and paused at the thing on wheels at his side. A moment later he said breathlessly, "Beefsteak!"

"What?"

"Do you remember what the Roman told us?"

"Sure, ten times around the Circle."

"But the exact words?"

"That's it, ten times around the Circle."

"He didn't say *walk* ten times?"

"Why, no."

"Ah!" The Tennessee Shad drew a long, comforted breath. He was saved. Then, carefully considering the inexperienced Skinner, he said carelessly putting one foot on the wheelbarrow, "Gee, if I could turn the laugh on the Old Roman! If I could get the best of him some way! They could fire me, I wouldn't care."

Skinner's glance in turn fell on the wheelbarrow.

"Eureka!"

"What is it?" said the Shad, wondering if he had taken the bait.

"I say! I have a wonderful idea. The wheelbarrow!"

"What about it?"

"We take turns, one gets in the wheelbarrow and the other wheels him around."

"Skinner, you're a genius," said the Tennessee Shad with great effusion. "It's the greatest joke ever heard. It'll kill the Roman. He'll explode. You're a hero, my boy. The whole school will cheer you on. How *did* you think of it?"

"Who'll start?"

"I will," said the Shad, hastily slipping into the wheelbarrow. "I weigh hardly anything, let her go."

Now the legs secreted behind the counter at the Jigger Shop belonged to Hungry Smeed, who as soon as the Roman departed, had gone scampering gleefully back to the Dickinson with the joyful tale of the Tennessee Shad's having been caught with the Uncooked Beefsteak. In one minute the entire house came rushing out to behold the humiliation of the crafty usurper of their own property. What they beheld instead was the lank limbs of the Tennessee Shad stuffed into the wheelbarrow that Skinner was trundling with an air of strained but supreme content.

"Well, I'll be jig-swiggered," said Macnooder ruefully.

"Can you beat him?"

"The Shad certainly is a wonder."

"How the deuce do you suppose he got him to do it?"

"Why, he's got the Beefsteak so hypnotized that he's grinning all over."

"He certainly is!"

"Boys, we can't help it, we'll have to give the Shad a cheer," said Macnooder. Overcome with admiration and soaring for once above the earthly line of dollars and cents in his enthusiasm for the artist, he said to himself, "I certainly must compromise, the firm has got to go on!"

"We certainly will."

The cheer that went rollicking over the campus, waking up the inmates of the Houses, encouraged Skinner wonderfully. He took it as a personal tribute. Startled by the unexpected clamor, the school came rushing to the windows, beheld the extraordinary voyage of the Tennessee Shad and sure of a sensation, came swarming out.

"Take it easy, Montague, old chap," said the Tennessee Shad. "Rest every half time around. Besides, we want the whole bunch to get on to us."

"Say, it's about your turn," said Skinner, happy but very hot.

"Never," said the Tennessee Shad firmly. "You're safe; you run no risks. But it's ten to one they fire me."

"I'll take the risk," said Skinner.

"No, you won't," said the Shad tragically. "Besides, it's a wonderful sell on the Roman, if I never touch foot on the ground. Oh, wonderful!"

"Still," said the Beefsteak doubtfully.

"My boy, the glory is all yours. You had the idea, you get all the credit," said the Shad, manfully resisting the temptation. "Hear that cheer? Look at the mob running over from the Upper—with cameras, too. It's the finest thing ever happened. Twice around now, that's a fifth the distance already. Keep a-going."

By this time the Circle was lined with rollicking, roaring boys, vying with one another who should cheer the loudest for the Tennessee Shad.

"Don't cheer me fellows, cheer the Beefsteak," cried the Shad, giving the high sign. "It's his idea, he thought it up. Cheer for the Uncooked Beefsteak."

And the school, gazing on the perfectly satisfied countenance of Skinner, understood the part it had to play. Immense cheers for the unsuspecting dupe rolled forth, jumping from group to group that before respective houses crowded down to the edge of the roadway.

The Uncooked Beefsteak, with every muscle strained, saw only the triumph in front, knowing nothing of the hilarious groups behind his back that locked arms and danced with joy.

"Isn't he wonderful?"

THE TENNESSEE SHAD STUFFED

INTO A WHEELBARROW THAT SKINNER WAS TRUNDLING.

"Look at the Shad's face!"

"How does he look so solemn!"

"And the Beefsteak thinks he is it!"

"Oh, joy!"

"Oh, rapture!"

"Cheese it. Here he comes again."

"Three cheers, fellows, for Beefsteak!"

The rolling accompaniment of cheers spurred Skinner on to supreme efforts. He was absolutely, airily happy. He beamed on the procession of excited faces that shouted forth their encouragement and at times was so convulsed with his own humor that he was forced to stop to let the gale of merriment spend itself.

He waited no longer than was necessary to rest the ache in his armpits, and then was off on the glorious journey. At the completion of the sixth round, the Tennessee Shad insisted that he should be massaged and a dozen hands fought for the honor; another crowd, with flapping handkerchiefs fanned air on his boiled complexion, while from all sides he heard the plaudits.

"Beefsteak, you're it!"

"The grandest scheme—"

"How did you think of it?"

"Keep it up."

"It's a record breaker."

"You're strong as an ox."

"All ready?' said the Tennessee Shad with maternal solicitude. "Here, wrap those handles with handkerchiefs, some of you loafers. Clear the way there, for Beefsteak!"

Intoxicated with the strong intoxication of the multitude, the seventh round was completed before he knew it. Then the roadway seemed suddenly to harden and strike his feet with the impact of every step. The Tennessee Shad began to grow to the proportions of P. Lentz and the circle to widen like the journeying ripples from a dropped stone. Four times he set down the awful burden and gasped for breath before the welcoming shouts went up.

"Eight rounds!"

"Only two more."

"Bully for the Beefsteak!"

"Strong as a blacksmith."

"More massage."

"Rub down the Beefsteak."

He began the ninth round; the chorus of shrieks and cheers was one steady howl in his ears, handkerchiefs and caps fluttered over his head, while dimly he heard new shouts.

"Go it there, you Beefsteak!"

"Show your speed."

492

"Hit up that pace."

"Make a record!"

Then he saw nothing but the interminable white space over the peaked head of the Tennessee Shad. Every fifty feet he set the wheelbarrow down to rest, doggedly resolved not to fail. Then the tenth round, the final triumph began. Ready to drop, paying for every yard gained by a hundred shooting pains, stopping, jerking along blindly, unheeding, he came at last to the supreme quarter and wheeled the Tennessee Shad straight to the entrance of the Kennedy House, set down the wheelbarrow and turned gloriously to view the triumph.

Suddenly he heard a shout wilder than all the rest and looking at the terrace of the Kennedy, beheld a sight that swept away the clouds of his illusion like a clap of wind. On the top step stood the Old Roman, a handkerchief at his eyes, doubling over with laughter, shaking hands, actually shaking hands, with the *Tennessee Shad*.

VII

FACTS LEADING TO A RECONCILIATION

AFTER THE Beefsteak's brief but disillusioning visit with the Tennessee Shad, Macnooder observed with satisfaction that while he had suffered—he had not improved.

Just what was the matter with the Uncooked Beefsteak was still a puzzle to the Dickinson House. It was quite evident that so long as he was oppressed and forced to the menial exercises of bootblacking and clothespressing, he was moderately inoffensive. It was equally evident that the moment the ban was lifted in the slightest and he was restored to human intercourse, he became absolutely unbearable. But the reason thereof was not to be found.

"What the dickens is the matter with him anyhow," said Turkey Reiter. "We have certainly given him enough exercise."

"Ah, he'll never learn," said the Egghead, who always took a gloomy view.

"He's all right when he is cleaning out the room," said Hungry Smeed, who had never enjoyed the luxury of a valet.

"We certainly treat him like a dog."

"We certainly do!"

"It's a crime!"

"Well, what are you going to do about it?"

"You'd think he would learn a thing or two."

"Well, at any rate," said Macnooder, "he's stayed on the reservation lately. No wandering from the fireside, and all that sort of thing. I'll bet the Tennessee Shad's tongue is hanging out every time the Beefsteak goes over to the village."

Macnooder spoke vindictively, harboring vindictive impulses toward the Tennessee Shad ever since the return of the souvenir toilet set to the Dickinson. Likewise the Uncooked Beefsteak, innocently acting on the artful suggestion of the Tennessee Shad, had returned to Macnooder, in the joyful belief of restoring a sacrificed heirloom, the football shoes which Flash Condit did *not* wear when

494

he crossed the Princeton goal line. As the restoration was made in private, Doc Macnooder accepted it with admirable gravity and saved thereby a public advertisement. But the blow told.

It would not do, however, any longer to risk open warfare with the Tennessee Shad, backed by the busy imaginations of Dink Stover and Dennis de Brian de Boru Finnegan. Another would have sought revenge. Not so Macnooder. His instinct was always financial. If he could not destroy, he would combine. With this idea in mind he began, introspectively and outwardly, to seek for some scheme worthy to offer to the Tennessee Shad as basis for a new treaty. After a season of wandering dreamily, straw in mouth, cap set ruminatively on the incline of his head, a fortunate conjunction developed an idea which almost resulted in a football riot and did produce a situation that should be brought to the attention of the omniscient body of rules-makers if only to avert a lurking danger which might turn a scholarly clash of gladiatorial universities into a shambles.

Macnooder, after a week of fruitless searching, was gazing hopelessly out of the window at the departing candidates for the House elevens, when a knock was heard and the voice of the Uncooked Beefsteak meekly sought admission.

Now for two days the ban had been lifted on the dispenser of Skinner's wealth, and Montague had been treated like a citizen; which, translated, means that the features of Turkey Reiter, the Triumphant Egghead, Macnooder et cetera, had once more returned to the hostile interiors of the Jigger Shop and Conover's.

"Come in," said Macnooder.

The Uncooked Beefsteak found his way through the litter of bottles and boxes and joined Macnooder on the window seat.

"Well, what's up?" said Macnooder critically, perceiving at once an air of importance and pride about his visitor.

"I say, Doc," said Skinner, heedless of the cold and antagonistic glance, "what do you say to injecting a little sporting life into this dead hole?"

"Oh, you think it is a dead hole," said Macnooder softly.

Skinner stifled a yawn and ran two fingers down the creases of his trouser leg.

"Come off, now. You know it's dead."

"Say, you must have an idea."

495

"I have."

"Touch her off."

"What do you say to getting up a book on the house games?"

"Gambling, Rollo?" said Macnooder, turning over the thought rapidly.

"Oh, rot!" said Skinner. "Don't josh me now."

"I'm thinking hard."

"It's quite sporty and heaps of fun."

"You've done this before?"

"Sure."

"But don't you think that was very wrong of you, Montague?" said Macnooder, who had not yet determined on a course of action.

"If you are talking like that—" said Beefsteak blushing a little, and rising.

"Sit down, sport," said Macnooder dreamily. "Elucidate a little on this here proposition of yours. Where would you begin?"

"I'd begin," said Beefsteak eagerly, "with the Kennedy–Woodhull Game next week."

"The Kennedy?" said Macnooder with a little start of interest.

"Why not?"

"But that's a cinch. No one would bet on that. Varsity men can't play this year and the Woodhull ought to win thirty to nothing."

"Bet on the score, then."

Macnooder took a long time before replying. His gaze traveled across and up to the eyrie of the Tennessee Shad, and rested there fondly.

Finally, smothering his enthusiasm, he said slowly, "Yes, I suppose that could be done."

"Same thing as betting to win and betting for place," said the Beefsteak in a sort of worldly way.

"But is this a square game?" said Macnooder.

"Oh, rather," said the Beefsteak. "Why, a bookmaker is the squarest thing a-going. I know a dozen of them."

"Now, he's off again on that eternal dead game sporting idea of his," said Macnooder to himself, mentally debating whether or not to consign him at once to the blacking brush. However, he temporized.

"Where do I come in?"

"You are an expert adviser," said the Beefsteak with just a touch of patronage. "You know the crowd better than I do. You'd better work up the bets."

"Oh, really!"

"And you get a third of the profits," said the Uncooked Beefsteak hastily.

"You supply the capital?" said Macnooder warily.

"Any amount!"

"It's most debauching!"

"Pooh! every gentleman places a little bet now and then," said the Beefsteak in his grandest manner.

At this moment a call resounded along the hall.

"Oh, you, Beefsteak, come here and press my pants!"

The gentleman of fashion disappeared in a twinkling. Skinner looked at Macnooder in a mute appeal.

"Better go," said Macnooder, thus relieved of all responsibility, "and tomorrow I'll give you an answer."

That night by recognized routes, Doc Macnooder journeyed in safety over to the Kennedy and the lair of Tennessee Shad. The conference was secret, complete, and satisfactory to all parties interested, and the first result was that the next morning the Uncooked Beefsteak was made happy by Macnooder's agreeing to act as a sporting partner in what was agreed should be a deliberate attempt to trim the Tennessee Shad.

Since the national game of football has been shorn of horns and hoofs, a little of the truth may be told of the joyful hecatombs of those earlier games in the nineties. Baseball on a professional field smooth as a billiard cloth, under the protecting vision of clubbed discouragers of assault and battery, is one thing; the same pastime on a back lot amid boulders and broken bottles, with opposing gangs waiting and willing on the lines, is quite a different risk—rated according to insurance tables.

Such was the relative position of the house games in the realm of football. They were strenuous affairs—rare opportunities when the best of friends could physically experiment on each other without an afterthought. Of course all this is changed, but it was a good school, though a rude one, for the masculine animal, who, refine him as you may, must somehow fight his way through this world.

Now, the Kennedy having four members of the Varsity, was ac-

497

cordingly weakened in its House eleven. The Tennessee Shad, who, as may be remembered, was thinner than his own shadow, was not exactly the most corpulent member of the eleven but a fair representative of the average. He was at quarterback, and Fatty Harris at center, a combination which looked very much like a cannon ball and a musket. Hungry Smeed, who even after he had consumed forty-nine pancakes, never weighed over one hundred and twenty, was at one end and Dennis de Brian de Boru Finnegan at the other. The guards weighed one hundred and forty and the tackles, the Gutter Pup and Lovely Mead, ten pounds less, and the situation is best understood when it is baldly stated that the team was so mortified that it had refused to stand up and be photographed.

The Woodhull team, on the contrary, was strong with second-team men, averaged over one hundred fifty pounds to a player, and was already conceded the house championship.

All of which made the conference of Kennedy enthusiasts on the evening before the game a most oppressively silent gathering.

"It's a joke," said the Tennessee Shad, reclining on P. Lentz's cushioned frame, to save himself for the morrow's fray.

"The faculty sprung this dodge about debarring Varsity members just to beat us out of a championship."

"Sure!"

"They're down on us."

"I'll bet Old Baranson at the Woodhull worked it through himself."

"I'll bet he did!"

"Well," said Lovely Mead cheerily, "they'll beat us about thirty-six to nothing."

"Fifty-six!"

"A hundred and six!"

"Never mind, I'll get a crack at Cheyenne Baxter," said the Gutter Pup, who came from the same town and loved his friend.

"I've got a few love pats for Butsey White myself."

"They outweigh us twenty pounds to a man."

"Why, if a wind should start up blowing we wouldn't stay on the field!"

"If you fellows would only spring some of my trick plays," said Dennis de Brian de Boru Finnegan, "they'd never get hold of the ball."

"What's your pet idea?" said Stover, yanking the Irishman to him by an ankle and a wrist.

"It's called the fan-wedge," said Dennis, who never resigned hope. "It's just like this, see! The quarter gives the signal, everyone on the team runs back and out in the lines of the spokes of a fan, and the center snaps the ball when they are on the run. The fan divides and sweeps toward each end and the quarter makes a long pass to whichever side looks best. See?"

"Dennis," said Stover severely, "go stand in the corner."

"It'll work, Dink, you see if it won't!"

"What idea is the Shad browsing on?" said Stover, squelching Finnegan by covering his head with a sweater.

"Oh, I'm kind of thinking of something," said the Tennessee Shad in a noncommittal way.

"Something that is good for thirty-six points?"

"My idea is a secret," said the Tennessee Shad loftily, "but if it works it will most certainly reduce the score."

At this came an interruption.

"Here comes Macnooder!"

"And the Beefsteak!"

"What's his game?"

"He's coming over to give us the laugh."

"Keep quiet," said the Shad quickly. "Don't get in a huff. Just let me draw him out."

There now appeared, followed by the Uncooked Beefsteak at a valet's distance, Doc Macnooder with a pair of uncased opera glasses strapped to his back, trailing a bamboo cane, a pencil over one ear and a note book in one hand. His approach was received in various ways; by the younger members with expectant grins, by the veterans with wary defensive looks, while the Gutter Pup openly and insultingly took the twenty-two cents that burdened his change pocket, counted them, and slipped them down his sock.

"Ah there!" said Macnooder, affably saluting with his bamboo cane. "Very pleasant evening, gentlemen. Nice day for ducks—white ducks, of course! Let me present to you Mr. Montague Skinner, my betting commissioner."

"Your what?" said two or three voices.

"I think I said betting commissioner," said Macnooder in his most inviting way. "Monte, did I say betting commissioner? I did. This, gentlemen, is a little betting account, called a book, that I finger thus between my thumb and my first finger. I am told there are a number of gents, called dead game sports, in this House, and I just dropped over to accommodate them. A little flier on the game, eh?"

At this there was a low, rumbling, portentous sound and Dink Stover, as President of the House, was about to order the proper measures when he suddenly beheld the left eyelid of the Tennessee Shad fluttering on his bony cheek.

"Now, little bounding boys," said Macnooder, genially poising a pencil, "we will do this in professional fashion; winner first, place afterward. Any Sporting Life eager to place a bet on the Kennedy to win tomorrow's game, step up. Step up, but don't crowd. We give you two to one, Woodhull to win. Did I hear a noise?"

"You are a dead game sport, you are," said P. Lentz sarcastically. "Why don't you ask us to give you the money?"

"Three to one," said Macnooder instantly.

"How generous!"

"Five to one."

"We're still listening."

"Six and seven to one. Eight to one. Dollars to doughnuts, in jiggers, in bank notes, in thousands. Come one, come all. Our capital is unlimited. Ten to one, then. Ten to one the Woodhull wins the game!"

"Ten to one the grass comes up in the spring," said the Gutter Pup sarcastically.

"Ten to one the earth goes around the sun."

"Ten to one *you* don't lose whichever way it comes out!"

At this, Doc Macnooder hastily changed the subject.

"Anyone want to bet on the score? Any dead game Kennedy sport got any feeling of confidence at all?"

"What do you want to bet?" said P. Lentz at last, stung into action.

"Even the Woodhull wins by fifteen points."

P. Lentz looked at Macnooder as Al at the Jigger Shop was wont to look when the charge account had been overstretched.

"Well, now, what's your idea?" said Macnooder professionally. "Speak up my man, speak up!"

"I'll bet you even," said King Lentz very slowly, "that they don't score over twenty-four points."

At this juncture a little lukewarm enthusiasm began to appear, and when Macnooder, after a whispered conference with Skinner, expressed his willingness, quite a number of wagers were recorded. The Tennessee Shad however, remained obdurate until thirty points had been conceded, when he at length responded, entraining in his fall Finnegan and the Gutter Pup.

"Say, it's a cinch," said Macnooder knowingly to the Uncooked Beefsteak, when they had returned to their rooms.

"Why, thirty points is nothing at all," said Skinner joyfully.

"Nothing!"

"Gee, I certainly wanted to get back at that Tennessee Shad."

"Sure you did. Well, you got him. He swallowed the whole fishing pole."

"But can we collect?" said Skinner, struck by a sudden horrid thought.

"Now, that's an idea," said Macnooder. "We must fix that. I tell you what. Give me your money, and we'll make Turkey Reiter stakeholder and I'll round up those paper collar sports in the Kennedy and make them plunk up tonight."

The Uncooked Beefsteak became so superhumanly unbearable under the stimulus of his new venture that the House in self defense was forced to set him to darning socks. So sure was he of his approaching victory over the Tennesseee Shad that not even this additional humiliation could disturb his equanimity. In the afternoon, after scrubbing off the degrading stains of blacking from his fingers, he slanted his pearl gray fedora at the proper rakish angle on his head, and, rejoicing inwardly, sauntered down to the third field to watch the preliminaries of the game.

The shivering line of the Kennedy was running through the signals in a weak discouraged way, while the well-nurtured, brawny team of the Woodhull, as though disdaining superfluous exertion, was languidly tossing the pigskin to and fro.

The Uncooked Beefsteak spread his feet, clasped his hands behind his back and, looking over the antagonists, smiled a thoroughly satisfied smile. About him reassuring comments went up.

"Say, it's a shame!"

"They'll never be able to count the points."

"The Woodhull ought to lend them a couple of men."

"They'll tire themselves out running down the field."

"Why, there won't even be a first class scrap in it!"

Macnooder came up, looking very canny.

"Say, Beefsteak, I've worked the Shad into doubling all his bets. How about it?"

The Uncooked Beefsteak wrung his hands furtively but with great feeling.

Jack Rabbit Lawson, referee, a fifth former with a flower in his buttonhole and a choker tie of several antagonistic shades, now passed languidly on to the field, and called the teams together, announcing in routine, half-hearted fashion, as he had done in a dozen games before, "Of course fellows, no roughing it."

"Oh, no!"

"Nothing brutal, nothing coarse!"

"Oh, dear no!"

"Remember, this is a gentleman's game."

"You bet we will!"

"I shall be very strict."

"Yes, Mr. Referee."

"The Woodhull wins the toss. The Kennedy kicks off. Are you ready?"

By common consent, the first line-up was devoted to a friendly exchange of amenities, with honors about even between Cheyenne Baxter and the Gutter Pup, who came from the same town, and Butsy White and Fatty Harris, who were too closely related.

With the second line-up the game began in earnest. There were many scores to wipe out between the two houses, and Ginger Pop Rooker at quarter for the Woodhull had no intention of losing the verbal opportunity of the present advantage.

"Oh, I say, fellows," he said in a careless, bored way. "What's the use of using the signals? Let's tell 'em where we're going. Ram the ball right through Lovely Mead and that little squirt of an Irishman! On your toes! Let her come!"

The humiliated Kennedy swarmed frantically to the point attacked, only to be borne back for a five-yard loss. The Woodhull came gleefully to its feet, laughing hilariously.

"Good eye, Ginger!"

"Tell them every time!"

"Poor old Kennedy!"

"All ready," said Rooker to the shrieks of the spectators. "Put it right through the Gutter Pup this time. Hard now!"

For thirty yards the outraged Kennedy was swept back before a fumble stopped the insolent advance. Cheyenne Baxter, at left half, for the Woodhull, owing to a retiring left eye, either saw imperfectly or with his battling right eye fixed on his chum, the Gutter Pup, momentarily forgot the technical presence of the superfluous football.

At any rate the Kennedy lined up, plunged at the opposing line and were carried back five yards to the accompaniment of derisive shrieks from the squabs of the Woodhull on the side lines.

There was a hurried consultation in which the Tennessee Shad was seen with his lips to Fatty Harris's ear, and then the team massed for a plunge on center. The ball was passed, there was a forward lunge, a churning movement; half the players went down in a heap and suddenly a report like a dynamite explosion was heard. Among the spectators a clamor arose.

"What the deuce has happened?"

"They've squashed Fatty Harris!"

"Fatty Harris is blown up!"

"Punctured!"

"Squashed flat!"

"Exploded!"

"No, it's the ball!"

"He's bust the ball!"

"He certainly has."

"Flat as a pancake."

"Fatty has smashed the ball!"

"Well, where *is* the ball?"

This last cry quickly communicated itself to the frantic Woodhull team, who, throwing themselves on Fatty Harris, rolled him over and discovered that the pigskin had vanished.

At this moment a wild, gleeful shriek arose from behind the Woodhull goal posts, and the Tennessee Shad was seen extracting from under his sweater the flattened pigskin. Instantly the field overflowed with the shock of waters, triumphant or frantic.

"Touchdown!"

"Robbers!"

"Touchdown for the Kennedy."

503

"Call him back!"

"Dead ball."

"Hurrah for the Tennessee Shad!"

"Muckers!"

"No mucker tricks!"

"The ball was down."

"Call it back!"

"Judgment!"

"Judgment, Mr. Referee!"

Jack Rabbit Lawson, hauled to and fro between the contending parties, found himself in the most serious predicament into which a referee can fall, when a decision must be given and either decision requires an escort of police. Moreover, each contending party, to clinch the judgment, had precipitated itself upon him and the struggle for his possession raged like the contention of Greek and Trojan over the body of Patroclus.

"Don't let those thugs bluff you, Jack!" shouted the Kennedy cohorts, in possession of an arm and a leg.

"Square deal, no cheating!" retorted the Woodhull with a commanding grip on the other extremities.

Fresh arrivals surged in, seeking to fasten on him.

"Touchdown!"

"No touchdown!"

"Square deal!"

"Justice!"

"No intimidation!"

"No mucker tricks!"

"Hands off," shouted Jack Rabbit Lawson. "Let go of me!"

"Mr. Referee," said the Tennessee Shad, artfully cool, "I demand that the game go on."

"The game must go on," said the referee, immensely relieved.

"Never," shouted the furious Woodhull.

"Mr. Referee," said the Tennessee Shad with magnificent impudence, "they know we've got 'em licked! I demand that the game go on. Settle the point afterward!"

At this, just as he intended, the Woodhull quite forgot that it was only a question of walking through the unresisting line in their fury at the trick sprung on them. With one accord they responded.

"We won't go on!"

"Don't give the robbers a point!"

"Don't you stand for it!"

"Judgment, Mr. Referee!"

"Let go of me, there, will you?" said Jack Rabbit Lawson for the tenth time. "I'll look it up in the rules."

Churning at his heels, the whole mass swept him on to the Upper, except where in spots little detached groups of enthusiasts sought their own solutions. At the Esplanade the crowd waited vociferously while Lawson went to his room, accompanied by the Tennessee Shad for the Kennedy and Ginger Pop Rooker for the Woodhull.

Lawson, having closed his collar and coaxed his necktie back into a normal position, looked sternly at Rooker and said, "Now, what's your argument?"

"My argument," said Ginger Pop turbulently, "is that a ball is dead when it is a dead ball! And furthermore, we are playing a game called football, and not 'Button, button, who's got the button,' or 'Going to Jerusalem,' or 'Post office,' or—"

"Hold up there," said Jack Rabbit magisterially, "that's enough. Your argument is a good one. Now, Shad, what's yours?"

"I have three arguments," said the Tennessee Shad, rising, with his thumb over the second button of his waistcoat. "First, the play had never stopped; second, you won't find anything against it; and third, this bunch of soreheads would have done the same thing if they had had a cute little boy like me."

"Your position is very strong," said Jack Rabbit Lawson, nodding to the Tennessee Shad. "I will now look it up in the rules."

He read through the fine print laboriously and solemnly and closed the book.

"Well?" said the rival counsels in a breath.

"There are things here," said Lawson judiciously, "that I want to think over. I will announce my decision in an hour."

At that time the mob gathered once more. Jack Rabbit Lawson appeared at his window and announced that he had read the rules again and was still deliberating, but that his decision would infallibly be given at five o'clock.

Suddenly, their fury having had a certain time to cool, the Woodhull all at once woke up and grasped the amazing fact of

505

their own blunder in not continuing a contest that could have but one outcome.

Consequently as the Tennessee Shad, camped on the Esplanade in the midst of the embattled Kennedy, was receiving congratulations, a suave delegation from the Woodhull headed by Ginger Pop Rooker with his blandest smile, approached, and the following conversation took place.

"Hello there, you foxy old Shad!"

"Hello, yourself."

"Say, you certainly worked a slick one over us."

"Is it possible?"

"Look here, it did make us rather hot at first, but we certainly have to take off our hats to you. That was a corking idea, a wonder, a peacherino, and perfectly square."

"Oh, don't make me blush."

"I say, old boy, we give in!"

"You do, eh?"

"Yes, we admit your claim. We'll agree to a touchdown. So now let's go back and finish the game."

The Tennessee Shad looked long and sadly at Rooker, then he laid his head on P. Lentz's shoulder and began to laugh. The laugh irritated Rooker and likewise alarmed him.

"I say, Shad, shall we play it over now or tomorrow?"

Then the Tennessee Shad spoke languidly, "No, dear boy, no. You had your chance on the field, and you refused, think of it, you *refused* to go on! Of course we'd have licked you to a scramble anyway, but, oh, well, we'll let it go at six to nothing."

"What, you won't play it over?" cried a dozen angry voices.

"Don't ask me."

"Why, you robber!" said Rooker, immediately changing his tone, "you low-down robber!"

"Thank you!"

"You little sneak thief!"

"A baby trick!"

"Mucker gag!"

"We'll appeal to Walter Camp."

"Do," said the Tenessee Shad, "keep on appealing. But you're licked, and remember this, that I rushed the ball right through you, right through the whole Woodhull line!"

This being a little super-insulting, the Kennedy took up a little stronger defensive position as the Woodhull advanced. The tension, however, was fortunately averted by the sudden appearance at his window of Jack Rabbit Lawson, who, having locked and fortified his door, now addressed the crowd.

"Fellows, I have read over the rules a third time, and I have come to a decision."

"Hurray!"

"Touchdown!"

"No score!"

"Woodhull!"

"Kennedy!"

"Shut up!"

"Let him talk!"

"Fellows, I have decided," said Jack Rabbit Lawson firmly, in the midst of a hollow silence, "I have decided TO RESIGN!"

And closing the window abruptly, he withdrew, nor could threats or cajolery ever draw from him an opinion on the case.

To avert a civil conflict, the Doctor at once appointed a faculty committee to render a decision within the half-hour. This committee, rejecting as immaterial the Woodhull's contention that the Tennessee Shad had used a sharpened nail, was guided by an almost analogous incident in the Harvard-Carlisle game, where, it may be remembered, a touchdown was scored by an Indian concealing the pigskin under the back of his jersey, and running the length of the field through the bewildered scholars. The tremendous classic prestige of Cambridge being decisive, judgment was rendered for the Kennedy, with this proviso: that the game should not be played over, and all adherents were ordered quarantined in their respective Houses for twenty-four hours.

The Uncooked Beefsteak, shocked and bewildered, went limply toward the Dickinson. Halfway, Turkey Reiter, stake-holder, accosted him.

"Hello there, Sporting Tootlets!"

The Uncooked Beefsteak stopped and feebly responded, "Oh, hello!"

"Rather bad day for bookmakers, eh?"

"I don't understand it at all."

"Well, I paid over the stakes," said Turkey Reiter mercilessly. "Say—rather expensive educating us, isn't it?"

Skinner shook his head.

"I don't understand. Where's Macnooder?"

"Doc? Over with the Tennessee Shad."

"With the Tennessee Shad!" said the Beefsteak, shocked. "Why, we got this up to trim him!"

"Look here, son," said Turkey Reiter, relenting a little, "you put this down from me—the only way to trim either of those weasels is to trim them together!"

Skinner took off his hat and slowly spun it on one finger, gazing stolidly at the windows of the Tennessee Shad.

"And now, Old Gazello," said Turkey, who enjoyed an occasional lapse into moralizing, "really you are not up to teaching these con men anything as yet, let alone sinful, wicked practices. *Savez?* Better sit down at our feet and pick up a few pearls."

The Beefsteak, incapable of reply, moved slowly away.

"Don't try to be a bad man," continued the moralist. "Don't listen too much to the chink of the coin in your pockets. Don't try to buy your way here, because it won't go—it won't go, my boy! But—if nothing will stop you, if you've got to get rid of the dough, for the love of Mike, give me a chance!"

VIII

THE BEEFSTEAK APPLIES FOR ADMISSION

FORTUNATELY FOR the firm, despite his previous trying experiences, it must be confessed that the Uncooked Beefsteak still clung to those sporting proclivities which, in more worldly communities, are regarded as the natural distinctions of a gentleman. Reduced by his disrespectful housemates to menial degradations as humiliating as endured by other kings in exile, the spirit of ambition was yet strong in him—the spirit to excel in some field, to rise from the mass at whatever cost, to be known as an individual and not a type.

Unfortunately, the field was limited. He was not an athlete and he lazily had no desire to be one. He neither sang nor was the cause of melody in instruments. He did not act nor was he given to journalism. All this was in the undeveloped area into which he had never ventured, satisfied with his own beau ideal of a man of fashion.

However, it did seem to the Beefsteak, despite certain disillusionment which he had encountered since his advent to Lawrenceville, that the school was sadly in lack of what is vulgarly known as a true gentleman-sport—the two names, in his mind, being complementary, if not synonymous. Of course, a number of the fellows rejoiced in the very common nickname of "Sport," but the title had certainly been conveyed without the slightest notion of its distinction.

To Skinner's critical mind a gentleman-sport was not only a disciple of that magnificent Englishman, Beau Brummel, but of that other distinguished Britisher, the Marquis of Queensberry, who, while laying down the full etiquette of the law, was always found at the side of the prize ring and never within it. Likewise, this ideal was one who never counted his change, never quarreled over a bill, who played with existence and wagered on the simplest turns of fate with anybody for anything. To be a gentleman-sport,

then, was to be magnificent, elegant and racy; and to be the first
gentleman-sport in the school was, in a word, the ambition to
which the Uncooked Beefsteak still clung, despite all reverses and
the combined educational efforts of his housemates.

However, his skirmishes with the Tennessee Shad and Doc Macnooder had instilled in him a spirit of canniness. He no longer
exposed his roll of bank notes, trailing it so to speak, on a string behind him. Instead, his first instinct when approached, was a convulsive movement toward the more secure buttoning of his coat. This
educational result of their efforts was not, it must be confessed, so
pleasing to Doc Macnooder and the Tennessee Shad, who, having
become reconciled, sought separately but fruitlessly to enlist the
Beefsteak in several schemes to humiliate the other.

Turkey Reiter alone was not suspected, for Turkey as President
of the House had undertaken a series of lectures on moral conduct.
These excursions into morality were delivered, strangely enough,
in only four places: at Laloo's, to the bubbling noise of the steaming
hot dogs; at Appleby's before the Turkish paste; at the Jigger Shop,
and at Conover's. Why the spirit should refuse to move elsewhere
went unnoticed by the Uncooked Beefsteak, who was immensely
flattered by the solicitude of the great Turkey Reiter, listened a
little and always begged the privilege of standing treat. The Beefsteak, still persistent, recurred to the Tennessee Shad and Doc
Macnooder.

"Gee, I'd like to get back at those bunco steerers," he said, digging his teeth viciously into an unresisting frankfurter.

"Be humble, son," said Turkey Reiter, with paternal im-
pressiveness.

"I'll get them yet."

"Others have tried," said Turkey Reiter, with a reminiscent
twinge. "Your game, young rooster, is to be humble."

"Well, now," said the Beefsteak, with a sudden access of frankness, as they were alone, "say just what is the matter with me
anyhow?"

"It's not just one thing, Old Gazello," said Turkey, comfortingly. "Though, of course, there is one thing that is dead against
you."

"What's that?"

"You're a billionaire."

The Uncooked Beefsteak stared very seriously at the can where the hot dogs were bubbling, and said, "I wonder if that is it?"

"Sure, you're fair game. You're the fresh meat for every hungry coot who is strapped and waiting for the first of the month to come around. Say, bub, do you know what I'd do if I were you?"

"What?"

"Burn the bank and strip to a dollar a week," said Turkey, rushing on enthusiastically, either because moralizing was apt to run away with his discretion or because the near approach of a recitation rendered impossible any further favors from the munificence criticized.

"Oh, I say—"

"Sure," said Turkey, become like many another, the victim of his own argument," these are wise words, sonny. Cut out the treating, get down in our midst, and let us educate you on proper lines. *Savez?*"

"What! Never treat?"

"Never."

"No one at all?"

"Well, only—" said Turkey, pausing a bit and clapping the Beefsteak on the shoulder in an extra amicable way, "only a fellow who's doing you good."

The Beefsteak watched Turkey Reiter go, chuckling, helter-skelter back to recitation and remained a moment in thoughtful meditation over the dubious interpretation of his last words. Then he paid the bill and went slowly up the village street.

Directly in front of him, in full possession of the walk, was a bulldog, of no more reassuring aspect than bulldogs usually are. As Appleby was at the window and several fellows lounging in the doorway, Skinner marched resolutely forward expecting the passage to be yielded. Ten feet away, as the maneuver only resulted in a certain disconcerting fixity of the brute's gaze, he made a wide detour and deferred to another day the issue whether or not the irreproachable aroma of trousers made at New York's most expensive tailor, would appeal to that sense of aristocracy which is said to be instinctive in the canine.

The dog, who was felicitously named Tough, was the property of Blimmy Garret of the Woodhull, who besides rejoicing in the distinction of having risen to six feet six, was, on account of his possession of a mustache and a real discouraging bulldog, generally regarded as filling the position to which Skinner longingly aspired —the premier dead game sport of the school.

The companionship of Tough had been rather expensive to Blimmy. Due to several cases of carelessness on the dog's part, he had been forced to buy the silence of Klondike, who shook up the beds in the Dickinson, and pay Blinky, the one-eyed purveyor of cigarettes, ten dollars and replace the shredded trousers.

Tough was supposed to inhabit a suite in the village, but being by nature inclined to good society he had learned at the sound of a professorial tread to retire under the window seat and remain until the danger had passed. Despite which, the All-Seeing Eye was decidedly fixed in the direction of Tough and waiting a logical excuse.

The Uncooked Beefsteak had no sooner completed the outer trail than a patter of feet and a slight asthmatic snort behind revealed the fact that the brute was deliberating at his heels. Now if the Beefsteak's courage had never been tested by a frontal attack, it was doubly uncertain when momentarily expecting a crisis behind. There was still twenty yards to the Jigger Shop and an acceleration of pace might have fatal results.

At this moment, the Uncooked Beefsteak, looking ahead, thankfully perceived the true cause of the commotion at his heels.

In front of Bill Orum's, the cobbler, another dog, with certain marks that would permit him for purposes of classification to be described as a setter, was rounding the corner with tail set and carefully poised step. The last animal was Henry Clay, the property of Bill Orum, who stoutly declared that his dog could annihilate anything that attacked him on the *left* side; the right eye having gloriously gone in a victorious career.

Just which side the bulldog selected in his forward movement would be hard to determine, but in another second the joined bodies were revolving in the dust much after the fashion of a giant pinwheel that has jumped its fastenings. At the uproar that fell upon the street, a crowd came rushing out while the rival owners, hastening up, finally secured possession of the hindquarters of their respective champions. Then it was found that the bulldog had a secure grip on the pride of the cobbler shop at the throat directly beneath the closed right eye.

In this *impasse* Al, from his wisdom, produced an ammonia

bottle and Tough yielded to science what he would not have yielded to nature. Blimmy Garret hastily smuggled the victorious Tough to a place of concealment while the crowd, drifting away, left a few to listen to Bill Orum's haranguing on the result and his repeated assertion that Tough would have been a dead dog by now if he had attacked on the *left* side.

"That dog of Blimmy's certainly needs a licking," said Al, whose eyes and throat had received their measure of the ammonia.

"He certainly does," said Skinner, in full agreement.

"A lot of reputation he's got," said Al contemptuously, "licking a lot of curs and a walleyed setter whose teeth have to be tied in!"

"I'd like to bring a real bruiser down here," said Skinner, with a knowing look.

"Go ahead."

"By jingo, I will," said Skinner determinedly as he walked home. "Or, at any rate, I'll find a pup who'll make mincemeat of that sassy coyote."

Now, the Beefsteak's mind did not as yet work with that instinctive flight toward a novel idea that was the characteristic of the veteran. As a consequence, it was only after having repeatedly expressed a desire to get even with the brute who had given him such a chilly few moments that the complete idea finally took shape.

He stopped as though he had stubbed his toe, overcome with the beauty of his inspiration. His first impulse was to rush with it to Macnooder and the Tennessee Shad with a request to be admitted into the firm. But though he had learned little, he had learned something. Bridling his enthusiasm he forced himself to go twice around the Circle, working out the details of his scheme.

"Gee, the greatest ever. I'll be a chief promoter myself, and get up a dogfight," he confidently proclaimed.

When the Uncooked Beefsteak approached the firm of Macnooder and the Tennessee Shad he did so with so much business discretion that the veterans were clearly amazed.

"I want a few words with you two," said The Beefsteak, with a certain manner. "No bluff—but an out-and-out understanding!"

"Why, Montague, how you have aged!" said Macnooder in soft surprise.

"It's no joke this time," said Skinner, waving the persiflage aside. "I've got a scheme and I want an understanding. Now I'll be frank."

"Hello," said Macnooder, who from constant use of this last assurance became suspicious of the words on another's tongue.

"You fellows are about the cutest thing out. You've flimflammed me, and you've done it well. I'm not kicking, only I've got my eyes open now. And you'll never get me again."

At this tempting challenge, Macnooder looked over the roofs of the houses, afraid to meet the eye of the Tennessee Shad.

"See here," continued Skinner, with more gravity, as he mistook their silence, "I'm for you fellows and I want to get into your game on the ground floor."

"What game?"

"Promoting."

"Bring us an idea," said Macnooder.

"I have."

"You've got me."

"The best."

"What is it?"

"Get up a professional dogfight, Blimmy's bull-pup and some other dog we'll get. Sell tickets and run it off in the woods at midnight."

Macnooder looked at the proud Beefsteak and then solemnly at his partner.

"Shad," he said, "extend to Monte the right hand of fellowship."

"We must get a dog, though, that will dine off Tough," said Skinner.

"I know one," said the Tennessee Shad dreamily.

"Where?" said the Beefsteak eagerly.

"Trenton," said the Tennessee Shad, "a long-haired dog, that's the game. Bulldogs are pie before long-haired dogs—can't get at the throat."

"The Tennessee Shad'll look after the challenge, then," glibly said Macnooder, who from old experience read aright the note of dreaminess in his partner's voice and knew something was brewing. "Who'll referee?"

"I will," said the Uncooked Beefsteak.

Macnooder glanced at the Shad and saw a little smile of satisfaction on those thin lips.

"I suppose I've got to be secretary and treasurer then," he said, with false weariness.

"That's the stuff," said the Beefsteak autocratically. "Besides,

I've seen a real fight and know the game."

"It's a good idea," said Macnooder after the vow of secrecy had been passed and the Beefsteak had gone, walking a little lightly on his toes.

"Yes."

"But, couldn't we put it over on the Beefsteak just once more—just one little final touch?" said Macnooder, to learn what the Shad was planning.

The Tennessee Shad remained a long time in cloudy speculation. Then he scratched his head, replaced his cap, and said carefully, "Tomorrow, Doc, I'll tell you all about it—tomorrow."

The Uncooked Beeksteak's eagerness to claim the limelight was quite in accordance with the plans of Macnooder and the Tennessee Shad. The more Skinner took upon himself, the more complacently they viewed the outlook. For some time it had become increasingly difficult for the firm of Macnooder to arouse any general enthusiasm for its speculative offerings. Particularly was this true of any attempt to collect before the fact.

Consequently, with great magnanimity, they assured the unsuspecting Skinner that the honor being his, they were determined he should have all the glory and suggested that whatever publicity was needed should come from him.

Skinner was allowed to announce the great event, to challenge Blimmy Garret in behalf of his champion and most important of all, to sell as many tickets as he could at the rate of fifty cents a head. Macnooder, modestly keeping in the background, received the receipts and safeguarded them, urging that no mention should be made of this trifling service.

By thus prominently displaying the Uncooked Beefsteak, they succeeded in working up a tremendous amount of enthusiasm in quarters which would have been decidedly lukewarm had the great sporting event borne the names of Macnooder and the Tennessee Shad.

When Skinner had collected and turned over to Macnooder the proceeds of thirty tickets, and had arranged the date and selected an ideal location in the groves that border the distant canal, he suddenly became rather panicky as to the mysterious champion whom the Tennessee Shad was to provide, and rushed all in a flutter to the Kennedy for reassurance.

"Be calm," said the Tennessee Shad, "I have the dog."

"Have you seen him?"

"I have."

"When?"

"This afternoon."

"Then he's near here?" said Skinner, surprised.

"I have him in training quarters," said the Tennessee Shad, with a mysterious wave of his hand. "Within a mile of where I stand."

"Training?" said Skinner, mystified.

"Feeding him on raw veal and mustard. You can spread the report that he's bitten two men in the last three days. That shows what he'll do to that china bull-pup of Blimmy's."

"You said he was a collie?"

"German Collie, a bruising ugly-tempered, rampaging collie."

"Supposing Tough licks him?" said the Beefsteak anxiously, contemplating a wager.

"A long-haired collie?" sad the Shad loftily. "Greatest fighter in the world. Why, Tough will never get his tooth in him. Put up all your money on it!"

"I wish I could see him," said the Beefsteak doubtfully.

"Course you do," said the Shad sympathetically. "But if you do, then Blimmy has a right to see. And say, if Blimmy sees this living death—it's all off. No bets, and no fight."

"Really?"

"Keep it quiet."

"By the way, what's the dog's name?"

"Dynamite."

The next afternoon the Shad arrived with a worried look.

"Say, Beefsteak, can't you put ahead the date?"

"What's the matter?"

"Why that brute of mine is chewing up everything in sight."

"No!"

"Fact. He tore the feathers off a duck and mangled a milk pail they left by mistake. We've got him boxed now."

"Supposing we pull it off tomorrow night."

"I don't think we can hold him any longer."

When Blimmy Garret heard the tales of butchery emanating from the opposite camp he was equal to the occasion.

"You go back, young stripling," he said imperiously to Skinner, "go back to whoever backs that ki-yi, and tell that old four-flusher

"YOU GO BACK, YOUNG STRIPLING."

that if his mongrel isn't any fiercer than that there won't be enough of him to line a pair of mittens!"

"They keep him shut up in a box," said the Beefsteak doubtfully.

"They do, do they? Well, you tell 'em we're holding Tough in a trunk with a couple of shot-laden trays over him too."

"They say he's even attacked a milk pail!"

"Oh, he has?" said Blimmy, growing indignant. "Well, tell them Tough is so wild, we've had to wedge his jaws."

"What for?"

"To keep him from wearing down his teeth when he thinks of that pup Dynamite," said Blimmy very seriously. "And say, go back and tell your friend that we don't want even another day. Pull the affair off tonight, or I won't answer for the spectators."

"All right," said Skinner, running off.

"Oh, I say!"

"What?"

"Tell him Tough will be there in a box, all right!"

"All right."

"And hold up, are you putting up a bet?"

"No—o," said Skinner, "I'm the referee. I can't."

When in the watches of the night, a shivering band of would-be sports bent on feverish dissipation gathered expectantly by the light of half-a-dozen lanterns in a distant and gloomy spot, the ferocious rumors from the rival camps had become common property and in certain quarters there was a marked impulse to seek places of security rather than the natural points of vantage.

"Have you ever been at one of these things?" said Shrimp Davis, who was the youngest allowed to qualify as a sport.

"No," said Peewee Bacon in the same woodland whisper. "It's pretty risky, isn't it?"

"There ought to be a ring with a high wall around it," said the Triumphant Egghead, who was always critical. "Something to protect the spectators."

"That's right."

"There's no telling what a dog will bite."

"And if his jaws set on you, they never let go."

"Say, this is a rotten place for a fight."

"Well, I wore leather boots and shin-guards."

Meanwhile, Skinner, dressed to kill in the flashiest of all his flashy vests and ties, checked suit and feathered fedora, was anxiously superintending the marking-off of the ring, and carefully selected a level glade among a clump of melancholy pines. Four stakes were driven in and several lengths of ropes stretched around.

"Say, the Beefsteak's quite the fellow, isn't he," said Peewee much impressed.

"He certainly has seen a lot of life."

The preparations for the safety of the public did not impress.

"What are they stringing up ropes for?"

"Huh, to keep us out of the ring."

"Is that all the guarantee we get?"

"And they say both pups haven't had a square meal in thirty-six hours."

"Oh, mother!"

"A dog's bite is poisonous, isn't it?"

"Sure, they burn you out with a red-hot poker."

"Oh, joy!"

"What's that?"

"Have they come?"

A series of yelps were now heard approaching from opposite directions and presently two wheelbarrows bearing sinister noisy boxes appeared out of the gloom. There was a rush in the direction of the Tennessee Shad and Macnooder, but all lingering incredulity was dissipated when the light of a lantern revealed behind the slats of an improvised cage, the dim head of a large collie —German or otherwise.

Macnooder, who had a strong dramatic instinct, was in sweater and high boots, a rag over his forehead and several crosses of black court plaster on his cheeks, which were at once taken to be proofs of the fighting qualities of the challenging Dynamite.

Both dogs, as a result of the exceedingly lumpy journey they had come, combined with the prodding received from two zealous owners, were in a humor more human than canine. As a consequence, no sooner had the full effect of their anger reached the crowd, than there began a curious shifting movement among the spectators; those in front slipping to the back while those who were promoted surrendered instantly their vantage.

519

The two boxes were placed at opposite sides of the ring, and the seconds summoned by Skinner met in the middle for conclave.

"So *you're* back of this!" said Blimmy comprehending Macnooder's connection for the first time.

"I'm slightly interested, Blimmy," said Macnooder with a smile.

"And you think you've got a dog can lick Tough, do you?"

"My dear old boy, we don't *think*."

"Are you backing your opinion?" said Garret furiously.

"It's all over. We don't want to *steal* your money!"

"Will you bet?"

"Wait," said Macnooder, who made a gesture to the Tennessee Shad, who immediately produced a spade.

"What's that for?" said Skinner, mystified.

"To bury Tough," said Doc, with a bland gesture.

"Begin," said Blimmy, in a rage.

At this there was suddenly heard a noise among the trees, like an army of squirrels. A third of the audience, their courage departing, were now seen making their way along overhanging branches.

Skinner, more thoroughly frightened than ever before in his life, remained alone in the middle of the ring, suddenly realizing the responsibilities as well as the glory of high office. Blimmy and Macnooder pushing the front of their boxes up to the ropes stood with their hands on the bolts.

"Stop!" cried the Tennessee Shad in a purposely tense voice. "Stop a moment."

"What's the matter?" cried a dozen alarmed voices.

"The Beefsteak must get out of the ring or I won't answer for the consequences."

At this another third of the audience took to shinnying up the most available trees, while the rest, including P. Lentz who couldn't, to have saved himself, lifted his two-hundred pounds from the ground, began to cast calculating glances to the rear. The Beefsteak, without a pause, retired outside the ropes while the tree dwellers with returning interest began to shout:

"Even on Dynamite!"

"I'll back Macnooder's dog."

"Goodbye to Tough."

"Stuffed dog tomorrow!"

"Ten to one someone gets chewed."

"What show has a Beefsteak got?"

"Jemima, they're fierce!"

"Give us the carnage."

"Blood!"

"Are you ready?" cried the Beefsteak, in a high falsetto. "Let 'em out."

There was a volley of cheers from the trees and a unanimous rushing movement to the rear on the part of the remaining spectators, a flight conspicuously led by Macnooder and the Tennessee Shad with well-acted fright.

The shutters dropped simultaneously, but only Tough bounded forth in furious solitary possession of the ring. From the released cage of Dynamite nothing stirred.

Conflicting shouts now sounded from the trees.

"What's the matter?"

"Where's Dynamite?"

"Why doesn't he come out?"

"Just wait till he does."

"When he makes up his mind, look out."

"Rats, he's afraid!"

"Go on, give him time!"

A full minute passed and still the only occupant of the ring was Tough with four legs stiffly planted, growling his defiance. From behind the tree trunks some of the most daring began to steal back to where the Beefsteak, puzzled, waited in suspense for the living destruction to burst forth.

Reassured, the crowd began to throng the ringside, shouting:

"Come on, Dynamite!"

"Sic 'em!"

"Poke him up!"

"Shake him up!"

"Kick the box!"

Acting on the hint, the Beefsteak shook the box with a thundering boot. A furious snarling, which momentarily restored confidence, answered him, but no Dynamite appeared.

"He's there all right!"

"What's the matter with him?"

"Hear him growl!"

"He's coming."

"The deuce he is!"

"He's gone to sleep."

"Where's the Tennessee Shad?" cried the Beefsteak.

The Tennessee Shad had disappeared.

"Where's Macnooder?"

The cry was taken up in vain. Suddenly the same suspicion seized the group of would-be sports who, rushing to the box, overturned it. At the same moment, Tough, springing forward, came to a disgusted stop, more in sympathy than in anger, before an aged, moth-eaten, toothless dog, who, emerging in snarling protest, sank immediately to a reclining position. At once it was a riot.

"Why, he's a billion years old!"

"No teeth!"

"No eyes!"

"Hair dropping out!"

"Even Tough wouldn't bite it!"

"Jemima, if it isn't Old Sally!"

"Sure, it is!"

"Belongs to Laloo!"

"Why, she is thirty years old!"

"A grandmother!"

"It's a put-up job!"

"Fraud!"

"Fake!"

"Skin game!"

"All bets off!"

"Murder!"

"Stop, thief!"

"Oh, what a bunco game!"

"Money back!"

"Give us our money back."

"Catch the Beefsteak."

"Hold him, boys!"

But that great sporting promoter, too amazed to think of flight, was gazing in dumbfounded horror at the blinking, ragged anemic specimen which the Tennessee Shad had advertised as Dynamite.

"Hold up, I say, it's the Tennessee Shad," he cried vainly, "catch Macnooder and the Tennessee Shad—they've got the money!"

Then the mob reached him.

IX

THE LAMB RETREATS

HAVING FOUND by successive disillusioning experiments with the firm of Macnooder and the Tennessee Shad that the school was neither impressed by his own worldly personality or ready for the launching of genteel sporting practices, Montague fell into a period of abysmal depression that was the more overwhelming in that he could see no guiding streak of light in the completeness of his darkness.

He had failed to impress. There was no doubt on that score. And as his moral education, by sharp processes, began to be accomplished, he himself began, curiously enough, to lose the zest for the ways and distinction of complete manhood and to long wistfully, unbeknownst of his comrades, for the simple frolics of a mere boy.

The trouble was that he was always an outsider. He perceived it despairingly as he perceived the vital truth, that a night feast on indigestible tinned food and dyspeptic root beer was still a banquet and a banquet that needed no more fortunate patron.

When Turkey Reiter had indiscreetly informed him that his fatal drawback was the reputation for billions, he spoke the truth, and he might have added that every billionaire in such an assemblage is held to be impossible, dudified and deserving of hard labor until he has removed the burden of suspicion.

Now the Uncooked Beefsteak could not comprehend this truth —he debated it, he meditated long thereupon in solitary tramps, he tried to comprehend it; but the traditions of his first sixteen years were too strong. It could not be so. It could not be that a generous open purse, a purse waiting to be called upon for the multifarious enjoyments of those he chose to signal out as his friends, could be a handicap. His theory could not be wrong, the blunder must have lain in indiscreet application. Some way there must be to win popularity and stop the humiliating and menial

services to which he was daily condemned by his paternally solicitous housemates. For, unable to perceive the larger good, the Beefsteak could see no useful purpose to be served in this course in
primitive tailoring, complete housework, and general bootblacking.

At times the House relented, hoping that the lesson had been
learned. Unfortunately, Skinner could not seize the subtle class
distinctions which forbade him, a mere bag of money, a noncom-
batant, what was permitted to the nobility of muscle and brain.

Of a consequence, no sooner was the ban lifted than he became
familiar instead of humble, boastful instead of inquiring, pushing
instead of thankfully receptive, and given to using nicknames,
which were reserved for those who had progressed to the second
degree. Upon which, the House would convene and agree that the
Beefsteak was still unfit for human intercourse and assign him back
to the boots and the clothes brush.

Now, in about the tenth period of this recurrent discipline, the
Beefsteak had suddenly a brilliant idea. The Easter recess was
approaching—he would invite Macnooder to spend the week with
him at his father's hotel and by dazzling him with its splendor and
magnificence, awaken him to a proper sense of the Skinner importance.

The result steadied him in his wavering belief in the theory of
the supremacy of capital. Not only was there an instant somersault
on Macnooder's part, a change accomplished between the blacking
of one boot and the withdrawal of the other, but the effect in the
House was electrical.

Half-an-hour after Macnooder had received the invitation, the
Triumphant Egghead smilingly appeared in the Beefsteak's room
with a genial manner. "Hello, Monte, old boy, not studying, are
you?"

"Come in," said the Beefsteak, chuckling inwardly.

"What a perfectly corking room, a peacherino!" said the Egghead, surveying for the first time the walls decorated with photographs of certain theatrical ladies who adorned but did not elevate
the stage, and chromos of national bruisers in boxing tights.

"You like it?" said Skinner carelessly.

"And gee! Look at the Dottie-Dimple-Toes! Say, you don't know
all these damsels, do you?"

"I'll put you next to any of them," said Skinner, relapsing into
the past.

"Gee, I'd like to meet a real live actress," said the Triumphant Egghead, slyly approaching his opportunity.

At this moment the door opened and the Waladoo Bird came hastily in. The Triumphant Egghead shot him a furious glance which was returned by one of suspicion and envy.

Then the Waladoo Bird, giant of the football eleven, sat down and, smiling on Skinner, said with directness, "Say, Monte, I've got to get a couple of suits bitten out for me in New York. You know the whole dressing game from A to Z. Give me a couple of pointers on what's the real thing. Look over my style of beauty and put me on. And say, what's the best hotel to stop at?"

The Waladoo Bird understood but one method of attack and that was a mass through the center of the line. But at this moment the door swung the third time and the Tennessee Shad entered, slightly out of breath, with a glance at the two visitors that sought to seize on the instant if he had been forestalled. Close on his heels came Dennis de Brian de Boru Finnegan, who beat to the threshold the Gutter Pup and Lovely Mead.

That night the Uncooked Beefsteak, who had been watched since luncheon by those who were most concerned in watching one another, went off to sleep more thoroughly happy than he had been in months. He had played the trump card and the stakes were his. No more would he lighten the burdens of Klondike, the houseman, no more would he bend in servile postures over the oozing muddy boots of striplings in knickerbockers, no more would he listen in enforced isolation to the whispered merriment of distant feasts; he would select with a ruthless and distinguishing finger his guests among the elite of his comrades; there should be a week of princely entertainment and then he would return, one of the chosen, a member of the crème de la crème.

At the same time Macnooder was saying excitedly to the Tennessee Shad. "See here, I've got the inside track—the Beefsteak will invite anyone I say."

"Little social secretary, eh?"

"Shut up. Do you know what I'm going to do? I'm going to sell excursion tickets, good for one week at the Regal Hotel, all expenses paid, and I'm going to soak each gazebo ten fat young plunks."

"Doc, it's glorious," said the Tennessee Shad, "you certainly will own Fifth Avenue. But say, how much longer do you think we can go on excavating in this here Beefsteak mine?"

"Very, very little. That's why we'll play this for a lalapazooza!"

"The trouble is we have assumed a moral attitude towards Monte," said the Tennessee Shad regretfully. "We are loosening his gold rocks but we are educating him."

"Yes, and when we get him educated and a proper self-respecting citizen—he'll be ungrateful."

"I fear so—I fear me much."

"On to the Regal Hotel!"

"On, Doc, on!"

About three o'clock in the afternoon of the opening of the Easter vacation there debarked at the Cortlandt Street terminal of the Pennsylvania Railroad a party of five in close marching order, consisting of Macnooder and Dennis de Brian de Boru Finnegan in advance, the Waladoo Bird and the Tennessee Shad supporting the center and the Triumphant Egghead guarding the rear.

"Halt," said Macnooder.

"What for?"

"We must consult. How shall we approach the Regal Hotel? On foot, in a swiftly moving trolley, or drawn by prancing horses?"

"Hire a hack, of course," said the Triumphant Egghead, who represented society. "You can't enter a hotel on foot."

"Why not?" said Finnegan.

"It isn't done."

"Rats! I'm for hoofing it. Show me the sights of Broadway and all that sort of thing."

"You're a hayseed and a jayhawker," said the Triumphant Egghead.

"Don't let's quarrel yet," said the Tennessee Shad soothingly, "I've only got sixty cents and I vote for the elevated."

"I think a barouche is an unnecessary expense," said Macnooder, who calculated on the Triumphant Egghead's buying the carriage.

At this moment the Waladoo Bird was discovered filling his pockets with peanuts.

"Merciful heavens," exclaimed the Egghead in horror. "You ignoramus, what are you doing?"

"Eating peanuts," said the Waladoo Bird, suiting the action to the word.

"Are you going through New York scattering shells like a hay-seed?"

"I am," said the Waladoo Bird who had the Western contempt for the abode of the unconvicted rich.

"I won't be seen with you."

"Don't."

"If he is determined," said Macnooder meditatively, "he had better work it off. Let's walk."

The Triumphant Egghead immediately engaged a coach and hid himself in the company of the Tennessee Shad whose exertions were always mental.

The Waladoo Bird, flinging out peanut shells with the regularity of a thrashing machine, strode defiantly, flanked by Dennis, who stepped from corner to corner to buy an extra, and Macnooder who showed a lively interest in the new attractions in the shop windows.

A matter of a block behind, at a patient walk, came the hired coach from the recesses of which the Triumphant Egghead gazed upon the offenders with wrath and disgust.

"I wonder what he thinks this Regal Hotel is?" he said furiously. "An actor's boarding house?"

"I know for a fact," said the Tennessee Shad to soothe and comfort him, "that the Waladoo Bird had only two dollars and thirty cents."

"Awful funny, ha! ha!" said the Egghead, who was in no mood for humor.

"He must get filled up sometime."

"If he don't, it's all off. Do you think I'm going to march into the foyer of the classiest thing in New York with an elephant ten feet high cracking peanuts?"

"How far is it uptown?"

"Five or six miles."

"He ought to get away with an awful lot of nuts by then," said the Shad, who began to share his anxiety. "So this hotel is rather flossy?"

"The flossiest."

"Lots of gilt and red plush and all that sort of thing."

"Sure."

"What's the fodder like?"

"The cuisine," said the Egghead elegantly, "is the most fashionable in the city."

"But the Beefsteak sets up for the grub?"

"Yes, you chump."

"Everything we get away with?"

"Sure."

"Perhaps if the Waladoo Bird knew that he would ease up."

The announcement, in fact, produced a decided sensation. The Waladoo Bird finished the last handful outside the carriage at the peremptory challenge of the Egghead and then jarred the carriage springs while Finnegan made the common demand for a show of speed.

When Montague Skinner, moving restlessly in the ante-room of the Regal Hotel, beheld the arrival of the overloaded coach, he was quite touched by the cordiality of the greeting he received.

"Leave it to me," he said, intervening between the reluctant purse of the Triumphant Egghead and the grinning coachman. Then with an ease that made the Waladoo Bird stiffen up and take notice, he summoned a footman and said, "Charles, see what the fare is and have the office attend to it."

"Here, I say!" began the Egghead, with not too much resistance.

"Oh now, Monte, this is ours!" said Macnooder more emphatically as he perceived an absence of danger.

"No," said the Beefsteak finally, but with the lightness that such a triviality merited. "From now on you are my guests."

The Tennessee Shad, who had sixty cents, exchanged a glance of delirious joy with the Waladoo Bird who had a two-dollar bill, and, being thrown together in their voyage toward the elevator, whispered, "It looks good to me."

"It certainly does."

"No expenses."

"None at all."

At this moment the Waladoo Bird was overwhelmed by a fearful thought.

"I say, he's got the bags."

"Who's got them?"

"The Buttons."

"Well, what of it?"

"We'll have to tip him."

"Well, tip him!"

"I've only got a two-dollar bill and a nickel," said the Waladoo Bird in a worried whisper.

The Tennessee Shad nervously shifted his sixty cents to an inner recess, maliciously enjoying the confusion of the giant who was wondering uneasily whether the elevator man would expect to be recompensed.

Macnooder, Finnegan and the Triumphant Egghead were escorted to their quarters by Skinner, after leaving the Waladoo Bird and the Tennessee Shad in the adjoining room assigned them.

The Buttons, having deposited the bags, was languidly busy straightening the window curtains and shifting the chairs with that perfect, expectant manner that is instinctive wih those whose fortunate mission in life is to be tipped.

"What'll I give him?" said the Waladoo Bird in a muffled roar.

"How do I know?"

"I can't give him a nickel."

"Never!"

"I say lend me a half a dollar."

"Can't. Macnooder's got my purse."

The Waladoo Bird, who had faced the Princeton Varsity without a tremor, quailed before the spruce representative of bellboys. For a moment his fingers hesitated over the plebian nickel and then, blushing with combined rage and embarrassment, he blurted out, "Here—take this."

And he thrust upon him the two-dollar bill.

The Tennessee Shad, who had the profoundest respect for capital, was furious.

"You jackass, what did you do that for?"

"I had to give him something, didn't I?"

"Yes, but, Holy Cats, you can *buy* a bellboy for two dollars!"

"Well, what was I to do?" said the Waladoo Bird, who, clutching his last nickel, began to feel the despairing loneliness of one who is stranded in the great city.

"Do, you blockhead? Ask him to get you some change."

"Ask him—" said the Waladoo Bird in stupid amazement. "Well, why in thunder didn't you tell me?"

"Humph! Thought you'd been weaned from the bottle," said the Tennessee Shad, who now felt a sense of personal loss.

"Well, by gravy, I'll do it now," said the Waladoo Bird, bolting into his coat.

"Hold up! What are you going to do?"

"I'm going to track that young highwayman down and shake it out of him!"

"Hold up! You can't do that."

"Can't I? Just watch me!"

"Hold up! You'll make a social blunder!"

"Beans!"

When the Triumphant Egghead with Macnooder and Finnegan entered the room they found the Tennessee Shad in an attitude of deep dejection with one ear trained for the outburst of an expected cyclone.

"What in blazes is the matter?" said Macnooder. "And where is the Waladoo Bird?"

The Tennessee Shad explained.

"My aunt's cat's pants, that is awful!" said the Triumphant Egghead with a shiver.

"Wriggling snakes, what do you suppose he's doing?"

"He'll smash the crockery!"

"Had we better tell the Beefsteak?"

"Never!"

"Why the deuce didn't you look after him?"

"What do you expect?" said the Tennessee Shad aggrieved, "Do I look like a tug-of-war team?"

"This is awful," said the Triumphant Egghead, wiping his forehead.

The door opened and the Waladoo Bird plumped in.

"Did you get him?" said the five in chorus.

"Get him?" said the Waladoo Bird in a rage. "Why, there are one hundred-and-fifty bellhops below, all hopping around, and every mother's son of them looks alike! Say, what color hair did that pirate of ours have?"

The Tennessee Shad promptly forgot.

"Look here, boy!" said the Triumphant Egghead. "This will never do. You'll queer the whole bunch."

"I gave him two dollars," said the Waladoo Bird, sitting down with a crash that brought a groan from the light furniture.

"And don't go making a woodpile of everything you sit on!"

"HOLD UP! WHAT ARE YOU GOING TO DO?"

"What's wrong?"

"You. You're wrong. You're not fit to come into the parlor. A nice time we'll have with you. Didn't you ever see a hotel before?"

"Are you speaking to me?" said the Waladoo Bird, rising.

When the altercation had subsided, another serious question arose.

"Where'll we dine?" said Finnegan who had been coached. "Supposin' we grub with the Beefsteak—private dining room, special dishes and all that sort of thing."

"I vote for downstairs," said the Waladoo Bird, who had been put in a contrary humor.

"Why?"

"I want to get a chance at a real bang-up menu."

"And I vote to put this guy in seclusion!"

The Waladoo Bird gave the Egghead an evil look and was about to reply when Macnooder suavely arose.

"The Waladoo Bird is quite right. We will dine in public."

"Everyone will be dressed to kill."

"Then we shall be taken for Western millionaires. But—I say *but*—we are going to pull off this thing in classy style."

"No social blunders," said the Tennessee Shad.

"And no trying to split the menu," said the Triumphant Egghead.

"We will pick out the daintiest dishes," said Macnooder, trying the power of suggestion on the Waladoo Bird, "the *recherché*, expensive dishes, and we will take little careless dabs at them."

"Fine!" said the others, with the unique exception of the Waladoo Bird.

"Tomorrow we'll rip the stuffing out of the bill of fare, we'll mangle it, we'll blow holes in it, tear it up the back and drive it to its corner!"

"Tomorrow!"

"Tomorrow! But tonight we'll go down in a bored sort of way. We'll put up an awful bluff, tired of caviar and nightingales' tongues and all that sort of thing. We've got to keep the Beefsteak in his place—remember that! Show him we're old birds."

"Righto," said everyone; that is, everyone except the Waladoo Bird.

"Just take a nibble here and there and then push the plate away," said Finnegan, wishing to be helpful.

"Righto!"

"And stretch your arms and yawn in a high-bred, classy sort of way."

"You chump!" said the Triumphant Egghead. "Where have you been brought up?"

"The last suggestion is now withdrawn," said Finnegan modestly.

"Now, we're all agreed," said Macnooder, with an expanding smile. "Our object is to take the wind right out of the Beefsteak's sails—to show him what! Nothing but short sprints tonight, all long-distance records postponed until tomorrow."

"All right!" said the majority, minus one.

The dinner passed without any exhibition of Gargantuan powers on the part of the Waladoo Bird, but this was due to no surrender to social prejudices but to the fact that, placed as he was to command a view of the foyer, his whole attention was concentrated on the perplexing passage of flitting bellboys.

The Uncooked Beefsteak was slightly disappointed by the reticence of his guests, but this sentiment was soon lost in the blissful enjoyment of his new social footing. Nothing, in fact, could have been more delightfully intimate than their bearing toward him. He was not simply a patron—he was one of them.

He took them to the theater, in a box, to a vaudeville performance over which a year ago he would have yawned himself weary. To his amazement, he found himself caught up in the general hilarity, wildly applauding slapstick comedians who caused Dennis de Brian de Boru to weep for joy. He applauded! He had never done such a thing before. He actually stamped his feet and rattled his cane, demanding renewed encores. And when the show was over and the Tennessee Shad proposed that, instead of dividing into two cabs, henceforth whenever they went they should all crowd into one and send an empty cab before them as a sort of guard of honor, he gleefully embraced the idea and balanced on the bony ridges of the Tennessee Shad, waving his hat to the crowds of Broadway with the zest of restored youth.

When, late at night, after the Waladoo Bird had consumed a terrifying number of oysters, Finnegan had eaten three Welsh rabbits, and Skinner had seen his guests to their rooms, he returned gorgeously to his private suite.

Bucks, the confidential valet, was in wait.

"How do Bucks? How are you?" he said languidly.

"Thank you, sir. It's good to see you back, sir."

"The old boarding house is still doing a fat young business?" asked Skinner, surrendering his coat and falling into the vernacular of the admired Turkey Reiter.

"I beg pardon, sir! Oh! Yes, sir," said Bucks, momentarily mystified. "I hope you enjoy the school, sir?"

"It is wonderful, Bucks, wonderful. Glorious times! Glorious fellows!"

"That Mr. Walader, sir, certainly is something of a man," said Bucks, with great respect.

"He could wipe the ground up with any cop in New York," said Skinner stoutly. "And at that you ought to see P. Lentz. He weighs two hundred and sixty."

Here the telephone began to buzz angrily.

"Hello," said Skinner, going to it.

"Hello. Is that you, Monte, old boy?" said the excited voice of the Tennessee Shad.

"Yes, here I am."

"Say, look here, the Waladoo Bird has gone clean through his bed!"

"What?"

"Punctured a hole clean through it! Say, fix him up, will you? He's in mine now!"

"All right," said Skinner, who, turning from the telephone announced with pride, "What do you think of that? He's smashed the bed, Bucks—couldn't hold him! See to it, will you?"

"Yes, sir."

"Get something very solid."

"Yes, sir."

"One of those things they rig up for cattle kings."

"Certainly, sir."

When the noiseless valet had slipped away, Skinner stood a moment in contemplation of the glorious feat.

"By George!" he exclaimed, "Won't old Fatty Harris be wild when he hears of it—he's only smashed a football. The Waladoo Bird is a wonder. By George, I never had a better time in my life! Gee, what a difference though it makes when you once get in!"

Then he sat down very seriously on the edge of his fragrant bed, staring at the toes that peeped forth from the gorgeous lavender silk pajamas.

"By George!" he said suddenly, with a great moral resolve. "I know what I'll do. I'll hire a tutor I will! I'll slave all summer. But I'll get to college with that bunch or I'll injure my health!"

When the stage had lumbered away after depositing the last returned convict, the inmates of the Dickinson House, exhausted and sleepless after that Easter period which the curriculum still persists in ascribing to rest and recuperation, foregathered once more on the steps and the young green banks in lively discussion.

The Uncooked Beefsteak from his room directly above, looked down with satisfaction, pausing in the process of arranging three new resplendent vests. It had been a never-to-be-forgotten week. His hospitality had gone beyond the limits where even a prince might hesitate. If there was a dish on The Regal Hotel public menu that Finnegan, Macnooder and the Waladoo Bird had not contended with, it was solely because the season outlawed it. They had neglected not a single theater, riding to and fro always with an empty cab ahead as an outrider. The totalled record of meals consumed and carriages provided had made Skinner pater blink with amazement and there had been a few words on the subject, including a cash offer if the visit could possibly be abbreviated.

But this was pure inconsequential persiflage and had been silenced at once by the announcement of Montague's highly virtuous intention to secure a college education.

The Beefsteak, fondly secure of the affections of his late guests, brazenly deployed an array of theatrical neckwear where it would most dazzle and astound.

Of course he had that admiration for the Waladoo Bird that d'Artagnan entertained for Porthos, Dennis de Brian de Boru fascinated him and the Tennessee Shad moved him to envy with the dark and devious strategy of his mind. But, after all, it was Macnooder, the financier, and the Triumphant Egghead, the representative of society, who really stirred his heartstrings, and they should be his special cronies, singled out from the multitude.

He finished the task of sorting his marvelous wardrobe and yielding to an impulse, boldly arrayed himself in his latest tailored creation, a noticeable concoction in large brown and green squares. He surveyed with genteel pride the thin, perfect line of the red silk necktie, passing his hand over the speckled vest with large white buttons. He liked to dress well, in perfect taste yet with distinction, and now at last he dared gratify this taste.

Secure as a Braddock in his complacent confidence, he went down the steps and burst in full vision upon the group.

"Well, old gazebos," said the Beefsteak, throwing back the sides of his coat, peacock fashion, "How do you like the spring styles?"

Turkey Reiter looked at Doc Macnooder and sadly shook his head, while in the group an ominous silence began to spread.

The Uncooked Beefsteak, all unaware, sauntered down to a position beside the Triumphant Egghead and clapped him on the shoulder.

"Egghead, old sporting life, tell the multitude about the classy food I corralled for you."

Then spoke Turkey Reiter, the czar, solemnly, "Beefsteak, there is a pair of old muddy boots, standing right in front of my wash-stand. The mud is rather hard and doesn't improve the boots a bit. Better go up now—quietly—and see what you can do with them."

"What!" said the Beefsteak, every hair of his head starting up with horror.

"Take great care of them," said Turkey Reiter softly. "They are my favorite boots."

"You don't mean it!" said the Beefsteak, turning desperately to Macnooder, "Oh, I say, not again!"

"It's for your own good, you blasted millionaire," said Macnooder sadly. "It hurts us more than it does you."

A great lump rose in the Beefsteak's throat. He turned wildly to the Triumphant Egghead.

"Yes, Macnooder is right," said this last hope. "We're really doing you good. So, Beefsteak when you finish the boots up nicely, come down on your tiptoes and brush up a few of my things. My clothes have been kept in such rattling good order lately that I should hate—"

But the Beefsteak zigzagging in his walk, had wabbled up the steps. He went to his room and sat down, steadying his head in his hands. And there at last the full light broke over him.

That evening as the House was gathered for supper, Butcher Stevens suddenly exclaimed, "For the love of Mike, look at the Uncooked Beefsteak!"

Around the corner came Skinner, clad in an ill-fitting pair of ink-stained corduroy trousers, a jersey in place of the loud vest and a slouch hat over his eye.

"Merciful heavens!" said the Triumphant Egghead, with a shock. "Beefsteak, where did you get that rig?"

"I traded it," said the Uncooked Beefsteak firmly. "Got it for my last $85 tailor suit."

"Dear boy, what does this mean!" said Macnooder, with a horrible misgiving.

"Read that!" said the Beefsteak, thrusting a paper on Turkey Reiter.

"What is it?"

"It's a telegram I've just sent home. Go on, read it!"

And Turkey Reiter read:

Joshua M. Skinner,
  The Regal Hotel,
    New York City.
  Cut my allowance to a dollar a week.

                                              Montague.

"Explain!" said the Tennessee Shad heartbroken.

"I will," said the Beefsteak militantly. "It means I am on, I'm wise. It means you've educated me and I know my lesson. From now on the bank is suspended. I'll start even. And remember this," he added, looking steadily at Macnooder, "I may still be a Beefsteak, but there's nothing uncooked about me—I'm done to a crisp!"

537

X

LAST HISTORIC EXPLOIT OF THE FIRM

Say did you pass? Then set 'em up!
  Good work, my brilliant brother.
Say, did you flunk? Then pass the cup!
  Hard luck! Let's have another!
It heightens all the joys of Greek,
  Soothes Mathematics' rigor,
In each event of life we seek
  The ever-flowing jigger.

Refrain

The jig, jig, jigger,
The jig, jig, jigger,
The jig, jig, jigger, the jigger,
But we, when waves of trouble roll,
We hie us to the jigger.

"FOR HEAVEN's sake, shut up, Goat! You're 'way off the tune," said the Tennessee Shad irritably.

Now, the Goat knew he was not off the tune and, likewise, perfectly understood the cause of the irritation. Wallowing gorgeously on heaped-up sofa cushions, breathing in the perfumed breeze at the open window, his chin in his hands, he looked down maliciously to where the Tennessee Shad, indolently on his back, retired under the brim of his sombrero, was nibbling at the pink-and-white petals that rocked languidly down. Then, with malice aforethought, the Goat's floating tenor resumed:

It cools in heat, it warms in cold,
  If sick it can restore us,
And when our health becomes too good,
  'Twill fix the matter for us;

So eat aplenty while you're small,
Eat more when you are bigger,
And lest we do not grow at all,
Let's take another jigger.

"Chorus now, Shad!"

The jig, jig, jigger,
The jig, jig, jigger,
The jig, jig, jigger, the jigger.
But we, when waves of trouble roll,
We hie us to the jigger.

Whereupon the Goat, seized with the idea, disappeared from the dormer window and presently shuffled out on the Esplanade.

"They're fresh strawberry jiggers, Shad," he exclaimed tantalizingly; "for the first time too."

The Tennessee Shad snored loudly.

"Would you like me to set you up?" said the Goat, frisking as near as he dared. "Would you like to forget the past and have a jigger on me—would you, Shad? My hair's long and curly now."

The Tennessee Shad was too wary to be caught by any such hypothetical invitation to which he knew very well the answer to his answer; so he snored again, but keeping an eyelid batting on the chance that the Goat would venture too near.

"Strawberry jiggers, nice, fresh, creamy strawberry jiggers!" said his tormentor. "My, I'm going to eat a dozen! Sorry you don't care about 'em. Ta-ta!"

The Tennessee Shad opened one eye and watched the Goat go gamboling toward the village, as goats should go who are glad to be alive in the best of all months, who have ravenous appetites and something jingling in their pockets to lay down on the counter.

The Tennessee Shad had all the requisites for perfect happiness except the last—there was nothing in his pockets to sound musically, not even one miserable nickel to strike against another. Not only was he devoid of credit, but, as the result of the education of Beefsteak, of the Criminal Club, and the search for German measles, he was not quite restored to that social standing which would warrant his approaching a past victim with the demand direct.

Despite these incontestable facts which should have allowed him to withdraw under the spell of his philosophy, one disturbing,

539

buzzing little sound persistently and mockingly persecuted him, "Fresh strawberry jiggers!"

Now, there are three great epochs in the annual of the school: the first appearance of the strawberry, the arrival of the raspberry, and that happy moment when the spoon plunges into the creamy jigger and strikes upon the juicy shreds of the peach. And, the greatest of these is the inauguration of the strawberry season.

The Tennessee Shad drew in his cheeks and ran his tongue over his lips until he could bear it no longer. He sat up, blowing the sprinkled apple blossoms from his coat, and began to consider seriously.

"I must see Doc Macnooder," he said at length, after a vain examination of his own artifices. He stood himself up by a process of jerks and, acquiring sufficient momentum by his first movements, entered the House, bumped around the corners and rubbed his way to Macnooder's room, where he gave the agreed signal. No answer returning, he applied his eye to the keyhole, and then, chinning himself, surveyed by way of the transom the deserted bottles, the stuffed owl and the dangling dried bats.

"Doc must be in the village," he said. "If he is in funds I certainly ought to be good for a touch there."

For those who knew the Tennessee Shad his gait told all. When under the magic of a possibly productive idea he went rapidly in a beeline, his thin legs seeming to shut and close with the agility of a tailor's shears. On the present occasion, being in a deeply meditative mood, he went in little stumbling steps, often stopping to change his stride, scratching his head and, being lonely, altering his stride to kick along some stone larger than the rest.

In this mode he suddenly perceived the plump, Capuchin figure and round head of Doc Macnooder sauntering toward him, hands sunk in his pockets, his glance wandering in the clouds. At the same moment Macnooder perceived him and the following colloquy ensued:

"Hello, there."

"Hello, yourself."

"I was looking for you, Doc."

"I was trailing for you."

" 'Em—you were?"

"I was."

"That means you are strapped."

"You don't mean to say you are?"

"Why, Doc, you're an old millionaire. I thought you—"

"My money's all tied up," said Macnooder. "Invested in stocks and that sort of thing."

"You were my last hope," said the Tennessee Shad, "If the firm's bust what are we going to do about it? We've got to find something."

"Let's see what's doin' first," said Macnooder. "Let's reconnoiter."

"We might try Laloo," said the Tennessee Shad thoughtfully. "I gave him the idea of hot dogs. He's made thousands on it."

But as they approached, Laloo, basking lazily at the entrance of the frankfurter palace, shifted his toothpick and ominously drew out a little memorandum.

The two stopped.

"There's gratitude for you," said the Tennessee Shad bitterly.

"You should have struck a bargain with him," said Macnooder, the banker: "ten per cent and your personal account."

"Shall we try Appleby?" asked the Shad.

"What's the use?" replied Macnooder.

They proceeded up the leafy street to where, before the Jigger Shop, a score of ravenous boys were clinking their spoons against their glasses. In front a huge placard announced:

FRESH STRAWBERRY JIGGERS

"Let's work the Hickey Flimflam on the bunch," said the Tennessee Shad, perceiving Turkey Reiter, the Goat, Butcher Stevens and the Gutter Pup.

"All right—I'm desperate," said Macnooder under his breath; "but wait till Turkey Reiter clears out. He's on."

"Turkey's a square sport," said the Shad; "he wouldn't give it away."

They reached the crowd on the steps and saluted.

"Pretty good, eh?"

"You bet your sweet life!"

"Nothing like the strawberry, is there?"

"Um-um!"

"How's the supply hold out?"

541

"Say, Doc," said the Tennessee Shad, closing one eye and cocking his head toward the counter where Al's steely glance was turned upon them, "do you think, could you be persuaded—eh, what?"

"What, *again?*" cried Doc in simulated astonishment.

Al's eye opened and his finger stole softly across his politician's mustache as he bent forward the better to listen.

"Oh, come on! There's always room for another," said the Tennessee Shad. "Just to be sociable."

"Why, you old gormandizer!" said Macnooder. "You'll swell up and bust!"

"Then you won't?"

"You bet I won't!" said Macnooder, loosening his belt. "And you're a bigger fool than I took you for if you do. However, go ahead and commit suicide if you want!"

"Well, I guess I won't," said the Shad softly, slipping his belt to an easier hole and sitting down. "I just wanted to be sociable, that's all."

They ensconced themselves in the group, chatting aimlessly for a quarter of an hour, with surfeited unconsciousness of the melting jiggers that circulated beneath their noses.

Finally, it being his turn to treat, the Beefsteak, in fancied security, maliciously addressed Doc Macnooder.

"How about it, Doc?"

Macnooder emitted a long whistle and said indifferently, "I oughtn't to, but if the Shad will take one, too, I'll be sociable."

"Only a single, Doc," said the Tennessee Shad; "I couldn't eat any more—I couldn't."

The Beefsteak, who not for the world would have offered to treat had he believed them ravenous and destitute, once persuaded that further jiggers might be accompanied by physical pain and exertion, insisted maliciously.

"How about it, Shad?" said Doc. "Come along, be sociable."

The Tennessee Shad in turn drew a long breath.

"Oh, very well," he said, "but only a single."

Al, in the act of filling the glasses, stopped and looked long at the Tennessee Shad.

"Now, what's the game?" he said to himself.

The Tennessee Shad looked indifferently into the coveted glass, stirred the solitary jigger a little with the spoon, nibbled without appetite and relapsed into conversation.

"Say, Shad, I'd like to bet you couldn't eat six doubles," said Doc facetiously, winking at the Beefsteak.

The Tennessee Shad snorted.

"You don't want a cinch, do you?" he said crushingly.

Turkey Reiter stopped, caught Macnooder's eye, smiled reminiscently and nudged the Beefsteak.

"I thought you'd bet on anything," said the Beefsteak.

"So I will."

"Well, I'll bet you can't do it right now!"

"Eat six double jiggers?"

"That's what I say."

The Tennessee Shad jingled his keys in his trousers.

"Why don't you pick my pockets?"

"You're a quitter," said the Beefsteak, warming at the thought of the many old scores he had to wipe off. "I'll bet you half-a-dollar even you can't do it, and the loser pays for the jiggers right now. And if you don't take it up you're a paper-collared sport and a bluff."

"That's pretty strong talk, Shad!" said Macnooder.

"It's all very well for you to talk," said the Shad angrily. "This is one of your put-up games!"

The Beefsteak, egged on by Turkey, insultingly flashed the half-dollar under the Tennessee Shad's nose, exclaiming:

"Oh, you bluff, you cheap sport! Will you take me? Will you?"

"You be hanged!" said the Tennessee Shad wrathfully. "If there ever was a cheap sport, it's you. You never would bet unless you had a cinch. Well, I'll take you—on one condition."

"What?"

Doc and Turkey looked surprised while Al at the counter, with his hand on the spigot, cocked his head slightly.

"That you make the same bet with Doc Macnooder."

Macnooder was on his feet protesting.

"Oh, I say, hold up. I'm not in this."

The crowd found against him.

"Hold up, there," said the Beefsteak, scratching his head. "That's a pretty big bet."

The Tennessee Shad saw the dawn of suspicion in the Beefsteak's eyes, and shifted his attack forthwith.

"Well, I'll make that bet myself," he exclaimed. "Who's the quitter now?"

543

The Beefsteak, reassured, stated the terms cautiously.

"Half-a-dollar even you can't eat six double jiggers—"

"Strawberry jiggers."

"Strawberry jiggers—in an hour."

"Let it go at an hour."

"Shake?"

"Shake!"

Then the Tennessee Shad turned aggressively on Doc Macnooder.

"Same thing goes with you?"

"Confound you!"

"Half-a-dollar even?"

"Well, yes."

"Shake?"

"Shake!"

"Al, serve 'em up!"

Then Doc and the Tennessee Shad, not too fast, but as with great physical effort, each ate six double jiggers.

The Beefsteak, whose hopes had been alternately raised and lowered with this comedy, paid sixty cents for the jiggers the Shad had consumed and sullenly tossed him the shining half-dollar. The Tennessee Shad, having lost to Macnooder, gravely transferred the coin, and Macnooder, rising, tendered it to Al, saying, "I'm a dime short, Al—but that's the price of admission."

"Keep it, my boy," said Al enthusiastically, putting the half-dollar away from him. "Keep it; it's yours. I'd be ashamed to touch a penny of it."

Turkey Reiter solemnly offered his hand to the Tennessee Shad, saying, "Old sporting print, I never saw it better done, not even by Hickey, God bless him!"

"Thank you!" said the Tennessee Shad. "Why, where is the Beefsteak?"

They crowded to the window and saw the Beefsteak, collar up, brim down, hands sunk in his pockets, deliberately tracking for home.

Half-an-hour later, the audience having shifted, they caught the Gutter Pup and repeated with equal success.

Arm-in-arm, fed to satiety, each with five nickels jingling in his pocket, Doc and the Tennessee Shad rolled hilariously back to the House.

"It was brilliant," said the Shad, thinking of future strawberry jiggers. "But it is limited, Doc. We were lucky to get the Gutter Pup."

"It leaves us about where we were."

"We've got to do something—something big—on a swipe scale!"

"We certainly have."

"You haven't anything up your sleeve?"

"Lots of 'em, Shad—but they're all on the flimflam order. This time we've got to produce some goods."

They proceeded, each searching inwardly until almost to the House. Suddenly from the north door Alcibiades, the waiter, with a splash of white linen over his arm, emerged and disappeared around the back. The Tennessee Shad stopped.

"Did you see him?"

"Who?"

"Doc, I've got an idea!"

"Fire away!"

"No—no," said the Tennessee Shad ruminatively, "not now, Doc; not just now. It needs thinking over. What time does it get dark?"

"Eight o'clock," said Macnooder mystified.

"Meet me at half-past eight, thirty feet behind the baseball cage —alone!"

The Tennessee Shad, on taking his seat at the table that night, fixed his gaze on Alcibiades, the waiter, in such a concentrated glare that that menial, in his nervousness, violently did offense to Slush Randolph's ear with the platter of incoming sinkers.

"Confound you, Shad," said Slush, "quit rattling Alcibiades. What's wrong with him, anyhow?"

The Tennessee Shad stared haughtily at Slush and addressed Hungry Smeed.

"What do you know about him?"

"Who? Alcibiades?"

"Yes, what's his real name?"

"Finnigan—Patsy Finnigan," said Smeed, who didn't know.

"Correct. Now does anything strike you as peculiar about him?"

"Naw," said Hungry Smeed, annoyed at being delayed in his eating and watching Slush from the corner of his eye to make sure he didn't beat him to a second helping.

"Look again."

"He looks like a prizefighter."

"Oh, you do see that, do you? Well, he was a prizefighter."

At this startling announcement Slush, Butcher Stevens, the Triumphant Egghead and Hungry Smeed raised their heads with a simultaneous jerk and gazed at the circling Alcibiades.

"Come off; he's too thin," said Butcher Stevens with a critical glance.

"Look at his jaw. Look at his bullet head. Look at those blood-shot eyes."

"Why, he's a feather!"

"Featherweight, that's it."

"Say, you old Tennessee Shad," said Butcher Stevens directly, "you know something. You've got something up your sleeve. Do you know he's a prizefighter?"

"Well, supposin' I do?" said the Tennessee Shad.

"A prizefighter!"

"It can't be true!"

"He does have the jaw."

"Shut up!" said the Tennessee Shad. "Do you want everyone to hear?"

"Say, Bub, what's doing?"

"I've got an idea," said the Shad with dignity, "a real imported, patent-applied-for idea, and I want you fellows to clear out and give me a chance. Mind, now, whatever you do, don't tell a soul what I told you!"

A moment later the astonished Alcibiades received from the hands of the Tennessee Shad, accompanied by a terrific look of mystery, a covert scrawl with a whispered: "Read at once."

At half-past eight, while Doc Macnooder, lurking in the gloom behind the baseball cage, was straining eyes and ears for the approach of the Tennessee Shad, suddenly, from the ground in front of him, a thin, black silhouette sprang up.

"What's that?" cried Macnooder, bounding back.

"Shh, Doc, it's me!" said the familiar nasal voice of the Tennessee Shad.

"Confound you! What do you mean by sneaking in on me like that?"

"Hush—I had to be sure you weren't a spy," said the Tennessee Shad, grasping his arm. "No one must know our errand here!"

"Well, what the deuce is our errand?"

"We are waiting for someone," said the Tennessee Shad mysteriously. "Sit quietly now and keep your fingers crossed, for if we pull this off, Doc Macnooder, we're going to buy a safe to stuff our spondulix in."

"Pull off what?"

"Silence!"

After ten minutes' tense breathing suddenly the Tennessee Shad spoke: "Doc?"

"Yes."

"Do you hear anything?"

"Not a sound."

"Well, I do—pebbles crunching over there. Now! Look!"

"Where?"

"To your right, squint down along the fence, just past where the moonlight hits the second tree. See?"

"There's someone coming."

"Hush!"

Presently the Tennessee Shad sent forth a cautious whistle. The approaching figure loomed larger, stopped, advanced, stopped and looked about defensively.

"He's carrying a stick," said Macnooder.

"It's all right," said the Tenneessee Shad, rising. "We'll go to meet him."

Advancing rapidly he exclaimed, "Mr. Finnigan, shake hands with Mr. Macnooder. Doc, shake hands with Mr. Finnigan."

"Why, it's Alcibiades!" exclaimed Macnooder.

"Of course it is," said Tennessee Shad. "Come, Finnigan, we're not safe here. Come quickly. Follow me."

"Where you takin' me?" said Alcibiades, planting the stick in front of him.

"Down by the pond in the woods where no one'll hear us."

"Thanks, but I'll stay here."

"Shucks, Alcibiades," said the Tennessee Shad soothingly. "All we want is to put a little sporting proposition to you."

"Well, you can put it here."

"Don't you trust us?"

"No, you young devils; you bet I don't. If you've got anything to say, say it or I'm going back."

547

The Tennessee Shad consulted with Macnooder and, taking a step toward Alcibiades, said firmly, "Finnigan, you're a prizefighter!"

"Huh?"

"You're an ex-prizefighter!"

"What's that got to do with it?"

"Are you?"

Alcibiades scratched his head and considered.

"And what then?" he said cautiously. "What's the answer?"

"I knew it!" said the Tennessee Shad joyfully. "Finnigan, give me your hand. I'm proud to shake it!"

The startled Alcibiades then suffered his right hand to be enthusiastically pumped by Macnooder, but kept with his left a convulsive grasp on the stick.

"Now, Finnigan," said the Tennessee Shad professionally, "here's the point. What would you say to putting on the mitts just once more?"

"No you don't!" exclaimed the little Irishman, springing back.

Macnooder and the Tennessee Shad gazed in astonishment.

"What the deuce is the matter with him Doc?"

"Guess he thinks we want to kidnap him and make him fight Turkey or Butcher."

"Don't be a fool, Alcibiades," said the Tennessee Shad sharply. "None of us wants to fight you."

"Well, what do you want, then?" said Alcibiades, still on the defensive.

"Do you know any of the profession down in Trenton?"

"In Trenton?"

"Yes. Could you get anyone from there to come up and go a mill with you?"

"Could I? You want *me* to find someone?"

"That's it. Do you know anyone there?"

"Oh, yes! Sure, I know a lot of men there. But what do I want to be puttin' on the gloves for, anyway?"

"Why, we put up a purse, of course."

"Well, now, why in the devil didn't you begin with that?" said Finnigan, dropping the stick. "That's talkin'. Sure I mistrusted you were tryin' to play a trick on me."

"So you think you could make a match, Finnigan?"

"Maybe so, maybe. I'm running into Trenton tomorrow morning. I might look around a bit. It all depends on the purse, you know. Now what might be your idea on that?"

Macnooder and the Tennessee Shad withdrew and whispered. Macnooder, as the man of affairs, continued the operations.

"Well, now, Finnigan, what would you say was a fair proposition? Come, now, speak right up!"

"For how long a fight?"

"Oh, fifteen good slashing rounds. Come, now, what would you say?"

"Well, I don't know what I'd say."

"How about fifteen dollars—dollar a round?"

"Sure you young bloods can do better than that."

"Well, twenty-five dollars—lump."

"There's the expenses from Trenton?"

"Five dollars more for the rig. Is it a go?"

"Well, I'll have to see a bit."

"Fix it up for tomorrow night if you can, and have your man here on the stroke of midnight."

"Well, I'll see what I can do."

"Twenty-five-dollar purse, five for the rig and fifteen good slashing rounds. That's the terms. All right? Put it here!"

The Tennessee Shad and Macnooder, having watched Alcibiades flit back into the far shadow of the Upper, withdrew to the secret banks of the pond where the lugubrious moon fell in a shining splash amid the mossy reflections of the wood.

"Shad," said Macnooder, breaking the silence, "this is a wonder. It is beautiful. I really am touched. As a bonanza investment it takes me back to the late lamented Hickey and his no-guarantee silver-gilt clappers."

"Let's reckon up," said the Tennessee Shad professionally. "First, expense account. Purse and rig from Trenton, thirty dollars. Hiring of baseball cage, nothing. Advertising, nothing. Bribing of police, nothing. Subsidizing press, nothing. Can you think of anything else?"

"I can't."

"Total expenses—thirty dollars. Now for the rub. What'll we make the admission—one plunk?"

"Two."

549

"That's pretty stiff."

"We'll make that for reserved seats, front row. Just before the fight we can issue ordinary admissions at one bone."

"Cash?"

"Absolutely."

"Now, Doc," said the Tenneessee Shad seriously, "we must look at all sides of this, and there's one snag and it's a big one."

"Which one?"

"Our past reputations."

"Um!"

"The Egghead's sore on me because that haircut before the Prom queered him with his girl, and the Gutter Pup for several reasons, but principally for my leading him into mumps instead of German measles. He had 'em bad, Doc, very bad."

"Well, I suppose we'd better cut 'em out, then?"

"On the contrary, don't you see, they're the only ones can help us to general confidence."

"I know it's a good one," said Macnooder somewhat puzzled, "but it hasn't quite got to me yet. How the deuce are you going to get those two yaps who are gunning for you to help you inspire general confidence?"

"I'm going to make them my officials—Gutter Pup shall be referee, and the Triumphant Egghead timekeeper."

"I see," said Macnooder enthusiastically; "salve them over with a few plunks apiece."

"Doc," said the Tennessee Shad from the heights of a loftier genius, "you are really only fit to be a money changer and a pawn-broker. When will you rise to the truths of high finance?"

"I am humbly listening," said Doc. "What is it?"

"I am not going to do anything so low-down, easy and common-place as to pay them to do what I've got to have done."

"No?"

"No! I'm going to make the Gutter Pup and the Triumphant Egghead give me the sanction of their re-spec-ta-ble names and I'm going to make 'em *pay me for doing it!*"

Doc Macnooder humbly knelt and struck the ground with his forehead.

"Oh wonderful Tennessee Shad! When you get into business let me be your office boy?"

"That's already promised," said the Tennessee Shad, pleased. "Turkey Reiter has the call. And now to biz. I let off a bit at the dinner table about Alcibiades being a prizefighter and told the boys not to breathe a word; so, by this time, it ought to be all over the Upper. The Gutter Pup'll be primed. Let's swoop down on him."

"If we pull this off," said Macnooder sadly "it'll be just about the last, Shad."

"Alas!"

"They'll never stand for another deal from us!"

"They've stood for a good many."

"Shad, here ends the firm of Macnooder and the Tennessee Shad."

"Perhaps, but Doc this is the great and only Lalapazooza. We may go down, but it'll be with the band playing and the dear girls strewing flowers!"

"Say, what are we going to call Alcibiades?"

The Tennessee Shad paused and reflected.

"Patsy the Brute."

"Then he ought to pad," said Doc doubtfully. "He looks more like chills and fever."

"Good idea. I'll see to that. The other fellow is the Trenton Terror."

The Tennessee Shad, accompanied by Doc, rapped softly and stole in as innocently as Br'er Rabbit. The Gutter Pup, alone, entrenched behind a desk, lifted the green shade from his eyes and looked at the intruder deliberately, with an appetizing, fox-eyed glance.

"Hello, you old Gutter Pup!" said the Tennessee Shad in a friendly way, while Doc slid to a seat. "Am I welcome?"

"You are not! Get out of here!"

"Does that little jigger episode rankle?" said the Shad, sidling forward. "Because I've come to pay you back."

"What!" said Gutter Pup, startled from his attitude.

"I've come to pay you back," said the Shad, jingling the three remaining nickels to sound like a pocketful; "that is, if—if you think it wasn't a square catch."

"Humph—that's the string to it."

"No, no, I'm serious. I want to be fair and aboveboard. If you think—well, what do you think?"

"Oh, you caught me all right."

"I'll tell you what I'll do," said the Tennessee Shad suddenly; "I'll help you to work it on Lovely Mead or the Egghead. I'll square it that way. What do you say? It certainly would be a corking sell on Lovely!"

At this astute appeal to frail human nature, the Gutter Pup's scowl of vanity gave place to a smile at the soothing thought of leading his dearest chum into the same trap into which he had fallen.

"Let her go at that."

"Good," said the Tennessee Shad, extending his hand. "No hard feelings. Gutter Pup, you're the sport of the bunch. Shake."

The Gutter Pup shook hands gravely.

"Now, Gutter Pup, we want your advice," said the Shad cheerily. "I've got an idea."

"No," said the Gutter Pup firmly.

"It's a beautiful idea."

"Never again!"

"Just hear it!"

"No and no!"

"What! Haven't you any curiosity?"

"I haven't!"

"But, Gutter Pup—"

"Not a word."

"It's just this—"

The Gutter Pup sealed his ears with his fingers and looked stonily at the Shad. The Shad looked at Macnooder, shrugged his shoulders and made a sign of capitulation. The Gutter Pup disdainfully maintained his attitude. The Tennessee Shad sat down, picked up a paper cutter and gazed at it with such set melancholy that, from sheer curiosity, the Gutter Pup released his ears.

"Gutter Pup," said the Shad pathetically, "do you realize that your conduct hurts me?"

"Glad of it."

"Do you realize that in a short month all we old friends are going away from here to part forever? Can't you understand that your conduct and Egghead's and all the rest hurts me and makes me feel bad? Don't you realize that I want to do something to wipe out the past and win back the friends, the good old friends again?"

"Yes, you do!"

"Yes, Gutter Pup, I do—I feel lonely. I want to be restored to the old feeling of confidence."

"Mumps!" said the Gutter Pup, blushing a little.

"That's just it," said the Shad instantly. "I wanted you to say that! That's just what makes me feel bad. I want to make amends; to give you fellows something that'll wipe off the slate. Now, my little idea."

Up went the Gutter Pup's fingers again. The Tennessee Shad looked very sad, sighed, rose and offered his hand in farewell.

The Gutter Pup, smiling scornfully, extended his.

"It was only a prizefight," said the Tennessee Shad hurriedly, clutching the hand in both of his. "Never mind. Goodbye! Come on, Doc."

He went toward the door; Doc did not rise.

"Hold up!" said the Gutter Pup.

"Well?"

"You said prizefight?"

"I did."

"What do you mean by that?"

"I meant a crocheting sociable, of course," said the Tennessee Shad. "That's what is always meant by prizefight! Well, goodbye."

"Wait a moment now; don't be so thundering touchy."

"I am touchy."

"Rats! Can't you take a joke?"

"Not some jokes. Come on, Doc."

"Look here, Shad," said the Gutter Pup, slipping past him and locking the door. "Say, I take it back. Go on, now, let me in on this. Who's the scrap between?"

The Tennessee Shad stared at Doc and then at the Gutter Pup.

"I said nothing about an amateur boxing exhibition."

"What do you mean?"

"I'm talking about a really professional prizefight."

"A prizefight between professionals—real professionals?"

"Exactly that."

"Then it's straight about Alcibiades?"

"Who told you?" cried Macnooder and the Tennessee Shad in simulated anger.

"No matter," said the Gutter Pup hastily. "I promised not to tell."

"Well, it is true," said the Tennessee Shad. "His real name is

553

Patsy the Brute and Doc and I have matched him to go fifteen rounds against a bruiser we're smuggling up here called the Trenton Terror. Now ask me to sit down, and put a soft cushion behind my back!"

The Gutter Pup, rendered weak by emotion, grabbed the Tennessee Shad's arm and clung to him. In his underform years (as has been related) the Gutter Pup had fought battles galore for the pure love of battling, and was now the President of the Sporting Club (*vice* Hickey once removed), an organization devoted to the scientific healing of animosities without recourse to debasing exhibitions of billingsgate. Likewise the Gutter Pup possessed on his wall, as the proudest ornament of the school, a signed photograph of John L. Sullivan. For all which reasons his clutch tightened, as though he were afraid the Tennessee Shad would slip away through the transom.

"Oh, Shad, do you mean it?" he said at last.

"I'm telling you."

"But how are you going to get them?"

"Of course we've got to raise a stiff purse," said the Tennessee Shad as an opening wedge, and then, observing the Gutter Pup thoughtfully replacing the key in the lock, he added: "but that's not what we came about."

"What then?" said the Gutter Pup, looking at him long and critically.

"We want your advice as the leading sporting authority in the school," said the Shad solemnly. "It's all a question of the referee. Doc's for Butcher Stevens and I'm for Turkey Reiter. What do you think?"

"Why not me?" said the Gutter Pup instantly.

Macnooder looked profoundly at the battling photograph of John L. reposing on the American flag—profoundly, with a concentrated glare. The Tennessee Shad climbed to his familiar roost on the back of the chair and replied with embarrassed reluctance, "Gutter Pup, I wish we could offer it to you. You really know more about such things than any of us. You're really it. I wouldn't hurt your feelings for the world; that's why I want you to understand our reasons before we ask anyone else."

"I don't see," began the Gutter Pup, cut to the heart.

"Now, let me put the case before you. We've got to pony up a stiff purse. You know professionals and you understand. If we could let the whole school in, why we'd have no trouble. We can't. This thing's got to be pulled off with terrific secrecy at midnight, down in the baseball cage. At most, we can't let in more than thirty or forty fellows. So the only way is to give the prime jobs to the fellows who'll put up for them. There you have it. Turkey and Butcher will uncork like a flash at the chance. Gee, who wouldn't? Do you see, Gutter Pup? You'll understand, won't you? You won't take it hard. We'll leave it all to you. Which one— Turkey or the Butcher?"

"I suppose you'd want a stiff contribution," said the Gutter Pup, his appetite in his eye.

"Pretty stiff," said the Shad with charming frankness.

"I could put up a fiver."

"I'm afraid that wouldn't do," said the Tennessee Shad sadly. "Don't think about it any more. Besides, we've got to have some bruiser like Turkey to keep things in order."

"Shad," said the Gutter Pup, now almost tearfully, "haven't I always kept things in order at the Sporting Club? Now, look here: Turkey's a mutt, and the Butcher—well, you simply can't invite a couple of real professionals unless you give 'em a referee who knows the rules; you simply can't."

"But what are we going to do?"

"See here," said the Gutter Pup desperately. "Make it eight! I'll borrow another three somewhere and somehow."

We rather counted on more," said the Tennessee Shad doubtfully. "What do you say, Doc?"

"Pretty cheap, Shad. Think of the glory of it!"

"I tell you how it might be done," said the Tennessee Shad thoughtfully. "If we could get someone to put up ten for timekeeper—"

"Leave that to me," exclaimed the Gutter Pup, grasping at the straw. "I've got just your man—Goat Finney. His father's a billionaire."

"I wonder if the Triumphant Egghead would put up five to be one of the seconds?" said the Tennessee Shad.

"Let me see him!" said the Gutter Pup enthusiastically. "Give me the chance."

"Well, on these conditions I am willing," said the Tennessee

Shad after sufficient deliberation. "If you can raise more, why, do it. How about it, Doc?"

"We always did want Gutter Pup to referee, you know."

"Get at it quick," said the Tennessee Shad, rising.

"You bet I will!"

"Cash," said Macnooder warningly. "Paid in five hours before the fight."

The Gutter Pup departed running.

At half-past ten that night, at the Tennessee Shad's dictation, Doc Macnooder entered in the joint account book the following items:

Goat Finney, for holding the stopwatch	$10.00
The Triumphant Egghead, for being permitted to rub down the Trenton Terror	5.65
Turkey Reiter, for being permitted to rub down the Trenton Terror	5.00
The Beefsteak, for the privilege of sponging off Patsy the Brute	3.75
Tough McCarty, for the privilege of sponging off Patsy the Brute	3.00
Slush Randolph, for the right to supply the sponges	2.50
Gutter Pup, for refereeing and procuring the above officials	8.00

Under cover of these confidence-inspiring names, Macnooder and the Tennessee Shad sold their tickets rapidly without a hitch, no questions asked.

At twelve o'clock the next day Alcibiades slipped the Tennessee Shad a note confirming the arrangements and guaranteeing the arrival of a local bruiser that night.

At seven o'clock each official eagerly presented himself in the Tennessee Shad's room and made cash payments. Meanwhile the subscribers for reserved seats were receiving from Doc Macnooder, in exchange for two dollars, a green ticket inscribed:

RESERVED SEAT
Doc Macnooder and the Tennessee Shad Offer
THE TRENTON TERROR
vs.
PATSY THE BRUTE

THE TENNESSEE SHAD

*For the Professional Featherweight Champion-
ship of Mercer County, in Fifteen
Slashing, Terrific Rounds
Under the Auspices of the Sporting Club
Present Ticket at 11:45 at
Baseball Cage*
$2.00

At ten o'clock a supplementary issue of one-dollar general admission tickets, open to all comers and presentable at 12:10, was eagerly snatched up.

At half-past eleven the Tennessee Shad and Doc Macnooder, armed with Legs Brownell's bull's-eye lantern, stole down by the pond to meet Patsy the Brute and the Trenton Terror. They found them side by side, amicably reclining under a tree, puffing vigorously on ill-smelling cigars. Doc Macnooder turned the lantern on the new arrival; the scrutiny was not favorable.

"Are you a prizefighter?" he said, discouraged.

"Why not?"

"You don't look it."

"I'm a better man than this fellow."

"Remember, they're featherweights, Doc," said the Shad.

"Well, give us the goods," said Macnooder. "Fight like demons. We want fifteen slashing rounds!"

"All right, boss."

"You're the Trenton Terror."

"That suits me."

"And, Alcibiades, you're Patsy the Brute."

"That's fierce enough. Where's the coin?"

"You'll get that in the cage."

"No you don't—we get it now."

"Don't you trust us?"

"I'd rather feel the coin."

The Tennessee Shad consulted with Macnooder and Doc paid over thirty dollars and stationed himself so as to command the retreat of the Trenton Terror. On the stroke of twelve they stole up to the cage and entered by the back by means of three large boards prudently loosened for the occasion to secure a retreat.

The ring was already roped off. Four dim lanterns at the corners lighted up the white sweaters and rat-like eyes of the silent, breathless crowd. Above, a swallow or two, disturbed by the unusual spectacle, were frantically scurrying among the rafters. At moments the door opened and a whispered recognition was heard.

Macnooder presented the combatants to the Gutter Pup and sent them to their corners to strip for action.

Murmurs of surprise began to rise from the amateurs as the ribs and collarbones of Patsy the Brute appeared from under the red flannels.

"Gee, he's thinner than the Shad!"

"He's wasted away."

"He must be awfully scientific."

"His blows wouldn't annoy a fly."

"Me for the Trenton Terror."

But at this moment the upper anatomy of the visitor was disclosed.

"Lord, he's thinner still!"

"I can look right through him."

"He looks more like a professor of chemistry."

"How many ribs can you count?"

"Featherweight? Paperweight you mean!"

The Tennessee Shad, prepared for such criticism, advanced swiftly to the middle of the ring and held up his hand.

"Ladies and gentlemen, before opening the festivities tonight I desire to say a few words in explanation. We are placing before you tonight, at much expense and great personal danger, one of the most unique, I may say *the* most unique, bona fide, high-class professional exhibition in the history of the school. I will say, for the benefit of a few experts on baby carriages and tiddledywinks who seem to be unusually vociferous tonight, that these gentlemen are not bloated middleweights. They are featherweights; each man is trained to the second; there is not an ounce of superfluous flesh on their bones. Each man is a streak of lightning, with muscles like whipcords, skilled in every trick and artifice of the game. We have tried to put before you not a lumbering exhibition of fatty degeneration, but a sizzling, rearing, tearing spectacle of fast, furious and sanguinary fighting. Are there any criticisms of the management?"

There were none.

Macnooder arose and made a sign to the seconds, and the contestants lumbered forward, Alcibiades girt with the school colors, his antagonist decorated about the waist with a blue-and-white pennant loaned by the Duke of Bilgewater.

"The contestants tonight," continued Macnooder in singsong, "are, on my right, Patsy the Brute, who will uphold the red and black; on my left, the Trenton Terror. Both men have ferocious reputations. In explanation I would say in confidence that Patsy's retirement from the professional ring was simply due to his having accidentally killed a man by a terrific wallop on the solar plexus, an accident which he profoundly regrets. The contestants are old enemies, they have already met three times in three bruising contests, and they do not want to conceal that this is a fight for blood! At their personal request the rules will be stretched so as to permit of the most deadly slaughter. The presence of our well-known sporting authority, the Gutter Pup, as referee, will, however, be a guaranty that this fight, though slashing, will be absolutely square and aboveboard! Rounds, three minutes each—one minute interim. Everyone be seated!"

The Gutter Pup whispered a moment to the contestants and then sprang back, crying, "Time."

The Trenton Terror and Patsy the Brute stood confronting each other, visibly embarrassed.

"Make 'em shake hands, Gutter Pup," said the Tennessee Shad quickly.

"Did you see that?" said Doc Macnooder, on the other side. "They didn't want to shake hands. Gee, but they've got it in for each other."

The first round was not exactly thrilling.

"The light and the ground bother 'em," said Macnooder. "Just wait till they get their bearings."

"Funniest style I ever saw."

"Why, they hold their fists down by their knees."

"Featherweights always have styles of their own."

"Don't see how they can strike from there."

"They're quicker than others. You'll see all right."

Round number two passed like the first.

"When are they going to begin?" said a voice.

559

"Push 'em together."

"Tie 'em together."

"They're sizing each other up," said Macnooder loudly. "Planning out the campaign."

In round three their gloves met twice.

"Each is afraid of the other's wallop," said Macnooder more loudly. "One blow'll decide it. Great footwork, wasn't it?"

Suddenly in round four, just as a few polite blows had been struck, a hoarse voice at the back whispered "Cheese it!"

Instantly the cage was plunged in darkness, while a confused murmur rose.

"It's the Doctor."

"We're trapped."

"We'll all be fired!"

"Let's get out."

"Silence!"

"Shut up, everyone. The Shad's gone to reconnoiter."

Presently the Shad's voice was heard, "Light up, there isn't a mouse stirring."

The lanterns flickered up again.

"Who yelled 'Cheese it'?" said Turkey angrily.

Everyone stood up and looked about.

"If anyone's afraid he can get out now quick," said the Gutter Pup. "We don't want to cheat the cradle."

Strangely enough no one availed himself of the opportunity.

Round four, being resumed, ended with the professionals clinched desperately. Then another delay arose. The contestants refused to fight unless the hat was passed for additional contributions. Macnooder calmed the angry crowd by explaining that the ground was so rough and the light so bad that the Trenton Terror was really running the risk of twisting his ankle. The hat showing only five dollars and twenty cents, the management was forced to add five dollars more before the fighters consented to go on. Macnooder having taken the precaution to hold up the bonus until one good round had been fought, the hopes of the whole company were raised by a few resounding thumps, accompanied by a great amount of prancing about the ring.

Toward the end of round seven, again the sepulchral voice was heard.

"Hi! Cheese it!"

Again every light was doused while everyone waited with calculated breath. Again the Tennessee Shad slipped out by the back, reconnoitered and angrily returned. This time everyone, slightly unnerved, made a determined search for the alarmist, accompanied by such inviting requests to show himself that it was no wonder the search was unproductive. They returned to the ring.

"This is getting on my nerves," said Goat Finney, blowing on his fingers.

"Wish the deuce it was over."

"The Doctor'll be sure to hear of it."

"Course he will."

"He always does."

"Why don't they hurry up?"

The next round, as the result of another strike, the hat was passed again. In round nine another alarm arose, with another fruitless search for the disturber. By this time the feeling of panic was becoming epidemic.

At the end of round ten an angry consultation took place in the middle of the ring. The Trenton Terror positively refused to continue unless the stakes were increased. Macnooder addressed the turbulent meeting, "Say, fellows, a word, one word, please. This is the situation. This fight is illegal. You don't realize that. If the police get the tip we might be jugged for a year. These continued fake scares are getting on the nerves of these gentlemen, naturally. They're the ones who're taking the risk and they feel they ought to be paid more for it. Now I'll leave it to you. Shall we pass the hat again or call it off now?"

At once a discussion broke out.

"No, no!"

"We want our money's worth."

"Do you call this a fight?"

"Gee, I've had enough."

"Call it off."

"Nothing of the sort."

"Go on."

"No baby act."

"Pass the hat."

The mysterious possibility of prison gave a thrill to the imagination that lifted the tame contest into the realm of the heroic. The Gutter Pup passed the hat.

Meanwhile, the Tennessee Shad and Macnooder were solemnly consulting.

"Gee, Doc, if this goes on another five minutes, where'll our profits be?"

"I know it."

"Each time it hits us harder."

"Well, what are you going to do about it?"

"Lord, if the Doctor would only come, Macnooder," said the Tennessee Shad in a solemn whisper. "He *must* come!"

The pair exchanged a deep, silent glance of comprehension. The Tennessee Shad smiled and disappeared carefully in the direction of the safety exit.

The collection was announced at three dollars and sixty cents. Public opinion forced from the ruthful Macnooder the disbursement of a sufficient sum to make up the stipulated ten dollars. Round eleven began with threats from all quarters directed against the management and the fighters.

Suddenly outside the gravel crunched under a firm tread and three startling knocks fell on the door. Everywhere the whisper went up:

"The Doctor!"

"Police!"

"Douse the lights!"

"Through the back, you chumps."

"Hurry!"

In less than a minute, amid a scurrying of frantic figures racing for the woods, the last vestige of the furious and terrific professional prizefight had vanished.

. . . .

The next afternoon, ensconced in the Jigger Shop, Turkey Reiter, the Gutter Pup and the Triumphant Egghead considered the reckoning of the night before.

"I'm out ten plunks," said the Egghead. "I got reckless when they passed the hat. How did you make out?"

"I'd hate to tell," said the Gutter Pup.

"Funny the Doctor didn't refer to it in chapel."

"Say, that was queer."

"What was the fight like?" said Al, who had listened.

"Frightful," said Turkey Reiter. "There was bad blood between them!"

"How long did it go?"

"Ten slashing rounds."

At this moment the Triumphant Egghead, looking out the window, exclaimed, "Hello!"

"What's the matter?"

"There they are!"

On the opposite sidewalk Alcibiades and the Trenton Terror were sauntering affably together.

"Is that what you call Patsy the Brute and the Trenton Terror?" said Al dreamily.

"Sure."

"Was this one of the Tennessee Shad's little parties?"

"Why, yes."

"Doc Macnooder, too?"

"Yes, he was in it."

"Hem," said Al thoughtfully, "I see where two back accounts get paid up."

"Al," cried the Gutter Pup, "what do you know? Do you know those fellows?"

"The Finnigan brothers? Rather—used to steal watermelons together."

"Brothers!" said the Gutter Pup with a gasp.

"Brothers!" said the Triumphant Egghead.

"Brothers!" said Turkey Reiter.

"But, Al, they *are* prizefighters, now, aren't they?" said the Gutter Pup desperately.

"Well, they have done a good deal of boxing," said Al, polishing the faucets.

"Ah, they have done that?"

"Oh, yes, down at Katzenbach's grocery. They used to box lemons."

.   .   .   .

The Gutter Pup, Turkey Reiter, Goat Finney, the Beefsteak and the Triumphant Egghead sat on the steps of the Esplanade, nursing their feelings and their pocketbooks. Boys with tongues in their cheeks looked at them as they passed, and snickered at a good safe distance. Others shouted to them, joyful, insulting gibes.

Presently the Tennessee Shad and Doc Macnooder loped up in a friendly manner and stood looking down at them.

"Hello, Turkey!" said the Shad hopefully.

Turkey's gaze remained set.

"Hello, Lovely!"

Lovely drew a breath and looked down.

"Aren't you going to say howdy?" pleaded the Tennessee Shad. "Egghead—Gutter Pup—oh, Gutter Pup?"

The Gutter Pup's lips moved and set again, while Macnooder was observed departing on tiptoes.

"I suppose you're sore on me," said the Tennessee Shad sadly. "Well, I don't blame you. I'll never forgive myself—never!"

He sat down opposite, took a handful of stones, juggled them in the air, sighed, and fell into their silence.

All at once he brightened, looked up and said, "Say, fellows, I've got an idea!"

Then they surged up and fell upon him.

"Macnooder! Doc, help there; stand by me! Ouch!"

But Macnooder, purely the spirit of commerce, scudding for the west, called back, "Sorry, Shad—can't do it; the firm's dissolved!"